OTTO KLEMPERER

Otto Klemperer, 1970. Photo: G. MacDomnic

OTTO KLEMPERER

HIS LIFE AND TIMES

Volume 2   1933–1973

PETER HEYWORTH

Published by the Press Syndicate of the University of Cambridge
The Pitt Building, Trumpington Street, Cambridge CB2 1RP
40 West 20th Street, New York, NY 10011-4211, USA
10 Stamford Road, Oakleigh, Melbourne 3166, Australia

© The Estate of Peter Heyworth 1996

First published 1996

Printed in Great Britain at the University Press, Cambridge

A catalogue record for this book is available from the British Library

Library of Congress cataloguing in publication data

(Revised for v. 2)

Heyworth, Peter, 1921–1991
Otto Klemperer, his life and times.
Includes discographies and filmography.
Includes bibliographical references and index.
Contents: v. 1. 1885–1933 – v. 2. 1933–1973.
1. Klemperer, Otto, 1885–1933. 2. Conductors (Music) – Germany – Biography.
I. Title.
ML422.K67H53   1983   785'.092'4 B   83–1992

ISBN 0 521 49509 1 (volume 1) hardback
ISBN 0 521 24488 9 (volume 2) hardback
ISBN 0 521 56538 3 (two-volume set)

All quotations from letters and notes by Otto Klemperer, Johanna Klemperer and Lotte Klemperer are copyright. They can be reproduced, distributed and communicated to the public only with the written consent of the copyright owner Lotte Klemperer or her heirs.

CONTENTS

	List of illustrations	page vii
	Publisher's note	ix
	Acknowledgements	x
1	Into exile	1
2	'A cloudburst of non-sequiturs'	20
3	Bread and work	39
4	In the wrong place	72
5	On the road to self-destruction	99
6	'Ajax fell through Ajax's hand'	124
7	Europe remains Europe	145
8	Behind the Curtain	172
9	Caught in the crossfire	190
10	A sea of troubles	220
11	The high ground regained	246
12	Ordeal by fire	269
13	Exit Legge	299
14	The shadows lengthen	321
15	The final years	338
	Notes	364
	Biographical glossary	386
	Discography by Michael H. Gray	394
	Klemperer on film by Charles Barber	461
	Bibliography	465
	Index	468

ILLUSTRATIONS

    Frontispiece   Otto Klemperer, 1970
1. Rehearsal for the first Viennese performance of the Berg Violin Concerto, 25 October 1936. Vienna Philharmonic Orchestra, conductor Otto Klemperer, soloist Louis Krasner, leader Arnold Rosé
2. Klemperer with his children Werner and Lotte on the beach, Los Angeles, 1935
3. Party at the Klemperers', Los Angeles 1935
4. Klemperer with Arnold Schoenberg and his daughter Nuria in Los Angeles, c. 1936
5. Klemperer and Johanna with children Werner and Lotte at Los Angeles railway station, c. 1936/7
6. Klemperer and Johanna at Lake Arrowhead, California, c. 1937/8
7. Klemperer in Los Angeles with bandaged head after an assault on him during the night of 13 March 1947
8. Klemperer with Yehudi Menuhin and Georges Enesco, June 1947
9. Klemperer conducting the Concertgebouw Orchestra of Amsterdam, late 1940s
10. Klemperer in Budapest, c. 1948
11. Klemperer with Aladár Tóth and Annie Fischer, Budapest, c. 1948/9
12. Klemperer rehearsing for his first post-war concert with the Berlin Philharmonic Orchestra, 30 April 1948
13. Walther Felsenstein and Otto Klemperer at a *Carmen* rehearsal, Berlin 1948
14. Klemperer in Rome, early 1950s
15. Klemperer, Johanna and Werner, early 1950s
16. Drawing of Klemperer by Willy Dreifuss, 1960
17. Klemperer with son Werner and grandson Mark, London, May 1960
18. Bruno Walter, Wilma Lipp and Otto Klemperer in Vienna, June 1960
19. Klemperer during *Fidelio* rehearsals with Elsie Morison, London 1961
20. Klemperer and Walter Legge, with Lotte Klemperer, at a recording session, London 1961

LIST OF ILLUSTRATIONS

21 Klemperer rehearsing in Philadelphia, October 1962
22 Klemperer in London, March 1967
23 Otto Klemperer, Lotte Klemperer, Jacqueline du Pré, Daniel Barenboim, March 1967
24 Pierre Boulez, Erwin Jacobi, Otto Klemperer, Anna Hesch (the Klemperers' housekeeper), Bayreuth 1967
25 Klemperer and his nurse Ruth Vogel in 1969
26 Klemperer being presented with his Israeli passport by the Director General of the Interior Ministry, August 1970
27 Klemperer and his cleaner's small son, Zurich, 21 March 1970
28 Klemperer with Lotte Lehmann, Lucerne, 22 July 1972
29 Klemperer with his daughter Lotte, Zurich, November 1972

Acknowledgement is made to the following for the use of copyright illustrations:
Frau Lotte Klemperer: 3, 5, 6, 7, 11, 14, 15, 25, 27, 28, 29; G. M. Cushing, Boston: 1; The Hearst Collection, Department of Special Collections, University of Southern California Library: 2; Studio Klein, Strasbourg: 8; Parlicam Pictures, Amsterdam: 9; Várkonyi Studio, Budapest: 10; Associated Press, London: 12; W. Dreifuss Archiv, Dept. of Prints and Drawings, Zentralbibliothek, Zurich: 16; Lotte Meitner-Graf: 17; Elfriede Hanak, Vienna: 18; Zoe Dominic: 19; EMI Records UK and G. MacDomnic: 20; Adrian Siegel, Philadelphia: 21; G. MacDomnic, Stanmore: frontispiece, 22, 23; K. Weiss, Jerusalem: 26

PUBLISHER'S NOTE

In October 1991, Peter Heyworth died suddenly, having completed all but the final chapter of this book. A few years earlier, after suffering a minor stroke, he had asked his colleague on the *Observer* John Lucas whether, in the event of his death, Lucas would be prepared to see the book through to publication. Sadly, it became necessary for this invaluable help to be sought, and Cambridge University Press and the Peter Heyworth Estate owe John Lucas a huge debt of gratitude for his work in preparing this text for publication. He wrote the second half of the last chapter, edited the entire draft typescript and checked innumerable details.

ACKNOWLEDGEMENTS

I could never have completed this biography of Otto Klemperer without the assistance of his daughter, Lotte Klemperer, who has provided me with a constant flow of family papers and other documents from her archive in Zurich. If at times she felt exasperated that I should be plying her with questions that Peter Heyworth had asked her already, she never showed it. Her generosity, encouragement and good humour have been boundless. I am deeply grateful to her.

I must also thank her brother, Werner Klemperer, who, in the course of two long and enjoyable meetings in New York, threw light on a number of obscure corners in the original typescript.

Others who have helped me include Jochen Voigt, who made available to me all Peter Heyworth's research files; Michael Allen, Peter Andry, Richard Armstrong, Otto Freudenthal, Sir Donald McIntyre, Gareth Morris, Karl Anton Rickenbacher, Eva Wagner-Pasquier and Ronald Wilford, who all provided new information; Joan Goldsbrough, who typed Peter Heyworth's original version – and then retyped it with my revisions; David Cummings and John Warrack, who both read the typescript; David Whelton, who gave me access to the Philharmonia Orchestra's archives; Penelope Souster of Cambridge University Press, who showed great patience over a task that took much longer than anticipated; and Peter Edwards, also of Cambridge University Press, who helped with the final editing of the book. I am most grateful to all of them.

Below is a list of acknowledgements that Peter Heyworth compiled before he died. Almost certainly there are errors and omissions that he would have attended to before publication, but, even as it stands, it provides testimony to his tireless and wide-ranging research.

John Lucas
London

Hans Adler, Pauline Alderman, Dorothea Alexander, Michael Allen, Leonard Amadio, John Amis, Richard T. Andrews, Peter Andry, Gustave Arlt, Verna Arvey, Douglas A. Asbury, Vladimir Ashkenazy, Lies Askonas, Felix Augenfeld, Loretta Ayerhoff.

ACKNOWLEDGEMENTS

Sol Babitz, Lotte Bamberger-Hammerschlag, Lady Evelyn Barbirolli, Boroslaw Barlog, John Barnett, Frau Bartsch (Berlin Philharmonic Orchestra), Gerth-Wolfgang Baruch, Oswald Georg Bauer, Mario Bayer, Anthony Beaumont, Pierre Béique (Montreal Symphony Orchestra), Margaret C. Beller, Lionel Bentley, Aurel Bereznai (Radio Free Europe, Munich), Martin Bernheimer (*Los Angeles Times*), Mario Beyer (Vienna Philharmonic Orchestra), Herta Blaukopf, Kalman Bloch, Thomas Blum, Massimo Bogianckino (Teatro Comunale, Florence), Ruth Bondy, Attila Boros, Philo Bregstein, Andras Briner, Marianne Brün, David Brunswick, Mark Brunswick, Natasha A. Brunswick, Samuel Brylawski (Library of Congress, Motion Picture, Broadcasting and Recorded Sound Division), Hugo Burghauser.

Jean Callow (Scottish National Orchestra), Stuart Campbell, Jacques Canetti, Olive Cassirer, Florence Caylor, Dorothea Chavanne (Gesellschaft der Musikfreunde, Vienna), Robert Chesterman, Evert Cornelis, Robert Craft, Dorothy Crawford, Paul Csonka, Caspar R. Curjel, Maria Curzio, George Cushing, Edmund A. Cykler.

Oliver Daniel, Susi Danziger, Lisl David, Henk de By, Michael de Cossart, T. de Leur (Royal Concertgebouw Orchestra), Peter de Mendelssohn, George de Mendelssohn-Bartholdy, Winton Dean, Olga Demetriescu-von Liechtenstein, Frau Deek (Vienna Symphony Orchestra), Leon Demeuldre (Société Philharmonique de Bruxelles), John Denison, Claire M. Deveney (Lahey Clinic Foundation), Felicia Deyrup (New School for Social Research), Peter Diamand, Thea Dispeker, Ian Docherty, Bertha M. Driscoll, Garrett, Earl of Drogheda, Vincent Duckles (University of California – Berkeley Music Library).

C.J. Earl, Joe Eckstein, John Edwards (Chicago Symphony Orchestra), Ruth Edge (EMI Archives), Georg Eisler, Herman Elbin, Sören Engblom (Archivist, Dagens Nyheter, Stockholm), Käthe Engi, Guy Erismann (Paris Radio), Morton Estrin, Diana Eustrati-Mittelstädt.

David Farneth (Kurt Weill Foundation for Music), Robert A. Fenn, Horace C. Ferris, Rudolf Firkušny, Richard Fisher (Royal Philharmonic Society), Ernest Fleischmann, Marius Flothuis, Eldon Fox, Francesca Franchi (Royal Opera House Archives, Covent Garden), David Frisina, Eleanore Fuhr (Westdeutsche Rundfunk Archives), Elisabeth Furtwängler.

Felix Galimir, Stephen Gallup, Lisel Gassyte, James Gibson, Cissie Gill, Bronislaw Gimpel, Johan Giskes (Gemeentearchief, Amsterdam), Hertha Glaz-Redlich, Michael Goldstern, Joan Gomez, Sir Reginald Goodall, Saul

ACKNOWLEDGEMENTS

Goodman, Eli Goren, Jane Gottlieb (American Music Center), Brigitta Graber (Vienna Philharmonic Orchestra), Ian Grant (Royal Festival Hall), Helmut Grohe, Sally Groves (Schott and Co.), Eric Guignard-Froebel, J. Larry Gulley (University of Georgia, Athens).

John Haag (University of Georgia, Athens), Monique Haas, P.G. Hadoulis, Maria Halbich-Webern, Clemens Hallsberg (Vienna Philharmonic Orchestra), Ida Halpern, Keith Hardwick (EMI), George, Earl of Harewood, Philip Hart, Diana Haskell (Chicago Public Library), Bert Heim, Eva Heinitz, Hans Heinsheimer, Norbert Henning (B. Schott Söhne), Hans Werner Henze, Piet Heuwekemeyer, Derek Hill, Ernst Hilmar (Wiener Stadtbibliothek), Eric Hirschler, Ira A. Hirschmann, Rosemarie Hohler (Lucerne International Festival), Harold Hort (Australian Broadcasting Corporation), Orvin Howard (Los Angeles Philharmonic), Axel Hubert, Walter Huder (Akademie der Künste, West Berlin), Anthony Hughes (Australian Broadcasting Corporation), Sir Ian Hunter, Frau Huwe (Berlin Philharmonic Orchestra).

Joan Ingpen.

Erwin Jacobi, William G. James, Walter Jellinek, János Jemnitz, Michael Johnson.

Philip A. Kahgan, Annelien Kappeyne, Judith Karp (Philadelphia Orchestra), Marres Kartegener, Jenny Keane (EMI Archives), Götz Klaus Kende, Louis Kentner, Milton Kestenbaum, Rolf Kienberger, Edward Kilenyi, J.M. Koerner, Olda Kokoschka, Gwen Koldovsky, Rudolf Kolisch, Bela Köpeczi, George Korngold, Louis Krasner, Herman Krebbers, Rhoda E. Kruse (San Diego Public Library), Veda Kuhule, Imre Kun, Adam Kurakin.

Eva Landé, Hans Landecker, Hans Landesmann, Beatrix Lang (Lucerne City Archives), Brenton Langbein, Thomas Lask, Norman Lebrecht, Dame Elisabeth Legge-Schwarzkopf, P. Alfred Leonard, Robert Levine, Charles Libove, Johannes Liese, Anthony C. Linick, Robert Lippmann, Erhard Löcker, Sir Joseph Lockwood, Daniel Luckenbill (UCLA Archives, Los Angeles), Miklos Lukács.

William McKelvey Martin, Eric McLean, Anna Mahler, Alfred B. Mann, Robert Mann, Manfred Mantner-Markhof, Jerilynn Marshall (Newberry Library, Chicago), George Martin, Erich Maschat, Erich Mauermann, Nicholas Maw, Micha May, J.F. Meakins, P. Mégy, Lord Menuhin, P. Thomas Michaels OSB, Marta Mierendorff, Marcel Mihalovici, András Mihaly, Nathan Milstein, Ray Minshull (Decca Records Co.), Donald Mitchell, Hans

ACKNOWLEDGEMENTS

Moldenhauer, Rosemary Moravac, Dan Morgenstern, Frederick Moritz, Gareth Morris, Lawrence Morton, Charles Moses, Henry T. Mudd.

Anita Naef, Jean-Michel Nectoux (Bibliothèque Nationale, Music Department, Paris), Frau Neunteufel (Salzburg Festival), Dika Newlin, Lulter Noss (Yale University), Helene Noltenuis, Jarmila Novotna.

Theo Olaf, Andrea Olmstead, Uwe Opolka, Martin Ormandy.

Manoug Parikian, Marie-Luise Passera (Deutsche Bibliothek, Department of Literature written in Exile, Frankfurt), Georgina Paton (University of California, San Diego), Jeane Paul (Occidental College, Los Angeles), Sir Peter Pears, Seymour Peck (*New York Times*), Jack Pepper, Ray Petch, Monika Petek (Austrian Cultural Institute, London), Klaus-Jürgen Peter, Martin Peters, Shabtai Petrushka, David A. Pickett, Henry Pleasants, Miss Pollard (Warburg Institute), James Poppen, Jutta Poser, J.W.H. Poth, Joel Prikin.

Anders E. Ramsey (Stockholm Philharmonic Orchestra), Jeanne Rains, M. Lanfranco Rasponi, Fritz Redrich, Kathleen Reed (University of Pennsylvania Special Collections), Sven Reher, Hans J. Reichhardt (Landesarchiv, Berlin), Gottfried Reinhardt, Virginia J. Renner (Huntingdon Library, San Marino), Regina Resnik, Clare G. Reyner (California State University, Long Beach), Sue Roach (British Library – Dutch Department), Don Roberts (Music Librarian, North-Western University, Evanston, Illinois), W.F. Robinson (Radio Free Europe, Munich), Charles Rodier (EMI Records), Josefer Rosanska, Gudula Rosenbaum, Deena Rosenberg, Margaret Rosenberg, Albi Rosenthal.

Richard Sachs, Harold E. Samuel (Yale University Library), György Sandor, Thomas Scherman, Hannelore Schmidt (Austrian Cultural Institute, London), Hans-Peter Schmitz, Karl Ulrich Schnabel, Walter Schneiderhan, Lawrence A. Schoenberg, Karel Schouten, Arthur Searle (British Library – Department of Manuscripts), Chris Sears (Philharmonia Archives), Egon Seefehlner, Irmgard Seefried, Wolfgang Seifert, Mrs Seligman, Elizabeth Sessions-Pease, William S. Severns, Nancy Shea (Clark Library, Los Angeles), Nancy Shear, Wayne Shirley (Library of Congress), Eric Simon, Zoltan Simon, Nicholas Snowman, László Somfai (Bartók Archives), Laszlo Somogli, Dorle Soria, Peter Stadlen, Wilfred Stiff (Ibbs & Tillett), B. Stillfried (Austrian Institute), Stephan Stompor, Gerald Strang, Ignaz Strasfogel, Otto Strasser, Hugo Strelitzer, George Stringer, Hilde Strobel, Rosamund Strode (Britten Estate), Hans Sulzer, Michael C. Sutherland (Occidental College, Los Angeles), Howard S. Swan.

ACKNOWLEDGEMENTS

Howard Taubman, Lawrence Taylor, Henri Temianka, Uri Toeplitz, Sir John Tooley, P.D. Trevor-Roper, Karl Trötzmüller, Gerald Turbow.

Werner Unger.

William Vacchiano, Hans van Leeuven, Gerard Verlinden, Jon Vickers, Gottfried von Einem, Alice von Hildlebrandt.

Friedelind Wagner, Wolfgang Wagner, Jeff Walden (BBC Written Archives, Caversham), Peter Wallfisch, William Weber (California State University, Long Beach), Karlheinz Weigand (Ernst Bloch Archive, Ludwigshafen), Henri Weill, Ronald Weitzman, Franzi and Ron Weschler, Mrs Victor White, Bruce Whiteman (McMaster University, Hamilton, Ontario), Christa Wichman (Wiener Library, London), Nicole Wild (Bibliothèque de L'Opéra, Paris), Ronald Wilford, Robert E. Wise (Lahey Clinic Medical Center), Jane Withers, Janet Wright (Swedish Embassy, London), Thomas Wright (Clark Library, Los Angeles), H. Wysling (Thomas Mann Archive, Zurich).

Frances Mullen Yates.

Frank A. Zabrosky (University of Pittsburgh Libraries), Maurice Zam, Dr Zimmermann (Stadtarchiv Zurich), Eugene Ziskind, Jaacov Ziso, Prinz Hubertus zu Loewenstein.

Archives Nationales, Paris; Amerikanische Gedenkbibliothek, Berlin; Gesellschaft der Musikfreunde, Vienna; Los Angeles Public Library – Music Division; *New Yorker* library; Städtische Bühnen – Musikbibliothek, Frankfurt a.M.; Stockholm Riksarkivet; Südwestfunk, Baden-Baden; Teatro alla Scala, Milan; UCLA Special Collections, Oral History Program.

All quotations from BBC internal memoranda are reproduced with the permission of the BBC Written Archives Centre. Quotations from EMI archival material are reproduced by permission of EMI Records Limited. Extracts from the letters of Arnold Schoenberg appear by permission of the Arnold Schoenberg Estate. The extract from a letter of Benjamin Britten is © The Britten–Pears Foundation and may not be reproduced further without written permission

1

Into exile

On 5 April 1933 Otto Klemperer arrived in Zurich from Berlin. His immediate concern was to inform the Berlin State Opera of his address, taking the view that he had done no more than absent himself temporarily during a difficult period. For the moment the opera house also continued to act as though that were the case. That he had in fact cut his ties with Germany was not clear, least of all to himself. On 7 April he wrote to his wife Johanna, giving details of the *Kur* he was undergoing at the Bircher-Benner clinic. He found the diet tasty, but to save money had taken a room at the nearby Waldhaus Dolder, in 1933 still a relatively modest hotel. Meanwhile, he told Johanna to make preparations to close the Berlin flat and come to Switzerland with the children, Werner and Lotte, and the family factotum, Fräulein Schwab, before the end of the month. Within about ten days they arrived in Zurich with money Johanna had baked in a cake. The nine-year-old Lotte was delighted to be free of schoolwork, but the move puzzled her. When her father explained that the family had had to leave Germany because he was a Jew, she had no idea what he was talking about.[1]

Zurich was full of refugees from Germany. Newcomers were spotted on the evening promenade on the Bahnhofstrasse, and the Hotel Baur au Lac was a favourite meeting place, at any rate for those with money. The unchanging ritual of a great Swiss hostelry brought a degree of reassurance. Among the acquaintances whom Klemperer encountered there was the celebrated Kantian philosopher Ernst Cassirer. He was astonished to be told by Klemperer that the guards whom the German authorities had placed on Jewish shops during the boycott of 1 April to discourage customers from entering were in fact 'archangels in Nazi uniform', whom God had put there to protect the owners. Clearly, the manic fires which had raged during his last days in Berlin had not abated.*

Unlike most of his fellow exiles, Klemperer was comparatively well placed to earn a living. In January 1933 an upheaval had occurred in the affairs of the Vienna Philharmonic Orchestra, as a result of which one of its members, the bassoonist Hugo Burghauser, had taken its helm. One of his first moves was to travel to Berlin to invite Klemperer to give a concert with

* Klemperer suffered throughout his life from manic-depressive illness.

the orchestra. Klemperer had conducted in the Austrian capital before, but not with the Vienna Philharmonic. He accepted Burghauser's invitation readily, for the orchestra had escaped the general decline in Austrian musical life that had occurred since the First World War. Within two weeks of leaving Berlin, Klemperer arrived in Vienna.

Apparently determined to ensure that his reputation as a radical should not prejudice his chances in a country ruled by Engelbert Dollfuss's conservative, clerico-fascist government, Klemperer gave an interview which appeared in the *Wiener Tag* on 22 April, the day before the concert. In it, he denied that he had ever been politically active and insisted that it was only his interpretations that had led him to be attacked in Germany as a *Kulturbolschewist*. The label, he declared, was as unwarranted as the slogan of *die Neue Sachlichkeit* that had earlier been hung around his neck.*

Klemperer chose to play safe by selecting Bruckner's Symphony No. 8, the score with which he had largely established his reputation as a concert conductor. Shortly before his first rehearsal, however, the city's Tonkünstler-orchester complained that it had already announced a performance of the work and asked the Philharmonic to change its programme. Klemperer was on the platform when the request reached him. Without hesitation, he agreed to substitute Bruckner's Fifth Symphony and set about rehearsing the work without even calling for a score. His memory and sang-froid much impressed the players.

The concert was a prodigious success. Klemperer's naturalness and directness delighted the orchestra.[2] The performance of Beethoven's First Symphony, which opened the evening, was widely praised for its chamber music-like quality; only Joseph Marx, composer and principal critic of the *Neues Wiener Journal*, found it reserved and doctrinaire. Marx also criticised the Bruckner as being melodically inexpressive. In particular, he considered that Klemperer's motoric rhythms in the scherzo lacked the ease and *Gemütlichkeit* of a *Ländler*. In Vienna, wrote Marx, who represented a pre-Mahlerian sensibility, Austrian composers should be given Austrian interpretations. But his remained an isolated voice. In the *Neue Wiener Presse* (25 April) Julius Korngold saluted Klemperer as a master of Brucknerian architecture. Rudolf Réti, critic of *Der Abend*, declared that he had rarely heard the Vienna Philharmonic play so impressively, and by implication

---

* The interview was given to Alfred Rosenzweig (1899–1948), a Viennese critic who subsequently emigrated to London, where under the pseudonym of Alfred Mathis he wrote a biographical study of Elisabeth Schumann. In the course of his introduction to the interview Rosenzweig observed that in his behaviour Klemperer gave no signs of the stresses to which he had been exposed in recent weeks. In a letter (1 September 1947) to Ernst Krenek, Rosenzweig subsequently claimed that he himself had written the interview to strengthen Klemperer's standing in Catholic circles. He also claimed that Klemperer had arrived in Vienna with recommendations to the Austrian hierarchy (Krenek Archives, University of California, La Jolla).

suggested that Klemperer was well fitted to fill the vacant position of the orchestra's permanent conductorship.³

Burghauser, who played in the concert, later recalled that

> In the finale ... the culmination of the double fugue had an impact it had never had in any previous performance. Until then, Furtwängler and Walter had been considered the outstanding conductors of Bruckner. With this ... [and subsequent] performances Klemperer demonstrated that he ... was the greatest and most impressive conductor of Bruckner's symphonies. And what was noteworthy was that he achieved greater expressiveness with performances that kept within the framework of a classical style and a clear, coherent rhythmic structure, in contrast to the performances of Furtwängler and Walter, whose extreme rhythmic freedom and irregularity romanticised and sentimentalised the works ... The feeling of the musicians was that Klemperer had provided a replacement for what had been lost with Weingartner and Strauss ... The entire orchestra was so impressed ... that he was engaged for the opening concert of the Philharmonic's series in September.⁴

Klemperer was equally delighted. Furtwängler had earlier told him that it was only in Bruckner that he would be able to form a real impression of the Vienna Philharmonic's unique qualities. Now, for the first time, he experienced 'the extraordinary beauty of its *Klangkörper*', which came to represent for him an ideal of orchestral sound.* At a moment when his entire future in Germany was in jeopardy, Klemperer had with a single concert won the admiration of an orchestra that in the matter of conductors was notoriously hard to please.

*   *   *

Although he had written to his wife shortly after his arrival in Zurich to assure her that 'I am now much quieter',⁵ that was not the case so far as his amorous inclinations were concerned. At the Viennese house of the American composer Mark Brunswick, he met Hilde Firtel, a young student of conducting who was also acquainted with Furtwängler. Asked by another guest, 'Haben Sie Feuer?' ('Do you have a light?'), he replied, 'Ich habe Feuer nur für Fräulein Firtel' ('I have fire only for Fräulein Firtel'). She was not the only young woman to take his fancy. On his return to Zurich towards the end of April, he found that Dorothea Alexander-Katz, a member of the Berlin Philharmonic Chorus, had also arrived in the city. Their regular meetings inevitably aroused Johanna's wrath, and tension rose in the small rented apartment that was intended to serve as a family home until Klemperer's future became clearer. When he invited the 21-year-old girl to accompany him

---

* Anderson (ed.), *Klemperer on Music*, p. 200. 'I think that the Vienna Philharmonic is much better than all the American orchestras ... I also prefer it to the Berlin Philharmonic' (Heyworth (ed.), *Conversations*, p. 88).

to Florence, where he planned to join the many distinguished musicians who were gathering for the first Maggio Musicale festival, Johanna chose to remain with the children in Zurich. From time to time Klemperer turned up on brief visits, so that contact between him and his wife was not entirely severed. But for the first time in fourteen years of married life they lived apart for three months.

'Il Nido', the villa he rented in Fiesole from American acquaintances, came complete with a cook, maid, chauffeur and car. It had a large garden and a terrace with a magnificent view over Florence and the Tuscan countryside. In these idyllic surroundings Klemperer wrote on 10 May 1933 to tell Johanna how foolish she had been to remain in Switzerland.

> Zurich, the lake, the attractive apartment, the fresh air – that's all very fine but ... basically quite superfluous. Here we have a house (where no one practises the piano) and what a house. What a garden, what a country. 'Race' certainly plays a part. I am – as a Jew – a man of the Mediterranean. You as a German [are] naturally not. Here it is as though – after forty-seven years of wandering in foreign parts – I have come home ... You (and the children too) will have to look on Switzerland as transitional, as I don't want to remain there.

A gathering such as the Maggio Musicale offered an opportunity to restore contacts that had been broken by his hasty departure from Germany and to make others that might pave the way for new engagements. Those attending the festival included Richard Strauss, Berg, Bartók, Kodály, Roussel, Milhaud, Krenek and Malipiero. One of the first visitors Klemperer sought out was Strauss. 'It will all come out all right', was the great man's bland comment on conditions in Germany. Visitors to 'Il Nido' included Rudolf Kolisch the violinist and brother-in-law of Schoenberg. The question of Schoenberg's safety in Berlin must have been raised, for it was on Klemperer's urging that Kolisch on 16 May sent the composer a cable: 'Change of climate urgently recommended.' That very day Schoenberg left for Paris.[6] Other regular visitors included Alma Mahler, who had arrived with her husband, the novelist Franz Werfel.

As usual in euphoric periods, Klemperer was composing furiously. In Zurich he had completed *1933*, a cry for revenge against the Nazis. When he played it to the art historian Bernard Berenson and his companion, Nicky Mariano, at their house outside Florence, they were amazed by the change in his attitude to the new regime in Germany; when he had last visited them, two months earlier, he had been euphoric about Germany under the Nazis.[7] Other guests, who included the critic Alfred Einstein and his wife, were surprised by Klemperer's openly amorous attitude to his embarrassed hostess. After dessert, he further disconcerted the company by calling for a glass of water to rinse his dentures. Two days later, when Einstein visited 'Il Nido', he found Klemperer in the garden shooting at portraits of Hitler, Goering and

Goebbels with an air pistol. Later, Klemperer played Einstein parts of a new opera, *Der verlorene Sohn* ('The Prodigal Son'), which he was composing as a prologue to *Bathsheba*, written the previous year. When Einstein questioned the wisdom of his plan to perform it in the open-air amphitheatre at Fiesole, Klemperer seized a poker and threatened him, 'not altogether in fun'.[8]

No one Klemperer encountered in Florence made so deep an impact on him as the philosopher Dietrich von Hildebrand. Born in Florence of Protestant parents, Hildebrand had, like Klemperer, earlier converted to Catholicism. They were immediately drawn to each other. In his unpublished memoirs,[9] Hildebrand describes Klemperer at that period as 'impetuous, incredibly impassioned and ambitious ... In addition to his great abilities as a conductor, [he] was a cultivated man ... The summer of 1933 was imbued with his presence.' However, there were aspects of Klemperer's character that disturbed Hildebrand. 'I unfortunately formed an impression', he recalled in his memoirs, 'that [Klemperer] hated the Nazis above all because they had dismissed him* ... the terrible doctrine, the worship of power, the idolatrous nationalism are not what primarily worry him.' Hildebrand and his guests were also appalled that a Catholic should have written a work so full of an Old Testament spirit of revenge as his *1933*, which Klemperer insisted on hammering out to them on an upright piano.†

*   *   *

Events in Germany had indeed brought about a transformation in Klemperer's political attitudes. The National Socialist government did not take long to react to his abrupt departure from Berlin. On the evening of 4 April, the day Johanna had bidden him farewell at the Anhalter Bahnhof on his way to Zurich, it was announced that he would not be taking part in the Berlin Festival that summer.[10] On the following day Hans Hinkel, a National Socialist who occupied crucial positions in the cultural life of the Third Reich, gave an interview in which he discussed various aspects of Nazi cultural policy. Asked specifically about Klemperer's future, he replied that no decision had been reached, but that his final concert with the Berlin State Opera orchestra, originally scheduled for 30 March, had been postponed 'in the

---

* Klemperer's dismissal was officially announced on 1 June.
† And when we are united
   And to power we return,
   Yes, then we shall repay you,
   As once you made us pay.

When you can fight no longer ...
Your houses will be burning,
Your cities will be sacked.

Twelve years later that vision was to be more completely fulfilled than Klemperer could have envisaged.

interest of the disciplinary development in Germany'. Such an event, he claimed, might lead to public disorder; 'in these days ... we need the SA and SS for purposes more important than to protect the hall for Herr Klemperer'.[11] As yet, however, there was no legal basis for dismissal. That omission was rapidly rectified. On 7 April the German government introduced a 'law for the restoration of the professional civil service' ('Gesetz zur Wiederherstellung des Berufsbeamtentums'), which enabled it to dismiss a public employee, a category into which Klemperer fell, on any grounds, such as non-Aryan descent, that rendered him or her undesirable.

Meanwhile the Berlin State Opera, eager to preserve a veil of legitimacy (it was still unclear whether the new regime would prove lasting), wrote on 11 April to enquire whether Klemperer would agree to his concert being given under another conductor, and whether in these circumstances the Berlin Philharmonic Chorus (of which he was still musical director) would be available to take part in the performance of Beethoven's Symphony No. 9 he had programmed. The letter ended 'with best wishes for your stay in Switzerland', for all the world as though he were there on holiday. Klemperer was, however, equally anxious not to burn his boats. In his answer he drily insisted that he was not in a position to enter into the issues the State Opera's letter had raised.

The report that Klemperer's name had been removed from the programme of the Berlin Festival was published as a decision taken by a committee of which Furtwängler was a member. Angered by this use of his name and doubtless disturbed by the contents of Hinkel's interview,[12] Furtwängler despatched on 6 April the first of many fruitless letters of protest to Hinkel's superior, Joseph Goebbels, the new Minister of Propaganda and Public Enlightenment.

> I allow myself [he wrote] to draw your attention to events in musical life that in my view are not a necessary part of the restoration of our national dignity which we all so gratefully and joyfully welcome.

Having thus distanced himself from opponents of the regime, Furtwängler continued,

> In the final resort I recognise a division only between good and bad art. Whereas the division between Jews and non-Jews ... is now drawn with unrelenting and theoretical harshness, even when the political behaviour of those affected has given no cause for complaint, the division between good and bad [art], which in the long run is so important, even decisive for our musical life, is all-too-much neglected ... It has therefore to be clearly said that men like [Bruno] Walter, Klemperer and [Max] Reinhardt, etc., must also be able to play their part in the Germany of the future ... I appeal to you in the name of German art, lest things should occur that perhaps cannot later be repaired.

It was bravely spoken, even if, by confining himself to the cases of three outstanding Jewish artists, Furtwängler made it plain that he was less concerned with the issue of racism than with the health of German cultural life. But Goebbels had little difficulty in rebutting his naïve attempt to draw a line between art and politics. In the *Berliner Lokal-Anzeiger* of 11 April (the same day as Furtwängler's letter appeared in the *Vossische Zeitung*), the Minister replied,

> Art must not only be good, it must be rooted in the people ... Art in an absolute sense, as liberal democracy knows it, is not permissible. To complain that, here and there, artists like Walter, Klemperer and Reinhardt are obliged to cancel concerts seems to me out of place in view of the fact that in the past fourteen years truly German artists have often been condemned to silence.

With that letter the regime made explicit its totalitarian claims in the field of cultural life. Furtwängler none the less remained unshaken in his belief in his ability, as Germany's leading musician, to influence its policies. Towards the end of April he wrote to Klemperer, urging him to return to Berlin, and offering to negotiate to that end with the authorities. By this time, however, Klemperer had acquired a firmer grasp of realities. From Fiesole he wrote to thank his colleague warmly for his support, but asked him on no account to intervene on his behalf.

True to Goebbels's promise, the National Socialist stranglehold on artistic life had already begun to tighten. On 27 April the Berlin State Opera revived *Tannhäuser*, not in Fehling's new production, which Klemperer had conducted the previous month, but in an old and more naturalistic staging. On the same day the head of the Frankfurt Museum concerts, which had earlier engaged Klemperer as conductor for the coming season, was curtly informed by the city's newly appointed Nazi burgomaster that 'the Opera House Orchestra cannot be made available for concerts under the direction of Kapellmeister Klemperer'.[13] In later years Klemperer declined all invitations to conduct in Frankfurt.

Such developments made it clear that he would not be able to fulfil his obligations as musical director of the Berlin Philharmonic Chorus, and he accordingly proposed to Furtwängler that these should for the time being be assumed by the Swiss conductor Ernest Ansermet. The suggestion was well calculated to discomfit the German authorities: the presence in Berlin of a conductor celebrated for his championship of Stravinsky and other 'decadent' composers would hardly have been welcome to the new regime, yet an open rejection of a distinguished Swiss conductor would have been embarrassing at a time when the regime was concerned to foster cultural relations with the outside world. Furtwängler seems to have nipped the proposal in the bud. But Klemperer persisted. Clearly savouring the embarrassment he was causing, he replied,

On the question of Ansermet, I cannot understand your position. Official declarations of the regime ... always emphasise how eager it is to engage foreign artists ... I esteem Ansermet greatly as an artist and at the moment cannot think of a more suitable conductor ... That he is French Swiss seems to me no disadvantage. In your open letter to Minister Goebbels you yourself, if I recall rightly, particularly emphasised that in art artistic ability must be decisive.[14]

On 14 May the Chorus loyally telegraphed verse greetings to Klemperer on his forty-eighth birthday. In less polished metres, he replied 'Grüsse gerne alle Damen. Wünsche Ansermet' ('Greetings to all the ladies. I would like Ansermet'). After the Ansermet project had come to nothing, Klemperer offered the position to Eugen Jochum, who declined on the grounds that 'the composition' of the Chorus (i.e. its predominantly Jewish membership) might cause him difficulties at the Berlin Radio, where he was musical director. The task was eventually assumed by Carl Schuricht. Within two years the membership of the choir had sunk to ninety-four. Later that summer, Furtwängler wrote again to acknowledge that any lingering hopes that Klemperer might be able to play a part in German musical life had vanished.[15] A projected meeting at St Moritz failed to materialise. Thereafter all contact ceased between the two greatest German conductors of their generation.

* * *

In March 1933, Klemperer had conducted the young Budapest Concert Orchestra for the first time and had been particularly delighted by 'the beauty and intensity'[16] of its Hubay-trained strings.* He made so deep an impression on the orchestra that it invited him to return in June to conduct it in the first Hungarian performance of Bartók's recently completed Piano Concerto No. 2,† and then to repeat it in Vienna, where the composer himself, who refused to perform in Budapest on account of what he considered to be the neglect there of his music, was to be the soloist. It was an engagement of special importance.

In spite of numerous reminders, Bartók's Viennese publishers failed to send a score to Fiesole. Klemperer thus arrived in Budapest towards the end of May ill-prepared to conduct a taxing work in an idiom largely unfamiliar to him. At his first encounter with the soloist, Lajos Kentner,‡ he made no bones about his unpreparedness, which was all too apparent in a chaotic opening

---

* The orchestra had been founded in 1930 by a group of young musicians who had recently left the Academy with the purpose of providing a counterbalance to the conservative programmes of the Philharmonic concerts. Jenö Hubay (1858–1937) was a celebrated teacher at the Liszt Academy for over fifty years.
† The work had been given its first performance at the Frankfurt Radio on 23 January 1933 with the composer as soloist. The conductor was Hans Rosbaud.
‡ Lajos (subsequently Louis) Kentner (1905–87) left Hungary in 1935 and later took British citizenship.

rehearsal. Klemperer's initial inability to master the bar changes rapidly led to tension.[17] There were disagreements with Bartók himself, and the leader of the orchestra, Tibor Ney, later contrasted Klemperer's 'loud and tyrannical' behaviour with the quietness of the composer, who sat in the auditorium with a metronome before him,[18] only at one point moving to the piano, so that, with Kentner conducting, Klemperer could listen to the balance.[19] Threatened with a débâcle, Klemperer set himself to mastering the score and, after no fewer than six rehearsals, conducted a performance which, like the work itself, was received with acclaim. The orchestra was so impressed that on the following day, 3 June, it invited him to become its permanent conductor.[20] Bartók, who was sparing with praise, later told his friend and champion, the critic Aladár Tóth, that he could not have conceived of a more complete account of the orchestral part of his concerto.[21]

The Budapest concert was, however, little more than a dress rehearsal for Vienna, where five days later Bartók himself took over the soloist's part. The conservative Viennese critics did not warm to a work outside their own tradition. In the *Neue Freie Presse* (9 June) Josef Reitler found the concerto lacking in melody and invention; the *Wiener Zeitung* (9 June) maintained that it offered nothing but 'motoric music, without emotion, forms or ideas other than that of movement'; in the *Neues Wiener Journal* (8 June) Joseph Marx dismissed it as deficient in ideas, themes, tunes and harmony. 'Taken as a whole', he concluded, 'it is an extremely modern, painfully dissident and musically unfruitful work.' Not for the first time, Vienna turned its back on music that broke new ground. In contrast, the visiting Hungarian critics hailed the work as a masterpiece.

In spite of the fact that he seems to have had little personal contact with the shy and withdrawn Bartók, Klemperer was enchanted by the sheer musicality of his pianism. 'The beauty of his tone, the energy and lightness of his playing were unforgettable. It was almost painfully beautiful.'[22] He was again impressed by the qualities of the orchestra's strings and at a post-concert party at the Ratskeller indicated that he might accept its invitation to 'become permanent conductor.[23] But, although Klemperer returned to conduct the orchestra in Budapest on several occasions in the next three seasons, nothing came of the idea owing to his commitments elsewhere. Not for another fourteen years, and in very different circumstances, did he find himself conducting the orchestra regularly.

*   *   *

Until the end of May 1933 Klemperer still clung to the hope that he would eventually be able to resume his career in Germany. However, on 2 June, the day of the Bartók concert in Budapest, Johanna telephoned from Zurich to tell him that a registered letter had arrived from Berlin giving him a month's notice of dismissal.[24] On 6 June the *Berliner Lokal-Anzeiger* reported that

> Generalmusikdirektor Otto Klemperer, who has been on the staff of the Berlin State Opera since 1927 has been notified by letter ... that his contract, which would have extended over a further four years, has been dissolved with immediate effect.*

The following day the *Vossische Zeitung*, flagship of the Ullstein press, which had preserved a vestige of its old liberal spirit, paid a tribute to Klemperer in terms that cannot have endeared it to the new rulers.

> In Klemperer, Berlin loses one of its most interesting musical characters. Much has been said and written against but also for his impact on Berlin. In any case he is a musician of really great stature, a spirit (*Geist*) that was always active and always activated the world around him.
>
> The State Opera am Platz der Republik [i.e. the Kroll] is closely linked to his name. It is still too fresh in the memory for it to be necessary to discuss the problems that it set out to solve ... a conception of combining a modern opera house with an opera house for the people was naturally not solved ... But memories of brilliant performances of *Oedipus Rex, Die Zauberflöte, The Marriage of Figaro* and other works will not be erased. And we shall also not forget what Klemperer achieved in the concert hall as an orchestral and choral conductor.

In its July number, the periodical *Melos*, which in the following summer paid with closure for its championship of contemporary music throughout the Weimar Republic, also saluted his achievements.

> Klemperer has been reproached for conducting too much modern music. In fact he gave only a few chosen works (Stravinsky, Hindemith) in performances that were recognised far beyond Berlin. His concert performances were exemplary in their blend of old and new ... His Bach and Bruckner performances remain a vivid memory.

In spite of these courageous tributes Klemperer's career in Germany was at an end. All that was left was for the lower echelons of the Prussian bureaucracy to tidy up the remnants. On 19 June the porter of the Linden Opera wrote to the backstage supervisor, asking if Herr Klemperer could return the keys he held. On the following day the question was raised of books and scores he had on loan. The tax authorities wrote to enquire of the day on which his dismissal would take effect. The State Opera replied that he would continue to be paid until the end of September 1933.[25] In that month

---

* Other Jewish members of the Berlin State Opera, notably the conductor Fritz Zweig and the soprano Lotte Schöne, were similarly dismissed. Exceptions were made for the conductor Leo Blech, and the singers Alexander Kipnis and Emanuel List, whose contracts expired in 1934. A few days earlier Schoenberg and Schreker were dismissed from their positions at the Akademie der Künste and the Hochschule für Musik.

Furtwängler, who had previously conducted at the Berlin State Opera only as a guest, was appointed its director.*

*   *   *

Klemperer considered the possibility of establishing himself in Vienna, the largest German-speaking musical centre still free of Nazi control. The child of an Austrian-born father, he was drawn to the city, its life and its musical tradition.† Vienna also seemed to offer a number of openings. The Philharmonic Orchestra was anxious to strengthen its ties to him. Announcing at a plenum meeting of the orchestra on 7 June Klemperer's engagement to conduct the opening and closing subscription concerts in the coming season, Burghauser stressed the importance of securing the services of a musician who was 'a great *Führernatur*' (the phrase was in the air).[26] On a more modest level, Klemperer was negotiating to give concerts with the Vienna Konzertorchester, a youthful group that had been founded the previous year, though nothing came of it. He was also involved in plans to set up a small touring opera company. Based in Vienna, it would employ a number of refugee artists and be modelled on Prince Reuss's Deutsche Musikbühne, which had so impressed him when he had attended rehearsals of Strauss's *Intermezzo* the previous summer.‡

It was not the only operatic opening that Vienna seemed to offer. In the summer of 1933 the State Opera was in the throes of one of its periodic bouts of intrigue. Clemens Krauss, its director, who had already been ousted as conductor of the Vienna Philharmonic Orchestra, was under attack, and his First Conductor, Robert Heger, had accepted an invitation to join the depleted staff of the Berlin State Opera. There were those in Vienna who considered Klemperer to be the man to succeed Heger, though whether there was any serious prospect of such an engagement is open to doubt: there was an unstated understanding in Austria that the number of Jews in such positions should remain limited.

In any case, Klemperer's behaviour did nothing to foster his chances of an appointment at the State Opera. In the last week of May he attended the dress rehearsal of a new production of *Die Zauberflöte* conducted by Krauss. He was in exuberant spirits and, according to Alfred Rosenzweig, uttered derisive comments from the stalls that Krauss could hardly fail to hear.[27]

---

* The contract was not signed until 16 January 1934 (Prieberg, *Kraftprobe*, p. 161).
† 'I like Vienna. Maybe it is an unhappy love, but I love it. I know the people are false ... [but] there is music, the greatest music, in the stones of the streets' (Heyworth (ed.), *Conversations*, p. 114).
‡ The Independent International Opera (UNIO), as it was at first called, developed into the Salzburg International Opera Guild, which toured in America and elsewhere. Sir Rudolf Bing (b. 1902), subsequently general manager of Glyndebourne and the New York Metropolitan Opera, was its administrator. Klemperer held auditions in Vienna in September 1933 and, together with Bruno Walter and Stefan Zweig, issued a statement of aims. But other commitments obliged him to abandon his original intention to act as artistic director.

Rosenzweig's account must, however, be regarded with reserve. Hilde Firtel, who sat beside Klemperer at the rehearsal, has said that he did indeed make unflattering comments, but doubted whether they were audible to Krauss. The following day Rosenzweig called on Klemperer at the Imperial Hotel to warn him against making himself a party to, as he put it, the conspiracy which was being organised against Krauss by Hugo Burghauser of the Vienna Philharmonic. Klemperer, who at that time had not yet received the sobering news of his dismissal from the Berlin State Opera, responded with loud abuse of Krauss in the public rooms of Vienna's leading hotel. On 17 June Klemperer was enraged to learn that the Austrian conductor Josef Krips* had been appointed to Heger's position at the Opera, while Fritz Busch and Bruno Walter had been invited to conduct guest performances.

Nevertheless, Vienna seemed to hold out promise of enough work for Klemperer to opt for 'pitching our tents' there, as he cautiously put it in a letter to the theatre director Natalia Satz on 27 July. Since 1918 the Austrian government had pursued a policy of renting accommodation in former imperial palaces to artists of outstanding merit, and Burghauser's official contacts enabled Klemperer to secure an apartment in the former imperial palace of Schönbrunn, in the south-western suburbs of the city. The accommodation, which was on the ground floor and gave directly on to the Kammergarten, had been occupied a century earlier by the Duke of Reichstadt, Napoleon's son by Maria Louise, Archduchess of Austria. The rooms were spacious, their outlook splendid. They were, however, ill suited to winter habitation. Such considerations did not deter Klemperer. Work was put in hand to install new heating and plumbing and the bills were met by Mark Brunswick, who had by this time fallen under the spell of his magnetic new friend. Felix Augenfeld, the architect engaged to supervise the alterations, found Klemperer 'irascible, erratic and domineering'. He was also struck by his lack of interest in practical and visual details. The workmen employed were, he noted, none the less fascinated by their strange and unpredictable client.†

*   *   *

In the course of 1933 Klemperer had come to realise that the world outside Germany was not necessarily well-disposed to victims of racial persecution. The first shock had been provided by the Zurich City Theatre. Eager to avail himself of the presence in the town of a conductor of world renown, its director, Karl Schmid-Bloss, had invited Klemperer shortly after his arrival

---

* Josef Krips (1902–74) lost his position in 1938 as a 'half-Jew', but was reappointed in 1945.
† Interviews with Felix Augenfeld (November 1977 and February 1981), who claimed that he never received payment from Klemperer for his services. Augenfeld (1893–1984) was noted for having 'created a special chair to accommodate the position that Sigmund Freud liked to sit in' (Obituary, *New York Times*, 23 July 1984).

in Zurich in April to conduct and stage a new production of *Fidelio* in the June Festival. In May Schmid-Bloss was obliged to inform Klemperer that the production had been postponed until the following season. That was less than the truth. On 3 May the Stadttheater's board of management had rejected his engagement as a guest artist.* No grounds were given.

Other blows followed. Shortly after returning to Fiesole at the end of June, Klemperer set out for Rome. His purpose was to urge his old acquaintance Cardinal Pacelli to intercede on behalf of the Jews in Germany. The Vatican's Secretary of State replied that the Church's aid had already been invoked from many sides. To Klemperer's amazement, he added that the differences between the Christian and the Jewish faiths could not be overlooked, as though to imply that the fate of German Jews was not an immediate concern of the Vatican. The Holy See had indeed other fish to fry: since the spring Pacelli had been personally involved in negotiating a concordat with the new rulers of Germany that was on the point of being initialled when Klemperer was in Rome. Pacelli procured an audience with Pope Pius XI, but beforehand cautioned Klemperer not to raise political issues, which the Holy Father did not care to discuss.[28] Klemperer was shocked by what he took to be the Vatican's unwillingness to engage itself on behalf of the Jews. Henceforth his attitude to the Church, though not to matters of dogma and faith, grew markedly more reserved.

The Vatican was not alone in its eagerness to reach an understanding with the Third Reich. After learning that he had been falsely listed as a Jew by Alfred Rosenberg's Kampfbund für deutsche Kultur, Stravinsky became apprehensive at the prospect of losing the earnings that German concert tours with the (Jewish) violinist Samuel Dushkin had brought him in the two previous seasons. In June 1933 he complained to his Berlin adviser, Fyodor Vladimirovich Weber, about the disfavour into which he had fallen in Berlin. 'I am surprised', he wrote, 'since my negative attitude to Communism and Judaism is – not to put it in stronger terms – a matter of common knowledge.'[29] By July, however, Willy Strecker, his German publisher, felt able to assure him that 'the danger has now passed' and that 'the guidelines set by the new music commission† will prove to be quite rational'.[30] Thus when in late August Stravinsky received an appeal from Klemperer, Bruno Walter and the writer Stefan Zweig asking for his support for the small opera company that Klemperer was attempting to establish in Vienna, his initial reaction was to avoid any action that might jeopardise his prospects in Germany. 'Is it politically wise', he wrote on 7 September to his Parisian publisher, Gavril

---

* Minutes of the Verwaltungsrat of the Stadttheater in the Zurich Stadtarchiv. On the day before the Verwaltungsrat made this decision, the *Neue Zürcher Zeitung* (2 May 1933) reported that the association of Swiss theatres had urged its members to avoid whenever possible the dismissal of Swiss personnel.

† Presumably the Reichsmusikkammer, established by Goebbels in September 1933.

Gavrilovich Païchadze, 'to identify myself with Jews like Klemperer and Walter ...? I do not want to risk seeing my name beside such trash as Milhaud [also a Jew] who have made their careers on the backs of others.' On reflection Stravinsky gave the as yet unborn company his blessing,[31] so that Klemperer never learnt of the initial unwillingness of the composer, whose music he had so resolutely championed at the Kroll, to lend support in his hour of need. But his mood darkened as he began to grasp the readiness of the world outside Germany to accommodate the barbarians in Berlin. 'Schreckliches wird geschehen' ('something terrible will happen'),* he wrote to Dorothea Alexander-Katz on 25 July as he sensed the growing menace in the air.

The German government had meanwhile found a new means of putting pressure on Jews who had escaped its clutches. On 26 July it introduced a *Reichsfluchtsteuer* (literally, a 'tax on fleeing the country'), whose effect was to tax emigrants with estates valued at more than 200,000 RM.† The sum demanded of Klemperer amounted to 4,550 RM. When he declined to pay on the grounds that he had not left Germany voluntarily, the authorities refused permission for him to export his possessions. He was, they informed him, free to live in Germany without work, as so many army officers had been obliged to do during the Weimar Republic.[32] A $50,000 life assurance policy he had taken out in 1926 was seized and in July 1934 a warrant was issued for his arrest in the improbable event of his return to Germany. The dispute dragged on until 1935, when he was informed that, after deductions for income and emigration taxes, a sum of $6,000 remained to his credit.[33] Owing to currency restrictions, the money could not, however, be transferred abroad.

These events further dispelled the blithe buoyancy with which Klemperer had sailed through his first months of emigration, and as his euphoria declined he turned again to his wife, whom he had scarcely seen since April. At the end of July, when his lease of 'Il Nido' expired, the family was reunited at St Jean-de-Luz. It proved, however, a brief holiday, for on 15 August Klemperer set out alone for Salzburg, where he was to make his first appearance at the festival.

* * *

The atmosphere in Salzburg was tense. From the day he had obtained power Hitler had declared that he intended to unite all German-speaking peoples in a single state: 'ein Volk, ein Reich, ein Führer', as the slogan had it. It was a policy that attracted considerable support within Austria itself,‡ and nowhere more so than in the Alpine provinces of the Tyrol and Salzburg,

---

* Slightly incorrect quotation from German translation of Wilde's text used in Strauss's *Salome*.
† Approximately £20,000 in 1933. On 18 May 1934 the sum on which tax was levied was reduced to 50,000 RM (£5,000), thus catching emigrants of even modest means.
‡ In 1919 even the Austrian socialist party, seeing little future in a rump State, had supported an *Anschluss*, though with a Germany very different from Hitler's.

whose inhabitants felt more kinship with the Bavarians over the frontier than with the more racially mixed and urban Viennese. In local elections in Innsbruck on 23 April 1933 no less than 41 per cent of the electorate had voted for the National Socialists. The following day the *Neue Zürcher Zeitung* described the mood in the frontier town of Salzburg as noticeably open to Nazism. Nowhere in Austria, it reported, was resistance to it so weak.

The new German government had already set out to destabilise Austria. Bombs exploded on the railways and in telephone booths. An Austrian *Freikorps* was established in Bavaria, to be deployed on the day of liberation. On 13 May Hans Frank, at that point of his career Bavarian Minister of Justice and Reichsjustizkommissar, addressed a Nazi meeting in Vienna without the permission of the Austrian authorities. When the Austrian government protested at this affront, Berlin responded by imposing a 1,000 RM tax on German visitors to Austria. The intention was to undermine the tourism on which the fragile Austrian economy was largely dependent. Its impact on the Salzburg Festival was calamitous. The number of Germans attending fell from 12,983 in 1932 to 796 in 1933. In a further attempt to undermine the festival, non-Austrian artists were warned that their appearance would result in the cancellation of their German contracts. Explosions continued to occur in the streets and Nazi leaflets were widely distributed, although the party had officially been banned in Austria.

Klemperer chose to stay in the Benedictine Abbey of St Peter, close to the Festspielhaus. The accommodation cost a modest three Schillings a night and he described it to Johanna as 'wonderful'. At the Café Bazar, the social hub of the festival, he ran into Richard Strauss, who, in spite of Berlin's ban on German artists taking part in the festival, had conducted the opening *Fidelio*. Klemperer was disgusted by Strauss's failure to enquire further into how he was faring.[34] He attended an open-air performance of Hofmannsthal's *Jedermann*, which was ruined by a downpour. The celebrated production, by Max Reinhardt, held little appeal for him. 'When one pursues the crassest naturalism', he wrote to Johanna, 'nature avenges itself.'[35]

To avoid repeating Bruckner's Symphony No. 5, which he had given four months earlier in Vienna, Klemperer elected to conduct No. 8 in Salzburg. In contrast to the almost unanimous enthusiasm he had evoked on the earlier occasion, his Salzburg concert on 20 August had a mixed reception. Although the *Wiener Zeitung* (27 August) described it as 'a triumph', the *Neues Wiener Journal* (23 August) found his account of the great Adagio lacking in warmth, while the *Neue Freie Presse* (22 August) noted a want of Brucknerian lyricism. Klemperer's austere and architectural approach to the music did not appeal to all Austrian ears, and he was not approached again by the Salzburg Festival until after the war.

On arrival in Vienna, he moved at once into a single room of the

Schönbrunn apartment and sent Johanna an ecstatic account of their new home.

> The apartment is indescribable. The couch appeared promptly on Monday afternoon. The piano was already there. I bought a stool for myself at Bösendorfer's. So I am 'set up'. The bed linen had already arrived from Zurich and I slept like a prince ('wie Gott in Frankreich') by an open window. In the morning a walk in the garden. I hope that the apartment's wonderful harmony will also affect you. It is really a great blessing for us all that we are able to live there. Please write to ... Schönbrunn, Vienna – that's sufficient.[36]

Visitors were as enchanted by these surroundings as was their host. But a darker side of Austrian life soon began to reveal itself.

* * *

In July 1933, Klemperer had been approached by Burghauser of the Vienna Philharmonic on a matter connected with the Church. Between 7 and 12 September a great ecclesiastical gathering was to take place in Vienna in commemoration of the two-hundred-and-fiftieth anniversary of the raising of the siege of the city by the Turks. The Allgemeine Deutsche Katholikentag had been planned the previous year, but had in the meantime come to acquire an unintended political significance. In reaction to National Socialist pressure the Austrian Chancellor, Engelbert Dollfuss, had dissolved parliament and on 21 May 1933 set up a 'Patriotic Front'. He had also sought and received support from Mussolini. As the British legation in Vienna reported that summer, 'Austria would appear to have avoided Nazi domination by accepting fascism.'[37] But, unlike its Italian counterpart, Austrian fascism had a strong clerical component. The Church was an essential pillar of the new 'Front', and the Katholikentag accordingly turned into a demonstration of that commitment.

The celebrations were planned on a massive scale. Ecclesiastical dignitaries from many lands attended. Trainloads of pious peasants were brought to the capital. There were processions and parades, and open-air masses were celebrated before vast congregations. There were endless speeches, including one in which Dollfuss, at a meeting of the Vaterlandische Front, denounced 'godless Marxism' and 'so-called democracy', and called for 'a renewal of the State' in an authoritarian mould.[38] He later rode in uniform around the Ringstrasse at the head of armed formations.

Music inevitably had a part to play. Among the events planned was a 'Geistliches ("spiritual") Konzert' to be given in the Musikverein by the Vienna Philharmonic Orchestra, and what conductor could be more suited to such an occasion than a convert who had not only made his home in Vienna but was widely supposed to have arrived in the city with influential recommendations to the Austrian hierarchy?[39] Klemperer readily accepted the invitation and at once informed Burghauser that the programme would consist of Palestrina's *Missa Iste Confessor* and Bruckner's Symphony No. 9, both works well matched to the occasion.

None the less, on 27 August he wrote to tell Johanna that he would not be conducting the concert.

> Reason: a friendly cleric, who recently spoke so warmly about the 'Führer' at a party at Frau Mahler's, has explained that owing to the *Schumann* affair (twenty years ago!)* the Katholikentag could not accept me. Nice, isn't it? Baptism, in which everything, even everything in the past, is wiped out, seems not to exist for this priest.

Meanwhile the Archbishop's Palace had let it be known that, in the circumstances, Cardinal Innitzer, who had planned to attend, would be unable to do so.

Klemperer was disappointed, but a *deus ex machina* appeared in the person of the financial administrator of the diocese, who had the cardinal's ear and procured an audience at which Klemperer was permitted to put his case. He argued, as he had done in the letter to his wife, that the general absolution he had received on entering the Church in 1919 had expurgated all his earlier sins. The cardinal conceded that he stood on strong theological ground and withdrew his opposition. In gratitude, Klemperer presented him with a copy of his biblical opera *Der verlorene Sohn*.

The concert was, however, less than a complete success. The Musikverein Hall was not full and Klemperer's rare incursion into the field of early music produced bizarre results. On grounds of authenticity he adamantly resisted all attempts to persuade him to include accidentals on leading notes in the Palestrina Mass. They were, he argued, not in the score.[40] To the astonishment of the critic of the *Neues Wiener Journal* (12 September), he omitted the Credo. Klemperer was vexed by his inability to obtain the services of the Vienna Boys' Choir (they were no doubt as usual singing at High Mass in the Hofkapelle on Sunday morning), as he was thus unable to give the Mass with boys' voices, as he had intended.[41]

Nor did his decision to give the Bruckner symphony in its original version, which differed in structure as well as instrumentation from the Löwe version in which it was still more usually performed,† meet with unqualified approval. Both Julius Korngold (*Neue Freie Presse*, 12 September 1933) and Max Graf (*Wiener Tag*, 12 September) maintained that the manuscript of the Adagio (the last movement Bruckner completed in 1894) was too sketchy to provide the basis for a performance. Yet one member of the audience was overcome by the peculiar intensity that Klemperer, the apostle of literalism,

---

* In 1912 Klemperer had eloped with the soprano Elisabeth Schumann.
† Robert Haas's *Urfassung* of Bruckner's Symphony No. 9 had only been heard for the first time in Vienna in the previous year, when it had been conducted by Clemens Krauss.

paradoxically brought to the music. Forty years later, Neville Cardus recalled that 'as he stood there, arms uplifted, ready to begin ... the audience was tense and dead silent. Before Klemperer's baton moved and before a note was heard, an elderly Viennese gentleman sitting next to me covered his face with his hands and burst into tears.'[42]

The Vienna Philharmonic Orchestra's opening subscription concert, which Klemperer conducted on 1 October, similarly failed to arouse the enthusiasm that had greeted his début in the spring. In his review of the 'Eroica' Symphony, which opened the programme, Joseph Marx, who had become the spokesman for Klemperer's decriers in Vienna,* returned in the *Neues Wiener Journal* (3 October) to his theme that his musical style was ill-matched to the Austrian classics. He was, Marx wrote,

> the type of energetic orchestral director who commands the formal construction of a work of art down to the last detail. This intellectual approach ... lends itself particularly to the performance of constructivist (*konstruierter*) contemporary music ... but it fails where music is an art of the soul, is involved in sensibility and feeling, as it is in classical Viennese music ... His gestures reflect this intellectual approach to the work ... Often one has an impression that he is taming the orchestra ... with ruthless and brutal movements. In spite of his strength of will, his seriousness and the passionate nature of his character, an immense coolness informs his achievements. It may be that he is a good conductor, but in no way does he succeed in luring us into the lovely, romantic terrain of art that is really felt, and it is just there that – for me, at least – great artistry begins.

Marx's review well expressed the reaction of a romantic sensibility allergic to Klemperer's rigorous musicianship. Other Viennese critics were impressed by the architectural grandeur he revealed in the 'Eroica', while the performance of Bach's Cantata No. 21, with which he ended his concert (Elisabeth Schumann was the soprano soloist), was widely praised. Yet a repetition of his earlier triumph had again eluded him.

None the less there remained much that bound Klemperer to Vienna. He had acquired splendid accommodation. He had established a close association with the orchestra he liked best, and there was a prospect of other work both in Vienna itself and in nearby Budapest. In Johanna's absence he lived more convivially than he had ever done in Berlin. He was a regular visitor to the Mahler-Werfels and to the Brunswicks, where occasionally he even contributed to musical evenings. The singers Jarmila Novotna and Rose Pauly, as well as Elisabeth Schumann,† were living in the city and he saw them

---

* It is hard to avoid the impression that in the matter of Klemperer, as in so much else, critical opinion in Vienna divided between Jews and non-Jews. At all events, his principal champions, Max Graf and Paul Stefan, were Jews, while his principal adversary, Joseph Marx, was not.

† In a characteristically generous gesture of support, Schumann included a group of Klemperer's songs in a recital she gave at the Queen's Hall in London on 28 November 1933. They elicited no more than a non-committal mention in *The Times* of the following day.

frequently. There were also new friends, among them Princess Marie Bonaparte,* a close friend of Mark Brunswick's wife, Ruth Mack. The princess was one of Klemperer's first visitors at Schönbrunn. Ten days later she returned with Freud and his wife.[43] Klemperer was deeply impressed by the character of the founder of psychoanalysis. What the great man thought of his host is unrecorded, but at some point Klemperer must have returned the call, for he later recollected the Indian artefacts that stood on Freud's desk.

Yet the outlook in Austria remained uncertain. Anti-Semitism was rampant, even within the hierarchy itself,[44] and Dollfuss's authoritarian regime lacked firm foundations. Would Austria prove able to preserve its independence of Germany? Would Klemperer's rigorous musicianship prove compatible to Viennese taste? Those questions remained unanswered when, on 2 October, the morning after his Philharmonic subscription concert, he set out on a two-week journey that was to take him to a remote and alien land.

* A lateral descendent of Napoleon I, Marie Bonaparte (1882–1962) married Prince George of Greece, younger brother of Constantine I in 1907. In 1925 she embarked on a training analysis with Freud, of whom she became a close friend and disciple. Thereafter she devoted her considerable wealth and talents to psychoanalysis. In particular, she used her royal status to rescue many of Freud's papers and some of his savings after the Nazi occupation of Austria obliged him to seek refuge in England.

2

'A cloudburst of non-sequiturs'

Klemperer had sought an American engagement several months before the National Socialists came to power in Germany. In October 1932 he had asked Willy Strecker of Schott's, who had been instrumental in procuring his initial engagement with the New York Symphony Orchestra in 1926, whether any openings were available in the United States. Later that year he had written again to Strecker, to enquire whether there might not be a vacancy in Chicago, where the orchestra's conductor, Frederick Stock, was said to be resigning (Klemperer was misinformed). With his reply (31 January 1933) Strecker enclosed a letter from America that stressed the difficulties orchestras there were experiencing during a period of acute economic depression, and instanced the Los Angeles Philharmonic Orchestra, whose precarious condition had led its conductor, Artur Rodzinski, to seek a position elsewhere.

With Hitler installed as Chancellor, the matter became more pressing, and on 25 February Klemperer wrote directly to Arthur Judson, the head of Columbia Artists Management, by far the largest American agency of its kind. In his reply of 15 March Judson repeated what Klemperer had already been told by Strecker: the slump had obliged many conductors to take cuts in their salaries. However, said Judson, there was 'a real future for you in America', though he advised Klemperer only to accept a position with one of the four first-class orchestras, by which he meant Boston, New York, Philadelphia and Chicago (the rise of Cleveland only occurred after the Second World War). Unfortunately, as Judson confirmed in a telegram on 13 April, there were no vacancies with any of them. In the event it was the Los Angeles orchestra that offered Klemperer work during the coming season.

The Los Angeles Philharmonic Orchestra had been founded only fourteen years earlier on the initiative of one immensely rich man, whose support in 1933 still remained the basis of its existence. Williams Andrews Clark had been born in 1877, the son of a senator of the State of Montana, whose wealth stemmed from copper deposits in Arizona. As a small child he had accompanied his mother to Paris, where he learnt French so well that on arrival in Los Angeles at the age of five he had difficulty in expressing himself in English. Shrewd investments enabled Clark to augment the fortune he in due course inherited and thus to indulge his artistic interests. From an early age he collected books and later built a library to house his acquisitions in the grounds of his mansion on West Adams Boulevard.*

Clark's other absorbing passion was music. As a boy in Paris he studied the violin under the Belgian pedagogue Martin Marsick, whose pupils included Jacques Thibaud and Georges Enesco. In 1911 Clark established the Saint-Saëns String Quartet in Los Angeles and himself played second violin. Eight years later he founded the Los Angeles Philharmonic Orchestra, which gave its inaugural concert on 24 October 1919. To accommodate its concerts he leased Cline's Auditorium in Pershing Square in the centre of down-town Los Angeles.[1] Los Angeles was, however, too remote from the hub of American concert life on the east coast to attract first-rate conductors. Until 1927 the orchestra was conducted by the British-born Walter Rothwell, who for a short period in 1895 in Hamburg had been assistant to Mahler. He was later dismissed as 'a comparative nonentity' by a local critic of repute, who went on to describe Rothwell's Finnish successor, Georg Schnéevoigt, as being 'tired, lazy and temperamentally unsuited', and Artur Rodzinski, who was only thirty-five on his appointment in 1929, as no more than 'an advanced beginner',[2] though a fellow critic subsequently claimed that Rodzinski had given the orchestra a degree of discipline and virtuosity it had previously lacked.[3]

After ten years, during which he had supported the orchestra virtually single-handed, Clark attempted in 1929 to hand it over to a committee, but public interest was so minimal that he was obliged to resume the burden.[4] However, his wealth had been so depleted by the slump that on 12 January 1933 he gave notice that he would cease to pay for the orchestra at the end of the current season. Two days later it was announced that Rodzinski had been released from his contract and that no successor would be appointed.[5] Should concerts prove feasible in the following season, conductors would be invited on an *ad hoc* basis. (Curiously enough, Klemperer's name was among those listed for consideration as early as February 1933, before any contact with him had been established.)[6] On 28 February an appeal for funds was launched, though by late April only $180,000 had been raised, which suggests limited public involvement in a conurbation whose population already amounted to 1,100,000. However, it was sufficient to persuade Clark to resume his support temporarily and to look for a conductor. Negotiations with Klemperer were opened in April, though at first they do not seem to have gone smoothly.† But by 10 June they were sufficiently advanced for Clark to

---

* His collection included twelve Shakespeare folios, four copies of the first edition of *Paradise Lost* and a unique assembly of writings by and on Dryden. He also collected material relating to Oscar Wilde, an unusual interest in the early years of the century. In 1926 Clark bequeathed his library and its contents to the University of California (Los Angeles).

† Klemperer later stated that the initial suggestion that he should conduct the orchestra had come from an American woman he had chanced to meet in Florence (Heyworth (ed.), *Conversations*, p. 71).

invite Klemperer to meet him in Paris. Klemperer felt that the salary offered was low, but Judson assured him that Los Angeles could not pay more.[7] Thus scarcely more than two weeks after his dismissal from Berlin he signed the offered contract. At least his immediate future was assured.

* * *

Klemperer set out for America on 2 October 1933 with a heavy heart. Johanna had only recently rejoined him at Schönbrunn after a separation that had lasted throughout much of the summer. As the tenderness and frequency of his letters from America reveal, they were again as close as they ever had been. Yet for the first time in their marriage they were now obliged to live at different ends of the globe for a period of over half a year. 'Don't be sad', Klemperer wrote from on board ship, two days after embarkation. 'When we decided that I should travel alone, we did so for the sake of the children.' On the *Ile de France* his spirits were raised by the lively company of the pianist Artur Schnabel. But his first glimpse of New York after an interval of six years did nothing to sustain them. 'After Vienna', he wrote to Johanna on 11 October, 'America seems even uglier than it did after Berlin.' In New York a discussion with Bruno Walter about the desirability of boycotting Richard Strauss's music, because of his acquiescence in the Nazi regime, led to a predictable disagreement. '*He* is going to perform it', Klemperer scornfully reported to Johanna. Klemperer determined not to do so for 'as long as I possibly can'.[8]

After a rail journey lasting three days and three nights, he arrived at his final destination on 14 October. At Santa Fe station he was greeted by a brass fanfare. There followed what the *Los Angeles Times* (22 October) enthusiastically described as 'a whirl of meetings, dinners, audiences and rehearsals' that reached its climax in a civic reception at which the comedian Eddie Cantor acted as toast-master and Grace Moore, Hollywood's leading songstress, sang arias. There were countless interviews. One journalist noted with amazement that Klemperer was unfamiliar with the names of some of Hollywood's best-known celebrities. Asked which director he admired, he cited the Frenchman René Clair and instanced *The Mother*, a classic of the Russian silent cinema, as a film that had given him particular pleasure.

Klemperer found Los Angeles every bit as strange as it found him. The place, he wrote to Johanna three days after his arrival, was really 'an enormous village. Lots of small low houses. Distances such as we can hardly conceive of. It takes me twenty-five minutes by car to the concert hall.' In the course of the past three decades the County of Los Angeles, which even in the twenties was larger than the State of Connecticut, had witnessed a prodigious boom, fuelled by the discovery of oil in 1892, winter tourism, real estate and, after the First World War, the establishment of Hollywood as the centre of the world's rapidly growing film industry. Between 1900 and 1930 the population had increased twelvefold. An average of 100,000 newcomers had arrived annually, so that by 1930 native-born Californians constituted no more than 20 per cent of the population. Half the population had lived in the region for less than five years. Farms and orange groves gave way to a vast suburban sprawl, in which shopping centres and petrol stations were often the only landmarks. A municipal ordinance of 1906 limiting the height of buildings to 150 feet had led development to spread horizontally.* Los Angeles, as Ogden Nash put it, was 'a cloudburst of non-sequiturs'.[9]

Klemperer's English was poor and his acquaintances were largely German-speaking. Southern California as yet contained no large colony of Central European intellectuals and artists, such as gathered there during the Second World War. Many Jews and opponents of Nazism still remained in Germany in the hope that the regime would not last,† while those who had emigrated had in the main moved to neighbouring countries, the intellectuals to France, the political refugees to Prague. Few could as yet bring themselves to believe that the world would permit the Hitler regime to overrun Europe. Such Central Europeans as already lived in Los Angeles were in the main associated with the film industry.

Among this group the screenwriter Salka Viertel played a central role. Klemperer found her 'a clever (*kluge*) woman',[10] and hers was one of the few *salons* he ever frequented. Among other acquaintances was the Austrian-born conductor Richard Lert, who had moved to America when his wife Vicki Baum, the popular novelist, had embarked on a career as a scriptwriter in Hollywood. Mark Brunswick's brother David and his wife also lived in Los Angeles and attempted to alleviate Klemperer's loneliness. 'A beam of light in this "intellectual desert"' was Rolf Hoffmann, professor of German at the University of California in Los Angeles.[11] Klemperer also met the pianist Richard Buhlig, who later became almost his only American-born friend in the area. But Klemperer's most regular companion in his first weeks in California was Max Reinhardt's twenty-year-old son Gottfried, who worked for MGM as an assistant to the director Ernst Lubitsch and thus formed a link between Hollywood and the immigrant writers and musicians. One evening Gottfried persuaded Klemperer to go to a movie at the Egyptian Theatre in Hollywood Boulevard, where the show was preceded by live music. When the band struck up the prologue to *I Pagliacci*, Klemperer leapt to his feet like a

---

* John Russell Taylor, *Strangers in Paradise*, p. 33. Until the ordinance was repealed in the sixties, down-town Los Angeles remained the only section of the city to be built to the height limitations it imposed.

† It was only in 1935 that the Nuremberg Laws formally deprived Jews of their citizenship and rights. Not until the *Kristallnacht* of December 1938 did physical violence against Jews become widespread and systematic.

man who had sat on a hornet. 'Leoncavallo!' he exclaimed. 'No movie will make me listen to that.'[12]

He was at first happy to be a guest in Clark's mansion on West Adams Boulevard, where, he wrote to Johanna (17 October), he had 'a beautiful bedroom with bath and every care'. But conversation was made difficult by his host's deafness. Clark also began to reveal disconcerting characteristics. 'Though Mr Clark is certainly very nice', Klemperer wrote to Johanna on 31 October, '... he is unfortunately addicted to alcohol and therefore often unbearable.' That was not Clark's only weakness. He was liable to appear naked at the breakfast table and on one occasion, similarly unclad, sat on Klemperer's bed and attempted to stroke his arm.[13] Scarcely three weeks after Klemperer's arrival, Clark suddenly announced that he would be leaving for Europe and closing his establishment while away. Though he had been led to suppose that he would be Clark's guest throughout his stay in Los Angeles and the expense of a hotel was unwelcome, Klemperer was relieved to move. 'Clark is basically a poor devil (in spite of his money)', he wrote to Johanna on 6 November. 'He should really be under supervision. And I think he is under bad influences ... I just wanted to get away from him ... as, to put it mildly, I found his behaviour offensive.'

In spite of its excellent acoustics, the Auditorium provided wretched accommodation for concerts. The building was the property of the adjacent Temple Baptist Church and on occasions the sound of hymns penetrated the hall. That was not the only disturbance. Traffic noises were audible and the seats squeaked. The primitive ventilation system could be heard during quiet music. There was no adequate ushering; late-comers, whose footsteps echoed on uncarpeted staircases, took their seats more or less as they pleased, sometimes to Klemperer's visible annoyance. The lavatories were abominable.*

Klemperer at first described the orchestra to Johanna, in his letter of 17 October, as 'very good and very nice'. Two weeks later he modified that praise. 'It is not all *that* good', he wrote on 31 October. 'I must not think of Vienna.' It was in fact something of a curate's egg. Clark had imported a handful of first-class principals at a high salary.† Other talented players had been drawn to Los Angeles by the high wages paid by the moving picture industry, but, as Klemperer was to learn, the Hollywood film studios also represented a drain on the orchestra. Personnel were constantly changing, in

---

* *Daily News*, 18 April 1934. Partly as a result of this article and a threatened boycott of a group of subscribers, it was announced five days later that the Auditorium would be refurbished. But it was not until thirty-one years later that Los Angeles provided itself with a purpose-built concert hall with the opening of the Dorothy Chandler Pavilion in 1965.

† Among these principals were Alfred Brain, a member of the British dynasty of outstanding horn players, Frederick Moritz (bassoon), Vladimir Druckner (trumpet), Henri DeBusscher (oboe), Sylvain Noack (violin), Emile Ferrir (viola) (Sven Reher, UCLA Oral History Program 300/191, p. 236).

part owing to the insistence of the musicians' union that instrumentalists should establish a year's residency in the area before they could apply for more remunerative employment in Hollywood.[14] In the opinion of Frederick Moritz, a long-time member of the orchestra who had earlier been a bassoonist in the Leipzig Gewandhaus Orchestra under Nikisch, the winds were better than the strings, whose back desks contained a good deal of dead wood.[15]

It took the orchestra some time to adjust itself to Klemperer's exacting methods and often sarcastic manner.[16] Tension rose at a rehearsal when he ordered a player to remove a piece of gum from his mouth. Klemperer, for his part, did not warm to American informality. The manager's wife, Caroline E. Smith, announced that they would call him 'Klempie'. 'You may call me', he snapped, 'but I shall not come.' Nor did he readily grasp that rehearsals could not be extended as and when he desired. Coming from a country where democracy stopped short of the concert hall, he stormed out of a rehearsal on discovering that two players had been released from their contracts to enable them to work in a studio.[17] Clark, who took it for granted that the orchestral management should 'not stand in the way of the men bettering their positions', regarded Klemperer's behaviour as 'childish'.[18] Nevertheless, Klemperer got his way and the players were persuaded to remain with the orchestra until the end of the season.

The opening pair of concerts on 19 and 20 October 1933 were sold out, at that time a rare event in Los Angeles.[19] Charles Chaplin and the film director King Vidor were both present at the first one. Klemperer's appearance on the platform was heralded with a fanfare and the audience rose to greet him. Although he had had no more than three days of rehearsal, his impact on the orchestra was already apparent in a programme that consisted of Bach's Toccata in C minor in Leo Weiner's arrangement,* Stravinsky's *Petrushka* and Beethoven's Fifth Symphony. José Rodriguez, the area's most perspicacious and literate critic, noted that it was the first time that he had heard the Los Angeles Philharmonic play 'as a genuine ensemble'.[20] His colleague, Bruno Ussher, concurred. 'The orchestra', he wrote, 'has not performed with such balance and clarity for a long time.'[21] Rodriguez described the Stravinsky as 'luminous and brilliant'; *Musical America* (10 November) found the Beethoven electrifying. Many reviews commented on Klemperer's sober manner of conducting.

The concert ended with ovations such as Los Angeles had rarely, if ever, extended to a conductor.[22] At first Klemperer was dismayed to hear the sound of whistling; only on returning backstage did he learn that in America this did

---

* In contrast to the more austere style of the Bach performances Klemperer had given in Berlin, for a few years after leaving Germany he frequently performed Bach in Weiner's orchestral arrangements.

not, as in Europe, indicate disapprobation.[23] However, the evening ended on a discordant note. In his dressing-room, Klemperer was startled to hear the strains of Sousa's *Stars and Stripes Forever* emerging from the auditorium. On returning, he discovered that Clark, who had sat among the first violins during the concert, was taking his turn to conduct the orchestra. Enraged, Klemperer ordered his employer to leave and Clark meekly obeyed.[24]

Much excitement was occasioned in publicity-struck Los Angeles by the huge stature of a 'Titan of Tone', who, in the words of one critic, 'looks as though he could whip Carnera'.* [25] But Klemperer's triumph proved more than an overnight sensation. Within little more than a month of his arrival the *Pacific Coast Musician* (25 November) reported that he had 'captured the imagination and musical admiration of the concert-going public ... Never in the fourteen years' history of the Los Angeles Philharmonic Orchestra have there been the ... large and immoderately enthusiastic audiences that have characterised [its] concerts so far this season.' Rodriguez wrote that 'it seems as if Klemperer has broken down the icy wall of [public] ... indifference which has hitherto spoiled the best efforts of the Philharmonic'.[26] The *Musical Courier* (12 December) reported that subscriptions had increased. Encouraged by this enthusiasm, the orchestral board announced two weeks later that it would be launching a drive to raise funds to replace the support that Clark had announced he would finally withdraw at the end of the season.[27]

This success cost Klemperer considerable effort. In Berlin, he had conducted no more than a handful of concerts each season, and at his guest engagements he had generally limited his programmes to familiar works. Now he found himself obliged to conduct a new programme each week over a period of six months. In addition, there were frequent Sunday matinées, often with different works, as well as a number of children's concerts, some of which he himself introduced in his halting English. As can be deduced from scripts he carefully prepared for these occasions, it was not a task he undertook lightly. Gaps in Los Angeles's experience of the classics facilitated his task; in the course of the season he was able to give the local premières of Haydn's 'Clock' and 'Farewell' symphonies. But he soon became uncomfortably aware that his repertory was too limited to sustain an entire season. In spite of the fact that he had already conducted more Debussy and Ravel than many of his German and Austrian colleagues, it was also too exclusively Central European to meet American taste. Thus in Los Angeles he found himself obliged to study a large number of unfamiliar works, a task made more burdensome by his slowness in learning and his insistence on conducting without a score.

Klemperer was not a musical snob, but some of the music he was asked

* Primo Carnera, an Italian heavyweight boxer of giant proportions.

to perform overtaxed his tolerance. He felt he had no alternative but to accede to Clark's request ('after all, he pays for everything') to conduct 'a very banal piece of Godard,* of whom he had a childhood memory'. 'In the rehearsal', Klemperer wrote to Johanna on 4 December, 'I was absolutely nauseated' ('hatte ich einen Riesenekel'). He then added, as though it had been a matter of cause and effect, 'I got a stomach upset, so the doctor ordered me to bed for a couple of days, and I was out of the mess.'

In spite of his lack of enthusiasm for César Franck's Symphony he found himself obliged to conduct it twice in the course of the season. Tchaikovsky came into a different category: Klemperer was by no means averse to his music and had already conducted it in Europe, if only on isolated occasions.† In Los Angeles, however, he found himself obliged to include the Piano Concerto, the Fifth and Sixth Symphonies and the *Romeo and Juliet* overture in his programmes. He also acceded to demands for Sibelius's First and Second Symphonies and *The Swan of Tuonela*.

The expansion of his repertory brought unlooked-for compensations. Among the composers Klemperer had not previously performed, none gave him so much pleasure as Berlioz. After conducting the *Symphonie fantastique* for the first time on 14 December 1933 he described it to his wife as 'a work of a hyper-genius'.[28] He wrote to Elisabeth Schumann (16 December), 'I have learnt here to understand the music of Berlioz better, while at the same time reading his immensely gripping memoirs. Do you know his Queen Mab Scherzo? It is a simply perfect piece.' He had conducted it for the first time two weeks earlier.

A number of factors limited Klemperer's choice of less familiar works. The management frowned on pieces by composers still in copyright on account of the expense of royalties. The orchestra could not afford to bring first-, or even second-class soloists three thousand miles to Los Angeles. When he determined to conduct a Bruckner symphony, he was obliged to choose No. 4 (which he had not previously conducted in public), for no better reason than that it was the only work by Bruckner in the orchestra's library. It was performed, uncut for the first time in Los Angeles, on 30 November 1933, but the hall was not full and the critics were predictably unenthusiastic. As the season progressed, Klemperer's lamentations about the restrictions grew more frequent in letters to his wife. His own refusal to perform any music by Richard Strauss represented a further limitation. Casting around for con-

---

* Benjamin Godard (1849–95), violinist and composer, mainly of salon music, which enjoyed a certain currency in France towards the end of the century. The piece was Godard's 'Sérénade à Mabel' from his *Scènes Ecossaises*.

† The Symphony No. 6 in Wiesbaden in 1926 and subsequently in Leningrad, where *Zhizn' iskusstva* (1 November 1928) had found him ill attuned to the music and the orchestral sound heavy and monotonous. When Klemperer conducted the Symphony No. 4 in Brussels in 1932, he admitted to Johanna that he had found it 'harder than I had expected' (letter of 2 November 1932).

temporary works that would be acceptable to a public largely unfamiliar with musical developments since the First World War, he fell back on scores that he had conducted with success at the Kroll, such as Stravinsky's *Apollo* and Weill's *Kleine Dreigroschenmusik*, which was greeted by hissing and silent disapproval.[29] American music was limited to Ernest Bloch's *Winter–Spring* (1904) and *Schelomo* (1916) and an early and unrepresentative piece, the *Black Maskers* suite, by Roger Sessions.

*   *   *

For the first time in his life Klemperer was condemned to spend months alone in a hotel room. In so far as a taxing rehearsal schedule and the need to study new scores permitted, he read avidly. He took special pleasure in Mozart's letters and Goethe's *Wilhelm Meister*. He also resumed riding, until compelled to abandon it by a recurrence of the back pains he had suffered during the previous summer. But he soon came to hate Los Angeles. In particular, he was oppressed by a sense of isolation. The place was 'an intellectual desert such as we don't know in our Europe ... Here one learns what a wonderful thing "a city" and "architecture" are ... And it's four-and-a-half days' rail journey from New York.'[30] 'My God, my God', he exclaimed in a letter (16 December) to Elisabeth Schumann, 'I didn't know that such a lack of intellectuality (*Geistigkeit*) existed.' Nor did the physical amenities of Californian life appeal. 'The rooms are pleasant, the service bad, the food ... unspeakable', he wrote to Johanna shortly after he had moved into a hotel. 'I live off eggs, potatoes, fruit and cheese. The vegetables are so appallingly (*sauschlecht*) prepared as to be uneatable ... And what heat! Tropical (a torment for me).'[31] The sheer remoteness of Southern California depressed him. 'It really is strange. There one stands and looks towards Japan',[32] he wrote to his wife after Clark had taken him to see the Pacific Ocean. 'I often long for Germany', he confessed to her on 15 December.

As a place to live in, Los Angeles did not warrant consideration. 'That I should remain (acquaintances suggest that I should bring you all here), my God, no!' he wrote to Johanna less than a month after his arrival.[33] When the orchestra announced its drive for funds to enable it to continue in the following season, Klemperer was unmoved. 'Even if it should continue to exist, I am far from decided to tie myself to it', he wrote to Dorothea Alexander-Katz on 23 January 1934.

In the solitude of his hotel room his mind turned constantly to his family in Vienna. Had Johanna been to the opera? Had she seen friends such as Elisabeth Schumann or Mark Brunswick? How was the Schönbrunn apartment, which he longed to see under snow? He was troubled about Johanna's deteriorating relationship with her friend and housekeeper, Louise Schwab, who had moved with the family to Vienna ('Don't insist on having your way in so many small things. The main thing is that Lotte should grow up in a *peaceful* home');[34] about his wife's tendency to take slimming pills to counteract the effects of her drinking ('You're not doing that, *Alter*, are you? Then I would prefer a womanly Bacchus'); about the failure of the marks left by Lotte's chicken-pox to disappear. Werner, now in his fourteenth year, was a cause of special concern. He was proving an idle pupil at the Teresianum, a well-known Catholic boarding school, and at weekends, which he spent at home, tension frequently rose between mother and son. But Klemperer was not convinced that his wife's robust approach to a rebellious adolescent was calculated to produce the desired result.

> I needn't say how much I disapprove of his laziness. In spite of that, it's better not to smack him, even on his behind... Last summer [when Werner had spent some weeks with his father in Fiesole] I discovered that an absolutely effective weapon was not to talk to him, not to answer questions, simply to ignore him. Then he is ready to make any concession. That he doesn't think so much of Steuermann* is no doubt due to the fact that he [Steuermann] is not very appealing and that the young Schnabel was naturally closer to him. But he was also lazy with him. I don't think that Werner will be a musician, so it's not all that important.[35]

Political developments in Austria also gave ground for concern. Before Klemperer had left for America his manic condition had made him blithely unaware of the threatening political developments that were taking place beneath the easy-going surface of Viennese life. Now reports of growing anti-Semitism, traditionally more endemic in Austria than in Germany, began to alarm him. 'Is it true', he wrote to Johanna on 6 November, 'that a strong anti-Semitic movement is afoot in Austria? If it takes a form similar to that in Berlin, I wouldn't want to stay in Vienna and think more and more of Italy. That is certainly the European country that will remain quietest (as long as Mussolini is at the helm).'† A suspicion began to dawn that his Viennese home was built on sand.

> I think about the future of the children. Let us suppose that Austria doesn't become Nazi. It will none the less remain so anti-Semitic that Jewish offspring will not get positions. Let us suppose that Werner wants to become a doctor. In Austria he will have *absolutely* no prospects... Unfortunately I think that your prognosis for Germany is wrong. It seems that everything is stabilising there.[36]

Klemperer's growing pessimism was strengthened by the haste of artists with whom he was on cordial terms to mend their bridges with the Third

---

* In Vienna Eduard (Edward) Steuermann had succeeded Karl Ulrich Schnabel in the unrewarding task of giving Werner Klemperer piano lessons. Steuermann (1892–1964), Austrian, later American, pianist, played in the first performances of *Pierrot Lunaire* and Berg's Chamber Concerto, as well as of almost every work by Schoenberg that contained a piano part.

† Anti-Semitic laws were introduced by Mussolini in 1938, largely to appease his German ally in the Rome–Berlin axis.

Reich. Lotte Lehmann, he bitterly complained to Johanna (4 December), 'has not only sung with Furtwängler but also has given a song recital in Berlin. Casella plays with Kleiber, etc., etc. It seems to be becoming the custom to give concerts in Germany "as though nothing has happened".'

Scarcely more than three weeks after Klemperer had voiced his fears about Austria, Dollfuss set out to crush the country's socialists, whose bastion in the working-class areas of Vienna was the sole remaining obstacle to the establishment of a fully authoritarian regime. On 12 February 1934 the combined forces of the police, the army and the fascist Heimwehr attacked the socialist Schutzbund, which had taken refuge in the huge housing estates that the Vienna municipality had built since the war. After fierce fighting, resistance was crushed. Klemperer was appalled. 'The terrible news', he wrote to Johanna on the following morning, 'weighs on me ... I don't think that we shall be able to remain in the beautiful city in which I should so much like to make my home.' 'What will happen here [i.e. in Los Angeles] is quite uncertain', he continued. 'So I *must* think of something else. Amsterdam offers a month. Russia a longer period. But everything still has to be negotiated.' In neither case did negotiations come to anything.

The Los Angeles orchestra's chances of survival had meanwhile worsened. Dismayed at his uncertain prospects in both continents, Klemperer at this point turned to the only American he could call a friend. On 8 February he wrote to ask the composer Roger Sessions to intervene on his behalf with Arthur Judson. News of Klemperer's impact on Los Angeles had doubtless already reached Judson's ears and he reacted promptly. On 12 February he wired Klemperer to tell him that he had 'a very important position in mind' and to ask for authority to act on his behalf. Klemperer was profoundly mistrustful of agents and he disliked Judson. 'I don't pay Judson to work for me', he later liked to claim. 'I pay him so that he does not work *against* me.'

But he could not have acquired a more powerful representative. Judson was in effect the tsar of American musical life. He worked from a handsomely furnished office on the top floor of the Steinway Building directly opposite Carnegie Hall, at that time New York's principal concert auditorium. The New York Philharmonic-Symphony Orchestra's administration was adjacent. On the floor below was the agency. To this power-house came an unending procession of petitioners. Tall, handsome, aloof, sleekly groomed and generally enveloped in cigar smoke, 'A.J.' radiated an aura of authority. He had strong views on conductors, based on their capacity to fit into the musical life of a community as well as on his assessment of their artistic ability. In Leopold Stokowski's view he was 'a natural enemy of new music'.[37] During the years when his power was at its height it was rare for an American orchestra to appoint a resident conductor without consulting him. Likewise, artists wishing to embark on an American career almost invariably first sought his advice and support.[38]

In spite of Judson's initial assurance that he had something 'important in mind', Klemperer heard no more from him for almost a month. When Judson finally wrote, it was only to tell his client that 'the conductorial situation is exceedingly complicated'.[39] Discouraged by this letter and by his failure to agree dates with the Concertgebouw,[40] Klemperer redoubled his efforts to find work elsewhere. He wrote to Dorothea Alexander-Katz in Paris to ask her opinion of the Orchestre Symphonique, which had not impressed him when he had conducted it in 1928 and 1931 but was holding out the possibility of an engagement.[41] He proposed himself to Stravinsky as conductor of the première of his most recent score, *Perséphone*. 'Where', he wistfully added, 'are the good times when we played one after another of your works at the Republic Opera in Berlin?'* But the composer chose to conduct *Perséphone* himself. Klemperer also approached Casella, who was director of the Venice Festival of Contemporary Music, to ask if there were any tasks he could undertake that autumn.[42] He even decided to accept the conductorship of the Vienna Concert Orchestra. The project came to nothing, but his willingness to conduct such a modest group is a measure of his need.

In fact Judson had not been inactive. At a meeting of the board of the New York Philharmonic Society on 28 February 1934 he had urged the need for a guest conductor who would combine new with standard works, so as to counter widespread criticism that had arisen in the course of the winter of the orchestra's conservative programmes.† Having thus skilfully prepared the way for Klemperer's engagement, on 10 April he formally proposed to the board that his client should conduct the first four weeks of the coming season. The proposal was accepted.‡

It was, on the face of it, exactly the American opening Klemperer sought. That Toscanini might shortly be bringing his tenure as conductor of the New York orchestra to an end was already a matter of discussion; Bruno Walter, who had conducted the remainder of the current season, had enjoyed only moderate success. New blood was needed and Judson had persuaded the board that Klemperer was its man. The offer was made more tempting by an

---

* I.e. the Kroll Opera (letter of 27 March 1935).
† Toscanini had done little to foster contemporary music since his appointment in 1926 as conductor of the New York Philharmonic. He had in particular neglected American music. When, early in 1934, the orchestra launched an appeal for $500,000, the composer Douglas Moore angrily asked, 'What for? The Philharmonic stands unalterably opposed to any progress in the new principles of music' (Shanet, *Philharmonic*, pp. 276–7). Such attacks were damaging to the appeal. Hence Judson's uncharacteristic concern with contemporary music.
‡ This was probably not the first time that Klemperer had been invited to conduct the New York Philharmonic-Symphony Orchestra. In 1930 both the *Berliner Tageblatt* (20 May) and the *Berliner Börsen-Courier* (21 May) reported that he had been offered the succession to Mengelberg, who had hitherto taken charge of that part of the season not conducted by Toscanini, but owing to his Kroll commitments had been unable to accept.

invitation to conduct the Philadelphia Orchestra (which Judson also managed) for seven weeks later in the same season. Yet, as so often at crucial moments in his career, Klemperer was stricken by misgivings. He had already written on 31 March to Johanna,

> New York is really thankless owing to the unique position that Toscanini (rightly) enjoys there. Apart from that I am respectfully aware of the distance that separates me from him. And then there is the disadvantage that one can only conduct what he *doesn't* want to ... Philadelphia, the only other place that still engages guest conductors, has the same wretched programme constellation. Anyway, no one has approached me in a binding way.

Klemperer must have written in a similar vein to Roger Sessions after Judson had officially informed him of the board's invitation, for on 15 April Sessions wired him in German urgently advising acceptance. 'The eventual succession to T. and W. is now much discussed ... Judson has strongly taken up the cudgels on your behalf and now needs co-operation on your part.' Later that day, Barbara Sessions wrote to amplify her husband's advice.

> This engagement has been secured for you with the very definite expectation that it should serve as an entry wedge for the future ... it should put you in an extremely favourable position when other dispositions are made, as they are bound to be in the near future ... The New York offer should be regarded in the light of its future possibilities, and these are great enough, we hope, to justify you in feeling that they offset whatever features of the arrangement may not satisfy you.
>
> Perhaps I should venture to add that Roger – and many others – would consider the possibility of your becoming the leading conductor of the Philharmonic as the best thing that could possibly happen in New York and that anything that might lead to that end would seem too important to ignore.

Klemperer overcame his reservations, and both the New York and Philadelphia engagements were made public on 21 April. According to the New York orchestra's announcement, he was to be 'the spokesman for the international modern composer'.[43] Olin Downes welcomed the engagement in the *New York Times* (6 May): 'The directors [have] discovered that ... a considerable body of subscribers, particularly of the younger generation, wish to hear the most important works of contemporary composers.' Klemperer, who 'was believed to be modern-minded', had accordingly been chosen to open the season. Within a year of fleeing from Germany, his openness to new music had unexpectedly served to gain him a singularly promising bridgehead in American concert life.

*   *   *

Meanwhile, Klemperer had discovered to his amazement that Los Angeles had never heard a complete cycle of Beethoven symphonies. For example,

'A CLOUDBURST OF NON-SEQUITURS'

No. 2 had not been played in southern California for fifteen years. He accordingly proposed that the unveiling of a statue of the composer in Pershing Square should be marked by such an event. The series, which extended over the early months of 1934, put a seal on his reputation in the area.* On 19 April the cycle came to a triumphant conclusion with the 'Choral' Symphony, which had hitherto been heard in Los Angeles only in the huge Shrine Auditorium, or in the even more vast outdoor arena of the Hollywood Bowl. At its close there were wild demonstrations. Yet, as Bruno Ussher sardonically observed in the *Beverly Hills Town Topics* (25 April), 'Musical Los Angeles has looked foolish before, but never more so than in connection with the Philharmonic orchestra's financing.' A gala concert at which Dick Powell crooned, Edward G. Robinson spoke and Miss Mario, described in the *Los Angeles Times* (17 April) as 'undoubtedly the queen of American songsters', gave her services, raised sufficient money to guarantee Klemperer's salary for the coming season.⁴⁴ There was, however, no certainty that there would be an orchestra for him to conduct, as the sums that had been raised by public appeals were hopelessly inadequate. On 15 April the *Los Angeles Times* claimed that the continuance fund, as it was called, amounted to no more than $4,000 (at that time about £1,000).

On 15 June 1934 William Andrews Clark died suddenly of a heart attack at the age of only fifty-seven. His will made no provision for the continuing existence of the orchestra, on which, it was estimated, he had spent some three million dollars since he had founded it fifteen years earlier. But Klemperer had already drawn his own conclusions about its prospects. On 2 May his lawyer, Walter Hilborn,† informed the American fiscal authorities that he 'has no present intention of returning to Los Angeles ... His employment next season depends entirely on whether or not sufficient monies are raised to continue the orchestra.' Indeed, as a men's glee club and brass fanfare sped him to the station after his final concert on 23 April, he must have doubted whether he would ever see the place again.

*   *   *

Klemperer returned to Vienna and at once threw himself into rehearsals for the last Philharmonic concert of the season, to take place on 13 May 1934. His programme, which consisted of music by Berlioz, Debussy, Stravinsky and Mendelssohn, raised the eyebrows of some Viennese critics. But, as the correspondent of the *New York Times* (16 June) acidly observed, only in

---

* A pirate recording of a concert that Klemperer conducted in Pasadena on 1 January 1934 gives a vivid impression of his approach to Beethoven at this stage of his careeer. His hard-driven account of the Symphony No. 5 is in its powerful coherence and unyielding tempi remarkably close to the Beethoven recordings that Toscanini made in the thirties.

† Walter Hilborn (1879–1976) remained Klemperer's lawyer in America. His papers concerning Klemperer's affairs are henceforth referred to as the Hilborn files.

Vienna could such a group of composers be considered a matter for comment. However, the concert was well received and Hugo Burghauser many years later recalled the performance of Mendelssohn's incidental music to *A Midsummer Night's Dream*, in which both Elisabeth Schumann and another old friend of Klemperer's, the actor Ferdinand Onno, took part, as 'an acoustical miracle'.[45] It was again left to the critic Joseph Marx to champion Viennese taste; he found the performances lacking warmth and dismissed *Petrushka* as a score that existed only in terms of its orchestral clothing.[46] Klemperer normally attached little importance to reviews, but on this occasion he was irked by what he regarded as a deliberate attempt to belittle the concert's success.

In spite of engagements in Warsaw, Budapest and Milan, his mind immediately turned to the new scores he would have to find for his New York concerts in the autumn. The first composer he turned to was living barely more than a stone's throw from Schönbrunn. Alban Berg and Klemperer were not strangers. As young men of exactly the same age they had met at rehearsals for the first performance of Mahler's Seventh Symphony in Prague in 1908. In spite of their common Mahlerian inheritance, Klemperer had, however, shown little interest in Berg's music. On the grounds that it would require more rehearsal time than he could provide, he had rejected *Wozzeck* for Cologne in 1923, when the composer had sent him a score of his as yet unpublished opera. Yet at the Kroll, where he was in a position to choose his repertory and to obtain as many rehearsals as he wanted, he had also failed to perform a single work by Berg. Not without reason, Berg had come to regard Klemperer's opera house as unsympathetic to his music.

Nevertheless, within a week of his return to Vienna, Klemperer wrote on 13 May to 'Verehrtester Herr Berg' to enquire about his most recent project. Only seven days earlier, Berg had completed his opera *Lulu* in short score. It had been composed with a view to a first performance at the Berlin State Opera under Erich Kleiber, who in 1925 had conducted the première of *Wozzeck*. But the arrival in power of a National Socialist government in Germany had raised doubts about the feasibility of such a plan and on 20 April Berg had written to Furtwängler (now director of the State Opera) to ask about the work's prospects. Meanwhile he planned to make a suite of excerpts, as he had successfully done in the case of *Wozzeck*, which would serve as a trailer for the opera and also earn royalties that had seriously diminished since the Nazis had boycotted his 'decadent' music. It was of this latter project that Klemperer had got wind. Could he, Klemperer now asked, perform the suite in October in New York? Three days later Berg, who was at the Waldhaus, his retreat in Carinthia, told Hans Heinsheimer, head of the opera department of his publishers, Universal Edition, that he would 'naturally reply positively' to Klemperer's request.

'A CLOUDBURST OF NON-SEQUITURS'

On 23 May Furtwängler informed Berg that, to his regret, an opera based on plays by Wedekind could not be staged in 'the Germany of today'. As there was now no prospect of *Lulu* being performed in Berlin, Berg wrote to inform Kleiber about the suite, which only a few days earlier he had promised to Klemperer, and to ask whether he would consider conducting its first performance in Berlin.[47] Kleiber immediately agreed to do so and in the following month confirmed that it had been fixed for a Staatskapelle concert on 30 November 1934. Meanwhile, in the last week of May Klemperer visited Berg at his flat in Hietzing, where the composer played him parts of his new score.* On 7 June he wrote to tell Berg, who had returned to his Carinthian retreat, that

> I look forward with the greatest expectancy to the completion of the *Lulu* suite. I only hope that I achieve really close contact with your new music and that it won't prove too difficult to learn. Will you be coming to Vienna in the coming weeks? Apart from the personal pleasure I should have in seeing you again, I would welcome the opportunity of going over your new score, which I am really extremely excited about.

It was not until Heinsheimer wrote on 26 June to tell Berg that Klemperer would include the suite in his opening concert in New York on 4 October, and would therefore have to take the orchestral material with him when he left for America in September, that the composer woke up to the fact that he had in effect promised the first performance to two conductors. Panic-stricken, he confessed to Heinsheimer on 28 June that, 'not without my fault', a terrible confusion had arisen. On the assumption that Kleiber would be conducting the opera in Berlin, he had agreed to Klemperer's request to perform the suite in New York. When the opera had fallen through, he had then promised Kleiber, to whom he was bound by ties of friendship and gratitude, the first performance of the suite, only to discover that Klemperer would be performing it almost two months earlier. Why, Berg protested, did Klemperer have to include it in his *first* programme? The question was disingenuous and irrelevant; Klemperer had from the start made it plain that he intended to conduct the suite in October. On 3 July Berg had to admit to Kleiber that he had made a *Mords-Pallawatsch* ('a frightful mess').

Universal Edition declined to save the composer's face. Heinsheimer observed cynically that the issue could be settled by the simple device of failing to meet the deadline of 1 September for the availability of the orchestral parts. But he added,

---

* Berg's diary contains no reference to a meeting that may well have been arranged at short notice. In a subsequent article (*Wiener Tag*, 21 October 1936), Klemperer referred to it as having occurred in 1935, when he himself was in Vienna only briefly and in early spring. It thus seems probable that 'the lovely summer's afternoon ... when I visited him [Berg] for the last time' was in 1934.

Whether or not we do so depends entirely and alone on you. We ourselves have never promised the first performance to Kleiber and we absolutely decline to tell Klemperer that we prefer a performance in Germany, where since 30 January 1933 [the day on which the National Socialists had come to power] not a single note of your music has been played, to one in New York. All the more so as no one knows whether Kleiber will be able to give the performance ... But you have conducted the correspondence with Kleiber and you must decide.[48]

On 9 July Heinsheimer told Berg that he still assumed that Klemperer would be conducting the work in New York.

It was, however, Klemperer himself who finally rescued the composer from the horns of his dilemma. As so often when veering towards depression, he had grown uncertain of his ability to do justice to a particularly complicated new score. His fears may not have been wholly irrational. In the mind of his friend Ernst Bloch, 'K[lemperer] has no special powers of conception [*Vorstellungsvermögen*], so that he easily gets a wrong picture, or no picture at all, from the scores of unknown works.'[49] Berg was aware of Klemperer's fears. On sending the score of the film music from *Lulu* to his publishers, he had advised Heinsheimer not to show him the most complex section of the opera at this stage, lest he take fright.[50] So far Klemperer's hesitations had been confined to the music. When, however, accompanied by the conductor Fritz Stiedry, he appeared on 10 July at Universal Edition's offices to inspect the Rondo, which Berg had only recently completed, he announced that, because of its text, he would in no circumstances perform the 'Lied von Lulu', Berg's closing threnody to the heroine of the opera, which is sung by her last lover, the lesbian Gräfin Geschwitz.[51] As in the case five years earlier of Brecht's libretto for *Der Fall und Aufstieg der Stadt Mahagonny*, the puritanical scruples to which Klemperer was prone when depressed had again come to stand between him and the opportunity to give the first performance of a major new work.

Weary of the vacillations of both composer and conductor, Heinsheimer at this point decided to act. On 20 July he wrote to tell Berg that 'on purely technical grounds' the orchestral material would probably not be available in time for Klemperer to take it with him to New York. Three days later, Berg, manifestly relieved, wrote to tell Kleiber that 'the affair is well on the way to being settled in your favour'. In early August, after inspecting the entire score for the first time, Klemperer informed Heinsheimer that 'owing to the calamitous condition of the material, [he] was not in a position to make anything of it'.[52] Thus it was Kleiber who finally conducted the first performance in Berlin, where the work met with predictable official disapproval. Five days later he resigned from his position at the State Opera; some weeks later he left Germany for good.

*   *   *

As the summer of 1934 advanced, Klemperer was increasingly troubled by bursitis in his right arm and on 23 July he travelled to Budapest to consult the physician who had successfully treated the complaint in the previous summer. Two days after he left Vienna, a band of Austrian National Socialists seized the Chancellery and assassinated Dollfuss. The coup failed and Mussolini's mobilisation of the Italian army forced the German government to dissociate itself from it. Klemperer's immediate reaction was that he and his family should leave Schönbrunn. 'The reasons lie more in feeling than reality', he admitted to his wife from Budapest on 27 July. 'It seems to me that (as a double foreigner in Austria)* I could easily experience unpleasantness in *this* apartment.'

On his return to Vienna from Hungary, he invited Dietrich von Hildebrand and his wife to dinner. Years later, Hildebrand recalled the occasion:

> It was still bright ... We ate in the garden in the front of the palace and the unique world of Austria, the world of rococo, the world of *Figaro* surrounded us. Schönbrunn as a whole is uniquely beautiful. But ... the little rose garden in the golden light of a summer (evening) was something quite special.[53]

But all present were painfully aware of the fragility of the evening's enchantment.

On 7 August Klemperer travelled to Zurich to have treatment at the Bircher-Benner clinic for the stomach pains that often plagued him when he was in low spirits. The expense of the *Kur* much worried him (another symptom of depression), but Switzerland, which only fifteen months earlier he had dismissed as a refuge, now presented itself in a different light. 'How lovely Zurich is, *Alter*', he wrote to his wife on the day of his arrival. 'The broad expanse of the lake. The cleanliness of the town and – above all else – the unpolitical atmosphere. In Vienna recently I felt as though I were living ... in torrid heat and violent thunderstorms that never produced the least relief ... I mean, morally, politically.'[54] The charms of the city in which he had made his home were wearing thin.

It was increasingly to America that his mind turned as he subjected himself to a variety of treatments fruitlessly ordained by Dr Bircher. As he had foreseen, it was proving difficult to devise New York programmes that would fit in both with Toscanini's prerogatives and with the restrictions imposed by Judson. The Philharmonic board had decided to dispense with choral works on grounds of economy. Even Toscanini was not wholly exempt. In anguish, Klemperer wrote on 12 August to Sessions:

> They have taken Mahler's *Das Lied von der Erde* from me and another programme ... has been refused on the grounds that a chorus would be too expensive ... I mustn't do Brahms, and Strauss I don't want to do. There are as good as no novelties. And yet I'm supposed to have success.

* As a Jew as well as a German.

At this point he delivered a bombshell:

> I have therefore decided to do Mahler's Symphony No. 2 ... Maybe you don't at all like the piece ... [But] it offers me as a *conductor* the possibility of a *great* success. More than anything else. It is *really important* for me to do this work ... You know how difficult it was (just on account of programmes) to decide to accept New York. Do please now help me with Judson.

Sessions was aghast. Klemperer seemed on the point of ruining his prospects in New York by insisting on performing a mammoth work that not only had little popular appeal but called for a large chorus such as Judson had already refused him. To a friend in Vienna (in all probability Mark Brunswick) he cabled in despair:

> Please explain to Klemperer utter impossibility of doing anything about programmes in New York. Situation controlled by musically ignorant men now intransigent. Feel that with patience and irony Klemperer can eventually win everything. Please use all influence.[55]

Perhaps as a result of Sessions's intervention Klemperer dropped his project for the time being. But he was not a man who easily abandoned an artistic ambition. A year later, he again confronted Judson with a demand that he conduct Mahler's Second Symphony, and on this occasion he carried the day. But it cost him his chance of succeeding Toscanini as the New York orchestra's permanent conductor.

3

Bread and work

Klemperer's ship berthed in New York on 28 September 1934. This time Johanna was with him. The following morning both the *New York Times* and the *New York Herald-Tribune* carried accounts of the difficulties he had experienced in finding the new works he had been asked to include in his programmes. 'All summer long', he told the *Times*, 'I read scores by contemporary composers, hoping to find something to play in my concerts here ... I do not care for music merely because it's modern; it has to be good first.'[1] The harvest was indeed meagre. In the absence of Berg's *Lulu* suite, the only score in his programmes that was new to New York (and to himself) was the symphony from Hindemith's unfinished opera, *Mathis der Maler*. Furtwängler had given its first performance six months earlier in Berlin.

Though Klemperer described it as the composer's most mature work to date, it failed to make much impact when he conducted it in his opening concert on 4 October. Nor did the other 'novelties' cause a stir. Olin Downes of the *New York Times* complained of 'the scents and oils' that Schoenberg had applied to Bach's Prelude and Fugue in E flat in his mammoth orchestral transcription of the work, and dismissed Stravinsky's *Symphony of Psalms* as 'arid'. Only Janáček's *Sinfonietta*, which Klemperer had introduced to New York in 1927, aroused real enthusiasm.

If the New York critics were not unduly impressed by Klemperer's contributions to the contemporary repertory, they agreed that he had matured as a conductor since his last appearance in the city in 1927. Lawrence Gilman wrote in the *New York Herald-Tribune*,

> Mr Klemperer returns to us somewhat less the singular and daemonic apparition who is remembered from other days. Time has subdued him. Yet the striking figure had last night lost none of its impressiveness, with its giant's height and stride, the hawklike orbs that seem to burn fanatically upon his players, the evidence of an ardent and vehement nature. But Mr Klemperer – who conducted without the benefit of podium, desk or score – is much more than a dramatic and spectacular figure, hovering above the front ranks of his players like some fabulous, gigantic man-bird of a legendary age: he is a musician of unchallengeable sincerity, a conductor whose skill and devotion and authority admit of no denial.[2]

Klemperer, who was well aware of how much hung on making a favourable impact in New York at a time when his future both in Vienna and in Los Angeles was uncertain, breathed a sigh of relief. 'Began yesterday', he wrote briefly to the violinist Bronislaw Huberman on 5 October. 'Thank God, everything went well. Was very warmly received.'

What seized the attention of both the press and the public were Klemperer's interpretations of the standard repertory rather than his contemporary offerings. Sibelius's Symphony No. 2, with which he ended his opening concert, won him a standing ovation. He even secured a sympathetic hearing for Bruckner's Symphony No. 9, which he gave for the first time in America in its original form on 11 October. It was, however, his Beethoven that made the deepest impact. Downes in particular praised 'the intensity of feeling, straightforward expression . . . and surprising variety of colour' that distinguished his account of the Fifth Symphony.[3] The performance of the Symphony No. 7 that brought his season to a close on 25 October was described by Oscar Thompson in *Musical America* (10 November) as 'eloquent, direct and unmannered'. The *Musical Courier* (3 November) found it 'authoritative and beautifully proportioned'. The classical poise that he had begun to reveal in his last season in Germany had become apparent to New York.

The only whiff of controversy arose from Downes's incautious observation in his review of the Fifth Symphony that Klemperer had made 'certain reinforcements of Beethoven's orchestration that modern opinion endorses'. Klemperer put the record straight in a letter to *The New York Times* published on 25 October:

> I assure you that I did not change a note. I only doubled the winds and horns on special occasions, but that because it serves only to give a good balance between the big strong orchestra of today and its winds.
>
> In former times I had the erroneous opinion one could change special moments in the instrumentation. But in recent years I know that the first condition of a good Beethoven performance is an untouched instrumentation. This is a kind of artistic credo.

Three days later Roger Sessions came to his support in a letter to *The New York Times*:

> For this writer the most remarkable technical feature of the performance lay in the fact that it followed so exactly . . . Beethoven's own indications.
>
> May I therefore suggest that if your critic found it 'a noble and fiery reading', this is due in part to the very fact that it was far more than usually true to Beethoven's intentions as he expressed these in the text of his work?

Two months later, when he conducted the Ninth Symphony in Los Angeles, Klemperer took the opportunity to explain his attitude to retouchings in more detail.

> I conduct [the Ninth Symphony] almost exactly as Beethoven wrote it. Almost all other contemporary conductors, Toscanini, Bruno Walter and others, conduct it with the changes made by Wagner. When I was younger ... I, too, conducted the Wagner version. But last year in Los Angeles and before that in Berlin, I conducted Beethoven's original score and I think it is better so. Wagner added an operatic flavour that was natural to him and never intended by Beethoven.
>
> Wagner wanted the world to think that he and Beethoven were blood brothers in music. That is not so. Beethoven was the musical son of Mozart and the line stopped with Beethoven. Wagner wrote good prose about Beethoven but ... his orchestrations ... were too thick.[4]

In a later review Downes made amends by emphasising that Klemperer's doublings in the woodwind were 'not to be construed ... as meddling with Beethoven's instrumental scheme. They represent necessary strengthening of wind parts to balance the modern orchestra's weight of strings.'[5]

After the final concert Klemperer wrote to tell Natalia Satz that he had conducted 'a wonderful orchestra with great success'. That was also the view of the press. In the *New York Post* (3 November) Samuel Chotzinoff wrote that, had Klemperer remained a little longer in the city, he would have emerged as a candidate to take charge of the entire first part of the following season, prior to Toscanini's arrival after Christmas.

*   *   *

Meanwhile, the Los Angeles Philharmonic Orchestra had been put on a firmer footing by a new group headed by Harvey S. Mudd, an engineer, whose wealth (like Herod the Great's) stemmed largely from copper mines in Cyprus, and Remsen D. Bird, president of Occidental College. On 10 October *Musical America* announced that the coming season was assured. A delegation had in fact already left for New York to open negotiations with Klemperer. An offer that would fill the gap between the end of his New York engagements in October and the start of his Philadelphia concerts in the following January was attractive to him. But it was only after Mudd and his associates had agreed to guarantee his salary that Klemperer asked the Vienna Philharmonic to release him from his commitments and signed a contract to conduct a six-week season.[6] On 5 November 1934 he accordingly set out by train for the west coast, though only on the following day was the orchestra in a position to offer contracts to the players.

That Klemperer was happier on his second visit to Los Angeles than he had been on his first was due largely to the fact that Johanna was with him. Her presence made it feasible to rent a furnished apartment in Beverly Hills and thus escape the loneliness and tedium of a hotel room and hotel food. He himself had to some extent begun to adjust to transatlantic ways, even to the extent of occasionally addressing the now matronly Johanna as 'my baby'. Though still heavily accented, his English had grown more fluent. He had also become more conventional in appearance. He did not rehearse in a bright green sweater, as he had done in the twenties. Ill-fitting glasses no longer tumbled down his nose when he was conducting.[7] But there was a deeper reason why Los Angeles had come to seem more tolerable. Klemperer was already seriously considering emigration and could no longer allow himself to reject out of hand a place that might shelter his family and himself in the troubles that seemed to lie ahead.

In spite of unseasonable rain the Auditorium was packed for his opening concert on 15 November. A brass fanfare again heralded his appearance, and orchestra and audience rose to greet him. One critic found the strings wanting in sweetness,[8] a common complaint at the time that is supported by the few surviving recordings of performances Klemperer conducted in the thirties. Another complained that the playing lacked 'the perfect finesse' it had attained by the end of the previous season.[9] The orchestra's unstable situation had clearly had its effect. But Klemperer's impact on Los Angeles was undiminished. Hal D. Crain wrote in *Musical America* (25 November):

> The new managerial set-up has done much to arouse general interest . . . and the sold-out house indicated that a new type of listener has been brought into the fold. The city's German contingent was out in full force and the language of the Vaterland was almost the language of the foyer and the corridors. The return of Otto Klemperer has obviously done much to create confidence in the success of the season, judging by the enormous ovation that was accorded him.

In the course of the season, Klemperer was able to include a number of works that had not previously been heard at Philharmonic concerts, ranging from Bach's Brandenburg Concerto No. 1 to Stravinsky's *Pulcinella* suite, and from Haydn's 'Drumroll' Symphony to Hindemith's *Mathis der Maler* Symphony. On 13 December he gave Schoenberg's *Verklärte Nacht* in the presence of the composer, and in the same concert conducted Reger's *Variations and Fugue on a theme by Mozart* and the second suite from Ravel's *Daphnis et Chloé*, both of them for the first time in his career. The programmes were far from conventional, yet it was generally agreed at the end of the season that audiences had been larger and more enthusiastic than ever before. The lady critic of the *Los Angeles Times* observed with astonishment that men were now attending concerts 'for the sole reason that they find keen pleasure in it'.[10]

Though the orchestra's finances were still precarious, Klemperer insisted that he would require a three-year contract if he were to make his home in Los Angeles. Fearful that he would lose his man, Mudd undertook personally to guarantee his salary. After a farewell performance of

Beethoven's 'Choral' Symphony on 28 December it was announced that Klemperer would indeed bind himself to Los Angeles for three years. Yet on that very day he wrote to friends, 'It is a big decision. I must admit that, as separation from Europe grows closer, I am filled with misgivings.'[11]

Under the terms of the contract he signed on 8 February 1935 he undertook to make himself available for thirty-two weeks in each season. His annual salary was to be $16,000. Changes in orchestral personnel were only to be made with his written permission. He was to have complete charge of programmes and choice of soloists and conductors. In most respects the terms of the contract were as good as Los Angeles could provide. Yet the existence of the orchestra itself was still unassured, so that the Southern California Symphony Association, which controlled the orchestra, undertook to notify him by 1 July 1935 whether the coming season would in fact take place. Klemperer now had three years of financial security ahead of him. He also had a firm springboard for an American career.

*   *   *

On 29 December 1934, Klemperer and Johanna left Los Angeles for Philadelphia, where he was to conduct the series of concerts that had been arranged for him by Arthur Judson. Three weeks earlier Leopold Stokowski had resigned as musical director of the Philadelphia Orchestra after a reign of twenty-four years and had agreed to conduct only as a guest during three months of the coming season. Thus Klemperer had reason to hope that success in Philadelphia might lead to a more permanent association.

When he had heard the Philadelphia Orchestra play in New York in the autumn, he had disliked the highly sheened quality of sound cultivated by Stokowski.* Yet as soon as he started work he became aware of the superbly responsive instrument he had at his disposal and in spite of his not undeserved reputation for abrasiveness, he won the orchestra over by the ease with which he got what he wanted without ruffling any feathers.

At his opening concert on 4 January 1935 it was observed that Klemperer had reseated the violins so that, contrary to Stokowski's practice, the first and second violins faced each other. Though the critic of the *Inquirer* found the playing lacking in finesse, the performance of the Fifth Symphony with which he ended an all-Beethoven programme won widespread acclaim. More than four decades later, a local critic recalled it as Philadelphia's first experience for many years of a classical German approach, 'cleaner, clearer and less sensational than Stokowski's'.[12] Klemperer's second

---

* Information provided by Roger Sessions (interview with the author, November 1977). Though Klemperer did not care for Stokowski's style, he admired his technique and energetic advocacy of twentieth century music. In his last years he was also (perhaps a little to his surprise) impressed by a performance of Beethoven's Symphony No. 5 that he saw on television in London. He and Stokowski were on cordial terms.

programme a fortnight later deepened that impression. Yet to some ears his directness seemed unseductive:

> If you like your music presented with honest style, scholarly orthodoxy and earnest fervour, you are going to line up very solidly in the Klemperer cheering section. If, however, your jaded senses demand a fillip of nuance, the flash of colour and the beguilement of grace, you are going to esteem Herr Klemperer greatly, but you are not going to fall in love with him.[13]

On 25 January a programme consisting of Mahler's *Kindertotenlieder* and Bruckner's Symphony No. 5, which had not been heard in Philadelphia since 1907, met with widespread incomprehension from critics and public alike. Klemperer was cast down. He wrote on 28 January to his wife, who had been obliged by the illness of both their children to return to Vienna,

> It wasn't full and, apart from a minority, the public doesn't like this music. Why do I do it? I don't want to make myself out as better than I am: it isn't only a desire to pioneer, but that everything [else] is so played out (*abgespielt*), and with this music I hope to attract more interest. The orchestra, which at first was not at all keen, now seems to take a certain pleasure in the music.

Four days later the orchestra visited New York, where it gave the same programme. Most of the New York critics were hardly less dismissive of the music than their Philadelphian colleagues. But Klemperer's performance of the Bruckner symphony won him an ovation and enthusiastic notices. Olin Downes described it as 'probably unsurpassable'. 'Mr Klemperer', he continued '... spoke with Bruckner's voice as though this were his own native speech, and conducted the orchestra from memory with an authority so complete and an understanding so vivid and profound that against all odds ... he carried his audience with him.'[14] For once Klemperer himself was gratified. 'The orchestra played even better than here', he wrote to his wife on 3 February after his return to Philadelphia. 'The public was warm and ... the Bruckner symphony was a really big success. The next morning I read none of the critics. Only after Schnabel had told me that Downes had written so marvellously did I dare to look at the *Times*.' The concert clearly bolstered his growing reputation in Manhattan, as did a second visit with the Philadelphia Orchestra on 19 February, when Winthorp Sargeant called a performance of the 'Eroica' Symphony 'noble, clear and straightforward'.[15]

Although a poll of Philadelphia subscribers had named Klemperer as one of the conductors most favoured to succeed Stokowski,[16] and his relations with the orchestral players were so cordial that he commented on the fact in a letter to Johanna (28 January), he doubted whether 'Philadelphia is interested in me in the long run'. His instinct was right. Three days later it was announced that Stokowski had made peace with the orchestral board. Henceforth Klemperer's hopes of establishing a foothold on the east coast were centred on New York.

He had come to like the city more than he had done during his first visits in the twenties. 'When I go to New York', he wrote to Johanna on 3 February, 'it is almost as it was years ago when I went from Wiesbaden to give concerts in Berlin. New York is beyond question the only really living city in America and its darker side is not so apparent on a short visit.' While there with the Philadelphia Orchestra he encountered many acquaintances and musicians he had known in Europe. Among them was Stravinsky, who was about to travel for the first time to California to conduct two concerts (on 21 and 22 February 1935) that Klemperer had arranged for him to give with the Los Angeles Philharmonic Orchestra.* Klemperer dined with the cellist Emanuel Feuermann and saw the pianist Lonny Epstein, an old friend from their student days in Frankfurt, who, like Feuermann, had emigrated to America. Sessions was also around and there were meetings with Schnabel, stimulating and provocative as ever.

Klemperer attended many musical events in New York, including the American première of Shostakovich's opera, *The Lady Macbeth of Mtsensk*, which much impressed him when he heard Stokowski conduct it on 2 February 1935. He also heard the Boston Orchestra under Koussevitzky. But the highlight for him was a Toscanini rehearsal with the New York Philharmonic-Symphony Orchestra. After it, Klemperer went to pay his respects to the great man:

> the Maestro himself was particularly nice to me ... he showed interest in me and spoke warmly of Bruckner (whose Seventh he conducted last week).† His eyes are as bright and clear as a young man's. He rehearsed Beethoven and Schubert. His appeal as a conductor is magical ... especially when he conducts unselfconsciously (*unabsichtlich*). That I think differently about many things is immaterial.[17]

However, the Philharmonic's management had yet to reveal whether it would offer Klemperer an engagement in the coming season and the uncertainty about his prospects on the east coast made it difficult for him to accept European engagements. Yet without them he could ill afford to retain

---

* Unlike Klemperer, Stravinsky was from the start enchanted by the west coast, where he was later to make his home. Klemperer also arranged for both Erich Wolfgang Korngold and Schoenberg to conduct the Los Angeles orchestra. Schoenberg's concerts (21 and 22 March), which he described as his first well-paid engagement in America (letter to D.J. Bach, quoted in Stuckenschmidt, *Schoenberg* p. 368), were not successful owing to defective orchestral material and the shortcomings of the composer's conducting technique.

† That warmth did not, however, prevent Toscanini from subjecting the work to severe cuts, which the *New Yorker* (9 February) described as 'well-calculated'.

the apartment in Vienna. It was thus in a state of some perplexity about the future that he embarked for Europe on 23 February 1935.

*   *   *

Klemperer's first stop was Rome, where he conducted the Santa Cecilia Orchestra. It 'played better than I expected', he wrote to Johanna on the day after the initial concert. He blamed himself for the shortcomings in the performance of Mozart's Symphony No. 40 in G minor. 'I still can't make [the Andante] poetic enough', he admitted. 'There is something that I always miss in the sound.'[18] Yet the reviews, he told Johanna, were 'kolossal', and he was moved by the visit backstage of the German ambassador, who came to offer congratulations.* It was a courageous gesture, considering that he represented a country that had forced Klemperer into exile.

Immediately after his second concert (10 March), Klemperer left for Milan to conduct the Scala orchestra in a complete cycle of Beethoven's symphonies. He was joined there by Johanna. After a separation of almost two months there was much to discuss, for decisions on the timing of the family's move to Los Angeles and on whether to keep the apartment at Schönbrunn had become pressing in view of the Los Angeles orchestra's insistence that he should conduct some of its summer concerts in the Hollywood Bowl. In the course of a fleeting visit to his home in Schönbrunn (he travelled to Vienna by aeroplane; his first flight ever), it became clearer than ever that in Austria 'everything was lost ... I felt that Hitler would come, if not that year, then next.'[19] Europe, he recognised, could no longer offer him and his family a secure future. He was also weary of the travelling he had had to undertake in the past two years. Yet by the time he set out on the return journey to America in early April he had still not resolved to abandon his base in Vienna.

*   *   *

Before Klemperer embarked from Gibraltar on 19 April 1935 he heard from Judson that he had been engaged to conduct the first three months of the New York Philharmonic-Symphony Orchestra's coming season. At a meeting on 14 January the executive committee of the orchestra's board had come to the conclusion that the current season was suffering from the employment of too many conductors for short periods and recommended that in 1935–6 one man should take charge of the opening months, prior to Toscanini's arrival in the New Year. Its initial preference was for Furtwängler. Six weeks later, however, Judson had again reported widespread feeling that the current

---

* Ulrich von Hassell (1881–1944), whom Klemperer had previously met on a visit to Barcelona in the twenties, was hanged on 8 September 1944 as a leader of the unsuccessful plot to assassinate Hitler on 20 July 1944.

season's programmes were giving 'insufficient attention to modern and American music' and urged the engagement of a conductor 'who will present modern music in a rather comprehensive survey'.[20] On 25 March he informed the executive committee that he was negotiating with Klemperer to conduct the first fourteen weeks of the coming season at a fee of $27,000. The committee gave its approval.

It was now clear to Klemperer that his future lay in America and that there was nothing to be gained by postponing the family's move to Los Angeles. Within three days of his arrival in California he took out naturalisation papers for American citizenship.[21] Johanna was still in Vienna with the children, but on 17 May he sent her characteristically meticulous instructions about their journey to Los Angeles and then passed to the disposal of their possessions.

> The furniture you will have to store so that either all or part can be sent here. That you can only decide here. In any event don't sell anything. Leave the piano with Bösendorfer, and also perhaps my parents' piano. I need my concert music, by which I mean the orchestral material and relevant scores, and all big and miniature scores. *No operatic* orchestral material, piano reductions, piano or chamber music. Also the manuscripts. Please pack my mementoes of my mother with particular care ... Books, the classics: Goethe, Schiller, Hebbel, Heine, Ibsen, etc. All that should go by slow freight via the Panama Canal ... It is much cheaper than by train via New York ... If I were you, I would take baggage only for six weeks ... and send all the big trunks with bedlinen, etc., by sea via Genoa ... Above all, *pax vobiscum* on the journey.* *Don't* allow either of the children to walk around the ship *alone*. [Werner was already fifteen years old!] You must be especially careful on the *sundeck* of the *Champlain*. It is rather smooth and slippy ... *Fahrt mit Gott!* I expect you here about the 15th [of June].

The decision had not been easily reached. 'We have gone to and fro over what to do now', Klemperer wrote on 22 May to a friend, Micha Konstam, from Los Angeles:

> In the long run Vienna is of course unthinkable. Here I am fairly sure of being engaged for four months of each year for the next three years. So there was a basis for moving. I was hesitant for a very long time. Now I hope that my decision will prove right in every way ...
>
> The landscape here is really wonderful ... [On the other hand] the schools are said to be very bad. But my son is unfortunately such a lazybones that even in Europe the results wouldn't have been up to much. Here he will at any rate have all the (social) possibilities he wouldn't have in Austria.
>
> My task here is that of a pioneer ... But the people are endlessly grateful and really love me ... About the life (and everything that goes with it) I still often

---

* A reference to the fact that relations between Johanna Klemperer and Fräulein Schwab had grown tense.

have doubts ... Recently in Vienna I was able to talk again at length with a friend, the philosopher Ernst Bloch ... I shall of course miss such a 'contact' (*Ansprache*) here. But how infinitely grateful I must be to the great America, which gives me bread and work – and, if God so wills, will also provide for our children.

On 15 June Johanna, the children and Fräulein Schwab arrived in Los Angeles as planned. Klemperer met them at the station in a chauffeur-driven Buick (he himself did not drive and never learnt to do so) and in unaccustomed splendour the family was swept to a large furnished house set in a spacious garden that Klemperer had rented in Funchal Road, Bel Air, a select residential area in the foothills of the Santa Monica Mountains with a panoramic view over the sprawling townscape below. It was an area favoured by film stars (Katharine Hepburn was a near neighbour) and was to remain their home for the next twelve months.

The future of the Los Angeles Philharmonic Orchestra was still uncertain, however. The beginning of July had passed without the Southern California Symphony Association being able to confirm, as it had committed itself to do, that there would be an orchestral season during the following winter. It was not until fifteen days later that Mudd, its chairman, was in a position to announce that the opening concert would take place early in January 1936 after Klemperer's return from New York.[22]

The administration of the orchestra had been put on a better footing. On 25 February 1935 the *Los Angeles Times* had announced the appointment as manager of Mrs Leland Atherton Irish. Of all the administrative figures whom Klemperer encountered in his long career, Mrs Irish, the wife of a wholesale tyre merchant, was the most unusual. Born in 1889 to parents who, it is said, had crossed America in a covered wagon, she was stout and exuberantly overdressed, but unfailingly good-natured. After making her mark in the area as a champion of water preservation, she had joined the Ladies' Committee of the Philharmonic Orchestra in 1923. For three years (1926 to 1929) she successfully managed summer seasons of concerts at the Bowl, where she instigated artists' breakfasts, at which she invariably forgot or mispronounced the name of her guest of honour.

Mrs Irish had a strong belief in publicity and outward appearances. When the shy and cerebral pianist Edward Steuermann first appeared as soloist with the orchestra, she insisted that he be photographed wearing a white apron and a chef's hat. Steuermann's protest that he was not opening a restaurant was swept aside. 'All musicians like to cook.'[23] On Hertha Glaz's arrival in Los Angeles in 1937 to sing in *Das Lied von der Erde* under Klemperer, Mrs Irish took one look at a face innocent of make-up and exclaimed, 'Well, my dear, we'll have to get you to a beauty parlour.'[24]

Mrs Irish was a formidable fund-raiser who, after hours at her desk, would sally forth 'beautifully groomed and fresh as a rose' to address schools and women's clubs.[25] She was, however, musically ignorant. On one occasion she urged Klemperer to omit the final movement of Tchaikovsky's 'Pathétique' Symphony, so as to bring a concert to a more invigorating conclusion.[26] Klemperer regarded her as a vulgar busybody. She was none the less totally devoted to him. The continuing existence of his orchestra owed more to her efforts than he may have realised.

Once he had committed himself to Los Angeles, Klemperer found himself obliged to make concessions to local conditions. His brief summer season of 1935 opened with a programme consisting largely of operatic arias sung by the celebrated American baritone Lawrence Tibbett in the vast Shrine Auditorium. In the interval begging bowls were passed round for the benefit of orchestral funds. A week later the soloist was the mezzo-soprano Gladys Swarthout, who took part in popular radio shows and could therefore be relied on to fill the house. On this occasion Klemperer assumed the unfamiliar task of accompanying arias from Thomas's *Mignon* and Charpentier's *Louise*.

When he had first come to Los Angeles in 1933 he had brusquely dismissed suggestions that he should conduct at the Hollywood Bowl with the comment, 'I am not a summer conductor.'[27] The vast natural amphitheatre in the hills behind Hollywood had first been used as a theatre in 1916, when Douglas Fairbanks senior and other luminaries of the young moving-picture industry had staged Shakespeare's *Julius Caesar* with a cast of three thousand. Concerts started in 1922, billed as 'Symphonies under the Stars', and programmes gradually grew more ambitious as opera and ballet were added to the usual diet of 'crooners, song stylists, harmonica players and dance orchestras'. In 1934 Max Reinhardt staged a celebrated production of *A Midsummer Night's Dream* with Mickey Rooney, at that time one of Hollywood's most celebrated child actors, as Puck. But in spite of such intermittent cultural achievements, the Bowl remained an annexe of showbiz.

> You love [ran a promotion leaflet] being in the midst of the largest audiences that assemble anywhere for symphonic music. You love walking up Pepper Tree Path, smiling at friendly faces, dropping your loose change into historical Golden Bowls ... You love watching the throngs stream in ... You love it when the lights go down, when an expectant hush smooths out trivialities and the Conductor raises his baton. You thrill to be part of ... this great civic achievement.[28]

Such ballyhoo was not calculated to appeal to Klemperer. A more serious obstacle was the Bowl's acoustical deficiencies. A decade later a local journal reported,

> Short of a loudspeaker system, which has not so far proved itself artistically in

Bowl-like conditions,* there seems to be no way of overcoming the alternating effects of distance upon sound ... By the time the sound waves have reached your upper perch, they will have lost much in intensity, in pitch, and in the special characteristics of color and timbre that distinguish one musical sound from another ... You learn to park your critical faculties with your car at the foot of Pepper Tree Lane ... And you must also remember that the imperfections of our economic system make adequate rehearsal time impossible.[29]

In 1934, however, the players of his orchestra had assumed responsibility for summer concerts at the Bowl,[30] and, as their musical director, Klemperer no longer felt able to distance himself from an undertaking that provided them with additional employment. He also needed the money. In 1935, at Johanna's urging, he had had to find $5,000 towards the expenses of emigration to Palestine of his younger sister, Marianne Joseph, and her husband. As he admitted to Johanna, he could ill afford to turn down concerts that would enable him to earn $2,000 in fourteen days.[31]

No fewer than 18,000 people attended his opening concert at the Bowl on 16 July 1935, thereby causing fearsome traffic jams. Hollywood was represented by Marlene Dietrich, Jeanette MacDonald and Josef von Sternberg among others, and the Lieutenant Governor made a lengthy speech. With what must have seemed wilful perversity, Klemperer chose to open a popular programme with a Bach suite, music matched neither to the dimensions of the amphitheatre nor the taste of his audience. Yet even when confronted by an unpalatable task (he was visibly irked by the disturbance caused by late-comers and early-leavers) he remained as exacting as ever; the great Jascha Heifetz† was among those summoned to Funchal Road for a piano rehearsal. Though the programmes of the five concerts Klemperer conducted at the Bowl in the course of the summer were in the main popular, they also included Beethoven's Symphony No. 9, Debussy's *La Mer* and excerpts from *The Ring*. At the end of the season it was estimated that he had drawn an additional 30,000 people to the Bowl.[32]

*   *   *

Meanwhile, Klemperer was under no illusions about the challenge he would be facing in New York in the autumn of 1935. Inevitably he would be subjected to direct comparison with Toscanini, who enjoyed almost God-like status in the city and who would, as usual, be returning to conduct the second half of the coming season. He was concerned at the prospect of preparing a different programme each week and repeating it three times, with further

---

* Loudspeakers were installed for a few concerts in 1936. Klemperer's view of them can be deduced from his reported observation to the technicians: 'You can conduct and I'll control the loudspeakers' (*Wiener Tag*, 21 October 1936).

† Jascha Heifetz (1901–87). Russian-born violinist, who had settled in Los Angeles, where he made a number of appearances with Klemperer.

changes of programme on Sunday afternoons, over a period of fourteen weeks. Feeling the burden to be more than he could sustain, he asked Judson to shorten the duration of his engagement. Judson was irked by his request, but, as a sop, held out the prospect of a week off in the middle of the period.[33]

When Klemperer, who was mistrustful of verbal assurances, asked for written confirmation, Judson back-pedalled: permission for a break would only be granted 'if absolutely necessary'.[34] A further difference soon arose. After Klemperer had with immense success conducted two performances of Mahler's Second Symphony in Los Angeles on 24 and 25 May, he returned to his earlier ambition of performing the work in New York. The project again met unyielding opposition from Judson, for the Philharmonic's board had by now ordered 'the complete elimination of choral works from the season of 1935–6 and 1936–7'.[35] An exception was made for a performance of the Verdi Requiem under Toscanini, but Judson undertook to try to persuade him to abandon even this. Klemperer was frustrated by this refusal to meet his wishes.

> It is [he wrote to Lonny Epstein on 9 June] miserable that I cannot do such a work (in spite of its weaknesses) in New York. But – on financial grounds – they refuse me the chorus and soloists ... They do nothing but make difficulties for me about the programme. What a joy! You can imagine how I am going to have to slave this summer.

Further troubles arose. Klemperer rejected three of the five soloists proposed by Judson for other works. To a friend he wrote,

> Spalding played with me last October ... The impression was not a good one. Iturbi is to [sic] much conductor ... I don't know Myra Hess, but I hear that she is the contrary to my musical imagination.* I wrote to the management ... that the characters of these soloists (without blaming them) would be to different of my own musical charakter [sic].[36]

On 19 May Klemperer authorised Judson to continue to act as his agent for a further two years.[37] But relations with Judson in his capacity as manager of the New York Philharmonic-Symphony Orchestra were badly strained by the time that Klemperer returned to New York on 28 September 1935 to embark on the marathon he dreaded, but knew to be crucial to his future.

*　　*　　*

Some of the city's most influential critics again greeted Klemperer as a conductor who would breathe new life into the orchestral scene. There was widespread awareness that the long reign of Toscanini was approaching its

---

* Albert Spalding (1888–1953). American violinist.
José Iturbi (1895–1980). Spanish pianist, who had started to make a career as a conductor.
Myra Hess (1890–1965). British pianist, of whom Klemperer subsequently formed a far more favourable opinion.

close and also concern about the healthiness of an orchestral scene that was dominated by a handful of star conductors. 'It is', wrote Downes, 'a disease that grows by what it feeds on ... Just three conductors in the East have come to mean box-office returns ... They are Koussevitzky, Stokowski and Toscanini ... What the three great orchestras of the Eastern coast will do when these three stop is an interesting question. New conductors will have to be developed. Where are the new men?' It was a question to which Downes himself proposed an answer. Klemperer, he wrote,

> does not work for the glory of the prima donna conductor, but the revelation of what he sees as the truth ... We remember no occasion when Mr Klemperer did less than his utmost for any composer he represented, or when he appeared to think that his ideas were more important for the audience than those of the man who wrote the music. That is a good deal to say in this day and age, when exhibitionism is often substituted, even in high places, for interpretation.[38]

Winthorp Sargeant found additional grounds for welcoming Klemperer's engagement. Toscanini was indispensable, but his repertory had grown limited and static:

> It becomes necessary to find a ... personality who is at the same time not so poor an artist as to suffer too much by comparison ... [Bruno] Walter, while he was a conductor of unquestioned ability, was hardly an ideal choice for this position.* His programmes tended to duplicate Toscanini's ... and the result was a serious lack of contemporary novelties and worthy revivals ... It is time that a cycle of pioneering began again. It is in this connection that Klemperer may prove of value. He is not only equipped to conduct Hindemith and Berg but he possesses psychological sympathy with the moderns and neglected romantics.[39]

The twentieth-century 'novelty' Klemperer chose for his opening concert on 3 October was not calculated to cause a stir: though new to him, Shostakovich's First Symphony was tolerably familiar to New York, as both Toscanini and Stokowski had already performed it. The concert as a whole failed to generate much excitement. The critic Paul Bekker found the evening 'colourless'.† B.H. Haggin complained of an excessive literalness in Klemperer's interpretations of Sibelius's Symphony No. 5 and Elgar's *Enigma Variations* and described the conducting in his second programme as no more than 'straightforward, sober and conscientious';[40] Marcia Davenport dismissed him as 'the best sort of German conductor, solid, precise, exacting'.[41]

It was an inauspicious start. Klemperer also managed to put his foot in

---

* Like Klemperer, Walter had conducted the New York Philharmonic for a month in the previous season, but had not been invited to return.
† *Die Staatszeitung* (New York), 4 October 1935. Bekker, former chief critic of the *Frankfurter Zeitung*, had emigrated to New York, where he had resumed his career on *Die Staatszeitung*, at that time the city's principal German newspaper.

it. On his arrival in New York he had talked to the press about some of the works he planned to conduct:

> I give Tchaikovsky because it is good music. Tchaikovsky has been the victim of the conductor. Year after year, interpretations ... have become more and more exaggerated, more and more hysterical and filled with false emotion, and inevitably his music has become a symptom of bad taste. But if you take the trouble to go to the source of the symphonies, to examine the life of the man and the actual notes of the scores, you find a sincere composer with a great melodic gift ... The bad taste is not in the music. It is in the people who have interpreted the music.[42]

The opinions were unexceptionable. But the critics chose to interpret them as an attempt by Klemperer to set himself above his colleagues and seized the opportunity to cut him down to size. Pitts Sanborn of the *World Telegram* listed some of the conductors (they included Mahler, Muck and Furtwängler) whom he had heard conduct Tchaikovsky in New York and added waspishly, 'in the matter of taste ... Mr Klemperer will have a good deal of proving to do'.[43] Perhaps as a result, the performance of the Fifth Symphony he conducted on 17 October was condemned by virtually the entire press. Sanborn dismissed it as 'the noisiest and in part the dullest' he had heard.[44] Winthrop Sargeant wrote that Klemperer's 'rigorous pruning of rubatos, violent changes of tempi and dynamic exaggerations' had deprived Tchaikovsky of 'the spontaneity and abandon' essential to his idiom.[45] Downes found the performance 'hasty, noisy, frenetic'.[46] The critics were also united in their rejection of the other main work in the programme, Schoenberg's Suite for String Orchestra, whose première Klemperer had given that summer in Los Angeles. Under the impression that the work was dodecaphonic, Downes described it as 'a pale monument to a lifeless theory'. Apparently unaware that Schoenberg had written it with a student orchestra in mind, Lawrence Gilman held up 'this Samson of the twelve note scale [sic]' to mockery as 'a harmless composer of salon music'.[47]

Criticism persisted, notably from B.H. Haggin, who wrote of lack of 'blitheness and geniality of spirit' in a performance of Haydn's Symphony No. 88 and of 'an insistence on the letter of the score even at the cost to the effect of the music' in Beethoven's Symphony No. 5, which formed the main works in Klemperer's fourth programme on 24 October.[48] The players were irked by the pernicketiness he was liable to show in rehearsal. In the course of preparing Ravel's *Tombeau de Couperin*, he insisted on dissecting the score bar by bar and discoursing on the detail, until Bruno Labate, the Italian-born principal oboist with whom something of a feud had developed, called out, 'Mr Klemps, you talka too much.'[49] Saul Goodman, the orchestra's timpanist, found Klemperer 'constantly on edge' and unnecessarily suspicious that 'people weren't giving him the attention he deserved'.[50] There was respect for his abilities, but relations with the notoriously hard-boiled New York orchestra failed to flower into the cordiality he had found in Philadelphia.

Half-way through his engagement, Klemperer took the week's leave he had earlier wrested from Judson. On 16 November W.J. Henderson acidly enquired in *The Sun* whether Klemperer's 'weariness' was not caused by his insistence on learning unfamiliar scores by heart. The shaft was not wide of its mark. Twelve days later Klemperer at last got round to conducting Berg's *Lulu* suite and, as he himself admitted in later years, had he not obliged himself to conduct the work without a score, he could have dispensed with the break that did much to undermine his relations with Judson and the board.[51]

Koussevitsky had already given the suite its New York première seven months earlier, on 4 April 1935. Klemperer's performance on 28 November drew only a small audience. In spite of what he described as 'a performance . . . of surpassing vividness and technical brilliance', Olin Downes denounced the work as 'involved trash . . . that will not outlast the decade that gave it birth'.[52] Only Lawrence Gilman spoke out unreservedly in its defence. 'In this music', he wrote, 'Alban Berg, brooding with compassion upon terrible, excessive things, has once more brought us close to those ultimate confrontations which are exalting, cleansing and restorative.'[53] Almost to his own surprise, Klemperer was impressed by the music. 'The suite of your pupil Alban Berg', he wrote to Schoenberg on 6 December, 'has in the meantime been launched, and adequately torn to pieces. But much of it sounded astonishingly well.'*

Klemperer had not in the meantime abandoned his desire to conduct a large-scale work with chorus, and to this end enlisted the support of Ira Hirschmann, an admirer and a prominent subscriber to the Philharmonic. Hirschmann, who later claimed to have spent 'hundreds of hours' trying to bridge the gap between Klemperer and Judson,[54] finally persuaded the two men to join him at lunch at the Plaza Hotel. Judson was condescending and supercilious, Klemperer silent and mistrustful. After some argument, Judson suddenly made a concession: Klemperer could do Beethoven's Ninth Symphony, a work that the conductor had also earlier proposed. Klemperer replied that, if he were to be allowed to give a piece with chorus, he would prefer to perform Mahler's Second Symphony, as he had originally suggested. Exasperated, Judson hurled his napkin on to the table and, turning to Hirschmann, exclaimed, 'I told you, one cannot work with this guy.'[55]

---

* Less than three weeks later Berg died in Vienna at the age of fifty. In that period he had written to Klemperer to ask whether he could help him to find pupils, whom he urgently needed in view of his drastically reduced income. Neither this letter nor Klemperer's reply has survived, but Klemperer refers to the correspondence in a letter to Lawrence Gilman (28 December 1935).

However, on 3 November it was announced that Klemperer would conduct the Mahler. He had got his way, but it was to prove a Pyrrhic victory.

Klemperer was aware that New York was unlikely to be more receptive to Mahler than it had been to Bruckner. 'Next week ... Mahler Two', he wrote to Schoenberg six days before he conducted the first of three performances in Carnegie Hall on 12 December. 'Cross your fingers! How they will pitch into it!' His forebodings were amply fulfilled. 'Mahler's Symphony No. 2', wrote the composer Marc Blitzstein, 'is very hard to stomach ... [His] melodic vein is here at its most trivial and lavishly empty. This is the hymn of the *petit-bourgeois* – it takes its heritage of passion and philosophical conviction with complacent faith, not quite at first hand.'[56] Others denounced it on less ideological grounds. Oscar Thompson declared that 'Mahler's aspiration far outran his achievements.'[57] The *Herald-Tribune* (13 December) saw in it no more than 'a tortured mind impotently seeking to break the bonds of a creative gift which never quite responds to the demands made on it'.

But even those critics who found Mahler's music hard to bear recognised that they had attended an outstanding performance. Winthorp Sargeant described it as

> so subtle, so breathtaking in its dramatic sweep that one wondered whether ... the widespread distaste for Mahler's music may not be due in part to the fact that it is so seldom performed with the insight that Mr Klemperer brought to bear on it ... Those who heard it ... can be assured that they have heard the finest Mahler performance that has graced New York's concert halls, at least since the days of Mengelberg.*[58]

Thompson, whose memory went back even further, saluted it as the best performance he had heard since Mahler had conducted the work in New York in 1908.[59] Paul Bekker, the author of one of the earliest (1921) studies of Mahler's symphonies, declared that with this account of No. 2 Klemperer had raised a monument to his master. America, he accurately predicted, would sooner or later have to confront the case for Mahler.[60] Even *Time* and *Newsweek*, weeklies that did not often review concerts, joined in the general paean of praise. But it was Olin Downes's notice in *The New York Times* (13 December) that gave Klemperer such satisfaction that he sent him a cable of thanks for 'this extraordinary review'.[61]

Downes was no more favourably inclined to Mahler than his colleagues were; indeed, he had urged Klemperer not to perform the work.[62] But the evening, he confessed in his review, had been 'overwhelming in its intensity and sweep of vision':

---

* Willem Mengelberg was co-conductor of the New York Philharmonic Orchestra, 1921–30.

> Mr Klemperer held the whole performance securely in his hand. When he sounded the first note he had the last in view. Conducting from memory, he did so with a master's grip upon everything – including himself ... He was never more excited than last night – one will not soon forget the towering figure, the flashing eyes, the features lit and working with the vision that possessed him – but this time he was sovereign. Every fibre of him went into the performance: not an ounce of feeling or energy was misdirected ... This performance was one of the historic musical occasions that ... will always appear significant in the musical annals of the city.

Among the audience were Alma Mahler and her husband Franz Werfel, who afterwards 'squirmed their way through a German-chattering mob' to Klemperer's dressing-room.[63] But if Klemperer supposed that Judson would regard this triumph as the vindication of his long struggle to perform the work, he was sadly mistaken. Later that evening Judson gave a supper party. The Werfels were invited; Klemperer and his wife were not.[64] After the third and final performance on 15 December, which *The New York Times* (16 December) described as, if anything, even finer than the first, Koussevitsky wired his congratulations on 'a great achievement'. But the house was not full, and Judson lost no time in informing Klemperer that the concerts had resulted in a substantial deficit.

Klemperer's two final programmes, before and after Christmas, were well received. The sonorous tone he was by this time drawing from the strings was cited by *The Sun* (27 December) as evidence of the rapport he had belatedly established with the orchestra and, at his final concert, which included *Verklärte Nacht* and the 'Eroica' Symphony, he was applauded by the players as well as the audience. But not a single voice in the press called for his return. In an article reflecting the general view of his achievements and limitations, the *American Hebrew* (3 January 1936) wrote,

> I am not one of those who consider Mr Klemperer an immortal of the baton, even though I admire many of his ... performances ... In certain works, he stands alone. I have already commented in these columns on his Mahler, Bruckner, his Alban Berg. Yet ... too many of his interpretations disclosed scabrous edges. Klemperer is not suited, for example, ... to Haydn and Mozart, his hand is too heavy for such delicacies. I find his Beethoven and some of his Brahms over-dramatised ... too frequently he finds difficulty in curbing his enormous vitality and almost primitive strength. He is a splendid musician, to be sure, an artist with more vigour than sensitivity, and more heroic brawn than tenderness. He is most certainly not a Toscanini or a Furtwängler.

Klemperer had excelled principally in music that New York audiences did not enjoy. He was not concerned to produce the tonal sheen they regarded as the hallmark of fine orchestral playing. His very manner of conducting lacked visual allure and his interpretations had an uncomfortable way of challenging accepted views of a piece of music in a city whose concert life had not been exposed to the purging fires of *die Neue Sachlichkeit*. That sense of discomfort was reflected in his social demeanour, his lack of small talk (even in his native language), his total inability to charm the wealthy dowagers who played (and still play) so prominent a role in the financing of American cultural institutions.*

Klemperer's resentment at his failure to conquer New York as he had earlier conquered Berlin, Vienna and the Soviet Union is apparent in an interview he gave immediately before leaving the east coast for California.[65] A city of seven million inhabitants that supported only one opera house and a single orchestra could not, he asserted, be described as musical. As though determined to burn his boats, on reaching Los Angeles he complained publicly of Judson's choice of soloists.[66]

*   *   *

On 2 January 1936 Stokowski again resigned as conductor of the Philadelphia Orchestra. On this occasion the board took him at his word and announced the appointment of Eugene Ormandy as his successor. In view of the success of the concerts he had given with the orchestra during the previous season, Klemperer was affronted to be passed over. 'After the decision of Philadelphia', he wrote to Hirschmann on 9 February, 'nothing will come unexpected and nothing will astonish me. The superficial music is "*en vogue*" (was *en vogue* and will be *en vogue* always) ... We are a minority.' Klemperer was not alone in his reaction. On 25 March *Musical America* questioned the choice and asked why Klemperer had not been engaged.

A far heavier blow followed. On his arrival in New York in mid-January, Toscanini confirmed his intention to resign from the Philharmonic and proposed Furtwängler as a possible successor.† In spite of Judson's

---

* Ira Hirschmann recounted to the author how Toscanini appeared at afternoon tea-parties offered in his honour by the lady subscribers on whom the New York Philharmonic so largely depended. He arrived immaculately dressed and was escorted to an upright chair in a corner, where tea was served on an adjacent table. One by one the ladies then advanced, as though to be presented to royalty. Toscanini gravely inclined his head to them and they moved on contentedly. Klemperer, in contrast, deposited himself on a sofa, open to assault from all sides. Every time an admirer advanced, he struggled to his feet, in the process sometimes upsetting his tea or putting one of his enormous feet on a precious plate. Having assumed an upright position, he would stand, towering above his would-be interlocutor, unable to find a word. Johanna, whose English was still virtually non-existent and who lacked social graces, was of little help in these ordeals.

† Harvey Sachs, *Toscanini*, p. 243. Toscanini's advocacy did not stem from friendly feelings for Furtwängler. The two men had clashed when they had both conducted at the Bayreuth Festival in 1931. At Salzburg in 1937 he turned his back on the German conductor after reproaching him for his temporising attitude to the Nazi leaders.

Furtwängler's view of Toscanini is apparent in the disdainful observations he put on paper after he had attended Toscanini's concerts with the New York Philharmonic Orchestra in Berlin in 1930 ('Toscanini in Deutschland', *Aufzeichnungen*, pp. 69–80). These comments stand in striking contrast to Klemperer's enthusiastic article of the previous year ('Der Dirigent Toscanini', *Über Musik und Theater*, pp. 49–50).

hesitancy,⁶⁷ the board accepted Toscanini's advice and at a meeting on 12 February charged a German-speaking member, the banker Felix H. Warburg, to open negotiations. Two days later Toscanini's resignation was announced. Furtwängler's appointment was made public on 28 February.

Klemperer had had no contact with Furtwängler since their relatively cordial exchange of letters in the summer of 1933. But in the intervening period he had grown increasingly critical of the inconsistency of his colleague's dealings with the German authorities. In many respects Furtwängler's behaviour had been creditable, even courageous. Aware that the Nazis regarded the composer with suspicion as a 'modernist', Furtwängler had conducted the first performance of Hindemith's *Mathis der Maler* Symphony in Berlin on 12 March 1934. In the course of the summer he had included the première of the opera in his plans for the coming season at the Berlin State Opera. Informed by Goering, who controlled the State theatres, that a stage production would require Hitler's personal assent, Furtwängler requested an audience with the Führer and, to ensure that Hitler should have prior notice of his views, wrote an article that appeared in a leading Berlin newspaper.⁶⁸ In it he argued that no composer of the younger generation had done more than Hindemith to maintain the reputation of German music in the world. Sensing a challenge, Hitler promptly cancelled the audience and on 3 December Germany's most celebrated conductor was informed by Goebbels that, unless he resigned forthwith from all his appointments, he would be subjected to the indignity of public dismissal.⁶⁹ Furtwängler chose to resign.

However, he then lost his nerve. On 28 February 1935 he called at his own request on Goebbels, and after the meeting issued a statement in which he expressed regret for any political inferences his article might have been thought to contain. On 10 April, immediately before leaving to conduct in Vienna, he was received by Hitler. After the meeting it was announced that he would conduct a charity concert at which the Führer himself would appear in the following month and, later in the summer, a performance of *Die Meistersinger* prior to the opening of the National Socialist party rally in Nuremberg.* Even Furtwängler's loyal secretary, Bertha Geissmar, later described his capitulation as 'a complete surrender in the eyes of independent observers'.⁷⁰

The news of Furtwängler's New York appointment unleashed a storm of protest in a city that contained by far the largest concentration of Jews in the world.† Klemperer was shocked by the announcement. On 1 March 1936

---

* Prieberg, *Kraftprobe*, pp. 227–9. Furtwängler characteristically attached importance to the fact that this performance *preceded* (and thus did not officially form part of) the rally, at which legal discrimination against the Jews purely on racial grounds was announced.
† In 1930 there were estimated to be 1.75 to 2 million Jews among New York City's population of almost 7 million. Jews were estimated to form more than half of the Philharmonic's audiences (Joseph Horowitz, *Understanding Toscanini*, p. 148).

the *New York Times* published a letter in which Ira Hirschmann contrasted the firm stance that Toscanini had from the start taken against the Nazis with Furtwängler's behaviour, and withdrew his support from the Philharmonic. The chorus of protest swelled when, within hours of the New York announcement, the Nazi authorities, anxious lest Furtwängler be lost to America, announced that he would be reinstated as director of the Berlin State Opera. It was not until 7 March that the Philharmonic board was able to publish a rebuttal by Furtwängler, who insisted that he would only conduct at the State Opera as a guest.

Two events occurred that day which together made a decisive impact on American public opinion: German troops reoccupied the demilitarised zone of the Rhineland and the *Manchester Guardian* published a letter from the violinist Bronislaw Huberman. In it Huberman cited Furtwängler as a prime example of the many non-Nazi German intellectuals who had contributed to the National Socialists' seizure of power by failing to resist them:

> Before the whole world I accuse you, German intellectuals, you, non-Nazis, as those truly guilty of... this lamentable breakdown of a great people... It is not the first time that the gutter has reached out for power, but it remains for the German intellectuals to assist the gutter to achieve success... They bow down and remain silent.

Although Huberman had written the letter from New York on 25 February, three days before Furtwängler's appointment was announced, he can hardly have been ignorant of its imminence. His letter was not entirely fair to Furtwängler, who had not 'remained silent', but it had its intended effect of arousing opinion, and on 9 March Hirschmann announced the formation of a committee to boycott the Philharmonic by bringing about a massive cancellation of subscriptions. Six days later the board published a telegram from Furtwängler in which he withdrew 'until the time the public realises that politics and music are apart' and complained of what he described as anti-German propaganda. That ill-timed attempt to lecture the Americans on their civic responsibilities cost him such support as he still enjoyed and the board accepted his decision without any expression of regret.

Klemperer's anger and resentment at the New York orchestra's attempt to engage Furtwängler are apparent in a letter he wrote to Lonny Epstein towards the end of April 1936:

> The protest [against Furtwängler's appointment] was absolutely justified... That the direction of the leading American orchestra should be placed in the hands of a Prussian *Staatsrat* I find insupportable. Not on political but on ethical grounds. (Although I gladly concede that art and politics have nothing to do with each other, I believe that art and morality are indivisible.) Herein lies the whole enormous error of condemning the National Socialist movement

politically, when it ought only and exclusively to be condemned on ethical grounds.

Further developments did nothing to appease his wrath. With Furtwängler's withdrawal, Klemperer considered himself a natural candidate for the post. But, although Hirschmann urged Toscanini to support Klemperer's appointment,[71] on 5 April the *New York Times* announced that no fewer than five conductors would share the coming season. Artur Rodzinski and John Barbirolli were to be responsible for the bulk of the concerts. It was clearly no more than an interim arrangement, but, as Klemperer's subsequent dismissive comment on Barbirolli suggests, 'He wasn't so bad, even if he wasn't so good either.'[72] Klemperer was affronted by the choice of conductors who were plainly not in the same league as himself. In his ire, he turned on Toscanini:

> The new conductors [he continued in his letter to Lonny Epstein] ... are Toscanini's fault. It was he who was decisive. I always have to think of the enormous, overwhelming and highly creative personality of Mahler as a conductor ... I swear to you that he conducted much better. That was never so apparent to me as a few weeks ago when I heard Beethoven Seven on the radio. I still have Mahler's performance in my ear!*

Whether Klemperer was right to hold Toscanini responsible for the new appointments is open to question, for some months later Toscanini was incensed at the appointment of Barbirolli as the Philharmonic's principal conductor in the teeth of his recommendation of Rodzinski.[73] But the brunt of Klemperer's anger was reserved for Judson. In a letter written in English from Los Angeles on 20 April, he accused his agent of having undermined his season in New York and done nothing to procure his re-engagement:

> Here are the details: for financial reasons I had not enough *soloists* and not enough performances with *choir*. In *twelve* weeks I had *two* soloists [Lotte Lehmann and Emanuel Feuermann]. Imagine, for next season you announce *thirteen* soloists for twenty-four weeks. So instead of *two* I would have had necessary at least *six* soloists in twelve weeks, and *two* choir performances. I asked you besides the Mahler Symphony for Beethoven's *Ninth* Symphony, because I knew that I had the utmost success in the whole world with this standard work and wished to do it in New York. You refused for financial reasons, so I did not have the necessary *material* to make my season so brilliant, as I would have done it *with* such material.
>
> You made it clear to me in different letters [now lost], that you wished to establish for me a *permanent* situation in New York, that the last season should be considered only as a through-way ... Because I was convinced that the situation would become for me a permanent one as musical direktor, that the

---

* Klemperer had heard Mahler conduct the work in Prague on 23 May 1908. The performance by Toscanini he heard on the radio was broadcast on 5 April 1936, the day on which the Philharmonic's arrangements for the coming season were made public.

society did not reengage me is the strongest *offence*, the sharpest *insult* to me as artist, which I can imagine. You see, I am no youngster. I have a name and a good name. One could not *use* me in a most difficult season and then expell [sic] me. This non-reengagement will have its very bad results not only for me in New York but in the *whole world*. ... This non-reengagement is an absolutely unjustified *wrong* done to me by the Philharmonic Symphony Society. The things for me in New York were decided in the moment I heard that a new musical direktor (Furtwängler) was engaged. ... Only the position of the *musical Direktor* could have any interest for me. As I told you before, I feel *very, very much offended* and I wish that the board reads this letter.

Klemperer usually confronted setbacks with stoical resignation: such an outburst of rage and resentment remained unique in his career.

*   *   *

Klemperer was in Los Angeles on 7 March, the day that Hitler's troops marched into the Rhineland. He had a concert that evening and, as was his custom, he had retired to his bedroom after lunch to rest. Werner was sent to wake him at 4.30 p.m. with the newspaper. Klemperer took one look at the headline announcing the news from Germany and said: 'This has to be the beginning of the end.' When he came downstairs he said nothing, but was clearly disturbed. Later, at the concert, he raised his arms vertically at one point as if to give an upbeat, but then dropped them just as suddenly and stopped conducting. Somehow the players managed to come in. The fifteen-year-old Werner was so moved by the incident that he burst into tears: he realised that his father had tried to express the hopelessness of the situation in Europe.

None the less, on 26 April, Klemperer and his wife sailed for that continent once more. After more than a year's absence, he was moved to see the cliffs of Normandy as his ship approached Le Havre.[74] A five-week tour took him to several cities that had been closely associated with earlier stages of his career. The first stop was Prague, where on 13 May he gave a Beethoven concert with the Czech Philharmonic Orchestra. He was joined there by his elder sister, Regi Elbogen, who, with her now ageing husband, was still living in Berlin. Together they visited the grave in the Jewish cemetery of their paternal grandfather, Abraham, whom neither of them had known. Because Klemperer as a Catholic could not say the Kaddish, the traditional Jewish prayer for the dead, his pious sister said it under her breath on his behalf.* Klemperer took the opportunity of their first meeting since he had left Germany to try to persuade her to leave as well. But Regi insisted that her husband, who was already in his sixties, felt unable to make a new life in a strange land.[75]

---

* The task is properly assumed by a male offspring.

After a brief stop in Budapest, where the strings of the youthful Concert Orchestra again delighted him, he set out for Moscow. Since his last appearance in the Soviet Union in 1929, he had received a number of invitations to return there. In the summer of 1933, for example, he had been offered a position as chief conductor at the Bolshoi Theatre.[76] Klemperer had in principle been eager to conduct in Russia again, but negotiations had repeatedly foundered on his insistence that he be paid in a transferable currency.

During the intervening years much had changed for the worse in Soviet musical life. In 1932 the Central Committee of the Communist party had merged the liberally minded Association for Contemporary Music and the anti-modern Russian Association of Proletarian Musicians into the Union of Soviet Composers. At the same time the organs of the two associations, *Musika i revolyutsiya* and *Proletarsky musikant*, were fused into a single periodical, *Sovyetskaya musika*, which henceforth became the union's mouthpiece. The foundations were thus laid for party control of musical life more complete than even the National Socialists achieved in Germany during the Third Reich. In the course of the following years Socialist Realism began to emerge as official doctrine, with formalism as the cardinal sin of bourgeois culture. A climax was reached on 28 January 1936, when *Pravda* attacked Shostakovich's opera *The Lady Macbeth of Mtsensk*. (At its première two years earlier in Leningrad, the opera had been favourably received.)

Klemperer conducted in Leningrad on 29 May. On the following morning he was taken by Ivan Sollertinsky and Fritz Stiedry, who since 1933 had been conductor of the Philharmonic Orchestra, to visit Shostakovich in his apartment on Kirov Prospekt. There the composer played his new Symphony No. 4,* whose orchestration he had completed only two to three days earlier. Perhaps on account of its strongly Mahlerian flavour, Klemperer was so delighted by the work that he asked Shostakovich for the right to give its first performance outside the Soviet Union.[77] In the following November, however, when already in rehearsal under Stiedry, the work was withdrawn and remained unheard until 1961. A cultural ice age was descending on the Soviet Union.

There was general agreement that in Beethoven (to whose music he confined himself on this visit) Klemperer's style had changed since the twenties. That in itself was not surprising; similar observations had been made in Germany three years previously, when his early fury was felt to have given way to a more classical approach. In Russia, however, reactions to this evolution in his style clearly mirrored ideological pressures. In *Sovyetskaya musika* (August 1936) Semyon Isaakovich Shlifshteyn claimed that Klemperer

---

* On more than one occasion Klemperer mistakenly claimed (e.g. letter to Olin Downes, 22 July 1942) that the symphony Shostakovich played to him was the Fifth. Shostakovich did not start work on this until April 1937, six months after Klemperer's last visit to the Soviet Union.

had lost his former 'spontaneity'. Matias Grinberg felt that the recapitulation in the first movement of the Ninth Symphony lacked 'the dramatic weight, the tremendous emotion and monumentality of earlier performances'.[78] Even Klemperer's most ardent admirers were perplexed. After hearing the first twenty bars of the 'Eroica' on the radio, the conductor Gavriil Yakovlevich Yudin recalled in his memoirs that he cried out, 'What has happened to Klemperer? Previously he was the young Schiller, and now – the old Goethe?'[79] In Yudin's view, with the end of the Weimar Republic Klemperer's Promethean and rebellious qualities had given way to a sense of resignation. Grinberg attributed the change to Klemperer's exposure to audiences in Europe and America who rejected a revolutionary view of the music. More crassly, Shlifshteyn blamed it on 'the climate of indifference to great art in the bourgeois West'.

It was left to Heinrich Neuhaus, one of Moscow's most respected musicians, to put the evolution Klemperer had undergone into perspective. In an article entitled 'Greetings to a master', he wrote:

> In the years since [his] last visit to Moscow much has changed in the consciousness and fate of the artistic intelligentsia of Western Europe. Much has also changed in Klemperer's creative manner. He has become notably more restrained ... [But] the great intensity of will, the artistic severity and clarity of thought remain the same. Busoni, too, as he grew older, became stricter, clearer and more intellectually inspired. Great masters never stop in the middle of the way – on the heights, the air becomes rarer, purer, colder ...
>
> Some comrades reproach Klemperer for a touch of academicism ... One should speak rather ... of an architectural approach, thought out to the last detail ... [so that] the performance is strictly subordinated to a spacious general conception ... An absence of contradictions – between part and whole, thought and feeling, integrity of conception and its realisation – is the fundamental ... feature of Klemperer's mastery.
>
> For us, Klemperer is one of the most noble, honest and steadfast representatives of the German intelligentsia, which is now deprived of its homeland.[80]

From Leningrad, Klemperer travelled to Austria, where on 7 June he opened the Vienna Festival with a Beethoven concert that similarly divided opinion, though in this instance on aesthetic grounds. There was praise for Klemperer's refusal to impose an 'interpretation' on the music, and for his ability to create tension, not out of rhetoric, but through thematic detail. There was, however, widespread criticism of the unpolished orchestral textures he seemed to favour. In an even-handed article, Max Graf summarised what to prevailing Viennese taste seemed to be Klemperer's shortcomings:

> As a conductor he is plain and without any of a star's ability to fascinate. He gives a strong beat with big gestures and is one of those fanatically objective conductors. The main element in the impact he makes is a rhythm that borders

on the mechanical. Subtleties of shadings, blendings of sound, nervous nuances – all that in which modern conductors seek to exercise their magic – are not his thing. In comparison to men like Walter and Furtwängler, Klemperer is coarse. Or to put it more politely: raw, manly and hard ... His Fifth Symphony is a construction of rough-hewn stone with great vaultings. Of romanticism – and with this Beethoven symphony the age of romanticism begins – ... there is no trace ... Architecture, logic and strength of will is certainly a side of Beethoven ... But it is only a side. It is not the whole Beethoven and least of all the Beethoven of Viennese tradition.[81]

On the morning following this Beethoven concert Klemperer held his first rehearsal for a Beethoven cycle in the Alsatian capital, Strasbourg, which in 1918 had reverted to France. Though almost twenty years had passed since he had been First Conductor at the opera there, he had retained special affection for a city that had played a crucial role in his own development. It was thus 'with visible pleasure that on entering the hall he looked round for old, familiar faces and greeted the assembled orchestra'. His feelings were not, however, universally reciprocated. Three months earlier, the Parisian musical journal *Le Ménéstrel* (5 March) had criticised the engagement of a German conductor in view of the fact that France, as the writer claimed, was herself so rich in this field. It was a theme to which the French Alsatian press returned in the course of reviewing the cycle. But if to some Strasbourgeois Klemperer was a *boche*, to others he was unwelcome as a Jew. In 1936 an autonomist movement was gaining ground among German-speaking sections of the population, part of which was sympathetic to the new Reich, whose dark expanses across the Rhine could be clearly seen from the top of the Minster. According to an eye-witness, Marguerite Hugel, a former pupil of Pfitzner and acquaintance of Klemperer, such elements were well represented in the city's orchestra. 'Klemperer', she recalled in her diary,

> starts the rehearsal with the Fifth Symphony, conducts two bars, stops, stares ahead for a moment, astonished and even appalled, considers, removes his coat and hangs it on a chair. The *corrida* can begin. With a sweeping gesture he begins once more, but after a few bars stops again. 'Together! ensemble!' he shouts, speaking a mixture of German, French and English ... Now the real struggle starts, as he gives everything he has to give, but demands from the orchestra efforts such as it is not used to making. Feeling grows against him which is certainly attributable to anti-Semitism ... Klemperer is like a young bear, rude and rough, the musicians increasingly resistant.

On the following day tension again started to mount:

> Just at the end of the last movement – the orchestra is being particularly recalcitrant – Klemperer suddenly stops to tell the leader how he should play.

Starts again; again breaks off. Klemperer: 'Don't you want to do it?' 'No.' Now Klemperer bursts into an unbelievable rage, and with good reason. 'If you don't want to play, you need not remain. Leave.' 'No, I shall stay.' 'Bon! alors moi, je pars et je ne dirigerai pas ... Unerhört.' *Nota bene*: all this had been in French. Now the violinist tries to speak German. Klemperer: 'Parlez français.' The violinist continues to speak German. Klemperer: 'Je veux que vous parliez français ...' He seizes his coat and leaves, as magnificent as Jupiter hurling his thunderbolts.

By the time peace had been restored, news of the dispute had spread around the city.

'The bear has made himself beautiful', noted Marguerite Hugel with heavy irony of Klemperer's appearance at his opening concert. 'The splendid locks have been brushed stiffly backwards. His tie has got hitched to the side, his trousers are short, his hair badly cut. In a word, he could not look worse. It is evident that his wife is not here.' In spite of his unpromising appearance, Klemperer once again revealed his astonishing ability to overcome the resentment he had provoked in rehearsal, even, as it were, to channel the resultant tensions into the performances. At each successive concert, enthusiasm grew, until the cycle culminated in a triumphant performance of the Ninth Symphony. The prodigal son had made good. At a party after the final concert Schnabel and Klemperer entertained the guests with Schubert piano music for four hands.* The following morning the two of them visited the Minster that had so gripped Klemperer's imagination as a young man and remained for him numinous as no other church.

Klemperer had originally intended to make a first visit to Palestine before returning to Los Angeles. His immediate purpose was to visit his younger sister, Marianne Joseph, who, together with her husband, had emigrated there in 1935. But originally there had been another reason for the journey. In the previous March, when he had played under Klemperer's direction in Los Angeles, Bronislaw Huberman had suggested that he should conduct the newly founded Palestine Symphony Orchestra. The project had come to nothing, almost certainly because in its early days the orchestra did not engage Jews who had converted to Christianity. Meanwhile, conditions in Palestine had deteriorated and on 12 June the British mandate authorities introduced emergency regulations. In these circumstances Marianne persuaded her brother to postpone his journey. Though Klemperer did not visit the Promised Land until fifteen years later, the concern with which he

---

* Marguerite Hugel was among those present. In her diary she contrasted Schnabel's 'Viennese friendliness' with the boorish way in which Klemperer turned his back on people to whom he did not want to speak. As a teenager she had attended a similar Strasbourg occasion in 1917 when Klemperer had played four hands with Georg Szell. Her attempt to remind him of it drew nothing but a grimace and the comment, 'That was twenty years ago.'

watched developments there is apparent from the letter (8 August) he wrote to his nephew, Herman Elbin,* a few weeks later.

> I wish that you were right about the innocence of the Jews in this conflict ... I am not sufficiently informed, yet I hear rumours of such provocative land speculation that reaction was inevitable. Maybe they are not true. Maybe the other side is involved in equally dubious business deals. But ... as long as the Jews fail to realise that the demands on them are *much, much* higher than they are on the heathen (and a great number of Christians are unfortunately still heathen!) ... the situation will not readily improve. I mean, the appalling sufferings to which they are exposed should help each individual to reflect on every step ... I hope that in these words you will only see a pro-Jewish attitude. I see only ... this path: the highest responsibility towards oneself.

After fourteen rehearsals and four concerts in Strasbourg within a space of ten days Klemperer was exhausted. But after a brief respite at the Bohemian spa of Marienbad, he and his wife set out on 8 July 1936 on their return journey to Los Angeles, where he had committed himself to conducting a further series of concerts at the Hollywood Bowl.

*   *   *

In late September Klemperer returned to Europe for a short tour that again took him to Vienna and Moscow. It was a long way to travel for no more than a handful of engagements. But now that his activities in America were confined to Los Angeles, he needed to preserve contact with leading European orchestras. An incident that occurred as he boarded the *Normandie* in New York harbour served to bring home his predicament. Alongside lay a German vessel, 'so close that I could have called across to it. When I saw the unconcerned faces and two blood-red flags carrying the swastika, I had a good mind to show the gentlemen my fists.'[82] That was part of the world from which he was now barred. Before many months had passed, it was to grow larger.

On 11 October he conducted the Vienna Philharmonic in another performance of Bruckner's Fifth Symphony, on this occasion in the recently published edition in which Robert Haas had restored the cuts and other retouchings imposed on the score by the composer's well-meaning but misguided disciples. Klemperer wrote to his wife from on board ship that some sections were so changed he had to learn them anew. In particular, he was concerned about the difficulty of sustaining the architecture of the finale, where Haas had restored a cut of 122 bars. The orchestra was also unfamiliar with the new version and most of the critics expressed a preference for the shorter form of the finale. Although Klemperer described the orchestral

---

* Herman Elbin (b. 1917), son of Ismar and Regi Elbogen, had, unlike his parents, already emigrated to America.

playing as 'indescribably good',[83] the performance failed to make the overwhelming impact of the one he had given in April 1933.

Klemperer's two other commitments in Vienna proved more controversial. One was to give the first Austrian performance of the Violin Concerto which Alban Berg had completed in the previous year, shortly before his death. The soloist was to be the American violinist Louis Krasner, who had commissioned the work and given its first performance six months earlier in Barcelona. Klemperer had also undertaken to conduct an *ad hoc* orchestra in a programme that was to include Webern's Symphony as well as Schoenberg's new suite, which had not been heard in Vienna before. Earlier that year Schoenberg himself had attempted to interest him in Webern's music.*

While he was in Vienna, Klemperer stayed at Mark Brunswick's villa, and it was there that he met Webern for the first time. The encounter did not go smoothly. Klemperer provocatively asked Webern what he thought of Puccini. Webern tersely answered, 'Nothing whatever.'[84]

Aware of the shortcomings of the performance of the Symphony that Klemperer had conducted in Berlin in 1931, Webern was understandably apprehensive. He therefore gladly accepted Klemperer's proposal that he play the work to him at his home. He also invited a number of friends to be present, among them a pupil of Schoenberg's, Josef Polnauer, to whom he wrote on 9 October, 'I am resolved to show and tell Klemperer everything, so far as that is possible.'[85] Two days later, the run-through took place in Webern's apartment outside the Viennese suburb of Mödling. It misfired badly. Partly out of nervousness, the composer played with 'an intensity and fanaticism' that seemed excessive to Klemperer, who, when the performance was over, coolly observed, 'I'm simply not able to bring such intensity to your music.'[86]

At the first rehearsal Klemperer was irritated by Webern's despairing attempts to indicate how passages should go by singing them to the leader. Klemperer himself was ill at ease and at the second or third rehearsal caused consternation by announcing that he could not perform a score he did not understand. The composer Ernst Krenek, who was present, reminded him that Webern's Symphony had been included because he had agreed only to perform music he had already conducted, and also warned that the National Socialist propaganda machine would make use of his withdrawal. Klemperer insisted, 'But I don't understand it'; to which Krenek replied, 'You don't have to; you only have to conduct it.'[87]

---

* On 27 August 1936 Schoenberg informed Webern that he had urged Klemperer to run through his friend's recently completed arrangement of the six-part Ricercare from *Das Musikalische Opfer* with the Los Angeles Orchestra. Webern's hope, expressed in his answer of 21 September 1936, that Klemperer would perform it remained unfulfilled. Louis Krasner (1903–95) told the author in an interview (February 1981) that Mark Brunswick, who was on friendly terms with Webern, had been instrumental in persuading Klemperer to conduct both the Webern and Schoenberg works.

Predictably, the performance made little impact. Joseph Marx led the critical assault. 'The orchestra clears its throat. Here a note, there an interval. Quick, slow, loud, soft. Beginnings of dissonant chaos. Silence.'[88] That description of the performance tallied with Webern's own reaction. Turning to the pianist Peter Stadlen, who was sitting beside him, the composer observed with bitter irony, 'A high note, a low note, a note in the middle – the music of a madman!'[89] Webern ruefully reported to Schoenberg, 'it is difficult for me to say much about the performance of my Symphony ... Manifestly, he [Klemperer] took trouble and also put many questions to me. But it was all in vain: the work remained closed to him.'[90] Six days earlier, however, he had expressed himself more explicitly to his friend, Edward Steuermann:

> Yes, Klemperer performed my Symphony ... Now, dear Steuermann, I know that Schoenberg is at the moment* on good terms with the man and I therefore don't want to condemn him absolutely. But I must say that what he did with my piece was bad beyond all measure, without sense or a glimmer of understanding. Better if it had not taken place.[91]

Klemperer's subsequent comment that the performance 'went quite well' must be accounted one of the few expressions of complacency he ever allowed himself.[92]

The preparations for the performance of Berg's Violin Concerto, which Klemperer conducted at a Philharmonic concert nine days later, also gave rise to difficulties, though of a different order. About a week before it was due to take place, Klemperer wrote to tell his wife that

> the management of the Vienna Philharmonic suddenly declared that advance booking for the Berg concert was so poor that they wanted to cancel it. There were some sharp discussions, in which I calmly stood by my contract, but – in order to show myself accommodating – declared my readiness to accept a reduction in my fee. (Herr Krasner, the soloist, has forgone his ...) At the same time I said that, should the concert *not* take place, they would have to pay me in full.[93]

Confronted with Klemperer's obduracy, the orchestra had little alternative but to agree to proceed with the concert, which attracted a larger audience than expected. However, the Philharmonic found a means of ventilating its lack of commitment to the work. In spite of the fact that the performance drew much cheering, most of the players ostentatiously left the platform immediately it was over. The veteran leader, Arnold Rosé, was one of the few to remain. Whether or not the applause was justified is hard to determine. Two of Berg's close friends differed markedly in their reactions to the performance. In the *Christian Science Monitor* Erwin Stein described it as

---

* The phrase 'at the moment' suggests that Webern did not expect that harmony to last. He was to be proved right.

1   Rehearsal for the first Viennese performance of the Berg Violin Concerto, 25 October 1936. Vienna Philharmonic Orchestra, conductor Otto Klemperer, soloist Louis Krasner, leader Arnold Rosé. Photo: G. M. Cushing, Boston

'brilliant', but Webern, in a letter to Schoenberg, insisted that it was 'finally no more than routine'.*

Klemperer was again full of enthusiasm for the Vienna orchestra. 'You should have heard *how* [it] played', he wrote to his wife on 28 October. But its behaviour before and after the Berg concert was symptomatic of a malaise that was in the process of undermining every aspect of Austrian life. Economic decline was only an outer manifestation of an inner sickness. In a one-party State politics had come to permeate cultural life. Inertia and provincialism were the order of the day. Such new works as obtained a hearing were in the main on a level that Mark Brunswick dismissed as

* Letter of 12 December 1936, in which Webern also expressed reservations about the performance of the Wood Dove's aria from *Gurrelieder* that Klemperer had conducted in the same concert as his Symphony.
  Like Webern and Berg, Erwin Stein (1885–1958) was an early pupil and close associate of Schoenberg. As an editor at Universal Edition, he was doubtless acquainted with the score of the concerto. So, too, was Webern, who started rehearsing the Barcelona première, a task he was eventually obliged to hand over to Scherchen.

'Alpine'.[94] 'Austrian musical life', he wrote, '[represents] the triumph of mediocrity and spiritual decline.' Within eighteen months of Klemperer's concerts in Vienna the rump State that had emerged from the Treaty of Trianon joyfully welcomed an *Anschluss* with Germany.

Owing to the cancellation of concerts in Budapest and Prague, Klemperer was at the last moment able to accept an invitation to return for the second time that year to the Soviet Union, where the authorities had a special task in mind for him. Since the revolution Moscow had lacked a concert orchestra commensurate with its standing as the new capital. In the summer of 1936 the 130-man USSR State Symphony Orchestra had accordingly been formed out of the best players of the All-Union Radio and Moscow Philharmonic orchestras.* Alexander Gauk was appointed conductor. Klemperer was to be artistic director. Precisely what his commitments were to be remains unclear. A puzzling feature of the appointment is that it was announced in the *Deutsche Zentral Zeitung* of 2 October, when Klemperer was still unaware that he would be in a position to return to Moscow later in the month. It may, however, originally have been intended to take effect only in the following year. On 10 October the German embassy in Moscow, which kept a sharp eye on the activities of emigrants (who were for the most part still German citizens), reported the news to Berlin, where it was personally noted by Goebbels.[95]

To Gauk's amazement, Klemperer spent much of his first rehearsal prowling between the desks, 'getting to know his musicians'.[96] He was less than satisfied with what he heard. To general annoyance, he cancelled two of the three programmes he was scheduled to conduct, so as to be able to devote no fewer than twelve rehearsals to the one that remained.[97] During these sessions the foyers of the Conservatory resounded to stamping, shouting and repeated cries of 'Noch einmal!' ('Once again!'). In the intervals the players emerged resentful and silent.[98] Harsh though they were, the methods produced the required effect. Gauk described the pair of concerts that Klemperer finally gave on 5 and 6 November, with the twenty-year-old Emil Gilels as soloist in Beethoven's Piano Concerto in C minor, as 'a triumph';† Moscow, it was generally agreed, had rarely experienced orchestral playing on such a level.[99]

Yet Klemperer's appointment as the new orchestra's artistic adviser evaporated as mysteriously as it had arisen. Before leaving he made what he described to Schnabel as 'a gentleman's agreement' to return for four weeks in the following year, and was sufficiently confident of that understanding to

---

* Klemperer had conducted the former in May 1936; the latter had been founded in 1931 out of the ashes of the ill-fated Sofil Orchestra that he had conducted in 1929, but had proved hardly more successful.

† The programme also included the *Tristan* prelude, Debussy's *Nuages* and *Fêtes* and Brahms's Symphony No. 1.

make reservations to sail from New York with his wife and Schnabel (with whom he was to appear) on 28 April 1937. Thereafter silence descended and his letters to Moscow remained unanswered. The German embassy there was also puzzled. On 30 March 1937 it informed Berlin that it was not clear whether Klemperer would be resuming his responsibilities.

Only in early April was he informed by telegram that the duration of his engagement had been reduced to two weeks. By that time, however, he had cancelled all his future commitments in Europe and thus had no alternative but to abandon his visit to Moscow. He was, as he wrote to Schnabel, 'really terribly sad'.[100] Later in the summer he also wrote to Ernest Ansermet, who had recently conducted what he referred to as 'my' orchestra, 'It's such a pity that people in Russia are continuously exposed to these unexpected alterations, so that it's difficult to come to *fixed* agreements.'[101] 'What', he asked Schnabel, ' is going on there? It is a mystery.'[102]

In fact Stalin's great purges were already taking their toll of Russian musical life. On 4 January 1938 Klemperer was informed by the Soviet authorities that to their regret they could offer him no engagements that year. The regime was no longer willing to countenance visits by foreign conductors.* Two months later German troops marched into Austria and by the autumn had established a stranglehold on a rump Czechoslovak State. Thus the spread of totalitarianism of the Left and Right finally brought to an end the chequered career Klemperer had been able to maintain in Europe since he left Germany five years earlier.

* Foreign conductors living in the Soviet Union were also feeling the effects. In August 1937, Fritz Stiedry was informed that a contract he had signed only three months earlier was no longer valid (Stuckenschmidt, *Schoenberg*, p. 386). 'I have been kicked out of Russia just as I was kicked out of Germany in 1933', he wrote to Schoenberg on 8 December 1937.

4

In the wrong place

Within a fortnight of returning to America from Vienna and Moscow, Klemperer conducted the opening concert of the Los Angeles Philharmonic's 1936–7 season. The programme included Dvořák's Cello Concerto, with Gregor Piatigorsky as soloist, and Berlioz's *Symphonie fantastique*. The season had almost not happened at all. The previous one had ended with a deficit of $156,000 and the orchestra's future had again looked uncertain.[1]

Klemperer's reaction to the crisis had been to request a meeting of the board, which he addressed on 31 July. He pointed to the artistic progress the orchestra had made under his leadership in the past three years, outlined his plans for the coming season, should there be one, and proposed that the money needed be raised by a 'voluntary music tax'. But that presupposed a widespread public interest that was far from evident. 'I hear [that] here in Los Angeles ... people are not interested in music', Klemperer noted in disbelief. 'Can that be true?'[2] Alas, it was all too true. Unlike its older counterparts in the east, the Los Angeles Philharmonic had no endowments. Even the ebullient Mrs Irish despaired. 'I am coming to believe', she confessed at a Bowl breakfast three weeks later, 'that those who are vitally interested in the continuance of the orchestra [are] but a few hundred loyal workers ... Only 1,600 people out of a population of more than 1,500,000 gave money to its support.* All year long we have worked on borrowed funds.'[3] On 12 August Klemperer wrote in disgust to Lonny Epstein: 'No certainty about next season. There won't be a "decision" until October. *Imagine* [in English]!'

José Rodriguez, the critic of *Rob Wagner's Script*, put his finger on what was wrong:

> Ever since the late William Andrews Clark Jnr ceased to guarantee the expenses of the Los Angeles Philharmonic Orchestra, this organisation has been in trouble. Every year it is a question of whether the orchestra can continue to operate; every year we see a fresh drive for money; every year we see a recurring alarm; our ears are filled with pitiful wailing and the cry for alms ... Why is it

---

* Los Angeles did not stand alone. In July 1936 *Musical America* estimated that, only a few years earlier, Manhattan's basic musical public amounted to no more than 16,000 people (Nicholas E. Tawa, *Serenading the Reluctant Eagle*, p. 128).

that people who do not hesitate to vote ... for a boulevard, a sewer or new school buildings will not assume a share of the orchestra's expense?

The root of its difficulties, he argued, lay in the manner in which it had come into existence:

> The Philharmonic was started ... [as] an incubator baby kept alive only by the Clark millions. It had a lonely childhood ... carefully sheltered from the rude world ... When it reached adolescence, it was suddenly told to go out into the world and make its own way.
>
> The inevitable happened. Deprived of its regular income, the Philharmonic began living on hand-outs grudgingly given ... Now people are getting tired of blowing artificial breath into it.

With a few honourable exceptions, Rodriguez continued, the financial backers of the Philharmonic regarded it as no more than an extension of their charitable activities. The supporters are mainly 'women of society', the orchestra itself a collection of 'excellent, good, indifferent and bad players. Its members were disillusioned, discouraged and suspicious.'

> In command of this rebellious and dispirited regiment is Otto Klemperer, a conductor of the highest achievements ... a man who considers his function to be simply that of performing the finest music in the finest manner. And here is the rub, for in Southern California, this is only half his job. His background ... has rendered him blind as a mole to the social aspects of his task. We need here a conductor who is ... able to make himself the people's leader in music as well as the Philharmonic's leader in performance ... one who will be loved as well as respected.[4]

In some respects this was unfair. Klemperer was far from interpreting his duties narrowly. Of all his obligations as musical director none was more irksome than having to take part in the annual Easter Sunrise Service, which in 1921 had been introduced at the Hollywood Bowl. In 1936 it was transferred to the Forest Lawn Memorial Park, immortalised by Evelyn Waugh in *The Loved One*. The *Los Angeles Times* (13 April) reported:

> High on a tree top, above a sleeping city, burned a huge cross. Silently, reverently, an endless line of worshippers ... wound its way towards the summit.
>
> Thus in the darkness, just before dawn, 30,000 persons found their way to the Tower of Legends in Forest Lawn Memorial Park, Glendale.
>
> As they moved quietly towards the amphitheatre atop a foothill of the Verdugos, only the faintest touch of pink lay across the distant Hollywood Mountains. Their silvered trumpets to their lips, the Philharmonic Trumpeters sounded a single long note into the East.
>
> And just as the last star faded, the gigantic congregation bowed their heads. It was Easter in the foothills.

To this bizarre celebration of the most solemn day in the Christian calendar, Klemperer and his orchestra contributed performances of the preludes to *Parsifal* and, as 'a victory paean at Eastertide', *Die Meistersinger*. The cold before dawn was so intense that the string players had to wear gloves while waiting to play. Afterwards, there was the added torment of breakfast and Easter eggs with the orchestral board in a down-town restaurant. The Sunrise Service was an occasion that deeply offended Klemperer's religious sensibilities. Yet, as long as he remained musical director, he had no alternative but to participate.

Other commitments to the community were more congenial. In the spring of 1936 he conducted a series of educational concerts at the University of California, Los Angeles (UCLA), that traced the development of music from Bach to the early twentieth century and which he himself introduced in halting English.* Together with Edmund Cykler, chairman of the music department of Los Angeles City College, he was also responsible for the formation of the Junior Philharmonic, made up of schoolchildren and students, and on several occasions rehearsed it. It was in part for such extra-curricular activities that, to his deep satisfaction, he was awarded honorary doctorates by two local universities, Occidental College in 1936 and UCLA in 1937. To the best of his abilities he also involved himself in fund-raising, attending 'an unbelievable number of *meetings and lunches*, at which there is an appalling amount of talk and as good as nothing happens'.[5] But his lack of social graces and the acute shyness in public of Johanna, whom the musical ladies regarded as 'a peasant',[6] made him ill suited to such activities. As Rodriguez had implied and he himself later put it, he was 'in the wrong place'.[7] 'It is strange here', he wrote the following summer to Lonny Epstein.

> The Pacific is certainly very beautiful ... But (what I much miss) no smell of the sea. The countryside is wonderful. But 'etwas fehlt' ...† What is it?
>
> ... Why doesn't the bread taste here as it does in Vienna? The wheat is the same. But it's not the same soil (in the widest sense of the word). Please don't misunderstand my reflections. There is much here for which I have to be grateful.[8]

*   *   *

To Klemperer's children, however, Los Angeles at first seemed a paradise. In Berlin and Vienna they had lived a sheltered existence. Care had been taken to ensure that they should not regard their father as in any way

---

* In the subsequent season Klemperer occasionally introduced the down-town Philharmonic concerts. The texts of a few of his somewhat pedestrian 'lecturettes' have survived, e.g. in Anderson (ed.), *Klemperer on Music*, pp. 178–81.

† 'There's something missing', a quotation from Weill's opera *Der Aufstieg und Fall der Stadt Mahagonny*.

'special'; Lotte, for instance, had no recollection of having heard him conduct in Berlin. That changed in Los Angeles. The fifteen-year-old Werner was at once struck by the publicity surrounding the family on its arrival from Vienna. As the schools were about to shut for the summer vacation, a young American student who spoke no German was engaged as tutor to the children, and by autumn they were sufficiently fluent in English to attend classes. To both of them, American schools came as a liberation, though fifty years later a classmate recalled Lotte as a thirteen-year-old girl who spoke with little accent, but kept herself to herself.[9]

Although Klemperer's own English had much improved, German inevitably remained the language at home, as on arrival Johanna (and Fräulein Schwab) could speak little else. Three years older than his sister and more outgoing, Werner was the member of the family who assimilated most rapidly to Californian ways. He already towered over his mother and, much to his father's disapproval, soon took to dating girls. Considered to be in need of discipline, he was in 1937 dispatched to a select boarding school in Santa Barbara. Klemperer, always concerned for his son's well-being, visited him on Sundays.

If by American standards Klemperer was an 'old-fashioned' father, the rages endured by orchestral players were never visited on his children. Unlike Johanna, who would on occasion manifest her anger with a slap, he was opposed to physical punishment. His sternest rebuke was silence. (In periods of depression, when he withdrew to his study, an oppressive quietness reigned in the house.) Yet, though a rather remote figure, he was none the less deeply concerned with the children's upbringing. This remained Catholic (although to a lesser degree than it had been in Europe); even at the age of sixteen Werner was expected to serve at Mass. Lotte at one point attended a convent school.

For Johanna, her husband remained the centre of her existence – and the most difficult of her children. Since the stormy summer of 1933, when they had lived largely apart for several months, they had grown closer than ever. 'I have reflected a lot', Klemperer wrote on 5 October 1936 while crossing the Atlantic, 'and I find our life together (in spite of mutual aggravations) natural and good. Even very good! Let us continue in peace and love to the end . . . On arrival I already look forward to my return.' Werner Klemperer later recalled family life as being more closely knit in Los Angeles before his departure to boarding school than at any other period of his childhood. Johanna's pathological jealousy remained undiminished, however. Suspicion of her husband's roving eye grew to a point where she would listen behind doors and open letters. Her drinking, which had already been evident in Berlin, also grew heavier; and by the thirties she had reached the stage of hiding bottles around the house. Later, when she was obliged by Klemperer's illness and incapacity

2   Klemperer with his children Werner and Lotte on the beach, Los Angeles 1935

to assume responsibility for the household, her drinking diminished appreciably.[10]

When the furniture and household goods had finally arrived from Vienna a week before Christmas 1935, Klemperer had rented another substantial residence in the elegant suburb of Bel Air, which, like the house in Funchal Road, was built in mock Spanish colonial style; it had large rooms and an extensive terrace with commanding views over the ocean and the Santa Monica foothills. Klemperer had his study in a large upper room, furnished with characteristic sparseness. The volumes of his Bach Gesellschaft edition stood in a bookcase. 'A big fireplace occupies one end and there is a long table for working on scores. Etchings by Rembrandt and Picasso are on the walls and a chair or two complete the furnishings, leaving space for pacing back and forth by a ... giant such as Klemperer', reported a local newspaper.[11] The furniture had arrived in a large disposable container, which Johanna adapted as a bungalow, positioning it on the beach, close to where Sunset Boulevard meets the ocean. The whole family, including Klemperer, who enjoyed swimming, spent much time there in hot weather. So far as material comfort was concerned, they had never lived better than in Los Angeles in the thirties.

The move did, however, bring about one change. Louise Schwab's role in the household had hitherto been crucial; without a housekeeper, Johanna would not have been able to pursue an artistic career. But now her career had ended.* Furthermore, Klemperer was no longer undertaking the lengthy tours on which she had in the past often accompanied him. With time on her hands, she increasingly concerned herself with domestic matters and grew resentful of Fräulein Schwab's influence on the household. In the autumn of 1937 Johanna insisted that her old friend and helpmate should leave. Klemperer was opposed to the break. Little though he warmed to Louise Schwab, he was well aware of her usefulness. As the children had come to occupy less of her time, she had added bookbinding to her attainments and applied herself to the task of repairing his broken-spined scores. Werner sided with his father; Lotte, as she was increasingly to do in family disputes, with her mother. Finally Johanna, seized by one of the rages to which she was prone, locked herself in her bedroom where she remained for several days. Only Lotte and a maid were permitted to enter with food and newspapers. Not until Klemperer had agreed to dismissal did Johanna re-emerge. Fräulein Schwab went to care for Klemperer's elderly cousin, the physician Georg Klemperer, who in the previous year had emigrated to near Boston.†

*　　　*　　　*

The precarious economic condition of the Los Angeles Philharmonic Orchestra and the unfamiliarity of its audiences with contemporary music made it hard for Klemperer to include unfamiliar works. That was one reason why in 1936 he finally abandoned his attempt to boycott the music of Richard Strauss.‡

When he addressed the Los Angeles orchestral board on 31 July 1936 Klemperer promised to provide 'the best American music I can find'. That was easier said than done. In Europe he had avidly attended important premières; he had also bombarded publishers with requests for new scores. At the Kroll he had been surrounded by younger men, such as Kurt Weill and Hans Curjel, who had assiduously drawn his attention to new works; the very air of Berlin, with its thirst for new experiences, had provided stimulus. In Los Angeles there was little new music to be heard, while American publishing houses were in the main weak and ineffectual. He himself had become an

---

* A song recital at the Urania in Vienna in April 1934 seems to have been her last public appearance. A project for her to appear as the soprano soloist in a performance of Schoenberg's String Quartet No. 2 in March 1936 in Los Angeles failed to materialise.

† In about 1940 Louise Schwab moved back to Los Angeles, where she kept house for Mark Brunswick's mother and also obtained a licence to deal in real estate. This she did to such good purpose that on her death in 1967 she left a substantial apartment block. A reconciliation with Johanna was effected in the early forties, but the relationship never regained its old intimacy.

‡ Strauss had on 13 July 1935 meanwhile resigned from his position as president of the Reichsmusikkammer.

isolated figure, physically and psychologically remote from the new energies that were beginning to make themselves felt in American musical life. He was now fifty and less willing to venture on to fresh territory.

In the mid-thirties a new school of American music started to emerge. The rising generation of composers, which included most notably Aaron Copland, turned its back on European models and, in an attempt to evolve a specifically American idiom, sought inspiration in native subject-matter. Such a development was not calculated to appeal to Klemperer's essentially European sensibilities. 'Pooh! I don't like that', was his reaction to *El Salon México* (1937), the earliest of Copland's populist scores.[12] Shortly after arriving in Los Angeles, Klemperer consulted Roger Sessions, one of the few American composers of his generation to remain aloof from the new trend, about the music of Roy Harris, a local composer whose self-consciously American music was in the ascendant.[13] Sessions was dismissive. Harris, he replied, was 'musically quite uneducated': in spite of a genuine talent his music remained 'fragmentary and uneven'. 'Such a case', he continued, is 'typically American ... Unfortunately there is very little music by Americans that is even presentable.'[14]

In 1935 Klemperer had conducted Harris's overture, *When Johnny Comes Marching Home*, based on the famous marching song, in both Los Angeles and New York, but it remained the only piece of its sort to find its way into his programmes. Sessions, whose intellectual idiom lay at the other end of the stylistic spectrum, fared little better. The *Black Maskers* suite, the early and unrepresentative score Klemperer performed in his first season in Los Angeles, was all he did of his friend's music. In the face of increasingly insistent demands that his concerts should include a larger quota of American music, he fell back on an older generation of composers who had been content to exist in the shadow of French or German models. As a result, the native works he performed in the seasons of 1936–7 and 1937–8 make undistinguished reading today.*

The issue reached a climax at the opening of the 1938–9 season, when Klemperer went out of his way to discuss his problems with the critic José Rodriguez. 'Where', Rodriguez reported him as demanding, 'are those American works?'[15] Rodriguez obliged with a list of scores by avant-garde figures such as Ives, Ruggles, Riegger and Varèse. These, he assured Klemperer, were 'works that are already proved in performance'.[16] Nothing came of Rodriguez's proposals, in part, no doubt, because Klemperer had

---

* They include Joseph Achron, Violin Concerto No. 2 (first performance, 19 December 1936); Ernest Bloch, *A Voice in the Wilderness* (first performance, 21 January 1937); Edward Carpenter, *Danza* (4 March); Louis Gruenberg, *Serenade to a Beauteous Lady* (20 November); Deems Taylor, Suite, *Through the Looking Glass* (15 and 16 April) and ballet music, *Casanova* (11 and 12 November); John Alden Carpenter, Violin Concerto (21 and 22 January 1938).

already made his programmes for the coming season. They included a larger proportion of American works than he had hitherto performed.* Time has, however, for the most part endorsed Rodriguez's description of them as 'inferior'. It was, he observed, as though Klemperer were saying, 'All right, here is your American music. I hope it chokes you.'[17]

It so happened that in August 1936 an American composer of unmistakable individuality settled in Beverly Hills. George Gershwin's original purpose in coming west was to compose songs for *Shall We Dance?*, a film featuring Fred Astaire and Ginger Rogers. But his horizons extended beyond the world of jazz and dance music. In 1927 in Vienna he had attended the first performance of Berg's Lyric Suite.[18] He had already shown his regard for Arnold Schoenberg by contributing to scholarships for his pupils at the Malkin Conservatory in Boston during the winter of 1933–4.[19] Contrary to what might have been expected of a composer wedded to the Austro-German tradition, Schoenberg was equally aware of Gershwin's stature.† Mutual regard led to a friendship bolstered by a common passion for tennis.

In spite of the fact that, shortly after he had attended a performance of *Porgy and Bess* in New York in October 1935, Klemperer had told an interviewer that 'Mr Gershwin has real talent',[20] he at first set his face against programming the music in Los Angeles, and a sharp disagreement ensued when Schoenberg attempted to persuade him to do so.[21] Klemperer was similarly annoyed when Oscar Levant, a successful jazz pianist who had briefly studied composition with Schoenberg, proposed that he should conduct a performance of Gershwin's Piano Concerto at a Philharmonic concert with the composer as soloist.[22] Levant nevertheless succeeded in bringing the two men together over lunch, at which Gershwin further increased Klemperer's resistance by questioning his ability to conduct the music. According to his own account of the incident, Klemperer replied, 'I've managed with Beethoven, so it'll probably be all right.'[23] Gershwin's doubts proved well founded. Though Klemperer finally agreed to proceed with Levant's project, he withdrew after two rehearsals for a concert scheduled for 10 February 1937.[24] Five months later Gershwin died at the age of only thirty-eight after an operation to remove a brain tumour. On 8 September Klemperer opened a memorial concert at the Hollywood Bowl with a performance (described by the *Musical Courier* of 1 October as 'careful') of an

---

* Daniel Gregory Mason's *Lincoln Symhony* (17 and 18 November 1938); Harl McDonald's Rhumba movement (20 and 21 January 1939); Gerald Strang's *Intermezzo* (9 and 10 February); William Grant Still's *Kaintuck* (17 and 18 February); Edward Burlingame Hill's Symphony No. 1 in B flat (23 and 24 February); Samuel Barber's Adagio for Strings and Essay for Orchestra, No. 1 (3 and 4 March); Joseph Achron's Violin Concerto No. 3 (first performance, 31 March and 1 April).
† In a draft version of a radio tribute, spoken after Gershwin's death, Schoenberg saluted him as 'a great composer', a term he did not employ lightly.

3 Party at the Klemperers', Los Angeles 1935
Left to right: José Iturbi, Otto Klemperer, Richard Lert, Henry Svedrofsky, Pietro Cimini, Bernardino Molinari, Arnold Schoenberg, Pierre Monteux, William Van den Burg

undistinguished orchestral transcription by Dave Broekman of Gershwin's Piano Prelude No. 2.* It was the net sum of their brief association.

Klemperer's contacts with composers of European origin had been inevitably closer. Among the many who were drawn to Los Angeles by the high salaries to be earned in the film industry and who had then settled in the area were two composers, Ernst Toch and Erich Korngold, whose music Klemperer had conducted in Germany. Klemperer became friendly with Toch and performed several of his works in Los Angeles. Klemperer found Korngold an entertaining companion, but performed none of his music in America. He had conducted Korngold's most celebrated opera, *Die tote Stadt*, in Cologne in 1920, but had found it a dispiriting experience.

* Twenty thousand people attended the concert in which Lily Pons, Gladys Swarthout, Al Jolson, Bing Crosby and Fred Astaire appeared. Levant played the Piano Concerto.

More celebrated composers arrived on visits, among them Stravinsky, who returned, again at Klemperer's invitation, to conduct the Philharmonic Orchestra in two concerts of his own music on 12 and 13 March 1937. The programme contained nothing newer than the suite from *The Fairy's Kiss* (1928). The remainder of both evenings was devoted to the *Firebird* suite and excerpts from *Petrushka*. Earlier Klemperer had made a fruitless attempt to persuade Stravinsky to appear with him as soloist in his Piano Concerto and *Capriccio*, as he had done in Germany. But the composer declined on the grounds that 'I have not played my concertos for two years and do not have the time now to refresh my memory.'[25] The real reason for his refusal probably lay in his awareness that Klemperer was in no position to offer the fees he could command. 'I doubt very much', Stravinsky wrote on 14 March to his German publisher Willy Strecker, 'whether Klemperer (whom I see here every day) could obtain the agreement of his committee for such a substantial sum. They are much poorer and more stingy here than you might suppose.'* A month before the composer's arrival, Klemperer telegraphed Stravinsky to ask his permission to give the first American performance of *Jeu de Cartes*,[26] which had been completed only two months earlier. That initiative also came to nothing. On the back of the cable Stravinsky scribbled a note (which doubtless formed the basis of his reply) to the effect that he was for the moment reserving his most recent score for his own concerts. *Jeu de Cartes*, which Klemperer eventually conducted on 17 and 18 February 1938, remained the only new score by Stravinsky that he presented during his six years with the Los Angeles Philharmonic Orchestra.

Another visitor was Paul Hindemith. After a period during which he had attempted to establish a *modus vivendi* with the Nazi State,† Hindemith had in March 1937 resigned from the Berlin Hochschule für Musik and in the following year emigrated to Switzerland. As fascism continued to spread across the face of Europe, so that even Switzerland seemed threatened, he embarked in 1939 on an extended visit to America. In Los Angeles his purpose was twofold, to investigate the possibility of providing music for Walt Disney's animated cartoons, and to take part as both soloist and conductor in

---

* It may have been on the occasion of this visit to Los Angeles that Klemperer tried, but failed, to bring Stravinsky and Schoenberg together. In *Dialogues and a Diary* (p. 106), Stravinsky dates his initiative as having occurred in February 1935. This is unlikely as Klemperer was then in Philadelphia. It is, however, probable that Schoenberg attended one of Stravinsky's concerts with Klemperer in March 1937. Schoenberg, having watched Stravinsky acknowledge applause with one of his characteristically deep and graceful obeisances, is said to have ruefully observed, 'That is something *I* cannot do.'

† Some German authorities (notably the Foreign Office) perceived that Hindemith's reputation might be of use to the Third Reich, which found itself short of representative composers, except for Strauss, and conspicuously failed to produce any. Hindemith was allowed to continue his teaching activities and at one point (1936) swore an oath of loyalty to the Führer. But rehabilitation never reached a point that permitted the staging in Germany of his opera *Mathis der Maler*.

a pair of concerts with the Philharmonic Orchestra.* On his first evening at supper Hindemith found the Klemperers 'living splendidly ... on the hills north of the town so that one looks down on an enormous sea of light beneath. [Klemperer] is quite unchanged ... Johanna is somewhat stouter, but otherwise she is also just as she was – there were even the usual disputes about whether she should have another glass of wine.'

In spite of small audiences Hindemith was well satisfied with the concerts and in particular with his own contribution.

> I played perfectly [he reported to his wife]. We rehearsed very thoroughly: for the two pieces we had almost eight additional hours, so that the playing was correspondingly light and transparent. The *Nobilissima [Visione]* suite, to which I added a couple of trombones and tuba on account of the large body of strings and doubled woodwind, went splendidly and, like *der gedrehte Schwan*,† had a greater success than ever before.[27]

His reaction to Los Angeles was less favourable:

> One can hardly speak of a musical life in this gigantic town apart from the movies. There isn't even a proper music school. Klemperer conducts the orchestra, but that stands as isolated as the famous tree in the Odenwald.‡ There is no sort of musically educated society ..., apart from the usual baggage-train of fat old women, board of trustees and the rest. I feel quite unwell, when (as I repeatedly saw) a dolled-up lump of flesh (*Fleischpatzen*) stands in front of the orchestra and deals with duties, wages and artistic matters.§ A conductor has nothing to say in all this! There is ... a Junior Women's Association, whose task is to meet this year's deficit of $15,000, partly out of its own handbags, partly by cadging. On Friday morning I had to spend a half an hour of the usual questions and answers ... Lert, who, even if not first class, was for years a name and conductor at the Berlin State Opera, conducts a sort of half-amateur orchestra in Pasadena. Schoenberg teaches harmony to beginners at the university (serves him right!), and for the rest all the one-time bigheads fumble around like a city music director in Kyritz an der Knatter.¶

Compassion did not temper the flow of Hindemith's malice. After his concerts, his room was besieged by

---

* In 1926 Hindemith had written music (since lost) for a silent cartoon of Felix the Cat; Disney did not, however, avail himself of his services. In the previous season Klemperer had conducted two of Hindemith's recent works, the *Funeral Music* (1936) and the *Symphonic Dances* (1937), on 3 and 4 February and 14 and 15 April 1938 respectively.

† Play on the title of *Der Schwanendreher*, in which the composer was the solo viola player. The suite from Hindemith's ballet score *Nobilissima Visione* was receiving its first American performance.

‡ 'Es steht ein Baum im Odenwald', folksong in *Des Knabens Wunderhorn*, edited by Clemens Brentano and Achim von Arnim, 1805.

§ The reference is undoubtedly to Mrs Irish.

¶ A small town in Mark Brandenburg celebrated as the epitome of provincialism.

all Berlin, as it lived and loved fifteen years ago and continued to do until yesterday!! Let us happily cross ourselves three times and sing loud allelujahs that we have nothing to do with it.

At dinner at the Lerts, where 'the Klemperer couple eagerly pursued their private and public duels, which ... Johanna with her constant but unsatisfied demands for alcohol almost always loses', Hindemith also met 'the silly movie-composer Wachsman with his racoonlike and Rilke-obsessed wife'.*

When in the following year Hindemith himself sought refuge in America, he did not return to what he described as 'a region of phantoms, illusions and demons', but settled at Yale University, where he remained until 1953.

*   *   *

Whereas Stravinsky and Hindemith were no more than birds of passage, Arnold Schoenberg had made his home in Los Angeles. In Berlin, where they had also been neighbours, he and Klemperer had seen little of each other. As Klemperer had shown only intermittent interest in Schoenberg's music, Schoenberg had come to regard him as a member of a hostile camp. In Los Angeles conditions were very different. Neither man was at first comfortable in the English language and in the early thirties the German-speaking colony was still small. Musical circles were even more limited. Both found themselves largely isolated among a population they found alien and philistine. They were thus thrown together by a common background and common interests.

During his first American winter on the eastern seaboard, Schoenberg had been plagued by asthma and bronchitis. A milder climate was necessary and on 1 October 1934, scarcely two weeks after his sixtieth birthday, he moved into furnished accommodation in the Hollywood Hills. Unlike Klemperer, he was at first delighted with his new surroundings. 'You cannot imagine how beautiful it is here', he wrote to Webern on 13 November in an uncharacteristic mood of lyrical abandon. 'It's like Switzerland, the Riviera, the Vienna Woods, the Salzkammergut, Spain, Italy – all in one place. And with that scarcely a day, apparently even in winter, without sun.' He was, however, less enchanted to receive an invitation to a banquet in honour of the very conductor who in his view had so shamefully neglected his music in Berlin and was now in charge of the only symphony orchestra within three hundred miles of his new home.

A lesser man might have swallowed his pride. But tactical considerations never prevented Schoenberg from giving vent to his resentment. He not only declined the invitation, as, two years earlier, he had refused to attend another banquet in Klemperer's honour in Berlin, but also wrote to Klemperer to make his position clear.

---

* Franz Waxman (1906–67). American composer and conductor of German birth.

I was yesterday obliged to decline an invitation in your honour. You know I have no reason to show you more respect than you have shown me. But that is not my motive in this case ... I find it outrageous that these people, who for twenty years have suppressed my music in this area, should now want to use me as a stage-prop, just because I happen to be here.[28]

Schoenberg's belief that his music had been 'suppressed' bordered on the grotesque: even to musical Los Angeles he was in 1934 scarcely more than a name. But Klemperer gladly seized on the intimation that he was not on this occasion the prime target of the composer's wrath and invited him to dine on 13 November. That did not prevent another attack in a letter Schoenberg circulated on 25 November to friends who had written to congratulate him on his sixtieth birthday. 'Klemperer', he complained, 'plays Stravinsky and Hindemith, but not a note by myself apart from Bach transcriptions.' As though determined to put Klemperer's behaviour in an unfavourable light, Schoenberg did not mention that he had scheduled *Verklärte Nacht* for performance in the following month. Nor did he take into account the limitations imposed on Klemperer's freedom of action by the orchestra's finances and the limited musical sympathies of its public. The stage was set for a stormy, yet curiously warm, relationship that endured until the composer's death in 1951.

In spite of his ambivalent attitude to much of Schoenberg's music, Klemperer never doubted his greatness, and in Los Angeles he set out to support him as far as lay within his power. During Schoenberg's first winter in the area he arranged for the composer to conduct a pair of concerts that were to have included the première of his new Suite for String Orchestra. When defects in the orchestral material obliged Schoenberg to abandon that project, Klemperer himself conducted its first performance later in the season.* The composer was delighted. 'The performance was good, on Klemperer's part even very good', he later reported to Webern.†

In Los Angeles Schoenberg came to accord Klemperer a respect he had shown him only spasmodically in Berlin. He quite frequently attended his concerts, including the performances of Mahler's Symphony No. 2 on 24 and 25 May 1935. Years later, in a letter to Olin Downes (21 December 1948), Schoenberg recalled that they had served to rekindle his interest in music which, he confessed, he had been unable to listen to with pleasure during the previous ten years – an indication of the disrepute into which Mahler's late romantic idiom had fallen in the heyday of neo-classicism. In March 1937

---

* 18 May 1935. The score bears a note in Schoenberg's writing: 'The spots on this score are Klemperer's drops of sweat.'
† The sentence occurs in a letter (7 July 1935) from Webern to Berg, in which Webern quotes from a letter he had received from Schoenberg. Stuckenschmidt (*Schoenberg*, German edition, p. 371) quotes directly from Schoenberg's letter, which the author has been unable to locate, and to which he gives the highly improbable date of 'late October'.

4   Klemperer with Arnold Schoenberg and his daughter
    Nuria in Los Angeles, *c.* 1936

Schoenberg attended rehearsals of *Das Lied von der Erde* (18 and 19 March 1937); the contralto soloist, Hertha Glaz, observed the close attention that Klemperer paid to his comments.[29] Never one to bestow praise lightly, Schoenberg wrote on 2 December 1935 to tell Klemperer that he had found a performance of Brahms's Symphony No. 2 that he had heard broadcast from New York 'extraordinarily beautiful'. On 30 July 1936, when recommending Klemperer to William Dieterle as musical adviser for a projected Beethoven film, he described him as a man 'who knows and understands Beethoven in a really outstanding way'.[30]

Schoenberg readily expressed his gratitude for Klemperer's support. 'I can't count on lessons', he wrote to Webern on 15 January 1936 at a time when he had no university appointment. '... If it were not for Klemperer, who now behaves admirably and with whom I have a very good understanding, I probably would not have got even this one Los Angeles concert, whose fee I so badly need. It does not seem to have been altogether easy for Klemperer to push it through.'* Though Schoenberg may still have been unaware of the fact, less than a fortnight earlier Klemperer had done him an even more substantial good turn. On learning that a vacancy had occurred in

---

* On 27 December 1935 Schoenberg had conducted the Los Angeles Philharmonic in a programme of his own works, which included the Suite and the first performance of his newly completed orchestral version of the Chamber Symphony No. 1.

the music department at UCLA, he had telegraphed from New York to urge that Schoenberg should be appointed, and on his return to Los Angeles hastened to confirm his recommendation in a letter to the President of UCLA, in which he described the composer as 'undoubtedly the most important among contemporary musicians'.[31] Partly as a result of Klemperer's intervention, Schoenberg took up an appointment that was to provide him until his retirement in 1944 at the age of seventy with the basic income he so desperately needed.

Klemperer's continuing failure to programme Schoenberg's mature music remained a source of tension, however. He was not in principle opposed to the twelve-note technique. 'It is not', he later maintained, 'just an abstract idea ... Used in the right way, the system can express a composer's intentions', even if 'Schoenberg sometimes went a little far, as in his ban on repeating notes.'[32] But few of the later dodecaphonic scores appealed to Klemperer, with the exception, subsequently, of the great String Trio (1946). After a private performance on 2 June 1935 of the twelve-tone String Quartet No. 3 that marked the conclusion of a course Schoenberg had given in his own home, Klemperer told Edmund Cykler that, while he could perceive the music's logic, he was not convinced of its expressive power.[33] Later that summer Schoenberg gave a six-week course on musical analysis at the University of Southern California. Klemperer dropped in on it. On one occasion he ventured to answer a question concerning Beethoven's Ninth Symphony. '*Falsch*, Klemperer', barked Schoenberg, as though he were rebuking a schoolboy.[34]

The earliest works he conducted readily enough. In addition to *Verklärte Nacht*, he included the Wood Dove's aria from *Gurrelieder* in a concert of mainly twentieth-century music he gave at UCLA in the spring of 1936. But such performances did nothing to appease Schoenberg's sense of neglect. Nor was it assuaged by performances of transcriptions such as the rarely heard Cello Concerto (1933), based on a keyboard concerto by the eighteenth-century composer Georg Matthias Monn. Klemperer was delighted by the work when he conducted its American première with Feuermann on 2 April 1936: 'the stupendously virtuoso treatment of the cello, and then the glittering orchestration!' he wrote in an undated letter to Schnabel. 'All in all, baroque as I like it (I am no purist!).' Schoenberg (Klemperer told Schnabel) had been 'very happy' with the performance. But what he wanted were performances of works that were in every sense his own.

The issue came to a head in the autumn of 1936, when Schoenberg was in the process of completing his Violin Concerto, the first major work he composed in America. Having read the first two movements, Klemperer wrote on 12 September to Elizabeth Sprague Coolidge, the great American patron of new music, informing her of the existence of what 'I think will become a very important work' and asking her to facilitate a first performance, but in a city other than Los Angeles, as 'the audience here is still not familiar with twelve-tone music'. The implication was that if Mrs Coolidge could find the money, he would conduct. Indeed, on 8 January 1937 the composer wrote to tell her that Klemperer was planning performances during the following season in Moscow, Paris and even Los Angeles. Yet nothing came of any of these projects. Mrs Coolidge's refusal to provide support, on the grounds that she was exclusively concerned with chamber music, may have contributed to their abandonment. In 1940 Klemperer again toyed briefly with the idea of conducting the still unperformed concerto. But when the work, which ranks among Schoenberg's greatest, was finally performed on 6 December 1940, it was Stokowski who conducted, with Louis Krasner as soloist. Thereafter Klemperer's interest in the work waned, as it did in almost all Schoenberg's serial music.

However, he continued to conduct Schoenberg's orchestral transcriptions. In agreeing that the use of four solo strings enabled it to qualify as chamber music, Mrs Coolidge helped to make possible the performances of the Concerto for String Quartet and Orchestra (1933), based on Handel's Concerto Grosso, Op. 6 No. 7, which Klemperer gave with the Kolisch Quartet on 6 and 7 January 1938. By this time Klemperer had conceived another, not dissimilar project. As he planned to end the 1937–8 season with a Brahms cycle, he invited Schoenberg to make an orchestral transcription of the Piano Quartet in G minor, Op. 25. Schoenberg welcomed the proposal with enthusiasm. He loved the work, felt that in performance the piano too often overwhelmed the strings, and set about transcribing it 'strictly in the style of Brahms and not going further than he himself would have done, were he still living today'.[35] The score, which he liked to refer to as Brahms's Fifth Symphony, was completed on 19 September 1937.

At this point, however, difficulties started to arise. Schoenberg insisted that the manuscript be sent for copying to his son, Georg, in Vienna and informed Klemperer that he expected the orchestra to bear the cost. Klemperer explained that the orchestra had no money for such purposes, but to resolve the matter gave Schoenberg a cheque for $200 on his own account.[36] He was accordingly surprised when Schoenberg informed him that he wanted the work to be given its première by one of the big east coast orchestras. In Klemperer's view, having himself instigated the work, he could expect to conduct its first performance.[37] But Schoenberg insisted that as there had been no commissioning fee there had been no commission. Klemperer, he maintained, had merely 'expressed a wish' (*gewünscht*) for such a work.[38] He (Schoenberg) was therefore at liberty to dispose of its first performance as he saw fit. 'As I had no publishers and ... had received no fee from Klemperer (who at first did not even want to pay for the parts), I offered it to others, among them Eugene Ormandy', who enraged him by declining to consider the work until he had had an opportunity to read the score.[39]

Schoenberg's attempts to secure an east coast première came to nothing: American interest in his music was at an even lower ebb than he supposed. It therefore fell to Klemperer to give the work its first performance in Los Angeles on 8 May 1938. Though praised by Rodriguez as 'a cunning and resourceful *tour de force*',[40] it elicited scarcely more interest than had Schoenberg's other orchestral transcriptions. Klemperer was, however, enthusiastic about a score that, on account of its composer's proximity to Brahms, is today generally considered to be the most successful of Schoenberg's exercises in the genre. Klemperer performed it no less than three times in the following season (once at the Hollywood Bowl) and included it in the concerts he gave in Mexico City in the following year.*

Although over the years something close to friendship developed between composer and conductor, there were nevertheless periodic squalls. At a dinner Klemperer gave to introduce Schoenberg to members of the Philharmonic board, the composer asserted that he could write to order like Bach. Klemperer sent for music paper and suggested that he make good his claim. Feeling himself to be challenged, Schoenberg banged his fist on the table so violently that he broke a glass.[41] The great man demanded unquestioning devotion from those who were admitted to his inner circle. He also had an overweening sense of his own importance. After Klemperer had failed to accept an invitation to visit him, Schoenberg wrote a letter of rebuke:

> I find it inappropriate that the extent of our meetings should be determined by you ... Anyone should consider it a pleasure as well as an honour if I enjoy seeing him often ... Do not suppose that I am not aware of the gratitude I owe you for your many successful efforts concerning my material affairs. I am very conscious of that, do not and shall not forget it, and will seize every available opportunity to express my thanks practically. But my sense of order tells me ... that every *Kulturmensch* ('civilised person') owes me tribute for my cultural achievements.[42]

At some point in 1938 what Schoenberg himself described as another 'angry exchange' took place between the two men. In a letter (2 April 1940) to Fritz Stiedry, he recalled,

> I reproached him [Klemperer] for the fact that in six years in Los Angeles ... he had not performed one single work with the exception of the Suite for *school* orchestra (which, though it was written by no less a person than Schoenberg, does not represent the sense of my historical task). He conducted *Verklärte*

---

* Thereafter the work remained for many years largely forgotten. Klemperer himself announced a London performance for 17 November 1971 in what proved to be his last season, but was obliged by failing health to cancel the concert.

Nacht, the Cello Concerto, the String Quartet Concerto, all in arrangements, even the Wood Dove [song from *Gurrelieder*] in an arrangement...

After the usual excuses: box office, board of directors, lack of rehearsal, difficulties with artists – all problems that are surmountable in the cases of Stravinsky and Hindemith – he was driven into a corner... and forced to admit that my music had become 'alien' to him...*

Some days later there was a reconciliation. I agreed to it, because he already looked suspiciously unwell and because earlier he had shown himself personally friendly – something that I shall not forget.

Schoenberg's ire generally subsided as rapidly as it had erupted. In 1936, less than three weeks after he had upbraided Klemperer for his failure to visit him, he accepted him as a private pupil. The lessons took place in April 1936 and Schoenberg, whose finances were at a particularly low ebb, accepted no payment for them. Klemperer later recalled,

He never said a word about the twelve-tone system. Not a word. He looked through what I had written and corrected it in a very wise manner, and we analysed Bach motets, but no so-called modern music. In my opinion the great thing Schoenberg taught us is that there is no real difference between consonance and dissonance.[43]

It does not seem, however, that Schoenberg had a high opinion of his pupil. Eight years later, in an angry outburst on the shortcomings of conductors, he singled out Klemperer as one 'whose incompetence became known to me... when I had to realise that he was unable to harmonise a chorale and to become acquainted with music without playing it on the piano'.†

In his diary for April 1936 Schoenberg noted three appointments with Klemperer, who before the end of the month had left for Europe. Whether the lessons were resumed on his return to Los Angeles in July is uncertain. Klemperer subsequently recalled them as numbering 'five or six'. Whatever their number, they remained for him 'among the greatest experiences of my life as a musician'.[44]

*   *   *

Disappointment at his failure to succeed Toscanini as conductor of the New York Philharmonic Orchestra did not cause Klemperer to abandon hope of other openings in the east. Early in 1937 he wrote to Claire Riess, founder and organiser of the League of Composers, a New York group that supported performance of new music, proposing that the Schoenberg and

---

* Yet only a few months later, on 26 January 1939, Dika Newlin, Schoenberg's young pupil, overheard Klemperer and another pianist playing a piano reduction of the Chamber Symphony No. 1 in a practice room at UCLA (Dika Newlin, *Schoenberg Remembered*, p. 77).

† Unpublished observations written in English on 11 August 1944. There is, however, ample evidence that Klemperer was an accomplished sight-reader, though this ability may not have extended to new works of exceptional complexity.

Berg violin concertos would make interesting novelties for New York and also raising the question of performing Hindemith's *Mathis der Maler* and Berg's *Lulu*, neither of which had been staged in America. After Berg's opera had scored a notable success in Zurich in the following summer, he put the question more directly: 'What do you think about a theatrical performance of *Lulu* in New York under my leadership?'[45]

Nothing came of the idea,* but more promising ventures were afoot. In the summer of 1936 Klemperer's friend and champion Ira Hirschmann had with Schnabel's support established a small concert-giving organisation, the New Friends of Music, to provide New York with the regular series of chamber music programmes the city had hitherto lacked. Such was the success of the first season that Hirschmann decided to spread his wings and set up a chamber group, the Orchestra of the New Friends of Music. Klemperer was his first choice as conductor.

In early December 1936 Klemperer sent Hirschmann concrete proposals. He suggested that the series, which could be conducted from the harpsichord, should include the six Brandenburg Concertos, performed with a small string band and original instruments. He would use baroque bows. He also suggested little-known Bach cantatas, to be performed with a small choir that would, if possible, include boys' voices, and less familiar Haydn symphonies with an orchestra of no more than thirty-one players. These proposals indicate how far ahead Klemperer was of most of his colleagues in his approach to the performance of eighteenth-century music at this stage of his career. It is also clear that Hirschmann's project appealed to him as a change from the conventional orchestral concerts in Los Angeles. In a letter (24 December 1936) to Artur Schnabel, Klemperer wrote that the direction of such a chamber orchestra 'would be nice for me'. What damped his interest remains a mystery, but by the following May doubts had clearly arisen in his mind. 'The orchestral idea seems to me a little to [sic] "Utopia"', he wrote disparagingly to Hirschmann. 'I know what time it takes to train an orchestra. And Haydn and Mozart is [sic] the most difficult. And it is too expensive.'[46] Klemperer thereafter proved elusive. 'He encouraged me in principle', Hirschmann later complained to Mark Brunswick. 'And after we got our plan organised . . . he held off a decision so late and then refused, so that it was necessary to take Stiedry.'[47]

It was not the only opportunity that came Klemperer's way. In the spring of 1937 he was invited to reconstitute the Pittsburgh Orchestra, which since 1927 had existed on an *ad hoc* basis, and to conduct its opening concerts in the following season. This time he did not hesitate, and in August set out on his new assignment. As he travelled eastwards the heat grew so intense that

---

* *Lulu* was not seen in New York until the Hamburg State Opera brought it to the Metropolitan Opera House in 1967.

5 Klemperer and Johanna with children Werner and Lotte at Los Angeles railway station, *c.* 1936/7

he could scarcely bring himself to leave the train at stations. He was also oppressed by the monotony of the landscape, which reminded him of the flat expanses between Warsaw and Moscow. 'We don't know how good we have it in California', he wrote ruefully to his wife on the day after his arrival in the grey and oppressively humid steel town, where he found 'a mediocre provincial orchestra'.[48] Such local instrumentalists as he auditioned were not of a sufficiently high standard to provide reinforcements. In New York, where he went a week later for further auditions, he was more successful in finding players of the quality he needed. By early October he was back in Pittsburgh for three weeks of intensive rehearsals and the three opening pairs of concerts. Klemperer was delighted with his new orchestra. 'I don't know if it is an apelike love for the child I have borne', he wrote to his daughter on 30 October, 'but sometimes it seems to me as though it plays better than that in Los Angeles.' Both the board of management and the players themselves were equally impressed and that winter Klemperer was offered the post of musical director of the orchestra at a salary reported to be $40,000, almost double what he was to earn under a new contract signed with Los Angeles a few months later. Although he toyed for a while with the possibility of combining positions in Pittsburgh and Los Angeles, he finally turned the offer down and Fritz Reiner was appointed in his place.

*   *   *

In February 1937 Toscanini accepted the position of conductor of the newly formed NBC Symphony Orchestra and appointed Artur Rodzinski his assistant. Klemperer's anger that his own claims to the subordinate post had been overlooked is apparent in the letter he wrote to Ira Hirschmann on 5 May:

> I have not words enough to tell you how disappointed, how bitterly disappointed, I am by the attitude of Mr Toscanini ... He chooses one man [Rodzinski], who has very limited music in his mind, to co-operate with him for NBC.
>
> I had the honour to watch a part of the life of Gustav Mahler, who was very different ... He looked for *talent* and *only for talent* ... You must not believe that I think that I would have been the right man for Mr Toscanini. But this choice! ... I know you are a friend of this great conductor ... But 'noblesse oblige' and talent obliges much more.

The experience of hearing the new orchestra for the first time on the radio in November revived his resentment. 'It seems to be a very good orchestra', he wrote to Hirschmann. 'Frankly spoken, I had some bitter feelings about the boycott, which the NBC uses against me in addition of the boycott of [the New York] Philharmonic.'[49] There soon proved to be no such boycott. On 26 January 1938 the *Los Angeles Times* reported that Klemperer had been invited to conduct three concerts with the NBC Symphony Orchestra between 5 March and 4 June, but had declined on account of prior commitments. Those commitments were real enough. The Los Angeles season did not end until 7 May 1938, and later in that month he was scheduled to conduct the *Missa solemnis* at the Florence Maggio Musicale.

In view of Klemperer's dislike of Los Angeles and the precarious condition of its orchestra, his failure within less than a year to seize at least two opportunities to escape remains puzzling, particularly as his contract was on the point of expiring. His own characteristically oblique explanation of why he acted as he did is significant. 'I did not feel very well', he later commented.[50] He had indeed been suffering again with his back, as he continued to do throughout the summer of 1938. But in this instance he was probably referring to his psychological condition. When Anneliese Reich, the daughter of his former doctor, Oskar Kohnstamm, saw him in Chicago, where he conducted three concerts with the Chicago Symphony Orchestra in the Christmas week of 1937, she found him depressed.[51] A letter Klemperer wrote to Johanna from Chicago also suggests low spirits:

The first rehearsal is over. Well, I don't find it agreeable. The orchestra doesn't *sound* well. Sour violins! It reminds me vividly (and with shudders) of certain German orchestras. I had quite forgotten that sound ... It is particularly difficult for me to work with such orchestras. There aren't – it must be said – enough Jews ... They have the *warmth* of tone that is indispensable for music. I don't think [the players] like me. They notice how disappointed I am. I can't change that. All in all, *mein Guter*, I don't think that this guest appearance will be of any significance (for the future).*

In the spring of 1938 Klemperer's elder sister, Regi, also perceived that something was amiss. 'Otto is not well', she wrote on 7 April to Marianne Joseph in Palestine. 'I can see it from his handwriting.'† As so often, depression and a feeling of being physically unwell went together, so that, once the season was over, his doctor insisted that he cease work. Klemperer accordingly cancelled his visit to Florence and in May 1938 went on holiday with Johanna, first to Catalina Island, off the Southern Californian coast, and then to Carmel, a quiet seaside resort north of Los Angeles, where the family rented a house for the summer.‡

*   *   *

By general consent, the Los Angeles Philharmonic Orchestra had improved under Klemperer's direction. On 10 March 1937 *Musical America* reported that it was playing with a new refinement of tone. Audiences in 1936–7 were also 10 per cent larger than they had been in the previous season,[52] in spite of programmes that had included a number of works unfamiliar to Los Angeles audiences. In the course of the season Klemperer had given the first performances in the area of Sibelius's Symphony No. 4 (7 January 1937), Mahler's *Das Lied von der Erde* (18 and 19 March 1937) and Bach's *Johannes Passion* (26 and 27 March 1937), the last without cuts. He had also performed for the first time his own transcriptions for strings of Bach's chorale prelude 'Nun komm der Heiden heiland' (10 and 11 December 1936) and of the aria 'Bist Du bei mir' (1 and 2 April 1937). Klemperer nevertheless felt that changes of personnel were necessary,§ and at the end of

---

* Letter of *c.* 21 December 1937. Klemperer conducted the Chicago Symphony Orchestra on 23, 24 and 28 December 1937, at a time when, under Frederick Stock, it had yet to reach the standards it later (1953–62) achieved under Fritz Reiner. Before the Second World War its personnel was so predominantly German that rehearsals were conducted in that language.

† Klemperer's elder sister was not the only relative to see an association between his psychological condition and his handwriting. In a letter of 3 October 1946 to Helene Hirschler, Georg Klemperer made a similar observation.

‡ Harvey Sachs's claim (*Music in Fascist Italy*, pp. 94–5) that Klemperer withdrew from Florence owing to the new racial laws is unfounded. These were not promulgated until 1 September 1938 and did not prevent Bruno Walter and Milhaud from taking part in the festival.

§ In autumn 1937 and in the face of union opposition he appointed as concert-master the Austrian-born violinist Bronislaw Gimpel (1911–79), who continued to lead the orchestra until 1942.

the 1936–7 season he auditioned a number of players. Instead of immediately dismissing the fourteen instrumentalists he intended to replace, he delayed a decision until shortly before the start of the new season, by which time it was too late for them to find new employment. The uproar that ensued in October 1937 reached the columns of *The New York Times* and seems to have taken him by surprise. Isabel Morse Jones, who in the *Los Angeles Times* rarely voiced even the mildest criticism, bluntly told him in a personal letter that the manner in which the dismissals had been made was 'inhuman'.[53] The board of directors was unhappy on other grounds. According to Klemperer, Mudd expressed concern lest there be too many Jews among the replacements. Klemperer was angered by what he took to be an expression of anti-Semitism.*

However, in spite of the resentments, the orchestra was aware that, as the critic José Rodriguez put it, 'no other candidate is fit to tie Klemperer's shoe laces ... Make no mistake, the man has perhaps one equal and no superiors in this country ... The loss of Klemperer would be a serious blow to our musical structure today.'[54] Furthermore, he continued to attract the public in steadily increasing numbers. In spite of economic recession, attendances in the 1937–8 season set a new record,[55] while audiences at the Hollywood Bowl for Klemperer's concerts were larger than for those given by other conductors.[56]

On 30 January 1938 the *Los Angeles Times* announced that Klemperer was about to renew his contract for another three years. He would conduct the orchestra for a minimum of twenty-four weeks at an increased annual salary of $24,000. As before, the board undertook to inform him each year by 1 May whether it would be in a position to present concerts during the following season. His salary would again be guaranteed by Mudd and another member of the board. Even if the orchestra's existence remained as precarious as ever, Klemperer and his family were assured of financial security for a further three years.

*   *   *

The value of that security grew steadily more apparent. Within two weeks of Klemperer's signing of his new contract on 28 February 1938, Austria capitulated to German pressure and in April Hitler made a triumphal entry into Vienna. After the Munich agreement in the following September,

---

* Heyworth (ed.), *Conversations*, pp. 98–9. In an interview with the author (1980), William McKelvey Martin, in 1937 assistant manager to the orchestra and a man whose devotion to Klemperer is not in doubt, stoutly refuted the implicit suggestion that Mudd was an anti-Semite. Be that as it may, it is perhaps not wholly irrelevant to note that, in a report (27 April 1937) to Berlin on Klemperer's activities and attitudes, the German consul in Los Angeles described Mudd, to whom he sold substantial quantities of copper, as 'on the whole well-disposed to Germany'. Should Klemperer adopt an anti-German stance, Mudd could, the consul advised, be relied on to 'show a wide understanding of the matter'.

6   Klemperer and Johanna at Lake Arrowhead, California, *c.* 1937/8

Czechoslovakia was obliged to cede its German-speaking areas to Germany. Six months later the Germans occupied the remainder of the country. On 9–10 November 1938 anti-Jewish riots were instigated throughout Germany. Hitherto, though deprived by the Nuremberg laws of their rights and citizenship, Jews had been able to go about such business as remained open to them without fear of organised violence. Henceforth they stood in physical danger. Up to this point immigration of Jews from Central Europe to the United States had been on a limited scale, so limited indeed that the German quota was not filled until 1939. Now, however, what had been a manageable stream was transformed into a flood that grew larger with every advance in the frontiers of the Third Reich. Like other refugees who had been fortunate enough to establish an early foothold in America, Klemperer found himself inundated with requests for affidavits, testimonials and jobs, because immigrants without work or other means of support required an affidavit that they would not become a charge on public funds before being admitted to the United States.

His most immediate concern was for his sister and brother-in-law, Regi and Ismar Elbogen. In May 1938 they belatedly decided to leave Germany and Klemperer provided an affidavit to enable them to enter the United States. He exerted himself assiduously also for Ernst Bloch,* who as early as spring 1937 was seeking a position in America that did not prove easy to find for a man who had never held an academic position, was a proclaimed Marxist (of a sort) and spoke no English. On his behalf (and that of others) Klemperer intervened on several occasions with the American Guild for German Cultural Freedom.† He provided a testimonial in support of his old friend's application for a Guild bursary and, after Bloch's arrival in New York in July 1938, pursued the matter in a letter in which he described him, a shade generously, as 'a second Spinoza'.[57]

In some cases his answers to appeals for assistance could only be discouraging. In February 1938 Fritz Stiedry arrived in New York from the Soviet Union and sought Klemperer's help in procuring work. Klemperer had to explain that he himself had no engagements to offer, and that the Hollywood Bowl was interested only in conductors with proven drawing power, which Stiedry, still virtually unknown in America, did not possess.[58] Similarly, the Viennese clarinettist Eric Simon had to be told that there were no vacancies in the Los Angeles orchestra. These difficulties weighed heavily on Klemperer's spirits.

Early in 1939 he began to experience alarming disturbances in his sense of balance. The orchestra noticed a decline in his hitherto enormous stamina and ability to maintain discipline in rehearsals.[59] In June he confessed in confidence to his old friend Helene Hirschler that 'already for quite a long time I have been in a condition that is not adequately described as exhaustion'.[60] Alarmed by reports of his condition, his 74-year-old cousin, the physician Georg Klemperer, flew for the first time in his life to Los Angeles, but after a stay of several weeks reached a conclusion that the symptoms arose from Klemperer's depressed state of mind.

Georg had proved a wise counsellor in earlier crises, and Klemperer accepted his diagnosis. But it did nothing to alleviate his sense of anguish. In a despairing letter (29 June) to his cousin he confessed that he had reached a point where he had come to doubt his own abilities. Georg set out to comfort him.

> Good Otto, take *one* piece of advice: don't make any assessments of your characteristics and abilities now or in the immediate future. In your present condition ... your view of yourself doesn't correspond to reality ... The only thing a doctor can do for you is to tell you time and again that your estimate of yourself is an expression of a pathological state of mind (*Seelenzustand*) and to

---

* In spite of Bloch's rather sour observation (letter to Joachim Schumacher, Prague, 17 October 1937) that Klemperer was not 'very philanthropic, unless the persons concerned are before him' ('wenn er die Menschen nicht sieht') (*Briefe*, pp. 524–5).

† Established in 1936 by Hubertus, Prinz zu Loewenstein (1906–84) to support scholars, scientists, artists and writers who had left Germany. Klemperer conducted a concert in its aid in Los Angeles on 23 September 1936. His association with the Guild attracted the attention of the German consul in Los Angeles.

tell you with the same certainty that this will pass ... Don't forget that you have already several times gone through this gloomy business. At the Kroll Oper you were for months just as indecisive and apathetic and spoke just as dismissively of your talents. And then one day you were yourself again ... You must not lose heart because this time the trouble is lasting so long ... Such cases ... often occur, but there is absolutely no case that doesn't recover completely ... The main thing is that you should not allow your false estimate of yourself to determine your behaviour. However hard it may be for you, you must force yourself to conduct in Mexico and at the Bowl. I have myself experienced how in the worst time in Berlin you conducted splendidly.[61]

Klemperer's symptoms continued to worsen, however. In the course of the summer a weakening of the right hand began to hinder his piano-playing. As he rose to speak at the annual fund-raising banquet for the Hollywood Bowl at Earl Carroll's Restaurant on 26 June 1939, he suddenly toppled across the table, upsetting a water jug.[62] Malicious tongues began to ask whether he had not acquired his wife's drinking habits. It was doubtless as a result of this incident that Klemperer consulted a neurologist, who confirmed Georg's diagnosis and recommended a course of swimming and massage. Yet after some weeks of the prescribed treatment at Arrowhead Springs, a nearby mountain resort, he admitted to Helene Hirschler that

> my walking ... has become very bad ... I lurch to and fro. I know that it comes from within. They call it hysteria, but what's to be done about it? I can still swim, though getting in and out is difficult. Every afternoon a masseur comes. I know that that is purely external. However, it's the only thing I can do at the moment.[63]

Shortly after Klemperer returned to Los Angeles, he was visited by Eric Simon, who on 1 August reported to Fritz and Erika Stiedry: 'I had an impression that mentally he is quite all right, but not physically. He gropes his way along a wall, lurches, walks quite slowly and looks as though he can move one side only with difficulty.' Simon's assessment proved more accurate than that of the physicians. The depression had in fact slowly begun to lift, so that by the time Klemperer set out for Mexico City, where on 11 and 13 August he conducted a programme that included Schoenberg's Brahms transcription, he was in better psychological shape than he had been for well over a year. 'Papa – fair!!' wrote Johanna to her daughter on their arrival. But for Klemperer the concerts were a torment. 'Imagine conducting with a constant feeling that one is falling over', he wrote to Helene Hirschler on his return.[64] The long walk to and from the platform at the Bowl, where he gave four concerts in the last week of the month, presented an even worse ordeal. At home he practised it in the hall, and in the amphitheatre William McKelvey Martin, the orchestra's assistant manager, held up a white handkerchief for him to steer towards. It was now painfully apparent that something was seriously amiss. But as Klemperer refused to make any reference to his disability, no one felt able to raise the matter.[65]

The conspiracy of silence was finally broken by a reference to Klemperer's condition in a radio broadcast by José Rodriguez. The board of the orchestra urged Johanna to take medical advice. She needed little persuasion, for, as she was aware, her husband's worsening physical symptoms could no longer be attributed to a depression that was now clearly on the wane.[66]

Klemperer was examined by a doctor, who advised him to consult his cousin in Boston. Johanna thought her husband seemed to be unnaturally laconic in the circumstances and found an excuse to return to the consulting room alone. The doctor told her that in his opinion Klemperer was suffering from a brain tumour that required immediate surgery and that the outstanding school for this speciality in America (and thus in the world) was in Boston, where Georg Klemperer was living.[67]

5

On the road to self-destruction

It did not prove easy to persuade Klemperer to leave his responsibilities in Los Angeles in order to travel three thousand miles for further investigations. Still unaware of his doctor's suspicions, he must have wondered why these could not be carried out locally. But Johanna dug her toes in and within a few days of his final concert at the Bowl they flew together to Chicago, where a freak snowstorm obliged them to continue their journey to Boston by train. There on 14 September 1939 he was admitted to the City Hospital. A preliminary examination led to the erroneous diagnosis of an intercranial tumour affecting the left side of the brain. Two days later he was transferred to the Lahey Clinic in the New England Deaconess Hospital, where the celebrated school of neurosurgery that had been established by Harvey Cushing was headed by his most distinguished pupil, Gilbert Horrax.* There tests proved the diagnosis to be incorrect: Klemperer was found to be suffering from a right-sided acoustic neuroma, a tumour on the nerve that transmits hearing and balance. This accounted for the increasing deafness he had suffered in his right ear since 1935. Meanwhile, his condition was deteriorating. His pulse had grown slower and he had begun to experience severe headaches. On 18 September Johanna was pressed to give her consent to an immediate operation. Initially she was unwilling to do so in the absence of Horrax, since she was eager that he himself should perform the operation. Georg Klemperer stressed the urgency of the situation, however, and she was about to give way when a nurse burst into the room. Horrax had returned a day earlier than expected and was already examining the patient. He confirmed the diagnosis made by his staff and that afternoon, in an operation lasting four and a half hours, removed a 'tremendously large',† slow-growing but non-malignant tumour on the eighth cranial nerve.

That night Georg Klemperer wrote to Helene Hirschler:

* Harvey Cushing (1869–1939) reduced the mortality in brain tumour operations from almost 100 per cent to 10 per cent and trained a generation of surgeons. Outstanding among these was Gilbert Horrax (1887–1952). An obituary notice (*Journal of Neurology*, No. 15, 1958, pp. 234–6) described him as unsurpassed 'in his mastery of the meticulous ... and brilliant ... technique essential to first-grade brain surgery'.
† Phrase used by Dr James Poppen in an interview with the author, November 1977. Poppen, who had been responsible for the correct diagnosis, assisted Horrax at the operation. He later succeeded him as head of the neurosurgical department of the Lahey Clinic.

> An acoustic neuroma the size of a small apple has been removed. Otto weathered ... the operation well. He is still unconscious, but pulse and breathing are satisfactory and so far the prognosis seems favourable. Both diagnosis and operation are brilliant achievements of the first order ... Otto's behaviour has been splendid.[1]

What Georg did not say, however, was that Horrax had been obliged to sever the seventh nerve, which controls the muscles of the face. As a result, the right side of Klemperer's face was partly paralysed, so that the right end of the mouth was dragged downwards. The right eyelid could not close and the consequent drying up of tears led to a sensation of a foreign body in the eye. The right side of the body was correspondingly paralysed. In varying degree these afflictions remained with him to the end of his life.

Four days later, Georg Klemperer wrote again to Helene Hirschler:

> It seems as though the shock of the operation has been overcome and that he is out of danger. Pulse this morning very strong, 80. Temperature, which had been up to 103° ... this morning 99.2° ... He is still under narcosis, but often wakes up and is then clear [in his mind]. He complains of headaches but is very patient ... The written report of the operation reveals how deep it went, but the tumour has been radically eliminated ... (Otto, who believed that death was certain, has shown himself a true philosopher.)[2]

> Without doubt [continued Georg on 26 September] he owes his life to the enormous skill of the surgeon, Dr Horrax. The German mortality rate for the removal of an acoustic neuroma was over 80 per cent, Cushing had 12 per cent, Horrax has 8!! ... The right-sided facial paralysis troubles Otto a great deal, but Horrax wants to repair that. He thinks that Otto should give up the whole of this season, but that he will probably be well enough to return to Los Angeles by the end of the year.

Klemperer's recovery did not go as smoothly as envisaged. Six days later, on 2 October, he began to run a high temperature and the headaches grew more severe. A lumbar puncture revealed meningitis. At a time when antibiotics did not exist, treatment consisted of sulphonamides, in themselves debilitating, transfusions of blood and other liquids, and up to five lumbar punctures daily. Performed without anaesthetics, these remained his worst memory. 'Prognosis uncertain, but in no way unfavourable', Georg Klemperer reported to Helene Hirschler on 5 October. A week later he wrote that the cerebro-spinal fluids were clearer, but that a raised pulse and temperature indicated the continuing presence of an infection in the brain. 'There is no clear sign of immediate danger, [but] prognosis *dubia*! ... It is a difficult time for all of us who love Otto.'[3]

From the day of the operation Johanna had warned the children not to divulge their father's condition: '*No one* must know about the operation ...

No one, dear Werner ... just say that Papa is under observation.'[4] Georg also considered, as he wrote to Helene Hirschler on 18 September, that the operation should not, at any rate for the moment, be made public, 'as a layman would believe that the brain is not functioning any more'.[5] But the news inevitably leaked out and on 30 September the *New York Herald-Tribune* reported that, according to Horrax, Klemperer was doing very nicely. Telephones started ringing and on 3 October Fritz Stiedry, having been informed by Rudolf Kolisch of the patient's condition, wrote to ask Schoenberg whether he could procure for him some of Klemperer's concerts in Los Angeles. On 4 October Walter S. Hilborn informed Mudd that his client would be unable to conduct during the coming season.* Because of the heavy drop in income involved, the lease on the house in Bel Air was not renewed.

Though there were alarming moments when his temperature flared up, Klemperer's condition gradually improved. On 7 November Regi Elbogen, who by now had settled in New York, wrote to tell her sister Marianne that their brother would be allowed out of bed for fifteen minutes on the following day. His ordeal had left him physically emaciated, but by the beginning of December he was well enough to undergo a further operation, in which Horrax unsuccessfully attempted to ameliorate his facial paralysis by in effect sacrificing the nerve controlling the tongue. The intervention resulted only in a further disability that persisted until the end of his life: henceforth a partial atrophy of the tongue caused him to speak indistinctly and have difficulty in swallowing. But by this time he was recovering fast. Indeed on 13 December Regi reported to Marianne that he was 'in good spirits'. The depression that was already lifting before the operation had yielded to a manic phase that was to prove among the most prolonged and destructive he ever experienced.†

At this point Klemperer dropped a bombshell. Reminding Johanna of an agreement they had made at the time of their marriage that she would raise no objection should he wish to spend a year on his own, he announced that on leaving hospital he would not return home, but live for an unspecified period in New York. Johanna was horrified. She sympathised with his unwillingness to show himself in Los Angeles until such time as his physical

---

* The season, which had as usual been in doubt until the last moment, was eventually opened on 30 November by Bruno Walter, who had recently settled in Beverly Hills. In an undated letter written shortly beforehand, Johanna told her children to attend the concert. They were not to make any comments, but should just 'keep smiling' (English in the original).

† Max Friedemann, who had been on the medical staff of Kohnstamm's clinic, which Klemperer entered in 1911 and on subsequent occasions, told the author (November 1977) that he had never previously known Klemperer so 'high'. This raises the question whether there was any connection between the brain surgery he had undergone and the period of intense euphoria that followed it. Neurologists and a psychiatrist consulted by the author are in agreement that Klemperer's manic-depressive illness may well have been exacerbated by brain surgery, so that a euphoria (or a depression) would tend to become more extreme than would otherwise be the case.

disabilities had become less conspicuous, but Manhattan in midwinter hardly seemed suited to the convalescence of a man in his condition. Separation was a cruel blow to a woman who had endured three months of great strain and was herself far from well; two months later she was to undergo an operation to repair a ruptured hernia. With the support of Horrax and Georg, however, she was able to persuade Klemperer on his discharge from hospital on 27 December to spend at least a month with her in a furnished apartment in Boston. There he busied himself with reading and studying the late Beethoven quartets. But, as Regi explained (in English) to Marianne, the plan to move to New York had become

> an *idée fixe* ... You know him, after the depression there is now the contrary, everything is rosy and there are no difficulties. I am very sorry that there is nobody who has influence upon him ... [The target of this comment was Johanna.] He is in high spirits, witty and so on, but bodily he is still handicapped. Well, let us hope that the result will be better than we think.'[5]

By good fortune, help arrived in the person of Gertrud Friedemann. Married to a distinguished physician, Ulrich Friedemann, she had been a piano pupil of Edwin Fischer and had sung under Klemperer in the Berlin Philharmonic Chorus. She now proposed that he should stay as a paying guest in her bungalow at Great Neck on Long Island. There he would be in a sympathetic environment and under a degree of medical supervision, yet only forty-five minutes' drive from Manhattan. 'A stone has fallen from my heart', wrote Johanna on 9 January 1940 to Gertrud Friedemann. 'After so long away I must return to the children, look for a house ... and also recover a bit myself.' Arrangements were made for Klemperer's young chauffeur, 'more student than servant', to live nearby, so as to be available to dress and shave him and also to drive him to New York.

On 2 February, the day before Klemperer moved to Great Neck, Georg wrote to brief Ulrich Friedemann on his cousin's condition:

> He has in general recovered, but the nerve channels that have been pressed on by the tumour are not yet functioning properly and will probably need exercising for a very long time. Added to that, there is a great feeling of insecurity and anxiety ... He must slowly learn to walk again by himself, to get up from a seat and sit down again without help, to read aloud, to practise writing and using his fingers on a piano ... It is particularly important to protect the cornea of the right eye, as at the moment the paralysis of the right side of the face prevents the lids from shutting.

In a second letter, written after Klemperer had spent ten days as guest of the Friedemanns, Georg went into more detail:

> I would ask you not to be too merciful ... Daily exercises are absolutely necessary. Should my cousin not do as you tell him, please write. I would then

try and persuade him to go to a sanatorium, where, if necessary, he could be more severely dealt with.

Under oath of *medical secrecy* I would like to explain the reason for the unconcern that leads him to neglect his exercises. Since his youth, he has suffered from cyclical periods of a manic-depressive condition that alternate with pauses extending over several years. Since he has grown older, he has been quieter, though in the past two years he has been very melancholy. A clear upward tendency has become evident since the operation. There is no doubt that he is in very high spirits and it may be that a sub-manic period is in the offing, in which, incidentally, his artistic genius and his amiability tend to reveal themselves to splendid effect.[6]

On 7 February Klemperer lunched with his sister and brother-in-law in New York. The following day Regi reported to Marianne: 'He walks very slowly, [even when] supported ... He eats with his left hand because the right hand is still weak. He wears dark spectacles ...' Three weeks later she wrote again, this time in German:

Otto is completely intact intellectually. But his mouth is still twisted and the eye troubles him ... His right hand is still very weak. His writing looks firm, but it requires a great effort. All his movements are very slow, but he *makes* them. He is very content with everything, absolutely not impatient. Astonishing! He would like to see people, but he rightly thinks that it would damage him professionally.[7]

At Great Neck Klemperer started to learn to type. With the help of Gertrud Friedemann and Lonny Epstein he also attempted to play the piano and together with his hostess tackled Bach organ music with his left hand.[8] His right hand would not respond. 'The whole right side is not good', he wrote to Anneliese Reich on 13 March. 'My face, my eye, my speech, my eating, my walking, my piano playing.' Fritz Stiedry, who visited him some weeks later, was shocked by his physical and psychological condition, and on 12 April wrote to Schoenberg:

The right eye, the right half of the face, right leg and right hand are more or less immobilised. Unless a miracle happens, it is hardly likely that he will be able to conduct here publicly before Christmas. His state of mind seems to me decidedly unstable. He is in extremely high spirits and full of plans. None the less, it isn't hard to perceive an inner restlessness and worry behind this manic elation.

Life at Great Neck was not without its consolations. Klemperer had what he himself described as a pleasant room. The house had a good library and looked on to woods. There were visits from Lonny Epstein and the Stiedrys, the Schnabels and the composer Paul Dessau. Best of all, Ernst Bloch came to see him.* However, he grew increasingly restive in suburban isolation. At night the household was disturbed by his incessant telephoning. He became hostile and aggressive to Gertrud Friedemann.[9] Inevitably, her well-meant attempts to restrain him led to a quarrel. On 26 April he left Great Neck and established himself in a one-room flat on the West Side of New York City.

A week later he travelled to Boston for a medical check-up. Horrax noted that, though the condition of the right eye was still causing discomfort, the upper lid could now be closed. Otherwise there was no improvement in the facial paralysis. The right hand was still weak, though Klemperer insisted that he would be able to conduct, despite his limited arm movements. Horrax made no reference to his patient's psychological condition. That evening Klemperer called on Koussevitzky, where he found the Stravinskys.† In her diary Vera Stravinsky noted, 'Klemperer comes in ... with a strange look in his eyes, as though he had risen from the dead.'[10] Georg Klemperer found his cousin's physical condition improved, 'even if', as he wrote to Helene Hirschler, 'it still leaves much to be desired'. In his judgement the manic condition was still within tolerable limits. 'If he can be kept in seclusion, so that his behaviour, which can be frightening for laymen, doesn't discredit him, the outlook for his future is, I think, quite good. He has survived worse attacks.'[11] But Georg's prognosis proved optimistic.

On 10 May, Maria Schacko,‡ a singer who until 1933 had been a member of the theatre in the small Saxon town of Altenberg, called on Klemperer, accompanied by her agent, Thea Dispeker. Her purpose was to secure an audition and Klemperer agreed to accompany her as best he could with his left hand in Schumann Lieder and 'Non so più' from *Le Nozze di Figaro*. Thea Dispeker then left. Maria Schacko remained.§ That evening she and Klemperer dined together. The following day they met again and worked on some of Klemperer's own songs. Thereafter they spent much of their time in each other's company, frequenting expensive French restaurants. On 14 May they celebrated his fifty-fifth birthday at lunch with his flame of twenty-eight

---

* Klemperer was disconcerted at his old friend's inability to find his feet in America or even to learn English. 'Bloch is someone who cannot help himself', he wrote to Helene Hirschler on 3 March, immediately after the visit. That same day he appealed on his behalf in letters to Thomas Mann and Hubertus Loewenstein, through whose joint intervention the American Guild for Cultural Freedom was persuaded to make a grant. Gertrud Friedemann arranged for Bloch and his wife to spend the coming summer on an estate in New Hampshire, where Klemperer later visited them (Klemperer's letter to Helene Hirschler, 20 March 1940).

† The composer was in Boston to deliver (in French) at Harvard University the Charles Eliot Norton Lectures, published in 1942 as *Poètique musicale*. Two months earlier he had married Vera de Bosset.

‡ The name would not have been unfamiliar. As a young student in Frankfurt, Klemperer had heard her mother, Hedwig Schacko (1867–1932), sing at the City Opera, of which she was a leading member from 1891 to 1912.

§ Accounts of the meeting given to the author by Miss Schacko and Miss Dispeker do not wholly correspond.

years earlier, the singer Elisabeth Schumann, who had emigrated to America after the Austrian *Anschluss* of 1938. Schumann was perturbed by his psychological condition. In a letter to a friend she questioned whether 'he will ever be himself again'.[12]

Maria Schacko, who was married to the conductor Maurice Abravanel, was thirty-five years old and 'a very pretty woman with fine features, beautiful complexion and eyes'.[13] She was swept off her feet by the attentions paid her by Klemperer, who in spite of his disabilities was still able to exercise considerable charm when so disposed. In Schacko's own words, 'a great love and a wonderful friendship' came into being.[14] On 17 May, after dining at Le Pavilion, they spent the night together, platonically, it would seem.[15] The following morning Klemperer rose early to hear Mass and later that day flew to Los Angeles. His departure suggests that at this point he was not disposed to take the affair more seriously than countless other fleeting associations he had entered into when manic.

Klemperer's presence in Los Angeles brought little comfort to Johanna, who only a few days previously had moved into a modest house she had bought in Brentwood. Immediately on his arrival he precipitated himself into a whirlwind of activity. On 21 May he instructed Walter Hilborn to sue Lauritz Melchior on account of remarks the tenor had supposedly made about their unharmonious collaboration in Buenos Aires in 1931. Two days later the Stravinskys arrived in the town that was to be their home for the next twenty-nine years. Klemperer met them at the station and immediately insisted on taking them on a tour of the area.[16] He also threw himself into the task of forming an amateur chorus, which was to be trained by Ingolf Dahl. A boil on his leg kept Klemperer in bed for a week, but it did not prevent him from composing. In early June he called on Bruno Walter to play some of his compositions. Walter expressed polite approval of some early songs, but, according to Klemperer's own account of the meeting, remained pointedly silent after he had given a one-handed performance of the postlude to *Bathseba*.

On 10 May the German army had invaded the Low Countries and thrust far across the plains of northern France, but Klemperer seemed unable to grasp the significance of events. On 30 May, as the British army was being evacuated from Dunkirk, he told Helene Hirschler that the situation did not worry him. A week later he wrote again, 'I can only repeat – don't worry. You cannot change things. In that sense I am an optimist.'[17] As the days passed, his mood grew more exalted. On 15 June he greeted the news that German troops had entered Paris as what he chose to describe as a miracle. On 26 June, four days after France had signed an armistice, he was delighted at the prospect that Britain would be obliged to do likewise. Thus fighting would cease and Europe would again enjoy peace.

In the middle of June, and with his sixteen-year-old daughter as chaperon, he moved to the clinic at Arrowhead Springs, where a course of baths and massages brought about some improvement in his physical condition. 'I can now walk without a stick', he told Helene Hirschler.[18] But his behaviour grew steadily wilder. No woman was safe from his advances. He squandered money with reckless abandon. At night he scarcely slept, and insisted that the clinic's swimming pool be lit so that he could use it at all hours. He wrote almost daily to Maria Schacko, often in a high-flown language, far removed from his usually sober manner of expressing himself. He also started to compose a cantata, at that stage entitled 'America'. Matters finally reached a point where the sanatorium authorities informed Lotte that, if her father did not leave of his own accord, he would be thrown out. Fearing a scene, she tactfully suggested that life in Santa Barbara might prove more entertaining. Klemperer took the bait and that same night they left by bus. He had, however, already invited Maria Schacko to join him at Arrowhead, where she arrived on 13 July to find that he had gone. When she eventually caught up with him in Santa Barbara, she proved no more able to restrain him than his daughter, who, after a quarrel, climbed out of her bedroom window and returned, penniless, to Arrowhead, whence the clinic director took the overwrought girl back to her mother in Los Angeles. She was, he suggested to Johanna, rather young to be responsible for a man in her father's condition.

From Santa Barbara, Klemperer moved to a hotel in Pasadena. There he insisted that the bar piano be removed to the staff dressing-room, where he proceeded to play his compositions. On another occasion he entered the swimming pool fully dressed.[19] Again, he was asked to leave. At one point he even turned up with Maria Schacko at his home in Los Angeles.[20] Enraged, Johanna left the house and threatened divorce. At this point Klemperer's sense of self-preservation momentarily reasserted itself:

> Please stay, don't leave at this moment or at least tell *me* where you are. There is no point in us both walking out. Be *at least* as good *to me* as you have always been over twenty-one years. Think of the time of my illness, when for four months in hospital you never left my side. Do you suppose I have forgotten that? ... I remain as close to you as I was twenty-one years ago when we married. That means with my *entire love*. I won't consider a divorce. I have not the least grounds for one.[21]

It does not seem to have occurred to Klemperer that Johanna had grounds for seeking a divorce from *him*.

At the end of July 1940 Klemperer returned with Maria Schacko to New York, where they took separate apartments on Riverside Drive. On 29 July he went to Boston for a check-up by Horrax. Though Horrax found that his physical condition had more or less stabilised, Georg Klemperer was alarmed at his cousin's psychological deterioration. To Helene Hirschler he wrote two days later:

> Your concern about Otto is unfortunately well founded ... His manic condition is at its peak ... The lack of critical perception (also in musical as well as in, alas, ethical matters) is dreadful, and ... on this occasion paranoid features are evident that I have not previously observed in his case. I have made him promise to see Paul Klemperer [a distant cousin, living in New York]. Although he is a pathologist, he has many medical connections and he is also a very clear-minded and sensible man ... I have asked him to make arrangements for a *psychiatric* consultation and, if possible, to get Otto into an institution immediately. I hope he succeeds and that Otto gets through the attack without hopelessly compromising himself. Purely physically, he is better and I don't think that the psychosis is connected with the tumour or the operation ... Let us hope ... that his mania is not again followed by depression. There is scarcely anything we can do other than ... to confide his fate to providence.

A consultation with Paul Klemperer resulted only in a course of short-wave electrical treatment, designed to strengthen his damaged side.

After three months Klemperer's association with Maria Schacko could no longer be regarded as a passing infatuation. In late August the couple spent a weekend with Ernst Bloch and his wife at their summer retreat in New Hampshire. The visit was not without its embarrassments. Unaware that Klemperer was bringing his mistress, Bloch accepted an invitation to dine at the big house of the estate he was living on. He wrote to the Hirschlers,

> You can imagine the difficulties ... with a lot of New England ladies. Finally, however, we had some music. The pretty singer sang Spanish folk songs, Schubert, Brahms and some of Klemperer's early things with an excellent voice. I don't think that it would be appropriate for me to get involved in the issue of Schacko, at any rate in letters ... The effect on Klemperer might be the opposite of what one intended. And then one has to consider whether one has the duty and the right to do so ... The main thing is that he should feel happy (*wohl*) and that life should be made easy for him. In any case, he doesn't ask for advice; quite to the contrary.[22]

On 2 September Klemperer returned to Los Angeles. Johanna was about to undergo another operation, this time for peritonitis. Eleven days later he had to take an oath of allegiance at his place of residence on becoming an American citizen. He was also eager to work with his new chorus, which Ingolf Dahl had been rehearsing since mid-July, and with the Hollywood Youth Orchestra, which Bronislaw Gimpel had established that summer. He did not make a happy impression on either. The orchestra was surprised when he sat on the floor in the middle of a rehearsal.[23] Dahl and his wife were amazed by his choice of the *Missa solemnis* for an inexperienced chorus and by his insistence that it should also perform his own composition, 'America', which on completion had been given a new title. '*Trinity*', wrote Etta Dahl, 'is, in the best American slangology, a scream ... It is inexplicable to both of us how a man who should certainly have better musical taste than all but a dozen others in the whole world should write such impossible stuff ... [but] no one dares to cross him.'[24] At about this time Klemperer burst into a lecture on music appreciation at the City College, where 'his whole aspect was that of a wild man'.[25]

Klemperer's behaviour had already occasioned much unfavourable comment. He now proceeded to destroy what remained of his reputation in Los Angeles. At night he would hire a taxi to visit a succession of night spots. In the early morning he would descend unannounced on friends, who were expected to provide breakfast and settle a sizeable cab fare.[26] 'Something seems to have damaged his self-control', wrote Vicki Baum. 'He tears around like a maniac, getting into conflicts with the police all the time; he is a Hoffmannesque figure with a black patch over one eye, his roaring voice, his paralysed walk and his tragic pursuits [*sic*] of every female that crosses his way.'[27] After he had returned to New York on 21 September, Johanna unburdened herself to her son:

> After Papa had left, I more or less broke down ... I feel weak as I have never felt before ... I left hospital too early ... [so as] to prevent Papa from giving a party for one or two hundred people ... the day before he left ...
>
> Papa squandered money here in an indescribable way. There wasn't a *single* night that he was at home – even during the operation. On the *second* day after my operation Mr Ruther (Union Bank) appeared at my bedside as he needed my signature, so that Papa could sell the bonds.* I was much too weak to resist for long and Papa had in any case to pay the bank debts. When I saw how he was running through the money, I made him ... put $1,500 in my account ... *Perhaps* he will come to his senses if he has no more money.[28]

* * *

It was agreed that Klemperer would not resume his duties with the orchestra until 1 January 1941, though his relations with its board were not helped when, against Hilborn's advice, he attempted to claim compensation for the part of the season he would be unable to conduct. Mudd tartly informed Hilborn that his client had over a number of years been earning at a level that should have enabled him to make savings.[29] Nevertheless, on learning of Klemperer's financial difficulties, Mudd did agree to advance him $2,000 from his salary for the coming season.[30] However, by this time news of his wild behaviour was spreading rapidly, and once he had left for New York

---

* In January 1939 Klemperer's savings amounted to $10,000 in a bank deposit account and $50,000 of US Bonds (Hilborn files).

on 21 September the board decided to dismiss him. Klemperer reacted with incredulous fury. He bombarded the unhappy Hilborn with telephone calls and telegrams, insisting that he stand on the terms of his contract. Aware that his client's legal position was untenable, Hilborn counselled caution. But Klemperer was not to be reasoned with. On 30 September he cabled what he described as 'my final condition': '12,000 dollars cash today until midnight Pacific time. 6,600 dollars eleven concerts per 600 dollars beside all financial things. I have right of occupation 1940–1 as musical director.' When Hilborn replied on the following day, 'Unable to make arrangement requested ... Believe I can secure present payment of ten thousand dollars for cancellation of contract', Klemperer wired, 'Proposition unacceptable will fight' and that same evening informed Hilborn in yet another telegram that he had engaged a New York lawyer, who 'will naturally represent me in my case'. On 2 October Hilborn cautioned his New York colleague, 'I do not know of any ground for suit against the Association.'[31]

Johanna was distraught. In a letter to Werner (3 October), she wrote:

> Papa has unfortunately behaved so impossibly here that in my view the Association has reason enough to break the contract ... At first I urged Papa to stick to [it], as I thought it would be terrible for him when he wakes up to find that he doesn't have a single engagement. But when one public scandal followed another and *no sort* of talking to him helped and he continued to destroy himself ... I urged him to accept the offer of $10,000 (which I think is very *decent*) and a guarantee of four pairs of concerts in 1942. But no amount of talking helps. He wants to sue as he did in Berlin, when he brought an action against the State – in a similar period – and lost! Only with the difference that this suit would cost our entire resources and would wash so much dirty linen in public, which would not be exactly advantageous for further engagements in America. Perhaps if he now sees no way of making do with his money, he will accept. I *cannot* send him any more ...
>
> When I think of the immediate future, my head whirls ... Let us say I have $2,000 in the bank. There are many bills for doctors and treatment.* I have declared my readiness to pay Papa's uncovered cheques. They amount to at least $800–900 – I fear even more. Among others there are cheques from the Hotels Miramar ... Ambassador and Biltmore, where Papa has taken rooms for the night. Apart from that he was also out on the town. *One* cheque alone for $300 ... *Many* $50, 45, 40, 30, 20 and so on. Several cheques for taxis, partly in Santa Barbara, partly in Los Angeles. Two Santa Monica Cab Co. cheques – one for $38, one for $15 – the men themselves were already here ... A telephone bill for $108. My hospital bill of $230 has to be paid. There is a bill from Shaw [Johanna's doctor] still to come. Whether I can now let the house in the winter is doubtful ... That means that by then $990 rental has to be put aside ... I

---

* Including – though Johanna did not mention it – $2,000 still owing to the surgeon, Gilbert Horrax.

again enclose $25 for you and the $20 Papa gave. Am very tired . . . Also there [New York] Papa *certainly* does not spend one night at home and certainly already has many debts – but *she* is not troubled about that . . . He will ruin his life and in doing so his conducting.

On 9 October Klemperer finally agreed to settle for $10,000, in addition to the $2,000 he had received the previous month as an advance from Mudd, the latter sum to be deducted from his fees should he be in a position to conduct in the seasons of 1941–2 and 1942–3. Five days later Klemperer's retirement as musical director of the Los Angeles Philharmonic Orchestra was announced in the press. The Association insisted that Johanna's position be safeguarded and, after some altercation, it was to her that the money was finally paid on 6 November; though Klemperer subsequently told Hilborn that, as the Association had refused to commit itself to engaging him for four pairs of concerts in 1941–2, 'the whole settlement is annihilated' and that he would accordingly return to Los Angeles to conduct his opening concert on 9 January 1941 under the terms of his old contract. In the following months Klemperer made a number of similar threats. Nothing came of them.

*   *   *

While still staying with the Friedemanns in Great Neck earlier in the year, Klemperer had busied himself with arranging concerts for the following autumn in New York: once it was settled that he would not resume his duties in Los Angeles until January 1941, he had no intention of remaining idle. In any case, he needed money. As his euphoria grew, so his fear of Schoenberg's mature music diminished, and he wrote to inform the composer that he planned to conduct *Pierrot Lunaire* and the as yet unperformed Violin Concerto that autumn in New York.[32] Schoenberg was far from pleased; he himself was planning to record *Pierrot Lunaire* in Los Angeles and then to perform it in New York. He was also still smarting from Klemperer's admission that his music had grown 'alien' to him, and on that account claimed to harbour doubts about Klemperer's ability to do justice to it, doubts that were ill-founded in view of his own declared satisfaction with the performances that Klemperer had conducted in Berlin and Los Angeles. He gave vent to his feelings in a letter to Fritz Stiedry:

> Although I nourish a full-grown grudge against Klemperer on account of his attitude to my music and . . . am convinced that he is unable to understand it, I don't want to upset him at the moment. Above all on humanitarian grounds: who knows whether he will ever be entirely restored to health. But also because . . . he has behaved in a very kindly way to me here and we live on friendly terms with his family* – and because I'm fond of him personally. But I can't

---

* A warm relationship had in particular grown up between the two wives. The Schoenbergs had also shown much kindness to Lotte, whom they had frequently invited to meals during her mother's four-month absence in Boston in the previous winter.

let such considerations be decisive in artistic matters. A musician for whom *Pelleas*, the *Gurrelieder*, the First String Quartet and the Chamber Symphony are 'alien' cannot be considered for performances of my more difficult works.[33]

In his reply Stiedry counselled moderation: 'It is impossible to stand in the way of a man who has been snatched from the jaws of death and is starting to make a plan for his life. For the foreseeable time he must be treated as a sick man.' Meanwhile *The New York Times* announced that Klemperer would conduct a performance of *Pierrot Lunaire* for the New Friends of Music in New York Town Hall on 17 November.

On 13 September Klemperer was a guest at Schoenberg's sixty-sixth birthday party in Los Angeles, at which Schoenberg, Steuermann, Leonard Stein and Felix Khuner took turns to participate in a four-handed version of a Mahler symphony. Steuermann performed the Piano Suite, Op. 25, and the festivities ended with Schoenberg's own version of 'Wien, Wien nur Du allein', after which he proposed a toast (in whisky) to 'the doom of Vienna'.[34] Two weeks later Klemperer got wind of Schoenberg's attitude to him and wrote from New York to protest.[35] Schoenberg's reply was unyielding:

> You are misinformed ... I have quoted word for word what you said in the course of an argument you will surely not have forgotten: 'Your music is alien to me.'
> That is not some of my works, but *all* my works.
> No further explanation should be necessary as to why I find that you should no longer perform my works ...
> That does not mean that I no longer take any interest in you; although I have no idea how the broken (artistic) bridges can ever function again.[36]

In his answer Klemperer indignantly denied that he had rejected Schoenberg's music in its entirety.[37] Nevertheless, on learning that Schoenberg was going to be in New York at the time of the performance of *Pierrot Lunaire*, Klemperer gave up his plan to conduct the work, even though he had already started to rehearse it, and handed the concert over to the composer.

That was not the end of the quarrel, however. On 22 November Schoenberg's publishers gave a party in the composer's honour in New York. Klemperer was not invited. 'This "non-invitation"', he indignantly wrote to Schoenberg two days later, 'means such a strong offence to me that after this incident everything is finished between you and me ... All personal relations are broken and I shall never see you again.'[38] The failure to invite Klemperer was doubtless due to an understandable fear that in his manic condition he might well have occasioned embarrassment. But, now that artistic issues were no longer at stake, Schoenberg at this point held out a hand of reconciliation,* and on 3 December Klemperer telegraphed to him in Los Angeles, 'Everything OK. Best wishes.'

*   *   *

Meanwhile, Klemperer had embarked on a series of Bach concerts at the New School for Social Research, which had been founded in 1919 in midtown New York as a centre of adult education by a group of left-inclined liberals associated with the periodical *The New Republic*. As early as 1933 its director, Alvin Johnson, had set up a 'University in Exile' as a graduate faculty for scholars who had been forced to leave Europe. In the autumn of 1940 those teaching in its music department included Hanns Eisler, the Russian-born conductor Jascha Horenstein, and Rudolf Kolisch. A joke was current among the students: 'Does the teacher speak English?'

Johnson was eager to take advantage of the presence in New York of many distinguished but underemployed musicians from Europe to promote chamber concerts, and Kolisch suggested that Klemperer be invited to conduct a series of Bach programmes, not dissimilar to those he had planned four years earlier for Ira Hirschmann's New Friends' concerts.† Klemperer duly auditioned a number of players and turned them all down.[39] It was left to Kolisch to assemble an orchestra of some twenty-five players and rehearsals began on 3 October 1940 under Thomas Scherman. Klemperer made his first appearance at a rehearsal only a few days before the opening concert, characteristically arriving in a taxi whose fare he could not settle. His first action was to place what looked like a revolver (it was in fact nothing more dangerous than a water pistol) on his desk. He then ordered that all Scherman's markings be erased, and insisted that, with the exception of the cellos, the entire orchestra should stand to play. (In an interview with *The New York Times* (3 November 1940) Klemperer subsequently asserted that small orchestras should always stand.) The players were alarmed by his wild appearance, but impressed by the command he exercised on the platform. Such rehearsals as Klemperer attended were continually interrupted by scenes. On one occasion a musician who had displeased him was chased on to the street. He frequently stormed into Johnson's office, threatening to leave, only to emerge smiling a few minutes later. In Scherman's view, the concerts would not have taken place without Johnson's diplomacy.[40]

The small hall of the New School was packed for the opening event on 16 October. Klemperer conducted without a baton,‡ and, as had been his

---

* Letter of 28 November 1940. On his carbon copy, he noted, 'I was at that time so sorry for him after the operation and the madness that followed it that I suppressed my personal feelings.'

† As Hirschmann was on the board of the New School, he may also have been instrumental in its decision to approach Klemperer.

‡ Though the aftermath of his operation had left him temporarily unable to wield a baton, he had in fact ceased to use one since *c.* 1935, partly under the influence of Stokowski's example (information provided by Lotte Klemperer).

practice in Berlin, used a mixture of new and old instruments, including viole da gamba, recorders and violino piccolo. In spite of a ragged start, the programme, which consisted of Klemperer's own arrangement of the chorale prelude 'Nun komm der Heiden Heiland', the Suite in B minor, the cantata 'Weichet nur, betrübte Schatten' with Elisabeth Schumann as soloist, and the Brandenburg Concerto No. 1, was well received. The playing had its roughnesses, but *The New York Times* (17 October), in particular, praised the 'wholesomeness and sanity' of the performances. Eva Heinitz, who had played viola da gamba for Klemperer in Berlin, found his Bach as natural, healthy and straightforward as it had been before.[41] To at least one musicologist, his approach to Bach seemed to be 'decidedly modern for its time'.[42] But there were disturbing incidents to which the New York critics discreetly made no reference. At one point during the concert Klemperer walked around within the orchestra; his 21-year-old son was so upset that he left the hall.[43] In the cantata a cellist forgot that the music had been transposed down. Klemperer grabbed her by the arm and yelled, 'E flat major'.

The three subsequent concerts went less well. On 30 October Klemperer took Bach's Concerto for two violins at such a pace that Kolisch and Felix Khuner had difficulty in keeping up. Klemperer himself played the continuo with one hand, 'occasionally striking a few chords or beating a few measures'.[44] In general his tempi in the Second and Third Brandenburg Concertos were thought to be rigid, his rhythms heavy-footed and the orchestral ensemble deficient in nuance and smoothness. 'The only consistent merit in the playing,' wrote Irving Kolodin in *The Sun* (31 October), 'consisted of a certain hearty vigour, a concern for fundamental verities of style and expression. Too often, though, this was manifested through scratchy tone and inaccurate intonation.' In the third concert, on 13 November, Klemperer conducted the Fourth and Fifth Brandenburg Concertos and the cantata 'Vergnügte Ruh', with Hertha Glaz as soloist; on 27 November Elisabeth Schumann was one of the soloists in the cantata 'Tritt auf die Glaubensbahn'. Hanns Eisler and the critic Theodor Adorno, who attended the concerts, later assured Ernst Bloch, who was still living out of New York, that Klemperer's 'enormous musicality ... has remained at its peak ("völlig auf der Höhe")'.[45] But the New School did not invite him to return.

Meanwhile, however, he had been invited to conduct another modest series of concerts in New York. In 1935 Roosevelt's Works Progress Administration (WPA) had established a Federal Music Project as a means of providing employment for musicians who had lost their jobs in the great slump or through the advent of the talkies. Within three years 2,642 musicians had been placed on the rolls of no fewer than thirty federally sponsored orchestras. The best of them was the New York City Symphony Orchestra, a dispirited band whose musicians had a reputation for recalcitrance.[46] Klemperer was the first conductor of any note to agree to work with it. As a means of keeping the players fully employed, the orchestra was allotted as many as nine rehearsals for each of its weekly appearances at the Carnegie Hall. Klemperer informed the management that he himself would take all of them, but he frequently failed to appear, and, even when he did so, it was often with a demand for money to pay off a taxi that he had kept throughout the night; on one occasion the musicians were obliged to pass round a cap to meet his debt. Once again he produced a water pistol.

The orchestra was not well-disposed to him.[47] Yet, in spite of the unpromising preliminaries, the first half of the opening concert on 27 October 1940 made a strong impression. 'Though the orchestra could not respond to all of Dr Klemperer's wishes ... [Beethoven's Fifth Symphony] emerged with a lucidity of form and the breadth and growth that only a master hand can summon', reported the *Musical Courier* (15 November). In *The New York Times* (28 October) Ross Parmenter praised Klemperer's 'admirable authority ..., attention to detail [and] sense of structure'. In Regi Elbogen's view her brother conducted 'just the same way he always did'.[48]

This favourable impression was, however, largely spoiled by the second half of the concert, which consisted of a choral version of the *Merry Waltz* and *Trinity*, the score Klemperer had composed in the course of the summer and rehearsed with his chorus in Los Angeles. Virgil Thomson,* the newly appointed critic of the *New York Herald-Tribune*, was comparatively forbearing. 'The *Merry Waltz*', he wrote on 28 October, 'is not especially merry ... but [it is] good-humouredly ironical in theme, and counterpointed with some wit.' *Trinity* lasted twenty-three minutes. It took as its starting-point the description of the day of Pentecost in chapter two of the Acts of the Apostles. But if the New York audience was expecting the musical equivalent of 'a rushing mighty wind' it was to be disappointed. The speaking with tongues was manifest in arrangements of the Austrian, French, British and American national anthems, with 'Drink to me only with thine eyes' and 'Au clair de la lune' thown in for good measure. When 'The Star-Spangled Banner' was reached, Klemperer invited the audience to rise to its feet and join in. Thomson described the accompaniment as 'a hubbub' redeemed in part by 'ingenious' harmony and 'some bright and brilliant' orchestration. Other critics were less merciful; the *World Telegram* (28 October) dismissed the piece as 'an orchestrated Tower of Babel'. A private recording of a brief

---

* Virgil Thomson (1896–1989). American composer, who between 1940 and 1954 established new standards of perspicacity, wit and literacy in music criticism in New York.

excerpt that is all that has survived suggests that *Trinity* lacked elementary musical coherence.*

The second engagement with the WPA orchestra also had its embarrassments. On arriving for a rehearsal, the soloist, Nathan Milstein, encountered Klemperer with a taxi at the stage door, owing $70 for an all-night rental in the usual way. Klemperer was in dress clothes, presumably because he had not changed since his concert at the New School the previous evening; they were liberally smeared with chocolate. At the start of the concert, which took place on 3 November, Klemperer turned to the audience and proceeded to read a statement. Two days earlier, *Aufbau*, the organ for German-speaking refugees in New York, had, he told his audience, published a letter accusing him of conducting works by anti-Semitic composers and conducting 'an official Eucharist concert in Vienna', doubtless a reference to the *Katholikentag* concert he had conducted in September 1933. As Klemperer began to defend himself, Horace Johnson, the director of the New York City Music Project, rushed down the aisle. Klemperer waved him aside with the words, 'Wait a minute – don't disturb me', and proceeded to read his statement to its end.† Yet in spite of everything the concert was an even greater success than its predecessor. Several critics commented on the great improvement in the orchestra's playing. Among the audience was the German conductor Wolfgang Stresemann, who had last heard Klemperer in his great days in Berlin. He was impressed by the way in which, 'under Klemperer's watchful eyes and ears', Brahms's Symphony No. 1 'took a compelling shape'.[49] Milstein, the soloist in Tchaikovsky's Violin Concerto, later recalled Klemperer's musicianship as being as 'straightforward and truthful' as ever.[50]

The third and final concert on 10 November was attended by Olin Downes. In the following morning's *New York Times* he wrote:

> Otto Klemperer conducted the WPA Symphony Orchestra of New York City last night in Carnegie Hall and achieved astonishing results ... Right there was the final answer to those who claim that the abilities of the conductor are but a secondary element in the success of an orchestral performance ... Dr Klemperer proved this by giving ... the most interesting orchestral concert we have heard this season at Carnegie Hall
>
> Dr Klemperer has transformed an orchestra which, under other conductors just a year or so ago ... was not worthy of consideration. Under these conductors

---

* Klemperer subsequently destroyed both scores, as he so often did at the end of a manic phase. The *Merry Waltz* was, however, rewritten as a purely orchestral piece in 1959. In this form it has continued to enjoy a small (and merited) degree of popularity.

† *New York Times*, 4 November 1940. In a letter subsequently published in *Aufbau* (15 November), he declared, 'I, Otto Klemperer, am a Jew and have never made any bones about it. I was indeed baptised many years ago, but I deny categorically that I have ever been active as an anti-Semite.' Like most Jews, he was, however, capable of caustic comments on other Jews.

the orchestra played like a set of farmers or worse. Under Dr Klemperer they performed with unfailing eloquence and distinction, with obvious respect for his leadership and a determination to give of their utmost . . .

We have rarely heard such spontaneous and masterful readings as Dr Klemperer gave of well-worn compositions which became fresh and inspiring under his baton. The '1812' Overture . . . is of its sort a masterpiece, as Dr Klemperer proved to us. The Brahms Haydn Variations . . . were given a penetrating and engrossing reading.

Haydn's Symphony (the 'Farewell') . . . was in classic style, but the classic style proved to be anything but dull and formal . . . The vigour and energy with which the main theme [of the first movement] strode across the orchestral background was notable. The opening of the slow movement was conspicuous for its grace and its lyrical symmetry.

It is unfortunate if this is to be the last of these concerts, as announced by the programme; unfortunate because of the quality of Dr Klemperer's performances and the evident hunger for them of the audience, which was greater than the seating capacity of the auditorium.

This review by the senior critic of the city's leading newspaper seems to have had its effect, because within a few days it was announced that after Christmas Klemperer would conduct a further series of four concerts with the orchestra in Carnegie Hall.

On 5 January 1941 there was again a capacity audience for the opening concert, which Ross Parmenter described in *The New York Times* (6 January) as 'stirring and beautiful'. Karl Ulrich Schnabel, who was in the audience, found Klemperer's performance of Beethoven's Symphony No. 7 'overwhelming'.[51] In the second concert on 12 January, which consisted of Mozart's G minor and Tchaikovsky's 'Pathétique' symphonies, both *The New York Times* (13 January) and the *Musical Courier* (25 January) commented on the astonishing improvement in the orchestra. Klemperer was prevented by flu from conducting on 19 January, when his place was taken by John Barnett, the orchestra's young assistant conductor. He did, however, start rehearsing for the final concert on 26 January.

The precise sequence of the events that followed is unclear. One night, Klemperer pushed his way into the apartment of Elizabeth Wysor, his soprano soloist, in an attempt to force his attentions on her.[52] At rehearsal the following morning he shouted at her so persistently that nervousness caused her to develop a heavy vibrato. Horace Johnson stopped the rehearsal and ordered Klemperer to leave the hall. There had, however, already been other difficulties between the two men. In an act of gratuitous officiousness Johnson had refused to admit acquaintances whom Klemperer had invited to attend a rehearsal. What, however, brought about a final rupture was Johnson's insistence that Klemperer should perform the *Siegfried Idyll* with full orchestra on the grounds that it was WPA policy to employ as many musicians as possible. Klemperer was adamant that the work should be played by no more than fifteen instruments and with solo strings, as it had been when Wagner himself conducted its first performance on Christmas Day 1870 on the occasion of Cosima's thirty-third birthday.* Johnson refused to give way and on 25 January Klemperer resigned.† As this was, however, by no means the first time he had walked out in a rage, Barnett confidently expected him to appear on the night of the concert. On this occasion, however, he failed to do so.[53] Thus ended an association that might have led to a comeback in New York. Henceforth Klemperer was not merely unemployed. He was widely regarded as unemployable.

*　　*　　*

There had been similar periods in his life, but earlier it had been possible to attribute his extravagant behaviour to youthful high spirits and an artistic temperament. In Berlin he had enjoyed an organised household and a substantial income; and Johanna was on hand to exercise a degree of restraint. In New York, his clothes were covered with stains and cigarette burns. He ate irregularly and had difficulty in directing food into his mouth. He walked lurchingly and with a stick. He had grown emaciated. With his huge height, booming voice, eye patch and changes of mood that were liable to switch from hilarity to rage within a few seconds, he could be a terrifying figure.

His days had a crazy rhythm of their own. In the morning he regularly went to Mass (religious observances being of particular importance to him in periods of euphoria). He wrote political articles, which he circulated to friends such as Bloch, who scathingly dismissed them as 'dirt';[54] the brutal assassination in Mexico City on 21 August 1940 of Trotsky, whom he had met fifteen years earlier in Moscow, obsessed him. He composed incessantly and badgered publishers to print his works. He visited agents and wrote to colleagues in a vain attempt to procure engagements. When in funds, he would appear in the Russian Tea Rooms, then as now a favourite meeting place for musicians; when broke, he would turn up in the hope of cadging a few dollars. In the evening he would go next door to the Carnegie Hall and stand at the back during concerts. Afterwards he would go out on the town. Harlem exercised a special fascination. Inevitably, he was involved in fights

---

* Klemperer was not entirely correct in his belief, which he maintained to the end of his life (see Heyworth (ed.), *Conversations*, p. 108), in the exclusive authenticity of the original performance. In 1871 Wagner conducted the work in Mannheim with an orchestra of over thirty players. In 1882 he conducted it in Palermo with a military band (Newman, *The Life of Richard Wagner*, IV, pp. 306 and 641). Klemperer's own 1927 recording sounds as though at least a small orchestra is involved. It is certainly not played by solo strings.

† Such, at any rate, is the account given in *The New York Times* (26 January 1941). In an interview with the author (11 February 1978) Barnett insisted that it was Klemperer's treatment of Elizabeth Wysor that brought about the final breach.

and scrapes with the police and on at least one occasion his wallet was stolen.*[55]

Tales of incidents spread – and grew in the telling.† At Bloomingdale's he ran up a bill for $376.50, which Ira Hirschmann, then president of the store, felt obliged to pay.[56] On another occasion, he attempted to charge a typewriter to his non-existent account; only Hirschmann's personal intervention averted his arrest.[57] He threatened secretaries and others who attempted to bar his way to their superiors.[58] On several occasions he appeared at the offices of *The New York Times* and demanded to see the music editor. Having finally penetrated to the library on the tenth floor, he held forth on the pernicious influence of female busybodies on American musical life,[59] a theme to which he returned in an interview published on 3 November 1940. There were also lighter moments. At a night club, Kay Kayser, a well-known band leader of the day, invited his audience to draw lots to conduct. Klemperer's number came up and he seized the baton to much applause. How, Kayser asked him afterwards, had he known what the band would play? Klemperer replied, 'All you have to do is to move the baton up and down as in the overture to *Figaro*.'

Even a friend as close as Ernst Bloch admitted that, 'Anyone else with Klemperer's symptoms would probably be considered mad ("ein Narr").'[60] That was precisely how most colleagues and acquaintances now regarded him. The few who tried to help got small thanks. Kurt Weill recommended him to a musician who was prepared to pay for conducting lessons, but after a few minutes Klemperer dismissed his pupil with the comment, 'You'll be all right.'‡[61] For several months he refused to correspond with Georg Klemperer and Helene Hirschler on the grounds that they had pressed him to enter a clinic. He wrote mockingly of Gertrud Friedemann in letters to mutual friends. Relations with Regi grew distant. Pious and prim, she was shocked by her brother's behaviour; he for his part dismissed her as 'too bourgeois'.[62] Not many former relationships survived. He saw something of Franz Werfel and Alma Mahler on their arrival in New York in October 1940. He also occasionally visited the French philosopher Jacques Maritain and the Catholic priest who heard his confessions. But his mainstays were a handful of old

---

* In the fifties Klemperer was moved to receive a cheque from a man who admitted having stolen money from him in New York. He donated it to Victor Gollancz's campaign against capital punishment.
† The author has for the most part included only such tales as could be substantiated.
‡ There was otherwise little contact or sympathy between Klemperer and Weill in America. Like most emigrants from Central Europe, Klemperer, who later described his former colleague as 'geschäftstüchtig' ('business-minded' – Heyworth (ed.), *Conversations*, p. 79) regarded Weill as having sold out to Broadway. On his first visit to Hollywood, Weill dismissed a concert he heard Klemperer conduct as 'very bad'. In a comment strikingly similar to Hindemith's rancorous outburst (see above, pp. 82–3), he also described Klemperer and Korngold, whom he met in the artist's room, as 'pretty disgusting' (letter to Lotte Lenya, 20 February 1937). In the United States Weill deliberately turned his back on his European past, with which Klemperer had at one time been so closely associated.

German friends who had settled in New York. Among those he was closest to were the gallery owner Karl Nierendorf and Elisabeth Schumann, who not only risked her professional renown by appearing in two of the four distinctly modest concerts that he conducted at the New School, but never denied him hospitality or money.

Inevitably, it was Maria Schacko with whom he spent most of his time, though they lived in separate apartments and their relationship seems to have remained largely platonic. That did nothing to dampen Maria Schacko's infatuation, however. 'I am now above all worried because Miss Schacko has so little good influence on him (or no influence at all)', wrote Ernst Bloch to Helene Hirschler on 11 November 1940. Johanna took a harsher view of her motives. 'From a love letter that I have, written by her to Papa', she wrote to Werner Klemperer on 3 October, 'her material egotism emerges clearly, as does the fact that Papa pays for everything, including singing lessons with Edyth Walker.* Three lessons cost $20 ... that is $80 a month before board and lodging, etc.' Maria Schacko was equally critical of Johanna, whom she supposed to be keeping Klemperer deliberately short of money. In fact there was scarcely any money there.

Johanna became further convinced of Maria Schacko's willingness to put her relationship with Klemperer to good advantage when on 4 December she gave a recital at the Carnegie Chamber Music Hall at which he accompanied her with one hand in a programme that included a group of his own songs. The *Musical Courier* (15 December) wrote that Schacko's voice 'disclosed color ... and was used with musicianly intelligence', but passed over Klemperer's accompaniment in silence, as did *Musical America* (25 December). Klemperer's one-handed piano-playing had an uncanny capacity to convey a work's essentials. But it was one thing for him to deploy this talent in private, and quite another to make a public demonstration of his disabilities. Appalled at the damage he was doing to his professional reputation, Johanna determined to make a final attempt to regain her husband and salvage what remained of his career. Towards the middle of the month she arrived with her daughter in New York, where they took a furnished apartment in a hotel.

Johanna attempted to explain to Maria Schacko that her relationship with Klemperer arose out of his manic condition and would surely end with it. For her part, Schacko assured Johanna that, should he wish to return to Los Angeles, she would put no obstacles in his path. Until such time, however, she had no intention of leaving him. At one point, when Johanna and Klemperer were together in a taxi, he suddenly put his head in her lap and

---

* Edyth Walker (1867–1950), celebrated American dramatic soprano, who sang Brünnhilde in Klemperer's first *Ring* in Hamburg in 1912. Maria Schacko did not find Walker a suitable teacher and the lessons were soon discontinued.

begged her not to abandon him; the euphoria would pass. Johanna was deeply moved.⁶³ But the incident, which lasted only a few seconds, had no effect on his behaviour. For six weeks he gravitated between his wife and his mistress. Bloch admired Johanna's forbearance: 'She treats him with gentle irony as always; it seems to do him good. As for Miss Schacko, she lets him do whatever he likes ("lässt ihm völlig freien Lauf").'⁶⁴ Georg Klemperer took a more critical view; like most of the family, he still regarded Johanna as unworthy of his great cousin. 'What he lacks', Georg wrote to Helene Hirschler, 'is a reliable and intelligent partner. Johanna certainly had and has the best of intentions, but she is not up to coping with *this* situation.'⁶⁵ Johanna probably reached a similar conclusion. Apart from providing regular meals, her presence in New York was achieving nothing, and towards the end of January she and Lotte returned to Los Angeles. Before doing so, however, she left a modest sum of money for emergencies with Karl Nierendorf. They were not long in arising, as Nierendorf wrote to inform her on 30 January 1941:

> He came the day before yesterday and demanded the money ... 'It is an emergency. How much have you got?' ... I gave him five dollars – and he was immediately content. He remained until almost midnight, quite quiet, even very reasonable ... But the following morning he already wanted two dollars more ... Then he came to lunch and again asked for money. He said he had debts. He returned in the afternoon, when I gave him ten dollars and told him that for the moment I couldn't give him any more ... When he heard that I was going to Chicago for four to six days, he wanted more money. I couldn't give him any. He didn't get angry, but became very downcast. 'Then what shall I do?' For a long time he sat in silence, sunk in himself. Today he came to lunch ... Then told me that I couldn't simply go off and leave him entirely without money. He absolutely had to pay fourteen dollars to a bank and needed three to four dollars a day ... So I gave him a cheque for thirty dollars ... Altogether since Tuesday he has had forty-eight dollars. I now have about twenty dollars of the money you left. How are we to go on?

*　　*　　*

As Klemperer's condition worsened, his friends began to discuss the possibility of persuading him to enter a sanatorium or even, as Georg Klemperer thought desirable, of having him committed to an institution, where he could at least be prevented from inflicting further damage on his reputation. Bloch was opposed to such a course. In view of Klemperer's wild antipathy to anything that smacked of regimentation, it could, in his view, only worsen his condition. 'Wasn't Kl. already in a sanatorium near Los Angeles?' he wrote to Helene Hirschler on 20 November 1940.⁶⁶ 'He told me about it, foaming with rage and manifesting real signs of craziness (*Wahnvorstellungen*) ... A sort of castration complex emerged. So long as there is no danger for others, Kl. must remain as long as possible "out of doors".' But it was Johanna who had to shoulder the final responsibility. Formal committal would, she realised, deprive Klemperer of the right to determine when he should leave. At nights she lay awake, desperately wondering what course to take, but finally always came to the same conclusion: he should be left free.[67]

Nevertheless Klemperer was persuaded by one of the many doctors he had consulted in New York to enter the Aurora Health Institute in Morristown, New Jersey, on 24 February 1941. Three days later he wrote to tell Helmuth and Marianne Joseph that it was 'nearly like Kohnstamm', in whose clinic in Königstein he had earlier taken refuge in times of trouble, and where he had already encountered his physician, Dr Hermann Weiss, if only in a personal capacity.* In Morristown, Klemperer disturbed his fellow patients at all hours by his noisy singing of a Bach sonata he was in the process of transcribing and on 27 February he was asked to leave.[68] After spending the night in New York, the following afternoon he entered of his own accord Wallingford House, Rye, in up-state New York, apparently unaware that, unlike the Aurora Health Institute, it was a mental home. That evening, at dinner with the medical director, Dr Daniel J. Kelly, Klemperer indicated that he required 'a room with much privacy ... a private telephone ... a key to the front and back doors and freedom for twelve hours in the daytime and twelve hours in the night-time'.[69] Learning that Kelly sang, Klemperer played some of his compositions to him on the piano. After dinner Kelly telegraphed Johanna in Los Angeles to ask her to sign committal papers. She refused.

Klemperer slept soundly that night.[70] At 8.45 the following morning he tried to leave the clinic in order to buy a newspaper but he found the doors locked. Kelly was summoned and insisted that Klemperer remain. In a manic phase the least opposition to his wishes was liable to trigger a terrifying outburst of rage. One such ensued. Realising that he had no power to detain his patient against his will, Kelly reluctantly allowed him to leave. But later that morning he informed the police, who at 1.55 p.m. issued an eight-State alarm, in which Klemperer was described as 'dangerous and insane'. The police message also advised that caution be used in apprehending him, as he carried a stick 'that he likes to use on policemen', though as a result of immediate protests by Klemperer's friends a supplementary message stated that he was 'only dangerous when aroused'.

Klemperer took a train to New York. There he went to Carnegie Hall, where Olin Downes was chairing a lecture, after which they had a long conversation. Downes later described him as talking with 'perfect reasonableness'. Klemperer then visited Nierendorf and explained that he had left Wallingford House as he had no intention of allowing himself to be confined.

---

* Weiss's mother had been a frequent patient at Kohnstamm's clinic (information provided by Mrs Anneliese Reich).

At 4.30 p.m. he turned up at Maria Schacko's apartment. From there he telephoned Kelly to make arrangements for settling his bill. Kelly at once informed the police, but by the time they arrived Klemperer had gone. A watch was put on places, such as Judson's office, at which he might appear. He had, however, already left New York, having decided to return to the care of the Aurora Institute while living in a nearby hotel. That night he ate late at Morristown, but, unable to find a room, then took the train to Newark, where he spent the night. The following morning, 2 March, he read, much to his amusement, the headline on the front page of the *New York Times*: 'Klemperer gone: sought as insane'. Werner Klemperer first learnt of his father's predicament from the paper of a fellow passenger in the New York subway.

That morning Klemperer returned by taxi to Morristown, eighteen miles away. As usual he was unable to pay his fare, and the cab driver complained to the police, who had no difficulty in tracing him to the small commercial hotel where the taxi had set him down. When two policemen entered his room, Klemperer reached for his stick, which was resting against the corner. His intention was no doubt innocent: he could not easily stand without it. But the patrolmen were taking no chances; one grabbed the stick, while the other hurled Klemperer on to the bed, where, they claimed, he continued to 'kick and protest'. At the police station, where he was put under protective custody, his briefcase was found to contain nothing but two 'operas', which, to judge from the descriptions given, were the two parts of his cantata *Trinity*. Klemperer had no money. In a basement cell measuring eight feet by six, he was visited first by a police surgeon, at whom he raged, and then by Dr Weiss, with whom he agreed to communicate only in writing. The deputy chief of police told the newspapermen who had by this time gathered that 'the very sight of a policeman's uniform is enough to make him shout and rattle on the bars of his cell'. The following morning the *New York Herald-Tribune* published a photograph of him, wild-eyed and with open shirt collar, clutching at those bars.

That afternoon Klemperer was examined by the resident psychiatrist of the New Jersey State Hospital, who pronounced him 'temperamental and unstrung', but saw 'no further reason for detaining him'. Regi Elbogen, who in her agitation had at first gone to Wallingford House, had by this time arrived and declared her readiness to assume responsibility for her brother, so that nothing now stood in the way of his release. Meanwhile, Johanna had heard the news from a newsflash in a coast-to-coast broadcast by Walter Winchell. She made immediate preparations to fly with Lotte to New York. Doubtless unaware of Regi's arrival on the scene, she telephoned before her departure to insist that her husband be released into her care only. Confronted with conflicting instructions, the police, who had earlier announced Klemperer's imminent release, decided to detain him for the night.

At Los Angeles airport, where the seventeen-year-old Lotte acted as interpreter, a distraught Johanna was besieged by reporters. On the following morning they were met at La Guardia Airport by Werner, who had protested to the press about Kelly's part in raising a police alarm and his father's subsequent arrest. The family took a taxi to Morristown, where they found Klemperer ensconced, like Eisenstein in the last act of *Die Fledermaus,* in the office of the local police chief and in the best of spirits.* On his release that afternoon he described his host and the deputy chief as his 'only friends in the world' and invited them to his next concert at Carnegie Hall. When asked whether he would be suing Dr Kelly, only a sharp nudge from Johanna prevented a reply that promised to be 'explosive'. But Kelly's ill-considered action had done damage to Klemperer's reputation that would take many years to repair.

* Klemperer himself was by no means unaware of the parallel. When later recounting the episode to friends in New York, he ended the story by singing 'Eisenstein wird eingesperrt' ('Eisenstein is locked up'), from a number in Johann Strauss's operetta (information provided by Mrs Mercedes Meyerhof).

6

'Ajax fell through Ajax's Hand'

If Klemperer regarded his 'escape' and arrest as an entertaining prank, the outside world took a different view of it. To colleagues and acquaintances it came as confirmation of what they had long suspected: brain surgery had left him mentally unhinged. 'People consider him totally mad', wrote Elisabeth Schumann to a friend,

> and things happen that are on the very brink of that ... I don't find him much madder than he was before, admittedly more uninhibited, more exalted – though as far as music is concerned: wonderful ... But ... no one wants him – he is too difficult for an organisation ... In addition, his financial prospects in the foreseeable future are frightful – his savings have been almost used up by the operation last year and his erratic life. It looks very black to me. Ah, how sad it all is.[1]

Klemperer had in effect become an outcast. 'None of Papa's friends, the Schnabels, etc., gives any sign of life', wrote Lotte Klemperer to Gertrud Schoenberg more than a month after the incident,

> I can understand that, because he really has been very offensive and nasty to everyone. But he didn't really know what he was doing ... I feel how it upsets him when everyone turns their back, [but] out of silly ... pride he behaves as though it were *he* who were offended ... He simply can't apologise. [But] does one have to apologise for an illness?[2]

Olin Downes alone gave public support. Two weeks after the Morristown affair he recalled the manner in which earlier in the season in his concerts with the New York City Symphony Orchestra, Klemperer had

> transformed that body, necessarily of the second or third rank ... into an ensemble of brilliantly effective qualities. He proved again that the first requisite of a significant orchestral performance is the conductor. It may here be added that if operations on the brain affected all conductors as they appear to have affected Mr Klemperer, it would be good for a number of them to hurry to hospital.[3]

Aware that only public success could effectively demonstrate that his artistic abilities were unimpaired, Johanna decided to throw most of her modest savings into making it possible for him to give a concert at Carnegie Hall on 21 April 1941. After a brief holiday at Miami Beach, during which both his walking and general condition improved, the family returned at the end of March to New York, where he at once set about assembling an *ad hoc* orchestra of seventy players. As Klemperer planned to perform the suite from Hindemith's *Nobilissima Visione*, he wrote to invite the composer, whose music he had so consistently championed in Germany, to attend. Johanna scribbled a brief postscript, 'Otto is very much better. Do please come if at all possible.'[4] Hindemith, who was teaching at Yale University, was unable to do so. Without troubling to disguise his relief, he informed his American publisher, Ernest R. Voigt, that 'It was easy enough to find an excuse. I was myself conducting the same piece that very evening.'[5]

The rehearsals gave rise to the usual tensions. At one point an enraged Klemperer chased off the platform a double-bass player who had inserted an appoggiatura in the slow movement of the 'Eroica' Symphony.[6] The violins and violas were obliged to play standing. None the less, as *Time* (5 May) put it, the concert successfully 'proved to the world that he is not crazy'. 'Whatever the vicissitudes of his recent life', wrote Irving Kolodin in *The Sun* (22 April),

> Otto Klemperer remains a challenging figure once he ascends a podium ... Last night at Carnegie Hall he asserted this fact again ... The indubitable musicianship of this gaunt figure was epitomised in his performance of *Nobilissima Visione*. It has been played here before ... but this latest revelation of its quality was even more rousing than the previous ones.

Other critics concurred and the remainder of the programme, which opened with the first performance of Klemperer's own transcription of what was described as Bach's Organ Sonata in E flat (presumably the Trio Sonata, BWV 525), was also well received. At the end of the evening he was accorded what *The New York Times* (22 April) described as 'a rousing vote of confidence from a large audience'.

But that did nothing to alter the unwillingness of managements to engage him. The New York Philharmonic was in the process of planning a centenary season in which leading conductors who had worked with the orchestra were to be invited to appear. They included Toscanini, Walter, Mitropoulos, Reiner and Efrem Kurtz, some of whom had been less closely associated with the orchestra than Klemperer, who was mortified to receive no such invitation.[7] In spite of the fact that his concert had resulted in a deficit of some $4,000,[8] he nevertheless announced a week later that he would conduct a series of ten concerts with the same orchestra in the coming season.[9] But it was no more than a gesture of defiance: the funds for such a venture did not exist and no more was heard of it. To all intents and purposes his New York career was at an end.

Lack of money also made it impossible for Klemperer to pursue a $200,000 suit he had filed against Daniel J. Kelly of the Wallingford House clinic. Kelly, he claimed, had 'wilfully and maliciously' raised the alarm that had led to his arrest and made statements that were untrue.[10] On 11 May Klemperer left for Los Angeles. Through the good offices of Walter Hilborn, Johanna had already attempted to persuade the Southern California Symphony Association to offer him guest engagements at the Hollywood Bowl.* The board at first played for time. 'Our organisation', ran a draft letter (26 March 1941) provided by the Association's legal adviser, 'is of the opinion that Klemperer would not be as well received as he should be if he were to be invited to conduct next summer, or until it is sufficiently demonstrated in other places that he has completely regained his health.'[11] Thus on his arrival Klemperer found his prospects in Los Angeles to be no better than in New York.

He began to look for other openings. The most promising was an invitation from Gustave O. Arlt, chairman of UCLA's committee on fine arts productions, to conduct three concerts with the local WPA orchestra at Royce Hall. When Klemperer called on Arlt in his office to finalise details, he was accompanied by 'a very large St Bernard dog', which proceeded to put its nose into the papers on the professor's desk. Arlt suggested that the dog be put outside. Klemperer replied, 'Dog? What dog? I don't have a dog.' It was, Arlt later recorded, difficult to persuade him to concentrate on the matter in hand.[12] He then became aware of a smell of burning. To his astonishment he observed that his visitor 'was smoking a large cigar, which he held between the middle and fourth fingers of his hand. It had burnt down ... so that you could actually smell the burning skin. Yet he didn't feel it.' His business completed, Klemperer rose to his feet and, with a line worthy of the Marx Brothers, demanded, 'Now, where's my dog?' 'We thought you didn't ...?' 'Well, of course it's my dog.'

Such behaviour was not a happy omen and at rehearsals Klemperer disturbed the musicians by his habit of starting a movement and then taking up a position within the orchestra from which he would sit and listen. He pestered women members, even pursuing one of them to the lavatory.[13] Breaking point was reached when Klemperer, who was conducting his own *Merry Waltz*, roughly reprimanded the orchestra for its inability to follow his beat. The rehearsal was abandoned and Arlt felt that he had no alternative but to cancel the concerts.[14] 'The last I saw of Klemperer', one young double-bass player recalled, 'was his vainly banging on the school door,

---

* The situation was complicated by a legal wrangle. Before agreeing to the settlement reached between Klemperer and the board in October 1940, Johanna had attempted to insert a clause whereby the SCSA would offer Klemperer guest engagements when his health permitted. Mudd never countersigned that rider, a deliberate omission of which Johanna became aware only when she at this point unsuccessfully attempted to impose it.

angrily shouting for more time with the orchestra.' His memory of Klemperer's musicianship was still vivid almost half a century later.

> His appearance was awe-inspiring, if not terrifying. But with no more ado, he led us through a Brahms First Symphony that in all my years ... has been unequalled ... He drove, as in a huge chariot, to the highest planes of expression, stopping not at all for corrections or interpretative advice. It was the essence of great conducting.[15]

Learning what had transpired during Klemperer's rehearsals, E.R. Hedrick, vice-president and provost of UCLA, wrote on 22 May to warn President Sproul that

> Dr Otto Klemperer ... has returned to this region after serious experiences in the East, to which you have had your attention drawn. It is entirely possible that you will be appealed to in connection with certain matters on this campus, and I think I ought to say that I have good medical advice that Dr Klemperer is still in a serious condition.

Another (unpaid) opening was offered by the Rehearsal Orchestra, an association of young instrumentalists who worked in the film studios and met on Sunday mornings for the pleasure of playing together under outstanding musicians, who included Schoenberg, Stravinsky and Bruno Walter. Klemperer gladly accepted an invitation to conduct a rehearsal on 8 June. Though the players were none too happy with his insistence on including some of his own music, the session went smoothly and the *Los Angeles Examiner* reported that his account of Beethoven's 'Pastoral' Symphony 'seemed to reveal a more flexible treatment of the music than in former years'.[16] Klemperer was invited to conduct another session on the first Sunday in July. Only belatedly was it realised that, owing to Independence Day, many of the musicians involved would be out of town, and the rehearsal was postponed. Enraged, Klemperer threatened to sue the orchestra, on grounds that remain a mystery.[17] Yet again, he had cut the ground from under his own feet.

Later in June, Klemperer and Maria Schacko went by car to Reno, where they remained for several weeks to enable her to file divorce proceedings. While there, they engaged a cook who could also drive. As a result of such extravagances, bills continued to arrive at Johanna's door. In the five months he spent in Los Angeles during the summer and autumn of 1941, Klemperer made only one public appearance and that in demeaning circumstances. On 29 September in the small hall of the Assistance League, a local charitable association that exists to help those in need of medical and psychological help, he accompanied Maria Schacko with one hand in three groups of songs (including some of his own), played the keyboard part in his own *Valse* for violin and piano, and provided the continuo in a performance of the Sixth Brandenburg Concerto. The programme also included a recently composed *Humoresque* for seven wind instruments, which, like the *Valse*, has not survived. The hall was packed by a public which had come 'to show Dr Klemperer that it has not forgotten his magnificent achievements as conductor of our Philharmonic Orchestra'.[18] But even well-wishers could not disguise the low level of the concert. 'The burden of the programme was borne by Miss Schacko, whose artistic efforts were handicapped by inadequate vocal equipment ... [and] by inadequate accompaniments played by Klemperer', wrote Hal D. Crain in the *Christian Science Monitor*. Klemperer's compositions were largely passed over in silence.

* * *

The previous month Klemperer had raised a loan on two small life insurance policies and, when this was spent, similarly raised another $5,000.* Johanna, who in spite of her straitened circumstances lent Schoenberg $500, recognised that the time had come to call a halt, if she were not to be reduced to penury. She had already used part of the money that had been paid to her under the terms of the settlement with the SCSA to buy a modest, four-room house with a small garden in Westwood, into which she and Lotte moved in June. One visitor described the house as being 'rather confining ... and miserably furnished' and 'a sharp contrast to [Klemperer's] sumptuous old home'.[19] Lotte had meanwhile abandoned her education at the age of seventeen in order to take a job as a sales assistant in a gramophone record shop. On the advice of Walter Hilborn, Johanna now steeled herself to impose a financial settlement on her husband. In spite of his vehement protests that he had earned the money she was proposing to ration, he was finally obliged on 17 October 1941 to sign a formal agreement. Under its terms Johanna retained sole ownership of the house. A trust fund was established with what remained. He would receive a weekly allowance of $50 as long as the money lasted.

After entering into the agreement, Klemperer set out for New York by car with Maria Schacko, who had only learnt to drive that year. After an accident in Arizona, their German accents and Klemperer's own behaviour attracted a hostile crowd. The police were called and on their appearance Klemperer drew his water pistol. Once again he was jailed, and only released after Maria Schacko had obtained legal assistance and paid a fine.[20] On 26 October Hilborn received a demand for money to meet the expense of car repairs. By the time that the travellers reached New York their journey had cost the trust fund an additional $290.[21]

---

* According to Maria Schacko (interview with the author, 8 December 1985), Klemperer at about this time made over a life insurance policy to a nurse who had taken his fancy.

Debts continued to pile up throughout the winter. In some instances Johanna was able to arrange for them to be paid in instalments. In other cases Hilborn had the disagreeable task of informing creditors that Klemperer could not meet his obligations, and in March 1942 summonses were issued by one of the many doctors Klemperer had consulted and also by *The New York Times*, in which he had almost a year earlier taken space to publicise his Carnegie Hall concert. Meanwhile he seems to have existed largely on loans.

In a letter to Marianne (7 December 1941), Regi observed that their brother showed no concern at his financial predicament. It was as though he were in a dream. 'I am not only out of funds, but also have no job', he wrote to Koussevitzky two weeks later, adding, 'I do not know what [has] happened.' All his attempts to find work fell on stony ground. A concert that he was to have conducted on 14 January 1942 was cancelled without explanation. He offered his services to a Treasury radio programme, *America Preferred*, in which foreign-born musicians expressed their gratitude to their new homeland by urging listeners to buy war bonds. He even appealed to Eleanor Roosevelt, the President's wife, in the hope that that indefatigable woman of good works would use her influence to procure engagements in army camps. An attempt to found an orchestra of his own predictably came to nothing.[22] So did a project for a production of Offenbach's *La Périchole*. On 17 January 1942 he conducted an orchestra of 55 players drawn from the New York Philharmonic in the first half of a Mozart concert at Carnegie Hall for the Mozart Festival Committee. In the second half of the concert Felix Wolfes conducted a performance of Mozart's one-act opera *The Impresario*. Klemperer's part of the programme included the 'Haffner' Symphony and the Sinfonia Concertante, K.364, with Mischa Mischakoff and William Primrose as soloists. The following day's *New York Times* reported that the audience had been 'large and demonstrative'.

It was the last conducting date that he had in his diary, though he did agree to rehearse the National Youth Administration's orchestra, which had been set up under Roosevelt's New Deal to provide training for young musicians at a pre-professional level. Forty-three years later a young member of the orchestra recalled the impact of his musicianship as well as his alarming behaviour:

> Klemperer raised his arms and proceeded to draw the most incredible sounds from these young players. His feeling for the music [the Prelude and Liebestod from *Tristan und Isolde*] inspired them to such passion and gorgeous sound that we who were listening and observing this phenomenon were completely captivated. Suddenly, during a long *crescendo* . . . the conductor exploded in a rage, alternately shouting and growling, his face beet-red and frothing at the mouth, flailing his arms to and fro, hurling the music stand to the floor and otherwise exhibiting the greatest outburst of anger any of us had ever witnessed . . . Then

the reason for this upheaval became apparent; the first cellist ... had exchanged instruments with another player in order to try out a different cello, only to discover, to his consternation, that it did not produce enough sound for Klemperer's demands and so laid down this instrument in order to retrieve his own.²³

As Ernst Bloch shrewdly observed, Klemperer's musicality stood like a fortress in occupied territory, the sole part of his character to resist the devastating impact of his illness.²⁴

Even Georg Klemperer gave way to despair. 'It is bitter to have to put it into words', he wrote to Helene Hirschler,

> But my feeling is that destiny would have been kinder, had he not survived the operation. Do you know Grillparzer's poem?
>
> > Was je den Menschen schwer gefallen,
> > Eins ist das Bittereste von allen:
> > Vermissen, was schon unser war,
> > Den Kranz verlieren aus dem Haar,
> > Nachdem man sterben sich gesehen,
> > Mit seiner eigenen Leiche gehen.
>
> (That is quoted from memory and probably contains mistakes.)*
> I don't at all want to hold Otto responsible for his actions ... But he has forfeited all remaining sympathy by cohabiting with a person while his wife and children are in straitened circumstances. I can't get over it, especially as he told me that he was living alone ... But no one can help him if his severely impaired conscience and moral judgement do not slowly recover.

On 19 April he returned to Klemperer's tragic predicament with another and even more sombre quotation from the German classics. 'I often think of Schiller's line', he wrote to Helene Hirschler. 'Ajax fiel durch Ajaxs Hand'† – 'Ajax fell through Ajax's hand'.

Meanwhile, Klemperer was offered a series of concerts in Mexico City, where his reputation was still intact. When the engagement was made public, a doctor who had the previous month served a summons for unpaid debts threatened to issue a subpoena, should he attempt to leave the country. Hilborn sorted out the problem and from the trust's fast-diminishing funds

---

* Letter of 4 April 1942. In fact the 77-year- old Georg's memory was remarkably good. The sense of the quotation (in which such minor errors as he made have been corrected) may be rendered as follows:

> Of all the pains that man must bear,
> One is the bitterest of all:
> To be deprived of what once was ours,
> To lose the crown upon our brow,
> After one has seen one's death,
> Then to walk with one's own corpse.

† Correctly, 'Ajax fiel durch Ajaxs Kraft' (*Das Siegesfest*).

gave Klemperer $200 for travelling expenses. The first concert on 6 May attracted a smaller audience than expected, owing in part to Schnabel's failure to appear as soloist. His absence led to a series of postponements, so that the next concerts did not take place until 5 and 9 June. In the audience on the latter date was Hanns Eisler, who subsequently described Klemperer's performance of Beethoven's Fifth Symphony as the best he had ever heard, in spite of the poor quality of the orchestra.[25]

Shortly after his arrival in Mexico City, Klemperer gave an interview to a local newspaper, *El Redondel* (3 May). After discussing his compositions, he was asked about his pleasures. 'I like very much to walk, ride and smoke a pipe', he replied, '... but, most of all, I like women.' Yet for the first time for more than two years there were indications of a change in his condition. He began to count his pennies, arranging to be paid from his fees only sufficient money to live on. He worried about the cost of telephone calls to Maria Schacko, who as a stateless person was unable to accompany him. He took the opportunity to buy a new suit, as tailoring was cheaper in Mexico than in America. By the time of his return he had saved $250 and was able to pay off some of his more pressing debts.[26] He also began to show concern about the state of his trust fund, which, as Hilborn informed him on 13 July, would provide his meagre allowance for only another nine months.

Bolstered by success in Mexico, on 20 June Klemperer requested Hilborn to remind Mudd of the agreement to engage him to conduct four concerts in the coming season in Los Angeles. Mudd was evasive:

> I think you will not misunderstand me when I say that we will have to satisfy ourselves that Dr Klemperer has completely recovered from his illness, that he will appear in public to advantage, and that he will be well received. It is a very difficult situation for all concerned and under all the circumstances I am compelled to add that we may not see our way clear to ask Dr Klemperer to conduct.[27]

Hilborn made further attempts to persuade Mudd that Klemperer's mental condition had improved, but Mudd remained unyielding. 'It would', he replied on 14 July, 'be infinitely better for him to conduct elsewhere than in Los Angeles at this stage of his career.' After a meeting of the orchestral board in September to discuss the coming season he wrote again, on this occasion in explicit terms, to inform Hilborn that 'the Association cannot see its way clear to offer him an engagement'.[28]

*   *   *

'For the past three days Otto was with us', wrote Regi to her sister on 9 September 1942.

> He has asked me to write to you, as he cannot bring himself to do so. That alone will tell you that he is depressed ... The situation is so similar to others in

the past that it would be laughable, were it not tragic. I don't need to tell you details. He has just suddenly woken up and sees things as they really are.

Klemperer had no money, no work and few friends. His first reaction was to ask his wife to take him back. But Johanna was bitterly resentful at the anguish he had caused her. He had lied to her so persistently about his relationship with Maria Schacko and his financial situation that she was scarcely more willing than Mudd to take on trust assurances that the manic period had run its course. She accordingly laid down conditions, which Hilborn communicated to Klemperer on 29 August. He was to make no further requests for changes in the financial arrangements they had made in the previous autumn; her agreement to his return was not to be taken as condoning his behaviour, should she subsequently wish to initiate divorce proceedings; he was to pay $30 a week from his allowance towards household expenses. Klemperer was outraged. To Johanna he wrote early in September,

> I am beside myself at the letter I have received from Hilborn. Such a private matter, which concerns only you and me, cannot be settled through a lawyer. The main issue, that no one else can disturb our life, has to be settled between us. You *cannot* expect me to sign this document. I feel *very* wretched. I'm afraid that *at the moment* I cannot come after all (that is the truth and not an excuse). But, as soon as I am able to travel, *please* receive me *warmly* and not with conditions.

To Hilborn he added on 2 September, 'I cannot accept the proposition that I should be admitted to a house purchased with money earned by myself as *a paying guest.*' As the depression deepened, Klemperer found himself increasingly unable to face the strains of a reconciliation with Johanna that would inevitably spell the end of his relationship with Maria Schacko. Once more he chose to retire again to the Aurora Clinic in Morristown, New Jersey, which he entered on 30 September, remaining there for two months.

When Lotte came to collect him in early December, she found him sitting in his room, surrounded by his baggage,* and even more skeletal than he had been a year earlier. On seeing his daughter, he burst into tears. He was eager to leave, but Lotte had to tell him that it would not be possible to do so until the following day, as she had had difficulty in finding rooms they could afford in New York. Until that moment she had found it hard to forgive her father for the suffering he had inflicted on her mother. Now for the first time she understood the profound pathos of his situation.

Persuaded that Klemperer's manic phase was now over, Hirschmann invited him to give a Bach concert with the New Friends Orchestra in New

---

* Among the personal belongings he had kept with him during the whole period of upheaval were letters his father had written to his mother during their betrothal, his mother's poetry album and a little bag, containing her passport photographs and an album 'just as she had left it' (letter from Regi Elbogen to Marianne Joseph, 9 January 1943).

York Town Hall. At first Klemperer hesitated, uncertain whether he could confront an orchestra in his depressed condition. Yet as soon as he stood on the platform he radiated authority. At the first rehearsal, he raised his hands and said no more than 'ein natürliches Tempo'. As one player recalled, there was an immediate sense of security and confidence.[29]

On the morning of the concert on 13 December, *The New York Times* published an article in which Klemperer outlined his approach to Bach.[30] It had scarcely changed since his years in Berlin. Bach, he insisted, should be played 'as simply as possible'. Dynamics should not be obtrusive, but rise and fall in accordance with the shape of the line. He favoured old instruments, provided that the performance did not take place in a large hall. As Olin Downes reported in *The New York Times* on the following day, these simple precepts were put into practice only in part at the concert. The solo instrument in the Suite No. 2 in B minor was a flute (instead of a recorder) and the strings had modern bows. Though gambas were used in the Sixth Brandenburg Concerto, they were different sorts of instruments, played with different techniques and, in Downes's opinion, their combination with modern strings had resulted in a 'muddy' ensemble.* In fact Klemperer never pursued the new ideas about performing practice. His approach to Bach stemmed from an instinctive dislike of the romanticised veneer that so many conductors of his generation imposed on music written with quite other sounds in mind. To this extent his Bach represented a half-way house between the old and the new. But with the passage of time interpretations that in Berlin in the late twenties had sounded disconcertingly 'modern' came increasingly to be regarded as old-fashioned.

Shortly after the concert Klemperer wrote to Johanna with characteristic directness,

> Now I come to the main point: my return to Los Angeles. I would very much like to live with you again. But you must understand my feelings about LA. I was once someone and am now *nobody* [English original]. In spite of everything, I intend to come to you with Lotte. Go on caring for me ('bleib mir gut').[31]

Johanna was by no means overjoyed. She was not convinced that her husband had finally broken with Maria Schacko and she dreaded the prospect of living with him in his depressed state. 'Don't leave me alone with him yet, Lotte', she begged her daughter, who had plans to move to New York.[32] Werner could do little to ease his mother's burden. Determined to follow a career as an actor, he had spent the past two years as a student at the Pasadena Playhouse drama school, but by now he had been drafted into the US Army.

---

* One of the gamba players, Eva Heinitz, pointed out in a letter to the author (29 November 1985) that in 1942 'no one was really aware of the doubtful results of mixing ... old ... and modern instruments'.

After basic training in Washington State, he had been assigned to the 44th Infantry Division and sent to Hawaii for further training as a combat military policeman. For all her reservations, Johanna was at the airport to meet her husband on his arrival on New Year's Day 1943. But reconciliation was to prove a longer and more painful process than either of them envisaged.

There was in any case an additional problem: how was he to earn a living? Before leaving for Los Angeles he had done what he could to find engagements. As one door after another was shut in his face, he became obsessed with the fear that he would never conduct again. On a visit to Judson's office, he was dismayed to observe that his portrait had been removed from the gallery of famous artists the great man represented.[33] All that Hirschmann could offer was a six-day provincial tour with a 40-strong *ad hoc* orchestra promoted by the New Friends of Music. It was not an enticing prospect, but on 17 February 1943 Hilborn warned that the trust fund contained no more than $25. It was the tour or nothing.

Early in March Klemperer returned to New York to start rehearsals. In Robert Mann* he had an outstanding young concert-master, but the uneven quality of the other players and the engagement for the opening concert of a singer of whom Klemperer knew nothing so depressed him that at one point he almost cried off. Johanna meanwhile bombarded her daughter with instructions: 'Don't forget to buy studs for the shirt collars. Are there enough white ties? Has Regi [with whom Klemperer had left most of his belongings] some white waistcoats – two are not enough ...? Don't forget the eau-de-Cologne. When you are packing Papa's case, put in two hand towels, handkerchiefs, shirts and a change of underwear, ties and comb.'[34]

The rehearsals were a torment. 'It has been a terrible time', Lotte wrote to her mother on 14 March, the day they left New York,

> I don't want to sound miserable, but, between ourselves, the whole tour is a *Schmiere* ('a provincial affair'). Papa is behaving splendidly in the circumstances. He conducts as formerly, drawing out of the musicians what they had certainly not previously [known they] had in them ... [But] the woodwind is so bad that I tremble each time in the trios of the Schubert and the G minor.†

The tour took in New Bedford, Massachusetts; Albany and Binghamton in New York State; Sandusky and East Liverpool, Ohio; and Danville, Virginia. It was still winter in north-eastern America and the wartime hotels were cheerless, the halls cold and ill-equipped. Travel between towns that were often hundreds of miles apart was mainly by bus. Klemperer was so 'withdrawn, preoccupied and indifferent'[35] that he often seemed incapable of communicating with the orchestra or of asserting himself when opposition arose among the players.[36] When Hirschmann suggested that with an

---
* Robert Mann (b. 1920), who in 1948 founded the Juilliard Quartet.
† Mozart's Symphony No. 40 in G minor and Schubert's Symphony No. 5 in B flat major.

additional rehearsal the orchestra could give a concert in New York at the end of the tour, Klemperer refused to participate. Later Klemperer wrote to Helene Hirschler, 'the conducting in small towns did not bring me any special satisfaction; nevertheless it is good to have something to do rather than nothing'.[37]

Before returning to Los Angeles, he went to Boston to see Horrax; he also consulted Georg, who afterwards wrote to warn Johanna of the difficulties he foresaw when Klemperer returned to her for good.

> He still has no firmness of will and suffers from great indecisiveness. That he is now coming to Los Angeles is at any rate a free decision that he has taken ... to make amends. But at the moment he is a prey to doubt and I have the impression that he regrets that decision. His illness makes him see everything that lies before him in a dark light. (He feels that in Los Angeles he will be totally deprived of stimulus and artistic openings.) I have done all I can to persuade him that he needs peace and quiet, which he cannot find in New York, where he would immediately fall under the fatal influence of that person ... He still does not seem to grasp that it is impossible for a wife to tolerate the existence of another woman, something that I put to him in the sharpest terms. If I may give you some advice, it would be best for Otto if you continued to treat him as a sick man, by which I mean that you should regard him as deprived of powers of free decision and of responsibility, and for the present handle him with the greatest care ...
>
> In spite of everything that has happened, I believe that (when well) he is a good and decent man. He often has a way of speaking and behaving that provokes you. But it would be best to ignore that and put it down to his illness. It will not be an easy task.[38]

Although Klemperer had visited Maria Schacko on his return to New York after the tour, he had spoken of her in such distant terms that Lotte felt able to assure her mother that the relationship had to all intents and purposes ended.[39] Georg's wise words also had an effect, so that when Klemperer returned to Los Angeles in early April Johanna welcomed him with a warmth she had not been able to summon three months earlier. Until the end of his life, he never forgot 'how she received me ... She said straight away, "Do you know, *Alter*, I specially drank nothing last night. It would never have done if I had met you with a hangover".'[40] It was an adroit means of switching attention from his shortcomings to her own.

As Georg had foreseen, it did not prove easy for Johanna. Whereas Klemperer had for the past three years been feckless, spendthrift and indiscriminately gregarious, he was now exacting and hypercritical, careful with money (in New York he had refused to take taxis to rehearsals for the Bach concert the previous December), impenetrable to strangers. Lotte had already given her mother a chilling foretaste of what to expect. 'One cannot get close to him. When I sometimes think that I begin to understand him, he has only to look at me with his cold, penetrating eyes for me to realise that he doesn't see me at all.'[41] His hours at home were rigorously scheduled. He rose early, studied scores, did finger exercises at the piano, read, took long solitary walks. He was so silent that days might go by without his uttering a word. His facial paralysis and false teeth plagued him. The right eye still burnt. Writing, not to mention playing the piano, was arduous. 'Worst of all', he wrote on 18 April 1943 to Helene Hirschler, 'is the apathy of the spirit. The New Friends have certain plans for next winter ... It's because of me that nothing has been decided. [But] it's unspeakably hard for me to suggest programmes.' Not surprisingly, the plans came to nothing. To Johanna he remained so cold and distant that she sometimes felt as though she no longer existed for him. She had experienced earlier depressions. But in Berlin in 1928 and 1932, and later in Los Angeles, he had had work and the support of colleagues and staff. Now he sat at home, bereft of inner or outer motivation.

Los Angeles had changed a good deal since he had last lived there, four years earlier. A new wave of immigrants had transformed what had been an intellectual desert into the temporary cultural capital of the German-speaking world. Thomas Mann, who had settled at Pacific Palisades, had assumed a quasi-ambassadorial role as spokesman for the German immigrants. Alma and Franz Werfel, rich enough to entertain after the prodigious success of *The Song of Bernadette*, had become the centre of a predominantly musical circle, into which Schoenberg was drawn. Brecht, at whose house guests sat on hard chairs and ate Helene Weigel's celebrated *Apfelkuchen*, attracted more radical spirits, among them Hanns Eisler, since 1942 profitably employed in Hollywood. The author Lion Feuchtwanger and his wife Martha drew another left-inclined group to their substantial and hospitable house. The theatre was represented by the actors Fritz Kortner and Peter Lorre, among others. Heinrich Mann and his notoriously inebriated wife, Nelly, eked out an impoverished existence with the support of his younger brother. It was a rich and varied scene. Small wonder that the hypochondriacal Thomas Mann complained that the stimulating company at hand frequently caused him to go to bed later than he would have wished.[42] But though these circles intersected at Salka Viertel's parties, the *émigrés* were far from forming a happy family party. There were rifts and feuds in abundance. What united the diaspora was dislike of American bread and American children, and a contempt for Anglo-Saxon cultural standards. Stravinsky, who had settled in Los Angeles in 1941, was exceptional in taking particular pleasure in his English friends, who included Aldous Huxley and Christopher Isherwood.

Klemperer occasionally attended the Evenings on the Roof chamber concerts,* at which he more than once heard Beethoven recitals given by his friend the pianist Richard Buhlig. But only rarely could he be induced to take part in social life, though he did attend Schoenberg's sixty-ninth birthday party on 13 September 1943, when such an animated musical discussion took place between Schoenberg, Thomas Mann and Klemperer that Mann noted the occurrence in his diary. Subsequently Mann referred to it in *Die Entstehung des Doktor Faustus*, his account of the genesis of the great novel he had started to write six months earlier. The novel led to a celebrated breach between Mann and Schoenberg, who considered that Mann had plagiarised his serial technique in his descriptions of the works of his composer-hero. But Mann's practice of drawing inspiration from real life did not stop there. Familiar with Klemperer's achievements in Berlin, he made him the conductor of the first performance of the apocalyptic masterpiece that forms a climactic chapter in the novel.

* * *

In the opinion of the critic Lawrence Morton, the Los Angeles Philharmonic Orchestra had deteriorated since Klemperer had left it.[43] But, far from seeking to avail itself of his services or even to offer him an occasional guest engagement, in August 1943 the Southern California Symphony Association announced the appointment as musical director of Alfred Wallenstein, who had not previously held a major conducting post. Wallenstein's arrival coincided with the resignation of Mrs Irish as general manager. Neither change was to Klemperer's advantage. Fortunately, however, Mrs Irish, whose devotion to him had never wavered,[44] continued to manage the Hollywood Bowl, where she was able to offer Klemperer a solitary concert in the summer of 1943. 'On 17 August', he wrote to Helene Hirschler on 7 July, 'there is even supposed to be a concert here. Do I have to tell you how I feel about it?' It was due largely to Johanna that he was at last persuaded to appear before a large audience that included Bruno Walter and George Szell. He was welcomed with prolonged applause. 'Though a bit tottery', wrote Richard Saunders, '... there was no question of any lack of control ... or of interpretative powers.'[45] Klemperer derived no satisfaction from the event. 'I would prefer not to describe my feelings while conducting', he wrote to Helene Hirschler on 31 August. Apart from an improvised concert for the troops in September 1943 he did not conduct again in public until the following summer. The contrast between the neglect Klemperer suffered at this period and the way in which the careers of other immigrant conductors prospered in America stuck in the throat of at least one observer. 'Bruno Walter, that windbag

---

* Established in 1939 in a successful attempt to provide Los Angeles with the adventurous programmes it had so badly lacked. Known later as the Monday Evening Concerts, when the programmes included several Stravinsky first performances, notably of *In Memoriam Dylan Thomas* (1954) and *Agon* (1957).

(*Seichbeutel*), blooms and flourishes', Ernst Bloch wrote on 6 May 1943 to Helene Hirschler. 'Where is God, as my philosopher great-grandfather used to ask?'

The two great composers living in Los Angeles were among the few who did what they could to help. On 12 November 1943 Schoenberg wrote to President Sproul of UCLA to suggest that Klemperer, whom he described as 'one of the most outstanding men in his field', be invited to hold conducting classes at the university. Nothing came of his initiative, however, perhaps on account of the warning Sproul had earlier received of Klemperer's instability. Three months later Stravinsky approached Leopold Stokowski:

> I would like to suggest the following idea which came to me recently. I have heard of your plan to found a new Symphony in the East.* I presume that you may desire a worthy and capable colleague, who at some time may be needed to share with you the conducting tasks. The conductor is none other than Otto Klemperer, who has now fortunately recovered and is in excellent shape. I take upon myself this suggestion in case you have not been *au courant* of his actual state of health.[46]

That approach also fell on stony ground. Klemperer again began to see a good deal of Schoenberg, who, as he later recalled, 'seemed to have grown milder'.[47] There were also visits to the Stravinskys. On 4 March 1944, Vera Stravinsky noted in her diary, 'Klemperers for tea. We are both very sorry for [them]. She tries to be brave and both of them appreciate the visit to us.'

With no openings in Los Angeles, there was nothing for it but to try his luck again in New York, and shortly after his visit to the Stravinskys Klemperer set out for the east by train, making the three-day journey without the comfort of a sleeping-compartment. But as on his visit twelve months earlier he met only with prevarication. Lunch with Artur Rodzinski, who had been appointed music director of the New York Philharmonic in succession to John Barbirolli, proved inconclusive. Stokowski was out of town and would not be choosing his guest conductors until the autumn. A meeting with Koussevitzky produced only confirmation of the fact that the trustees of the Boston orchestra preferred young American conductors. Judson promised to look around, but had nothing concrete to offer. '*Guter Alter*', Klemperer wrote to Johanna on 3 April, 'I am so ashamed to tell you these details.' There were also personal affronts. He wrote on 5 May to Helene Hirschler,

> I was at a benefit for the Poles, at which Huberman played the Szymanowski concerto very beautifully ... in the interval I saw the publisher Knopf and his wife.† I had previously known them quite well, once even sailed to Europe with

---

* The New York City Symphony Orchestra, not to be confused with the orchestra of the same name that Klemperer conducted in 1940–1 and was disbanded in 1943.
† Alfred (1892–1984) and Blanche (1894–1966) Knopf, co-founders in 1915 of the celebrated publishing firm that bears their name.

the wife. You wouldn't believe how unfriendly they were. They hardly greeted me. That isn't a matter of my imagination. It also struck a friend of mine (who also knew them). Something like this upsets me terribly ... Do you really think that people have taken my unconstrained behaviour of two years ago so badly?

Lotte, who had travelled with her father in order to look for a permanent job in New York, found him a room large enough to accommodate a piano for $14 a week. 'Much too much', he at first wrote to Johanna.[48] The shabbiness of the room depressed him. Together he and Lotte searched for something better, but, as Lotte reported to her mother, he continually missed more suitable accommodation through his inability to make up his mind. One room seemed more agreeable, but had no bath and was noisy. Another became free in the building Lotte was living in, but it was not possible to play the piano there. Without work and lacking a comfortable base, Klemperer spent much of his time at rehearsals and concerts. He heard recitals by Schnabel and was impressed by a chamber group under Adolf Busch. He attended Rodzinski's rehearsals for the first American performance of Shostakovich's new Eighth Symphony, but liked only the scherzo and slow movement. Zinka Milanov's singing particularly pleased him in a performance of Verdi's Requiem Mass, 'very well' conducted by Bruno Walter. He also heard Leonard Bernstein conduct his own *Jeremiah Symphony* with the New York Philharmonic. He 'has talent', Klemperer wrote to Johanna, 'even if he doesn't appeal to me all that much'.[49]

New York had nothing to hold him, and a visit to Maria Schacko proved that his feelings for her were dead, 'so that matter is settled'. 'Ah, *mein Alter*', he wrote to Johanna on 22 March, 'you know that what I would like is to come home and be quite passive.' Yet a month later he was still in New York, unable to reach a decision about his future. Johanna was also torn. During his years of euphoria Klemperer had cruelly humiliated her. Now his icy remoteness prevented the wounds from healing. 'I cannot and will not force him to live with me', she wrote bitterly to Lotte on 8 May. 'It could well be that he would be better living there [i.e. in New York] alone, rather than here with me.'

By the time Klemperer finally returned to his wife in early June 1944, the estrangement between them had deepened. Less than three weeks later, Johanna sent Lotte an anguished and despairing letter:

> Yesterday he was in a wretched mood. Or was I so aware of it because on our twenty-fifth wedding anniversary the day before yesterday ... he had pulled himself together so that he was *completely* normal? Not that he was in any way tender, just that the hate he certainly feels for me was not so apparent as usual. Ah, my Lotte, to you I can write as I feel, you are the only person I have – sometimes I think it's quite pointless to go on living. Papa recently said that in autumn he would return to New York and in that case I *certainly* will not live

with him again ... He uses me only as cook, nurse and maid. He doesn't have *any* feeling for me, such as would make this life a little easier. On the contrary, I see only the hate and mistrust that (I believe) Schacko and Regi have sown in him ...

... I can't go on like this. It is also not good for him. He himself doesn't want to live with me and, if he had more money, he certainly would not have come back here. You mustn't suppose that we have scenes. Not at all. But this sort of living alongside each other is hell for a person like me. I must and will end it. He is a great man and a great artist. Only the combination with me was wrong – I think for both parties. I really knew that when I married him. But he was so strong and I was so in love.[50]

Yet that love somehow survived. And when tension arose between Klemperer and his daughter, Johanna was the first to remind Lotte of her father's qualities:*

From long experience I know how it is with Papa. One is repelled yet equally strongly drawn to him, and who is *for* him, loves him *entirely*. I know of no man who is so *worthy* of love (I mean on account of his *human* qualities, out of which his artistic qualities arise). You will understand that later, my little one. You will come to love him and will be proud and happy to have this man as your father.[51]

That summer Mrs Irish provided Klemperer with two further concerts at the Hollywood Bowl, which he conducted successfully, in spite of his usual protestations that they had brought him 'neither pleasure nor satisfaction'.[52] Perhaps impressed by the warmth of the press reaction, Wallenstein invited him to conduct the Los Angeles Philharmonic Orchestra during the coming season. A little-known Brazilian pianist, Bernardo Segall, had already been engaged as soloist in Francisco Mignone's Brazilian Fantasy No. 1,† and though Wallenstein attempted to persuade him that it was an 'effective' piece, Klemperer remained sceptical. In the same programme Schoenberg had as a seventieth-birthday tribute been invited to conduct his Theme and Variations, Op. 43b, which he had composed in the previous year for military band, but subsequently rescored for symphony orchestra. The concert was, however, postponed when in December 1944 Klemperer contracted bilateral pleurisy. This entailed a stay in hospital, where the infection was successfully treated with the new wonder drug, penicillin. A month later Schoenberg was also taken ill. Thus the way was free for Klemperer to conduct the entire concert.

---

* A year earlier, Georg Klemperer, who had been moved by the nineteen-year-old Lotte's close resemblance to her mother as a young woman, had observed that Klemperer was prone to lecture and find fault with his daughter. She for her part, having experienced his behaviour when manic, was not disposed to accept moral instruction now that he was depressed and puritanical.

† Francisco Mignone (1897–1986), a prolific composer of Italian origins, whose music is influenced by South American rhythms and folksong.

Besides the Mignone Fantasy, it included Beethoven's Fifth Symphony and Schoenberg's Chamber Symphony No. 2, which Klemperer substituted for the Theme and Variations; it had not been heard in California before. The programme was to be given four times in all, twice in Los Angeles and once each in San Diego and Pasadena. As the day approached Klemperer began to suffer from stage fright.[53]

The house had long been sold out when on 8 February 1945 he appeared at the Auditorium for the first time for almost six years and was greeted with 'applause so spontaneous and sustained that he had to acknowledge it several times before the programme could get under way'.[54] Apart from the Fantasy, which the critic Lawrence Morton dismissed as 'rowdy claptrap', the concert was an overwhelming success. Not given to hyperbole, Morton wrote,

> Standing before the orchestra like a giant, with his left hand carving out gestures of magnificence and mastery, [Klemperer] made the ninety men and women play like gods. Correctness of speed and intonation and phrasing and dynamics — all of these were part of the Klemperer readings. But beyond them are the intangibles — qualities of heart and mind, depth of understanding, the wisdom that comes from long experience and meditation and study.[55]

Another critic wrote, 'If Mr Wallenstein was in the audience ... he had an opportunity to hear how the orchestra can play ... If, however, he took it for granted that it sounds as well when he conducts, that would be a mistake.'[56] Even Klemperer himself grudgingly admitted to Helene Hirschler that 'it went relatively well. People even talk of a success.'[57] He did not, however, warm to Schoenberg's Chamber Symphony. 'Especially in the second part, the music is quite alien to me', he wrote on 26 February to Lonny Epstein, thus perhaps unconsciously echoing the very word that had so offended Schoenberg when he had applied it to his music seven years earlier.

After the concerts Klemperer continued to sit at home, sunk in despair. An Easter Sunrise Service (fee $250) did nothing to raise his spirits. Nor did an unpaid American–Russian friendship concert at the Shrine on 16 May, when he shared a programme with Stravinsky, and the actor Edward G. Robinson delivered an impassioned address. Among the works he conducted was Prokofiev's cantata, *Alexander Nevsky*, which he had trouble in learning and found 'very weak'.[58] That summer there were two more concerts at the Bowl, where the crudeness of the amplification continued to disturb him. In nine months he had earned only $3,250. Thus when he was approached by a prosperous business man, who wanted conducting lessons, he felt he had no option but to agree, sceptical though he was of their value.* Accordingly, from September to December Klemperer gave instruction to Jacques Rachmilovich (1895–1956), who, much to his teacher's surprise, in 1945

---
* 'What one can teach ... is so minimal that I could explain it to you in a minute' (Heyworth (ed,), *Conversations*, p. 110)

founded the Santa Monica Symphony Orchestra and later made recordings. In a draft income tax return Klemperer declared the fees as ranging from $10 to $20 a session.[59] In Lotte Klemperer's recollection the true figure was $25 – at all events a far from princely sum.

More welcome was an invitation to inaugurate the Los Angeles Music Guild with two Bach programmes in October 1945. This small organisation had been brought into existence during the previous winter through the initiative of Alfred Leonard, proprietor of a local gramophone record store, in order to provide the area with a series of classical music concerts. Thanks to the presence in Hollywood of many outstanding instrumentalists, it was possible to assemble a first-rate chamber orchestra. The violinist Henri Temianka and the harpsichordist Alice Ehlers were engaged as soloists. Sol Babitz, who prepared the orchestral material, found Klemperer unconcerned with musicological niceties, but insistent on clarity and unequal notes.[60] Because he shared the widespread dislike of Bach trumpets at that time, Klemperer substituted E flat clarinets for them.[61]

Though the orchestra of twenty-six players was of high quality, the rehearsals did not go smoothly, as the instrumentalists were frequently unavailable owing to studio commitments. 'They simply go where they can earn most money', Klemperer wrote scornfully (6 October 1945) to Helene Hirschler. But even before the rehearsals began the air was full of thunder; Alice Ehlers had been reported in the press as defending Furtwängler's role in the now defunct Third Reich. In the middle of the night Klemperer delivered an ultimatum to Leonard on the telephone: he would not appear if Ehlers did. Leonard reminded Klemperer that he had himself spoken of including Strauss's recently composed *Metamorphosen* in a future concert. Klemperer retorted, 'Furtwängler didn't compose *Der Rosenkavalier*.'[62] The deadlock was resolved by a motor accident in which Alice Ehlers strained several fingers. On learning that Ingolf Dahl had been invited to take her place, she refused to lend her harpsichord, which was one of the very few in the area. The Violin Concerto in A minor with Temianka as soloist was substituted for the keyboard concerto originally announced. Two hours before the first concert, it was discovered that the orchestral parts had been left in Pasadena, where a public rehearsal had taken place the previous evening. To general amazement, Klemperer sat calmly in his dressing-room marking quantities of miniature scores so as to provide substitute material should the police fail to rush the missing material to the Auditorium in time.

The event was attended by many of the prominent musicians in the area. Klemperer received an immense ovation. The *Los Angeles Times* (26 October) wrote that those whose knowledge of Bach was confined to transcriptions for full orchestra could have no conception of the clarity of the performances. Ingolf Dahl described the second concert as 'one of the most beautiful' he had ever heard or taken part in.[63] Lawrence Morton wrote that he had 'left the concert in a state of the highest exaltation ... In matters of tempo, phrase and dynamics, [Klemperer] was as correct as a judge, as sensitive as a poet.'[64] After the concert Stravinsky, who had sent flowers, came to congratulate Klemperer in his dressing-room. In her diary Vera Stravinsky noted 'a wonderful Bach concert'.[65] Klemperer commented bleakly to Helene Hirschler, 'The Bach concerts have taken place. I enclose a criticism. About my own reaction, I prefer to say nothing. Stravinsky came round and seemed very satisfied. I found that very nice.'[66]

Werner also attended the concert. He was still in uniform, but his discharge from the Army was imminent. On discovering that he had been at drama school, the military authorities had transferred him to Special Services, and for two years he had been touring Pacific combat areas, directing and acting in plays that ranged from *Macbeth* and *Hamlet* to *Blithe Spirit* and *Arsenic and Old Lace*. Now he planned to go to New York to pursue a career in the theatre.

Following the success of his Philharmonic concert Klemperer was asked to give another one in the new season. This time he was allowed to choose his own programme, though he complained that 'I can't decide myself and it's not easy for anyone to help me.'[67] Eventually he resolved to give the first west coast performance of Berg's Violin Concerto. But in spite of an outstanding soloist, Joseph Szigeti, the work itself failed to appeal to him as it had done when he had championed it nine years earlier in Vienna. To Helene Hirschler he confessed, 'I am in a curious position with this piece (as with most modern pieces). The music certainly impresses me in its logic, and I don't want to resist the *Zeitgeist*. But I can't go along with it any more ... That makes me very sad.'[68] Depression no doubt played a part in this reaction. But he was now sixty and the caution that had always tempered his radical sympathies had grown more pronounced with the years.

At Christmas 1945 Klemperer travelled to Salt Lake City, where he gave a mammoth performance of *Messiah* in the Mormon Tabernacle before an audience of 12,000, relayed by a public address system to the multitudes outside.[69] A few weeks later he was in Vancouver, where on 3 February 1946 he was obliged to conduct *Tod und Verklärung* with a piano in place of a harp, because the harpist had previously accepted an invitation to play at a wedding. 'That is something I have not done before', he drily observed in a letter (1 February) to Johanna. However, he could not allow the incident to prevent him from agreeing to return in the autumn, as conductor for the entire season. In 1945 his gross income, including interest of $268.50 on the few government bonds that he still held, amounted to $7,843.50.[70] It was a considerable improvement on his earnings in the previous year. But it was clear that he could not hope to do more than survive in Los Angeles.

By the beginning of 1946 musical life in Europe was slowly reviving, at any rate outside a devastated and divided Germany, and Johanna was eager that he should return there as soon as possible to seek work in a continent still unaware of the disruption of his career in America. Klemperer was still so depressed that all decision seemed beyond him and for weeks he resisted her urgings, though to Helene Hirschler he gloomily admitted on 18 January, 'I will probably *have* to go.' In the meantime, however, Johanna had taken matters into her own hands and approached Judson's agency, Columbia Artists, which had no difficulty in putting together a tour that would mark Klemperer's return to Europe after an absence of almost ten years. On 2 March he and Johanna left by train for New York. A week later they sailed to England, whence they took a plane to Stockholm.

7

Europe remains Europe

Klemperer's first concert with the Stockholm Philharmonic Orchestra took place on 20 March 1946. The speed at which he took the finale of the 'Haffner' Symphony raised a few eyebrows, but at the end of the evening the public responded with enthusiasm. In the audience were Aladár Tóth, a Hungarian critic, and his wife, the pianist Annie Fischer, who had fled to Sweden when German troops had moved into Budapest in 1940. Tóth had had reservations when he had last heard Klemperer conduct in Budapest in May 1936, but now detected 'a great mental change'. In an undated letter to his friend the conductor László Somogyi, Tóth wrote,

> The 'Haffner' Symphony was not only the most beautiful performance of the work we have ever encountered ... From a stylistic point of view it was perhaps the most perfect Mozart conducting we have heard. The Fifth Symphony was wonderfully beautiful, incredibly rich (and for this reason instructive), especially on the second night.

Tóth was less enthusiastic about the performances of Brahms's Symphony No. 3 and Schubert's No. 9 that Klemperer gave in his second Stockholm programme on 27 March. Both seemed to him to suffer from a coldness and rigidity that was untrue to the spirit of the music. But when the two men met afterwards at the house of Johannes Norrby, the director of the Stockholm Konzertföreningen (Concert Society), they were immediately drawn to each other. 'It hurts one to look at this man', Tóth continued in his letter to Somogyi. 'His face, or rather his mouth, is pulled to one side, his right arm is half paralysed and completely rigid when conducting. He also drags his right foot. But what a deeply honest, charming and good man this Klemperer is and what a "straight soul".' The conversation continued until the early hours of the morning and Tóth was touched by the readiness with which Klemperer, on learning that Norrby was rehearsing an amateur choir in Bach's B minor Mass, went through the work with him at the piano. A personal bond had come into existence that was to play a crucial role in Klemperer's career.

The next day Klemperer flew to Italy, where over the following six weeks he gave concerts in several cities. In Milan, Franco Abbiati, the senior critic of the city's leading paper, *Corriere della Sera* (9 April), hailed him as 'a real master'; he had transformed the orchestra of La Scala into 'a miraculously alert and disciplined body'. A number of concerts followed with the Santa Cecilia Orchestra in Rome, where Klemperer gave two performances of Bach's *St Matthew Passion* and set the hall 'in delirium' with Brahms's First Symphony.[1] Klemperer also appeared in Florence, Turin and Naples. He was disappointed by the poor state of string-playing 'in the land of Vivaldi, Veraccini and Corelli [sic]',[2] but by the time he left Italy on 13 May, he had made sufficient impact to be invited the following year.

Next came concerts in Paris, where he conducted both the Conservatoire Orchestra and the French Radio's Orchestre National. Klemperer did not attract large audiences, but he made a far deeper impression on the critics than he had done on his pre-war visits. After a Beethoven programme on 19 and 21 May, Claude Rostand saluted him in *Le Figaro* as 'a very great conductor'.[3] Klemperer was delighted to find the city outwardly unchanged. 'How much we would love to live here', he wrote wistfully to his old friend and legal adviser, Fritz Fischer.[4]

While in Paris, Klemperer was invited by the military authorities to conduct in the French occupied zone of Germany. In contrast to the British, who in the north-west were largely preoccupied with establishing law and order and feeding the huge industrial conurbations of Hamburg and the Ruhr, and the Americans, who in the south were pursuing the chimera of 'denazification', the more far-sighted French had launched an active cultural policy in the comparatively small and rural area they occupied on the borders of France. At Baden-Baden, headquarters of the French forces, a radio station had been set up, the modest *Kur* orchestra had been expanded to symphonic proportions and the critic Heinrich Strobel, who before 1933 had been one of the Kroll Oper's most committed supporters, had been appointed musical director. It was doubtless Strobel who invited Klemperer to conduct in Baden-Baden at a time when the remainder of the country was still closed to artists from abroad.

Not all Klemperer's friends were happy at his willingness to return to Germany. 'This entire people', Fritz Fischer wrote to him, 'has turned its back on us as we have on it, and so it must remain.' Klemperer was unconvinced. 'For all time?' he replied, questioning the finality of such an attitude.[5] Two days later, on 24 June, he crossed the Rhine, the first of the great *émigré* musicians to return to his native country. He found the atmosphere of the undestroyed spa town 'magical'.[6] Asked on arrival whether he would prefer an oboist who had been a member of the National Socialist party or a less good one with irreproachable political credentials, he replied, 'The Nazi, of course.'[7]

On his first appearance the orchestra stood and applauded. Contrary to his habit of launching into a rehearsal without so much as a 'Guten Tag', he first addressed the players. 'I have come to Baden', he told them, 'to try to heal the wounds made by this terrible time. I believe that music is one of the powers that can heal those wounds. I beg you to regard my presence in that spirit.'[8] Such words were balm to a populace uncomfortably aware of its isolation from the outside world and eager to clasp a hand held out in a spirit of reconciliation. The concert, on 30 June, was a triumph. Hilde Strobel wrote to her brother, 'I couldn't believe it was our orchestra, the men played so fabulously.'

Immediately after the concert Klemperer returned to Paris to make some records. Before leaving for Europe he had been visited in Los Angeles by a Hungarian immigrant, George de Mendelssohn-Bartholdy, who in spite of his impressive name was not related to the composer. Mendelssohn had heard Klemperer conduct in Berlin before the war and now invited him to record for Vox, the small company he had set up at the end of the war. Its resources were limited, but a contract was signed that was automatically to be renewed unless terminated by either party. Klemperer agreed to make four records a year and not to record for any other company without prior agreement. Because costs were lower in Europe, it was agreed that the recordings would be made in Paris, and in the first week of July Klemperer started to record the Brandenburg Concertos, *Eine kleine Nachtmusik* and two of the Bach transcriptions he had made ten years earlier in Los Angeles. A Bach keyboard concerto and Klemperer's *Merry Waltz* were also recorded but not released. Rehearsal time was restricted, the technical level of the recordings was not high and weak distribution resulted in disappointing sales. But the players of the Pro Musica Orchestra, an *ad hoc* ensemble, were good and Mendelssohn was impressed by the assurance and rapidity with which Klemperer worked. For the first time since 1932 he had established a modest foothold in the recording industry.*

* * *

From Paris, which had done much to restore his spirits,† Klemperer moved to the Dutch seaside resort of Scheveningen, where four concerts he gave with the Hague Residentie Orchestra between 10 and 19 July were greeted with acclaim. But the climax of his tour was the concert he gave on 26 July with the Amsterdam Concertgebouw Orchestra at Interlaken in Switzerland. He was moved when at the first rehearsal the manager, by way of introduction, declared, 'Now that Klemperer is here, we know the war is really

---

* During the economic slump negotiations with Electrola had collapsed in February 1932 on differences on fees and repertory (EMI archives, Hayes). He had made no records in America.

† In a list of the dates of the depressions and euphorias that Klemperer later in the year prepared for a Los Angeles psychiatrist, he gave May 1946 as the month in which this long-lasting depression started to yield.

over.'⁹ An affinity was established between him and the orchestra from the start. Those who had not seen him since he had last conducted it in 1929 were shocked by his appearance. But as Hubert Barwahser, the principal flute, later put it, as soon as he mounted the platform 'something happened'. It was not, Barwahser recalled, with his arms but with his eyes that Klemperer seemed to conduct. His impact on the orchestra was so great that those members who were not playing in the performance of Bach's Suite in D that opened the concert crowded into the hall in order not to miss it.¹⁰

In the *Basler National-Zeitung* (29 July) Otto Maag called the account of Brahms's First Symphony 'an unforgettable experience'. Klemperer was overjoyed to find himself again at the head of a great European orchestra, which had clearly taken him to its heart. In an interview published in *Time* (5 August) the orchestra's manager asserted, 'Klemperer is one of the very few great living conductors. He can be compared only to Toscanini, Bruno Walter and – let us say it without political prejudice – Furtwängler.' After years of obscurity in America, he had at last begun to rebuild his career.

Inevitably there were painful reminders of the recent past. In Stockholm a German soprano who had been a member of the Kroll Oper wrung his hand and declared that, to show that she was no Nazi, she had after the war adopted a Jewish child. 'Why now?' asked Klemperer. A self-exculpatory screed by Furtwängler, 'Why I stayed on in Germany', that chanced to come into his hands was, he felt, uncomfortably reminiscent of the defence speeches of the accused at the International War Crimes Tribunal at Nuremberg.¹¹ The spirit of reconciliation he had shown at Baden-Baden did not outlast the summer. 'I never met anyone who said he was a Nazi ... They all said they had been persecuted', he told an interviewer on his return to North America. 'The Germans are sorry they lost the war – period! They do not say, "we lost the war because Hitler was the aggressor".'*

Yet he was overjoyed to be in the Old World. In Holland the North Sea, so familiar from his Hamburg childhood, enchanted him as the Pacific could not. 'Europe remains Europe', he declared in a letter to Helene Hirschler from Interlaken, where his bedroom window looked out on the glistening peak of the Jungfrau. 'Bloch was right when he wrote to me that it is the old Antaeus,† from whom we all stem.' 'Naturally Europe is in a very bad situation', he wrote to Olin Downes on the same day. 'The food question, the money question are terrible. But I think it will change in a short while

---

* Interview with Pierre Berton in *The Sun* (Vancouver) of 27 September 1946. Klemperer's change of heart may have been connected with the revelations of the Nuremberg trials, which took place that summer and much preoccupied him. Furtwängler's screed is not among his papers in the Zurich Zentralbibliothek.
† A wrestler in Greek mythology, who drew new strength whenever his feet touched the earth (his mother Gaea).

and Europe will develop again, especially musically. For instance, the Concertgebouw Orchestra, I think ... is even better than it was.'[12]

After concerts at Vichy and Zurich (where only a misunderstanding about dates prevented a visit to Strauss, who was staying in nearby Baden),[13] Klemperer returned to Paris to complete the Vox recordings he had started in July. It had been a rewarding and enjoyable summer. Both he and Johanna would dearly have liked to remain in Europe. A house in Los Angeles and commitments to conduct there and in Vancouver made that impossible, but they took comfort from the fact that the invitations that had poured in from all sides would make possible an even more extended European tour in the following spring. When they boarded an aircraft for New York on 30 August, Klemperer's prospects looked better than at any time since he had left Europe for America in 1936.

* * *

On arrival in America Klemperer and his wife travelled to Boston to visit cousin Georg. They also saw Ernst Bloch, who reported, 'Klemperer is here, miraculously restored, having won Paganini-like triumphs in Rome, Zurich, Paris, Stockholm – and Baden-Baden.'[14] However, in spite of his eighty years and failing health, Georg was not deceived by his cousin's new-found buoyancy. 'In my view there can be no doubt that he is clearly at the start of a manic period', he gloomily advised Helene Hirschler on 5 September.

> If that develops everything he has recently achieved is in jeopardy. I did all I could to influence him, but he is not at all responsive. The only person who could *perhaps* help is his wife, whom he has again started to treat badly, as he always does in manic phases. Johanna is basically good-natured, but she is overwrought – she does not seem to have had an easy time in Europe. Unfortunately she isn't intelligent enough to exercise her influence, which can occasionally be very effective, at the right time and in the right way.

Regi Elbogen, whom Klemperer had visited on arrival in New York, formed a similar conclusion. 'He was very excited, so that, by the time he left two-and-a-half hours later, I was ill, really ill!' she wrote on 8 September to Marianne. 'At the end I spoke very seriously to him ... But it was all quite useless ... Hanne [Johanna], whom I telephoned, said that it was only recently that he had become so excited.'[15]

On his return to Los Angeles Klemperer threw himself into a round of purposeless activity. In spite of sedatives prescribed by his cousin, he slept for no more than three hours at night. Within ten days he made two journeys to Santa Barbara to visit Lotte Lehmann, whom he had not seen for years. He insisted on taking Schoenberg's fourteen-year-old daughter Nuria to Mass. He began to compose again. He talked incessantly. His appearance grew increasingly neglected. Observing the familiar symptoms with dismay, Johanna persuaded him to consult Dr David Brunswick, a psychiatrist practising in Los Angeles and brother of his friend Mark.

Brunswick observed what he described as an 'impairment of judgement'. Believing that it might respond to shock treatment, he referred Klemperer to a colleague, Dr Eugene Ziskind, who had diagnosed Gershwin's fatal brain tumour. Ziskind saw Klemperer on 17 September. He found him voluble, lacking in reserve and prone to laughter without apparent cause. But he could discern no flight of ideas; what his patient said was not only coherent, but on a high intellectual level. He did, however, observe some curious obsessions, which included a preoccupation with incest and an *idée fixe* that at a sanatorium he had briefly stayed in six years earlier in Santa Barbara he had been offered a beautiful nurse to sleep with as an inducement for him to remain. Ziskind thought that such notions indicated impairment of judgement. But an electroencephalogram proved normal, and he accordingly advised that any decision about treatment should be postponed until Klemperer had fulfilled engagements in Vancouver for which he was due to leave Los Angeles on 26 September.[16]

Johanna was exhausted from the strains of the European tour; her presence in any case served only to aggravate Klemperer. It was therefore agreed that the 23-year-old Lotte should accompany him. It was to prove a traumatic experience for her.

Klemperer's opening concert in Vancouver on 6 October was an uncharacteristic concoction of his own choosing. The first half consisted mainly of arias by Mozart and Beethoven sung by the young Austrian soprano Regina Resnik. After the interval came Schoenberg's transcription of the Brahms G minor Piano Quartet. Two days before the concert Klemperer, in spite of his physical handicaps, accompanied Resnik at a piano rehearsal 'as if he had eight hands'.[17] At half past one that night she heard a knock on her door. It was Klemperer, who had returned from a concert given by Lionel Hampton, the famous jazz band leader. He 'wanted to talk' and proceeded to do so for over two hours without, however, making any advances. Twenty-four hours later he disappeared and was nowhere to be found until he turned up more than an hour after the final rehearsal should have begun, so that there was time only for a run-through of the programme. Shortly before the concert itself, he was found wandering in the foyer of the hall. In spite of these unpromising preliminaries, Resnik forty years later recalled Klemperer's conducting as 'one of the most sublime moments of my life'. After the concert there was a reception at the house of Amy Buckerfield, the wealthy chairman of the orchestral board. Klemperer led his hostess's young daughter into the garden. 'As we stopped at an apple tree', she recalled, 'I was suddenly clutched in a vice-like grip by Klemperer, who exclaimed, "Ach

– Adam and Eve and the apple." It was only with difficulty that I extricated myself.'[18]

The next day Klemperer flew to San Francisco, where Resnik was to sing the role of Fidelio under an old acquaintance, the Austrian-born conductor Paul Breisach. He attended rehearsals and offered loud comments, at one point even suggesting that he should take over. At a party afterwards he played much of *Rigoletto* by heart on the piano and persuaded the singers present to join in, among them the celebrated American tenor, Jan Peerce, and Hertha Glaz. By the time he returned to Vancouver on 16 October his condition had deteriorated. 'Every night', wrote the distraught Lotte to her mother two days later,

> we are up until about four or five in the most miserable bars. He runs after every woman, smokes like a madman and gets excited about everything. When he sits at the piano or conducts he is wonderful. But unfortunately only then. Otherwise he is completely manic and (in my opinion) absolutely not responsible for his actions . . . It can't go on like this.
>
> . . . Naturally he has clear moments . . . [But] if one tries to stop him he becomes furious and hateful . . . Only once have I forgotten myself and that was yesterday afternoon, when he walked out [on the whole engagement] and I was frightened that he was going round the bend. Then I had to scream at him that . . . he must listen and control himself. He was naturally livid, ran out of the office and roamed around the town for hours. I was absolutely desperate and just longed to faint and become unconscious. But then in the evening . . . he rang up and . . . asked me to eat with him.
>
> . . . At one o'clock in the morning we went on to a club and danced until three. When we got home he still wasn't tired. He said that he would go for a moment to get a drink from the night porter as that would make him sleepy. I . . . just let him go . . . Everyone here says that I'm the only one who can calm him. But I have my limits . . . and I'm becoming ill . . . Nothing is more agonising than to watch a man like Papa destroy himself.

Johanna's awareness of her husband's spendthrift habits when manic added to her desperation. In an undated letter to him, she wrote,

> The fact that you haven't sent money either to me or to the bank probably means that you haven't got any. What is going to happen? How are you going to pay for the journey to Europe? Or your debts? Ah, my Otto, you write and telegram that you owe everything to me. [But] . . . it seems that everything that has been achieved with *such difficulty* is once again to dissolve into nothing. What a vain labour of love – that is all I can say. 'Was soll werden, wie soll's enden?'*

---

* 'What will come, how will it end?' Quotation from *Gebet* (1915), text and music by Klemperer.

Yet at moments he would converse with lively intelligence about books, music and ideas. There were also sessions of chamber music in his hotel apartment. The Vancouver concert-master, Albert Steinberg, would be summoned at all hours to perform Beethoven violin sonatas in which, to the ears of one listener, Klemperer's one-handed accompaniment always seemed to predominate.[19] With the help of the hotel staff Lotte in vain planted sleeping tablets in her father's soup. She found herself obliged to collude with the night porter to arrange for the comings and goings of the women Klemperer had picked up on his nocturnal wanderings. There were scenes galore in rehearsals for the programme of French music, consisting of a suite from Rameau's *Les Paladins*, Bizet's incidental music to *L'Arlésienne* and Berlioz's *Symphonie fantastique*, which he conducted on 20 October. The local press was enthusiastic, but the orchestral board was beginning to wonder whether the game was worth the candle, and its doubts increased when Klemperer presented a series of demands and threatened resignation if they were not met. Some of his requirements were reasonable attempts to improve unsatisfactory conditions. Others, such as a request that he be provided with a villa and swimming pool for the duration of his engagement, were preposterous. Mrs Buckerfield, whose panic-stricken board members had on one occasion hidden themselves under the stairs when Klemperer had announced his intention of attending a meeting, finally indicated to Lotte that she would be happy to cancel his contract for the remainder of the season. Klemperer was persuaded that he was in need of a rest and on 22 October he flew to Los Angeles, unaware that he would not be returning. The following day his resignation was announced.

* * *

Klemperer was now more intensely manic than at any other time in his life. Hitherto his euphoria had been contained within a vestige of rationality. Now he seemed at moments 'beyond sanity'.[20] On 27 October he invited the soprano Jarmila Novotna to accompany him to Mass. Afterwards he proposed a swim at the Ambassador Hotel, where she only with difficulty prevented him from entering the pool fully clothed.[21] The question of shock treatmant, left in abeyance on his departure for Vancouver, now recurred. Klemperer was fiercely resistent to the suggestion. But Ernst Toch's psychiatrist wife, Lilly, suggested that he should enter a clinic outside Chicago, run by Julius Steinfeld, a psychiatrist with whom both she and Helene Hirschler had for many years been on friendly terms and who had successfully treated her husband for depression. Steinfeld, in Lilly Toch's view, had two merits. He was not, as she put it, 'a tabulating American', but a man of vigorous intelligence and broad culture, whose 'European mentality' would appeal to Klemperer;[22] and he was not committed to the use of shock treatment in cases such as his.

Klemperer was intermittently aware of the seriousness of his condition and he agreed to put himself under Steinfeld's care. In the first week of November Johanna took him to the Forest Sanatorium for the treatment of mental and nervous disorders, situated in flat, desolate country near the small town of Evanston on Lake Michigan, some twenty miles to the north-west of Chicago. On arrival Steinfeld told her to leave without saying goodbye to her husband. As he had foreseen, Klemperer became so excited that his legs and arms had to be strapped to his bed.[23] For three days he maintained an attitude of 'aggressive opposition',[24] refusing all food. Once his patient became quieter, Steinfeld gave him what he described as 'modified sleeping treatment', followed by psychoanalytical sessions. Within two weeks Klemperer had in Steinfeld's view greatly improved. Thereafter he spent much time composing and playing a piano that had been put at his disposal.

After tests and investigations Steinfeld reported to Ziskind. 'I do not know', he wrote on 14 November,

> whether we are justified in diagnosing him as a manic-depressive. It is my impression that he has some sort of a beginning dementia. It is possible that the operation and its sequels are the cause for this dementia, which is expressed by disturbance of memory, lack of criticism and judgement, euphoria, etc. What puzzles me is ... that he has been on a successful concert tour through Europe, which of course is not in accordance with a state of dementia. On the other hand I am positive that his thinking impairment cannot be explained by his manic state.

A physiological investigation on 18 November tended to confirm Steinfeld's view. It found a degree of memory impairment and 'perseveration', a condition in which it is hard to escape from a recurrent idea, feeling or action, and also raised the question of whether the removal of the tumour and its aftermath had not caused a degree of brain damage. Ziskind did not wholly agree. Acknowledging receipt of Steinfeld's report on the neurological investigations, he replied on 9 December that in his opinion 'although there were a few features that were not common in the average manic-depressive patient, I thought he was in a hypomanic attack'. At this point Steinfeld decided on a course of insulin shock therapy.* To the end of his days Klemperer remained unaware that he had received such treatment. To reassure Lotte, Steinfeld invited her to witness a treatment, which proved as peaceful as he had claimed it would be. After an injection Klemperer slept for about ten minutes and on awaking assumed that he had dozed off. The only after-effect was a temporary loss of memory.

By early December Steinfeld considered his patient sufficiently improved

---

* In 1933 findings had been reported on the use of insulin, first isolated in 1922, to diminish over-active states. Because of its danger, the therapy was largely succeeded in the 1940s by electro-shock treatment. Phenothiazine drugs were a later development.

to be treated as an out-patient, and Lotte went to live with her father at a nearby hotel that accepted the clinic's out-patients. When her father appeared, he seemed as excitable as he had been six weeks earlier in Vancouver, but Steinfeld insisted that, whatever her initial impression might be, the worst was over.

Steinfeld would have preferred to keep what he regarded as an unusually complicated case under observation. He was, however, convinced that work would prove therapeutic, and he was also aware how urgently necessary it was for Klemperer to earn some money.* He accordingly allowed him to leave with his daughter on 20 December for Salt Lake City, where, as in the previous year, he conducted Christmas performances of *Messiah*. The day before Klemperer's departure Steinfeld wrote at length to Helene Hirschler:

> What disturbs me about K is the fact that I consider his intellectual capacity to be somewhat damaged. Whether it is a matter of incipient senility or whether the month-long meningitis is the cause is difficult to determine. But the many investigations I have both made myself and had made reveal a disturbance in abstract thinking. That need not be evident to laymen or affect his conducting activities. But I would be surprised if he were to prove able to absorb new works as before and did not have to live mainly on old stock.

On Christmas Day Johanna telephoned Salt Lake City with the news that Georg Klemperer had died at the age of eighty-one. To Lotte's surprise, Klemperer received the news with apparent unconcern, even though the old man had wanted him to know that his thoughts had been with him to the end. With his will Georg left a note, headed 'Otto'.

> You can be absolutely sure that you will be entirely well again . . . Things are *not* as you see them. You are musically absolutely capable and able to meet any demands. Your future is assured. Bear the burden of anxiety patiently. It is a trial you are destined to shoulder and you have often come through. Use your reason to overcome your feeling of anxiety. The Lord will not leave you and you will soon be freed from it.

It was Georg's view rather than Steinfeld's that finally proved to be the more accurate.

*   *   *

On his return to Los Angeles Klemperer's first engagement was to conduct the Philharmonic Orchestra on 6 January 1947 in a concert in aid of its pension fund. At his insistence the programme contained Stravinsky's recent Symphony in Three Movements, which, though composed in Los Angeles, had yet to be heard there.† Klemperer was convinced that the work was

---

* In February 1947 his account was to all intents and purposes empty. Ziskind's fees had still not been settled in 1951.
† The composer had conducted its first performance in New York on 24 January 1946.

a 'masterpiece': to Stravinsky he described it (in English) as 'a great and mature work'.[25] But it was to prove an unhappy choice. The audience was small, so that the orchestra's fund failed to benefit, while the work itself was received by the local press with a notable lack of sympathy. Richard Saunders found a lack of 'inspiration',[26] while the *Pacific Coast Musician* (18 January) dismissed the score as little more than 'a succession of unpleasant noises having neither purpose nor direction'. Even Lawrence Morton, the only Los Angeles critic to be admitted to Stravinsky's circle, was less than wholehearted in his enthusiasm. Though he hailed the first movement as 'Stravinsky's greatest achievement', he remained uncertain about the second and dismissed the finale as 'spotty and episodic'.[27] However, it may have been the performance, and not the work itself, that accounted for the symphony's failure to make a greater impact.

In a letter to Helene Hirschler, written on the following day, Lilly Toch attributed any shortcomings to Klemperer's unwillingness to prepare himself adequately.

> When it is a matter of *Messiah* in Salt Lake City or the 'Pathétique' here yesterday, he can afford not to do so. A performance such as that of the Stravinsky symphony ... would, I think, anywhere else be taken amiss. Here it was a triumph.
>
> On the platform he looked like old prints of Paganini as 'the devil's fiddler', so tall, so thin, so bent. Everyone close to him was relieved it went as well as it did.

Thomas Mann, with whom Klemperer, Johanna and Lotte dined on 14 January, found his guest 'noisy' and 'temperamentally unbalanced' to an extent he described as 'rather terrible'.[28] Meanwhile, Regi raised the question whether the lying that had been such a disturbing feature of his last manic phase had not started to recur.[29]

It was probably on some nocturnal excursion that Klemperer received a wound in the lower part of his leg that kept him in bed for a week before the Bach programme he conducted for the Music Guild on 22 January and obliged him to sit for much of the concert. Klemperer never told his family what had happened, although for some days he uncharacteristically insisted on making his bed, lest Johanna or Lotte should find traces of blood on his sheets. But the shock of a wound that seemed to have been caused by a knife or a broken bottle had a sobering effect.[30] Hitherto he had adamantly refused to consider putting himself again under Steinfeld's care. Now he elected to return to the Forest Sanatorium.

Steinfeld, who found Klemperer's explanation of the wound 'contradictory and nonsensical',[31] recommended that he should proceed with his plans for a second European tour. But, having witnessed Klemperer's intense irritation with, and sometimes unpleasant behaviour towards, Johanna and

7   Klemperer in Los Angeles with bandaged head after an assault on him during the night of 13 March 1947

Lotte, he advised that it might be better for him to travel on his own. To the Tochs, he had written a month earlier (10 January),

> He must live separately from the two women and be *forced* to rely on himself. I know that is probably not feasible because he is childishly dependent. He is still

... fixated on his mother, who kept him in great dependency ... and thus in constant rebellion against her. That is the pattern of his behaviour and he seems to fall into the same role with the two women with all the ensuing complications. He is certainly a manic-depressive type, but his basic (*uralte*) neurosis is stronger than the psychotic part and makes all attempts [to treat him] patchwork. I hope he will soon fall into a depression, as that is his 'happy' time when he can work.*

In spite of Steinfeld's opinion that Klemperer might be better on his own, Johanna decided that in his current condition it would be too risky to allow him to travel alone. It was therefore agreed that Lotte would accompany her father to Europe.

Before leaving America, Klemperer returned to Los Angeles to gather his belongings and on 12 March gave a final concert there with the Music Guild, a point he underlined by ending it with Haydn's 'Farewell' Symphony. The following evening he was as restless as ever and, ignoring all requests that he stay at home, insisted on taking a taxi down-town. The next morning he was brought back by the police with a bandaged head. His clothes were filthy and his shirt was covered in blood.[32] On 15 March the *Los Angeles Times* reported that at a bar Klemperer had encountered two men, who had offered to drive him to another bar but on the way had beaten him up and robbed him of $30 dollars. Shortly before dawn he had been found lying in the street and had been treated in hospital for what the *Herald-Express* (14 March) described as 'severe lacerations'. The next day the *New York Herald-Tribune* carried a headline, 'Dr Klemperer beaten and robbed ... in quest of American jazz'.

The incident may account for the fact that, on his arrival in New York two days later, Regi found her brother quieter than he had been six months earlier. But it did not keep him from similar nocturnal excursions in New York. He also took the opportunity to resume contact with Maria Schacko. Meanwhile, Johanna wrote to urge Lotte not to forget to buy her father galoshes and to take food in view of the shortages in Europe. But she could not bring herself to write to him. After the strains of the previous six months she was exhausted and embittered. She had had to raise a loan on the security of her house to pay for air tickets, well aware that in his present frame of mind there was little prospect that he would remit much of his earnings in Europe. Alone and now nearing sixty, she had been left with a pile of unpaid bills and no means of support beyond the interest on the modest sum she had been able to invest after the settlement Klemperer had received from the Southern California Symphony Association six years earlier.

* It is not easy to square Steinfeld's view that Klemperer's troubles were largely neurotic in origin with his earlier opinion that they were, at any rate in part, caused by brain damage sustained in the course of the tumour operation and its aftermath.

Although Klemperer had conducted in Baden-Baden during his previous European tour, he had not been able to visit Austria or other parts of Germany. Early in 1947 his New York agent applied for permission to visit both countries. But when the passports were returned they contained no such validation and it required a cable signed by the US Under-Secretary of State, Dean Acheson, to persuade the American occupation authorities in Vienna to approve a visit to Austria. No permission to enter Germany was forthcoming.[33] However, Klemperer had more than sufficient engagements to keep him fully occupied for the coming six months.

His plans to begin his tour in London had to be abandoned owing to an acute fuel shortage in Britain, and on 19 March he and Lotte left New York for Vienna. Owing to engine trouble they were obliged to spend the night in Frankfurt, where they had their first glimpse of the devastation inflicted on German cities by Allied bombing. Lotte was aghast at the sea of ruins and the hungry, frightened faces in the streets. Klemperer, however, was not in a frame of mind in which anything troubled him. He sat at the hotel's piano and played a series of tunes. 'What were they?' he asked the blank faces that had gathered round. Only later did Lotte realise that every piece he had played was by Mendelssohn. Nazi censorship had effectively deprived the Germans of a part of their inheritance.

In Vienna they were boarded in a hotel reserved for American personnel. Though elections had taken place and an Austrian government had been established in the early winter of 1945, the country was still in effect ruled by a quadripartite High Commission. Industry (50 per cent of which was in the Russian zone surrounding Vienna) and agriculture were in ruins. Communication between the four occupied zones was so circuitous that it was easier to travel to Czechoslovakia than to the Allied zones in the south and west of the country. In Vienna the cathedral, the opera house, the Burgtheater and the principal museums were in ruins. It was the era of Carol Reed's memorable film, *The Third Man*: there was a severe shortage of fuel and food and the black market thrived.

The Viennese press gave Klemperer a fulsome welcome. In *Die Welt am Abend* (27 March) the producer Oskar Fritz Schuh recalled his achievements at the Kroll, 'which have become as much a part of theatrical history as has the period of the Vienna Opera under Mahler'. But a certain reserve became apparent in the critics' reaction to the two programmes he gave with the Vienna Symphony Orchestra within a few days of his arrival. Helmut Fiechtner was impressed by the grandiose structure of his performance of Bruckner's Symphony No. 7, but found it lacking in detail,[34] a view also held by a member of the orchestra who had played under him before the war.[35] The critic of the *Wiener Kurier* considered the performance of Bach's *Johannes*

Passion on 3 April overdriven and lacking in inwardness.[36] To the *Wiener Zeitung* (16 April) it sounded like 'a successful improvisation'.

Klemperer had arrived in Vienna without plans to appear at the State Opera, but shortly after his arrival he was invited to conduct two performances of *Don Giovanni*. Though he had in the past been unwilling to conduct repertory performances that he had not himself prepared, and though he was in any case shortly to leave for Italy, the opportunity of working again in the theatre after an interval of more than fourteen years proved irresistible. Lotte's objections were brushed aside and the Italian leg of his tour was jettisoned.

Following the destruction of its own house, the Vienna State Opera was enjoying a brief golden age in the historic Theater an der Wien, where *Fidelio* had had its first performance. Travel was still difficult, and for those artists who had still to be 'denazified' impossible. The vast majority of German theatres were in ruins and in any case had no foreign currency to pay guests from other countries. With the collapse of the Third Reich, many Austrian singers had returned to their native country, while a number of leading German artists had been granted Austrian citizenship to enable them to leave Germany (and in some cases political associations they were glad to forget) and become members of the Vienna State Opera. Thus for a number of years the city boasted an ensemble of outstanding singers, such as it has never since proved possible to maintain, there or elsewhere. Even by the standards of the time, Klemperer was provided with an outstanding cast: Irmgard Seefried (Zerlina), Elisabeth Schwarzkopf (Elvira), Ljuba Welitsch (Anna), Paul Schöffler (Giovanni), Erich Kunz (Leporello), Anton Dermota (Ottavio), Ludwig Weber (Commendatore) and Alfred Poell (Masetto).

In the concert hall the manic Klemperer was prone to neglect rehearsals. But in the theatre his condition could lead to incandescent performances, as it plainly did on 10 and 12 April. 'The fire of his musical will ... burst more strongly and more individually than in his two concerts', wrote Peter Lafitte in the *Wiener Kurier* (11 April), '... the work was given an almost feverish tension which pushed the demonic into the foreground.' Though the orchestra was dismayed at Klemperer's insistence on himself accompanying the recitatives,[37] all reviews agreed that he had stamped a deeply personal mark on the performances and held the singers under his spell. But when the board of the self-governing Vienna Philharmonic Orchestra (whose personnel is largely identical with that of the State Opera orchestra) met later in the year to choose conductors for the following season, Klemperer's name was not among those under consideration.[38]

*   *   *

On 22 April Klemperer arrived in Stockholm to conduct Beethoven's

'Choral' Symphony. His return visit to the city aroused high expectations, but it did not go smoothly. In rehearsal a timpanist hit his instrument as a joke. Klemperer was angered and made an unflattering observation about the player's competence. Hardly had tension subsided than Klemperer slipped and, under the impression that some members of the orchestra had laughed, stamped off the platform. By the time he had been persuaded to return, the orchestra had decided that it would not play for him.[39] The quarrel was patched up, but seven years were to pass before Klemperer was again invited to conduct in Stockholm.

After a concert in Copenhagen, he travelled to Paris, where, as the first German conductor to appear at the Opéra since the war, he was to conduct four performances of *Lohengrin*. At the first rehearsal he objected to the fact that in the scene prior to the hero's arrival in Act One only the front rank of the women in the chorus sank to its knees while the remainder continued to stand. When the house producer, Pierre Chéreau,* refused to amend his staging, Klemperer delivered an ultimatum: Georges Hirsch, the director of the Opéra, must choose between Chéreau and himself. Hirsch tried to resolve the difficulty by advising Klemperer to produce a medical certificate that would enable him to withdraw and yet be paid. Klemperer's riposte was to send a doctor's statement that he was 'in perfect nervous equilibrium' and a notification that he would be suing the Opéra for $25,000.[40] Some Parisian newspapers supported his stand and *Time* (17 May) declared that he had fallen foul of a chorus 'well known for its ability to act like something left over from the Reign of Terror'. Johanna also considered that he was justified. 'I know exactly the passage he means', she wrote to Lotte. 'It is a marvellous effect when Lohengrin ... appears backstage and in front the women sink *as one* on to their knees.' But in an interview in *France Soir* (20 May) Hirsch maintained that Klemperer's withdrawal had nothing to do with difficulties between him and the chorus: 'Unfortunately in the course of the rehearsal I observed that Otto Klemperer was no longer "the giant" whom I had admired and that his physical condition would not allow him to conduct at the Opéra.'† The statement damaged Klemperer's reputation, but his financial situation made it impossible to proceed with his intention to sue. He was never again invited to conduct at the Opéra.

After ten days in Paris, during which he slept only fleetingly at night, telephoned friends in the small hours to discuss a book or to borrow money, walked around the town in a suit and sandals, disturbed performances at the

---

* No relation to Patrice Chéreau, the producer of Bayreuth's memorable centenary *Ring* of 1976.
† A well-informed article that subsequently appeared in the *Basler National-Zeitung* (3 June) maintained that Hirsch had told Klemperer, 'You cannot conduct, as the chorus refuses to sing under your direction.'

Opéra Comique and elsewhere, attended Mass at Notre-Dame in the morning and spent his evenings in Montmartre,[41] he arrived on 27 May at Baden-Baden, where he was to give a concert with the South-West German Radio Orchestra. In rehearsal it rapidly became evident that he was hopelessly at sea in Martinů's Cello Concerto. To avoid embarrassment, the soloist, Pierre Fournier, agreed to substitute a Haydn concerto.[42] The 21-year-old Hans Werner Henze, who was studying composition with Wolfgang Fortner in nearby Heidelberg and had hitch-hiked to Baden-Baden to hear a rehearsal under a conductor whose name for the young was already legendary, was amazed that Klemperer was interested only in rehearsing his own recently composed string quartet and Johann Strauss's waltz *Wiener Blut*.* After the concert on 1 June the *Badener Tageblatt* (6 June) complained that Klemperer's 'regrettable nonchalance' had caused it to fall below an acceptable level. Strobel, hitherto one of his most committed supporters, swore that he would never again engage him to conduct at the Südwestfunk, and never did so.

The next stage in this unhappy odyssey was Strasbourg, where on 8 June Klemperer conducted the opening concert of the city's first post-war Bach festival. Georges Enesco played for the first time since the war with his pupil, Yehudi Menuhin, in the Double Violin Concerto. But what should have been a happy reunion was marred by Klemperer's sarcastic tongue. Two weeks earlier Furtwängler had conducted in Berlin for the first time since he had been absolved by a denazification court of having lent his prestige to support the Nazi regime and had been greeted by an immense ovation. Ten days earlier, Menuhin had let it be known that, as a gesture of reconciliation, he would appear with him as a soloist.† Doubtless riled at a Jewish colleague's readiness to draw a veil over the past, Klemperer turned to Menuhin in rehearsal and rasped, 'I hear you play only with Nazis.'‡ If intended as a joke, the remark was not taken as such.

Klemperer was no less prone to cause difficulties with old friends. Believing that Artur Schnabel was making excessive use of the sustaining pedal in a rehearsal of Beethoven's Fourth Piano Concerto for a concert with the Hague Residentie Orchestra at Scheveningen on 18 June, Klemperer

---

* Interview with Hans Werner Henze, 17 May 1974. When, some six weeks earlier in Vienna, the Schneiderhan Quartet had attempted to give this (or maybe another) string quartet a private run-through for Klemperer's benefit, the project had been abandoned as some parts extended over considerably more bars than others (interview with Wolfgang Schneiderhan, 8 October 1984).

† *New York Times*, 15 May 1947. He did so at Salzburg, Lucerne and Berlin in the following August and September.

‡ Fearing that an encounter with Furtwängler himself might lead to some such incident, Johanna had written a few days earlier to Lotte to warn her to 'prepare Papa for that. He should be reasonable ... I find tolerance a good thing' (undated letter). When the two conductors were both in Salzburg later in the season, Klemperer studiously avoided any encounter (Lotte Klemperer, communication to the author, 1 August 1984).

8 Klemperer with Yehudi Menuhin and Georges Enesco rehearsing the Bach Double Violin Concerto at the Strasbourg Bach Festival, June 1947. Photo: Studio E. Klein, Strasbourg

stared persistently at his feet. Schnabel stopped and asked what was wrong. 'Are there no pedals?' Klemperer enquired with heavy sarcasm. Schnabel was so angry that the concert was at one point in danger of cancellation.[43] The visit to Holland was marred by a series of such incidents. As was now his habitual practice, Klemperer demanded to be paid in advance. He arrived late at rehearsals; on one occasion a search at his hotel found him lying comfortably in his bath. Whenever he needed cigars he simply seized them and told the shopkeeper to charge them to the orchestra's management. Angered by a slip in rehearsals he told the players that they were 'communists'. Only with difficulty were they dissuaded from walking out.[44]

At his second Scheveningen concert on 20 June Klemperer arrived on the platform to find that the wrong Brandenburg Concerto had been placed before him. In full view of the audience he hurled the score into the orchestra, where it struck a cellist. Such behaviour inevitably affected the playing. The performance of Bruckner's Symphony No. 4 with which he ended the concert seems to have been a rough-and-ready affair, though press reactions differed markedly. For Leo Hanekroot (*De Tijd*, 21 July) it was as though Klemperer 'were taking the orchestra through a sight-reading ... without tension, warmth or atmosphere ... This conductor's matter-of-fact approach has gone too far ... [He] is no longer to be included among the conductors of the highest class.' However, in spite of the trials they had endured, many of the orchestral players found themselves spellbound by Klemperer, though the management was less than wholly enchanted.

* * *

From Holland Klemperer travelled for the first time in fifteen years to London, where he had been engaged to give two concerts with the London Symphony Orchestra on 23 and 26 June at the Harringay Arena, a covered stadium that seated some ten thousand people and was better suited to the ice hockey, boxing and wrestling it generally housed. The music was interrupted by the noise of shunting goods trains, which in the slow movement of Beethoven's Violin Concerto proved so distracting that Klemperer momentarily stopped the performance.[45] The soloist, Ida Haendel, was surprised that he did not ask for a run-through with piano, or even a meeting, before the final rehearsal on the morning of the concert. It was indeed strange behaviour for a conductor who in London had acquired a reputation for painstaking preparation. Relations with the orchestra were at one point so bad that only Anna Mahler's intervention prevented a walk-out.* Yet Ida Haendel noted that 'the players seemed to understand his intentions by the mere raising of his eyebrows'.[46] The second Harringay concert included the 'Eroica' Symphony, and arias by Weber and Wagner sung by Joan Hammond. The critic Alfred Rosenzweig reported that though Klemperer's condition was 'very sad', there was still 'an enormous power in him'.[47] Yet his appearances attracted so little interest that of the largest daily press in the world only *The Times* (28 June 1947) seems to have reviewed either of the concerts.

Klemperer was due to make a third appearance at the Harringay Arena on 3 July, this time with the French Radio's Orchestre National, in a programme consisting of Beethoven's Eighth Symphony, *Petrushka* and Rachmaninov's Third Piano Concerto, with Moura Lympany as soloist. After holding initial rehearsals in Paris, Klemperer informed the concert director, S.A. Gorlinsky, that he did not intend to conduct the Rachmaninov work and proposed Mozart's D minor concerto as its replacement. According to Rosenzweig, Gorlinsky replied that 'Mozart ... is not a box office attraction here', whereupon an enraged Klemperer left London to conduct a concert in Vienna. On his return four days later a telephone call from his daughter in Vienna informed him that a cable had arrived from London cancelling his

---

* Anna Mahler (1904–88), Mahler's only surviving child, with whom Klemperer had been on friendly terms since the twenties. It was during this stay in London that she made her remarkable bust of what she described to the author as 'the mad Klemperer' (interview of 16 December 1985). The original stands in the Dorothy Chandler Pavilion in Los Angeles.

appearance with the Orchestre National. Malcolm Sargent, who conducted in his place, invited him to share the programme, but Klemperer declined to do so.

The concert in Vienna was the final event of an international festival of contemporary music that had been established in an attempt to resuscitate the Austrian capital's languishing reputation in this field. During the previous autumn Klemperer had himself proposed that he should give what would be the first public performance in Europe of Stravinsky's Symphony in Three Movements.[48] Shortly before leaving for Europe, he had been persuaded to include as well the Violin Concerto that Erich Wolfgang Korngold had written in the previous year for Heifetz. Both performances misfired. At the first rehearsal with the Vienna Symphony Orchestra it was discovered that Stravinsky's publishers in London had sent the wrong symphony.* Meanwhile, Klemperer had turned against Korngold's glib attempt to resuscitate the rhetoric of the romantic concerto and demanded that it be removed from the programme. That was a concession the festival's director, Egon Seefehlner, could not make; in an American-occupied city it would have been politically embarrassing to withdraw a work by a former Austrian who was both a Jew and an American citizen.

The critic Helmut Fiechtner dismissed Korngold's concerto as 'inconceivably empty and styleless'.[49] The *Wiener Tageszeitung* mischievously commented that a score that had been 'composed for the Caruso of the violin, had in Bronislaw Gimpel [the soloist] found its Jan Kiepura'.† On Klemperer's insistence, Tchaikovsky's 'Pathétique' Symphony was substituted for the Stravinsky. Whatever its merits, it did not provide a festival of contemporary music with a suitable close. It was also strange behaviour for a conductor who in the current number of the *Oesterreichische Musikzeitung* had proclaimed his belief that the music of living composers could stand comparison with that of earlier periods.

*   *   *

Communications and travel were still so difficult in Central Europe that concerts were frequently arranged at short notice. As Klemperer had returned to Vienna after the collapse of his last London engagement and had a few days to spare, he agreed to conduct a concert with the Vienna Symphony Orchestra at the Graz Festival on 10 July. The Australian-born pianist Kendall Taylor, who also took a part in the festival, recalled that Klemperer

---

* Klemperer himself may have played a part in the confusion. In an article he wrote on contemporary music for the *Oesterreichische Musikzeitung* (July–August 1947), he referred to Stravinsky's 'three-movement symphony in C major', conflating two separate works, an error that is reprinted without correction in Anderson (ed.), *Klemperer on Music*, p. 207.

† Jan Kiepura (1902–66). Polish tenor who in the latter part of his career had abandoned opera for the movies.

wore a pair of high rubber boots throughout his visit, and even kept them on for his concert. Among those who travelled there expressly to hear a conductor he knew only by reputation was Herbert von Karajan. On the morning after the concert Karajan offered Klemperer a lift back to Vienna. The encounter between the *Wunderkind* of the Third Reich and a pillar of the Weimar Republic did not prove rewarding: Klemperer seems to have slept for most of the journey.[50] Karajan, who was still banned by the Allied authorities from conducting in public,* formed an impression that 'He was angry. I didn't know why ... OK, I had been a Nazi. But we were all Nazis, Furtwängler, Böhm, me.'[51]

On the same day Klemperer set out for Salzburg, where he was due to start rehearsals for the première on 6 August of a new opera, *Dantons Tod*, by the 29-year-old Austrian composer Gottfried von Einem. The festival city was overflowing with Sudetendeutschen refugees. Accommodation was short, public transport rudimentary; though street lighting had been restored, some areas were still without gas. The festival, which before the *Anschluss* had been of unmatched splendour, was still struggling to re-establish itself. Many of the names on which its reputation had been built were dead, had not yet been denazified or had not returned to Austria: in 1947 Bruno Walter preferred to lend his prestige to Salzburg's new rival, the Edinburgh Festival. Thus the appearance of Klemperer to conduct the first performance of a new Austrian opera assumed special importance.

The initial approach had come from the opera's producer, Oskar Fritz Schuh, shortly after Klemperer's arrival in Vienna earlier in the year. The young composer was summoned to sing and play the work, which, according to Klemperer's own account, he did to such good effect that after only a few minutes Klemperer declared himself willing to conduct it. Aware that the project to perform a new opera at the Salzburg Festival was under attack from, among others, Karajan, he went to the length of stressing in print the 'great impression' the opera had made on him.[52] It was an unusual testimonial from a conductor who was usually reticent in his public advocacy of new works. But on his arrival in Salzburg three months later it was painfully apparent that Klemperer had done nothing to prepare himself for a task for which he now showed no appetite whatever. A festival that had yet to rid itself of the taint of the recent past could not afford to dismiss a famous conductor who was also a victim of National Socialist persecution and an American citizen. It was accordingly announced on 1 August (though the agreement had been reached two weeks earlier) that Klemperer was in need of a rest and would hand over to the Hungarian conductor Ferenc Fricsay, who

---

* In addition to his prominence in the musical life of the Third Reich, Karajan, though himself an Austrian citizen, had joined the German National Socialist Party in April 1933. The ban was lifted after denazification proceedings in the autumn of 1947. He had, however, started to record for Walter Legge a year earlier.

was then little known in the West. As a peace offering it was agreed that Klemperer would conduct a single performance of *Figaro* when he returned to give a concert later in the festival.

Klemperer now had free time on his hands. Having obtained local permission to enter Germany, he visited Hitler's Alpine retreat in the Obersalzberg, close to the Austrian border, and then drove to Munich, where he sought out Hans Pfitzner. Life had not treated his old master kindly. In spite of the fact that Hitler seems to have visited Pfitzner as early as 1923, presumably in the hope of securing an ideological ally, the Nazi regime had shown less interest in his music than Pfitzner had himself expected.*

Klemperer found the 78-year-old composer living in an old people's home in the suburbs of Munich. The room was tiny and Pfitzner sat on a stool, while Klemperer draped his huge frame on a narrow bed.† As a tribute to his old teacher, Klemperer brought a canon, one of whose themes was drawn from *Palestrina*, which he inscribed, 'To Hans Pfitzner in deep respect (*tiefer Verehrung*)'. The old man was delighted to see his former pupil and colleague, and conversation and reminiscences flowed for two hours.[53] As Klemperer later recalled, Pfitzner 'inveighed with undiminished acerbity against all things contemporary';[54] only on the question of Walter Abendroth's biography of the composer did any difference of opinion arise, though there might have been more serious discord had Klemperer been aware that, a year earlier, Pfitzner had informed Bruno Walter by letter that their close mutual friend Paul Nikolaus Cossmann, former editor of the right-wing and separatist *Süddeutsche Monatshefte*, had died 'naturally' in Theresienstadt concentration camp.[55]

Klemperer offered Pfitzner any necessary help with money (though how, in view of his own finances, he proposed to give it remains unclear). The only help he would welcome, Pfitzner replied, would be a production of his last opera, *Das Herz*, which had been rarely staged since Furtwängler had conducted its first performance in 1931. Klemperer regarded it as 'a very bad piece' and he never attempted to oblige, nor indeed subsequently to perform any music by Pfitzner.[56]

* Such success as Pfitzner enjoyed in the Third Reich was largely in German annexed and occupied areas rather than in Germany proper. In 1940 he returned in triumph to Strasbourg, where he had lived for a decade, to conduct a concert of his own music. A Pfitzner week took place there in 1943. In 1942 the Berlin State Opera took a production of *Palestrina* to the Paris Opéra. Pfitzner's friend and patron, Hans Frank, Governor-General of occupied Poland (a rump State that consisted of such parts as had not been annexed by Germany and the Soviet Union) arranged concerts in Cracow, where Pfitzner was on more than one occasion his guest. After Frank had been condemned to death by the International War Crimes Tribunal at Nuremberg, where he was hanged in October 1946, Pfitzner sent him a letter of commiseration (Prieberg, *Musik im NS-Staat*, pp. 215–25). Whatever his other failings, Pfitzner was wanting neither in loyalty nor courage.

† When, later that summer, Klemperer also visited the 83-year-old Richard Strauss, he found him, in contrast, in the best of spirits, 'sitting in the best hotel in Pontresina' (Heyworth (ed.), *Conversations*, p. 46).

When later in the year Pfitzner was brought before a denazification tribunal on the charge of having been a major offender, he asked Klemperer for a testimonial. Although Klemperer regarded the charge as ridiculous, the document he provided was non-committal. In a covering letter (23 December 1947) he explained that, as he had 'unfortunately not been in Germany at the time', he could say nothing about Pfitzner's activities in the Third Reich. Schoenberg, Alma Mahler and Bruno Walter proved more forthcoming, and, in spite of the fact that Pfitzner had accepted the Nazi title of Reichskultursenator, he was acquitted on 31 March 1948, in large part because he had not been a member of the party.

* * *

Tales of the scenes and scandals that had occurred at almost every city where Klemperer had appeared soon spread. The Concertgebouw Orchestra was particularly concerned about reports it had received of his visit to Scheveningen. After the previous summer's triumph at Interlaken, the orchestra had engaged him not only to conduct it there at the end of July, but also to take over four weeks of its coming season in Amsterdam. Klemperer's Dutch agent sought from Lotte assurances about her father that she found hard to give.[57] Eventually, at Lotte's suggestion, it was agreed that the Interlaken concert should be treated as a trial run. Only if it proved satisfactory would arrangements be finalised for the fifteen further concerts Klemperer was to conduct in the autumn. Johanna was horrified to learn of the threat to her husband's most substantial engagement in the coming months and even suggested in a letter to Lotte that it might be better for him to cancel his immediate commitments in order to undergo psychiatric treatment. 'For the first time I am without hope for Papa', she wrote on 10 July. 'Against everyone, I have never lost hope. But now?'

Although so much hung on the Interlaken concert, Klemperer's appearance on arrival there was anything but reassuring. In spite of the heat he was dressed in a heavy, ankle-length cloak whose hood he kept over his head. On the promenade, dressed in a dark jacket, shorts, socks and suspenders, he gave the impression of a man who had forgotten to put on his trousers. He caused a fire in his hotel room, again demanded to be paid before he started rehearsals and substituted the 'Eroica' Symphony for Schubert's Symphony No. 9. He showed little interest in rehearsing it. After running through the opening bars of each movement, he dismissed the orchestra. 'Gentlemen, you know this piece. I know this piece. Sometimes it rains. Sometimes it's sunny. Let us hope the sun shines this evening. Good-day.'[58] Such behaviour was not calculated to calm the fears of an apprehensive management.

Even at the height of a manic phase Klemperer was capable of delivering a great concert if he had at his disposal a fine orchestra and was himself at ease with the music. The switch he made in the principal work on the programme may have been prompted by such a consideration. Whereas he remained apprehensive of the Schubert symphony until the end of his life (though his 1960 recording of it is outstanding), the 'Eroica' was a work in which he rarely failed to impress. If that was his calculation, it proved well founded. In the unanimous recollection of surviving players forty years later, the concert on 28 July 1947 was as fine as that he had given with the Concertgebouw Orchestra in the previous summer.[59] In the *Basler National-Zeitung* (30 July), Otto Maag described the performance of the 'Eroica' as 'triumphant ... a packed-out hall was gripped to its innermost being by a sense of form and measure that is becoming increasingly rare in the world today'. Those were qualities singularly lacking in the conductor's daily life. At a dinner after the concert members of the orchestra were disconcerted to observe him knocking the ashes of his pipe on to the plate from which he was eating. But no more was heard of the cancellation of the concerts he was to conduct during the coming season in Amsterdam.

With three weeks to pass before he was due to return to Salzburg, Klemperer moved to the Hotel Waldhaus in Sils-Maria, where he had spent a number of summer vacations before the war, pausing only briefly in Zurich to borrow money. News of his eccentricities had, however, reached news editors eager for a good story during the silly season and he was pursued to Sils by a reporter from *Time*, who on 1 August filed an account of his investigations:

> I watched him return from a day's outing. He emerged in the hotel lobby in bright green corduroy shorts ... his naked thin white legs in striped silk socks and black shoes. Under one arm he carried a towel, a tennis racket, a folding draught board and the music of Roy Harris's new Symphony.* His black hair was combed only by the wind, one lock falling over an eye ... He looked like a possessed prophet with his haggard, convulsive face and dark, deep-set eyes.

The correspondent reported that Klemperer passed his days in walking, reading and composing.

> In the bar of the hotel he is a regular and very late guest, drinks benedictine with mineral water. The barman said, 'Yesterday I sent him to bed. He always stays so long and alone.' It may happen like last night, that towards midnight he puts his coat over his dinner jacket, takes his crumpled hat and walking stick and launches out into the ... night with his dark glasses on, driving to St Moritz to have a look at night life in the famous bar of the Palace Hotel ...
>
> His room, when I went in to see him, was in a state of complete disorder, drawers pulled out, clothes, books, papers, music sheets scattered over the floor, a half-finished meal on top of his laundry. He swept his unpressed trousers from

---

* Presumably Harris's Symphony No. 3 (1937), which Klemperer was to conduct at his coming Salzburg concert.

the chair to let me sit down, then let himself flop on to a red plush sofa, right on top of a heap of sheets of his last compositions.[60]

His behaviour was so bizarre that former associates assumed him to be insane. He played tennis by himself, hitting the ball over the net and then walking to the other side of the court to return it. He turned up uninvited at the rehearsals of a new piano quartet, consisting of Schnabel, Szigeti, Primrose and Fournier, which was preparing for its (hugely successful) début at the first Edinburgh Festival later in the month, and proceeded to tell Schnabel that his playing was too loud. No young woman was spared his attention. To protect his female pupils, Fournier described them as sisters and daughters of his colleagues. But that did not deter Klemperer. On an evening when the quartet was attending a concert given by the Romanian pianist Dinu Lipatti, he roamed the village, knocking on the doors of houses in which the girls were staying. At some point he was obliged to leave the Waldhaus and move to the Suvretta House in St Moritz. There he appeared at a formal dance at the Palace Hotel arrayed in *Lederhosen* and a Tyrolean hat as well as the customary socks and suspenders. Early one morning he burst unannounced, and similarly attired, into the bedroom of Irene Eisinger, a former member of the Kroll ensemble, who was staying at the same hotel.[61]

Yet, as *Time*'s correspondent observed, Klemperer still exuded an aura of 'fascinating personal greatness'. The reporter also noted that he was intellectually alert. Asked his opinion of von Einem's opera *Dantons Tod*, Klemperer criticised the libretto for not following Büchner's play more closely, and dismissed the music as lacking in tragic stature. 'The French Revolution', he observed, 'was not . . . agreeable . . . at least not for those who were beheaded.' As he was to conduct Mahler's Fourth Symphony in Salzburg, he wrote to the publishers in Vienna, requesting them to provide a score with the little-known instrumental amendments that the composer had made in the final year of his life.* It was not the action of a man wholly beyond reason.

Once in front of the Vienna Philharmonic Orchestra in Salzburg on 24 August, he again proceeded to demonstrate that his musicianship and authority were unimpaired. Though Harris's symphony did not fire the Austrian critics, there was unanimous praise for his interpretation of the Mahler symphony, which was widely described as the outstanding event of the festival.[62] Klemperer, who had not conducted the score since 1930, also

---

* Letter to Alfred Schlee, Sils-Maria, 31 July 1947. Klemperer may have learnt of these unpublished revisions, most of which were made in July 1910, when he attended rehearsals in Munich for the first performance of Mahler's Symphony No. 8. Although Mahler conducted the Fourth Symphony with these amendments in New York on 17 January 1911, they were not incorporated into the score published later in the year after his death. They were thus virtually unknown in 1947, when Universal Edition was not in a position to fulfil Klemperer's request (letter of 12 August 1947).

found himself stirred by it. Mahler's time would come, he wrote to a correspondent shortly afterwards, perhaps unconsciously paraphrasing the composer's own remark. It was not a widespread view of music that had yet to make its mark in either the Anglo-American world or Central Europe.

During the last week of the festival Paul Hindemith arrived to hold a course at the Mozarteum on 'Problems of Music Theory'. In his lectures the 52-year-old composer, who was on his first post-war visit to Europe, propounded the reassertion of tonality he had made in his *Unterweisung im Tonsatz*, which had been published in Germany before his emigration, but had as yet made little impact there or in Austria. To many in Central Europe it seemed to offer a basis for what *Melos* under Strobel's editorship proclaimed as 'a new firmly-grounded world-wide style'.[63] Only at a modest summer school, founded that year in Darmstadt, had the first intimations of dissent among the young and of a revival of interest in Schoenberg's twelve-note technique become evident. But in Salzburg Hindemith was the man of the hour and his lectures were attended by, among others, Ernest Ansermet, Herbert von Karajan and Eugen Jochum.

Klemperer was also in the audience and *Die Presse* (6 September) commented on his 'extremely practical and concrete observations on, for instance, the value of the twelve-note technique'. When, however, Hindemith at the end of a lecture called for questions, Klemperer raised his arm and called, 'Where is the lavatory?' His immediate intention was doubtless to fulfil a need and to raise a laugh. But beneath the jest may have lain a desire to mock the composer's latter-day dogmatism. Klemperer regarded with growing distaste the campaign that Hindemith had begun to wage with increasing virulence against modernism in all its guises. An admirer of Hindemith's earlier music, Klemperer later deplored the drastic revision to which, 'much to its disadvantage', the composer subjected his opera *Cardillac* in 1952. He found *Die Harmonie der Welt*, which Hindemith intended as his *magnum opus*, 'terribly dull' when he heard it shortly after its first performnace in Munich in 1957.[64] Of Hindemith's later works, only his last opera, *The Long Christmas Dinner*, aroused Klemperer's interest. He continued to perform a limited number of Hindemith's pre-war works, notably the suite from *Nobilissima Visione*. But, though relations remained overtly amicable, there was little further contact between him and the composer he had championed so assiduously at the Kroll.

When Hindemith's course ended on 29 August, Klemperer was still vainly awaiting a visa to enable him to travel to Budapest,[65] where he had been invited to conduct by Aladár Tóth, who was now director of the State Opera in the Hungarian capital. With time on his hands, he at first toyed with the idea of visiting his sister Marianne in Palestine. But funds were lacking and on 8 September he left Salzburg for Paris. On 22 September he wrote to tell a friend that he would be departing the following day for Hungary.[66] His passport indicates that he did indeed cross from Switzerland into Austria on 24 September, but it was not until 8 October that he emerged from the Arlberg Express at Budapest's east railway station. A new chapter in his odyssey had begun.

8

Behind the Curtain

Shortly after he had heard Klemperer conduct in Stockholm in March 1946, Aladár Tóth had returned with his wife Annie Fischer to Budapest where, owing in part to the influence of the composer Zoltán Kodály, Tóth had been appointed director of the State Opera with effect from 1 September 1946. Though never a Communist, Tóth had by his wartime emigration and early opposition to fascism established credentials that, at any rate in the immediate post-war years, strengthened his hand in dealing with a government that was to become increasingly Marxist. The theatre itself, a handsome, late nineteenth-century edifice, modelled on its grander counterpart in Vienna, had suffered only minor damage in the war. But many voices were worn and weary after years of hardship, there was a shortage of adequate instruments, the repertory was limited, the productions in the main fusty. A number of artists had left a country that already lay under the shadow of Communism.[1]

Aware that only drastic measures could restore the Opera House to its former level, Tóth made it a condition of his appointment that he should be empowered to engage a guest conductor of international repute,[2] and on 16 November 1946 he wrote to invite Fritz Busch, Bruno Walter and Klemperer to take part in a Mozart cycle later in the season. Nothing came of his approaches to Busch and Walter, while his letter to Klemperer, who was under Steinfeld's care, failed to reach its destination. But Tóth persisted. He sent a second and more pressing invitation and, as soon as Klemperer returned to Europe at the end of the winter, dispatched an emissary to Vienna, where a contract was signed on 30 March 1947. It was agreed that during the following autumn Klemperer would conduct two performances each of three Mozart operas, as well as two concerts. He would be paid in dollars. In a letter written two days later Tóth urged him to extend his visit to Budapest for 'as long as possible'. Though well aware of the problems that he would incur with the engagement of Klemperer, Tóth was convinced that he had found a conductor worthy to stand alongside Mahler and Nikisch, both of whom had worked earlier at the Budapest Opera.[3]

Hand-to-hand fighting between the German and Soviet armies in the winter of 1944–5 had devastated the city. The bridges that linked Buda and Pest on opposite sides of the Danube had been destroyed. The streets were grey and shabby. Food and fuel were scarce. Yet in spite of these hardships the country was enjoying a brief respite from foreign intervention. The German invaders had been expelled, but the question of whether Hungary would form part of a Soviet bloc had yet to be resolved. In free elections in November 1945 the anti-Communist Smallholders' party had polled no fewer than 57 per cent of the vote (only 17 per cent voted Communist) and, as a result, headed a coalition government. However, with Russian support, the Communists secured the crucial position of Minister of the Interior and, after the secretary-general of the Smallholders' party had 'confessed' to anti-Soviet activities, their leader, Ferenc Nagy, fled in the summer of 1947 to Switzerland, where he resigned. In elections in August 1947 the Smallholders' power was shattered and the Communist party and their left-wing socialist allies (fused ten months later into a single Hungarian Workers' party) polled 35 per cent of the vote. An extensive programme of collectivisation was forced through parliament, although the ground had not yet been fully prepared for a Communist takeover.[4] Thus, to outward appearances, Hungary was still a relatively free and independent country when the 62-year-old Klemperer arrived there in October 1947.

Since Tóth was away in Moscow, Klemperer was met at the station by Annie Fischer and Miklós Lukács, secretary-general of the Opera House, who were surprised to discover that their guest, who was sporting his high rubber boots, had no baggage apart from a dispatch case. Surprise turned to consternation when Klemperer announced that he would conduct Bruckner's Seventh Symphony at his opening concert four days later. Informed that that would not be possible, he turned on his heels as though to re-enter the carriage from which he had descended a few minutes earlier. He then thought better of it.[5]

His immediate task was to conduct *Don Giovanni* at the Opera House on 10 October, only two days away. Like all operas in Budapest, it was to be sung in Hungarian. Tóth had assembled a cast that included many of Budapest's leading singers, including Júlia Osváth (Donna Anna),* Mária Gyurkovics (Zerlina),† Endre Rösler (Don Ottavio), György Losonczy (Giovanni) and Mihály Székely (Commendatore).‡ At his first rehearsal Klemperer brushed aside introductions and abruptly indicated the opening tempo to his répétiteur, András Korodi, who then went through the first act while Klemperer busied himself with cleaning his pipe with a knitting-needle. Only at crucial moments did he pause to make a small gesture.[6] An attempt to communicate in his few words of Russian with those orchestral players who did not speak German did nothing to win sympathy. Tension rose further

---

* Júlia Osváth (1908–94), soprano who had sung under Toscanini at the Salzburg Festival before the war.
† Mária Gyurkovics (1913–73), distinguished coloratura soprano who never sang outside Eastern Europe.
‡ Mihály Székely (1901–62), bass who appeared regularly at Glyndebourne and the New York Met.

when he roughly criticised individual members of the cast before himself angrily storming out of the theatre, whereupon three singers declared themselves indisposed.[7] The substitute Donna Elvira, who had to be hauled out of the hairdresser's, insisted that she could not appear in a role she had not sung for several years without an additional rehearsal. As a result the performance had to be postponed for forty-eight hours. Further difficulties were created by Klemperer's insistence that he should himself accompany the recitatives, in the teeth of Tóth's attempts to dissuade him. Since he could in effect only use his left hand, his playing was limited, while his total ignorance of Hungarian was apt to result in an alarming lack of synchronisation with the voices. The ensuing confusion was frequently ended by the leader of the orchestra giving the cue for the next number.[8]

Yet such was the spell of Klemperer's musicianship that opposition soon evaporated. For the most part he conducted sitting. But, as Mária Gyurkovics subsequently recalled, 'When this huge man stood up and opened his arms, he made the whole stage leap with dramatic excitement in a way that I cannot put into words.'[9] György Losonczy was at first thrown by the 'dizzy' tempo that Klemperer set for 'Fin ch'han dal vino': 'When I heard the few bars of introduction, I felt that I would not be able to follow him. But he carried me along with the eyes of a demon, so that, forgetting everything, I was able to sing at this crazy speed.'[10] Both the *Don Giovanni* and the performance of *Così fan tutte* that followed on 15 October made an immense impression. There was, however, sharp criticism of Klemperer's accompaniment of the recitatives. 'By fulfilling that function', wrote István Szenthegyi in *Kis Ujság* (17 October), 'he deeply embarrassed both singers and audiences. The recitatives and the chords in the score never once coincided.'

Owing to the postponement of *Don Giovanni*, Klemperer's first appearance in Budapest was at a concert with the Municipal (previously Concert) Orchestra on the very morning of the day he eventually made his bow at the Opera House. It was a feat that might have overtaxed the energies of a younger and fitter man. But in spite of his frail appearance his appetite for work seemed to know no bounds; it was as though a spring long under restraint had been released. When Klemperer entered the Erkel Theatre for his first rehearsal for the concert, the orchestra rose to its feet. But he had no time for courtesies, shouted 'Beethoven Seven' and raised his arms. Caught unawares, the players joined in piecemeal, and Klemperer continued to conduct without interruption until the end of the work. 'It was only a rehearsal', recalled the leader, Vilmos Tátrai.* 'But I still remember it as the most successful and grandiose performance of my life.'[11] In the finale, Ede Banda, the leader of the cellos, wondered how Klemperer would be able to cap the power of his first crescendo. When the moment came, without beating

---

* Vilmos Tátrai (b. 1912), leader of the eponymous string quartet.

time, he slowly raised his arms until, as though of its own volition, the music rose to an immense climax.[12]

*   *   *

Within a few weeks Klemperer had conquered the city. At every appearance he was greeted with tumultuous ovations. Long queues formed at the Opera House twenty-four hours before he was due to conduct. Young people established syndicates, whose members took it in turns to stand for three-hour shifts, even during the icy winter of 1947–8, when the Danube froze. One of these was the composer György Ligeti, then a student of composition at the Academy, who later described the performances he heard Klemperer conduct in the late forties as among his greatest musical experiences.[13] Klemperer himself seemed to be everywhere. When not conducting, he would look in on his colleagues' rehearsals and performances. His conspicuous figure was seen in hotels and restaurants, often accompanied by a woman he had met in Salzburg during the festival and subsequently brought to Budapest, nominally as his secretary, though she was wholly lacking in abilities such as might have enabled her to fulfil that role. He would sit until the small hours in cafés, surrounded by intellectuals and artists and whoever cared to join in, discussing music, politics and whatever other topics arose. In night-clubs he would sit himself next to any woman who took his fancy or move to the piano and play excerpts from operettas and other light music.

Orchestral players were at first sceptical of a conductor who seemed so uninterested in rehearsal, rarely uttered a word and made no more than a few small gestures. Yet they soon changed their minds about him. Players testified to the ease with which he could launch the finale of Beethoven's Symphony No. 1 with a flick of his fingers.[14] Others related how, while attending a rehearsal of a colleague who was having difficulty with the opening bars of Strauss's *Don Juan*, Klemperer, without mounting the platform, gave an almost imperceptible movement of his hand that enabled the orchestra to achieve what was required.[15] Only in some twentieth-century scores did his technical limitations become apparent.

Singers were at first alarmed by Klemperer's appearance and ecentric behaviour. Yet they found him surprisingly easy to follow. Only two matters continued to cause difficulties – his insistence on himself accompanying the recitatives in Mozart, and his alarmingly fast tempi.*

---

* As the Hungaroton recordings confirm (see Discography), these tempi sometimes bordered on the unsingable (*Fidelio*, Act Two finale, and *Die Meistersinger*, Act Two finale). Comparisons between the Budapest *Don Giovanni* and the EMI studio recording that Klemperer made in London in 1966 are revealing.

	Budapest	London
Overture	4'50"	6'50"
Sextet	6'50"	8'50"
Il mio tesoro	4'00"	5'05"

See also *Fidelio* timings on p. 201.

Because funds were scarce and materials in short supply, Tóth was unable to provide the new productions Klemperer would normally have demanded. Working conditions thus bore no resemblance to those he had enjoyed at the Kroll Oper in Berlin. Like all Central European opera houses of the period, Budapest's was run as a repertory theatre with a wide range of works that changed nightly. It was the system against which Klemperer had inveighed during his galley years in Hamburg and Cologne. But its limitations now troubled him far less than they had done. What he wanted above all else was an opportunity, such as had been denied him since 1933, to conduct regularly in the theatre. In a manic condition he had little interest in the careful preparation of which he was liable to make a fetish when depressed. In his first season in Budapest his rehearsals rarely amounted to much more than a run-through. The performance itself was everything, as is indeed evident in the live recordings which have survived from this period and which, for all their lack of polish and technical shortcomings, provide evidence of the dramatic excitement that Klemperer generated in the opera house at this stage of his career.

His behaviour could be disconcerting, however. He frequently conducted (and afterwards took his bow) with the trousers of his dress clothes stuffed into his boots. He refused to begin a performance until his 'secretary' had been permitted to take her seat wearing her fur coat, rather than leaving it in the cloakroom as was the practice.[16] Arriving late to conduct *Così fan tutte*, he took over the off-stage band and left his twenty-year-old assistant, Tamás Blum,* to conduct the opera for the first time in his career. When, in a performance of Bruckner's Seventh Symphony that was also being broadcast, the percussionist omitted the cymbal clash at the climax of the slow movement, Klemperer's yell of fury was audible on the radio as well as in the Great Hall of the Music Academy.†

*   *   *

In the autumn and early winter of 1947 Klemperer was only intermittently in Budapest. Indeed, within a fortnight of his arrival he had left for Belgium to conduct three concerts for the Brussels Philharmonic Society. It was only on 29 October, twenty-four hours before he was due to conduct a solitary performance of *Die Entführung aus dem Serail*, that he was back in Budapest, this time without visa as well as baggage, so that Tóth, who had come to meet him at the airport, was obliged to telephone the Minister of the

---

* Thomas (Tamás) Blum (b. 1927), répétiteur and conductor at the Budapest National Opera, 1945–53 and 1958–72. Since 1972 musical director of the Zurich Opera Studio.
† Vilmos Somogyi, *Világ*, 26 September 1948. The player was doubtless using the Haas version, in which the cymbal clash is omitted. As this version had only been published in 1944, Klemperer may not have been familiar with it.

Interior, László Rajk, to enable him to re-enter the country.[17] Owing to insufficient rehearsal the *Entführung* did not go smoothly.[18] On 8 November he gave a concert in Milan with the Scala orchestra that included the first performance in Italy of Stravinsky's Symphony in Three Movements. It was not warmly received. 'The best thing about the Stravinsky was the opposition', Klemperer observed sardonically.[19] Back in Budapest for a stay of less than a week, he gave hastily prepared performances of *Der Rosenkavalier* (13 November) and *Otello* (15 November). Both suffered from insecure ensemble, while his phrasing in *Otello* was considered Germanic. One critic found both evenings 'spiced with concentration, power and intelligence',[20] but Klemperer seems to have been less satisfied. On leaving the orchestra pit after *Otello*, he was heard to mutter, 'That will have to be worked on' ('Das muss man einstudieren').[21]

There was, however, no time for that. Two days later, and still in high boots, Klemperer arrived in Amsterdam to fulfil a month's engagement with the Concertgebouw Orchestra, whose management's doubts had been stilled by the success of his Interlaken concert in the previous summer. The manic phase, which had now gripped him for over two years, showed no sign of waning. He sat up half the night in cafés and bars, where he improvised from Viennese operettas until the early hours of the morning. He spent wildly and then demanded that his fees be paid in advance. Friends and acquaintances were obliged to escort him to brothels. Prostitutes were invited to attend rehearsals at the Concertgebouw. He appeared dressed in pyjamas in the foyer of his hotel and demanded that a woman, who should be blonde, be sent to his room. Inevitably, he was requested to leave the hotel; Calvinist Amsterdam was not yet the swinging city of the sixties. The secretary from the Concertgebouw, who packed his belongings, found boots in the bed, burns in the linen and the remnants of meals spread around the room. At another of the three hotels to which he moved in the course of four weeks he inisisted on being massaged in his room. When the hotel objected he tried to persuade the pianist Maria Curzio, who was in hospital, to agree to the massage being performed in her room. Arrangements were finally made for an unoccupied operating theatre to be made available for this purpose. There, to the surprise of the staff, he was later discovered, naked and sleeping soundly.[22]

In such a frame of mind he showed little interest in rehearsals, often bringing them to an early close. Inevitably, the concerts themselves were uneven. In Peter Diamand's words, 'Some were great; some were badly prepared and not good; some were badly prepared and yet had glorious moments.'* At Klemperer's own request the programmes included Berg's Violin Concerto, whose first Dutch performance at Klemperer's opening

---

* Peter Diamand (b. 1913), director of the Holland (1948–65) and Edinburgh (1966–78) Festivals.

concert on 19 November failed to evoke much enthusiasm in either the public or the critics. The Dutch première of Stravinsky's Symphony in Three Movements on 10 December was more warmly received. But the cuts Klemperer made in the coda to the finale of Mendelssohn's Scottish Symphony on 23 November, and his insistence at the concerts on himself playing the continuo in a Bach Brandenburg Concerto and a Handel Concerto Grosso, were widely attacked. So were the all-too-evident disagreements about tempi with his soloist, George van Renesse, in a performance of Mozart's Piano Concerto in D minor. 'Such fights', commented one critic, 'would be better confined to rehearsals.'[23] Klemperer had yet to establish the unchallengeable position he came to occupy in Holland in later years.

Critics differed in their reactions to performances of the classics that stood in sharp contrast to the romanticised interpretations they had grown used to during the half-century (1895–1945) in which Willem Mengelberg had reigned over the Concertgebouw Orchestra. Yet, as Bertus van Lier, the critic of *Het Parool*, observed after Klemperer's opening concert, if his 'Eroica' was not 'our' Beethoven, in his choice of tempi and firmness of pulse it was probably closer to 'Beethoven's Beethoven'.[24] In the course of the visit references in the press to the public enthusiasm he evoked grew more frequent, while Klemperer himself responded warmly to an orchestra as much at home in contemporary idioms as in the classical repertory. 'I will never forget my season in November and December 1947 . . . [with] one of the best . . . perhaps the best . . . orchestras in Europe', he wrote half-way through his month in Amsterdam.[25]

The Concertgebouw engagement completed, Klemperer planned for the second time that year to visit his younger sister, Marianne Joseph, in Palestine. At the last minute, however, a telegram advised him not to come on account of the tense internal situation in the country.* Klemperer decided to spend Christmas 1947 in St Moritz, where he set himself up in style at the Hotel Carlton. Within a few days he found himself unable to pay his bills. In the absence of Johanna, who was in Los Angeles, and Lotte, who was trying to make a life for herself in Paris, he cabled an urgent request for $100 to Maria Schacko in New York. By the New Year he had moved into a *pension* costing little more than a tenth of what he had been paying at the hotel. But the money he owed at the Carlton was still outstanding in 1951.[26]

*   *   *

* Marianne's concern was well founded. Following Britain's decision to hand back the mandate under which it governed Palestine, the United Nations on 29 November had approved a plan to partition the country. On 12 December a meeting of Arab rulers announced the setting up of an Arab Liberation Army, which at once launched assaults on the Jewish quarters of Jerusalem, where Helmut and Marianne Joseph lived.

9   Klemperer conducting the Concertgebouw Orchestra of Amsterdam, late 1940s.
     Photo: Maria Austria, Parlicam Pictures, Amsterdam

On 8 January 1948 Klemperer returned to Budapest, this time with the intention of remaining for several months. Tóth could thus bring to fulfilment his long-cherished plan to mount a cycle of the five principal operas of Mozart's maturity,* and to do so with a conductor he considered without equal in his generation as a Mozartian. It was the first (and last) occasion on which Klemperer conducted such a series, and to the end of his life he remained deeply grateful to Tóth for enabling him to do so. On 11 January much cheering greeted his reappearance, after an interval of almost two months, to conduct *Don Giovanni* with a virtually unchanged cast. At the second performance a week later the roles of Don Giovanni and Leporello were taken (in German) by Paul Schöffler and Erich Kunz, who had appeared in the two performances of the opera Klemperer had conducted in Vienna in April 1947; the rest of the cast sang in Hungarian. *Die Entführung* and *Figaro* were added on 17 and 24 January. The performances were not without blemishes. *Világ* (13 January) noted with surprise that Klemperer himself accompanied some bars of Don Giovanni's Serenade – on a piano. There was as usual disagreement about his tempi. While *Kis Ujság* (14 January) found some so fast as to be scarcely singable, the composer and teacher Endre

---

* *Idomeneo* and *La Clemenza di Tito* did not at that time rank as part of the canon.

Szervánzky went out of his way to praise them.²⁷ At a performance of *Così fan tutte* on 29 February Klemperer suffered a lapse of memory, so that the performance came to a momentary stop.²⁸ But such incidents did little to detract from the impact of the cycle as a whole.

His centre-piece was a revival of *Die Zauberflöte*, which (for the first time in Budapest) he rehearsed for several weeks. The opera preoccupied him as perhaps never before. 'Mozart's music is strange', he wrote to Fritz Fischer on 18 February, three days before the first night. 'One never seems to have finished with the interpretation. I think that is because [it] is so perfect. How can an interpretation convey [such] perfection?' 'He didn't say much in rehearsals', László Nagypál, who later sang Tamino, recalled,

> [But] we learnt things that it was thereafter impossible to conceive otherwise . . . He aimed for a sober, even puritanical, manner of performance. He could be nice and would compliment the orchestra and singers when he was satisfied. But he also knew how to make scenes! If he felt it to be necessary, he would be unimaginably rude to get what he wanted.²⁹

The public also felt the lash of Klemperer's tongue. He had wanted the dress rehearsal to be closed to the public, because he was unhappy about certain aspects of the production and he knew that there would be a good deal of stopping and starting. The Opera House board, on the other hand, wanted the rehearsal to be open, and invited friends and relatives of the artists, as well as some regular opera-goers, to it. In an attempt to meet Klemperer's objections, the first six rows of the stalls were left unoccupied. It was evident from the start that the compromise did not please him. The opening scene was marked by his 'almost inarticulate shouting'. He called for the designer, Gusztáv Oláh, then for the répétiteur, Tamás Blum, and he continued to interrupt the performance until the end of the first act when the lights were raised. At this point people who had been standing at the back hurried forward to occupy the empty seats. In a rage, Klemperer insisted on their withdrawal.³⁰ Several hostile accounts of the incident appeared in the Budapest press, one paper criticising him for 'discourteous and egotistical behaviour'.³¹

Tóth stood by Klemperer. There were, he ruefully admitted, all manner of scenes and difficulties. 'But even if there were explosions, there was never a breach, thanks to the irresistible charm of his personality, his deep seriousness and a native humour that he was also able to turn against himself.'³² To Klemperer, Tóth remained not only a loyal friend, but 'an administrator of artistic culture and understanding such as I have never experienced before or since'.³³

Always a light-hearted city, Budapest was entertained by the eccentricities

10   Klemperer in Budapest, *c.* 1948. Photo: Várkonyi Studio, Budapest

and extravagances that had shocked provincial Los Angeles. As the stories of Klemperer's rages, witticisms and escapades with women circulated and grew in the retelling, he rapidly became a celebrity even in non-musical circles. He himself warmed to the liveliness of the inhabitants and their unconcern with convention. He enjoyed the city's intellectual vitality and its still plentiful food.

Even before his Mozart cycle was complete, Klemperer had turned his attention to Wagner. On 5 February 1948 he conducted a revival of *Lohengrin*, a work he had not performed since 1925. The Hungarian tenor József Simándy, who sang the title-role, found the rehearsals disappointing; for much of the time Klemperer appeared to be dozing. Only when mistakes occurred would he suddenly come to life and shout in a German that even those members of the cast who spoke the language found difficult to understand. But at the first performance he was transformed and, in the words of one witness, 'his glowing eyes cast a spell over the orchestra. He bewitched us. We forgot the oddities and eccentricities and the jokes. A great conductor stood before us, a genius who radiated music ... It was impossible to do other than what he wanted.'[34] *Tannhäuser*, which Klemperer revived on 4 April without the cuts habitually made in Budapest, made an equally deep impression. At his first piano rehearsal he played the entire work to the assembled cast from memory, though he had not conducted it for fifteen years.[35]

In addition to his opera appearances Klemperer also regularly conducted concerts with the city's three principal orchestras. Nothing created a greater impression than the performance he gave of Beethoven's Ninth Symphony at the Music Academy on 11 March 1948. Though free, as he had not been in Los Angeles, to conduct more or less whatever he chose without bowing to box-office pressures, Klemperer's Budapest programmes contained relatively little new or recent music. He was now in his early sixties. When manic, he had in any case little appetite for learning new scores, and, as Steinfeld had foreseen, he may also have been experiencing difficulty in absorbing new or unfamiliar works.

Richard Strauss's *Metamorphosen*, which he conducted for the first time on 12 March 1948, was in a long-familiar idiom and posed no special rhythmic challenges. But Stravinsky and Bartók were another matter. In *Jeu de Cartes*, which he substituted for Stravinsky's recently composed Concerto in D, he left an impression of no longer being fully conversant with a score he had conducted eleven years earlier. In *Szabad Nép* (16 April) Endre Szervánszky described the performance as rhythmically insecure and lacking in colour. The non-committal reviews of Bartók's Second Violin Concerto, which Klemperer conducted with Endre Zathureczky as soloist, and the subsequent comments of the leader, Vilmos Tátrai,[36] suggest that the performance was not wholly convincing. Henceforth Klemperer increasingly withdrew into a repertory that extended from Bach to Mahler. On the rare occasions he ventured outside it, he no longer enjoyed the successes he had achieved before 1933.

*   *   *

BEHIND THE CURTAIN

11   Klemperer with Aladár Tóth and Annie Fischer, Budapest, *c*. 1948/9

On 8 February 1948, four months after Klemperer's arrival in Budapest, Tóth wrote to inform the Minister of Religious Affairs and Culture that Klemperer would be willing to sign a long-term guest contract and to emphasise the gain to the National Opera, were he to make it the centre of his activities. In the 1948–9 season he would be ready to conduct forty performances at a fee of 3,000 forints each. That, Tóth stressed, was not as much as he received in Amsterdam, even if far above levels current in Budapest. László Bóka, the Ministry's senior official, noted on the letter, 'Yes. Prepare documents for the Minister, urgently', and on 30 March Klemperer signed a contract on the terms Tóth had specified. Fourteen days earlier he had also bound himself to conduct a number of concerts. For these he would be paid 2,500 forints a concert, with an additional 1,500 forints for a public dress rehearsal or a repeat concert. By international standards the fees were by no means exorbitant. But measured against the low salaries prevalent in Hungary and the weakness of the forint they were embarrassingly high.*

---

* As leader of the Concert Orchestra, Vilmos Tátrai earned 1,600 forints a month (information provided by Attila Boros). A répétiteur at the Opera House was paid about 900 forints a month. George Cushing, later professor of Hungarian literature at London University,

Now that he had committed himself to Budapest, it became necessary for Klemperer to find more permanent accommodation, and at the end of March 1948 he moved from the hotels he had hitherto occupied into a small flat in Csengary utca, only a few blocks from the Opera House and, as it happened, less than a stone's throw from the ever more powerful ÁVO secret police headquarters. 'There are three unfurnished rooms', he informed Fritz Fischer on 28 March, 'and I have bought some furniture – a couch, two cupboards, two chairs and a table – relatively cheaply.' The apartment itself looked down on a dark and dingy courtyard, across which reverberated the noise from surrounding flats. It was not luxurious accommodation, but in post-war Budapest living space was at a premium. There he was visited by a reporter.

> Main staircase, second floor. A sombre entrance and we are in a room that is at once Klemperer's dining-room, study and bedroom. An agreeably warm room with a brown, earthenware stove, a bed in a state of disorder, a small table on which are lying a teapot, cups, jam, sugar, butter and rum. Against the wall is a kitchen dresser, covered in books and manuscripts. Near the door a pair of miraculously well-cleaned boots ... on the ground a raincoat rolled into a ball, a scarlet tie, a waistcoat. A suit hangs on a peg on the side of the dresser. On a table in front of the stove a radio sits buried behind books. The walls are bare except above the bed, where an opera poster is pinned, while above a piano close to the window is fixed a picture postcard of Mozart. Everywhere books, papers, manuscript scores. And still more books. I fish some out haphazardly: the Bible, Riemann's *Musiklexicon*, Madách's *The Tragedy of Man*.*
>
> A distant memory of students' lodgings revives, of the eternal nostalgia for youth and freedom ... and of discussions into the dawn.
>
> In those quarters of indescribable disorder lives a sixty-year-old student ... Yes, Klemperer is now one of the inhabitants of Budapest.[37]

News of Klemperer's earnings travelled fast. Within five days of Tóth's letter to the Ministry, Endre Gaál attacked their scale in *Magyar Nemzet* (13 February), a daily newspaper that retained a degree of independence of the ruling left-wing coalition, and went on to describe him as a 'neurotic and a sick man', unfitted to meet the Opera House's need for a music director. There is no evidence that Tóth ever intended to appoint Klemperer to the position of music director, to which in his manic condition he would in any case have been ill-suited, but Gaál's article was a warning shot. In the coming weeks a debate about the preferential treatment accorded to Klemperer raged with increasing acrimony in the press. There was resentment of his high fees and discontent over the disadvantageous effect his presence was said to be

---

recalled that as a student in Budapest during this period he survived on a monthly grant of 200 forints.

* Imre Madách, highly esteemed if today rarely read Hungarian playwright and poet (1829–64), much translated into German.

having on the careers of the Hungarian conductors on the theatre's staff. That meant first and foremost on the career of the Opera House's First Conductor, János Ferencsik.* Tóth, however, did not look with favour on Ferencsik's claim to advancement.

On 10 April Tóth defended his policy of binding Klemperer more closely to the Opera House in an interview with the weekly *Szivárvány*. He argued that, whatever the tensions and problems arising out of Klemperer's presence, only a conductor of his calibre could restore to the Budapest State Opera its former international reputation. Both Mahler and Nikisch had left the house after a comparatively short period. 'I should not like that to repeat itself', Tóth added warningly. 'We should now atone for all that was done against Mahler. After all, Klemperer is his greatest heir.'

At this point the Ministry of Culture also made an ill-judged intervention in support of Klemperer's engagement. On 14 April *Magyar Nemzet* reported that a letter from Bóka had been posted on the Opera House's notice board. In it he cited a performance he had attended of the recent revival of *Tannhäuser* as an example of the contribution Klemperer was making to the theatre. Such direct official interference seems to have irritated the Opera's works committee, which met shortly afterwards and urged Tóth not to appoint Klemperer on a permanent basis.[38]

The pro-government press thereupon entered the fray. On 20 April the social democrat *Népszava* accused *Magyar Nemzet* of exploiting differences within the Opera House in order to make political mischief. On the following day *Szabad Nép*, the official organ of the Communist party, attacked the bourgeois press for having named Ferencsik as the leader of the malcontents, so as to set him up against Klemperer. *Magyar Nemzet* did not take the attack lying down. On 25 April Gaál welcomed the stand of the works committee on what, he insisted, had become a matter of public concern and went on to comment on the deficiencies that had revealed themselves in some of Klemperer's recent appearances in the Opera House and elsewhere, notably in the performance of Stravinsky's *Jeu de Cartes*. Why, Gaál asked snidely, had Klemperer failed to secure such a long-term contract elsewhere?

On 5 May, in an attempt to correct the widespread impression that there was personal rivalry between Klemperer and Ferencsik, *Szabad Nép* published a two-part interview in which both Tóth and Ferencsik discussed the points at issue. Tóth rebutted the allegation that Klemperer's engagement was to the disadvantage of Hungarian conductors at the Opera House and listed the works that Ferencsik had conducted during the season, notably *Peter Grimes*, 'the most successful première of the year'. Ferencsik himself insisted that he was on the best possible terms with Klemperer, whose work

---

* János Ferencsik (1907–84). From 1927 until his death répétiteur and conductor at the Hungarian State Opera. From 1953–7 musical director.

he greatly admired. The dispute was finally resolved when, at the end of the season, Ferencsik signed a contract to conduct exactly the same number of performances at the Vienna State Opera as Klemperer had agreed to conduct for Tóth.[39] Though he at no time held any permanent post in Budapest, Klemperer's position was henceforth unchallengeable and unchallenged.

*   *   *

Communication between Klemperer and Johanna had more or less ceased since he had left Los Angeles more than a year earlier in March 1947. Such letters as he had written were brief and uninformative and she was too bitter to answer them. Even after he had sent money at Christmas that enabled her to make payments towards the more pressing debts he had left behind, her reply made no reference to the possibility of any future reunion.[40] Steinfeld had repeated his advice that, come what might, Klemperer would be best left to his own devices. Johanna accordingly set about trying to rebuild her life as best she could in her straitened circumstances.

Financial worries engulfed her. Bills that her husband had earlier incurred in America continued to descend. The loan she had raised to enable him and Lotte to travel to Europe was still outstanding, and so were Steinfeld's and Ziskind's fees for psychiatric treatment. Monthly payments towards rates and her life insurance premium had to be met. There were also unforeseeable expenses; the disposal of a branch from a tree in the garden would, she wrote despairingly to Lotte (8 November 1947), cost $10–15. 'I wake up and anxiety ... overwhelms me.' She sold Klemperer's piano and, though now nearing sixty, started to look for a job. Unable to find one, she decided to move into even more modest accommodation, but in the post-war housing boom failed to find anything within her meagre means. Instead, she raised another loan to pay for alterations that would enable her to let half her small house. As the loan proved insufficient, her daughter, Carla,* sold the fur coat her mother had given her in more prosperous days. It was not until 12 February 1948 that Johanna was able to tell Lotte that, after adding a kitchenette, she had been able to rent out two rooms for $75 a week. Even if she was herself without a bath, she could now meet her immediate needs. Money was not the only problem; she was obliged to inform the Collector of Internal Revenue that 'due to circumstances beyond my control it has been utterly impossible for me to obtain the necessary information to prepare the return'.[41] It had not crossed Klemperer's mind to furnish an account of his now substantial earnings, on which as an American citizen he was obliged to pay American tax.

---

* Carla Metzner, née Geissler (1906–63) was born before Johanna met Otto Klemperer. Until her marriage in the early 1930s she lived with the family and in 1936 she and her first husband joined them in LA.

As he started to put down roots in Budapest, Klemperer occasionally threw out a casual hint that Johanna should join him there. The prospect did not appeal. On 12 February 1948 she wrote to Lotte, who was still in Paris, 'There is nothing in his letters that would encourage me to start life with him again. I'm too old and too *weak* to be able to pick up that hectic way of living again.' She also had reservations about making her home in a country under Russian domination at a time when relations between the United States and the Soviet Union were rapidly worsening. With her practical sense she did not share her husband's and young daughter's dislike of America or their sunny view of prospects in Soviet-controlled Hungary. 'You know how I feel', she continued in her letter to Lotte.

> There is filth everywhere... But in *this* country there are more *possibilities* than elsewhere for things to develop in the 'right' way... It's also not quite right for the writer you quote (isn't his name Ehrenburg?)* to say that people here *worship* machines... The truth is that the Russian housewife would be glad of much of the equipment we have... I, for example, because I have to make do with so little, am aware of the affluence and luxury that even people of *modest* means enjoy here. I go every eight days to a shop where there are thirty Bendix washing machines. For 25 cents (*soap is free*) I can put in the washing, go round the corner and do the shopping and in half an hour it comes out wrung *out* and absolutely clean... I hang it in a lovely gentle *sun* (Joy No. 1) in our own *garden* (Joy No. 2) after I have driven back in my *car* (Joy No. 3). Tiger and Micky [the cats] play in front of me on the grass (Joy No. 4). All this and a *nice* house (Joy No. 5) I can afford here on a *very* small income.
>
> You rightly ask, where are the intellectual pleasures? Those lie within oneself and are independent of *where* one lives, my little one. People, in case one is dependent on them (which thank God I'm not), are the same everywhere... I'm not interested in concerts, as neither Toscanini nor Klemperer is to be heard here. What I do miss, my dear one, is you.

Once Klemperer had obtained a flat and even acquired a few sticks of furniture, his requests that Johanna should join him became more insistent. She at first thought in terms of a visit only. Eventually, however, she succumbed to the urgings of both Lotte and Aladár Tóth that a home, such as Klemperer was quite unable to provide for himself, might bring a degree of stability into his life. But she remained full of misgivings. 'I never thought it would come to this', she wrote to Lotte on 29 March, 'and I am still not quite sure whether I am doing the right thing.' It became clear that, owing to his wild extravagances, Klemperer was not in a position to pay for her travelling expenses or to settle his more pressing debts in America. He was accordingly

---

* Il'ya Ehrenburg (1891–1967), Soviet writer and publicist, who did not originally support the October Revolution, but in the thirties adapted himself to Stalinism. After Stalin's death, however, he was in the vanguard of the short-lived political relaxation of Khrushchev's early years, which he heralded in his novel *The Thaw* (1954).

obliged to turn again to Harvey Mudd, who lent $2,000. In gratitude for this help, Johanna gave Mudd one of the family's few surviving treasures, a letter in Mendelssohn's hand. On 13 May she cabled Lotte to tell her that she would fly to Paris in early June, so that they could travel together to Budapest.

On 3 June 1948 Klemperer, clutching a huge bunch of roses, was at the airport to greet them. Moved by his haggard face and shabby appearance, Johanna could only say, '*Alter*, I shall have a job feeding you up.'[42] But the happiness of reunion was short-lived. The flat in Csengary utca proved so dirty and inadequately furnished that the family was obliged to move temporarily to a hotel. Four days after her arrival, Johanna scribbled a postscript to a letter Klemperer had dictated to Fritz Fischer. 'He is more or less unchanged, unfortunately. *No one* can help him – well-meant advice only enrages him. Lotte and I are in despair.'

*   *   *

Klemperer had been composing furiously throughout the first winter in Budapest. Among other items later destroyed in the cold light of depression were a waltz intended as an interlude in *Die Fledermaus* but never used, a string quartet and a coloratura waltz that formed part of a programme of his compositions given at the Radio on 15 April. On this occasion Klemperer spoke a few words of introduction to his music, which, he insisted, was written in the spirit of Haydn and Mozart. He also accompanied some songs. The concert failed to impress. In spite of his cordial relationship with Klemperer, Sándor Jemnitz, a composition pupil of both Reger and Schoenberg and one of Budapest's most respected critics, did not mince his words. 'The music', he wrote in *Világosság* (18 April), amounted to 'childish caricatures'. Such works, he continued, might have been performed before a few close friends, but not before an audience of several hundred people. Why had the excellent musicians taking part not had the courage to prevent Klemperer from making a public exhibition of himself? 'It is impermissible to make a great if naïve master ridiculous just for the sake of a small sensation.'

But, when riding high, Klemperer was impervious to criticism. He was in any case engaged in a more extensive venture, a setting of Heine's poem *Die schlesischen Weber*, written in 1844 after a number of Silesian weavers had been killed in the course of riots against their conditions of employment. The work, which Klemperer entitled *Die Weber*, was written for unison chorus accompanied by simple instrumental ostinati in a manner reminiscent of pre-war political *Kampfmusik*. The score has not survived. At some point in May 1948 Klemperer turned up at the Budapest Radio in order to record a short extract from the cantata, which he intended to offer to Johanna on her approaching sixtieth birthday. In the studio he took from his pocket a crumpled manuscript and, to his own accompaniment, began to bellow an extract 'like a wounded lion in its last hour'. For the second side of the shellac recording he croaked his own setting of Heine's 'Ich weiss nicht, was soll es bedeuten' in a curiously moving voice. At this point, he had doubts as to the suitability of the present and also, no doubt, about the artistic result. He turned to Tibor Polgár, head of the Radio's music department, who had been supervising the recording. Klemperer suggested that perhaps his wife might prefer money. Though unaware of Johanna's straitened finances, Polgár ventured to suggest that cash might indeed be more welcome, whereupon Klemperer abandoned the project, leaving the record behind him.* *Die Weber*, however, was not abandoned. On 13 August Klemperer conducted its first performance in Budapest, where, at a time of year when the city was empty, it received scant attention. Less than three months later he gave two further performances in far more exposed conditions in East Berlin, where it served to underline his increasingly radical political sympathies.

* Polgár, who later went to Canada, recounted the incident in *Magyarság* (Toronto, 3 January 1987). The recording is still in the possession of Hungarian Radio.

9

Caught in the crossfire

At the beginning of March 1948, Klemperer left Budapest for four days to give a concert in London with the Philharmonia Orchestra, which had been founded three years earlier by the record producer Walter Legge. The concert, given on 5 March at the Royal Albert Hall, was promoted, not by Legge, but by the British conductor Richard Austin, who as a student had heard Klemperer conduct in Germany before the war. In an attempt to provide London with better-rehearsed and more adventurous programmes than it enjoyed in the immediate post-war years, Austin had set up the New Era Concert Society. In November 1947 he had travelled to Amsterdam to engage Klemperer to give the opening concert. Thus Klemperer first came to conduct the orchestra with which his name was later to be so closely associated. At that time, however, the Philharmonia was still in its early days and he was not impressed by it at rehearsal.

The first half of the concert, which consisted of Bach's Suite No. 3 and Stravinsky's Symphony in Three Movements, does not seem to have gone well. Among the small audience was William Glock, one of the few London critics of the day thoroughly conversant with Stravinsky's recent music. He was also familiar with the composer's own recording of the symphony. In *Time and Tide* (13 March) Glock described Klemperer's performance of it as 'an agony'.

> It was not even adequate in the ordinary matter of time-keeping, let alone in balance of tone, in intensity, in understanding of any kind. I don't think that Otto Klemperer was much to blame. A dozen rehearsals would be necessary to play ... properly [this] masterpiece of musical logic, orchestral writing and harmonic invention.

The Times (6 March), however, found the performance 'brilliant' and Tom Carter, the leader of the orchestra, subsequently claimed that the Philharmonia had enjoyed working under a conductor who 'so clearly understood the complexities of the score'.[1] Klemperer himself seemed content with what he had achieved. The work itself, he wrote on 8 March to Fritz Fischer, '*gains* on repeated conducting'. But Glock was not alone in his low opinion of the performance. Walter Legge, who attended the concert in the company of

William Walton, later described its first half as 'an unhappy occasion. My orchestra seemed unable to understand Klemperer's beat, the Stravinsky was new to them. Walton and I left at the interval.'[2] Legge thus failed to hear Klemperer conduct the 'Eroica' Symphony in the concert's second half. It was that performance which attracted attention elsewhere. In spite of Legge's lack of interest, EMI decided later in the year to open negotiations for Klemperer to make a single recording on its modest Parlophone label.[3] Even the BBC began to consider an engagement.

Up until this point the Corporation had shown remarkably little interest in Klemperer as a conductor. As early as 26 February 1930 Kenneth Wright, a member of the BBC's music department, had advised his superiors that Klemperer, 'who does a lot of rehearsing' and was reputed to be difficult, would not be suited to conducting the newly founded BBC Symphony Orchestra. Six years later it was the same story. On 13 April 1936 Julian Herbage, then a programme planner in the music department, reported that the music panel 'felt it to be doubtful whether [Klemperer] would materially add to the scope of next season's programme scheme'. A single studio concert was eventually proposed for the following November. But Klemperer either could not or would not accept an offer that could hardly be regarded as other than a put-down.

In January 1946 Klemperer's London agent, Ibbs and Tillett, wrote to the BBC, asking if it would give him a concert. When the letter was read to the artists' committee of the music department, one of its members recalled that on his last pre-war appearance in London Klemperer 'had been in a state of nervous tension bordering on eccentricity and there was trouble with the orchestra'. The committee concluded that it 'could see little opportunity of offering him an engagement'.[4] There the matter rested until in the summer of 1946 Klemperer met Sir Adrian Boult at Scheveningen and expressed his interest in conducting the BBC Symphony Orchestra. Boult, who was the orchestra's chief conductor, lost no time in informing the music department.[5] But the project was again nipped in the bud. In an undated memo, Kenneth Wright, who by now was acting Director of Music, informed Boult that 'preliminary enquiries do not suggest that we are anxious to put ourselves out to include Klemperer, or even to include him at all, but in preparing our next quarterly schedule let us take into account that he will be available if we want him'.

After the 'Eroica' with the Philharmonia Orchestra the BBC's attitude towards Klemperer underwent a dramatic change. Wright admitted that there could be no question of 'the brilliance of his conducting' and another official, Eric Warr, described Klemperer's account of the symphony as 'wonderful'. Boult dictated a memorandum: 'I would say that he *should* be engaged ... but ... I think I, or somebody, should make a firm date for all rehearsals and performances and simply step in if anything goes wrong with him.' He added in pen: 'He has been conducting magnificently in Holland recently, I hear.'[6] Wright undertook to make further enquiries and on 24 March reported his findings:

> The matter is naturally rather delicate ... there is no doubt that even [in Holland] ... the actual concerts were very fine. He did not change his rehearsals, but walked out of them early when he felt there was no more need to work. The chief difficulty was his constant demand for advanced payment against his fee, and he invariably exhausted these advances by lavish spending before the concert date and then declared he could not proceed with the concert because he had no money ... In spite of eccentricities, the Concertgebouw has engaged him for the complete Beethoven cycle next season. Mrs Beek [the wife of Klemperer's Dutch agent] feels it essential that someone should look after him constantly while he is here.

Eventually the Corporation decided to give Klemperer a single studio concert in the following December. In the event he was unable to get to London because of fog and a further year was to pass before the proposed studio concert could take place.

Klemperer's meagre reputation in Britain at this period is evident from the press reactions to his solitary Philharmonia concert, which occurred at a period when both Erich Kleiber and Wilhelm Furtwängler were making their first triumphant post-war visits to London. In February 1948 Kleiber had made such a deep impression in three concerts with the London Philharmonic Orchestra that he had at once been invited to return for a more extensive period in the following season and was later engaged at Covent Garden. On 29 February, at the first of no fewer than ten concerts with the LPO in London and the provinces, Furtwängler had also been accorded an enthusiastic reception. In an article in which he compared the return of the three great musicians from Central Europe (and criticised the lamentable condition of conducting in Britain), Desmond Shawe-Taylor found Kleiber 'the most masterly'. In no more than a brief comment he commended Klemperer's performances of the classics as 'clear, authoritative and restrained'.[7] The *Music Review* dealt at length with the Kleiber and Furtwängler concerts, but failed to refer to Klemperer. The *Daily Telegraph*, traditionally assiduous in its coverage of musical events, also ignored his concert.

Though not generally prone to jealousy, Klemperer could not but be aware of the disparity between the receptions accorded to himself on the one hand and Kleiber and Furtwängler on the other. Kleiber he had never liked, but as a young man he had been on friendly terms with Furtwängler. However, he had been angered by what he regarded as Furtwängler's conciliatory attitude to the rulers of Nazi Germany and also by the triumphant ovations he had received on resuming his career in 1947. At a time when

Klemperer's own career lay under a shadow, his great rival had regained his position as Germany's leading conductor, as though the Third Reich and his role in it had been forgotten.

Klemperer was under no illusions as to his colleague's stature. Prior to Furtwängler's reappearance in Paris on 24 January 1948, he wrote to urge Lotte, who was living there and had never heard him conduct, not to miss the concert.[8] But in an answer to a letter in which she described her impressions, he made his own attitude plain.

> I know him very well (*sehr genau*), as a conductor as well as a man. That he conducts better than Walter is no compliment. I don't deny that he achieves what he sets out to do. But what he wants is so hateful to me that I cannot speak of it in parliamentary language.[9]

There is no doubt that Furtwängler would have welcomed an approach from Klemperer, particularly as they were staying in the same London hotel.* But Klemperer was determined to avoid any such encounter, and on later occasions he would send his wife or daughter to reconnoitre in order to ensure that no chance meetings should occur in hotel lobbies or elsewhere.[10] From the time of this visit to London a new asperity creeps into Klemperer's references to colleagues who had remained in Germany. In particular, he attributed his inability to obtain an engagement at the Salzburg Festival to the influence again wielded there by former National Socialists, such as the actor and theatre manager Gustav Gründgens and Herbert von Karajan.[11] 'Only fascists are being engaged this year', he wrote bitterly to Lonny Epstein from Budapest on 13 March. 'Musical direction is in the hands of Furtwängler and Karajan.' In fact, such influence as Furtwängler exercised at the Salzburg Festival did not exclude the participation in 1949 of Bruno Walter and George Szell, both Jewish emigrants. In 1948 Karajan was in no position to determine who would or would not be engaged. As Klemperer became increasingly aware of the extent to which his behaviour had made festival directors and others wary of engaging him, the more prone he became to attribute their caution to political and even racial motives.

Yet his attitude to colleagues with National Socialist affiliations varied. On more than one occasion he turned down Edwin Fischer as a soloist, perhaps because Fischer, though a Swiss citizen, had continued to live in Berlin until 1942 and to participate in official occasions.[12] He took a more lenient view of another pianist, Walter Gieseking, though he never appeared with him after the war. 'I consider [him] such a great pianist that I overlook his political views', he wrote at the same time as he refused to appear with Fischer.[13] Perhaps because he felt that younger artists who had only come into

---

* Opinion expressed by Furtwängler's widow in a letter (19 November 1986) to the author. In another letter (9 December 1986) Elisabeth Furtwängler said that her husband felt closer to Klemperer as a musician than he did to Walter.

12 Klemperer rehearsing for his first post-war concert with the Berlin Philharmonic Orchestra, 30 April 1948. Photo: Associated Press, London

prominence during the Third Reich had had little alternative but to curry favour with it, he was in general less censorious of their behaviour. Told – after the event – that the concert he had given in Vienna with Wolfgang Schneiderhan was Schneiderhan's first public appearance after denazification proceedings, he laughed.[14]

*   *   *

In May 1948 Klemperer conducted his first concerts in Berlin since 1933. His arrival coincided with rising tension between the Allied and Soviet occupiers, who, in accordance with the terms of the Yalta Conference, had governed the city since its fall. Alarmed at the determination of the Soviet Union to impose Communism on Eastern Europe and at the threat this seemed to pose in particular to Western Germany, the Allied powers on 23 February had called a security conference in London, to which the Soviet Union was not invited. As though to confirm the fears of the West, the Czechoslovak Communist party seized power in Prague virtually simultaneously. The President, Eduard Beneš, was forced to resign and on 9 March Jan Masaryk, the Foreign Minister, fell from a window in mysterious circumstances. Four days earlier, Lucius D. Clay, the military governor of the American zone of Germany, had warned Washington of what he regarded as 'a subtle change in Soviet attitudes'. His apprehension proved well founded. On 20 March the Soviet representative walked out of the Allied Control Council, thus effectively bringing four-power rule of Germany to an end. Ten days later the Soviet forces imposed restrictions on road and rail communications with the Western sectors of Berlin.[15] These restrictions probably account for the postponement of a visit Klemperer had originally planned for early April. His sudden arrival at the end of the month came as a surprise even to the agent who had arranged it.[16]

Klemperer's return to the city of his pre-war triumphs was regarded as an important event and the acting burgomaster put an official car at his disposal. He was appalled at the scale of the city's devastation. His old home in the Maassenstrasse was in ruins, as was the entire area surrounding it. No painter, he told a Hungarian interviewer, could have conceived a more terrible vision of the Last Judgement. But he was happy to be back in Berlin. He observed ironically in what was doubtless a reference to the re-emergence of Heinz Tietjen, who was shortly to be appointed Intendant of the Berlin Städtische Oper, that he found it surprising to be greeted with friendliness by men who had taken an active part in expelling him from German musical life fifteen years earlier.*

During the visit Klemperer conducted three concerts with the Berlin Philharmonic Orchestra, which took place at the Titania Palast, the cinema in suburban Steglitz where the orchestra performed until the new Philharmonie was opened in 1963. There were no difficulties at rehearsal, but when Klemperer appeared at eleven o'clock on 2 May for the first concert, one critic was struck by 'the almost mistrustful glance at the audience'.[17] Those who recalled him from earlier years were surprised by the restraint of his gestures. 'Nothing in his demeanour betrays a world-famous star', wrote Walther Harth. Other critics found that he had matured.

> He is less passionate, even if in Mozart's D major ['Prague'] Symphony the tempi remain as fast as they always were in his Mozart (*Don Giovanni*). But the relentlessness with which he formerly clung to dynamics and tempi is no longer so fierce and unyielding. His movements – he has in the meantime dispensed with a baton – are the exact opposite of Furtwängler's. All the drawn-out gestures that in Furtwängler's case help to create gradations of orchestral sound are absent. [Klemperer's] cues are so abrupt that they almost endanger precision. None the less, once we had got used to it, his Mahler [Symphony No. 4] held us enthralled.[18]

Klemperer got back to Budapest on 8 May with only an hour to spare before he was due to conduct *Die Zauberflöte* at the Opera House; the performance

---

* 'Berlini impressziók' ('Impressions of Berlin', *Népszava*, 24 October 1948). Klemperer's agent, Hans Adler, in an interview with the author, recalled that during his visit Klemperer dictated a diatribe (now seemingly lost) against Tietjen and Furtwängler.

was on the verge of being called off. The magazine *Képes Figyelö* (18 May) spoke of hiccups in the overture and the first act. A week later he embarked on a series of performances of *Die Fledermaus*. Two of them were given on an outdoor stage at the zoological gardens. When a nearby steam locomotive let out a prolonged whistle, Klemperer gesticulated in its direction. The noise ceased abruptly, as though at his command. He turned to the audience and remarked, 'Aren't I somebody?' ('Wer bin ich?').[19]

There was much praise for his unmannered approach to the piece, but rehearsals produced the usual upsets. Angered by Klemperer's far-reaching alterations to the production, Gusztáv Oláh withdrew his name.[20] Another fuss occurred when Klemperer, dissatisfied with the ballet in the second act, simply dispensed with it,[21] much to the fury of the prima ballerina, who dared to point out his ignorance of her art ('I beg pardon, Herr Direktor, but dancing you do not know').

As though his manifold activities were not sufficient to consume his manic energies, Klemperer next grasped an opportunity to involve himself in the spoken theatre. During a late-night discussion at his favourite haunt, the Café Arányi, he learnt from Tamás Major, the director of the National Theatre, of plans for a new production of Shakespeare's *Midsummer Night's Dream*. Major was to direct it himself. Klemperer urged him to use Mendelssohn's complete incidental music and offered to conduct it. Major had reservations about the feasibility of using a romantic score in a modern production; in any case he lacked the funds for such an ambitious undertaking. But Klemperer persisted and agreed to forgo a fee.

Temperamentally incapable of taking a back seat in any theatrical enterprise, in rehearsal he interfered in every aspect of the production, often, as Major conceded, to good effect. To general surprise he was found to be as familiar with the play as with the music.[22] Although the two together extended over four-and-a-half hours, the production was an immediate success, and between 11 June and 29 July 1948 Klemperer conducted no fewer than twenty-two performances, followed by eight more early in the following season. Few undertakings in his entire career gave him such delight as an opportunity to direct in the theatre a score that he referred to as 'dieser Glücksfall' – 'this stroke of luck' – in German music.* It provided a gratifying conclusion to his first season in Budapest.

* * *

Before the next season started Klemperer returned to Berlin, this time at the invitation of the Radio, to conduct the Berlin Philharmonic Orchestra in three

---

* Letter to Fritz Fischer, Budapest, 8 July 1948. Klemperer believed the quotation to stem from Nietzsche, but it has not proved possible to verify this. A subsequent projected collaboration with Tamás Major on Offenbach's *Orpheus in the Underworld* at the Magyar Theatre came to nothing.

performances of Mahler's Second Symphony on 18, 19 and 20 September. It was a work in which he had always excelled. The eminent critic Hans-Heinz Stuckenschmidt described the concert he attended as 'the greatest musical experience of recent years ... Klemperer ranks among the greatest conductors of the present day.'[23]

During his previous visit to Berlin Klemperer had gone out of his way to stress that he was not bound exclusively to Budapest; what he would most like, he had explained to an interviewer, would be to divide his time between the two cities.[24] Now the critics were loud in their insistence that he be invited to resume the crucial role he had played in its cultural life during the latter years of the Weimar Republic.

Between the concerts in May and September 1948 conditions in Berlin had, however, materially altered. On 18 June the Western Allies had introduced a separate currency in West Germany, thus finally breaking with any lingering pretence that occupied Germany was governed as a unitary State. On 24 June the Soviet Union responded with a total land blockade of West Berlin in the belief that, cut off from sources of food and fuel, it would fall into its lap. That expectation was eventually confounded by the Anglo-American airlift, but in September the prospects for West Berlin looked grim. The airlift as yet provided no more than 40 per cent of the barest necessities. Meanwhile the Soviet and East German authorities seized every opportunity to undermine the morale of the beleaguered population, and, when Klemperer arrived in mid-September, the fate of the city's Western sectors still hung in the balance.

Currency reform and blockade between them brought about far-reaching changes in Berlin's artistic life.* In the immediate post-war years culture had been a means of assuaging the manifold miseries of daily living; theatre and concert tickets were one of the few amenities that could be bought with a currency that otherwise had become almost valueless. The reform reversed the situation overnight, at any rate as far as the Western sectors were concerned. A population that had hitherto been deprived of most of the necessities of life was more concerned to acquire the goods that suddenly appeared on the open market than to spend their very limited resources in the new currency on cultural events. Theatres and concert halls that had been packed were suddenly ill attended.

The blockade also had the effect of dividing the city into two increasingly distinct cultural communities, particularly after the non-communist municipal representatives withdrew from the City Assembly in the Eastern sector and on 7 December elected Ernst Reuter as burgomaster of West Berlin.

---

* After the introduction of a new currency in East Berlin that also circulated in the Western sectors, the Western Allies likewise introduced the new West Deutsche Mark. Thus the city had in effect two currencies.

Free movement between the two parts of the city continued throughout the blockade, as indeed it did until the construction of the wall in 1961, but Westerners were disinclined to attend cultural events in the part of the city under Soviet control, while the strength of the new Deutsche Mark made it disproportionately costly for Easterners to visit the West. Western newspapers that had hitherto covered cultural events beyond the Brandenburg Gate now became less willing to do so. As food and fuel became short in the West, increasing tension inevitably gave rise to cultural reprisals. In October the American authorities (with the support of an overwhelming majority of its members) banned the Berlin Philharmonic Orchestra, which was domiciled in the West, from playing at the Soviet-controlled Radio in the East.[25]

In such circumstances artists increasingly found themselves obliged to choose between the two parts of a divided city. In Klemperer's case the cultural authorities in the Soviet sector proved the more welcoming, perhaps in part because Klemperer was domiciled in Soviet-occupied Hungary. At the end of the war the theatre administrator Ernst Legal, with whom Klemperer had worked amicably at the Kroll Oper, had succeeded Tietjen as Intendant of the Berlin State Opera, which was now in the Soviet sector of the city. On 16 October 1948 the American-licensed *Neue Zeitung* carried a report that Klemperer would be conducting there later in the season, though for unknown reasons he did not do so. It was not the only invitation he received. In 1947 a second opera house, the Komische Oper, had been brought into existence in East Berlin under the direction of the Austrian producer Walther Felsenstein. He and Klemperer met for the first time when Felsenstein attended one of Klemperer's performances of Mahler's Symphony No. 2.[26] Klemperer saw Felsenstein's staging at the Komische Oper of *Orpheus in the Underworld*, which he later described as 'enchanting'.[27] Discussions took place, during which Klemperer, on learning that the Komische Oper was about to stage *Carmen*, proposed himself as its conductor. He also enthusiastically endorsed Felsenstein's plan to give the work in its original form with spoken dialogue rather than with orchestrally accompanied recitatives, which was the usual practice at the time.*

East Berlin held other attractions for Klemperer. Although his innate scepticism stood in the way of any overt political commitment, he remained essentially a man of the left and his sympathies had been strengthened by his distaste for American cultural life as well as by the warm welcome he had found in Budapest. Many of Germany's leading left-wingers had rallied to what was to become the German Democratic Republic and had made their home there. Among them were Bertolt Brecht and the composers Hanns

---

* In an interview (*c.* 1972) with Philo Bregstein, Felsenstein claimed that it was Klemperer who persuaded him to stage *Carmen*. In view of the fact that the production had been announced in July 1948, two months before the two men first met, this seems improbable.

Eisler and Paul Dessau. Ernst Bloch was shortly to move to Leipzig, where he had been appointed professor of philosophy. These – and there were others – were friends and acquaintances of many years' standing.

Back in Budapest, Klemperer lost little time in ventilating his sympathies. In an article published in *Népszava* on 24 October he blamed shortages in West Berlin, not on the Soviet blockade, but on the black market.* The Western sectors, he claimed, gave the impression of a city 'prior to evacuation'. Artists from East Berlin were treated as 'lepers' in the West and its orchestras were prevented from performing on the radio there. Fortunately, these utterances by an American citizen do not seem to have attracted the attention of the United States legation in Budapest.

On the same day that the article appeared, Klemperer was involved in an extraordinary fracas at the Budapest Opera House during a performance of *Lohengrin*. It was the culmination of a long-running dispute between conductor and public over the matter of encores. Klemperer was opposed to them, but Budapest opera-goers, closer to their Italian than to their German counterparts on the matter, regarded them as a right hallowed by tradition. During a performance of *Don Giovanni* the previous season, Klemperer, infuriated by demands for a repeat of the Don's 'champagne' aria, had left the pit and had refused to return until silence had been restored.

The *Lohengrin* incident was a more serious trial of strength. During the second act Klemperer had already been visibly irked by the noisy applause that had greeted Ortrud's curse, 'Entweihte Götter!' In the last act prolonged cheers broke out after József Simándy had sung the Grail narration, 'Im fernen Land'. Klemperer refused to stop and the applause continued throughout the ensuing chorus, at the end of which the Elsa, unnerved by the hubbub, missed her cue. Enraged, Klemperer turned to the audience several times in an attempt to silence it. He eventually succeeded in doing so, but by this time he had had enough and brought the performance to a halt. After shouting 'Frechheit' ('impertinence') he left the rostrum. Only after a pause of some minutes could he be persuaded to continue the performance.† As he was about to start, a man sitting in the front row of the stalls leaned forward and said to him, 'Spielen Sie doch die Gralserzählung nochmal!' ('What about playing the Grail narration again!') Klemperer was greatly amused by the interjection.[28]

Usually tolerant of Klemperer's foibles and ready to defend him in almost all circumstances, Aladár Tóth on this occasion rebuked him for leaving the pit. On the following day *Népszava* published an article, in which

---

* In fact the currency reform introduced in the West had virtually abolished the black market.
† The incident can be heard on a Hungaroton recording (LPX 12436) of excerpts from the performance, which was broadcast.

Klemperer defended his (undoubtedly justified) belief that applause was out of place in Wagner, but also obliquely apologised for his behaviour.

> At the end of the Grail narration, which had been very well sung by József Simándy, there was the usual applause. Last year this applause ceased after a short while. That was not the case yesterday. The clapping continued . . . so that I had the impression that the audience wanted to compel a repetition of the narration. I must make it clear that I repeatedly turned to the audience to ask it to stop applauding. But without success.
>
> In my view it is impossible to repeat anything in Wagner's operas . . . I therefore indicated to the orchestra that it should continue. But because of the continued loud applause I broke off and left the conductor's desk. At the exit to the pit I was asked to conduct the performance to its end, which I did. When afterwards, and contrary to my practice, I appeared before the curtain together with the singers, we were met by jeers, hisses and whistling from a part of the audience. That part . . . is mistaken if it supposes that I disapprove of applause on principle. I also do not at all disapprove of applause of operatic arias that can be repeated.*
>
> I am sorry that, on account of what I regarded as a provocation, the performance was broken off. But I attempted to make good this error in as much as I immediately returned to the conductor's seat and continued. I also attempted to atone for the incident by later appearing before the curtain. I regret that the incident occurred.

A few days later Klemperer told a reporter from the magazine *Független Magyarország* (1 November),

> I have just received a letter from a retired member of the Opera House orchestra, who writes that Gustav Mahler . . . had a warning put up in the foyer of the Vienna Opera House. It read, 'We ask the audience not to interrupt the flow of the performance'. All I can say is, it's a pity that Mahler could not have had that warning nailed up on the walls of the Budapest foyer as well!

In fact, Klemperer's wish was granted, for at subsequent performances of *Lohengrin* notices were posted in the Opera House, requesting the audience not to applaud.

Meanwhile Klemperer was deep in rehearsals for a revival of *Fidelio*, to open on 8 November 1948. Cuts of some 40 per cent imposed earlier in the season on the Opera House's budget had made it impossible to provide him with a new production, as had been intended.[29] But rehearsals that stretched

---

* At concerts, Klemperer was known to take a more flexible view. At a performance of Tchaikovsky's 'Pathétique' Symphony with the Scottish Orchestra in Glasgow in the following year, and to the evident surprise of the *Glasgow Herald* (31 October 1949), he even implicitly encouraged the audience to applaud after the rousing third movement, because he felt it to be more appropriate there than at the end of the work. On another occasion in 1949 he himself led applause for Annie Fischer at the end of the first movement of the 'Emperor' Concerto in Amsterdam.

over several weeks enabled him to put his stamp on both staging and musical preparation to a degree he had not previously achieved in Budapest. He insisted that all members of the cast be present, even when they were not required to sing. In spite of his inability to speak Hungarian he intervened even in the manner in which the dialogue was accented.[30] Perhaps anxious lest he incur another expression of public displeasure, he defended his decision to omit the Leonore No. 3 Overture, traditionally included in Budapest. It was dramatic nonsense, he argued in a newspaper article, for Florestan to be rescued twice, first on the stage and then in the overture.[31] In a second article, published in the theatrical paper *Pesti Músor* on the day of the première, he explained the two principles that underlay his approach to music theatre. The first was Mahler's observation that all relevant stage instructions were implicit in the score – all one needed was an ability to read between the lines. The other was Mozart's dictum that the text should be the handmaiden of the music.* In both cases, the moral was *prima la musica*.

To István Szenthegyi in *Kis Ujsák* (10 November) the impact of the performance sprang 'not so much out of changes of scene as out of changes in psychology ... Klemperer produced, not from without, but from within, [so that] the audience was held spellbound by a drama of the emotions.' The trumpet entry at the prisoners' cry of 'Freedom!', said Szenthegyi, was like a great 'flash of light' in the prevailing blackness. In later years, Bence Szabolcsi, the Hungarian musicologist, recalled the scene in which Leonore had helped Rocco to dig the grave intended for her husband: 'it was as though hell were about to swallow up humanity'.[32] In rehearsals the tempi seemed at times so fast as to be unsingable.† Yet the performance had such intensity that, as one of the young people in the audience later recalled, 'at the end ... we applauded until our hands were red and felt that the entire opera should have been repeated there and then'.[33] Jemnitz wrote that the performance finally revealed the full significance of Klemperer's presence in Budapest.[34]

---

* It has not proved possible to trace the occasion of Mahler's observation, which may have stemmed from a remark made in Klemperer's presence. (Klemperer seems to have missed the irony that Mahler lent his authority to the old tradition of including Leonore No. 3.) Mozart's well-known dictum, which Klemperer frequently quoted, derives from a letter to his father *à propos* the first performance of *Die Entführung aus dem Serail*.

† Their speed can be gauged by comparing Klemperer's timings for the Budapest première (recorded on Hungaraton LPX 12428–29), a private recording of a performance he conducted at Covent Garden in 1961, and his EMI recording of the opera made in 1962.

In spite of the startling differences, the relationships *between* the tempi are remarkably constant. The relative slowness of the EMI recording in comparison with that made at Covent Garden can doubtless be attributed to the impact of a live performance on a conductor who never ceased to be a man of the theatre.

	Budapest	Covent Garden	EMI
No. 3 Act I quartet (canon)	3′27″	4′00″	4′35″
No. 8 Pizarro/Rocco duet	4′20″	4′53″	5′25″
No. 14 Act 2 quartet	4′17″	4′55″	5′25″
No. 16 Finale	12′04″	13′42″	14′36″

On the day after the première Klemperer left Budapest to give three concerts in Brussels with the Belgian National Orchestra; Claudio Arrau was the soloist in Beethoven's Third Piano Concerto. From there he went to Berlin to begin rehearsals for the *Carmen* with Walther Felsenstein and also to conduct two concerts at the Komische Oper on 26 and 29 November. On each occasion the long programme, which included Mozart's 'Jupiter' and Tchaikovsky's 'Pathétique' symphonies, ended with Klemperer's new cantata, *Die Weber*. It attracted critics from both sides of the city. Though Klemperer uttered a few introductory words in which he somewhat gratuitously insisted that he lived in Communist Budapest purely for musical reasons, the work was inevitably regarded as a political statement and reactions to it varied accordingly. *Neues Deutschland* (28 November), the official organ of the East Berlin Communist party, approved of the cantata as an affirmation of Klemperer's 'opposition to capitalism, fascism and war threats'. *Der Abend* (27 November), published in the Western sector, dismissed the work as 'a primitive, political marching song'. In *Die Welt* (27 November) Kurt Westphal described it as 'too crass for the concert hall and, for a great musician, too unscrupulous in its means'. One way or another, Klemperer had embarked on a course that was to endanger his entire career in the West.

* * *

Felsenstein's Komische Oper was not the first Berlin theatre to bear that name. Its forebear had been opened by Hans Gregor in 1905 with the aim of bringing higher standards of production to the lighter end of the repertory. After the end of the Second World War the Soviet occupation authorities revived the idea to bring opera to a wider public, and on 23 December 1947 a resuscitated Komische Oper opened its doors in the Metropol Theater. Its opening productions were of *Die Fledermaus*, Offenbach's *Orpheus in the Underworld* and Orff's chamber opera *Die Kluge*. The *Carmen*, announced on 30 July 1948, was its most ambitious project to date. Felsenstein set about preparing a new German translation of the text, which, he stressed, he intended to perform without cuts.

For the first time since 1933 Klemperer found himself working with a man whom he regarded as 'a producer of genius'.[35] Only occasionally was he irked by Felsenstein's tendency to 'overdo things'.[36] In particular, he objected to his partner's readiness to subordinate musical to theatrical ends, as when he obliged artists to sing into the wings when it seemed dramatically appropriate.* Inevitably there were moments of tension between two such self-willed characters. But both men later recalled the collaboration as

---

* Klemperer disapproved of the practice. In a letter (Budapest, 6 April 1950) to Diana Eustrati, he wrote, 'Sing out *forwards*. Always!'

13   Walther Felsenstein and Otto Klemperer at a *Carmen* rehearsal, Berlin 1948

harmonious. For Felsenstein it remained a high point of his career. 'Otto Klemperer', he wrote in the last year of his life, 'was one of the greatest and most uncompromising artists with whom I have worked, a fanatical and extraordinarily intelligent musician, a conductor for the theatre.'[37]

The première on 4 January 1949 was attended by almost everyone of importance in the city's musical life. Though Klemperer himself counted it 'a very great success; chorus, orchestra and production excellent',[38] the critics were not uniformly enthusiastic. There was much praise for the knife-like sharpness of the orchestral playing. 'The accents', wrote Stuckenschmidt, 'were hard, clear, even cruel.'[39] In the *Tägliche Rundschau* (6 January) Karl Laux described the musical interpretation as 'taut and unyielding'. There was praise for Elfriede Trötschel (Micaela) and Heinz Sauerbaum's robust Don José, but the Carmen was found so inadequate that at Klemperer's insistence the role was sung in the two remaining performances he conducted by her stand-in, Diana Eustrati, a Greek singer to whom he had grown much attached during the weeks of rehearsal. Admiration for Felsenstein's production was tempered by criticism of his decision to perform the work in its uncut original version, which resulted in a performance that on the first night lasted some four-and-three-quarter hours, though this may also have been due in part to a time-consuming scene change between the third and fourth acts.[40]

During his weeks in East Berlin Klemperer stayed at the once famous Hotel Adlon, now largely a ruin, but close to the Komische Oper. In the evenings he frequented Die Möwe, a night-spot favoured by artists and intellectuals, often in the company of Hanns Eisler, who earlier in the year had been deported from the United States after interrogation by the House of Representatives Committee for Un-American Activities. On New Year's Eve they were joined there by Brecht, who was rehearsing *Mutter Courage* at the Deutsches Theater, his first production after his return to Berlin. Alfred Kantorowicz, another member of the party, left an account of the evening.

> The conversation covered all periods and places: art, music, philosophy, theatre, America, Russia and world affairs. There was a discussion about Charlie Chaplin. Brecht was taunted about the effectiveness of the rebuff he had administered to the snoopers on the American Congressional committee. There was much polished malice about our poet laureate, who had seen to it that his own verse had been published in an edition one-and-a-half times as large as that of ... Brecht's. 'That is a cup (*Becher*) we shall all have to drain', observed Brecht grimly.*

The evening recaptured the intellectual stimulus Klemperer had relished in pre-Nazi Berlin. For a while he even toyed with the idea of moving back to Berlin. 'If conditions here don't get much worse', he wrote on 28 December to Micha May, 'we're considering moving entirely to Berlin in the coming year. In the final resort I belong to Germany. Now more than ever.' Yet when Felsenstein invited him to become the Komische Oper's musical director, he refused.[41] That decision was not due to any opposition on the part of the American authorities, though they would hardly have welcomed the prospect of an American citizen occupying so prominent a position in East Berlin. His motives were almost certainly artistic. In Budapest a privileged position gave him power without responsibility. At the Komische Oper he would inevitably find himself playing second fiddle to a director who ruled his house as an absolute sovereign and in a theatre whose vocal standards were at best uneven. His native caution may also have begun to assert itself. To accept an official appointment, as opposed to a temporary engagement, would have been to make an irretrievable political commitment.

*   *   *

---

* Alfred Kantorowicz, *Deutsches Tagebuch*, Vol. One, pp. 559–60. The 'poet laureate' in question was Johannes Becher (1891–1958), distinguished Communist poet and novelist. Originally an expressionist, Becher ended as an upholder of Socialist Realism. On his return to Berlin in 1945 after ten years in the Soviet Union, he was appointed to the influential position of President of the Academy of the Arts in the eastern sector; hence Brecht's pun on his name.

On his return to East Berlin from emigration, Alfred Kantorowicz (1899–1979) became editor of the left-wing intellectual periodical *Die neue Weltbühne*, a position he held until his appointment in 1950 to a professorship at the Humboldt University. In 1957 he fled to West Germany.

Klemperer's visit to East Berlin lasted twelve weeks. On the morning after his return to Budapest on 15 January 1949 he threw himself into rehearsals for his next major undertaking, a revival of *The Tales of Hoffmann*. Apart from a solitary occasion at the Kroll in 1929, when he had stood in for Zemlinsky, he had never conducted the work before, nor was he to do so again. But his love of Offenbach, which went back to the very start of his career when in 1906 he had conducted *Orpheus in the Underworld* for Max Reinhardt, was deep and lasting.

In Budapest, as he observed in a letter to his Berlin Carmen, Diana Eustrati, to whom he was now writing almost daily, there was, alas, 'no Felsenstein'.[42] He thus felt obliged to produce the opera himself. As well as opening traditional cuts, for the first time in Budapest, he placed the Munich scene before the Venetian one, as Offenbach intended, rather than the other way round. This involved a longer scene-change than usual and, to give the stagehands more time, Klemperer composed some variations on the famous Barcarolle, which would serve as an extended prelude to the Venetian scene, now in the third act. These were rehearsed but not, it seems, performed, probably on account of Tóth's intervention.[43] Costumes and full lighting were used at all rehearsals.[44] Owing to his belated return from Berlin, these were fewer than Klemperer would have wished, but they sufficed for him to put his own unmistakable mark on the work. To one critic the textures had a Gallic lightness, the rhythms were 'living and tangible'. Boros recalled something 'terrifying and fantastic' about the performances.* After the dress rehearsal Klemperer felt the undertaking to be in need of further rehearsing, but subsequently conceded in a letter to Diana Eustrati that the première had gone 'quite well'.

In contrast to the hastily prepared *Hoffmann*, Klemperer was able to devote several weeks of rehearsal to his next major operatic assignment, a revival of *Die Meistersinger* (again performed without cuts) on 27 March. There were a good many rows during the preparations.[45] At the final dress rehearsal, he called a member of the orchestra 'an idiot'. After the interval, the leader demanded an apology, whereupon Klemperer retired to his room, declaring that he would on no account give one. Tóth attempted to mediate; a doctor brought Klemperer a sedative secreted in a glass of water. After much discussion he was persuaded to accompany Tóth to the room in which the orchestra was angrily debating the situation. Klemperer marched in boldly and asserted that his comment had referred only to a single player. He looked round the room. '*There* he is', he shouted. '*That's* the man I called an idiot –

---

* Boros, pp. 84–5. A very lo-fi (and hence unpublished) radio recording of the performance conducted on 2 April 1949 confirms those impressions. Klemperer casts a macabre and menacing light over the drama without depriving the music of its sparkle and wit.

and an idiot he is.'[46] The orchestra burst into laughter and returned to work. Such a character was hard to resist.

Insisting that the work was to be approached as a comic opera, Klemperer held up Richard Strauss's light-handed and brisk interpretation of it as the ideal.[47] His own tempi were at moments so fast that the last act, timed in a recording made two weeks later, was fifteen minutes shorter than customary.[48] Yet reminiscences are unanimous in stressing the splendour of the opera's great moments. Júlia Osváth, who as Eva at each performance watched him conduct the prelude from the wings, later recalled the shiver of excitement she always experienced as it reached its climax. Pál Varga, the chorusmaster, similarly recollected the grandiose power of the chorale 'Wach auf', though he found the musical flow that Klemperer achieved in the conversational scenes no less remarkable. Klemperer himself later paid tribute to the outstanding contribution of the chorus, and there were those who found a new suppleness in his own conducting. In the first interval of the première, Árpád Szakasits, the country's president, presented Klemperer with the officer's cross of the order of the Hungarian Republic.

* * *

By March 1949 Hungary had fallen into the grip of a totalitarianism that was modelled in almost every respect on the dictatorship that Stalin had established twenty years earlier in the Soviet Union. When Klemperer had first arrived in Budapest eighteen months earlier, the Communist party, which felt obliged to move cautiously owing to the limited support it commanded, was still advocating freedom of opinion. But the situation was transformed after the Communist seizure of power in Prague in February 1948. Then, on 26 June 1948, only three days after the inauguration of the Berlin blockade, the Tito regime in Yugoslavia was denounced by the Soviet Union as 'deviationist'.

Such events in countries on its northern and southern frontiers inevitably had far-reaching repercussions within Hungary itself. In a series of moves that the Communist leader, Mátyás Rákosi, described as 'salami tactics', his party rapidly established its grip on the levers of power. On 25 March 1948 all concerns employing more than a hundred workers were nationalised. Confessional schools were abolished on 11 June, and four days later the Communist and Socialist parties were merged. Tito's expulsion from the Comintern brought a further sharp turn of the screw, for the possibility of a 'nationalist' brand of Communism posed a threat to the Muscovite leaders of the Hungarian party. On 5 August László Rajk, the only prominent Communist leader who had not entered Hungary in the wake of the Soviet army, was transferred from the crucial position of Minister of the Interior to the Foreign Ministry. Thereafter, the process of change through force quickened. On 26 December 1948 the Cardinal-Primate, József Mindszenty, was arrested. Less than two months later, while Klemperer was preparing *Die Meistersinger*, he was sentenced to life imprisonment.

After the performances of *Die Meistersinger*, Klemperer went to Amsterdam for three weeks for a Beethoven cycle with the Concertgebouw Orchestra. He wore the decoration he had received from the Hungarian President, though he was not to keep it for long. Johanna, as usual more worldly than her husband, made sure that it 'disappeared', though she would never say what she had done with it. The fate of the order caused a good deal of family hilarity. Klemperer maintained that Johanna had thrown it into the sea. The Dutch visit ended on 12 May with a performance of the Ninth Symphony, which was described in *Het Parool* by Bertus van Lier as being 'a volcano of essential energy ... stripped of routine and sentimentality'. Confronted with the Concertgebouw's heavily marked conductor's score, Klemperer had flung it aside with the remark, 'That isn't a score, it's a novel.' At his insistence, all retouchings were removed.

Three days later, elections held in Hungary on a single-party list produced a majority of 94.6 per cent for the Communists. Now that all power lay in his hands, Rákosi was able to move against Rajk. On 19 June Rajk was arrested as a member of a 'Trotskyite, Fascist, Zionist gang' and in the autumn subjected to a show trial on a pattern established twelve years earlier in the Soviet Union. After confessing to having been all along an American agent and supporter of Tito, Rajk was hanged on 15 October.

Unlike many artists, Klemperer followed political events with keen interest.* Those who knew him during his years in Budapest are agreed that he was well aware of developments within Hungary. Why then did he allow himself to become an ornament of a totalitarian regime at the very time when he was so sharply critical of Furtwängler's failure to dissociate himself from the Third Reich? His lack of sympathy for America undoubtedly played a part. 'I could not identify myself with American cultural life', he told a Hungarian interviewer. 'Its artistic atmosphere did not inspire my imagination. I am not interested in jazz or in Gershwin's music [see, however, p. 79]: it is an alien world to me.'[49] In particular, he disliked the commercialism rampant in American musical life. Asked how he could live in a country where Socialist Realism was the order of the day, he replied, 'I prefer arguing about whether *Aida* is a love story or a political drama (naturally, I think it's a love story) to discussing whether Heifetz's fee should be ten or twenty thousand dollars.'[50] His lively memories of the warmth with which he had been received in Moscow and Leningrad before the war also inclined him at first to look favourably on things Russian.

But, although he was sympathetic to Marxism, the Stalinist trials of the

* 'He talks politics all the time' (Sándor Jemnitz's unpublished diaries, 6 April 1949).

thirties had long since caused him to outgrow any early tendency to regard the Soviet Union as a beacon of hope for humanity. '*Den* Bösen sind sie los, *die* Bösen sind geblieben' ('*That* evil one they are rid of, the others remain'), he had written to Helene Hirschler at the end of the war in Europe, quoting from Goethe's *Faust*.[51] Nor had he even then the least sympathy for Soviet cultural dogma: 'Is there such a thing as socialist, capitalist or democratic music? I think there is only good or bad music.'[52] In particular, he regarded attempts to make composers toe an aesthetic line with abhorrence. On learning that Shostakovich had been rebuked by Soviet officialdom for the ironic flavour of his Ninth Symphony, he described such behaviour as 'ridiculous'.[53] He wrote on at least two occasions to tell the composer of his admiration for a work he frequently conducted in the early fifties. Both letters remained unanswered, perhaps because they never reached their destination.

These views had been expressed while Klemperer was still living in Los Angeles, but there is no evidence that residence in Budapest led him to look more favourably on Soviet cultural policies. But for the moment he was happy as he had not been since his time as musical director in Wiesbaden during the mid-twenties. On his return to Budapest after a brief absence in the late autumn of 1948, he told a reporter that it was 'as though I were returning home. I feel well in Budapest. I feel as though I am part of it.'[54] In a sense he was able to enjoy the best of both worlds. His high earnings sheltered him from the material want increasingly suffered by the general populace. The regime saw to it that in the summer of 1949 he and his family were allocated a spacious flat overlooking the City Park and, when the area was subsequently set aside for another privileged segment of society, a substantial villa in the bosky outskirts of the old city of Pest was put at his disposal. Yet as an American citizen he was free to come and go as he chose. 'For opera directors', observed Bloch ironically, 'there seems to be no silken curtain.'[55] But more important to Klemperer than all these privileges was the fact that in Tóth he had found a director able to provide him with working conditions such as he had not enjoyed for some time. It was this more than any other factor that at first inclined him to turn a blind eye to a deteriorating political situation.

But there was a price to be paid. He was living in what, intellectually and politically, had become a closed society. A controlled press and radio inevitably reflected a Soviet view of the world. Many of the people he mixed with to a greater or lesser extent shared that viewpoint and nowhere more so than in East Berlin. It is probably not mere chance that after his visits there his attitudes became increasingly partisan, and this expressed itself in a sharpening of his animosity towards musicians whose careers were again flourishing as they had done during the Third Reich.

In November 1948 the news that the Chicago Symphony Orchestra was negotiating to engage Furtwängler for eight weeks in the coming season unleashed a storm of opposition among leading Jewish musicians, several of whom threatened to boycott the orchestra. As he was not in the United States, Klemperer was not asked for his support. That did not, however, prevent him while in Berlin from publicly urging that Furtwängler be prohibited from conducting in America.[56] His intervention put paid to any lingering hopes of a reconciliation between the two greatest German conductors of their generation. It also effectively ended any possibility that Klemperer would be invited to conduct at the Salzburg Festival, where Furtwängler was again influential in the choice of artists.*

Sometimes Klemperer's actions appear to have been motivated purely by jealousy. Three weeks earlier, on learning that Erich Kleiber was about to conduct in Budapest for the first time since the war, Klemperer seems to have denounced him to the authorities as a fascist. The accusation was quite unfounded. Kleiber, who had left Nazi Germany in 1935, heard of Klemperer's machinations and almost cancelled his engagements with the Radio, though he was persuaded not to do so.† On the other hand, there is no doubt that Klemperer did identify himself increasingly with the 'anti-fascism' that was one of the main planks of Communist propaganda. Evidence is provided by his reaction to the death of Georgi Dimitrov, the Bulgarian Communist leader, on 2 July 1949 in Moscow. As a token of his admiration for Dimitrov's courageous appearance for the defence in the Reichstag fire trial, Klemperer attended a memorial ceremony held in his honour at the Budapest Opera House later in the month. His action was not reported in the press, but the appearance of a citizen of the United States on such an occasion was not calculated to appeal to the American authorities at the height of the Cold War. He was to pay dearly for this and other indiscretions.

*   *   *

During his visit to Amsterdam in the spring of 1949 Klemperer was still spending money so recklessly that he had drawn five-sixths of his not insubstantial earnings before he returned to Budapest in mid-May.[57] In other respects, however, his euphoria was on the wane. In a letter (2 May 1949) to Lotte, Johanna noted with relief that he was no longer disappearing at night. At the height of his euphoria his encounters with women were fleeting, and consequently played no real part in his life. As he grew more stable, however,

---

* Elisabeth Furtwängler, letters to the author, 19 November and 9 December 1986. A sad aspect of this incident is that Furtwängler, as yet unaware of Klemperer's intervention, had in a statement issued three days later welcomed the fact that Klemperer, like Walter, had declined to associate himself with the boycott.

† Article by Tibor Polgár, *Magyarság*, Toronto, 3 January 1987. Though no other documentation of the incident has come to light, many witnesses have attested to the fact that something of the sort occurred. Johanna disapproved of her husband's action.

he regained his ability to form a real attachment, such as came into existence in the course of that summer.

On his way to morning rehearsals at the Budapest Opera House, Klemperer frequently dropped into a nearby café for breakfast, where he became well known to the waitresses. One of them introduced him to her sister, Erzsébet, a woman already in her early thirties and not particularly pretty. Klemperer was enchanted by her simple manner and transparent honesty. She accepted no presents and when he provided tickets for the opera refused to go backstage to see him after the performance. The only favour she asked for was help in finding a place at school for her young brother, who, as a child of lower middle-class parents, was disadvantaged against the offspring of proletarian families. Through his contacts at the Ministry of Education (which also controlled cultural affairs), Klemperer was able to intervene successfully on her behalf. As Erzsébet spoke very little German, written communications were effected through Oszkár Kaufman,* with whom Klemperer had become friendly. Though there was probably no physical intimacy, a genuine love came into existence. Johanna was saddened, but grateful for the calming influence exercised by the attachment. Erzsébet and Klemperer continued to see each other until he finally left Budapest a year later. Months afterwards, Kaufman wrote to Klemperer at her request to inform him that she was engaged to be married. Thereafter all contact ceased.[58] In a real sense, Erzsébet was his last love, though by no means his last affair.

*   *   *

In late May 1949 Klemperer conducted two concerts in Rome with the Santa Cecilia Orchestra. He also had an audience with Pius XII, who as papal nuncio in the twenties had been an enthusiastic supporter of the Kroll Oper. Klemperer asked him to provide papers for Fritz Fischer, who, though living in Italy, was stateless. The Pope obliged. Most of the remainder of the season Klemperer spent in Budapest. At its close he and Johanna set out for Australia. They had to fly there via London, where they spent a week. 'No eggs!' Klemperer wrote to Helene Hirschler on 25 July, contrasting conditions in Budapest with the severe rationing that still prevailed in Britain. That he was prepared to travel so far suggests that engagements outside Budapest were not proving easy to find; according to Sir Charles Moses, general manager of the Australian Broadcasting Commission, which promoted the tour of nineteen concerts, Klemperer was engaged for a fee lower than Malcolm Sargent would have commanded.

Johanna at first reacted favourably to Australia. It was, she wrote to

---

* Oszkár Kaufman (1873–1956), architect of the reconstructed Kroll Theatre in Berlin, had returned to his native Hungary in 1945.

Lotte (16 August), 'American in a good sense. People simple, not snobbish.' But she soon wearied of the British-style hotels and found the food 'atrocious'. Of the four cities they visited, only Adelaide ('I could live here') pleased her. Klemperer was irked by the Anglo-Saxon Sunday that still prevailed in Melbourne. 'Not only are all the shops closed but the restaurants as well. Only the churches are open and people pour into them, *faute de mieux*.'[59]

He was, however, agreeably surprised by the general standard of the orchestras, and the players warmed to his lack of egotism and the caustic humour that lurked behind a forbidding exterior. Interrupted in rehearsal by off-stage hammering, he advised, 'Play more softly; you'll disturb the carpenters.' Rehearsals passed without incident. However, an animosity towards Elisabeth Schwarzkopf, his soloist in a number of concerts, soon became evident. At his opening concert in Sydney on 11 August he deliberately set out to embarrass her by launching into an aria while she was still acknowledging the audience's applause and then setting a tempo so fast as to be barely singable.[60] Johanna observed that, at rehearsals for the first performance in Australia of Mahler's Symphony No. 4, in which Schwarzkopf was the soloist,

> Papa was oddly animated – scolded the singer far too much and too often ... It was also the first time that I found Papa not so good – his conducting was somewhat stiff and the orchestra didn't sound full enough to me.[61]

Any animosity that Klemperer may then have felt towards Schwarzkopf, with whom he frequently appeared in later years, did not prevent him from inviting her to dance with him at a supper party given by Sir Charles Moses after his opening concert. Schwarzkopf declined. His host's daughter was then escorted to the floor, where Klemperer made clumsy attempts to kiss her. '*Please*, Dr Klemperer', the young woman remonstrated. 'Not *here*!' '*Where*, then?' came the reply.[62]

The tour went well. After the opening concert Lindsay Brown of the *Sydney Morning Herald* (12 August) wrote that Brahms's First Symphony had been played 'with an astonishing breadth of vision and dramatic concentration. The force of its tragic ideas was communicated with driving directness.' Five days later the same critic wrote, 'It is difficult to recall another Australian-made concert in which character, drive, great-hearted fidelity, zeal and knowledge have been so powerfully compounded.' In the view of Wolfgang Wagner, the critic of *The Canon*, the orchestral playing 'surpassed everything we have heard hitherto'.[63] Klemperer's success in Melbourne, where he conducted Bruckner's Seventh Symphony, was no less striking. At his final concert in Sydney on 10 October, he gave his own neo-classical *Little Overture*, which he had performed two-and-a-half months earlier in Budapest.

The work received no more than mildly respectful notices, but the evening ended with an ovation described as one of the biggest ever accorded to a conductor in the city. Before leaving Klemperer accepted an invitation to return at the end of the coming season.

On his way back to Europe, he stopped off in Los Angeles, where he saw both Schoenberg and Stravinsky. In New York on 19 October he visited his sister Regi, whom he had not seen for two-and-a-half years. Though irritated by his constant politicising, she was relieved to find him relatively quiet. 'He is now on a good middle path, if only it lasts', she wrote to their sister two days later. Johanna also perceived an improvement. 'Thank God, he is *much, much* better', she wrote to Lotte on 2 November. 'Everyone says so.' By now Klemperer and Johanna had reached London, where, on 3 November, he succeeded at last in conducting a studio concert with the BBC Symphony Orchestra.* He also gave concerts in Glasgow and Edinburgh with the Scottish Orchestra. On 8 November, at the Royal Albert Hall, he conducted the Philharmonia Orchestra for the second time, again under the auspices of Richard Austin's New Era Concert Society. To the flautist Gareth Morris, who was playing under him for the first time,

> He seemed a terrifying personage ... He looked odd and he had a disconcerting habit of walking in the midst of the orchestra even during a concert with his tie unknotted and an almost wild look in his eye ... Yet I at once felt that I was in the presence of somebody supremely out of the ordinary who was lost in the music. So when before the concert I was summoned to his room I was full of nervous fear that I had not pleased him. He was standing with a score: 'This note must be *very* loud. Goodbye, we shall meet at the concert.' We shook hands and I was his slave.†

The programme consisted of Beethoven's *Grosse Fuge*, Bartók's Piano Concerto No. 3, which Klemperer conducted for the first time, with György Sándor as soloist, and Brahms's First Symphony.

For Richard Capell in the *Daily Telegraph* (9 November) the Brahms symphony 'spoke of ripe experience'. The anonymous critic of *The Times* (9 November) was less enthusiastic about it. Klemperer, he wrote,

> made the first movement dull, the second rather more eloquent and, like many another conductor of the finale, got its fluctuating tempi wrong. The trouble began with that *accelerando* just after the big tune which is not marked in the score but which most conductors make ... This put the rest of the movement

---

* The programme consisted of Bach's Suite No. 3, Stravinsky's Symphony in Three Movements and Beethoven's Symphony No. 7. Klemperer said later that he had been impressed by Boult's orchestra (*ABC Weekly*, 12 August 1950).

† Contribution to the programme book of the Klemperer Memorial Concert, conducted by Rafael Kubelik in the Albert Hall on 14 January 1974. Morris (b. 1920) was principal flautist of the Philharmonia and the New Philharmonia Orchestras (1948–72), and a member of the board of the latter (1964–72). No British musician came closer to Klemperer.

too fast, although the *largamente* marked at the return of the big tune was observed, but the horn tune had no space to turn round in and, by the time the brass chords were reached in the coda, the symphony was bolting down hill and came to the end too soon.

* * *

By mid-November Klemperer was back in Budapest. A month earlier, on 12 October 1949, the United States legation there had forwarded to the Department of State in Washington a translation of a news item that had, it said, appeared five days earlier in *Magyar Nemzet*. According to this report, Klemperer had cabled from Australia a substantial contribution to a Hungarian State loan as an expression of his loyalty to the People's Republic. Up to this point, the legation had either been unaware of, or turned a blind eye to, his political sympathies. On this occasion, however, it meaningfully reminded Washington that his passport was due to expire on 26 February 1950. 'The above information', the letter continued, 'is being furnished to the Department for its use in considering future applications by Otto Klemperer for passport services.' The State Department reacted promptly. A note, headed 'Refusal', was placed with Klemperer's papers to ensure that any request for an extension or renewal of his passport would not be granted.*

Blithely unaware of these developments, Klemperer gave an interview, in which he first described his journey to Australia and then proceeded to give his impressions of the West. He was reported as follows:

> War hysteria is at its height in the West. The capitalists' individual and collective mistrust against everybody and everything coming from the People's Democracies can be called a panic. In consequence of irresponsible and unrestrained agitation in the Press, people are frightened of war instead of understanding that the only true and sincere aim of the Soviet Union and the People's Democracies is peace. Having now at last seen with my own eyes what goes on on the other side, I must declare in the full knowledge of my responsibility: we, the German emigrants from Hitler's Germany in 1933, to whom America gave citizenship, visas, bread, positions and security at that time, cannot share the anti-Soviet attitude of America today, in spite of the gratitude we are bound to feel ...
>
> A real musician can only work seriously in a cultured atmosphere. As culture in the Hungarian People's Democracy is today in the process of reaching an extraordinarily high level, one can perhaps work nowhere else as well as one can here.[64]

A translation of the interview was forwarded to Washington on 1 January 1950 and duly attached to Klemperer's papers, where it lay like a time bomb.

---

* In fact his current passport was not due to expire until 16 November 1950. The information above was made available to Lotte Klemperer in 1980 under the US Freedom of Information and Privacy Acts.

Whether Klemperer ever expressed himself in such terms is open to doubt. He was no ideologue. But the interview illustrates the degree to which he had come to accept an Eastern view of a world caught in the Cold War. So, too, had Lotte, who in Budapest had come to embrace Marxism with all the ardour of youth, so much so that even the patient Johanna reproached her daughter for being 'frightfully one-sided', as she put it in an undated letter written in May 1950: 'You feel yourself above all these unenlightened Westerners ... because you have found the key to the universe ("das Alleinseligmachende"). The Catholic Church claims the same. But what is truth? No one *can* know.' Yet Johanna had also to some extent come to share her husband's sympathies, if in a more prudent and realistic manner. A few days after she had rebuked Lotte she had second thoughts. 'I have a slightly bad conscience about my last letter', she wrote. 'What is truth? is a big question. However I am in no doubt which side at the moment comes closest to it.'[65]

Far from having reached 'an extraordinarily high level', as Klemperer claimed, cultural life in Hungary had entered an ugly phase. After Tito's severance of his ties with Moscow, the Soviet Union set out to prevent other potential schismatics from following his example. Every aspect of Hungarian life was subjected to a systematic process of Russification, and special attention was given to culture. This sphere was placed in the care of the poet József Révai, who on 10 June 1949 was appointed Minister of People's Culture as part of the government changes that occurred at the time of Rajk's arrest.

Though totally unmusical, Révai was a man of culture and subtle intelligence, who in his younger days had been a literary critic of repute. As minister, however, his task was to enforce Stalinist standards in the arts and he proceeded to do so with inflexible energy. One of his first acts was to extract from his former teacher, the philosopher György Lukács, a recantation of his relatively liberal interpretation of Marxist-Leninism.[66] Though Révai himself is said to have continued to receive each new work by Thomas Mann on publication, he permitted little Western literature to enter the country. American films were banned. Soviet standards increasingly prevailed.*

In the field of music the course to be followed was that laid down by a resolution of 10 February 1948 of the Central Committee of the Communist party of the USSR. In it, leading Soviet composers, notably Prokofiev and Shostakovich, were censured for having written music that reflected 'formalist distortions and anti-democratic tendencies alien to the Soviet people'. They were also accused of having fostered 'atonality and dissonance' and 'renounced melody'. Henceforth Soviet composition was to develop in 'a

---

* 'Let us learn from Soviet Culture ... the most advanced in the world' (Révai, *Szabad Nép*, 18 December 1949, quoted in István Csicsery-Rónay, *The Russian Penetration of Hungary*, p. 40).

realistic direction', with due recognition of 'the deep organic connection between the people and their songs and music'. 'High professional art' was to be 'combined with simplicity'. This programme was duly approved by the First All-Union Congress of Composers, which met in Moscow from 19 to 25 April and appointed Tikhon Khrennikov, a composer of no distinction, as its secretary-general.

Within a few weeks these principles, which had been inspired by Zhdanov, Stalin's commissar for the arts, were obediently echoed in Hungary. On 9 May 1948 *Szabad Nép* announced that the new Hungarian Workers' party, which was about to be formed by an amalgamation of the Communists and left-wing social democratics, 'rejects the reactionary bourgeois ideals of *l'art pour l'art*. It seeks for a high level of realism, which should reflect the life and struggles of our people ..., hail the victories of popular democratic ideals and be optimistic in outlook.' As the new party strengthened its grip on every aspect of life these guidelines were enforced with increasing zeal, and 'experts' descended from Moscow to ensure that cultural life developed in the required mould. Khrennikov was among the visitors.

As the least overtly political art, music was less immediately exposed to pressure than literature, theatre and painting. Even so, as an example of the way the wind was blowing as early as February 1949, Sándor Jemnitz had already been instructed that reviews of 'bourgeois events', such as solo recitals, were not required.[67] The Opera House inevitably came in for attention. In *Szabad Nép* (5 February), Géza Losonczy, Révai's Secretary of State at the Ministry of Culture,* made plain that its repertory did not adequately reflect the party's cultural policies. Losonczy had a long list of complaints. National operas, such as Erkel's, were neglected. There was too much Wagner. Bartók was condemned for 'decadence and formalism' and his ballet *The Miraculous Mandarin* singled out as 'unsuitable to the moral and aesthetic education of the Hungarian working class'. The Opera House was also rebuked for having in the previous season performed *Petrushka*, 'a totally formalist work by the white *émigré* Stravinsky', while operas by truly Russian composers were 'not performed in appropriate relationship to their significance'.† Productions lacked realism and detail. The Opera House itself

---

* Losonczy's brief but chequered career exemplifies the changing fortunes of the leaders of the party in the late forties and early fifties. Appointed a member of the Central Committee at the age of only twenty-nine, Losonczy (1917–57) continued to serve as Secretary of State until 1951, when (together with János Kádár) he was arrested. In 1956 he became editor-in-chief of *Magyar Nemzet* and a member of Imre Nágy's government. After its collapse, he was again imprisoned and died before he could be brought to trial.

† The only works by Wagner in the repertory (all conducted by Klemperer) were *Tannhäuser*, *Lohengrin* and *Die Meistersinger*. In 1950–1 the repertory included five Russian operas – three by Mussorgsky, Borodin's *Prince Igor* and Tchaikovsky's *Queen of Spades*. Bartók's ballet *The Miraculous Mandarin* was not performed after 9 December 1950. By March 1952 the

sheltered too many fascists, 'dollar worshippers', friends of America and reactionaries. Such an onslaught was aimed at Tóth's artistic policies. Klemperer naturally supported his friend and intervened on his behalf at the Ministry, but at one point Tóth was on the point of resignation.[68]

It was not long before a series of minor irritations brought home to Klemperer the extent of the changes that had occurred during his four-month absence in Australia and Britain. Perhaps as a result of having seen Schoenberg, he had returned to Budapest with the intention of performing his Theme and Variations, Op. 43b, an unproblematic score, close to Reger in its tonal idiom and busy counterpoint. But by the autumn of 1949 Schoenberg had been branded as a formalist and his music in effect banned in the Soviet Union and its satellites. Permission therefore had to be sought from the Ministry of Culture, where the responsible official was Miklós Csillag.* On 29 November, Jemnitz noted in his diary, 'Klempi would like to do Schoenberg, but they want to stop him.' Within two days of that entry Klemperer, who had access to Révai, saw the minister himself,[69] and it is hardly conceivable that he would not have taken the opportunity to raise the matter. But permission was not forthcoming.

There was no redress; once the Ministry had spoken, even Tóth, himself now under attack, was powerless. Klemperer did, however, refer to the matter obliquely in an interview he gave to the official *Szabad Nép* on 25 December. Asked about 'formalism' in music, he sucked his pipe and then observed ironically, 'Anything that people cannot understand can be classified as formalist.' Music, he continued, was moving towards a new kind of classicism. Bartók's Third Piano Concerto, which he had just conducted in London, was classical in spirit; so was Schoenberg's Theme and Variations.

There were other annoyances. A week before Klemperer's return to Budapest, Vasily Ivanovich Vaynonen, a well-known Soviet choreographer, had descended on the Opera House. His mission was to bring Hungarian dance up to the standards prevailing in the Soviet Union and to found a ballet school in Budapest. For three months the stage was largely occupied by rehearsals for a production of *The Nutcracker*. Klemperer was not used to taking second place in the Opera House. Nor did he warm to the first task he had been induced to undertake: a new production of Mussorgsky's opera *Sorochinsky Fair*, with choreography by Vaynonen, the première of which was planned to celebrate Stalin's seventieth birthday. The first night, on 25 December, was attended by the President of the Republic, the Soviet

---

repertory consisted of sixteen Russian works, as compared to five Italian, four Hungarian and two German (Csicsery-Rónay, p. 24).

* Miklós Csillag (b. 1906). A pupil of Kodály who was Head of Music, Arts and Artistic Instruction at the Ministry during the years (1949–53) when Révai was Minister and Stalinism was at its height. When questioned by the author on 20 October 1986, Csillag was unable to recall the incident.

ambassador and Révai. 'Klemperer hates this piece', Jemnitz noted in his diary, 'though I cannot understand why.' Before going on to conduct, he whispered, 'If I fall asleep, wake me up.' The opera did not prove popular and Klemperer conducted no more than three performances.

His work at the Opera House proved increasingly frustrating. A projected new production of *Aida* came to nothing, while a revival of *Salome* failed to materialise, partly on account of the disfavour into which Strauss's music had fallen and partly on account of casting difficulties. A preliminary rehearsal did, however, yield an incident that rapidly made its way round the city's coffee houses. Having missed his entry at the very start of the opera, the tenor singing the role of Narraboth sought to excuse himself by explaining, 'I used to be a Jew' (i.e. one of the group of Jews in the work). 'So did I', retorted Klemperer. A new production of *La Traviata* had to be postponed until the summer on account of Vaynonen's activities.

* * *

As Europe split into two increasingly hostile camps, Klemperer found himself on the wrong side of the political fence and fewer invitations came from the West. Negotiations with the Berlin Philharmonic Orchestra foundered on disagreement about fees; like its counterpart in Vienna, the orchestra regarded an invitation to conduct it as an honour, and set its fees accordingly. A plan for Klemperer to conduct the Brandenburg Concertos with a group of leading instrumentalists in West Berlin collapsed when he walked out, apparently because some of the players failed to appear at his first rehearsal.[70] On 31 March 1950 he conducted an isolated performance of *Carmen* at the Komische Oper, where he also gave a concert on the following day. He secured an engagement in Vienna in June, but was forced to cancel it because of a minor prostate operation.

Thus his only major undertaking outside Hungary in 1950 was to conduct and produce a new staging of *Die Zauberflöte* at La Scala, Milan. The programme first credits Mario Frigerio with the production, but Johanna's letters indicate that the final responsibility was Klemperer's. He disliked Ludwig Sievert's* designs so intensely that Johanna, who had remained in Budapest, was concerned lest a fracas at Italy's leading opera house might jeopardise further engagements. On 2 May she wrote to Lotte with her usual shrewdness:

> Papa shouldn't upset himself about the ... sets. It's *impossible* to impose one's ideas as a guest ... *Whatever* Papa does, it will *for the moment* be held against him ... He must be very careful and considered in all his dealings. Toscanini always was. I can still see the appalling sets he brought ... to Berlin and yet the

---
* Ludwig Sievert (1887–1968). Though at first influenced by Appia, Sievert turned to expressionism during his period under Carl Hagemann at Mannheim (1914–19).

performances were *unforgettable* and *unique* because he conducted. *That's what it all depends on.*

She was also concerned that he might upset the singers. 'Be a good fellow, Otto', she wrote in an undated letter. 'Be patient. Artists sing more freely, and thus better, for someone they like.'

On this occasion her fears proved groundless. The rehearsals went smoothly and the performances themselves were in the main warmly received. Klemperer himself was particularly delighted by his Pamina, Margherita Carosio, and the cast also warmed to him. At a party given in honour of his sixty-fifth birthday on 14 May by the theatre's director, Antonio Ghiringelli, there was a cake with candles, and Luigi Infantino (Tamino) and Giuseppe Taddei (Papageno) presented him with a ring inscribed with their names.

Among those who travelled to Milan for the occasion was Maria Schacko, who had returned to live in West Germany. Klemperer took a room for her at a different hotel from that in which he and Lotte were staying and provided tickets. But such brief notes as he sent made plain his determination to keep her at a distance, though he did provide her with a letter of recommendation, typewritten in English.* The day before he returned to Budapest they met for the last time, though an intermittent correspondence continued for a number of years.

While Klemperer was in Milan, Johanna wrote to tell him that 'rumours are going round the town that we are all leaving Budapest'. In fact he may already have reached a decision to do so before he had set out for Italy, for on 6 May Johanna, luxuriating in the spring in her suburban garden, wrote wistfully that it was perhaps the last she would enjoy in Budapest. The time had come to move. For Klemperer, the internal political situation held no appeal; he was a rebel by nature, but he was not a revolutionary. Language had also become an irksome limitation. In Milan he had conducted *Die Zauberflöte* in Italian; in Budapest, in Hungarian. Would he, he asked sadly, ever again do so in German?

On his return to Budapest from Milan Klemperer flung himself with enthusiasm into hurried preparations for the postponed production of *La Traviata*, a work he had not conducted since 1912. After no more than a week of rehearsals the first night took place on 26 May. But his Verdi failed to convince; in the view of one critic, he had brought to the score a dramatic vehemence that might have been more appropriate to *Otello* and in doing so deprived the work of its lyrical pathos.[71] On 4 July and in tropical heat he conducted a performance of *Don Giovanni* that, unbeknown to the audience, was to be his last appearance in the Opera House. Open-air performances of

---

* 'To Whom It May Concern. Herewith I recommend very highly Miss Maria Schacko for Opera and concerts. She is an excellent mezzosoprano, vocally and musically. Her interpretation is superb. Budapest, 21 April 1950.'

Die Fledermaus and the 'Choral' Symphony followed on 15 and 18 July respectively. Two days later he left for his second tour of Australia.

The news that he had it in mind to leave Budapest for good must have spread, for shortly before his departure he was summoned by Révai himself and asked to return the following season. Klemperer refused to commit himself.[72] He may still not have reached a final decision, for it was not until two months later that he wrote from Sydney to tell Tóth that he would not be coming back, at any rate in the foreseeable future.

> Please believe that it is very painful for me to give you this negative answer ... My interest in your achievements and in the Budapest Opera remains unaltered. Though our ways must for the moment part, I am quite sure that we shall come together in the future.[73]

Though Klemperer and Tóth met from time to time until the latter's death in 1968, they never again worked together. But Klemperer never ceased to feel deep gratitude to a friend who had shown confidence in his abilities at a time when the rest of the world had turned its back on him. Klemperer could hardly have survived in Budapest without Tóth's unfailing support. Tóth provided him not only with work, which he both needed and enjoyed, but also with a base. As a result, Klemperer regained his self-confidence and self-respect, and by 1950 was in far better shape physically than when he had arrived in Hungary three years earlier. Now the time had come to re-establish himself in the West. It was not to prove an easy task.

10

A sea of troubles

By the time Klemperer and Johanna arrived in Australia at the end of July 1950 it was clear that neither of them was well. Klemperer had begun to suffer from intermittent stomach pains, which an X-ray in Sydney suggested might stem from his gall bladder. Johanna complained of chronic fatigue. 'Every little thing taxes me', she wrote to Lotte on 4 August. 'I have pains in my shoulders, chest and arms . . . It must be my nerves.' In fact it was *angina pectoris*, a condition that was to end her life six years later.

Ill health inevitably cast a cloud over a ten-week tour that would have strained a younger and fitter man. 'His entire life', wrote Johanna, 'consists of standing on a platform, lying in bed and sitting in a car.'[1] He was hard to please. Orchestras that had passed muster twelve months earlier now failed to do so. He no longer found pleasure in the company of the people he had previously enjoyed meeting. In Johanna's view he was not depressed, though the mania that had possessed him during the three years in Budapest had diminished appreciably.

He conducted twenty-seven concerts, however, and included in the programmes two works that he had intended, but failed, to perform in Budapest – Schoenberg's Theme and Variations, Op. 43b, and Stravinsky's Concerto in D. The tour's climax came with the four performances of Mahler's Second Symphony he conducted in Sydney between 19 and 25 September. The work was unfamiliar to Australian audiences, yet, as Lindsay Brown wrote in the *Morning Herald* (23 September), Klemperer received 'probably the most excited and most grateful ovation ever accorded a musician in Sydney. Long after the house lights were switched off, the audience was still on its feet applauding thunderously.' The performances became legendary for all who attended or took part in them, a legend substantiated by a recording in the archives of the Australian Broadcasting Commission.

* * *

After the tour ended in mid-October, Klemperer flew with Johanna to Los Angeles, where he visited both Schoenberg and Stravinsky. He was disappointed that Schoenberg seemed uninterested in the performances of the Theme and Variations he had given in Australia. But the 76-year-old composer was already a sick man; it was to be their last meeting. Stravinsky was as usual more affable. On arriving for lunch, Klemperer noticed that the composer's amanuensis, Robert Craft, was carrying a score by Schoenberg's former pupil, Gerald Strang. Seizing it, Klemperer pointed to the opening notes, counted up to twelve and announced in a stentorian voice, 'Nowadays no one is doing anything else.' Such words were liable to be regarded as an affront in a household where mention of Schoenberg's technique was enough to provoke its master's wrath, for in 1950 Stravinsky was still composing in a tonal, neo-classical style and was ill-disposed to serialism. But if the composer heard his guest's observation, he did not react to it. After lunch, at which conversation was in German, he showed Klemperer the first act of his new opera, *The Rake's Progress*. A week later Stravinsky wrote to his publisher in New York: 'Otto Klemperer – whom I met here a week ago – is so enthusiastic about the whole thing that I prefer to leave to him the conducting even for the première and give all my energies to the supervision of the rehearsals.'[2] The plan was soon abandoned. On 24 January 1951 Stravinsky agreed to conduct the première himself in Venice in the following September for the then huge fee of $20,000.* Meanwhile Klemperer's enthusiasm for the work had cooled.

To take advantage of Klemperer's brief stay in Los Angeles, a Bach concert was arranged at short notice at the University of California's Bovard Auditorium, where on 29 October he conducted a group of twenty-three players in a programme consisting of the Brandenburg Concertos Nos. 1, 3 and 5, and the Suite in B minor. The house was only half full, but Klemperer was warmly received. One critic commented on the change he seemed to have undergone since he had last conducted in Los Angeles three-and-a-half years earlier at the height of a manic phase: 'He is quieter and more considerate in rehearsals. To his commanding stature as a person and a musician there seems to have been added a very humane quality, which has seemingly grown as his physical powers have grown since his illness of a decade ago.'[3] Among those present were Stravinsky and Craft, who in his diary that evening wrote that, though the tempi were fast, 'at least this music, new in its time, does not sound artificially archaic'.

That evening Klemperer flew to Montreal for two pairs of concerts in what was still a musical outpost. It was all his New York agent could procure for him in North America. On arrival Klemperer questioned the manager, Pierre Béique, about the orchestra; Stravinsky, he said, had told him that it was so bad that he should not have accepted the engagement.[4] Les Concerts Symphoniques had indeed had a chequered history since it had been

---

* Vera Stravinsky and Robert Craft, *Igor Stravinsky in Pictures and Documents*, p. 407. According to Robert Craft (letter to the author, 3 May 1979), the payment was intended as an addition to the original commission fee and was paid to Stravinsky in this guise to obviate the need to share it with his librettists, W.H. Auden and Chester Kallman.

established in 1936. Only with the appointment in 1940 of the Belgian-born conductor Desiré Defauw as artistic director, had the orchestra been put on a regular footing with seasonal contracts for the players. By North American standards it was still a second-rate body, whose current lack of a musical director was reflected in slack discipline. Public interest was at a low ebb.

Klemperer's fears proved ill founded, however. From the first rehearsal he caught the players' imagination.[5] In a Beethoven concert on 31 October, they 'played beyond themselves and excitement spread ... like a charge of electricity', Eric McLean, the critic of the *Daily Star*, later recalled. 'In the unison scale passage which opens the triumphant presto finale of the Leonore overture [No. 3] Klemperer stepped right into the cello section, as though he would dig out the sound with his own two hands.'[6] After a second programme on 14 November McLean described the playing as more inspired than any he had experienced in the city.[7] Even Klemperer was satisfied. In a letter to his daughter he described the orchestra as 'very competent'.[8] Not surprisingly, he was invited to return in the following autumn.

*   *   *

Between engagements in Montreal, Klemperer went to New York, where he applied for an extension to the American passport that had been issued to him in Brussels in November 1948 and had now expired. The renewal was granted, but only for seven months. He would thus be obliged to return to America once he had completed his European engagements.

The State Department took the opportunity to pass his papers to the Federal Bureau of Investigation. Klemperer's name had already come to the FBI's attention in connection with his membership of the advisory board of a Musicians' Congress that had been held in Hollywood in February 1944 and been suspected of being a Communist front organisation.[9] In view of his deeply depressed condition at the time, the implication that he was involved in subversive activities bordered on the grotesque.* An even more extraordinary example of official paranoia had occurred in August 1946, when the German Ministry of Propaganda's dossier on Klemperer came to light in the ruins of occupied Berlin. On forwarding these papers to the FBI on 5 December, a State Department official raised the question of whether Goebbels's Ministry had not considered using Klemperer 'for propaganda work during the war period'. It is hard to conceive of a less probable hypothesis, yet it was taken seriously enough for Klemperer's dossier to be put before the Bureau's director, J. Edgar Hoover, with the suggestion that an

---

* These and other papers were subsequently made available under the US Freedom of Information and Privacy Acts. Their value is much reduced by the illegibility of much of the material and the many erasures made to protect sources of information.

inquiry be initiated. That within so short a period Klemperer should have come under suspicion of subversive activities on behalf of both the Nazi regime *and* the Communist International throws light on the confusion of mind reigning in some official circles even before the notorious Senator Joseph McCarthy had made his mark on the political scene. Thus Klemperer had come to be regarded with mistrust by the American authorities long before he blotted his copy-book in Budapest. On 17 November 1950 an inquiry into his activities was duly instigated. Its 'ostensible purpose' was described as 'passport security'.[10]

Meanwhile, with the outbreak of hostilities in Korea, the world seemed on the brink of global war and political attitudes hardened accordingly. Klemperer set out to restore his reputation by giving a stridently anti-Communist interview to a New York radio station that caused Lotte (who had remained in Hungary) considerable embarrassment when it was subsequently broadcast to Hungary by the Voice of America.[11] He turned down an invitation to conduct in Budapest, it was said, in protest against a Hungarian ban on several of its leading artists, including János Ferencsik, appearing in the United States.[12] He also began to worry about the possible repercussions in America of a commitment to conduct a new production of *Der Freischütz* that Felsenstein was staging after Christmas at the Komische Oper in East Berlin.

*　　　*　　　*

On 17 November Klemperer and Johanna flew to Paris, where for Vox he recorded Schubert's Symphony No. 4 ('an indescribably beautiful piece', he wrote to Lotte) with the Lamoureux Orchestra, and then four days later travelled to Brussels where he had concerts. The issue of where they should settle continued to dominate their minds and the decision increasingly seemed to hinge on the East Berlin engagement. The plans for *Der Freischütz* were already far advanced. Felsenstein himself was to direct, the sets were to be designed by Caspar Neher and Klemperer's participation had been announced. Earlier in the autumn Felsenstein had written to ask him for his metronome markings, adding, 'you cannot conceive of the expectation and misgiving with which our *Freischütz* is awaited'.[13] In an attempt to bind Klemperer to the Komische Oper, he not only held out the prospect of further collaborations, but offered to put the direction of the theatre's concert series in his hands.

The question of whether Klemperer should fulfil the engagement led to differences with Johanna. If Klemperer was anxious to distance himself from his earlier anti-American stance, the more Johanna saw of life in the West the less she liked it. She was also irritated by the way he continued to speak well of his years in Budapest in private, while attacking Communism in public.* In particular she jibbed at his readiness to jettison his commitment to the Komische Oper for no better reason than that it had become politically embarrassing. Why, she asked, should they not settle in Berlin; after all, Felsenstein lived in the West while working in the East.

In this instance, Klemperer showed a sharper awareness of the situation than Johanna. Unlike Klemperer, Felsenstein was not an American citizen, but an Austrian, and hence technically neutral. Nor did Felsenstein at that time also work in the West, as Klemperer had every intention of doing. The end of the Berlin blockade had not brought about a relaxation of tension in the city. On the contrary, by the winter of 1950–1 an effective ban on artists working on both sides of the city had come into existence.[14] Thus to conduct at the Komische Oper would be to risk becoming *persona non grata* in West Berlin and hence inevitably in the new German Federal Republic, as well as incurring American wrath.

The longer Klemperer delayed a decision, the more his innate caution asserted itself. 'Whether I conduct at the Komische Oper is still uncertain', he wrote to Lotte from Brussels on 22 November, only a week before he was due in Berlin. 'But I'm afraid I won't.' A chance engagement seems to have tipped the balance. Eduard van Beinum, Mengelberg's successor as principal conductor of the Concertgebouw Orchestra, was taken ill and Klemperer agreed to conduct his Amsterdam concerts in the second week of December, an engagement that clashed with his obligations to Felsenstein. On 29 November Klemperer flew to Berlin as planned, but the rehearsals for *Der Freischütz* started under another conductor.

Hardly had Klemperer arrived in Amsterdam than the Concertgebouw learnt that the conductor Rafael Kubelik would be unable to fulfil his commitments with the orchestra in January and February 1951, and Klemperer agreed to return for a further three weeks after Christmas. Altogether he was to work in the Netherlands for more than twelve weeks in the 1950–1 season. Yet, although Klemperer was by now less manic than he had been when he had conducted the Concertgebouw Beethoven cycle in 1949, he was not to repeat the success he had enjoyed on that occasion, at any rate so far as the Dutch critics were concerned.

The main work in his first concert on 10 December was *Das Lied von der Erde*, with the English contralto Kathleen Ferrier and the Dutch tenor

---

* The discrepancy between these attitudes was more understandable than Johanna allowed. Such sympathy as Klemperer had ever felt for Communism as practised by the Stalinist regimes of Eastern Europe had long since evaporated. In a letter to Helene Hirschler (18 March 1951) he was ready to admit that George Orwell's attack on Soviet totalitarianism in his novel *Nineteen Eighty-Four* was justified. In the same letter he referred to Ernst Bloch, who had moved to the German Democratic Republic, as being 'condemned' to live there. On the other hand he never ceased to be grateful for the conditions of work he had enjoyed in Budapest.

Frans Vroons as soloists.* It was a score with which he had always met with success, but on this occasion the press, with one exception, ventilated its dislike of the performance. *De Waarheid* pronounced it restless and agitated. The *Nieuwe Rotterdamsche Courant* was of the same opinion and criticised the choice of Klemperer as a replacement for van Beinum. Even the sober-minded Piet Tiggers in the *Algemeen Handelsblad* described it as overdriven and lacking in nuance. Bertus van Lier stood alone in praising an interpretation that had, he claimed, matched musical severity to an almost demonic intensity.[15] In Amsterdam, Klemperer's approach to Mahler came as an affront to critics raised on the more indulgent interpretations of Mengelberg, whose long association with the composer had caused his view of the music to be regarded as authoritative.

Three days later, the second of the programmes that Klemperer had taken over from van Beinum was no better received. It opened with an account of Schumann's Symphony No. 4 that was widely dismissed as fast and unfeeling. Nor, predictably, was Klemperer felt to be at his best in a performance of Poulenc's Piano Concerto with the composer as soloist. It was not his sort of music, as he made amply clear after the concert. Asked by a French diplomat how he had found the concerto, Klemperer called out to Peter Diamand, 'Sagen Sie, was heisst Scheisse auf französisch?' ('Tell me, what's shit in French?')[16] Poulenc, however, was clearly unaware of Klemperer's views. He gave him a score of his *Aubade*, inscribed 'pour monsieur Klemperer avec toute ma sympathie artistique'. To Matthijs Vermeulen, the idiosyncratic critic of *De groene Amsterdammer* (23 December), who was to lead the pack against Klemperer in the coming months, what his conducting above all lacked was colour. But even Vermeulen had to concede that the performance of the 'Jupiter' Symphony, which ended the concert, was masterly.

After a Christmas break in Berlin, where he recorded three Mozart symphonies for RIAS (Radio in the American Sector),† Klemperer returned to Amsterdam on 3 January 1951 for the series of concerts he had agreed to take over from Kubelik. By this time the Concertgebouw, however, was troubled by more than conductors' cancellations. In his search for replacements, its artistic director, Rudolf Mengelberg,‡ had invited Paul van Kempen to conduct two performances of Verdi's Requiem Mass on the fiftieth anniversary of the composer's death at the end of the month. Van Kempen was a controversial figure in Holland. Though Dutch-born, he had worked in

---

* The programme also contained Mozart's Piano Concerto in C major, K.503, which he had not previously conducted, but had taken over from van Beinum with the Dutch composer, Hans Henkemans as soloist.

† Nos. 25, 29 and 38. The two earlier works henceforth figured frequently in his programmes.

‡ Rudolf Mengelberg (1892–1959). German-born nephew of Willem Mengelberg, composer and from 1935 until 1954 artistic director of the Concertgebouw Orchestra.

Germany since 1916, had taken German citizenship in 1933 (of all years) and in the following year had been appointed conductor of the Dresden Philharmonic Orchestra. At the end of the war he had returned to Holland and attempted to reclaim his Dutch citizenship, which had still not been granted in 1951. Though van Kempen had been cleared politically and had since 1949 been chief conductor at the Dutch Radio at Hilversum, he had not hitherto appeared with the Concertgebouw and his engagement aroused a storm of protest. On 9 January the Communist *Waarheid* denounced the board, made up of an autonomous group of well-to-do burghers, for supporting 'collaborators'. There were stormy debates, both in Parliament and in the Amsterdam city council, where the Left enjoyed a majority, and ten days later the influential *Parool* joined the attack. In the *Groene Amsterdammer* Vermeulen also assailed what he described as Rudolf Mengelberg's policy of engaging German artists, among whom he instanced Klemperer.

The Concertgebouw players expressed opposition to the engagement of van Kempen, who was described as 'a controversial figure', though they did not at this stage refuse to play under him.[17] Klemperer had no need to enter the fray, and it might in any case have been expected that a man who, less than two years earlier, had appeared before an Amsterdam public wearing a decoration of the Hungarian People's Republic, would align himself with the forces of 'progress'. But, whatever his political sympathies, Klemperer had no time for democracy in the concert hall; in this respect he was very much a German conductor of the old school. Rudolf Mengelberg was in any case a friend whom Klemperer had known since he had first conducted the Concertgebouw Orchestra in 1929. Klemperer may also have been piqued by Vermeulen's attack on his own engagement. Whatever his motives, on 19 January he gave an interview to *De Telegraaf*, in which he criticised the campaign against Rudolf Mengelberg and deplored the way in which politics were being brought into artistic matters: 'In short, I think it is ridiculous when artistic life is disturbed by party politics.'

The intervention was to cast a shadow over Klemperer's relationship with certain elements in the orchestra. He had, however, left Amsterdam by 28 January, when noisy demonstrations interrupted van Kempen's performance of the Requiem and members of the orchestra left the platform. After they had refused to return, they were dismissed forthwith.[18] The dispute was soon settled, but in the course of negotiations, in which both the government and the city council took part, it was agreed that the powers of the board would at the end of the 1951–2 season be vested in a new foundation, on which both the State and the players would be represented.[19] Rudolf Mengelberg was obliged to resign.

* * *

A SEA OF TROUBLES

14   Klemperer in Rome, early 1950s

On 10 February 1951, Klemperer arrived in Rome to begin rehearsals for a production of *Fidelio* he was to stage as well as conduct. Three days later he withdrew. There had already been difficulties over the scenery, which the Rome Opera proposed to borrow from the Scala.* He therefore arrived

---

* On 19 December 1950 Klemperer had written to ask Tóth to send photographs or sketches of the sets by Oláh that were in use in Budapest to Rome as an example of what he had in mind. He had also submitted sketches by Casper Neher that remained unacknowledged (letters to Fritz Fischer and Nelly Failoni, 11 and 12 January 1951).

with reservations about the entire undertaking and these were reinforced when, at his first piano rehearsal, he encountered in Christel Goltz a singer who, as he later put it, 'incorporated an interpretation of the role of Fidelio that musically and spiritually was completely opposed to mine'.[20] An immediate cause of tension was her insistence that her husband (who was also her singing teacher) be present at the piano rehearsals. The breach came when Klemperer took exception to her rendering of 'Abscheulicher', whereupon Goltz observed, 'You bring *me* something new and I bring *you* something new.'[21] Klemperer withdrew from the production. A year later, as if in justification of his action, he wrote to Tóth, 'Nothing is so hateful to me as the modern prima donna opera conductor. However opera is a unity ... [and] the conductor must be the pulse of the whole undertaking.'[22] Such was the principle that had prevailed at the Kroll Oper, but it was to prove increasingly hard to realise in the post-war world. Asked whether he had deserted opera, he bleakly replied, 'No. It has deserted me.'[23] A decade was to pass before he conducted in an opera house again.

With free time on his hands, Klemperer took the opportunity to make his first visit to Israel and on 15 February he cabled his younger sister, Marianne Joseph, to announce his arrival on the following day. On the morning of his departure for Jerusalem, Klemperer, accompanied by Johanna and Lotte, had another audience with Pope Pius XII, who asked him how old he was. Sixty-five, replied Klemperer. 'That's nothing', said the Pope, 'I am already seventy-four.' Johanna, who had been very quiet, suddenly spoke up. 'You wouldn't think it', she told the supreme pontiff. 'You look much younger. But then men with strong features like you and my husband always look much younger.' Klemperer was touched and amused by the spontaneity and unaffectedness of her remarks and often recalled them in later years.[24] Once in Israel, he learnt of the existence of the 35-man orchestra which the Israeli Radio maintained in Jerusalem and at once expressed a desire to hear it. As its standard of playing was not high, efforts were made to dissuade him, but he was not to be put off. An official of the Radio, Shabtai Petrushka, went to visit him at his hotel.

> Upon entering his ... room, I found him busy writing music. I introduced myself and he remarked that he was just composing a mass, adding point-blank, almost challengingly: 'You probably know that I am a Catholic. Does this disturb you?' 'Not at all', I replied. 'Good', he continued, 'but I am a Zionist. Does this strike you as paradoxical?' 'No', I answered, 'I know of quite a few Christian Zionists: Balfour, Churchill, Wingate ...' This he dismissed with: 'Oh, these eccentric English ...'[25]

The next morning Klemperer attended a rehearsal of the orchestra. After conducting it for a few minutes, he declared that he would like to give a concert. A Mozart programme was hastily arranged, which Klemperer conducted twice in Tel Aviv as well as in Jerusalem. Marianne, who had not seen her beloved brother for eighteen years, was overjoyed about the visit. 'It was unbelievably marvellous', she wrote after his departure. 'Otto ... felt *very* happy here and everything stood under a good star. The concerts were completely improvised, the orchestra ... played as though bewitched.'[26]

* * *

The introduction of the long-playing record in America had led to a boom in sales,* and earlier in the year George de Mendelssohn-Bartholdy had written to urge Klemperer to undertake a series of recordings which, he claimed, would not only prove more financially rewarding than concerts, but would help to restore his reputation in the United States.[27] Klemperer agreed to embark on the project and, shortly after his return from Israel, travelled to Vienna, where he began with the 'Pastoral' Symphony, which was completed within five hours. The *Missa solemnis*, Bruckner's Fourth Symphony and Mahler's *Das Lied von der Erde* followed. The orchestra was the Vienna Symphony Orchestra.

On 24 March 1951, Klemperer returned to Amsterdam for a further series of concerts with the Concertgebouw Orchestra. Two days earlier Willem Mengelberg had died in exile in Switzerland at the age of almost eighty. He may have been politically disgraced, but for more than half a century he had been the dominant figure in Dutch musical life. For Klemperer, he was above all the conductor who more than any other had championed Mahler's music during the composer's lifetime. On the morning of 31 March he accordingly attended a Requiem Mass in memory of the dead conductor, though he clattered out in mid-service, apparently bored by the address.[28] That afternoon he conducted a memorial concert at the Concertgebouw. The programme included the *Abschied* from *Das Lied von der Erde* and the 'Eroica' Symphony. Once more, Klemperer's artistic allegiances had taken precedence over political issues.

Klemperer remained in Amsterdam until the first week of May. There were times when he goaded the orchestra beyond endurance. Yet to some of its leading members it was as though he had only to stand before them for their playing to be transformed. The source of his fascination was hard to explain. 'It bordered on the mystical how an aura suddenly settled over the orchestra and the hall', Karl Schouten later recalled. 'I am a sober man and have constantly asked myself how this was possible. I observed him very intensively. What I saw before me was this magician with his big, clumsy movements and his dark, burning eyes.'[29]

Criticism of Klemperer persisted, however. Some of his failures can be

---

* LPs had been introduced by CBS in June 1948, but only started to replace 78s after Victor belatedly followed suit in January 1950.

attributed to the fact that he had been persuaded by Rudolf Mengelberg to take over works programmed by other conductors. Besides the Poulenc concerto, they included Bartók's Viola Concerto, which Klemperer gave for the only time in his career (with William Primrose as soloist), and Falla's *Nights in the Gardens of Spain*, which was widely felt to lack Spanish atmosphere. Many critics found his concerts uneven in quality. The Dutch composer Marius Flothuis recalled a superb account of a Mozart symphony that was followed by a performance of *Tod und Verklärung* so rough and ready that it was hard to believe that they had been conducted by the same man.* Van Lier similarly described Klemperer as a 'showery' conductor, meaning that he was as unpredictable as the spring weather.[30] Other critics were harsher, none more so than Vermeulen. Why, he asked, had Klemperer so often been invited to stand in for other conductors, why had he been allowed to conduct an occasion such as the Mengelberg memorial concert – and why had it contained no Dutch music? Not only was Klemperer past his best, his presence did not harmonise with the policies which the Concertgebouw Orchestra should pursue in the future.[31]

There were evenings at which Klemperer received great ovations. But Amsterdam's critics, used to the highest standards of orchestral playing, were less tolerant than their counterparts in Budapest of the lapses that were liable to occur in a manic phase.† In particular the Beethoven cycle of 1951 met a more mixed reaction in the press than had that of two years earlier. He was still far from commanding the veneration he later came to enjoy in Holland.

After his six weeks' stint in Amsterdam Klemperer returned to Vienna on 12 May, where he immediately embarked on more recording sessions, beginning with Mahler's 'Resurrection' Symphony. As the fortieth anniversary of the composer's death fell on 18 May, Klemperer persuaded Mendelssohn to mount a public performance in the Musikverein. There was much wry comment in the press that it had been left to a small American recording company to promote a concert in memory of a composer who had played so prominent a role in the city's musical life and whose own music was so deeply rooted in the Viennese symphony. Even so, the hall was far from full and the critics in the main were dubious of the music's value. Roland Tenschert, for one, thought that the gap between Mahlerian nostalgia and the modern world was unbridgeable.[32] There were, however, no such reservations about the performance. Klemperer, wrote Peter Lafitte in the *Wiener Kurier* (19 May), was less at home than Walter in the Schubertian second movement, but elsewhere had shown himself to be his equal as a Mahlerian. Klemperer was deeply stirred by the occasion. 'It was quite shattering', he wrote to Helene

---

* Interview with Philo Bregstein, *c*. 1972. The symphony was probably No. 29 in A, which preceded Strauss's work at a concert in The Hague on 21 April 1951.
† It seems that the manic phase which was declining in the autumn of 1950 flared up in the spring of the following year.

Hirschler a week later, 'when one reflects ... on what happened to Mahler during his period as opera director and how he stuck it [here] for ten years. The Habsburgs treated him well; they sensed who he was. What drove him out was the hostility of the mediocre. Even today these people are our *true* enemies.'[33]

Less than two months later, on 11, 12 and 14 July at the Holland Festival, Klemperer again conducted the 'Resurrection' Symphony, in performances to mark Mahler's anniversary. The rehearsals were stormy. Kathleen Ferrier, who was also the soloist in the performances of *Kindertotenlieder* that preceded the symphony and who had not yet fully recovered from an operation for the cancer that was to end her life less than two years later, found the going rough. 'I hate to work with Klemperer', she wrote. 'I find he shouts like a madman ... Perhaps his Mahler comes off sometimes, because he wastes no time nor sentiment – but ohh!!!! whattaman!!'[34] On this occasion the performances indeed 'came off'. Their impact was overwhelming and undoubtedly contributed to the revival of interest in Mahler's music that was to gather momentum in the course of the fifties.*

*   *   *

On 3 May 1951 the official opening of the Royal Festival Hall marked the first stage of the development of London's South Bank as an arts centre. It was also regarded as a key event in the Festival of Britain, whose purpose was to celebrate the country's post-war reconstruction. The Arts Council organised a seven-week series of concerts in the hall featuring all the main British orchestras. The programmes included a liberal sprinkling of British works. For the Philharmonia Orchestra's two concerts Walter Legge had originally intended to engage George Szell as conductor with Artur Schnabel as soloist. Szell turned out to be unavailable, however, and, according to Legge, Herbert von Karajan proved to be unacceptable to the Festival's organisers as his replacement.[35] It was at this point that, on the suggestion of Schnabel, Klemperer was engaged.

Over the years *The Times* had been distinctly sparing in its praise of Klemperer, but its anonymous critic was full of enthusiasm for his first concert, an all-Beethoven concert:

> Rare indeed are the occasions when great music is allied to a performance that can claim to have taken its measure fully and unquestionably ...
>
> If a single unison chord may be said to foretell the course of things to come, it was Mr Klemperer's sustained F at the opening of the *Egmont* overture. From this to the glorious C major ending of the fifth symphony there was not a moment when tension sagged ...

---

* The performance of 12 July 1951 was broadcast and later released both on LP and CD by Decca.

> Mr Klemperer's grasp of the music's innermost significance was evident from the perfect fusion he achieved of its dramatic, epic and lyrical elements. Here, indeed, is a musician whose emotional intensity is wonderfully matched by an impressive intellectual force ... And rarely has a conductor made so few movements to so great effect.[36]

Schnabel had had to withdraw because of illness and Myra Hess played the 'Emperor' Concerto in his place. It was, said *The Times*, 'one of the great moments of her career'. Klemperer may have had doubts about Hess in the past, but on this occasion he was delighted by her performance, which, he told Aladár Tóth, reminded him of Eugen d'Albert, whom he had heard play the concerto 'particularly beautifully' at the turn of the century.[37]

Klemperer's second Festival of Britain programme, on 29 June, was to have included the Enigma Variations, but he got cold feet and decided that he would conduct the 'Jupiter' Symphony instead. It was not that he disliked Elgar's work – he knew it well, for he had conducted it in America. Simply, he felt that he could do more justice to the 'Jupiter' on what was, after all, an important occasion for him. The Arts Council was most put out, though it could hardly accuse Klemperer of anti-British bias, since he was opening the programme with Walton's *Scapino* Overture. There was, however, a general feeling of resentment that he should have refused to conduct a favourite British score. Frank Howes, chairman of the Arts Council's music panel, insisted that Klemperer should make a statement through the Council explaining his actions.[38] This Klemperer did, but instead of giving the real reason for the substitution, he claimed that he had made it because the dry acoustic of the new hall was 'not so well suited to the sonorities of Elgar's masterpiece'. When *The Times* printed the statement two days before the concert, Howes, now wearing his other cap as the paper's chief music critic, added a footnote to it, in which he rebuked Klemperer for presuming 'too much on the tolerance of the British public'.* Howes's intervention provoked a good deal of finger-wagging from his more complacent colleagues. 'Manners, manners, Herr Klemperer!' chided Richard Capell, the senior critic of the *Daily Telegraph*.[39] Had not Klemperer on occasions been compelled to perform works in less than ideal circumstances, Capell asked, as when he had conducted *Figaro* in a theatre as large as the Kroll or Stravinsky's Symphony in Three Movements in the over-resonant Albert Hall? 'As for Klemperer's Elgar, we have probably lost little or nothing. He was always a dry conductor, best suited by Hindemith and the like.' To its credit, however, *The*

---

* Howes chose to ignove the fact that the Variations had been given in the concert series already, by Barbirolli on 25 May. Klemperer had known of Barbirolli's performance for some time (letter to Klemperer from Johanna, Bad Ischl, 24 April 1951), which may have been another reason why he felt justified in not conducting it himself. Howes (1891–1974), a champion of British music of the early twentieth century, was chief music critic of *The Times* from 1943 to 1960 and exercised much influence behind the scenes.

Times quickly forgot its hostility over the programme change. The performance of the 'Jupiter' Symphony, said its critic, 'glowed with exhilarating vigour ... Dr Klemperer's headlong pace in the finale lent excitement to the momentous contrapuntal argument, since it was brilliantly, responsively, played.'[40]

Walter Legge did not attend the first of the Festival of Britain concerts and arrived at the second in time only to catch the finale of the 'Jupiter' from the wings. But what he heard was sufficient to transform his attitude. At least one member of his orchestra was similarly impressed. As Marie Wilson passed Legge on leaving the platform, she put her hands on his shoulders and said, 'I feel like a tart, taking money from you for making music with a man like that.'[41]

By 1951 Legge had established a unique position in British musical life. He was running the Philharmonia Orchestra as a personal fiefdom and, with Herbert von Karajan as principal conductor, was in the process of turning it into an exceptionally fine instrument. Simultaneously, as artistic manager of Columbia Records,* he had taken advantage of the collapse of the German recording industry after the war to engage almost every Central European artist of note, including some who were still prohibited from appearing in public on account of their Nazi affiliations.[42] But Legge was more than a tycoon with a nose for quality. He played a crucial role in the recordings made by his artists, including those of his wife, Elisabeth Schwarzkopf, and more than any other man was responsible for establishing the producer as a key figure in the recording studio. As he himself liked to put it, his role was that of 'a musical midwife'. By these means he built up a catalogue of recordings unequalled in their time in Europe. His two spheres of activity were complementary. His prominent position in the recording industry enabled him to procure contracts for his orchestra that assured its financial viability (as long as Legge remained at its head the Philharmonia received no public subsidies), while EMI benefited from the availability in London of an orchestra of international calibre.

Legge combined a flair for business with sharp ears and a sense of quality that deserted him only in the field of twentieth-century music, where his tastes were philistine. A waspish tongue, autocratic ways and a high opinion of his own talents ('I have nothing to be modest about') did not make him popular. He was, however, a more sensitive, even emotional man than he appeared to the outside world. Partly because of his abrasive manner, he remained an outsider in British musical life. But he was a man of power. A contract to record with Legge was a passport to an international reputation.

On the day after the second Festival Hall concert Legge invited

---

* One of EMI's two major classical labels (the other being His Master's Voice). Not to be confused with its American rival, CBS (Columbia Broadcasting Systems).

Klemperer and Johanna to dinner at his house in Hampstead. A car was ordered to take the guests home at 10.30 p.m., but when the hour arrived Klemperer, hugely entertained by the often scurrilous brilliance of his host's conversation, declined to leave. Johanna curled up on a sofa and slept while the two men talked until 4.30 a.m. Four hours later, the telephone rang by Legge's bedside. It was Klemperer. 'Since you turned me out while I was in the middle of a sentence', he chided, 'I want now to finish what I was saying.'[43]

The spark that had been struck never developed into friendship. Much though he had enjoyed the evening, Klemperer was irritated by Legge's airy dismissal of the artistic policies he had pursued at the Kroll Oper; his mistake, Legge informed him, had been to perform so much new music. There was also something about the man himself that aroused mistrust. On the way home, as he later recalled, he observed to Johanna, 'That is a very dangerous man. He knows a lot, yes. But he is dangerous.'*

That Klemperer's standing in the musical world at the time was modest is illustrated by the fees paid to conductors at the 1951 Holland Festival: Stokowski received 2,500 florins, Kubelik 2,000, Szell 1,250, Klemperer 1,000.[44] Legge lost no time in engaging him to conduct two concerts with the Philharmonia Orchestra during the next season. He also recommended him to EMI, but did not suggest that he should record for Columbia. Instead, it was agreed that he would 'try to get Klemperer for popular repertory on HMV Plum',[45] a cheap label reserved for artists with limited drawing power.

The offer was less than flattering, but Johanna was delighted. As part of what was then Europe's largest recording concern, His Master's Voice represented a big step up from the diminutive Vox. Klemperer himself was uncomfortable. He was still under contract to Mendelssohn, who had paid him substantial advances. He also felt disinclined to break with a man who had enabled him to make recordings at a time when no one else had shown any interest in doing so and now had more ambitious plans for the future.†
What he hoped for was that EMI and Vox would be able to reach what he described as 'a gentleman's agreement'.[46]

In August 1951 it was agreed that Legge would send him an exclusive three-year contract, but a week later Johanna wrote to tell Lotte that it had not yet arrived. Legge later claimed that Klemperer had proved reluctant to proceed on account of 'the moral obligation' he felt towards Mendelssohn. Whatever the reason, the matter had not advanced by the time that Klemperer and Johanna set out later in the month on a South American tour.

* When this observation was published (Heyworth (ed.), *Conversations*, p. 105) in 1973, Legge was deeply offended. He held Heyworth responsible as editor and on that ground henceforth declined to discuss Klemperer with him.
† These included a number of classical symphonies to be recorded with the Berlin Philharmonic Orchestra (letter from Mendelssohn to Klemperer, New York, 3 July 1951). It is far from clear how a company with such limited resources would have been able to engage so prestigious an orchestra.

15   Klemperer, Johanna and Werner, early 1950s

Before leaving Europe, Klemperer attended the funeral in Switzerland of Artur Schnabel, who had died on 15 August. He wrote to Schnabel's widow: 'With Artur there departs not only a great artist and a great human being who was close to us, but one of the last representatives of an entire generation that is slowly disappearing.'[47] Schoenberg had died a month earlier at the age of seventy-six. 'The circle around me grows steadily smaller', he wrote gloomily to Lotte on 27 August. Fritz Busch's sudden death on 14 September must have come as yet another loss. Klemperer conducted a concert in his memory in Buenos Aires. From Argentina he travelled by ship to Venezuela. Such engagements, which involved much wearisome travel and work with indifferent orchestras, provided little satisfaction. But he badly needed the money they earned. Only in August 1951 had Johanna been able to settle Swiss hotel bills incurred four years earlier.

At the end of the tour Klemperer and Johanna flew to New York, where they arrived on 12 October 1951. On the following morning Klemperer flew on alone to Montreal. Owing to a misunderstanding, Pierre Béique, the manager of Les Concerts Symphoniques, was not at the airport to meet him. Before taking a taxi into town, Klemperer went to buy some pipe cleaners. On leaving the shop, he missed his step and fell heavily. At the Royal Victoria Hospital, where he was taken in great pain, an X-ray examination revealed that he had fractured the neck of his left femur. In the course of a five-hour operation on 16 October a Smith-Petersen nail and plate was hammered into position. Breathing difficulties necessitated a bronchoscopy to clear the blocked air passages.[48] By the end of the month Klemperer was eating well and in general surprisingly good-humoured, though he was confined to a wheelchair. The surgeon had made it plain that he would be unable to work until the spring.

While in hospital Klemperer learnt with astonishment that among the recordings Vox had issued that autumn under his name in America was one of Mendelssohn's 'Scottish' Symphony. He had indeed embarked on such a recording, but had left it uncompleted on leaving for a Greek tour with the Vienna Symphony Orchestra on 13 June and had not subsequently returned to Vienna. In an angry letter he told George de Mendelssohn-Bartholdy that the recording represented 'a gross public deception' and demanded its instant withdrawal.[49] Mendelssohn conceded that the objection was valid and agreed to withdraw the record (which he did not do).* But he insisted that Klemperer had only himself to blame for what had occurred.

> As you will recall, I was in Vienna when you had finished in one session . . . the complete first movement . . . I left with the understanding that the following week . . . an additional session would be set up to complete the Scotch [sic] Symphony, particularly . . . as you had actually rehearsed . . . the second movement. It never occurred to me that you would refuse to finish the recording . . . without telling me a single word about it . . . It was therefore quite natural for me to assume that you yourself had continued to finish the recording.

Only when he returned to Vienna, Mendelssohn continued, had he discovered, quite by chance, that the recording had been finished, not by Klemperer, but by the Austrian conductor Herbert Haefner.†

Meanwhile, prompted by the generally favourable reviews that the Vox recordings had received in America, Legge belatedly sent Klemperer a draft contract. It offered ten recording sessions a year over a period of two years. The works to be recorded were to be selected by EMI, which would exercise exclusive rights over Klemperer as a recording artist. This last condition troubled him in view of the obligation he continued to feel towards Mendelssohn. But his scruples vanished when, within days of receiving Legge's contract, he learnt of the deception that Mendelssohn had practised in the matter

---

* Still attributed to Klemperer, it remained on sale for a number of years.
† Letter from George de Mendelssohn-Bartholdy, New Haven, 15 November 1951. Thirty-five years later, Mendelssohn presented a materially different version of events, according to which it was he himself who, in Klemperer's presence and with his active approval, had completed the slow movement. Haefner had then recorded the remainder of the work with Klemperer similarly at his side (letter to the author, New York, 9 December 1986). Mendelssohn died in 1988 before the author had an opportunity to confront him with the discrepancies between his two versions of what had taken place. Mendelssohn also failed to explain how it came about that a recording issued under Klemperer's name did not include the cut he invariably made in the finale.

of the 'Scottish' Symphony. By 18 November Legge was able to inform EMI that he was in negotiations with Klemperer. But they did not reach agreement easily. Klemperer insisted that soloists should only be engaged with his consent. Legge wanted a change in one clause because, as he put it, 'There is always the danger that K may have a recurrence of his old malady ... it may take the form of violent insanity or complete paralysis',[50] an illuminating example of the wild rumours about Klemperer current at this period of his life, even among well-disposed associates. Only on 10 May 1952 did Klemperer finally sign on the dotted line.

*   *   *

During the long period of hospitalisation books were, as ever, a solace, and Klemperer's reading extended from St Augustine and Pascal to Dickens and Fontane. He also took the opportunity to acquaint himself with recent compositions. He found Bartók's Concerto for Orchestra 'good, if not overwhelming', which may account for his failure to perform it. More predictably, Prokofiev's recently published Symphony No. 6 failed to appeal. No new work so preoccupied him as *The Rake's Progress*, which earlier that autumn had had its première in Venice. The more he studied the vocal score, the more his reservations grew. 'I don't at all reproach ... the way Stravinsky's music borrows from earlier styles. I just find his *ideas* in this respect too thin', he wrote to Fritz Fischer. He was particularly critical of the libretto. 'I cannot understand how a musician like Stravinsky ... could have composed such a concoction.' Indeed, his earlier enthusiasm for Stravinsky, the contemporary composer he had so long felt closest to, seemed to be on the wane. He had already confessed to Fritz Fischer that he had begun to feel equivocal about the Symphony in Three Movements and later in the year he was to turn down the Concertgebouw Orchestra's request that he include the *Symphony of Psalms* in his programmes. There had always been an element of ambivalence in Klemperer's attitude to contemporary music. 'You know what I would most like to conduct', he confessed to Fischer wistfully. 'Just Bach and Mozart.'[51]

The tedium of his days was broken by occasional visitors. Among them were Joseph Szigeti and the Montreal critic Eric McLean, who brought scores. On 24 November, the violinist Henri Temianka and four colleagues performed Schubert's C major String Quintet in his room. Another discovery was Mozart's Clarinet Quintet. But his convalescence went less smoothly than had been expected. In December 1951, and again in the following month, he suffered from bouts of pleurisy and pneumonia that yielded only slowly to repeated courses of antibiotics and left him weak. He also started to suffer from acute stomach pains that eluded diagnosis. Could they, Lotte wondered, be due to anxiety about the heavy medical expenses he was incurring at a time when his only earnings were the royalties on his Vox recordings? Though these amounted to $5,900 in 1951, they were insufficient to cover his debts to Mendelssohn. On 27 January 1952 while suffering from a recurrence of the lung infection that had necessitated yet another course of antibiotics, he described himself to Fritz Fischer as 'comme ci, comme ça'. It was an expression he sometimes used to indicate to close friends that all was not well in his psyche and, little more than a month later, Lotte informed Helene Hirschler that, though physically much better, 'he is somewhat depressed, very disheartened and sees the present as well as the future in the bleakest light'.[52]

The depression was not to be compared in intensity with the one he had endured between 1942 and 1946, but inactivity exacerbated it. Of the handful of offers he received, all he felt able to accept were two pairs of concerts in Montreal, and even they gave rise to difficulties. Only after a trial rehearsal did he finally agree to conduct the opening concert on 22 April 1952, for it required a huge effort of will for him to confront an orchestra and to communicate his wishes.[53] These were torments he had braved in past depressions, but there was now the added indignity of having to appear on crutches. To spare him embarrassment, a curtain in front of the platform was raised only after he had seated himself before the orchestra. Once he started to conduct, however, his fears left him, and the Montreal critics were unanimous in saying that the concert was every bit as good as the one he had given eighteen months earlier.

The following morning Klemperer learnt to his sorrow of the death of Elisabeth Schumann, to whom he had spoken on the telephone only a few days earlier. Apart from Johanna, no woman had been closer to him. It was not the only event to lower his spirits. He suffered a recurrence of prostate trouble, and a urologist incorrectly diagnosed malignancy and recommended an operation, pending which he put Klemperer on regular doses of female sex hormones as a means of containing the condition. These, however, had the effect of deepening his depression. Then, in early May 1952, Johanna, who had been in poor health herself for the past year, suffered a coronary spasm and found herself unable to hold a glass. The disability had righted itself by the following morning, but she had suffered a slight stroke. The strains of the past twelve years were indeed beginning to take their toll; henceforth she tired easily and was never really well.

Once Klemperer had been discharged from hospital the question arose of where the family, which had been living out of suitcases since leaving Budapest, was to live during his convalescence. Los Angeles was out of the question; the house there was let and he had in any case come to loathe the place. New York was expensive and oppressively hot in summer. In Montreal there were doctors and physiotherapists familiar with his case and he was on good terms with the orchestra. An inexpensive flat with a large terrace that provided an area in which he could practise walking on crutches was accordingly rented for six months.

Klemperer's only other engagement for the remainder of the season was to conduct the Chicago Symphony Orchestra in a series of eight concerts at its annual alfresco summer festival at Ravinia Park. Again he appeared on crutches and sat throughout the performances. There was only one rehearsal for each programme and at first the Chicago players seemed coolly disposed towards him. However, the opening concert on 22 July, which included the 'Eroica' Symphony, won an enthusiastic reaction in the press, and the success grew from evening to evening. At the final concert, which ended with a series of orchestral excerpts from *Lohengrin, Tristan* and *Die Meistersinger*, the players joined in the audience's ovation. On 7 August Lotte wrote to Ernst and Lilly Toch, 'I have *never* heard my father conduct so splendidly.' It was a remarkable achievement for a man still so physically handicapped that he had difficulty even in turning to acknowledge applause.

Meanwhile problems had begun to arise over the recording contract he had signed a few months earlier with EMI. Because orchestral players in the United States were paid at far higher rates than their counterparts overseas, an increasing number of American companies, of which Vox was one, had taken to recording in Europe. The American Federation of Musicians determined to protect its members from this threat and in June 1952 its president, James C. Petrillo, forbade his members to conduct 'foreign-staffed orchestras'.[54] Lotte appealed to the union for her father's exemption on the grounds that his EMI contract pre-dated the ban. But on 21 August Petrillo himself informed her that 'the Federations's restriction on foreign records is in full effect. Members of the Federation will not be permitted to make records with foreign musicians.'

Aware that if he did not abide by the union's ruling, he would be unable to perform in the United States and Canada, Klemperer wrote to ask Legge for what he termed 'a friendly solution' of his contract.[55] To his dismay, Legge reacted in a manner that was anything but friendly. He pointed out that Klemperer was by no means the only artist to be affected by 'this dictatorial fiat', warned that he would regard any attempt to break the contract as 'actionable' and referred the matter to EMI's legal department.[56] There wiser counsels prevailed.[57]

Apart from five further pairs of concerts in Montreal,* where he was still living, and isolated guest appearances in Quebec and Toronto, Klemperer had no other engagements that autumn. Meanwhile the prospects of his being

---

* At the second pair, on 28/29 October 1952, the 27-year-old Pierre Boulez, on his first visit to North America, was present in the audience. Thirty-six years later he recalled the intensity that Klemperer radiated in spite of his immobility (Philo Bregstein, interview with Boulez, *L'Orchestre*, May 1988).

able to embark on a European tour in January 1953 had improved. Supported by a single stick in the place of crutches, he could now walk short distances on his own. Because his passport had expired a year earlier he applied at the American consulate in Montreal on 4 November 1952 for an extension to it.* He could hardly have chosen a more unfavourable moment. On the very same day the Republicans won the Presidency with a sweeping majority after an interval of twenty years. Hitherto the Democrat President Truman had vetoed much of the more extreme anti-Communist legislation passed by a Republican Congress. Now Truman had been defeated in the election by General Eisenhower.

After Klemperer made the application, a long silence ensued. 'We still haven't got our passport extension, although it should have arrived long ago, which makes me particularly nervous', wrote Lotte to Ernst Toch on 5 December. Three days later the consul-general in Montreal was informed by Washington that 'passport facilities' for Klemperer, his wife and daughter had not been approved. Furthermore they were cautioned that, if they failed to return to the United States by midnight, 23 December 1952, they stood to lose their American citizenship. Though the Montreal apartment had been rented until the middle of January, they were obliged to move to New York, where they took a small apartment in a cheap West Side hotel.

The shortness of the passport extensions he had been granted since leaving Hungary should have warned Klemperer of possible trouble. He was in any case aware that naturalised citizens were obliged periodically to resume American residence if they were to retain American citizenship. But, as he explained to his sister Marianne,

> Of course we knew that one couldn't be away for longer than five years. But that wasn't taken so literally and, particularly in the case of artists, quite short stays were sufficient to enable one to leave again for a longer period. At least that was our impression. But now, owing to a new law (the Immigration and Nationality Act)† which is retrospective, everything is taken very precisely. The expression 'continuous residence' has a new legal interpretation. Thus my absence from the States is considered to date from 1946 – long beyond the permitted time.[58]

On arrival in New York on 16 December 1952, Lotte made a sworn statement that, though the house in Los Angeles had been let since 1948, the family had maintained it as their American residence. But that cut no ice with Mrs R.D. Shipley, director of the Passport Office, who on 14 January 1953 informed her

---

* Originally issued in November 1950, it had on 24 April 1951 been extended for a further six months by the US consulate in Amsterdam.

† The notorious McCarran/Walter Bill had been passed by the Republican Congress on 11 June 1952. Vetoed by President Truman, it had been passed again by Congress with the two-thirds majority necessary to overrule the President and came into force on 24 December 1952, two weeks *after* it was applied to Klemperer on 8 December.

that 'evidence has not been submitted to this Department that would indicate that your cases would come within the scope of any of the exceptions of the law mentioned'.

The repercussions were far-reaching. For the second time in fifteen months a foreign tour had to be cancelled at short notice. More serious still, there was now no question of Klemperer being able to fulfil his EMI contract, which was already jeopardised by Petrillo's campaign to prevent American conductors from recording in Europe. He felt obliged to ask Legge to release him from it so as to be free to record in the United States in the unlikely event of his being invited to do so. As an interim solution Legge agreed on 6 March to postpone for twelve months the date on which the contract would enter into effect.

For much of the time Klemperer sat in his dark, shabby apartment, reading and studying scores. Occasionally, he visited his elder sister, Regi, now widowed. From time to time he attended rehearsals. But he was hard to please. When Bruno Walter made a characteristically broad rallentando at the entry of the second subject in the 'Haffner' Symphony's first movement, he whispered loudly 'Warum?' ('Why?')[59] In February he attended two rehearsals of *The Rake's Progress*, which was receiving its American première at the Metropolitan Opera under Fritz Reiner. Though Klemperer sent Stravinsky a telegram for the first night, 14 February, wishing him 'all success for your great opera' and subsequently claimed to have been 'deeply impressed by the last act',[60] three months later he told Fritz Fischer that the rehearsals he had attended had only confirmed the disappointing impression he had had from the score, adding, 'I am very sorry that the work says nothing to me.'[61]

To old acquaintances like Lotte Lenya he was so distant that, when they met at the dress rehearsal, he appeared not to recognise her.[62] As always in depressive periods, he presented a bleak and remote face to the outside world. He was also bereft of all motivation and power of decision. 'Frankly ... I don't want to appear any more in public', he wrote on 4 February to Micha May. That was more than a passing whim. On 5 June Regi reported to her sister that she had only with great difficulty been able to dissuade him from cancelling such few engagements as he had.

It was at about this time that another acquaintance, the actress Käthe Schröder,* wrote to Furtwängler to ask his help in finding Klemperer a position in Germany. The suggestion did not fall on fruitful ground. In his reply of 19 June 1953, Furtwängler wrote,

> I have followed Klemperer's activities with constant concern in recent years. Earlier, and especially as a young man, I had a good personal contact with him,

---

* Käthe Schröder-Aufrichtig (?–1980). Actress and theatre critic who with her Jewish husband emigrated to Rome, where she died. She seems to have known Klemperer during his years in Cologne.

> which with the passage of time became weaker. Recently I haven't seen him at all.
>
> Through his clear Communist sympathies he has unfortunately made things harder for himself in West Germany than they were already through the effects of his illness. And I fear that in West Germany, whose confines are so narrow and in which our own musicians no longer find anything like the scope that they did formerly, there is little [Furtwängler crossed out the 'no' he had earlier dictated] place for a man like Klemperer, who has for so long been abroad, even if as an artist he may still have much credit.
>
> Life, particularly professionally, is today ... harder for us 'old ones', because to the change of generations must be added the change of entire classes and political upheavals.
>
> For my part, I will gladly again look round in Germany, though, as I have said, as far as I know the ground I am sceptical.

Furtwängler clearly considered his colleague to have no special claim to sympathy in Germany. It does not seem to have occurred to him that Klemperer's long absence from the country of his birth had not been voluntary. None too subtly, he indicated that his primary concern was the difficulties that the aftermath of the war had brought German musicians such as himself. If Furtwängler, who was well placed to procure engagements with the Berlin Philharmonic Orchestra and the Salzburg Festival, ever 'looked around' on Klemperer's behalf, no trace of it has come to light.

* * *

Meanwhile, American engagements had proved hard to secure in mid-season, especially for a conductor with a reputation for erratic behaviour, and Klemperer's only work during the first seven months of 1953 was a handful of concerts in Chicago, Pittsburgh and Montreal, and a return visit to Ravinia in July. After Ravinia, where he was irked by the lack of rehearsal and failed to repeat the success he had enjoyed there twelve months earlier, he and Johanna travelled to Los Angeles, which at least provided a refuge from the New York summer. It also presented an opportunity for him to consult Dr Ziskind, whom he had not seen since the height of his manic phase in the winter of 1946–7. He had, he told Ziskind, 'lost all courage for life'. 'His one wish', Ziskind concluded in his notes of 7 August, 'is to lie down and not to work.' However, Klemperer forced himself to conduct twice at the Hollywood Bowl, on 1 and 3 September, when huge audiences rose to greet him, though the critics were not overly enthusiastic. They were to be his last appearances in Los Angeles.

A few days later he was back in New York, where he continued to busy himself with the arrangements for a European tour in 1954. But it did not always prove easy to reinstate engagements that had been cancelled twice already. The BBC told Klemperer's agent, 'We are now completely full up during the periods you mention.'[63] A more serious blow was the failure of the Concertgebouw Orchestra to offer any engagements. Conditions in Amsterdam had changed; in the autumn of 1952 Guillaume Landré, together with his assistant, Marius Flothuis, had succeeded Rudolf Mengelberg as the orchestra's artistic directors. Both men embodied a conscious break with the *ancien régime*. Both were French rather than German in aesthetic orientation. As composers, both felt Dutch music to have been neglected hitherto in the orchestra's programmes. Jan Bresser, at that time leader of the orchestra, later recalled that the new directorate, having known Klemperer only in a manic condition, was concerned with the difficulties he might cause.[64] An element of personal animosity may also have been involved; Landré is said to have been vexed earlier by Klemperer's failure even to open a packet of Dutch scores he had sent him. Be that as it may, his terse comments in the margins of letters from Klemperer's Dutch agent suggest that he was less than keen to engage him.[65]

A much greater obstacle to the tour was the fact that Klemperer still had no passport, even though ten months had passed since he had applied in Montreal for an extension to his old one. As a result of Senate investigations into the role of Communist sympathisers in both government and the field of the arts and entertainment, officials such as those in the Passport Office were finding it prudent not to incur suspicions of undue liberalism. In July 1953, on the suggestion of Bruno Walter, Klemperer had engaged a New York lawyer, Victor Jacobs, who advised that he should write a personal letter to Mrs Shipley, the Passport Office's director. In the letter Klemperer said that he had understood from previous discussions that in time his application would be reconsidered. In view of the need to make arrangements for the tour, it was important to know whether or not he and his family would be allowed to travel to Europe.

Jacobs himself took the letter to Washington. On it an official noted, 'To be handled on citizenship basis only. Consider as clear from security standpoint.' Bureaucratic wheels began to turn, though only slowly. The Passport Office called for evidence that Klemperer and his family had neither residence nor assets in Europe. On 3 September Klemperer wrote to assure Mrs Shipley that on his return from the tour at the end of June 1954 he intended to take up residence in Los Angeles: 'All our roots are here in the United States and we have no ties in Europe, and it is our hope and intention to live permanently in the United States.' That assurance was a good deal less than the truth. By 2 December, when he again wrote to Mrs Shipley, passports had still not been issued. And when they finally were sent on 23 December, two weeks before his intended departure for Europe, they were valid for less than seven months. Klemperer's own passport was stamped with the words 'shall not be extended without the express authorisation of the Department of State'. Mrs Shipley had taken him at his word that he would be resuming residency in the United States in July 1954.

The protracted negotiations over the passport took their toll. In spite of his improved physical condition, Klemperer remained as depressed as ever. Money was short and Johanna was not well. In October 1953 he embarked on yet another series of concerts in Montreal. After the opening concert, which in Johanna's view he had conducted 'really splendidly', he suffered what she described as 'a terrible attack of self-doubt'.[66] He continued to make heavy weather of the least problem. Though he had recorded Schubert's Symphony No. 4 three years earlier and subsequently performed it on several occasions, he huffed and puffed about including it in his second Montreal programme a fortnight later on the ground that it was 'technically difficult'.[67] Similarly he tried, but failed, to get out of Dvořák's Symphony No. 8 because he had never conducted it before and in his depressed condition felt unable to learn it within a few weeks.

He also had strong doubts about a single concert in November in Portland, Oregon, which involved a 3,000-mile journey to conduct an orchestra of doubtful quality, but there was no question of breaking his contract.* Apart from anything else he needed the money. The Portland Symphony Orchestra turned out to be a good deal less than a full-time professional body. All its seventy players held other jobs, so that rehearsals could only take place in the evenings or on Sundays. The first rehearsal was 'a nightmare'.[68] Klemperer was annoyed to discover that all the parts had not been corrected in accordance with the instructions he had sent in advance. He also discovered that most of the players had never before performed Beethoven's Seventh Symphony. They for their part were bewildered by his slurred and heavily accented speech, which became more incomprehensible as he grew angrier. In the first rehearsal they got no further than the opening movement. To the manager, Philip Hart, Klemperer insisted that 'with such an orchestra I cannot give a concert'.[69] Back at the hotel he lamented to Johanna, 'I'm not up to it any more. We must cancel.'[70] Yet in the course of the second rehearsal communication was somehow established. By the third, the players were at his feet. 'Just how he achieved this', wrote Hart, 'is difficult to explain, for his gestures were often imprecise and he continued to gesticulate and shout

---

* The engagement was secured for Klemperer by Ronald Wilford (b. 1927), then a young concert agent in New York, who had the responsibility of finding conductors for the Portland orchestra's 1954–5 season. Besides Klemperer they included Dimitri Mitropoulos, Fabian Sevitzky, William Steinberg and Stravinsky. Wilford recalls that Klemperer was 'paid more than anybody else, because he needed it' (interview with J.L., New York, December 1993). Later Wilford joined Columbia Artists and in 1970 succeeded Judson as its president, Klemperer always remained grateful to Wilford for having faith in his abilities during a particularly difficult phase of his career.

wildly as he lost his temper over the players' failure to follow his ... directions.'

At the concert itself, Johanna noticed on his entry that, for the first time since his fall, he was walking with new confidence, as though buoyed up by an awareness of what he and the orchestra had achieved in rehearsal. Recalling the evening, Hart wrote,

> After it was over, every player was ... convinced that he had participated in an extraordinary performance. Klemperer conducted ... as if oblivious of audience and orchestra alike. Most of the time he hovered over the score like a giant crab in white tie and tails, rising now and then to his full height ... when carried away by a climax.[71]

Thirty years later, he recalled the Beethoven symphony as 'for all its imperfections, one of the most extraordinary performances I have heard'.[72] On the day after the concert Johanna wrote, 'Believe me, Lotte, even in the best performances in Chicago or Montreal he did not conduct like that. The audience ... was beside itself.' Yet Klemperer was as implacable as ever. After the concert he refused to receive visitors, making an exception only for members of the orchestra, and even they did not escape unscathed. As Hart was about to drive him back to his hotel, the first oboist nervously tapped on the window of the car to apologise for a mistake. After he had gone, Klemperer observed bleakly, 'He shouldn't apologise. He should stop playing.'

On his return to Montreal, Klemperer visited the urologist he had consulted in the previous year. The prostate had grown smaller and he was advised that an operation would not be necessary.[73] There was a brief and unsatisfying visit to Buffalo for two concerts with an orchestra that Johanna described as 'miserably mediocre and unenthusiastic'.[74] For the remainder of the time Klemperer sat, sunk in gloom and almost without work, while little more than a mile away the New York Philharmonic Orchestra desperately sought replacements for its musical director, Dimitri Mitropoulos, who had been taken ill. The prospect of the coming European tour continued to fill him with apprehension.

11

The high ground regained

On his arrival at Amsterdam airport on 7 January 1954 Klemperer seemed a changed man to those who remembered him from past visits. He was so thin that his clothes hung loosely on his huge frame. His mask-like face was remote and expressionless. Annelien Kappeyne, daughter of a former director of the Concertgebouw, 'had an impression that he was no longer fully alive'.

Members of the Hague Residentie Orchestra, who had last played under him in 1947, noticed there were no longer jokes and witticisms in rehearsal, yet his command of the orchestra seemed to them even more complete than in the past. Even so, few could have guessed that Klemperer, who was now in his sixty-ninth year, was about to enter one of the most fruitful periods of his entire career. After a successful opening concert in The Hague on 13 January, Klemperer three days later took the orchestra to Amsterdam, where the Dutch critics acclaimed him with a unanimity they had not shown on his previous visit to the city. Inevitably, they wanted to know why the Concertgebouw Orchestra had not also engaged him.

After concerts in Paris and Copenhagen, Lotte reported to Helene Hirschler that 'artistically Papa is in quite special form'.[1] So he also proved to be on his next engagement, with the Essen City Orchestra on 5 February, though his appearance caused consternation. Alfons Neunkirchen, critic of the *Duisburger Nachrichten*, noted (10 February): 'The side door opens ... A physically broken man supported on a stick makes his way to the conductor's desk and then, held by nearby musicians, lets himself fall into a chair.'

Three days later Klemperer conducted the North-West German Radio Orchestra in Cologne. After the first rehearsal on 6 February Eigel Kruttge, who had not seen Klemperer since he had acted as his assistant at the Cologne Opera in the twenties, noted in his diary, 'From the first bars the lion's claws'. Kruttge was now in the Radio's music department and was able to procure further engagements for his old chief. Before leaving for Berlin, where he conducted the RIAS Symphony Orchestra on 14 and 15 February, Klemperer visited his parents' graves in the Jewish cemetery (as he continued to do whenever in Cologne). The place was so overgrown that they were hard to find. According to Jewish custom he left a stone as a token of his visit and made arrangements for the site to be cared for.² By 17 February he was back in Cologne for an additional concert that had been arranged at short notice after his success earlier in the month. Kruttge found 'everything absolutely right' in a programme that ended with Mahler's Fourth Symphony.

The Zurich Tonhalle was far from full when on 28 February Klemperer appeared there with the Winterthur City Orchestra. But among those present was Willi Schuh,* the respected critic of the *Neue Zürcher Zeitung*. A precise and scholarly man, Schuh was as little given to hyperbole as the newspaper he worked for. On this occasion, however, he let the trumpets sound. The concert, he wrote on 5 March,

> must be counted among the finest and most impressive we have experienced for a long time. Klemperer may have changed ... – the former champion of the new today prefers classical programmes – but the immense artistic intelligence and spiritual power ... are unaltered.

Schuh was particularly taken by the performance of Mozart's Symphony No. 29. He had, he claimed, never heard a performance of it as satisfying. In the 'Pastoral' Symphony he singled out Klemperer's ability to combine a basic tempo with expressive detail and fresh and lively textures.

The next stop was Florence, where Klemperer's second concert with the Maggio Musicale Orchestra, which consisted of Brahms's Symphony No. 3 and the 'Eroica', was described by *La Nazione* (8 March) as one of the most elevating artistic experiences the city had enjoyed in recent years. Before leaving for Rome, Klemperer was invited to conduct a production of Weber's *Euryanthe* in April. It clashed with engagements in Milan, but as he wrote to Johanna, 'I think that it would be better in any case for me *not* to conduct any opera this year.'³ His appearance continued to shock those who had not seen him since before the war. After Klemperer had dined with the art historian Bernard Berenson at his villa outside Florence, his host noted in his diary, 'Klemperer, once such a handsome male that while kneeling in prayer in Cologne Cathedral he was mistaken for a romantic hidalgo, now hobbles, conducts seated ... looks wretched and *hurt*.'⁴

The time had now come to return to London, where Walter Legge had engaged him for two more concerts with the Philharmonia Orchestra. There had been changes for the better in the city's musical life, and artists aspiring to international celebrity now had to make their mark there. Occupied Berlin and Vienna, both of them now standing on the periphery of Western Europe, were no longer the great centres of musical life they had been. Paris's principal musical institutions were in a state of decrepitude. *Faute de mieux*, London increasingly found itself in a central position. Many of its concerts

---

* Willi Schuh (1900–86). Critic on the *Neue Zürcher Zeitung* from 1928, its music editor 1944–65. Author of *Richard Strauss: A Chronicle of the Early Years (1864–98)*.

were as ill-rehearsed, and their programmes as conventional, as ever. But with no fewer than five full-scale symphony orchestras competing for the public's favour, the new Festival Hall alone housed more concerts than the city had ever enjoyed before. Also, owing in large part to Legge's flair and energy, London had become the hub of the recording industry in Europe.

Klemperer's first programme, on 19 March 1954, consisted of the *Egmont* Overture, Brahms's Second Piano Concerto, with Géza Anda as soloist, and the 'Jupiter' Symphony. To the author, who was hearing Klemperer for the first time, the dominant mark of his style was 'a rare capacity to see a work as a whole. The parts are there in all their fullness; but, like Toscanini, Klemperer is able, with no stretching or pulling of tempo, to give them their proper place in the general structure of a work.'[5] Klemperer himself was less than happy with what he had achieved. Legge provided only two rehearsals and he did not find the Philharmonia Orchestra as good as he had been led to expect.[6]

After further appearances in Amsterdam and Cologne, Klemperer returned to London for an all-Beethoven concert on 9 April. At rehearsal, at the start of the slow movement of the 'Eroica', Klemperer barked at the orchestra, 'Gentlemen, this is a *march*. *Without* sentiment.' Among the handful of critics who attended the performance was John Amis, who wrote,

> It was a great evening and it is difficult to think of any other conductor ... who so gets to the heart of Beethoven as Klemperer. One talks of this or that conductor's Beethoven, but with Klemperer it is Beethoven's Beethoven ... There is no distortion of the text, there is passion and drama without hysteria, an extraordinary natural sense of rhythm and the music is stamped with a sense of Homeric grandeur. The Eroica had an architectural proportion that controlled the music from first note to last.[7]

Given the successes he had had in Europe, it had become necessary for Klemperer to consider his future. His American passport was only valid for six months. To return on its expiry to the United States, where McCarthyism was rampant, would be a risk, and in any case he would be unable to earn enough money to live on there. But if he were to remain in Europe, on what passport would he travel? Swiss nationality would be hard to obtain without a long period of residency. His feelings about the new West German Federal Republic were at best ambivalent. 'There's hardly anything to compare with the German woods and the changing seasons', he had earlier written to an old friend who, like himself, had fled from National Socialism. 'In spite of that I can well understand your unwillingness to return.'[8] As a former German citizen he could, however, qualify for a Federal Republic passport by going through the formality of establishing temporary residence in Germany. On 12 April, Lotte Klemperer wrote to Hanns Hartmann, the Intendant of the West German Radio in Cologne, who had helped her with enquiries, to tell him that her father would reach a decision on his future before the end of the month.

The reason for the delay was that Klemperer and Legge were to meet to discuss his situation in the last days of April in Milan, where Klemperer had concerts and Legge would be recording *Norma* with Maria Callas. When Legge attended the second of Klemperer's concerts on 30 April, he found the Teatro Nuovo depressing and the audience 'small and apathetic'. But he was so enchanted by the performance of Mozart's Symphony No. 29 that Klemperer drew from a scratch chamber orchestra that he decided there and then that the work would be among the first he would record with him.

That evening, Legge, who enjoyed food and wine, invited Klemperer to dine at a quiet restaurant that specialised in chicken on the spit. To his surprise, his guest ordered nothing but two boiled eggs and a glass of milk. After this austere repast, Klemperer explained his predicament. If he were to abandon America and reclaim German nationality, he would need some form of steady income, as he could not for long stand the strain of the continual travelling he had been forced to undertake since his return to Europe. Legge replied that neither he nor EMI could guarantee Klemperer an income, but he could offer enough concerts and recordings to ensure him of at least £2,000 a year. The following morning Lotte telephoned to tell Legge that her father had decided to remain in Europe.[9] The die had been cast.

On 7 May 1954 Klemperer wrote to inform his American agent, Siegfried Hearst, that he would not be returning to the United States. He explained that he needed to be free to travel and had been advised that there was no way of telling when or whether the regulations that obliged naturalised American citizens to return periodically to the United States would be lifted. That made it impossible to enter into long-term commitments. American union policies also prevented him from recording in Europe as long as he remained a citizen of the United States. Finally, repeated journeys across the Atlantic were a financial and physical burden he could no longer support.

To establish German residency, Klemperer and his wife and daughter were registered as sub-tenants in Eigel Kruttge's flat in Cologne. Within a little more than a week the formalities had been completed and when Klemperer left Germany on 29 May he was in possession of a German passport.* While he travelled to give concerts in Lisbon and Oporto, Johanna went to look for an apartment in Zurich, which offered the advantages of being German-speaking and having excellent communications. In the Seefeldstrasse, close to the north side of the lake, she found a three-room flat and took it for a year. Nearby she also rented a small studio flat for Lotte.

---

* Though he continued to travel on his American passport until it expired in July. He may have done so because it was not until October that he informed the US Consulate in Zurich that he, Johanna and Lotte had taken German citizenship.

Towards the end of the summer season, Lotte wrote from Scheveningen, where her father was again conducting the Residentie Orchestra, 'For the first time in years our affairs are in order. We have somewhere to live and the future looks good . . . I can hardly wait to get my things together at last and to be able really to unpack.'[10]

That was not the only good news. On 30 July Klemperer was notified that the German authorities had granted him an annual retirement pension of DM8,400, payable from his sixty-fifth birthday in 1950 and subject to yearly increments. Johanna, who was also granted a retirement pension of DM2,880 on the same terms, had meanwhile discovered to her surprise that, as a member of the Deutsche Bühnenverein, which she had joined in 1903 when she became a member of the chorus at the Hanover opera house, a sum of DM18,000 had accumulated to her credit. This she used to buy furniture for their new home. Meanwhile Klemperer's claim for compensation for the dissolution of his contract with the Berlin State Opera in 1933 and seizure of his life insurance policy was still outstanding.* For the first time since 1939, he had work, a roof over his head and a degree of financial security.

Yet that did nothing to lessen the depression that had now held him in its grip for more than two years. Quoting a passage from Goethe's *Faust, Part Two* that he had read forty-three years earlier, when he had been in a similar condition, he compared himself to the character of Sorge ('Care'): 'Der Entschluss ist ihm genommen' ('the power of decision is taken from him'). 'These words', he wrote to Fritz Fischer on 6 August 1954, 'will tell you how I am . . . I occupy myself as best I can, [but] have a deep dread of the coming season.'

Rightly believing her father's star to be in the ascendant, Lotte now set out to order his life. She wrote to a friend, Loli Matvány,

> The constant worry, humiliation and almost hopelessness of my parents' situation made me resentful, furious and (truly a novelty for me) ambitious. I became absolutely determined that [their] last years should be as they justly deserved. By this I mean above all that my father should be able to work with the best available materials and do only what pleases him . . . Money, success and all those vanities are not my main concern . . .
>
> When we left the States last January, we left with nothing. My father's stock professionally had gone down considerably. The general consensus . . . was – Klemperer is through, let's go and see the remnants! With second-rate orchestras, sceptical audiences and the usual colleagues ready to do damage at the slightest . . . provocation . . . he came through with miraculous success.
>
> But it was a new battle in every city. Shortly after our arrival in Europe my mother became ill . . . [My father] was in a constant state of indecision about anything and everything. The tour was terribly planned. There was not one day

---

* A payment of DM20,000 was finally authorised in February 1959.

of rest. Hardly finished with one concert, I was already packing and we were off to another climate.

When John Beek's contract as Klemperer's manager in Europe came up for renewal on 1 July 1954, Lotte urged her father to confine Beek's activities to Holland only and to delay signing a new contract with EMI, so that Beek, who was based in The Hague, would not be able to collect 5 per cent of the recording royalties he had done nothing to earn. Lotte supported her father's wish not to commit himself to EMI for more than a year at a time. She took other important decisions.

> When it came to the next season, my fun really began. Without the slightest inhibitions I scratched out all those engagements which I did not consider worthwhile. Soloists unknown to my father are from now on taboo. In London, Amsterdam and Italy I insisted on higher fees – and got them. You should have seen my father during these sessions! He was almost frightened and would occasionally mutter, 'Findest Du nicht, dass Du etwas milder sein solltest?' ('Don't you think you should be a little milder?')
>
> But for me it was now or never. The next season is all set. There will be less – but only the best artistically and financially ... As things are planned I shall do most of the travelling with my father, as my mother has not been so strong lately.[11]

As a result of Lotte's efforts, the following four seasons came increasingly to centre on three cities: London, Cologne and Amsterdam. Werner was the only member of Klemperer's immediate family still living in America. Since 1946 he had been struggling as a stage and radio actor in New York, but now, at last, he had made a breakthrough, playing alongside Tallulah Bankhead in the comedy *Dear Charles*. It was to enjoy a long run on Broadway

After spending the remainder of the summer in Switzerland, Klemperer began the 1954–5 season by conducting the Berlin Philharmonic Orchestra. The concert, given at the Titania Palast on 1 October, was well received by both press and public, but it led to no further dates with the orchestra in the following two seasons. The reason for this is uncertain, but it is possible that Klemperer rejected the low fee habitually offered by an orchestra that, like its counterpart in Vienna, regarded an engagement as an accolade.

After Berlin, Klemperer travelled with Lotte to London for his first recording sessions with the Philharmonia Orchestra, which were supervised by Legge and his assistant, Walter Jellinek. The 'Jupiter' Symphony was recorded on 5 and 6 October. The morning of the 7th was to be devoted to Hindemith's Horn Concerto with Dennis Brain,* who four years earlier had given the work its première and had begged Legge to let him record it.

---

* Dennis Brain (1921–57). The greatest horn player of his generation. He died in a road accident when driving from Edinburgh to London shortly after he had played in a concert conducted by Klemperer.

Klemperer had agreed to accompany, though he was unfamiliar with the score.¹² In the mid-morning break Brain complained to Legge of Klemperer's slow tempi and slack rhythms. Klemperer declined to alter his tempi, whereupon Brain, usually 'the gentlest of men', as Legge described him, refused to come to the evening session at which the recording was to have been completed. Sensing trouble, and well aware of how much hung on her father's association with the Philharmonia, a white-faced Lotte arrived unannounced that afternoon at Legge's office. Equally eager to avert trouble, Legge suggested that the Horn Concerto be dropped in favour of the suite from Hindemith's *Nobilissima Visione*. Face was saved on all sides and recordings of the Hindemith suite, as well as Mozart's Symphony No. 29 and Brahms's Variations on a theme of Haydn, were completed without further difficulties. Later, in 1956, Brain recorded the concerto with the comnposer conducting.

By mid-November Klemperer was back in London to record a group of Beethoven overtures and Bach's four orchestral suites. Before the end of the sessions Legge felt that 'Klemperer and the orchestra, so to speak, had fused'.

> He was always at the hall early and sat on his rostrum watching each player's arrival with baleful eyes. He worked carefully, stopped rarely and used few but explicit words. He usually played a whole movement through, then rehearsed all his wants in detail. Slowly he thawed a little . . .

Klemperer's gift for impromptu witticisms helped to break the ice. As Legge recalled,

> The first, I think, was when the sub-principal violin looked repeatedly at his wrist-watch because Klemperer was rehearsing a moment or two over time. Klemperer at first feigned to ignore this, then stopped the orchestra, leaned over to the player and asked mock-solicitously, 'Is it still going?' and continued rehearsing.¹³

This and other stories of the grim-looking old gentleman's ready wit started to spread around London and did much to win the players' affection.

A good working relationship also came into existence between Klemperer and Legge, whose sharp musical intelligence he learnt to respect. In November 1954 Legge invited Klemperer to the EMI studios in Abbey Road to hear the first batch of recordings he had made earlier that autumn. Depressed and hypercritical, Klemperer at first wanted to remake them, but, aware that this would hardly be feasible on financial grounds, he finally agreed to leave the decision to Legge. That continued to be his practice: henceforth he listened to playbacks at recording sessions and made retakes when asked to do so.¹⁴ It was a method of working that functioned well, if only because, while Legge was passionately involved in every aspect of recording, for Klemperer it remained at best a source of income and on occasions a welcome opportunity for additional rehearsals before a concert.

Legge's commitment to Klemperer was, however, still limited. In each of the seasons of 1953–4 and 1954–5 he invited him to conduct no more than two concerts with the Philharmonia. In 1955–6 the number was raised to three. Thus Klemperer was still open to approaches from other London concert-giving organisations and on 14 and 28 November 1954 he appeared at the Festival Hall with the London Symphony Orchestra. In spite of a popular programme, there were empty seats at the first concert: in London his name was still no guarantee of a full house. But the second, which included Mahler's Symphony No. 4 (still a comparative rarity in Britain), was better attended. Two more engagements with the Philharmonia occurred when Rodzinski withdrew at short notice and Legge invited Klemperer to take his place. At the first of these on 30 November he opened the evening with the slow movement of the 'Eroica' Symphony in memory of Wilhelm Furtwängler, who had died that morning at the age of sixty-eight.

By the time Klemperer returned to Zurich he was clearly unwell. In spite of his insistence that he was suffering from a mere stomach upset, Johanna, rightly suspecting appendicitis, telephoned a doctor, who arranged for him to be taken to hospital, where in the middle of the night an emergency operation was performed. While he was on the operating table the appendix perforated, so that Johanna's prescience may well have saved his life. At first Klemperer recovered well, but soon after returning home on 10 January 1955 he began to be troubled by a bladder infection, owing to the prostate condition from which he had intermittently suffered since 1950.* Contrary to the diagnosis made in Montreal in 1952, an investigation revealed a large but benign tumour.

Its removal on 4 March brought about a rapid improvement in his general health. It was thus a visibly stronger man who returned to London in April 1955 for engagements with the Royal Philharmonic Orchestra as well as the Philharmonia. His collaboration with the former on 20 April seems to have been less than harmonious:[15] John Warrack was not the only critic who thought that Beecham's orchestra had played 'below its best'.[16] None the less, Bruckner's Symphony No. 4 caused what Neville Cardus described as 'quite a scene among the large audience at the end',[17] in itself an event in a city that had hitherto shown little enthusiasm for such music. But it was once again a Beethoven concert with the Philharmonia four days later that evoked the most enthusiasm. 'Everything went wonderfully', Lotte wrote to friends. 'He has never had such success there, not only with the public, but also with the press and the orchestra.'[18] On 14 May Klemperer celebrated his seventieth birthday. It passed unnoticed in London, but, largely as a result of Eigel Kruttge's

---

* Among other inconveniences, the condition had obliged him to forgo liquids for several hours before conducting and occasionally necessitated catheterisation (communication from Lotte Klemperer, 11 November 1989).

efforts, it was marked by several events in Cologne. On 9 and 10 May Klemperer appeared at the head of the Gürzenich Orchestra* for the first time since he had left the opera house in 1924 in a programme that included Bruckner's Symphony No. 7. However, the principal celebrations took place at the Radio, where on 17 May he conducted a concert performance of *Don Giovanni*. At the first entry of the trombones in the supper scene, he rose in the excitement of the moment to his full height and continued to conduct standing until the end of the performance. In his diary Kruttge described it as 'a great evening'. Klemperer himself was less than wholly satisfied. An international cast proved more uneven than it had looked on paper,† and he found the Cologne Radio Orchestra less good than in the previous season. The occasion also served to confirm his doubts about concert performances of operas. Though he later conducted several such evenings in London, at heart he remained a man of the theatre, for whom opera without a stage was a contradiction in terms. After a week's break he embarked on rehearsals for Beethoven's *Missa solemnis*, which he conducted on 6 June. Although he had recorded it in 1951, he had not performed it in the concert hall for twenty-two years.

* * *

Meanwhile, Klemperer had been asked to conduct the Amsterdam Concertgebouw Orchestra once more. After the success he had enjoyed with the Hague Residentie Orchestra a year earlier, Marius Flothuis, who was on the point of succeeding Landré as the Concertgebouw's artistic director, had had little alternative but to pocket his pride and offer an engagement. At first Klemperer was by no means eager to accept. Lotte demanded – and got – a substantially higher fee than the Concertgebouw had previously paid.[19] Two concerts were planned for the winter of 1954, but had to be abandoned owing to Klemperer's ill health. Thus it was not until 7 July 1955 that, after an absence of four years, he again appeared at the head of the Concertgebouw with a programme consisting of the 'Pastoral' Symphony, the suite from Hindemith's *Nobilissima Visione* and Schoenberg's *Verklärte Nacht*. Even the critic Matthijs Vermeulen admitted that he had never heard the strings of the Concertgebouw play with such intensity and such a range of colour and nuance as they had in *Verklärte Nacht*.[20] The public enthusiasm was immense and more concerts were planned for the following season. The rift with the Concertgebouw's management seemed to have been repaired.

* * *

---

* The name used by the Cologne City Opera's orchestra when it appears in the concert hall.
† It included George London as Don Giovanni, Ludwig Weber as the Commendatore, Hilde Zadek as Donna Anna, Leopold Simoneau as Don Ottavio and Rita Streich as Zerlina.

In October 1955 Klemperer returned to London to record Beethoven's Third, Fifth and Seventh Symphonies. When issued in the following year, they did more than anything else to re-establish his reputation in America as well as Britain. But such work gave him little satisfaction: 'the recordings have begun well', he conceded to Johanna. '[But] making records is always a bit of a problem. For me, the *essential* thing, the *personal* is lacking.'[21]

It is a measure of Klemperer's growing reputation that the BBC, which hitherto had felt unable to offer him more than an isolated studio concert, now engaged him for a period of three weeks in December 1955, during which he was to conduct six concerts, one in the Festival Hall and five in the studio. The preliminaries did not go smoothly. Baulked of his original wish to do Beethoven's Ninth Symphony, Klemperer settled for Brahms's German Requiem, but insisted on the engagement of a 21-year-old Dutch baritone soloist with little experience. Maurice Johnstone, the BBC's deputy controller of music, informed Klemperer's London agent that 'his selection ... has been very badly received here ... I hope that, on future occasions, he will pay a little more respect to the professional judgement of his English colleagues.'[22] On this occasion, the BBC's concern had turned out to be justified.

When the producer in charge of the programmes requested a staff car to take Klemperer to and from the BBC's Maida Vale studios, he was told sharply that 'an artist is expected to provide his own transport'.[23] Yet for all its bureaucracy, the BBC provided a welcome opportunity to do works that Legge would not allow him to conduct with the Philharmonia, for example Debussy's *Nocturnes*. *The Times* (8 December) praised Klemperer's performance of them, though it was what it described as an 'exuberant, exalted' account of Brahms's Fourth Symphony that made the deepest impression. In the opinion of Erwin Stein only the soloists marred the fine studio performances of the Brahms Requiem on 9 and 10 December.[24]

At the end of the engagement, the producer in charge reported:

> Klemperer, for all his reputation, proved astonishingly easy to work with, thanks to his daughter's help and his greatly improved state of health. He also produced a most stimulating difference of opinion among musicians, half of whom found his performances intolerably rough and truculent, [while] the other half ... found in them the same magic as ever.
>
> I feel both [views] are well justified, for undeniably he retains much of his old drive, the ability to build wonderful climaxes, and his instinctive grasp of a great work's architecture. On the other hand, much of his work seemed to lack humanity and warmth ... Many of his tempi were too fast for expression to be balanced with excitement, and his implacable tendency to over-rehearse did not endear him to the orchestra or chorus, whose Brahms Requiem seemed to me thoroughly stale ... I hope Klemperer can return to us some time

to provide further healthy controversy, but I hope not in preference to Schuricht.*

For all the success that Klemperer was beginning to enjoy in London, there were those who remained in two minds about him.

*   *   *

The following month Klemperer conducted the RIAS orchestra in Berlin, which he found disappointing; it lacked 'real sound', he said.[25] As her father entered the hall of the Berlin Hochschule for the first concert on 10 January 1956, Lotte overheard a woman seated immediately behind her in the auditorium ask her companion, 'Is he a Jew?'† To her amazement, Lotte subsequently learnt that her neighbours were none other than Dr Gerd von Westermann, the Intendant of the Berlin Philharmonic Orchestra, and his wife.[26] When Westermann heard of his wife's *faux pas*, he attempted to put matters right; only a week after the incident, Klemperer received an invitation to conduct the Philharmonic Orchestra that autumn at the Berlin Festival, which Westermann also ran. It so happened that Klemperer was already committed to another engagement, but Lotte's answer made it clear that he would not have accepted, even had he been free to do so. 'My father', she wrote on 18 February 1956, 'does not wish to appear at this year's Berlin Festival.' Having failed to mollify Klemperer, Westermann resorted to a little German-style diplomacy. On 1 March he wrote at length to explain to Klemperer that Lotte had unfortunately not heard his wife's rider to her original question. As he himself distinctly remembered, after asking whether Klemperer was a Jew, she had at once added, 'He doesn't look like one.' Klemperer read the letter with incredulity.

Peace was patched up when Klemperer and Westermann met by chance in the following year, and Klemperer returned to conduct the Berlin Philharmonic on 23 March 1958. But the coolness between him and the orchestra was so evident that one critic even commented on it.[27] In contrast, when he conducted a Beethoven programme at the Radio six days later, the RIAS Orchestra rose on his entry and joined in the applause at the end of the concert. It might not have been a first-class orchestra, but, as Klemperer wrote to Helene Hirschler, he got more pleasure from conducting it than he did from the Berlin Philharmonic. Another six years were to pass before he returned to the city.

*   *   *

New Year, 1956, found Klemperer in Cologne, where the Gürzenich Orchestra

---

* Michael Whewell, BBC internal memo, 4 January 1956. Carl Schuricht (1880–1967), though highly respected, was not generally considered a conductor of Klemperer's calibre.

† The German, 'Ist das ein Jude?' has a more pejorative flavour. Literally, 'Is that a Jew?'

failed to satisfy him in a Mozart programme on 7 January. 'Above all it lacks the charm that is all-important in Mozart',[28] he wrote to Johanna during rehearsals. For much of the early summer of 1956 Klemperer was again in Holland. In May he gave another Beethoven cycle, the success of which far outstripped its predecessors of 1949 and 1951. To his surprise and joy, Aladár Tóth turned up when his wife Annie Fischer was the soloist in the Third Piano Concerto on 2 May. The two men had not seen each other since Klemperer's departure from Budapest six years earlier. Tóth did his best to persuade his old friend to return to Budapest as a guest, but Klemperer refused to commit himself. That autumn Tóth lost his position at the Opera in the upheaval of the Hungarian uprising against the Russians, so that the question of a return to Budapest lapsed, at any rate for the time being.

Later in the summer Klemperer returned yet again to Amsterdam to conduct a Mozart programme (12 July) for the Holland Festival. For the first time in many years the family was able to be together. Werner was on a visit from the United States. Johanna was enjoying a few days' respite from the strains of moving house. As the flat she had rented two years earlier in Zurich had proved unexpectedly noisy, she had taken another in the nearby Dufourstrasse. It was to remain Klemperer's home until his death.

*   *   *

In outward appearance Klemperer was by 1956 transformed from the emaciated and dejected figure who had returned to Europe two years earlier. 'You wouldn't recognise my father', Lotte wrote to Ernst and Lilly Toch on 28 January 1956.

> Since May, he conducts standing (at rehearsals, recording sessions, everything), has put on weight, again has a normal colour and artistically is in the best possible form. Psychologically, he is quiet and serious, no longer so depressed, though still completely antisocial. He is doing his thing more than well and is working with concentration and discipline, so on journeys we live a very strict but also satisfying life.

Despite Lotte's impression that her father's depression was no longer as intense as it had been, his letters continued to be full of complaints and lamentations. In particular he had again become exaggeratedly self-critical. Even the Philharmonia had failed to satisfy him entirely when he had conducted it in a Beethoven programme on 23 March 1956. 'Everyone finds this orchestra particularly good, but I'm not quite of that opinion', he wrote on the following day to Helene Hirschler.

After their return from Holland in July 1956 Klemperer and Johanna, who in the course of the last four years had grown close again, remained in their new Zurich apartment, while Lotte retired to a sanatorium near Munich to recover from a gruelling season. But life in a three-room flat with a man still in the throes of depression proved exhausting and after four weeks of 'vacation' Johanna felt as weary as ever. She decided to take a *Kur* in the Austrian spa of Bad Gastein, while Lotte accompanied her father to London. Johanna's journey on 15 September proved unexpectedly exhausting. Having almost missed her connection in Innsbruck, she was obliged to sit for several hours with her baggage on the floor of the guard's van. Two days after her arrival she developed a feverish cold.[29]

On 30 September Johanna suffered a heart infarct. The following morning Klemperer and Lotte flew from London to Vienna, whence they took a taxi to Bad Gastein. There it was decided to move Johanna to Munich, where Klemperer had a concert with the Bavarian Radio Orchestra on 18 October. The journey overtaxed her strength, but, once in hospital, her condition at first seemed to improve, so that she was able to listen to a broadcast of the concert. By the end of the month Klemperer was already overdue in London for the recording sessions he had postponed on learning of Johanna's illness. Considering the constant presence of a depressed husband to be of little benefit to his patient, the doctor advised Klemperer to fulfil his obligations, and on 28 October he accordingly flew to London with Werner, who had earlier arrived from America. Klemperer had already almost completed recordings of three of the Brahms symphonies when on 1 November Lotte telephoned to tell him that Johanna was failing. The next day he and Werner returned to Munich.

Johanna had been barely conscious all day, but, as he entered her room, she opened her eyes and in a clear voice called out, 'Alter'. It was the last word she spoke. The following day she lapsed into a coma and that evening died at the age of sixty-eight, prematurely worn out by the stresses and strains of thirty-seven years of married life. Klemperer's debt to her was immense, as even Regi Elbogen, by no means always charitably disposed to her sister-in-law, acknowledged in a letter to Marianne Joseph:

> We owe Hanne [Johanna] eternal gratitude. Fortunately you don't know all that happened after the operation [in 1939] . . . On several occasions the doctors demanded that he be put in a closed institution and he would never have come out of it. But she stubbornly refused to commit him. Her agreement was indispensable. And then just think of it – this rise in Europe. She was so proud of him.[30]

For a while Klemperer sat alone by Johanna's bedside. At one moment he suddenly emerged from the room and called for a doctor; he had imagined that she was still breathing. He insisted on making the funeral arrangements himself. As music, he chose two pieces by J.S. Bach, 'Bist Du bei mir' and 'Wenn ich einmal muss scheiden'. That, however, required permission from the municipal burial office, where an official explained that, left to their own devices, people were liable to make unsuitable choices. The funeral took place in Munich on 6 November according to the Catholic rite. The conductor Eugen Jochum* and his wife were the only mourners apart from Klemperer and his two children. As the grave was some distance from the chapel, special permission was given for a car to enter the cemetery. But Klemperer insisted on walking behind the coffin. The next morning he, Werner and Lotte flew to London, where rehearsals were due to begin on the following day. Thereafter he scarcely ever referred to Johanna, though the following spring, after a concert in Rome, he suddenly looked up and exclaimed to Lotte, 'If only I knew where to telephone now!'[31] When not with Johanna, he had invariably telephoned her after a concert.

* * *

By the start of the 1956–7 season Klemperer was the only active member of the group of celebrated German conductors who had been photographed with Toscanini on the occasion of his visit to Berlin with the company of La Scala, Milan, in 1929. Furtwängler had died in 1954, Erich Kleiber in January 1956. Bruno Walter, now eighty, was living in semi-retirement in Beverly Hills. Toscanini had also retired.

The death of Furtwängler, in particular, had widespread repercussions. In 1955 Karajan, hitherto the keystone of the Philharmonia in the concert hall as well as the recording studio, succeeded him as conductor for life of the Berlin Philharmonic Orchestra. When in the following year Karajan was also appointed director of both the Vienna State Opera and the Salzburg Festival, it was clear that he was moving out of Legge's orbit. As a result Legge turned increasingly to Klemperer. In the 1956–7 season he engaged him for five Festival Hall concerts that included a cycle of the Brahms symphonies. For the following season he planned an extensive Beethoven cycle that would also be recorded.

News of Klemperer's successes in London and elsewhere in Europe inevitably reached America, where his recording of the 'Eroica' Symphony was received with almost as much enthusiasm as it had been in London. In September 1956 Legge, eager to foster Klemperer's transatlantic reputation, judged the moment opportune for him to reappear in America. Klemperer reacted coolly, but Legge approached the American agent Arthur Judson and after much correspondence the New York Philharmonic Orchestra invited him to conduct a Beethoven cycle in December 1957.

Lotte rejected the offer on behalf of her father: he was not free at that time (in fact, he was) and could, in any case, not undertake more than three

---

* As Chief Conductor of the Bavarian Radio Orchestra (1949–60), Jochum had been responsible for inviting Klemperer to Munich for concerts in April and October 1956.

concerts in a week. As Klemperer was aware, the New York Philharmonic habitually performed each programme four times in as many days, a practice he had found burdensome when, as a much younger and fitter man, he had conducted the orchestra in the thirties. The fee was also unacceptable.[32] The orchestra met both objections. But Klemperer refused to take the bait. The memory of the humiliations he had suffered in America was still vivid and, now that he had re-established his reputation, he was not prepared to wag his tail as soon as he was offered a bone. But more was involved than wounded pride. When Judson revived the project twelve months later, Klemperer hesitated for a day before refusing the offer, claiming, again untruthfully, that he had other engagements. 'Basically', Lotte wrote to Louise Schwab, 'he has a great fear of New York.'[33]

*   *   *

Klemperer's first London engagement in the 1956–7 season was to conduct the *Missa solemnis* on 29 September at the Festival Hall in celebration of the tenth anniversary of the BBC's Third Programme. 'It was not a perfect, but a noble and inspiring, performance', wrote the critic of *The Times*, who complained that the Benedictus had been 'spoiled because Mr Paul Beard [the leader] would not see eye to eye with Dr Klemperer about its natural pulse'.[34] Desmond Shawe-Taylor wrote in the *New Statesman*,

> Klemperer is now happily enjoying a return of good health and a sort of Indian summer of reputation: people are beginning to talk of him, I note, as the leading Beethoven conductor of our time. This is interesting, because he represents a swing of the pendulum away from the most admired Beethoven interpreters of recent days ... He does not linger and sentimentalise, as Furtwängler did; nor does he, like Toscanini, subordinate everything to architecture and vital rhythm. His conception of the Mass is noble, intensely musical and satisfying; when set beside that of Toscanini, however, it is often a little tame. Under Klemperer's beat, the famous difficulties in the vocal parts seemed almost to melt away.[35]

There was a repeat performance in the BBC's Maida Vale studio on the following day. Among those present was the Philharmonia's leader, Manoug Parikian, who went to congratulate Klemperer in his dressing-room, but found him in no mood for compliments. 'Do you think I am a fool?' Klemperer asked and waved his visitor aside.[36]

A Brahms cycle (2, 9 and 16 November) with the Philharmonia aroused a good deal of enthusiasm, but Klemperer's Mozart continued to divide London's critics. Martin Cooper described the tempi in performances of the last three symphonies on 22 March 1957 as 'absolutely rigid', the sound as 'colourless', the general approach 'unsmiling' and 'schoolmasterly ... If this is the new fashion in Mozart, Bruno Walter and Beecham must look to their laurels, for their Mozart and Klemperer's have nothing but notes in common.'[37] *The Times*, in contrast, wrote, 'The overriding impression was that ... Mr Klemperer was dead right, every time and in every symphony, that is to say, tempo, balance, phrasing, dynamic level, were all of them right.'[38] But *The Times* boasted a rota of anonymous critics, famously diverse in their opinions. When, a year later, Klemperer gave another all-Mozart programme, consisting of the symphonies nos. 25, 38 and 40, it complained of 'an inner lack of warmth'.[39] If, in London, his Beethoven had come to be regarded as authoritative, as a Mozartian he remained controversial.

* * *

Although London and the Philharmonia Orchestra were well on the way to becoming the centre of Klemperer's activities, it was the Amsterdam Concertgebouw Orchestra, which combined German discipline and splendour of sound with superb French-style woodwinds, that he enjoyed conducting more. In addition it was more generous with rehearsal time than Legge could afford to be. It was also familiar with a far wider range of music than the Philharmonia, though the only major contemporary score Klemperer included in his Concertgebouw programmes in 1957 was Stravinsky's Symphony in Three Movements, which he conducted on 20 and 21 February. The audience's reaction to it was so cool that Klemperer angrily threatened to perform the entire symphony again as an encore.*[40] It proved to be the last occasion on which he conducted the work in public.

In every other respect the visit was a success and on the day of his departure the orchestra's artistic director, Marius Flothuis, invited him to conduct another Beethoven cycle in May of the following year. A month later, however, Flothuis wrote to inform him that, owing to foreign tours and recording sessions, the Concertgebouw would be unable to invite him to conduct the cycle in 1958 after all.[41] Lotte reacted angrily. Her father, she insisted, regarded the verbal agreement reached in Amsterdam as binding. 'Your behaviour', she wrote to Flothuis on 27 March, 'has greatly affronted my father and deeply annoyed him.' In view of this he would not fulfil the earlier agreement to conduct the Concertgebouw for two weeks in January 1958. In fact, the orchestra had no commitments that would have ruled out a Beethoven cycle.[42] Confronted with the prospect of losing Klemperer for both periods, Flothuis wrote to Klemperer on 10 April to inform him that it would be possible to invite him to conduct the Beethoven cycle after all and asked if

---

* This coolness can hardly be attributed to the performance. A private recording shows that, despite measured tempi, the opening movement developed formidable momentum. It was the work itself that the conservative Concertgebouw audience failed to warm to.

he might come to Zurich to discuss details. Lotte replied tersely that all communications should henceforth be in writing.[43]

A week before he was due to return to Amsterdam on 2 May 1957 to begin rehearsals for a performance of the *Missa solemnis*, Klemperer intimated that he did not wish Flothuis to meet him at the airport.[44] In Amsterdam he rejected all attempts to heal the breach; it was, after all, not the first time the orchestra's management had given him grounds for resentment. 'Because of how I feel at the moment', he wrote to Flothuis on 9 May, 'I do not wish to reach any decisions about the coming season.' Thus relations between Klemperer and Flothuis reached a low ebb. Difficulties had already arisen about singers (Klemperer had rejected Peter Pears as tenor soloist in favour of Jószef Simándy, whom Flothuis considered unsuitable) and instrumentalists (he had insisted that the Concertgebouw's leading woodwind players should play in all three performances). Klemperer was also dissatisfied with the Tonkunst Chorus. In Flothuis's view he was out to make difficulties. In the circumstances the performances on 17, 19 and 21 May, the first that Amsterdam had heard since 1936, were surprisingly successful. But Klemperer again felt that the work had eluded him. Back in Zurich, he wrote to Aladár Tóth, 'It is enormously difficult to translate into reality a work that doesn't take reality into account.'[45]

Disagreements continued to dog Klemperer's relationship with the Concertgebouw Orchestra, though he returned to Amsterdam in January 1958 and again in the following May, when he conducted a Beethoven cycle. By now there were widespread rumours that the visit might well be his last. Lotte had earlier relayed her father's wish that, in view of his relationship with the Concertgebouw's management, there should be no public celebration of her father's seventy-third birthday on 14 May. But when Klemperer raised his hands to begin the morning rehearsal with the overture to *King Stephen*, the orchestra burst into the old German salute 'Es lebe hoch' and broke into cheers. Klemperer's quarrel had never been with the players and, in acknowledging their greeting, he told them what a privilege it was for him to conduct Willem Mengelberg's old orchestra.[46]

Van Lier considered that some of Klemperer's tempi in the Beethoven cycle were slower than in the past; the Symphony No. 7 in particular, had been performed 'with the brakes on', a criticism that could not have been made of performances in earlier years.[47] But *De Telegraaf* (1 June) wrote that at the end of the final concert the audience clapped, stamped and shouted as bouquet after bouquet was brought on to the platform. Yet in spite of the success there were no plans for Klemperer to conduct the Concertgebouw again. Public indignation at the continuing failure of the orchestra's management to reach agreement with Klemperer led to the formation in the autumn of 1958 of an 'Action Klemperer' movement, which in September 1958 issued a pamphlet urging concert-goers to make their feelings known.[48] Six weeks later, the management announced that negotiations were in progress for a Beethoven cycle in the 1959–60 season, but they came to nothing and Klemperer did not appear at the Concertgebouw again until 1961.

*   *   *

After Johanna's death in November 1956 Lotte had moved into her father's flat in the Dufourstrasse. During that winter Klemperer saw even fewer people than usual. Only on special occasions, such as the stage première of Schoenberg's *Moses und Aron* at the Zurich City Opera on 6 June 1957, did he venture out. Though much in the work impressed him, as a whole it left him unmoved.[49] To avoid having to answer questions about it, he refused to leave his seat in the interval.* Two months later he heard another new opera, when a visit to Munich coincided with the première of Hindemith's *Die Harmonie der Welt*. To his dismay, he found himself seated in a box alongside the composer's wife and was hard put to it to find suitable words about a work that he later described as 'terribly dull'.[50]

Lotte had suggested that they should as usual spend their summer vacation in a hotel. But, aware of the burden she had been bearing since Johanna's death, Klemperer opted to go to a sanatorium on Lake Constance, so as to enable her to spend three weeks on her own. The sanatorium failed to come up to expectations and within four days he was back in Zurich. On 21 July Lotte returned, alarmed by the news that he had fainted. A passing circulatory disturbance was diagnosed, and two days later he seemed well enough to set out for Salzburg, where he was to conduct the festival's opening concert. But on arrival there on 24 July he again felt so weak that on doctor's advice he returned to Zurich.

Within two weeks he had recovered sufficiently to start rehearsals for concerts he was to give with the Bavarian Radio Orchestra at the Edinburgh Festival on 23 and 25 August. Four days later at the festival he conducted the Philharmonia in a programme that included *Das Lied von der Erde*, a work he had not previously performed in Britain. On this occasion he opted to give it with a baritone instead of the usual contralto, as he had done when he had first conducted the work in Cologne in 1921 with Friedrich Schorr as soloist. In spite of Dietrich Fischer-Dieskau's fine singing, Klemperer's decision was widely criticised, notably by Desmond Shawe-Taylor, in whose opinion two male voices deprived the work of contrast and sensuous appeal.[51] Klemperer had, however, already reached a similar conclusion,[52] and never repeated the experiment.

---

* Helmuth Plessner, interview with the author, Zurich, January 1974. For a similar reason, when expecting a visitor, Klemperer would have any new scores he might be studying removed, so as to avoid being drawn into discussion of them.

Shawe-Taylor found 'little rapture or heartbreak or consolation' in Klemperer's interpretation, while *The Scotsman* remained 'quite unmoved'.⁵³ Klemperer was to some extent in accord with his critics. Back in Zurich on 1 September, he admitted in a letter to Helene Hirschler that 'the piece formerly moved me more than it does now'. But the roots of the general disenchantment in the press lay deeper. Klemperer's approach to the work stood in sharp contrast to Bruno Walter's, which Edinburgh had heard in 1947 and which was still widely accepted as authoritative. Whereas Walter stressed the nostalgic and consolatory side of the music, Klemperer brought out its inner anguish. In 1957 Edinburgh was no more ready to accept such an approach than Amsterdam had been seven years earlier. Klemperer was not usually troubled by unfavourable criticism, but in this instance he was still licking his wounds a month later. 'The London papers attacked me in an extraordinary way over *Das Lied von der Erde*', he wrote to Lonny Epstein on 2 October. 'They found that it didn't have enough feeling. There's little I can say to that. I did it as well as I could.' Some years were to elapse before Klemperer's Mahler interpretations gained widespread acceptance in Britain.

*   *   *

At the end of September 1957 Klemperer returned to London to conduct the Philharmonia in an extensive Beethoven cycle and also to record the symphonies.* From the opening concert on 11 October, which ended with the 'Eroica' Symphony, it seemed as though in Beethoven he could do no wrong. Among those who afterwards came to pay tribute was Herbert von Karajan, who told him, 'I have only come ... to say that I hope I shall live to conduct the Funeral March as well as you have done.'⁵⁴ *The Times* (4 November) praised what it described as 'a blazing account' of the Seventh Symphony. In the *Evening News* (9 November) Mosco Carner confessed to being 'transported' by a performance of the 'Emperor' Concerto, in which Claudio Arrau was the soloist. Arrau later recalled the quite special impact of the opening chord and described Klemperer's accompaniment as perhaps the finest he had ever experienced in the work.†

---

* Except Nos. 3, 5 and 7, which he had recorded two years earlier. To provide him with additional rehearsal time, the recordings were to be made before the concerts, a practice to which Legge increasingly resorted.

† Claudio Arrau (1903–91), celebrated Chilean pianist; interview with the author, London, 21 June 1977. He was, however, markedly less enthusiastic about their collaboration in Chopin's E minor Piano Concerto in Cologne on 25 October 1954. But his later claims – 'I had almost to *teach* Chopin to Klemperer. He had never conducted it. He had never even played Chopin himself' (Joseph Horowitz, *Conversations with Arrau*, p. 125) – are unfounded. In earlier days Klemperer frequently played Chopin for his own pleasure. He had conducted the E minor concerto in Los Angeles in 1937 and recorded it in Vienna in June 1951, on both occasions with Guiomar Novaes as soloist. Arrau did, however, admit to finding Klemperer more accommodating in Cologne than he had been thirty years earlier in Wiesbaden.

Legge was jubilant. 'The concerts are going like wildfire', he wrote to Dorle Soria of Angel Records in New York on 1 November.* 'There has been nothing like this in London's musical life since Toscanini in the 1930s.' Four days later, he reported again. 'Klemperer goes from strength to strength. When we have completed the Ninth I shall have given you a Beethoven cycle on records that will be prized as long as records are collected.'

For the Ninth Symphony, Legge had a special card up his sleeve. He had long nursed an ambition to form a choir to match his orchestra and in August 1956 had invited Wilhelm Pitz, with whose work at Bayreuth he was familiar, to train a chorus of two hundred amateur voices with professional stiffening. Auditions took place that autumn in London and rehearsals started in February 1957. Though Britain prided itself on the quality of its big choirs, the impact of the Philharmonia Chorus on its début in performances of the Ninth Symphony on 12 and 15 November 1957 was sensational. 'The finale', wrote *The Times* on 13 November, 'exceeded in grandeur and brilliance and human exhilaration all that the foregoing movements had implied, for the Philharmonia Chorus can really sing the music . . ., sing it accurately and with full, musicianly tone in every vocal part.' Mosco Carner described the performance as 'the triumphant climax to a series of concerts which will go down in the annals of London music as one of the most memorable in recent years'.[55]

There were some dissenters. Desmond Shawe-Taylor found the performance 'impressive' and 'solid', but less moving than others he had heard.[56] In the *Daily Telegraph* (13 November) Martin Cooper complained of a lack of 'lyrical tenderness' in the slow movement. But the overwhelming consensus of critical opinion was voiced by John Amis. 'The performance of the Ninth Symphony', he wrote, 'was something to remember for ever . . . It may be doubted whether we shall hear [its] like . . . when Klemperer has gone.'[57]

'The cycle came . . . to an indescribable conclusion', wrote Lotte a few days later. 'There was jubilation as never before.'[58] The orchestra and chorus presented Klemperer with a silver dish, inscribed 'in affection and gratitude'. Legge gave him a set of handsomely bound full scores and orchestral parts, complete with his markings, of the Third, Fifth and Seventh Symphonies. The London County Council commissioned a bust by Jacob Epstein for the Festival Hall. As Klemperer left the hall an hour and a half after the final concert had ended a hundred people or more were still standing in the cold outside the stage door and lined the path to his car.

Yet, as always when depressed, he could not bring himself to admit to satisfaction. 'Outwardly', he wrote to Helene Hirschler, 'it was probably a very great success', as though to call that success into question.[59] However, on

---

* Angel Records had been set up by EMI to distribute Legge's and other recordings in the United States.

the day after the final concert, he wrote a letter of congratulation to the Philharmonia Orchestra and Chorus: 'May I thank you with all my heart for the precious gift which you gave me yesterday evening. I thank you not only for your gift, but above all for your artistic achievements ... I am very proud of all of you.' Hitherto most orchestras had regarded Klemperer with a mixture of admiration and fear. With the Philharmonia, however, a bond had come into existence that was to endure until the end of his career. 'They really love him',[60] exclaimed Lotte, perhaps not without a trace of wonderment, for no one was more aware of the difficulties he was capable of provoking, when so disposed.

Virtually overnight, Klemperer came to be regarded as the last of the 'great' conductors. In an internal EMI memo, urging that his contract be renewed without delay, Legge described Klemperer as, 'with the possible exception of Karajan, the most valuable property we have among conductors'.[61] The telephone rang incessantly at the Hyde Park Hotel as agents, managers, journalists, promoters and other camp-followers of musical life attempted to climb on the bandwagon. But Klemperer was not a man easily swept off his feet; in the ups and downs of his own life he had learnt how fickle success could be. During all manner of discussions, he remained, said Lotte, 'as though lost in the clouds, occasionally descending to murmur, "I will think about it"'.[62] Now that he could pick and choose, he had no intention of allowing himself to be rushed into ill-considered commitments.

Lotte discovered that celebrity had its comic side. Because, in the past, she and her father had never been met at the airport in Vienna, she did not bother to inform the Gesellschaft der Musikfreunde of Vienna of their time of arrival when Klemperer flew there at the end of February 1958 to give three concerts with the Vienna Symphony Orchestra. As soon as they landed, she noticed something unusual:

> Who is that standing there with an enormous lilac bouquet? Why, the Director [of the Musikfreunde], together with his secretary and a cascade of sugary welcoming phrases. Papa looked astonished ... At the customs ... I was at once approached by an official who asked me to identify the baggage. 'I have instructions to get you through quickly.' When I wanted to change money, they were quite shocked. 'You can have as much as you want.' I said that a thousand Schillings [approximately £14] would be enough, whereupon they promptly gave me five thousand. Papa, who doesn't like rehearsing before 10 a.m., asked when the rehearsals would be. 'As you determine, Herr Professor' ... He then asked if they would take place in the same hall [as the concert]. 'We wouldn't *presume* to put you in another hall.' At that, Papa turned to me and with an expression of mock gravity asked, 'Did you hear that, Lotte?' The next morning I was sent six ... bottles of wine from the director 'mit Handkuss' ('with pleasure').

All this has nothing to do with love. They want a Beethoven cycle next year and the Brahms Requiem at the festival this June.[63]

As far as Lotte was concerned, Vienna was 'a beautiful stage set . . ., on which mediocre actors are performing a bad play'. Klemperer was more indulgent; he had what he himself admitted to be 'an unhappy love'[64] for a city which for him was so closely identified with Mahler. The visit went well. Heinrich Kralik, the city's senior critic, praised his conducting of Bruckner's Seventh Symphony and saluted him as the last survivor of a great generation of conductors.[65] Klemperer was gratified by the Vienna Symphony Orchestra's evident devotion to Bruckner. Before he left, he visited the wing of Schönbrunn Palace which had been his home from 1933 to 1935 and (as Lotte had foreseen) agreed to return in June for the Brahms Requiem.

*   *   *

Following Klemperer's triumphs in London and elsewhere, the young German Federal Republic decided that the time had come to present its citizen with one of its highest decorations, the Grosses Verdienstkreuz mit Stern.* He was at first in two minds whether to accept. 'You can imagine how I feel about it. Germany is a very dubious matter. We cannot and should not forget', he wrote to Helene Hirschler three days before he was due to receive the honour at the West German London embassy on 8 April 1958. To Lotte's relief, when the day came, her father was on his best behaviour. 'After the Ambassador had given an endless speech in which the word "German" recurred constantly . . ., my father thanked him and replied, ". . . Speaking is not my business. I would just like to say that all my life I have tried to give *good* music in *good* performances, and I will continue to do so".'[66] He was relieved when Helene Hirschler wrote to assure him that he had been right to accept the honour. But only a few days later, he began to have further doubts. He was disturbed by a newspaper report that a West German schoolmaster had been applauded by the local population after he had been sentenced to a year's imprisonment for anti-Semitic utterances.[67]

After two concerts in London on 7 and 10 April, Klemperer travelled to Stockholm. In contrast to the wild and unpredictable figure the city had last seen eleven years earlier, he now impressed the orchestra with his air of quiet authority. After the final concert it played a salute and the audience joined in with a standing ovation. At the age of seventy-three, he had within little more than three years succeeded in re-establishing a reputation at least as great as that he had enjoyed in Germany before 1933. The high ground had been regained. Physically he was in better shape than at any time since before the

---

* Walter Legge subsequently claimed (*Daily Telegraph*, 15 May 1974) that the award had been made as a result of his lobbying.

war. Best of all, the depression that had plagued him for six years had lifted. Lotte wrote to her friend, Loli Hatvány, from Stockholm on 17 April:

> a psychological balance has established itself, such as *I* have *never* known. He is good-humoured and cheerful, eats and sleeps well, doesn't sweat at night (as he has done for the last four years) ... works well ... and gets on with everyone. His wit and sense of mockery have also returned ... He is also conducting better than ever ... Everyone says he looks ten years younger. Our meals and being together have become a pleasure for me. We haven't laughed so much in a long time ... I had come to believe that it would never again be like this.

Perhaps in an attempt to disguise from herself what lay ahead, Lotte had, for once, misjudged the way the tide was flowing.

12

Ordeal by fire

In the spring of 1958 Klemperer had started to show a renewed interest in religious observances. He had again begun to compose. Both activities heralded a manic phase. In such periods he was prone, as Lotte put it, 'to spend money like a drunken sailor'.[1] In the past there had been little money for him to spend. In recent years, however, his earnings had been substantial, and Fritz Fischer urged him to give Lotte a power of attorney. He at first reacted angrily, but eventually accepted what proved to be sound counsel.

On 9 June Klemperer set out for Vienna, where six days later he conducted a performance of Brahms's German Requiem with the Vienna Philharmonic Orchestra and the Singverein of the Gesellschaft der Musikfreunde. Wilma Lipp and Eberhard Wächter were the excellent soloists. 'We have heard [the Requiem] a dozen times in recent years and from conductors of the calibre of Schuricht, Furtwängler and Karajan', wrote the *Express*.[2] 'Yet yesterday in the Musikverein we seemed to be hearing it for the first time.' Klemperer was delighted with the orchestra, which he had not conducted for ten years, and agreed to return during the following winter to conduct a Beethoven cycle. A Mozart cycle and a series of concerts of contemporary music were to follow in the 1959–60 season.[3] Operatic projects were also afoot. In the autumn of 1956 Klemperer had been invited by the general administrator of Covent Garden, David Webster, to conduct *Fidelio* in London. After some hesitation he finally refused on account of his heavy concert commitments and the unsuitability of the old sets. But Webster promised to return when Covent Garden could afford new ones, and in November 1957 he proved as good as his word.[4] Klemperer was still unwilling to commit himself. But, after a flying visit to Vienna, Webster was able to announce that Klemperer would both produce and conduct a new production of Beethoven's opera at Covent Garden in March 1960.

In April 1958, Klemperer had summoned Peter Diamand, the director of the Holland Festival, to London and told him that he would like to conduct *Tristan und Isolde* in the following year with the Concertgebouw Orchestra in the pit and Wieland Wagner as producer. Aware of New Bayreuth's debt to the Kroll Oper,[5] Wieland lost little time in inviting him to conduct any opera he chose at Bayreuth. Klemperer opted for *Die Meistersinger* at the 1959 festival.[6] He also agreed to conduct and produce *Tristan und Isolde* at the Metropolitan Opera in New York in December 1959. Thus, after decades during which most of the world's leading opera houses had seemed scarcely aware of his existence, no fewer than four new productions lay ahead, two of which he would stage himself. To outward appearances his career was flourishing as never before. But Lotte was worried. Her father, she wrote to a friend from Vienna,

> is again very high ... In January the depression lifted and there followed three perfect months during which he was absolutely balanced. Then in Amsterdam in May came the first unmistakable signs of a mania ... He is again blissfully happy and for all his seventy-three years enjoys life in every way. He looks splendid, has put on 15 kg. since December, is able to take a bath without help, then at about 6.30 a.m. comes beaming into my room and talks without drawing breath.
>
> Wherever we are, he is always on the move, rushing around without in fact doing anything. There are no evenings without people or the theatre, and at night he goes off to the most dangerous localities. You can understand how much all this worries me ... He only has to slip ... or to fall into bad hands with God knows what danger of blackmail ... The possibilities are endless.
>
> ... He is quite aware of his condition, and also that he can't really do anything about it though he tries to and that is much. ... He has a great desire to smoke but doesn't ..., so that at least there isn't the continual danger of fire, as he has no inhibitions about falling asleep anywhere. He's on sedatives, but these seem to me of scarcely any use.[7]

After the visit to Vienna, Klemperer took advantage of a break in his schedule to visit his younger sister, Marianne, whom he had not seen since 1951. The Israel Philharmonic Orchestra got wind of his presence and invited him to conduct a concert at short notice in Tel Aviv. In spite of Lotte's protests and the intense heat, he accepted, only to be obliged to cancel after he had fainted in the corridor of his hotel. That did not prevent him from turning up at a rehearsal four days later and for his own amusement running through the first movement of Beethoven's Symphony No. 7. Meanwhile his restlessness was growing more intense. He spent days in theological discussions with a Dominican priest who heard his confession and gave him communion. At night he was out on the town. By the end of a fortnight of ceaseless activity, he was exhausted. But before leaving for Zurich, he agreed to return in the winter to give four concerts with the Israel Philharmonic. Agreement on programmes proved hard to reach, however, and the tone of the management's letters grew sharp as it became apparent that Klemperer had no intention of signing a contract before the differences had been settled to his satisfaction.[8] Ill health then obliged him to cancel the concerts.*

After a few days in Zurich, Klemperer and Lotte left on 14 July 1958 for a summer holiday at the Waldhaus Hotel at Sils-Maria in the Swiss Engadin. Klemperer spent much time composing, among other items a waltz for the hotel's trio, which was performed in the lounge for the benefit of the guests.[9] The Waldhaus also boasted a chapel, where he occasionally attended Mass. 'My father's recent rediscovery of Catholicism', wrote Lotte ironically,

> would shame the Pope ... He has become friendly with a priest ... to whom he constantly tried to explain theological issues, above all the freedom of the will (which my father categorically denies – a position that isn't exactly Catholic) ... At the moment he is travelling with a two-volume Old Testament, a New Testament, Luther's Bible, the Psalms in Latin and German, also in Hebrew (which he can't read), Thomas à Kempis – and the Koran ... And of course a missal together with a four-volume breviary.[10]

To provide Lotte with a much-needed respite, it was agreed that Werner, who had joined his father at Sils-Maria, should accompany him to London, where on 17 August he was to begin rehearsals with the Philharmonia for concerts at the 1958 Edinburgh Festival.

* * *

The first reports from London were not encouraging. On 20 August Werner telephoned Lotte with the news that his father was cutting short rehearsals and seemed basically uninterested in work. At nights Klemperer would go off on his own and only return in the small hours. On one such excursion, he insisted that Peter Diamand, who had come to London to discuss arrangements for the Holland Festival *Tristan*, should accompany him to the Stork Club, a plush night-spot much favoured at the time. Having signed himself in as Mr Black, and his embarrassed companion as Mr White, he announced that he would have a blonde and Diamand a brunette. Hostesses were produced and Klemperer danced. But when the ladies made it plain that their task was confined to such services, he called for the bill and indicated his ill humour by slowly and noisily counting the notes on the table. Outside, he announced that he was going to Bayswater, where he would find what he wanted. When Diamand refused to go with him, Klemperer bundled

---

* Illness had also forced him to cancel two previous invitations to conduct the Israel Philharmonic, in 1952 and 1955. This, together with the orchestra's unspoken assumption that as a Jew he owed it a favour, subsequently led to rather strained relations, as is illustrated by the following (possibly apocryphal) story. Klemperer had expressed disappointment that the orchestra had not approached him earlier. The manager replied that, as a Jew who had converted to Catholicism, he was a heretic. Klemperer pointed out that the same could be said of Koussevitzky, who had conducted the orchestra. 'Yes', replied the manager, 'but without a fee'. Klemperer: 'I'm still Jewish enough not to do that.'

him into a taxi. He himself returned some hours later, yet the following morning appeared punctually at rehearsal.[11]

Lotte became increasingly fearful. 'It is really terrible to look on as he destroys himself', she wrote on 24 August to Helene Hirschler,

> And there's ... as good as nothing one can do about it ... It's just not possible to put someone who has to appear in public under care ... I reflect how many years of patience and perseverance, effort and work, were necessary to achieve what, almost miraculously, has been achieved ... And can so easily be destroyed at a single stroke. These are terrible thoughts.

By the time Klemperer reached Edinburgh, where he had concerts on 24 and 26 August, he had become infatuated with an attractive young red-haired cellist who had recently joined the orchestra. The festival had taken rooms for him and Werner at a centrally situated and comfortable hotel; the orchestral players were as usual lodged in a spartan university hostel on the city's periphery. On arrival, Klemperer informed Robert Ponsonby,* the festival's director, that he wished to stay at the hostel too. Without checking, Ponsonby rashly replied that it was full. But Klemperer, who had ascertained that a room (no. 38) was vacant, was not to be easily outmanoeuvred. Early on the following morning, on arriving at Waverley Station to meet an artist from the night sleeper, Ponsonby was startled to see the conspicuous figure of Klemperer attempting to get a lift from a passing motorist. Ponsonby found a cab and told the driver to take Klemperer to his hotel. Klemperer however insisted on going to the hostel.

At midday he turned up without warning in Ponsonby's office and gave instructions that a pair of letter-scales be put between them. They were, he told Ponsonby, to debate the question of where he would stay and weights would be added to either side of the scales according to which of them won points in the argument. A compromise was eventually reached, according to which Klemperer would sleep in his hotel, but during the day would compose in the hostel, on the grounds that it was quieter there. Later that day Ponsonby received a letter in English, which Klemperer had apparently typed himself.[12]

> Now the scales of justice shoed [sic] me that I *won*, I hope that No. 38 is now available. If it should not be ... it WILL BE VERY GAD [i.e. bad] for the authorities of Edinburgh and you. In other words I warned you.
>   With best and cordial regards,
>   Your sincere friend,
>   Otto Klemperer.
> East Suffolk Street, No. 38.

---

* Robert Ponsonby (b. 1926). Artistic director of the Edinburgh Festival (1956–60), Administrator, Scottish National Orchestra (1964–72), Music Controller, BBC (1972–85).

Klemperer's manic phases had their comic moments. But neither his Edinburgh concerts nor those that followed in Lucerne on 3 and 10 September with the Berlin Philharmonic and Philharmonia orchestras respectively earned the sort of plaudits in the press that had become usual since his return to Europe.

From Lucerne the Philharmonia went to Vienna, where it was to record the *Missa solemnis* with Karajan. Klemperer, keen not to lose sight of the red-headed cellist, elected to join it. There were anxious moments for Lotte and Werner, who went with him. Karajan gave orders that no visitors were to be allowed into the recording sessions, which were being held in the Grosser Saal of the Musikverein. Security was tight. Clem Relf, the Philharmonia's librarian and Klemperer's right-hand man at the orchestra, was alarmed to hear one morning that Klemperer was in the building's basement and apparently trying to find his way into the hall. Relf eventually tracked him down in the gloom of a storeroom. 'Stick 'em up!' Klemperer called out in English, and there was a flash as he flicked his lighter at Relf. Unfortunately he had failed to get the lighter completely out of his pocket and there was a strong smell of burning. Having made sure that Klemperer's suit was not alight, Relf escorted him up to the hall.[13]

*   *   *

In London, Klemperer was to give no fewer than twenty-one concerts with the Philharmonia during the coming season. He was to open the Leeds Triennial Festival with Beethoven's *Missa solemnis*. He was to conduct *Tristan* in Holland and there were to be Beethoven cycles in Vienna as well as London. As Walter Legge wrote later, 'No season had looked rosier.'[14] It might have daunted a man half Klemperer's age. But in a manic phase his energies were boundless. In any case, as he wrote to an old friend, 'I have conducted these things so often that I won't have to work too much.'[15] On his return to Zurich from Vienna he was almost always out at nights. He had again begun to smoke. Attempts to persuade him to consult a psychiatrist were met with the outraged protestation that he had rarely felt so well balanced. Lotte thereupon decided that the time had come to call a halt. The result was a furious quarrel: for three days father and daughter did not speak. On 25 September, however, exhausted by the life he had been leading, he felt unwell and remained in bed. It was only then that he admitted that a few days earlier he had had a bad fall, since when his right lung had been paining him. By the evening he had developed bronchitis and as a result had to cancel the *Missa solemnis* in Leeds, as well as a projected visit to Venice to attend the first performance of Stravinsky's *Threni*.[16]

By the evening of 30 September 1958 the temperature was down and Werner left for America. Lotte set her alarm clock for 3 a.m. in order to check that her father was comfortable. On entering his bedroom a terrifying sight met her eyes: his bedclothes were on fire.

> There were already big flames. He ... had his feet on the floor and was struggling to get free. I extinguished the flames on him as he lay on the floor ... Then I cut away everything from his body. He was conscious and kept calling out, 'Water, water.' But I knew that he mustn't be given any.[17]

What had occurred was what Lotte had long feared. Klemperer had fallen asleep while smoking his pipe and woken to find the bedclothes smouldering. Half asleep and panic-stricken, he had seized the nearest liquid – a bottle of 75 per cent proof spirits of camphor that had been used to massage a neuralgic area of his neck. This highly inflammable fluid he had poured over the bed-linen, which had at once burst into flames.

A rapid examination at Hirslanden Hospital revealed that a good 15 per cent of his body had suffered second- and third-degree burns. Worst affected were his chest, left arm, armpits and neck. The right side, including his face, was also burnt. He was suffering from intense nausea. Inevitably, the bronchitis flared up. Two days later, on 3 October, loss of body fluids caused kidney failure. The only available kidney support machine was in the Cantonal Hospital, but by this time Klemperer was too ill to be moved. That night Lotte was advised to sleep in the hospital, as it was feared that her father might not survive it. For three days he hovered between life and death. Then on 6 October his kidneys started to function. The immediate crisis was over.[18]

Klemperer was unaware of how close to death he had come. The doctors and nurses were astonished by the stoicism with which he supported the intense pain of the burns he had suffered. Worst of all was the agony of the daily changing of the bandages in which he was swathed. In an effort not to cry out, his whole body trembled, yet not once did he accept morphia.[19] It was some weeks before the doctors decided skin grafts would be necessary and an operation was performed on 13 November. By mid-December the wounds seemed to have healed. Dressings were no longer necessary, and it was thought that he would be able to return home with a nurse before the end of the year and even to begin work in February or March 1959. Yet he failed to gain strength as expected. A few steps cost him a great effort, even when supported on either side. Conversation with visitors left him exhausted. Two wounds on his chest reopened.[20]

Lotte had at first supposed that the shock her father had suffered would put an end to his euphoria, as indeed at first seemed to be the case. But, with the New Year, the manic phase began to reassert itself. The doctors hoped that this might revive his normally formidable powers of recuperation, but by mid-February his general condition was basically unchanged. As Lotte reported, 'He spent most of his time in bed, still had to be fed and was incapable of taking a step on his own.' It was none the less decided that he should return home with day and night nurses. Once there, he went straight to his piano, only to discover that what since his brain tumour operation he had regarded as his 'good' hand was now the 'bad' one. He still lacked the energy to get up and, if persuaded to do so, returned to bed exhausted after half an hour. Yet the longer he remained bedridden, the more debilitated he became. In March a return of the cystitis that intermittently plagued him left him weaker than ever. More wounds were reopening and his condition appeared to be deteriorating.[21]

By 16 March the entire chest was covered with wounds. 'None of the many treatments has had any effect', Lotte wrote despairingly in one of the regular bulletins that she sent out to friends and relations. Klemperer dubbed them *Hirtenbriefe*, or 'pastoral letters'.

> ... In other words the situation is now critical. If we go on as at present, it can only mean an ... increasingly distressing and painful wasting away ... Therefore a last attempt *must* be made. The doctors know the risks involved and you should be aware of them too. There is no other choice but with God's help he will pull through and be spared for a few short but fruitful years.
>
> It was decided yesterday evening that a fresh attempt should be made to transplant new skin on the chest. Therefore the day after tomorrow we go with an ambulance and two nurses to the Cantonal Hospital in Solothurn.[22]

There the chest was scrubbed with cooking salt compresses in order to remove the granulated tissue that had formed wherever the grafts had not taken. The following day a large area of skin was removed from Klemperer's right thigh and pressed in small pieces on the chest. Eight days later, the same treatment was used in an attempt to close the few small places still open. This second operation proved unsuccessful but, once the major grafts had taken, other wounds started to heal of their own accord. With that came a slow but steady improvement in Klemperer's general condition and by 8 May 1959 he was strong enough to return home.[23]

*   *   *

After the fire the press had been told that Klemperer was suffering from bronchitis 'with complications'. The Beethoven cycle he was to have conducted in London in October and November 1958 was cancelled, and twenty recordings with the Philharmonia were postponed. To maintain his morale, Klemperer was at first allowed to believe that he would be able to fulfil engagements later in the season, even though there was little possibility of his doing so. Walter Legge, on a visit from London, found it 'a chilling experience to have to lie to this huge, fearless and determined old man, now helpless, bandaged and prostrate, knowing perfectly well that even if he recovered he had months of suffering ahead'.[24] Klemperer at first accepted the situation. But as the manic phase revived he grew restive.

He looked forward eagerly to Bach's *St Matthew Passion*, which in May 1959 he was due to record and perform in London. Choral rehearsals under Wilhelm Pitz had already begun when, on 7 April, Lotte informed Walter Legge that her father would not be able to fulfil the engagement,[25] though at this point Klemperer did not know it. Later in the month, Klemperer, who was still in hospital, informed his surgeon that 'even at the risk of my life, I'm going to conduct that *Matthew Passion*'. 'I don't think you will be risking your life', the surgeon replied, 'but you may well be risking your career.'[26] Shortly afterwards Lotte broke the news that she had cancelled the engagement.

Klemperer finally returned home on 8 May. The start of the *Tristan* rehearsals in Holland was less than three weeks away. Lotte had long harboured strong doubts about the feasibility of the project and had asked Peter Diamand to come to Zurich to persuade her father to withdraw. For moral support, Diamand brought with him Hans van Leeuwen, the concert manager of the Concertgebouw, with whom Klemperer was on cordial terms. On arrival they found him studying the score of *Tristan*. Before they could broach the matter, Klemperer proceeded to go through the entire work, dictating detailed instructions. When he had finished, he made it clear that the interview was over. Back in Holland, Diamand took the precaution of engaging Ferdinand Leitner as deputy conductor.[27]

Meanwhile, to celebrate his seventy-fourth birthday on 14 May, Klemperer engaged a local orchestra to play through some of his recent compositions. Lotte at first opposed such a costly project – the family finances had already been severely depleted by his extravagance and the expenses of a long illness. On reflection, however, she came to the conclusion that if he were going to collapse while conducting, it was better that he should do so in his home town, rather than in the glare of an international festival.[28] In fact the event, on 21 May, went better than she had dared hope. Once confronted with an orchestra, Klemperer seemed a new man; for three hours he worked intensively without showing fatigue or suffering after-effects.[29] Somewhat reassured, Lotte set out on 27 May with her father and a nurse, Sister Käthi Egli, for The Hague and *Tristan*.

At first all went well. Klemperer was strongly affected by music he had not conducted since his years in Cologne. In Wieland Wagner he found a sympathetic collaborator* and he was well satisfied with a cast headed by

---

* The two men had taken to each other at their first meeting in the previous winter at Klemperer's hospital bedside, when Klemperer is said to have opened the conversation by asking 'What was it like sitting on the Führer's knee?' (Hitler, an old friend of Wieland's British-born mother, Winifred, had been a frequent visitor to Wahnfried, the family house in Bayreuth.)

Martha Mödl and Ramon Vinay. A young Hungarian, Peter Erös, was hired to conduct the backstage orchestra and play the piano at rehearsals. As is customary when speaking to a senior German conductor, he addressed Klemperer as 'Herr Generalmusikdirektor'. 'Don't call me that', he was told sharply. 'I am neither the general of the army nor the director of a bank. I have a name: Dr Klemperer. K-L-E-M-P-E-R-E-R.'[30] Two rehearsals with the singers and lunch with Wieland Wagner on the day after his arrival left Klemperer exhausted. But by the following morning he had sufficiently recovered to work with the singers with all his old concentration. That evening he attended Wieland's first stage rehearsal and made detailed comments with unusual diplomacy. 'If all goes well', wrote Lotte on 30 May, 'the performance should be something special.' After the first two days of Klemperer's orchestral rehearsals, Ferdinand Leitner prepared to leave, convinced that his services would not be needed.[31]

On 5 June, however, a few small wounds reopened on Klemperer's chest and his general condition began to worsen. Five days later Lotte wrote to tell friends that

> As a result of the pain and the infection he is much more easily tired and could hardly get through the rehearsals. Naturally the results were also weak. He spared himself and hardly moved, [but] ... the last two days' rehearsals have been disastrous and since then I've been urging him to withdraw. He cannot and must not risk ... a spread of the infection.
>
> After a long, calm discussion he has now come to see all that. Of course, he is very cast down ... But, believe me, it is best so ... It was a grandiose ... effort (*Versuch*).[32]

At the same time Klemperer also withdrew from *Die Meistersinger* in Bayreuth, where he had been scheduled to go for rehearsals after Holland. Later that summer Wieland Wagner sent him a facsimile of the autograph score of *Tristan* and wrote, 'I know that your *Meistersinger* would have been a musical event ... whose impact on Bayreuth and the interpretation of Wagner as a whole would have been of incalculable importance.'[33]

On 11 June Hans van Leeuwen accompanied Lotte and her father to Amsterdam airport. In the waiting-room that had been set aside for them, Klemperer took out his rosary and photographs of his parents and Johanna. It was, van Leeuwen felt, as though he believed his career was over.[34]

Treatment at the Cantonal Hospital in Solothurn proved so successful that by 1 July 1959 Klemperer was well enough to return home. Three days later he travelled to St Moritz with Sister Käthi and a wheelchair. When Lotte joined them there on 11 July, she found him almost miraculously improved. Thanks to the efforts of a masseur he had abandoned the chair and was quiet and cheerful. He was no longer composing, though at Lotte's suggestion he did write out the full score of the *Merry Waltz*; the original had been lost. He found it a therapeutic project. Meanwhile, Klemperer had been obliged to postpone the *Fidelio* he was to have produced and conducted at Covent Garden in the coming season, though he assured Legge that he would be well enough to conduct two concerts with the Philharmonia Orchestra at the Lucerne Festival in early September.[35]

*   *   *

Legge was doubtless relieved to receive that news, for during Klemperer's long absence he had found himself in difficulties. For various reasons Herbert von Karajan had grown impatient with EMI, and in January 1959 had signed a contract to record with the Vienna Philharmonic Orchestra for Decca. Two months later he had made his first recording with Deutsche Grammophon. When, after interminable wrangling, Karajan finally renewed his EMI contract in August 1959 for a further two years, it yielded little more than a handful of pot-boilers. The biggest fish had got away.

Fortunately for Legge a replacement was at hand and he cast round for means of binding Klemperer more closely to the Philharmonia. On 17 August 1959 he told him that he proposed to appoint him its 'principal conductor for life'. In accepting this largely spurious title, Klemperer told the orchestra that he looked forward to an association of many years. One of the players observed that, to judge from Klemperer's appearance, it 'looked as though it might only last a few weeks'.[36]

*   *   *

Klemperer conducted his two concerts in Lucerne as promised. The first was an all-Tchaikovsky programme; the second was devoted to Mozart. They went off without incident, though Lotte noted that her father had emerged from the fire and the tribulations that followed perceptibly aged.[37] Indeed, by the time he arrived in London on 30 September 1959 for an arduous series of recordings and concerts, his health was again causing concern. After two days of rehearsals for *Don Giovanni*, which was to be recorded and then given two concert performances at the Festival Hall, an unexplained high temperature obliged him to withdraw from both projects.* Lotte was even more disturbed by her father's lack of interest in his work. 'I don't want to alarm you, but I doubt whether he will be able to fulfil his commitments', she told friends on 5 October.

> If he were twenty years younger, I would now say to him, 'Come along, free yourself for a while from all engagements' ... But ... one cannot ... force

---

* The recording was taken over by Carlo Maria Giulini, the concert performances by Colin Davis, who enjoyed a success that eventually led to a series of important positions in British music.

[such a step] on a man ... who is after all in his seventy-fifth year, because by doing so one would be depriving him of the only thing for which he lives.

An electrocardiogram indicated pericarditis (an inflammation of the membranes surrounding the heart), not in itself a serious condition, but one that was liable to recur. Though Klemperer's temperature soon returned to normal, the doctors insisted that he withdraw from his sole remaining operatic commitment, *Tristan* in New York, where rehearsals were due to begin in early December. Only fear of undermining his morale further prevented them from similarly urging him to abandon the Beethoven cycle due to start in London on 26 October. A week earlier Lotte had written, 'The last two days have increased my anxiety ... [Papa] moves with great effort ..., says little, looks drawn and white, and sleeps a great deal. I have the impression of a seriously sick man, though clinically everything is in order.'[38]

It might indeed have been better for Klemperer's reputation in London had he at this point done as his doctors wished and abandoned the cycle. Mosco Carner found the first two movements of the 'Eroica' lacking in tension and dynamic drive.[39] Neville Cardus wrote that the Symphony No. 4 was 'rather staid and deliberate'.[40] The 'Pastoral' was better received, if only because, as *The Times* (17 November) delicately suggested, it was suited to a conductor who had now 'reached a less vehement time of life'. David Cairns (using the pseudonym Adam Bell) found the Ninth Symphony lacking the fiery spirit of the performances he had given two years earlier.[41] 'It is no use pretending out of sympathy for Dr Klemperer', wrote *The Times* (30 November) at the end of the cycle, 'that his intellectual grasp of Beethoven any longer soars above ... his physical infirmity.'

*   *   *

Yet in spite of his infirmity, Klemperer was very active in London. On 7 November he attended a rehearsal of Stravinsky's *Oedipus Rex* under the composer. Six days later, he uncharacteristically donned a dinner jacket for a performance of *Salome* at Covent Garden. On 18 November he attended a Brecht evening at the Festival Hall, whither he returned a few days later to hear Beecham conduct Haydn's Symphony No. 99, which he enjoyed greatly, and Offenbach's rarely performed Cello Concerto. At the end of the month Lotte noted in her diary that her father was smoking again. On their return to Zurich in early December they learned that Werner's wife, Susan, had given birth to a son, Mark. He was Klemperer's first grandchild. Delighted by the news, Klemperer wrote to the parents in English, congratulating them and asking about the baby's weight. He ended the letter, 'The best wishes for you three! Your father, father-in-law and grandfather, O.K.'[42]

As Lotte was unwell, Hilde Firtel, whom Klemperer had got to know in

16   Drawing of Klemperer by Willy Dreifuss, 1960

Vienna in the summer of 1933, undertook to accompany him on his next visit to London, where, together with a nurse, they arrived on 16 January 1960. On the following evening he went out in search of a night-club and only returned in the small hours. The doctor prescribed sedation and for a day or two he was quieter. But the restlessness soon reasserted itself and, in the absence of Lotte's restraining hand, Klemperer's life became increasingly frenetic. In the daytime he was kept busy by recording sessions and rehearsals, but most evenings he was out and about. Within the space of a few days at the end of January he attended another Brecht evening, heard an act of *La Traviata* at Covent Garden with Joan Sutherland ('an extraordinarily beautiful voice and an extraordinarily bad actress'),[43] was present at Sadler's Wells' new staging of *Oedipus Rex* and a concert given by Yehudi Menuhin at the Festival Hall. On 25 January he attended a rehearsal with Annie Fischer and afterwards took her to supper at the Savoy Hotel, where he ran up a large bill and took to the dance floor with Hilde Firtel.[44] At the Hyde Park Hotel he received an unending flow of visitors, including Arthur Koestler, with whom he became friendly.* At the invitation of Covent Garden's chairman, the Earl of Drogheda, he saw *Lucia di Lammermoor* from the royal box and was only with difficulty restrained from leaving in the first interval. Afterwards he went to supper at the home of the Earl of Harewood,† where he and Hilde Firtel played Schubert.[45] After dinner with Neville Cardus and Else Mayer-Lismann, he drew a bundle of papers out of his coat pocket and proceeded to read a short story he had written about a visit to a prostitute.[46] Cardus persuaded Klemperer to dictate his memories of Mahler, which later in the year were published in German.‡ It was a strenuous existence for a man of almost seventy-five, who had undergone a protracted illness, and was also working hard. In the circumstances it is not altogether surprising that a Brahms cycle in early February failed to arouse much enthusiasm.

That same month, Klemperer, who was an avid newspaper reader, discovered that the almanacs of the Verein Deutsche Tonkünstler und Musiklehrer (Association of German Musicians and Music Teachers) had in successive years failed to mention the anniversaries of the births of Mendelssohn and Mahler. On 13 February, enraged by what he took to be a deliberate slight to two composers of Jewish blood whose music had been banned during the Third Reich, he sent the association a letter of protest:

> One has the impression that the years of the shameful regime of 1933 to 1945 are back ... Has the VDTM forgotten that the Gewandhaus [Orchestra] and the Vienna Opera were renewed by Mendelssohn and Mahler ...?

---

* Arthur Koestler (1905–83). Hungarian-born journalist and writer. Author of *Darkness at Noon* (1940).

† Earl of Harewood (b. 1923). Held various posts at Covent Garden, 1951–72. Managing director of Sadler's Wells (later English National) Opera, 1972–85. Artistic adviser, New Philharmonia Orchestra, 1966–76.

‡ These were published in Britain in 1964 in a somewhat expanded version with the title *Minor Recollections*. Klemperer was highly entertained by the review in the *Sunday Times* (1 November 1964). 'Dr Klemperer's *Minor Recollections*', wrote Desmond Shawe-Taylor, 'are just that.'

> But I am doing the association an injustice. Probably the Communists are to blame ... They are the scapegoats to whom all evils are attributed ...
>
> I hope that the irony of my words is apparent ... We immigrants – Jews, Catholics and Protestants – know very well where all this comes from: not from the Communists, but from the Fascists who still occupy leading positions in Germany. The rule of law which was overturned by Hitler must be reinstated. That would be justice in the name of art.
>
> Perhaps I should end this letter with the words:
>
> With treudeutschem Gruss,* 'Heil Hitler'.
>
> Dr Otto Klemperer.

The association protested its innocence. But, like many intellectuals whose sympathies lay on the left, Klemperer had become suspicious of what he regarded as the increasingly conservative face and growing power of the young Federal German Republic. Within a few days he found further ground for concern. On 23 February *The Times* reported that the German defence ministry was negotiating with General Franco's government to establish depots and training areas in Spain, which Klemperer chose to regard as 'a last step before a great world catastrophe'.[47] One way and another, West Germany continued to preoccupy him. 'I am truly pleased that I have nothing to do in Germany in the coming season', he wrote to a friend in Israel.[48] Taken gently to task by a German friend for resorting to the sort of generalisations to which the National Socialists had been so prone, he explained his position in more considered words:

> I was born [in Germany] and regard Hamburg, where I went to school and grew up, as my home town. I am well aware that there are good people in all countries. I have no intention of maintaining my attitude for ever. I very much hope that political circumstances will alter and that I too shall be able to alter [my position]. But at the moment I am so enraged by what has happened in Germany ... since Christmas† that for the moment I do not want to go there.[49]

*　　　*　　　*

After a short visit to The Hague in March 1960 to visit his elder sister, Regi, who had settled there to be near her son, Klemperer returned home to Switzerland for a six-week break, during which he conducted three concerts, all of them in Zurich. Back in London at the end of April, he gave an all-Tchaikovsky programme, consisting of the 1812 Overture, the First Piano Concerto and the 'Pathétique' Symphony, a work he had not conducted there before. David Cairns found the first half of the concert 'heavy going'.[50] But

---

* The phrase does not mean 'a true German greeting', as it was mistranslated in the *Observer* (21 February 1960). *Treudeutsch* is a pejorative expression, meaning simple or dim-witted. *Mit deutschem Gruss* was a much favoured way of ending letters in the Third Reich; Klemperer was making a play on words.

† Conceivably a reference to the desecration of a Cologne synagogue on Christmas Eve, an incident followed by similar outrages elsewhere in the Federal Republic.

17   Klemperer with son Werner and grandson Mark, London, May 1960

there was widespread admiration for an interpretation of the symphony that made up in architectural strength for what it lacked in brilliance and excitement. In comparison, three Mozart programmes later in the month were coolly received.

An undercurrent of discontent with Klemperer's increasingly stereotyped programmes in London also became evident. The Tchaikovsky concert apart, he had conducted nothing but symphonies and concertos by Beethoven, Brahms and Mozart during the season. Legge's need to recoup the losses he had suffered during Klemperer's eighteen-month absence from the Festival Hall was no doubt partly to blame. But Desmond Shawe-Taylor regretted that a musician who 'in his young days [had been] a highly successful champion of what was then new and good ...' should be

18 Left to right: Bruno Walter, Wilma Lipp and Otto Klemperer in Vienna, June 1960. Photo: Elfriede Hanak, Vienna

turned into 'a mere purveyor of handsomely . . . boxed sets of the World's Classics'.[51]

In contrast to his seventieth birthday, Klemperer's seventy-fifth was widely celebrated. Messages of congratulation poured in from far and wide, including one from the President of the Federal German Republic. On 11 May EMI gave a reception at the Dorchester Hotel at which the British soprano Heather Harper sang eight of Klemperer's songs. *The Times* (14 May) found them 'muscular and thoughtful, [though] rather old-fashioned in idiom for one who was best known in his younger days as a champion of Schoenberg, Stravinsky and Hindemith'. Werner, now pursuing a successful film career in Hollywood, flew to London for the occasion with his wife Susan and their baby son. Klemperer, who had not seen his grandson before, expressed his pleasure in a small piece of music he composed specially for his daughter-in-law. Among the many tributes was an elaborate encomium from Wieland Wagner: 'Classical Greece, Jewish tradition, medieval Christendom, German Romanticism and the realism of our time are all combined in this man and make Klemperer the conductor a unique artistic phenomenon.'[52]

On 25 May Klemperer flew to Vienna to conduct a complete cycle of Beethoven symphonies with the Philharmonia. The change of scene seemed to bring about a sudden revival of his energies. The critics marvelled that so frail a body could deliver performances of such power. Their doyen, Heinrich Kralik, wrote that the second concert had confirmed and strengthened 'an impression of truly authentic Beethoven',[53] even if the tempi were sometimes slower than those Vienna was used to. On 7 June the Ninth Symphony brought the cycle to a triumphant conclusion. The chorus was the Singverein of the Gesellschaft der Musikfreunde; the quartet of soloists Wilma Lipp, Ursula Boese, Fritz Wunderlich and Franz Crass. Karl Löbl, the critic of the *Express*, could not recall a performance to equal it: 'Klemperer hardly conducted ... Sometimes he seemed only to be listening. But what tension and intensity, what virility in the organic growth of the movements ..., what clarity of structure, what melodic expressiveness in the slow movement and hymn-like ecstasy in the finale.'[54] Bruno Walter was also in Vienna, to conduct a farewell concert with the Philharmonic Orchestra. Klemperer attended his rehearsal of Mahler's Fourth Symphony. It was the last time the two conductors met; Walter was to die in California less than two years later.

After recording Brahms's Violin Concerto with David Oistrakh in Paris, Klemperer took his vacation for the second year running in St Moritz, where he set about composing a biblical opera, *Thamar*.* Lotte found him for the moment quiet and cheerful.[55] The improvement proved short-lived. A few days after his return to Zurich on 17 August, he resumed his nocturnal excursions. Fearful lest he might injure himself or get into trouble, Lotte on one occasion decided to follow him:

> I went to the café he usually goes to first and sat ... at a table with a good view ... Then he came in. He was walking uncertainly and slowly. He had his glasses on and he saw me. He stood only a yard away, stared at me ... for about thirty seconds (I stared back) and then slowly moved off. He had absolutely failed to recognise me.[56]

* Tamar, daughter of David, who was raped by her brother, Amnon (2 Samuel 13). Only the funeral march from the opera and its libretto have survived.

That a manic phase had reasserted itself was all too apparent at a concert he gave with the Philharmonia in Lucerne on 1 September. One critic claimed that Klemperer hardly had the strength to hold together Bach's Brandenburg Concerto No. 1. Another reported that in *Das Lied von der Erde* the orchestra seemed not to be paying attention to its conductor, so that 'a typically English fog lay over the performance'.[57] In rehearsal Klemperer's beat was so vague that Hugh Bean, who had been leading the orchestra for three years, resorted to indicating entries as best he could. To Rudolf Firkušny, the soloist in the 'Emperor' Concerto four days later, Klemperer seemed to be having difficulty in rehearsal in indicating what he wanted. The performance went better.[58] Even so, the critic of *Die Stadt* (6 September) found the orchestral playing in the *Coriolan* overture limp and lacking in precision, and the 'Eroica' deficient in detail and tension.

Lotte found her father's personal behaviour equally disturbing. Usually aloof to the court liable to cluster around a great conductor, in Lucerne he seemed to bathe in the adoration of fans who, as Lotte scornfully put it, 'hang on his most trivial observations as though he were Socrates in person'.

> I have never known him so vain and eager for attention. Sometimes I cannot believe my eyes and ears. He repeats his old stories, recommends his own records as the 'best', is willing to be photographed by anyone and at any time and runs down his colleagues as never before. In me he sees only a middle-class spoilsport and worrier, etc., etc. In addition I am written off on account of my lack of Catholicism and aversion to Mahler's music.[59]

Fortunately the phase only lasted for a short time.

*   *   *

The standard of Klemperer's performances during the 1959–60 season may have been uneven, but as far as London's concert-going public was concerned he had inherited Toscanini's mantle as 'the great conductor' of the day. EMI was not slow to perceive the implications. 'In view of Dr Klemperer's outstanding popularity with the record-buying public and of his rather uneven health', ran an internal memo, 'the current policy is to make as many recordings as possible while he is available to us ... According to the figures available, Dr Klemperer is the most profitable of our orchestral conductors currently recording.'[60] An increase in the number of recordings and concerts with the Philharmonia Orchestra made it possible for Klemperer, who was finding travel even more burdensome, to centre his work on London. During their increasingly lengthy visits, he and Lotte made a temporary home for themselves in a suite on the top floor of the Hyde Park Hotel.

On 25 September 1960 Klemperer arrived in London for a stay that, with a three-week break at Christmas, was to extend until the following May.

After recording the Brandenburg Concertos, he opened his Festival Hall season on 17 October with a performance of the *Missa solemnis*. On this occasion Legge ensured that he had an orchestra, chorus and soloists far superior to those the BBC had provided four years earlier. Yet the performance failed to take fire. 'The trouble', wrote David Cairns,

> lay with Klemperer's conducting. For the first time the heroic struggles he has waged to master sufferings which would have felled a weaker will seemed seriously to constrict his interpretation of Beethoven instead of deepening it, and one was aware of them as physical handicaps. The experiences which made his Ninth Symphony incomparable ... have not issued in an equal illumination of the Mass.[61]

The critics now began to write with increasing frankness about concerts that fell mostly far short of those Klemperer had given in the mid-fifties. There were complaints about the imprecision of the accompaniments to concertos. *The Times* criticised a 'lack of physical vigour' in Bartók's Divertimento for strings, which Andrew Porter claimed had lasted over half an hour as against the composer's own timing of 22 minutes 13 seconds.[62] Porter also drew attention to 'un-Philharmonia-like mishaps, none too serious on their own but mounting up, [that] have been besetting these concerts'.

A programme on 4 December consisting of the six Brandenburg Concertos drew especially heavy fire. *The Times* (5 December) described Klemperer's readings as 'a curious mixture of modern loyalty to history and traditional suet pudding'. On the one hand, he had used an appropriately small band and one player per part in Nos. 3 and 6. As against that, he had preferred flutes to recorders in Nos. 2 and 4, and the harpsichord continuo had been so over-amplified that it had sounded as though played on the treble register of a modern grand piano. The only trills permitted were those written out by Bach himself. There were massive rallentandi. 'Much of the music', concluded *The Times*, 'sounded humdrum, or uncharacteristic of Bach's thought as our age conceives it.' Attempts by the harpsichord player, George Malcolm, to decorate the continuo part met with Klemperer's fierce disapproval.[63]

There were some high points none the less. Bruckner's Seventh Symphony on 7 November aroused enthusiasm and, in spite of the diffidence with which Klemperer to the end of his life approached Schubert's Symphony No. 9 in C major, the performance of the work he conducted on 1 December was described by Legge as 'a sensation'.[64] Klemperer recorded both symphonies and agreed to be interviewed by John Freeman for the BBC television series *Face to Face*, when he talked with uncharacteristic freedom.[65]

After spending Christmas 1960 at home in Zurich, Klemperer returned to London to start rehearsals for his postponed production of *Fidelio* at Covent Garden. On arrival Lotte went to inspect the backstage amenities of the Royal Opera House. 'It's terribly old', she reported, '... with spiral staircases and all manner of possibilities for a fall ... I almost had to crawl on all fours to get into the orchestral pit ... It's going to be very, very difficult for him.'[66] Klemperer insisted on attending all piano rehearsals. The cast found him easy to work with. He knew precisely what he wanted, though he was willing to accommodate singers with small changes of tempi. The only passing difficulty arose from his dislike of what he felt to be Jon Vickers's exaggerated style of acting as Florestan. (Vickers later described him as a conductor who 'understood singing and singers'.)[67] On 8 February, Lotte wrote,

> Up to now everything is going *very* well. Papa is working quite marvellously, knows [the work] unbelievably well and is obviously so happy to be doing it again that he's really blossomed. Even in the piano rehearsals the production is splendid. He could really have been an actor. Time and again he leaps up without his stick and runs ... around to show what he wants. I wouldn't have thought it possible.
>
> ... The piano rehearsals last almost four hours with hardly a break and afterwards he's still fresh! The atmosphere is *very* agreeable. Everybody takes the greatest trouble and one feels that they really enjoy the work. He himself is unusually nice and patient and doesn't spare himself. No detail escapes him.[68]

There was considerable excitement at the first night on 24 February 1961; few members of the audience had ever experienced Klemperer in the theatre. He himself was more than usually nervous: he had not conducted a staged performance of an opera for eleven years. At the interval he was upset when Legge came backstage to inform him that the first act had been found disappointing.[69] But Klemperer was not a man to turn tail. After the house lights had dimmed, the woodwind chord that introduces Florestan's recitative, 'Gott, welch Dunkel hier', rang out like a great cry of anguish. With the aria, wrote John Warrack, 'an authentic Klemperer force began to shake the performance'.[70] The dungeon scene was followed by a gripping account of the Leonore Overture No. 3. The jubilance of the final scene was matched by the ovations that followed after the curtain had fallen. Klemperer had triumphed as he had not done in London since the Beethoven cycle of 1957. There was also praise for a production which Desmond Shawe-Taylor described as 'sober and sincere, straightforward and solid'.[71] 'Everything on stage', wrote Mosco Carner, 'sprang directly out of the music.'[72]

There was, however, widespread criticism of Klemperer's decision to perform the Leonore Overture, a practice that David Cairns denounced as 'barbarous'.[73] Such had indeed been Klemperer's own view in Budapest thirteen years earlier, when Tóth had vainly tried to persuade him to include

19 Klemperer during *Fidelio* rehearsals with Elsie Morison, London 1961. Photo: Zoe Dominic

it. To Tóth he now confessed a little ruefully, 'I did Leonore No. 3 . . . I know it's illogical, but one has to put up with that.'[74] He was never much concerned with charges of inconsistency.

Few events in his career gave Klemperer as much satisfaction as his Covent Garden *Fidelio*. He publicly expressed his appreciation of 'Sir David Webster's wise and understanding manner [that] made everything possible that . . . I could desire'.[75] To Lotte Lehmann he wrote, 'Everything went well, thank God, and even the press has been positive. [Sena] Jurinac was very good as Fidelio . . . Do you know Hans Hotter? There's a really fine performer. He sang Pizarro.'[76] After the final performance on 17 March Webster presented Klemperer with a laurel wreath on stage. On an accompanying card he wrote, 'You have conquered Covent Garden.'[77] Klemperer carried the card on him for a long time afterwards.

On 8 March Walter Legge wrote to David Bicknell, his superior at EMI, 'All Klemperer's performances of *Fidelio* at Covent Garden were sold out within twenty-four hours of the opening of the box office, which seems . . . to justify serious reconsideration for recording this opera with Klemperer [rather than Karajan].' With the intention of ensuring maximum international sales, Legge proposed that only Vickers and Gottlob Frick (Rocco) should be retained from the Covent Garden cast. Birgit Nilsson, he said, should replace Jurinac as Leonore,* Nicolai Gedda should take over Jaquino from the British tenor John Dobson, and either Anneliese Rothenberger or Elisabeth Söderström should sing Marzelline instead of Elsie Morison. Legge also wanted Franz Crass as Pizarro instead of Hotter. 'If I can get this cast', he told Bicknell with a hyperbolic flourish, 'we cannot fail to make one of the supreme recordings in the whole history of the industry.' Since the Philharmonia was already under contract to EMI, it was to be used instead of Covent Garden's orchestra. EMI duly approved the project, but Klemperer was not impressed. He wrote to Legge, in English:

> I am not willing to record *Fidelio* unless I can do so with the cast, orchestra and chorus of my performance ... of 24 February 1961.
>
> You must understand. I feel myself as a Pygmalion, who formed the whole group to his wishes. You know yourself that ... 'ensemble' in ... opera does not exist any more. In these three weeks of preparation ... I could at least show the way to a good ... performance. If I would now make a recording with a so-called star cast, I would ... have to go against my own convictions. Therefore, I shall not record *Fidelio* unless as stated.[78]

But after Legge had explained that only a recording with a cast such as he proposed would be commercially viable,[79] Klemperer accepted that he had no alternative but to give way.

On another matter he proved less yielding. When, shortly after his success at Covent Garden, Klemperer asked to see a copy of his contract, Legge at once suspected that he had been approached by another company. Such was indeed the case: Decca was prepared not only to pay substantially higher royalties, but also to record *Fidelio*. As a result EMI was forced to raise the royalty rate of 'the last of our big conductors with a name'[80] from 5 to 7.5 per cent for orchestral recordings (and rather less for large works with soloists). Karajan had for some years been receiving no less than 8 per cent for orchestral recordings.

*   *   *

On 19 March, two days after the last *Fidelio*, Klemperer rehearsed the Philharmonia Orchestra for a recording of Brahms's German Requiem with Elisabeth Schwarzkopf and Dietrich Fischer-Dieskau as soloists. In the course of the session he conducted the funeral march from the 'Eroica' Symphony in memory of Beecham, who had died on 8 March. He also contributed a perceptive and appreciative obituary of the British conductor to the *New*

---

* Legge felt that Jurinac, who had been chosen by Klemperer himself for the stage production, lacked the requisite dramatic stature for the role.

Statesman and Nation.* He had already conducted a public performance of the Requiem with the same forces at the Festival Hall on 3 March. Fischer-Dieskau found Klemperer's gestures disconcertingly vague and was shocked by the deep yawn he emitted at the end of the work.[81] Thereafter, Klemperer's concerts increasingly drew critical fire. Two performances of *Messiah* on 2 and 4 April aroused the same sort of response as had met his Brandenburg Concertos earlier in the season. Yet even after a dull evening the wit still flashed. Urged by a correspondent of the *Jerusalem Post* to conduct the work in Jerusalem, Klemperer drily asked, 'Didn't you have a bit of trouble with the Messiah?'[82] Reactions to a performance of Mahler's *Das Lied von der Erde* on 13 April, with Christa Ludwig and Fritz Wunderlich as soloists, were mixed. John Amis, who had been among the first to perceive Klemperer's stature on his return to London in 1954, wrote:

> Now that the Battle of Klemperer has been won ... everything he does is wildly applauded. At which, of course, perverse critics like ourselves ... start saying that not all Klemperer's performances are great and that recently they have not been up to his own high standards. Take this latest concert, for instance.
>
> The *Freischütz* Overture, Mozart Clarinet Concerto and *Das Lied von der Erde* which made up the programme provided marvellous moments, but ... on the whole this was pretty ragged playing, without proper weight, rhythm or form. The Philharmonia Orchestra seems to have lost the confidence that, whatever happens, the performance will somehow pull through and come off.
>
> The Weber sagged, the Mozart rarely bloomed ... and the Mahler was so determinedly anti-Walter as to avoid practically any sentiment ... For *Das Lied* to leave one almost entirely unmoved, something must be wrong and I am convinced that it was Dr Klemperer. I guess that he was off form.[83]

An all-Mahler programme on 24 April opened with the Adagio from the unfinished Tenth Symphony in Krenek's realisation, the first German performance of which Klemperer had given thirty-seven years earlier in Berlin.† Later he admitted that, while in 1924 he had found 'some beauty in it', in London his impression of the Adagio had been 'fully negative'; he now thought it 'much too long'.[84] On 1 and 3 May two concert performances of *Die Zauberflöte* brought an unprecedentedly gruelling London season to an unremarkable conclusion.

It was not only in London that success proved elusive. Three weeks after his return to Zurich, Klemperer gave two performances of Beethoven's Ninth

---

* It appeared in the issue of 17 March 1961. Beecham had conducted the Philharmonia Orchestra's inaugural concert on 27 October 1945.

† Klemperer may have been induced to conduct the Adagio as a result of the interest aroused by Deryck Cooke's interim edition of the entire symphony, first performed in the studio under Berthold Goldschmidt and broadcast on 19 December 1960. Goldschmidt, who had been acquainted with Klemperer in Berlin before 1933, tried to interest him in Cooke's version, but Klemperer rejected it: 'It's impossible. I mean, if Cooke were another Mahler, it might be all right' (Heyworth (ed.), *Conversations*, p. 36).

Symphony with the Tonhalle Orchestra on 30 May and 1 June. A local critic wrote that large sections of the first one 'had made a really dull (*matt*) impression'.[85]

*   *   *

Much of Klemperer's spare time in London during the spring of 1961 was devoted to composing. On 6 March he engaged the Philharmonia and invited friends and colleagues to a private concert of his music in Battersea Town Hall. The programme consisted of the Fugato for strings (1958), whose first performance he had conducted at the Zurich Radio on 24 April 1960, a new version of the *Merry Waltz* and the Symphony No. 1. When, after an interval of three years, he returned to the Concertgebouw Orchestra on 22 June 1961, it was on condition that he might give this symphony its first public performance. Though he received a tumultuous welcome from the audience, the visit left an unhappy impression. The critics' reactions ranged from polite murmurings to open embarrassment. Would Klemperer, several of them asked, have programmed such a work, had it not been by himself? To Harold Schonberg, the chief critic of *The New York Times* (23 June), the climax of the second movement, where the 'Marseillaise' rises out of an orchestral tumult, 'sounded like Charles Ives in one of his wilder moments'.

The other principal work in the programme, Bruckner's Sixth Symphony, also proved disappointing. In *Het Parool* (23 June) Lex van Delden regretted that Klemperer's conducting had amounted to little more than an occasional intervention at crucial moments. Others went further:

> What was once a firm grip on the orchestra and the score has – let us be honest – been lost ... Klemperer is now obliged to conduct sitting. But in that position he can no longer see the players and most of them cannot see him. That at least must be the conclusion when a conductor who was once painstakingly precise ... descends to music-making that is frankly sloppy ... On an evening such as this Klemperer must be driven to the painful realisation that he is no longer able to conduct.[86]

The concert was given as part of the Holland Festival. Three months later Klemperer and the Philharmonia brought the 1961 Edinburgh Festival to a conclusion with a late-night concert of dances and marches by Offenbach, Johann and Richard Strauss, Berlioz and Klemperer himself. It was, wrote the critic Christopher Grier,

> a case of setting a giant to catch butterflies. The great man sent up regular signals with his left hand to the orchestra, which bumped and thumped its strict-time way, oom-pa-pa oom-pa-pa, through the music as if it were involved in some ... session in a German beer garden.
>
> As the 'Emperor' Waltz churned on and on and on at a steady *forte*, and still

more so when the *Rosenkavalier* waltzes were strait-jacketed, the evening gained a surrealist flavour; when finally the Philharmonia dared to get out of step in a One-Step [from *Das Ziel*] by the conductor (intended to be danced by patients in a sanatorium) one half expected to see Dr Caligari himself lurking at the back of the platform.[87]

*   *   *

After the success of the Covent Garden *Fidelio*, Herbert Graf invited Klemperer to produce and conduct four performances of the work at the Zurich City Theatre, only a few hundred yards from his apartment in the Dufourstrasse. The cast was to include Sena Jurinac, and the American tenor James McCracken as Florestan. Klemperer made one condition. The Tonhalle Orchestra consisted of two entities, one of which gave concerts, while the other served the theatre. The concert orchestra was the better of the two and Klemperer insisted that certain of its key instrumentalists should play in *Fidelio*. Nobody from the theatre warned him that this could lead to difficulties. Inevitably the implication that some members of the theatre orchestra were not good enough for him put noses out of joint and from the first rehearsals the atmosphere was unfriendly. Relations deteriorated to a point where he walked out of a rehearsal and refused to return until the orchestra gave him a declaration of confidence. Graf was only able to extract this by promising the orchestra's representatives that once the *Fidelio* performances were over, they would never be asked to play under Klemperer again. Klemperer was not informed of this deal.[88]

The opening night on 27 September 1961 went well, so well indeed that Graf asked Klemperer to conduct an additional performance to mark the opening of the Zurich Festival on 1 June 1962. Klemperer agreed to do so, provided he could be assured of a dress rehearsal with the same cast and orchestra. On 24 October 1961 the theatre confirmed the rehearsal. There, for the time being, the matter rested.

*   *   *

On 16 October 1961 Klemperer returned to London for another marathon of recording sessions, opera performances and concerts that was to last virtually without interruption until the following May. He began with a Beethoven cycle, which, it was generally agreed, reached a much higher level than that of the previous year. The playing of the celebrated German pianist Wilhelm Backhaus in the Third and Fifth Piano Concertos won unanimous praise. Though he and Klemperer were contemporaries, and as students had competed in Paris for the Rubinstein prize (which Backhaus had won), they had never met. Legge had tried to persuade Klemperer to work with him before, but Klemperer had shown no eagerness to do so, on account of the favour Backhaus had enjoyed in Germany. But he was so impressed by a recital he heard Backhaus give in Lucerne in September 1960 that he relented and asked Legge to engage him. Some while before the Philharmonia concerts Backhaus got in touch with Klemperer; he had discovered that they were both staying at the Hyde Park Hotel. Klemperer felt he had little option but to invite him to tea. Klemperer was in one of his most taciturn moods and after the introductions there was silence, while Lotte offered sandwiches. Suddenly, Klemperer asked in a matter-of-fact voice, 'Tell me, Mr Backhaus, is it true you were Hitler's favourite pianist?' Backhaus hummed and hawed, apparently out of modesty. 'I wouldn't like to say that', he answered finally, 'but he did like my playing very much.'[89] Klemperer was enchanted by Backhaus's naïve honesty. Thereafter they got on splendidly, on and off the platform.

Klemperer invited Ernst Bloch to London for the start of the cycle. The philosopher was Klemperer's oldest surviving friend and the only man with whom he was *per Du*. After Bloch had lost his Leipzig professorship as a 'revisionist' in 1957, Klemperer had tried to persuade him to leave the German Democratic Republic, and Bloch finally did so in August 1961 when, by chance, he found himself on holiday in West Germany as the Berlin Wall was going up. Although Klemperer had been an early admirer of Bloch's work, in later years he began to have doubts, in particular about Bloch's ideas on music. 'His manner of speaking belongs to a vanished epoch', Klemperer wrote in 1959. 'His brand of Expressionism was an essential part of the twenties, but isn't any more today.'[90] The friendship survived, however. Klemperer commissioned an article from Bloch on *Fidelio* for the Covent Garden programme, but then rejected it for the curious reason that it was 'purely aesthetic' (i.e. non-political). A passage about the opera from Bloch's *magnum opus, Das Prinzip Hoffnung*, was used instead.

In London the two saw a good deal of each other, though in conversation they often pursued separate trains of thought – Klemperer's mainly philosophical, Bloch's mainly musical.[91] The only discord that arose stemmed from Bloch's failure to hit it off with Arthur Koestler, which was hardly surprising, as Bloch remained a Marxist of a sort, while Koestler, who had contributed to a collection of anti-Commmunist essays, *The God that Failed* (1950), was a militant apostate.

In November 1961 Klemperer at last completed a recording of the *St Matthew Passion*. From the start the undertaking had been beset with problems. The first sessions had taken place the preceding winter in a resonant neo-Gothic church, but, because of a damp atmosphere, had had to be transferred to the EMI studios in Abbey Road, the acoustics of which proved too dry for a large choral work. Finally the recording was made in the Kingsway Hall, where the acoustics lay midway between the two extremes. Klemperer instinctively adjusted his tempi to these varying conditions.

20 Klemperer and Walter Legge, with Lotte Klemperer, at a recording session, London 1961. Photo: G. MacDomnic

According to Legge's assistant, Walter Jellinek, the opening chorus lasted fourteen minutes in the church, ten-and-a-half minutes in the studio and twelve-and-a-half minutes in the hall.[92] As the sessions depended on the availability of a number of eminent soloists, the work had to be recorded in dribs and drabs, a practice that Klemperer abhorred. There were also interpretative differences. Peter Pears, who was singing the Evangelist, found Klemperer's tempi unduly slow, and was upset by his insistence on conducting the recitatives.[93] (Once Klemperer's back was turned, these were re-recorded without his knowledge or permission.)[94] Klemperer for his part disliked the pathos that both Pears and Dietrich Fischer-Dieskau brought to their singing; in his view the Evangelist's role was to relate a story. Similarly, he insisted that the chorus 'Truly, truly, this was the Son of God' should be regarded, not as a spiritual meditation, but as a dramatic expression of the Centurion's sudden recognition of Christ's divinity.[95] When Klemperer conducted the work at the Festival Hall three months later, it was greeted by the usual complaints that the only trills and appoggiaturas allowed were those written in the score.* And yet, wrote *The Times*, 'the sheer honesty and

---

* The soloists included Agnes Giebel (deputising for Elisabeth Schwarzkopf), Christa Ludwig, Franz Crass, Peter Pears, Nicolai Gedda and Walter Berry – a characteristic Legge all-star cast. The performance took place on 25 February 1962.

conviction [of many passages] made one think twice before declaring the reading unstylish'.[96]

*   *   *

Most of December 1961 was taken up with rehearsals for Klemperer's second project for Covent Garden, a new production of *Die Zauberflöte*. When it had been first mooted, Lord Drogheda had suggested that the Austrian-born artist Oskar Kokoschka be invited to design the sets. Klemperer accordingly wrote to invite the painter to visit him in Zurich, but added, 'The difficulty is that for me the word *modern* at the same time means *mo*dern ["to putrefy"].'[97] When they met on 12 May, Klemperer opened the proceedings by telling Kokoschka that he would have preferred Picasso, adding for good measure, 'I really don't know any of your paintings.' Unperturbed, Kokoschka came back with the information that Furtwängler had wanted him to design the opera for Salzburg, but, sadly, the conductor had died before the production could take place. The meeting ended inconclusively.[98] A week later Klemperer wrote to explain why collaboration would not be possible. 'You have to be your own producer. Your sets demand that ... But I must also be my own producer. Two producers won't work. One cannot serve two masters. You know yourself that there's no democracy in art.'[99]

For a while Klemperer toyed with the idea of using Schinkel's celebrated designs, made for Berlin in 1821. Eventually, he settled for the Austrian-born painter Georg Eisler, son of the composer Hanns Eisler, who had had no previous theatrical experience. His sets, which Legge dismissed as resembling 'a provincial monumental mason's junk yard',[100] were panned mercilessly in the press.

The first night, on 4 January 1962, aroused little of the enthusiasm that had greeted *Fidelio* a year earlier. Philip Hope-Wallace detected 'a faint miasma of boredom' in the house.[101] Peter Branscombe described Klemperer's production as 'respectable and unobtrusive in an old-fashioned way'.[102] Desmond Shawe-Taylor found the sets and costumes 'disastrously bad'; the musical performance, he said, was 'clear, warm and humane, though lacking in sparkle'.[103] To accommodate Joan Sutherland, who did not endear herself to him by appearing in street clothes in her final scene in a dress rehearsal that was running over time,[104] Klemperer allowed both the Queen of the Night's arias to be transposed downwards, the first by a semitone, the second by a tone. However, differences of opinion about rhythm and tempo resulted during Sutherland's first aria in an all-too-public trial of strength, which, as David Cairns noted, she lost.[105] All things considered, Sutherland's performance had not lived up to expectations.[106] By general consent the most successful performance was that of Geraint Evans as Papageno, to whose numbers Klemperer brought a liveliness and humour lacking elsewhere. Cairns suggested that a performance that on the first night had in part been 'cold and lifeless' would subsequently warm up. In fact, the reverse seems to have occurred. On 18 January Andrew Porter found the fifth performance 'sometimes in danger of disintegration' and lacking 'any sense of secure ensemble'.[107] Legge was so disconcerted by these and other unfavourable notices that in a confidential memo to David Bicknell of EMI he questioned 'whether we should go ahead with the idea of recording this opera [with Klemperer] . . . I feel that, with an eye to the future, it would be politically and economically more prudent to offer [it] to Karajan.'[108] Bicknell concurred, but a month later changed his mind. EMI could not afford to lose Klemperer.[109]

On 3 February, only twelve days after the seventh and final performance of *Die Zauberflöte*, Klemperer began to record *Fidelio* at the Kingsway Hall.* It turned out to be one of the most inspired recordings of his career. Yet when he returned to Covent Garden in April to conduct two further performances of the opera, again with Sena Jurinac and Jon Vickers, his efforts aroused little enthusiasm. After the second performance on 9 April, Klemperer flew home to Zurich with Lotte for a short break. It clearly did him good, for on his return to London he scored an unexpected success with the *Symphonie fantastique* of Berlioz, a composer with whom he had previously been little associated in Britain. The performance, on 4 May, was described by the critic of *The Times* as 'grandly mature, rich in body, abundant in detail, and considered with loving care . . . Dr Klemperer's tempi were deliberate, but they were not sluggish; the steady March to the Scaffold was ominously thrilling.'[110]

Three days later Klemperer was back at the Festival Hall for a programme that included the first public performance in Britain of his Symphony No. 1, or Symphony in Two Movements, as he now preferred to call it. Some months earlier he had sent copies of the work to a number of composers and conductors, asking for their comments. Among those who troubled to send more than a bare acknowledgement was Benjamin Britten. After apologising for the lateness of his answer, he wrote,

> I must warn you . . . that being a composer myself, I have perhaps rather narrow views of contemporary music! We all have to face the same problems today, and each of us, rightly or wrongly, feels that we are solving them in the only right way! That may make my comments rather narrow-minded, and not so interesting to you. And there is another great difficulty: your score is very clearly, but rather inaccurately, written, and I am not always sure what you mean . . .
>
> My great aim as a composer is to find exactly the right notes to say what I

* Walter Legge's original plan to have Birgit Nilsson as Leonore, Nicolai Gedda as Jaquino and either Anneliese Rothenberger or Elisabeth Söderström as Marzelline came to nothing. On the recording the roles are taken by Christa Ludwig, Gerhard Unger and Ingeborg Hallstein respectively.

have to say ... I feel that your ideas are often very good ... But, dear Doctor, I am not always so sure that the notes you have chosen are always the exactly right ones to express what is so clearly in your mind.[111]

Unpalatable truth could hardly have been more deftly expressed.*

The *Times* critic who attended the performance of the symphony was more blunt: 'The disappointment is that a musician so brilliantly endowed with insight into the musical structures of others shows so little original architectural gift in this work of his own.'[112] But Klemperer did not allow himself to be discouraged. On 19 May he rented the Festival Hall and, with the Philharmonia, ran through more recent scores, which included his Symphony No. 2, which Hinrichsen had agreed to publish, and two sets of variations that Klemperer subsequently destroyed.

Three days earlier Klemperer had gone to the Kingsway Hall to complete a recording of Stravinsky's Symphony in Three Movements. Gareth Morris, the Philharmonia's first flute and one of the conductor's most loyal supporters in the orchestra, had an impression that he was no longer able to beat the fast music. Among those present at this session, and at the run-through of Klemperer's own works, was Albert Simon, a musician he had known in Budapest. To his surprise, Simon heard critical comments from Legge, as well as from members of the Philharmonia Orchestra. One player went so far as to claim that Klemperer was living off his reputation.[113] When he flew to Zurich on 21 May there were those who wondered if he would be back for the 1962–3 season.

---

* During the winter of 1961–2 Klemperer busied himself with a new opera, *Juda*, 'this time (sadly!) without a rape', as he informed Lotte Lehmann (letter, 25 October 1961). With a few days to spare in January 1962 he flew to Frankfurt with Hilde Firtel, to whose piano accompaniment he sang all the roles in *Juda* to Harry Buckwitz, Intendant of the Frankfurt city theatres. Buckwitz was polite but non-committal.

13

Exit Legge

On his return to Zurich, Klemperer found himself at the centre of a row occasioned by the single performance of *Fidelio*, with which he was due to open the 1962 Zurich Festival on 1 June. Herbert Graf had failed to tell the Tonhalle Orchestra about the performance. When the players first heard about it in February 1962, they were incensed, because only five months earlier Graf had promised them that he would never ask them to work under Klemperer again.

When their representatives reminded Graf of his undertaking, he attempted to argue that the performance was no more than an extension of the previous autumn's run and thus did not represent a new engagement. If that were the case, the players retorted, a dress rehearsal would be unnecessary. They accordingly gave notice that they would perform on 1 June under protest, but would not be available for the rehearsal. They also demanded that Graf should inform Klemperer of the deadlock. When he declined to do so, the Zurich branch of the Swiss musicians' union, the Schweizerische Musikverband, wrote to Klemperer on 1 May to inform him that the orchestra would not be available for a rehearsal. Lotte replied on her father's behalf that he was withdrawing from the performance and, for good measure, added that he would never again conduct the Tonhalle Orchestra.[1] Klemperer later sent a copy of the union's letter to the editor of the *Neue Zürcher Zeitung*, which published it on 23 May.

Once the matter was public property, tempers started to rise. Most of the press considered the orchestra's behaviour unwarranted. A critic who took its part was rewarded with a torchlight procession and an alfresco performance of a Mozart serenade outside his house.[2] The city president tried to mediate, but without success. At a press conference the union denounced Klemperer's treatment of the orchestra as 'unworthy, indecent and unacceptable',[3] which led Rafael Kubelik to withdraw from performances he was to have conducted both at the Tonhalle and the City Theatre,[4] and to call on his colleagues to show solidarity with Klemperer.[5] Though the recording of *Fidelio* that Klemperer had made in London had not been released yet, Legge had an advance pressing sent to Zurich, where Swiss Radio broadcast it on the evening the festival performance was to have taken place. On 7 June

Klemperer was met by a great ovation when he appeared in the Tonhalle at the head of the Philharmonia Orchestra, which by chance had been invited to give a concert at the festival. A few days later the Tonhalle Orchestra, which *Der Bund* (13 June) described as 'the worst-behaved orchestra in Europe', was roundly booed at the Stadttheater. Several newspapers contrasted the smoothness with which Covent Garden had staged *Fidelio* with the tumult in Zurich. On 9 June Herbert Graf, who had increasingly come to be seen as primarily responsible for the mess, resigned. On 15 June the theatre announced that it was suing the orchestra for damages, whereupon the Tonhalle revoked its contract with the theatre.

The Zurich *Opernskandal* provided a picture of provincial life at its most animated. As the *Neue Zürcher Zeitung* observed on 5 July in its report on a debate in the city council, no one had come well out of the fracas. Klemperer had failed to treat the orchestra with due respect, but the behaviour of the musicians' union had left him with no alternative but to withdraw. He himself remained silent, his sole intervention consisting of a lawyer's letter requesting that he be paid his fee of 4,000 Swiss francs for the cancelled performance. Four months later the theatre offered three-quarters of the sum, which Klemperer declined. It was not until 1965 that Rudolf Kempe, on being appointed artistic director of the Tonhalle Orchestra, arranged for the fee to be paid in full. Klemperer at once agreed to conduct a concert with the orchestra in the following season.

Klemperer spent most of July 1962 on holiday in Annecy, where he had what Lotte described as 'some manic days'. He read a good deal of Shakespeare and composed an opera (long since vanished) based on *The Merry Wives of Windsor*. The restlessness had also revived. On 25 July he returned from a nocturnal excursion having clearly suffered a nasty fall.[6]

It was not until early September that Lotte observed a renewed and this time decisive swing towards what was to prove the last intense depression Klemperer was to suffer. By the last week of the month it had grown so deep that the psychiatrist he consulted in Zurich advised him to cancel a series of concerts he was due to give with the Philadelphia Orchestra in the following October. Aware that work was her father's only refuge in such a period, Lotte insisted that the seven-week visit to America should go ahead as planned.

On 29 September Legge made a flying visit to Zurich. He was not slow to grasp the significance of Klemperer's psychological condition. 'He is a completely changed man', he wrote to Bicknell on 4 October. 'The euphoria which has reigned over the last 4½ years has completely passed and he has entered the depressive phase, which means that he will work with greater intensity, though probably more slowly. This fortunate state of affairs almost guarantees him a triumph with the Philadelphia Orchestra.' In this respect, at any rate, Legge's confidence proved exaggerated.

EXIT LEGGE

21   Klemperer rehearsing in Philadelphia, October 1962. Photo: Adrian Siegel, Philadelphia

The American visit had been arranged by Ronald Wilford,* who eight years earlier had secured for him the much-needed concert in Portland, Oregan. Contracts were signed in September 1961. Klemperer, who had not visited America for almost eight years, wrote to the Philadelphia Orchestra's musical director, Eugene Ormandy, to say how much he was looking forward to the trip.[7] 'It is late, but not too late', he told Arthur Judson, who was still president of Columbia Artists.[8] There were to be concerts in New York, Washington and Baltimore, as well as in Philadelphia itself. There was also a plan, which Klemperer endorsed enthusiastically, for him to record with the Philadelphia Orchestra for American Columbia. At first EMI was nervous, for its contract with Klemperer was due to run out before he reached America, but Legge guessed, correctly, that Klemperer would not want to prejudice his future relations with EMI.[9] Eventually a compromise was reached. Klemperer

* By 1962 Wilford had become Judson's associate with responsibility for the management of conductors represented by Columbia Artists, and was thus well on the way to becoming the most powerful agent of his generation.

could record with the Philadelphia Orchestra, provided he did not duplicate works he had recorded already for EMI. In the event the plan collapsed, because, in his depression, Klemperer refused to change his concert programmes to include suitable works that fell into this category.* To Ormandy's disappointment he even reversed an earlier decision to include his own Symphony in Two Movements.[10]

On 4 October 1962 Klemperer flew with Lotte and a nurse to New York, where he remained in his rented apartment for a week of acclimatisation, obsessively studying the long-familiar scores in his programmes. He always suffered from stage fright and on this occasion he was particularly nervous about appearing before American audiences again. He barely ate, found it hard to sleep and refused to see any visitors apart from Werner and a handful of old friends, such as Lonny Epstein and Mark Brunswick. On 11 October he travelled to Philadelphia, where rehearsals began two days later. At his opening concert on 19 October he conducted a programme consisting of Beethoven's Third and Sixth Symphonies. The local press made respectful noises, though the *Philadelphia Inquirer* (20 October) noted that 'tempi were a bit slower and a shade more deliberate than those to which audiences in this country are accustomed'. Four days later in New York the same programme won him an ovation the like of which, said *Time* (2 November), 'conductors rarely hear'. But the critics were less enthusiastic. 'The evening dragged relentlessly', complained Jay Harrison in the *New York Post* (28 October). 'Every note was inspected, mulled over ... Every phrase was ... viewed through an aural telescope.' Paul Henry Lang in the *Herald-Tribune* (24 October) described the performances as turgid. Even Werner Klemperer later recalled the evening as being disappointing.[11] Only Winthrop Sargeant reminded his readers that Klemperer conducted in a style to which they had become unaccustomed since Toscanini had become the measure of all things. His performances of both symphonies, Sargeant insisted, had 'unmistakable grandeur' and were remarkable for their clarity of detail.[12]

As the tour progressed to Washington and Baltimore the press grew marginally less dismissive. But it was Eric Salzman of *The New York Times* who expressed a majority view when he described the performances as having 'the aura of ... a religious rite. The public was awe-struck, the critics mainly sceptical.'

By the time Klemperer returned to Zurich on 22 November, he had lost no less than 25 kg. in weight. He was also physically unwell, but the worst of his depression was over. A fortnight later he flew to London, but soon after

---

* The works Klemperer agreed to conduct in America were Bach's Brandenburg Concerto No. 1, Beethoven's *Egmont* Overture and Symphonies Nos. 3, 6 and 7, Brahms's Symphony No. 3, Mozart's 'Jupiter' Symphony and Schumann's Symphony No. 4.

his arrival there a sudden fever caused by chronic cystitis obliged him to cancel the first two performances of a revival of *Die Zauberflöte* at Covent Garden.

Klemperer began 1963 by conducting the last three performances of the run of *Die Zauberflöte* and then embarked on an arduous series of recordings, beginning with Tchaikovsky's Fifth Symphony. The art historian Gertrud Bing reported to the Hirschlers that several members of the Philharmonia had told her that he was now working more intensely than at any time since the fire. That was also Legge's view. 'Klemperer', he wrote to Bicknell on 22 January, 'is now in such form as I have never known him. He is working with an intensity and concentration that inspire awe and the Tchaikovsky Fifth results are hair-raising.'

The London critics concurred. After Klemperer had conducted his first London concert for nine months on 10 February, in a programme that included the Prelude and Liebestod from *Tristan und Isolde* (with Christa Ludwig as soloist), David Cairns wrote that he had

> never heard this music move on grander tides of rhythm, its form more continuously implicit in its phrases, its phrases more nobly moulded, its orchestral polyphony more precisely articulated.[13]

The performance of Bruckner's Symphony No. 4 that followed made an equally strong impression.

Klemperer's next major project was a new production of *Lohengrin*, to open at Covent Garden in 1963. When it had been discussed two years earlier, Klemperer had wanted Wieland Wagner to produce, but unfortunately he had other commitments. So had Klemperer's second choice, Walther Felsenstein. Covent Garden then proposed Sam Wanamaker, but, on learning that he was not familiar with *Lohengrin*, Klemperer turned him down. Instead, he told David Webster, he would produce the opera himself as well as conduct it.[14] In view of the length of the work and the state of Klemperer's health, the proposal did not commend itself to Covent Garden's board.[15] At this point Georg Solti, the company's musical director, pressed the merits of Josef Gielen, senior producer at the Vienna State Opera. When Klemperer had seen Gielen's production of *Idomeneo* (which Solti had conducted) at the 1951 Salzburg Festival, he had described it as 'terrible'.[16] But time was now pressing and, after the persuasive Webster had visited him in Zurich, Klemperer unwillingly agreed to Gielen's engagement. However, Klemperer got his way over the designer, Hainer Hill, who had been responsible for the Covent Garden *Fidelio*.

No sooner had the question of the producer been settled than casting began to cause problems. Klemperer wanted Maria Callas for the role of Ortrud. He had been impressed by a concert he had heard her give in the

Festival Hall on 27 February 1962. Later, Legge took her to one of Klemperer's concerts. After it, the following exchange took place:

> Klemperer: Your Lucia is marvellous. Your Aida ... your Norma. But your Alceste, forgive me for saying so, is not good. ... We must do something together.
> Callas: It would be an honour.
> Klemperer: What would you like to do?
> Callas: Alceste, of course, Maestro.[17]

An artist able to hold her own in repartee was much to Klemperer's taste.

Two weeks after the encounter Legge informed EMI that he was hoping to set up a recording project that would bring Callas and Klemperer together.* However, when Legge told Callas that, for the recording to be feasible, she would have to accept a lower royalty than usual, she gave a reply that, Legge thought, was 'better not put on paper'.[18] Callas, who earlier in her career had sung Isolde, the *Walküre* Brünnhilde and Kundry, seems to have taken Klemperer's invitation to sing Ortrud seriously, but nothing came of it. On 7 April 1962 Klemperer informed Webster that she had written to him to turn the role down.† It went instead to Rita Gorr.

Klemperer also told Webster that he was doubtful if the Spanish soprano Victoria de los Angeles was the 'right type' for Elsa and suggested that Régine Crespin should take the part instead.[19] The matter was eventually resolved when de los Angeles herself decided to withdraw two months before the first night.[20] At short notice Crespin agreed to take her place, though because of other commitments she was unable to attend all of Klemperer's rehearsals; she also proved unfamiliar with the cuts that Klemperer had opened in accordance with his usual practice. When Webster wrote to inform Klemperer that Sandor Konya had withdrawn from the title role and that Hans Hopf would replace him, Klemperer felt he had had enough. 'Your letter of 6 February', he wrote in English to Webster two days later,

> brings me in a very serious situation ... I agreed to Mr Hopf in an emergency situation, i.e. for the last two performances. Now you are engaging him for all performances, and this I cannot accept ... I will wait until the end of next week before making any definite decisions, but unless a miracle happens, I do not know whether I can participate. You know that only if I can take the responsibility in good artistic conscience can I do it. In addition, I must think of my

---

* In a memorandum to J.D. Bicknell (13 March 1962), Legge suggested that the pieces to be recorded should include 'Non mi dir' from *Don Giovanni*, Sextus's two arias from *La clemenza di Tito*, Beethoven's 'Ah, perfido!', 'Ocean! thou mighty monster' from *Oberon*, and the Liebestod from *Tristan und Isolde*.

† Callas's letter has not survived. She may have felt unable to sing Ortrud in German. She had performed her previous Wagner roles in Italian.

strength and nerves, because even under ideal circumstances *Lohengrin* – a work of three-and-a-half hours – is for me quite an undertaking. Therefore, the more difficult the situation becomes, the harder is the work for me.

The miracle duly occurred. Konya was persuaded to sing in three performances. Piano rehearsals began on 26 February. Most of them took place in Klemperer's suite at the Hyde Park Hotel. Reginald Goodall acted as his assistant and James Gibson, head of Covent Garden's music staff, played the piano for them.

The first night was on 8 April, a week later than originally envisaged. The production was dismissed as tame and conventional, but the critics were unanimous in their praise of the musical side. Desmond Shawe-Taylor warmed to its 'fine dramatic sweep and feeling for structure'.[21] Martin Cooper singled out 'a quite extraordinary splendour of tone and fineness of detail'.[22] The *Times Educational Supplement* (3 May) described the occasion as one of the greatest Wagnerian evenings Covent Garden had experienced since the war: 'For once, the opera *sounded* so wonderful that one really did not mind how it looked.' For reasons best known to itself, the BBC failed to transmit a performance, so that no record survives of Klemperer's last great operatic achievement.

The effort left him exhausted, which may explain the general disappointment with two Philharmonia concerts he gave in the Festival Hall in early May. But by the middle of the month he was back on form. *The Times* (13 May) found his account of Bruckner's Symphony No. 9 a 'monument of majestic, often awe-inspiring sound, perfectly proportioned and therefore never a moment too long'.

Yet Klemperer was in low spirits and weakened by recurrent cystitis. On 7 June he set out, 'very, very unwillingly',[23] for Vienna, where six days later he conducted a performance of Mahler's Symphony No. 2 with the Vienna Philharmonic that was greeted ecstatically by the press. On 16 June the success of the Beethoven concert he gave with the Vienna Symphony Orchestra was so great that, as Lotte ironically commented, 'even he seemed aware of it'.[24] There were family pleasures, too. On 21 June, Klemperer learned that he had become a grandfather for the second time when Werner telephoned from America to say that his wife had given birth to a daughter, Erika.

*   *   *

During the summer of 1963 Klemperer was plagued by eye and tooth troubles, but on his return to London on 15 September he at once plunged into a back-breaking series of recording sessions. On 10 October he embarked on yet another Beethoven cycle at the Festival Hall, at the end of which David Cairns wrote, 'Klemperer is on such superb form this season that everything he touches glows with vigour and freshness.'[25] However, on his return to Zurich for a Christmas break he was tired and dispirited. To Lotte he seemed to have aged visibly.[26] But back in London at the end of January 1964 his run of successes continued. He began to record *Das Lied von der Erde* and, as was his custom, took the opportunity to attend other people's performances, for example *Rigoletto* under Georg Solti at Covent Garden. On 26 February he turned up at the Festival Hall for Pierre Boulez's first appearance in London as a conductor.* Klemperer was aware of Boulez's significance as a composer: Hans Curjel, the former *Dramaturg* of the Kroll Oper, who lived close by in Zurich, had played him a tape of *Le Marteau sans maître*, the work that more than any other established Boulez as the leading composer of his generation. Klemperer had reservations about what he took to be its expressionist roots, which he considered 'passé'.[27] Boulez's programme at the Festival Hall included Webern's Variations and Beethoven's Fourth Piano Concerto, with Clifford Curzon as soloist. Klemperer was not enthusiastic about Curzon's playing, but the conducting must have impressed him, for the following morning he telephoned an astonished Boulez to ask if he might attend rehearsals for his next concert. He sat in the BBC's Maida Vale studio, saying little but following the scores of Webern's Six Pieces, Op. 6, Stravinsky's then little-played Symphonies of Wind Instruments and Boulez's early cantata *Le Soleil des eaux*. On the following day he attended the concert itself at the Festival Hall.

The experience marked the start of his admiration for Boulez, whom he considered 'the only man of his generation who is an outstanding conductor *and* musician ... Without doubt ... a man of his time in the best sense of the word'.[28] In some respects Klemperer looked on Boulez as his successor, in so far as he stood against self-indulgent and romanticised interpretations and regarded a conductor as having a special obligation to the music of his own time. He also saw 'a great danger for Boulez's future' in the increasing proportion of his energies that he was beginning to devote to conducting. 'What is important for him, in my opinion, is to develop as a composer. That he conducts splendidly – my goodness, that shouldn't be so terribly important to him.'[29]

*   *   *

On Monday 9 March 1964, the author was enjoying a late supper at the Hyde Park Hotel when a huge figure loomed over the table. It was Klemperer, who without ado exclaimed, 'I have no orchestra more.' That very evening he had, he said, learnt that the Philharmonia Orchestra was to be 'indefinitely suspended'. He was manifestly shocked.

Klemperer may not have been aware of it, but the Philharmonia had

---

* The orchestra was the BBC Symphony, of which Boulez became chief conductor (1971–5).

been facing a variety of difficulties for a number of years. Though Walter Legge's formal position in the EMI hierarchy was less senior than he liked people to think, his energies and artistic flair had in the post-war years made him a dominant figure in the recording industry, who exercised almost complete independence and brooked no interference from his nominal superiors. In the late fifties, however, conditions had grown less favourable to him. On becoming chairman of the international combine of Electrical and Musical Industries in 1954, Joseph Lockwood was disturbed by the independence exercised by producers like Legge. To curb over-production and overlapping, and to ensure that the recording programmes should be economically viable, Lockwood in 1958 set up the International Classical Repertory Committee, whose prior agreement was needed before a recording could go ahead. Legge himself was a member of the committee, along with the other EMI producers and the principal marketing managers, but he did not welcome the reduction of his freedom of action and the obligation to justify his actions to others. When, in his absence, the committee approved a proposal that Barbirolli should record Mahler's Symphony No. 9, Legge was angry:

> I was in Paris recording with Callas when the above proposal was discussed at the I.C.R.C.
>
> Both the proposal and its acceptance have the appearance of [a] curious lack of understanding of the loyalty and consideration we owe our best-selling conductor and to the record business.
>
> Our two Mahler recordings with Klemperer [the Second and Fourth Symphonies] are extraordinary in quality and we have good reason to believe that they will sell well. Klemperer is generally acknowledged the greatest living Mahler interpreter. I have great regard for Barbirolli – it was upon my urging that EMI made a contract with him last year – but neither I nor anyone else in his senses would expect Barbirolli either to record a performance comparable to Klemperer's or likely to sell as well.[30]

In a sharply worded reply Bicknell reminded Legge that Barbirolli had signed his contract only on condition that he could record the symphony in question. He also pointed out that Legge had not previously proposed that Klemperer should record it, though he added that Barbirolli's recording did not 'preclude the possibility of doing another one with Klemperer at a later date'.[31]

There were other disputes. By the end of the fifties the success of Decca's recording of *Das Rheingold*, which John Culshaw had made in Vienna with dramatic sound effects, had made Lockwood nervous that Decca, EMI's principal competitor in Britain, had again stolen a march on its more cumbersome rival, as it had earlier done with the introduction of LP records and stereophonic sound. Legge's approach to recording was purely musical; in his view sound effects were a vulgar intrusion. But early in 1962 Lockwood began to agitate for their introduction in Klemperer's recording of *Fidelio*. Legge reacted with contempt. He proposed that another producer should be given a tape of the dungeon scene: 'Let him and the ... people who want sound effects ... show by a demonstration of their "improved" version to Dr Klemperer and me what we should have done.'[32] A tape complete with sound effects was sent to a number of critics, who rejected it unanimously, and as a result the experiment was dropped.[33] Legge had won his point, but he recognised that a warning shot had been fired across his bows.

On 27 June 1963 he gave EMI twelve months' notice of his resignation. Later he confessed that once it had been announced he imagined that 'every gramophone company in the world would be on my doorstep'. That proved an error. 'There was nothing, nothing at all.'[34] But, as he explained to *The New York Times*, it had been impossible 'to continue working in an organisation in which I cannot maintain the standards associated with my name ... Nor do I believe that artistic policy can be handled by a committee.'*

Legge had other troubles. In the early sixties conditions in the recording industry began to grow more difficult. During the 1960–1 season EMI had been unable to use the Philharmonia for all the sessions for which it had been contracted. This signalled a threat to the very existence of an orchestra whose earnings stemmed in large part from recordings. In future it would be more dependent on concert work. But here, too, there were problems. In December 1960, following sustained criticism that standards of performance at the Festival Hall were often low, and that too many programmes were stereotyped and repetitive, T. Ernest Bean, the hall's general manager, called a meeting of the representatives of the four London orchestras† to discuss what might be done to improve matters. Legge attended, though it went against the grain for him to do so. Bean subsequently claimed that his aim was limited to preventing programme clashes, but the memorandum he produced as a basis for discussion suggested that his longer-term intention was to encourage the orchestras to show that they were 'capable of planning and carrying through a far higher standard of concert, more embrasive [*sic*] in their range of programmes, conductors and artists ... than London could hope to enjoy under the present system of ... freelance promotions'.

Legge was enraged. Who was Bean to pass judgement on the standards of the Philharmonia? Even Bean's wish to avoid programme clashes would

---

* *New York Times*, 8 March 1964. In spite of his talents, Legge was not greatly mourned by EMI. A month before his resignation from EMI was due to take effect on 30 June 1964, Bicknell wrote to a senior colleague, 'As recently he has gone out of his way to offend almost everyone with whom he has worked ... , I think it is out of the question to organise anything in the nature of a valedictory lunch' (EMI internal memo, 29 May 1964).

† The London Symphony Orchestra, the London Philharmonic Orchestra, the Philharmonia Orchestra and the Royal Philharmonic Orchestra. The BBC Symphony Orchestra fell into a different category. It could afford to be adventurous in its programmes because the Corporation met its deficits in full.

necessitate agreement among the orchestras as to which of them should give, for instance, a Beethoven cycle in the coming season. Why, Legge argued, with the greatest Beethoven conductor of the age at his disposal, should he be obliged to give way to a rival orchestra? But the independence he treasured grew harder to sustain as the Philharmonia became increasingly beholden to box-office receipts, and by the season of 1963–4 he found himself obliged to accept a guarantee of £15,000 from public funds. To obtain it, he had to submit his plans to his new benefactors. As John Culshaw, Legge's counterpart at Decca, later observed, 'What had started as a quest for perfection was turning into a battle for survival.'[35]

In August 1963 Legge, with EMI's encouragement, made a fruitless approach to its main continental rival, Deutsche Grammophon,[36] in the hope that it might make use of the Philharmonia. Increasingly desperate, he crossed the Atlantic that winter to try and interest the big American recording companies. Again he got a negative response. 'The news I received from everybody in New York', reported Bicknell, not without a trace of *Schadenfreude*, to his counterpart in Capitol Records on 24 January 1964, 'was that Walter was touting round in all directions but at the end of his visit had failed to land anything.'

Meanwhile, Klemperer was becoming a source of concern. Since his visit to America in 1962 he had shown little eagerness to renew his EMI contract and, when he eventually did so on 18 January 1964, he refused to commit himself further than 2 May, the date on which the Philharmonia's contract with EMI also expired. In any case he was no longer willing to give EMI the exclusivity it had hitherto enjoyed. As a result of the success he had enjoyed in Vienna in June 1963, the Vienna Philharmonic expressed a desire to record with him.[37] The idea appealed to Klemperer. It also appealed to EMI, which approached its Austrian agents to see what might be arranged.[38] What Klemperer wanted was a contract that allowed him to record with other companies those works that EMI did not want from him, for example *Die Meistersinger*, which EMI had recorded already with Kempe, and Mozart operas.[39]

*   *   *

On Sunday evening, 8 March 1964, Legge invited three senior members of the Philharmonia* to his house in Hampstead, where he informed them that he would be 'indefinitely suspending' the orchestra and chorus at the end of the season. Jane Withers, the orchestral manager, was also present. The news would not be made public until late on Tuesday 10 March, so that the players could be informed by letter beforehand.[40] In fact many of them learnt of it from the radio before the post arrived. Klemperer first heard what was

* Hugh Bean (leader), Gareth Morris (first flute), Bernard Walton (first clarinet).

afoot when, on the afternoon of 9 March, Jane Withers telephoned Lotte, shortly before he was due to set out for a recording session for *Messiah* at the Kingsway Hall.⁴¹ There he at once confronted Legge, who confirmed the news he had not had the courage to communicate directly.* At first Klemperer found it hard to take in. He could not believe it was true. Legge, he thought, was bluffing for some reason that was not immediately apparent.

On Wednesday 11 March the London newspapers carried Legge's statement. In it he asserted that it was 'no longer possible ... to maintain the standards that have been [the Philharmonia's] hallmark since I founded it'. He then listed some of the factors that had forced him to this conclusion. There was an insufficient number of players in Britain to staff two really first-class orchestras.† London suffered from a surfeit of inadequate orchestras. The record industry was contracting and the general public was only interested in the most celebrated artists. No mention was made of Klemperer, the orchestra's principal conductor for life. In a comment on Legge's statement, the music critic of *The Times* (11 March) observed that, even if London were unable to support four symphony orchestras, it was no solution to disband the one that had 'uninterruptedly maintained an exalted standard of executive artistry' since its foundation. There was a widespread sense of outrage at what had happened. Before the start of a concert with the Philharmonia on 23 March the usually undemonstrative Sir Adrian Boult turned to the Festival Hall audience and asked, 'Do you want to see a great orchestra snuffed out like a candle?'⁴² Questions were asked in Parliament, appeals were made to leading politicians and a group of Labour Party back-benchers tabled a motion demanding an immediate government grant to ensure the Philharmonia's survival – all to no effect.

Salvation came from within the orchestra. On 18 March it was announced that the players had elected a governing body to run the Philharmonia themselves. Legge may not have bargained for such a move. He treated the reconstituted orchestra ungenerously, refusing to sell the players its own music library and subsequently disposing of it instead to the Bournemouth Symphony Orchestra for the modest sum of £300.⁴³ On the grounds that he

---

* It was on his return to his hotel later that evening that Klemperer told the author what had occurred. Both Legge (*On and Off the Record*, pp. 105 and 190) and his wife, Elisabeth Schwarzkopf (interview with the author, 2 April 1989), subsequently insisted that Klemperer had already been informed of the orchestra's suspension, and that it was only after he had agreed a statement that the news was broken to the three members of the orchestra mentioned above. Lotte Klemperer insists that Legge's claim is 'absolutely untrue' – 'OK was not consulted and heard about it ... at a *Messiah* session on 9 March 1964' (communications to the author, 26 July and 27 November 1990). Having himself witnessed Klemperer's shock on his return from that session, the author has little hesitation in preferring Lotte Klemperer's version of events.

† A reference to the difficulties the Philharmonia had been experiencing in matching the terms of employment that the BBC had been offering since 1962 in an attempt to raise the standards of its own symphony orchestra.

might want to use the Philharmonia Concert Society as a vehicle for future promotions, he tried (unsuccessfully) to persuade Edward Heath, then President of the Board of Trade, to refuse to allow the orchestra to register the title of the New Philharmonia.* Klemperer felt too old to continue as the orchestra's principal conductor,[44] but agreed to become its president and undertook to give it ten dates in the coming season of 1964–5. His support was to prove crucial to its future.

Though the *Evening Standard* (12 March) reported Klemperer's anger at the manner in which Legge had disposed of his orchestra, and though during a recording session Legge's assistant, Suvi Raj Grubb, overheard irate exchanges between them in the control room,[45] relations between Klemperer and Legge at first remained outwardly correct. But tension began to gather when on 17 March Legge forwarded to Klemperer a letter from EMI's German offshoot, Electrola, questioning the wisdom of Klemperer's intention to record *Die Zauberflöte* later in the month without dialogue.[46] Legge urged him to compromise by using the dialogue, but in a drastically curtailed form. Klemperer retorted that he considered dialogue superfluous in a recording, adding, 'As I take responsibility for these records I must use my own judgement.'† Legge forwarded Klemperer's response to Electrola with the comment, 'There is no fool like an old fool.'[47]

The first recording sessions for *Die Zauberflöte*, on 24, 25 and 26 March, passed smoothly. But when they were over, Legge informed Klemperer that he intended to be present at the piano rehearsals with individual singers that Klemperer planned to hold in his hotel suite after the Easter weekend.[48] For Klemperer there was a clear distinction between a recording session, at which the producer presided, and piano rehearsals, which were the conductor's province. He accordingly told Legge that his presence would not be needed and, to avoid misunderstanding, later telephoned to confirm what he had said.[49] Legge had not attended such rehearsals in the past, but thought it important to do so on this occasion because it was to be the first stereophonic recording of *Die Zauberflöte*. As he later put it, 'I could not involve myself in and take responsibility for such an important and expensive undertaking without having personally supervised the rehearsals, least of all with a conductor whose hearing was by then evidently impaired.'‡

---

* Michael Johnson, letter to the author, London, 31 July 1984. In February 1968 EMI purchased Legge's 97 per cent holding of the Philharmonia's shares for £53,000 in order to acquire its royalties, which had previously been paid to Legge's Philharmonia Concert Society, i.e. Legge (Pettitt, *Philharmonia*, p. 130).

† A subsequent attempt to persuade Klemperer to change his mind proved equally fruitless. On 5 May 1964 he wrote to Peter Andry, 'The dialogue is based upon the scene and on the gesture. Therefore, without the visual effect it is ridiculous.' Curiously, Legge was being inconsistent in siding against Klemperer. There is no dialogue in either of the two previous recordings of *Die Zauberflöte* that he had produced – Beecham's and Karajan's.

‡ Legge/Schwarzkopf, p. 191. It is probable that Klemperer, who had suffered from deafness of the right ear since the mid-thirties, had by 1964 begun to hear less well with the left ear. This

On 28 March Klemperer sent a telegram to EMI asking 'whether my contractual duties as a conductor oblige me to hold purely musical piano rehearsals in the presence of producer'.⁵⁰ He asked for a reply in writing by the following evening. It came in the form of a telegram from Legge himself: 'I have already informed EMI that irrespective of their wishes I will not attend rehearsals or recordings of *Zauberflöte* or any other work at which you are present.'⁵¹ Thereafter all contact ceased until at the very end of Klemperer's life Legge wrote to enquire about his health. A visitor to Legge's house shortly after the break commented on the absence of Epstein's bust of Klemperer from its usual place of honour. 'We have moved it to a smaller room', said Legge.⁵² Klemperer's final assessment of Legge was not flattering: 'He likes to think of himself as an incomparable musician ... He is a very gifted connoisseur and a very good record producer – *c'est tout*.'⁵³

The *Zauberflöte* sessions were completed in mid-April 1964. A month later Klemperer went to Berlin, where he conducted his first concert with the Berlin Philharmonic Orchestra since 1958. The programme, which was given on three successive days, consisted of Bach's Suite No. 3, Mozart's Symphony No. 29 and Beethoven's 'Pastoral' Symphony. It did not prove a happy visit. Klemperer took against Scharoun's new Philharmonie, which since its opening earlier in the season had been widely hailed as the most imaginative concert hall to have been built since the war. Relations between him and the players remained cool on both sides. In the view of its Intendant, Wolfgang Stresemann, the 'singing style' of Karajan's orchestra was fundamentally incompatible with what he described as Klemperer's 'non-espressivo' approach.⁵⁴

Differences came to a head when, as in London, Klemperer wanted a more forward woodwind sound in the 'Pastoral' Symphony. As usual when he had a special request to make of individual players, he summoned the first flute and first oboe to his room in the interval of the second concert. Believing the trouble to lie in Klemperer's deafness, they refused to present themselves, which Klemperer not unnaturally regarded as an affront. The concert proved less than a great occasion and his ill humour was all too evident when at Lotte Klemperer's suggestion the author visited him in his dressing-room and found him sitting bolt upright in a dressing-gown, surrounded by apprehensive officials. The opportunity to cause embarrassment

---

was, however, not Legge's only attempt subsequently to cast aspersion on Klemperer's faculties at this period. On p. 87 he wrote, 'At a greater distance of time I doubt if I shall so carefully conceal ... my conviction that when I decided to give up the Philharmonia Orchestra, his – to me – evident falling off as a conductor was a contributing factor.' That comment might indeed be considered applicable to the Klemperer of the years immediately after the fire. In the seasons of 1962–3 and 1963–4, however, all the evidence (which includes Legge's own comments – pp. 515, 518) suggests that he was in better form than at any time since 1957–8.

was too good to be missed. 'What are *you* doing in this frightful city?' he shouted across the length of the room.

*   *   *

The New Philharmonia Orchestra made its first public appearance on 27 October 1964 at a concert in aid of its own funds at the Royal Albert Hall. Klemperer conducted Beethoven's Symphonies Nos. 1 and 9 without a fee. For the first time in his career he agreed to a concert being televised, in spite of his dislike of the heat and glare of the lights, not to mention the inevitable close-ups of the conductor.* But he was aware how urgently the new orchestra stood in need of support and publicity. A film of the event shows a man in complete command of the orchestra before him in spite of the paucity of his gestures. The huge audience gave Klemperer a standing ovation, but the London critics were divided. Klemperer was himself dissatisfied. 'The concert gave me no sort of pleasure', he wrote to Fritz Fischer on 11 November. 'I could easily blame that on the hall, as its acoustics are really bad, but if there was a feeling of restraint, it lay within myself.'

By this time Klemperer had won the affections of the players to a degree unprecedented in his career. Laurence Taylor, a young American violinist who joined the orchestra in the autumn of 1964, was struck by the absence of tension at rehearsal. 'It was relaxed, congenial ... yet utterly professional.' 'Old Klemp', said Taylor, 'was very earnest ... and Olympian in the grand Germanic manner.' The players had indeed come to realise that 'old Klemp' had a bark that was worse than his bite. Unlike most continental orchestras, the New Philharmonia was not intimidated by his formidable exterior and would even on occasions indulge in a little gentle ragging. Taylor noted that 'whenever Klemperer became a bit too demanding, they just ... joshed him back ... Klemperer would huff and puff a little and then laugh himself.'[55] And he was able to give as good as he got. After a ragged entry in a recording of Beethoven's Eighth Symphony, Raymond Clark, the principal cellist, called out, 'Dr Klemperer, will you please give us a very clear beat at this point and we will get it together for the first time in musical history.' 'In *British* musical history', came the reply.[56] As he was waiting to go on to the Albert Hall platform, the leader, Hugh Bean, drew Klemperer's attention to the fact that his fly was open. 'What has that to do with the music?' he asked.

In December 1964 Klemperer returned to Germany for a concert with the Cologne Radio Orchestra. Six weeks later he went to Munich to give two performances of Mahler's Symphony No. 2 with the Bavarian Radio Symphony Orchestra. Once more the work made a great impact under his direction. During a brief stay in London he conducted a Brahms programme

---

* After watching a few moments of the *Face to Face* interview, he was so horrified that he insisted on turning it off (Lotte Klemperer, Diaries, 8 November 1964).

in the Festival Hall on 3 February 1965. There was disagreement among the critics about the standards of the New Philharmonia's playing; Andrew Porter found it 'not as flawless as that of the old Philharmonia at its best'.[57] Otherwise there was virtual unanimity about what Desmond Shawe-Taylor described as 'a glorious concert... There was serenity here, but no dawdling; drama, but no hysteria; strength, but no violence.'[58]

In mid-February Klemperer set out for Rome, but four days after his arrival there he went down with influenza and had to cancel one of his two concerts with the Santa Cecilia Orchestra. Before leaving for Italy he had seemed depressed. He had written to his old friend, Helene Hirschler, asking her not to join him in Florence, his next stop after Rome:

> The reason? For some while now I haven't felt well, as you know. I now need about five times as much time for my work as I did. I have rehearsals every day and have to use what remains for rest and study.
>
> ... when a friend such as you wants to visit me, I must have time for her. That is not possible in this case. I have all sorts of the afflictions of old age... If I should recover, which can't be taken for granted, I would love to see you.[59]

While he was in Florence, Klemperer was saddened by news of the death in New York of Lonny Epstein, who had been a friend since they had been students at the Hoch Conservatory in Frankfurt sixty years ago. However, taken as a whole, the Florence visit gave Klemperer a good deal of satisfaction. His schedule allowed him more time for sightseeing than usual and he enjoyed working with the Maggio Musicale Orchestra, which responded to him with enthusiasm. The performance of Mahler's Symphony No. 2 on 12 March won him another tumultuous ovation.

*   *   *

At the beginning of April 1965 Regi Elbogen, Klemperer's elder sister, died in Holland at the age of eighty-two. Klemperer's eightieth birthday, on 14 May 1965, approached, and he began increasingly to brood on the approach of his own death. Feeling off colour in Florence, he had suddenly observed, 'Well, I'm simply a week older.'[60] Six days later, he dreamt that two hands were pressing down on his shoulders and so vivid was the sensation that on awaking he time and again turned his head to make sure there was no one behind him. Asked by Lotte what he supposed the dream to mean, he replied, 'My strength is leaving me, of course.'[61] His thoughts often returned to Johanna's death, and in particular to whether she had been aware that she was dying. With irony he recalled 'the good advice I always gave Mama, that there was no point in thinking about it – and here am I doing just that'. The following day he suddenly observed, 'What a wonderful song Schubert's "Die

Krähe"* is', and went on to recall Egon Pollak's death while conducting *Fidelio* in Prague.

Klemperer celebrated the birthday in Stockholm, where he conducted four concerts and was joined by members of the family, including his two grandchildren, as well as by Paul Dessau. By now Werner had embarked on playing his most celebrated role, that of Colonel Klink, the bumbling German commandant of a prisoner-of-war camp in the hugely successful television comedy series *Hogan's Heroes*. It was to run for no fewer than seven years and would win him two Emmy awards and five nominations. Later Werner arranged for his father to see two episodes at a studio in Zurich. Klemperer was amused by them. 'You're very good', he told Werner, 'but who is the *author* of this piece?' Werner replied that a large group of writers was involved. Clearly, Klemperer could not imagine how such an arrangement could work, but he expressed his pleasure that his son should be enjoying such a financially successful career. Eight days after his birthday he flew to Copenhagen, but his concert there had to be cancelled when he developed severe intestinal troubles, which had to be treated in hospital. When he returned to Zurich on 29 May he was still feverish. On 17 June Lotte noted in her diary that it was hard to tell which of his symptoms were real and which were due to persisting depression. This year there was no Alpine holiday; he preferred to spend the summer quietly at home in Zurich. He again wrote to postpone a visit from Helene Hirschler: 'I haven't been feeling well for a fairly long time ... I'm not a good companion at the moment and would like to put off our seeing each other until the second half of August. Perhaps I'll be feeling better by then.'[62]

*   *   *

Klemperer was still weak when, after spending two weeks in London recording Haydn and Mozart symphonies, he embarked on a long-awaited recording of the *Missa solemnis* on 30 September 1965.† As so often, work proved the best therapy and the sessions culminated in a triumphant public performance in the Festival Hall on 17 October. It was the fourth occasion within nine years that he had conducted the work in London and this time, in the opinion of some critics, he came closest to surmounting its formidable challenges.

After a very necessary two-and-a-half month break in Zurich Klemperer returned to London in the New Year. On 30 January 1966 he accompanied Yehudi Menuhin in a performance of Beethoven's Violin Concerto after they had recorded it. Klemperer found Menuhin's playing 'very disappointing.

---

* The crow is a symbol of death in *Winterreise*.
† EMI had earlier postponed permission for a recording on the grounds that 'the profit situation is still not considered satisfactory' (Michael Allen, EMI internal memo, 9 October 1963).

Although I had four recording sessions with him, there was no sort of development in his tone.'[63]

In the early months of 1966 Klemperer again conducted a number of concerts in Germany, starting with an all-Beethoven programme on 17 March with the radio orchestra in Cologne. Two weeks later a concert with the Bavarian Radio Orchestra in Munich consisted of Schubert's Unfinished and Bruckner's Fourth symphonies. For once Klemperer himself was satisfied. 'I have the happiest memories of the concert', he wrote to the orchestra's manager. 'Especially the Unfinished, which I can hardly conceive of better played.'[64]

Next, in late April, came Hamburg, where he gave a concert with the North German Radio Orchestra. Inasmuch as Klemperer had a *Heimat*, it was this Hanseatic city, from which his mother's family came, and where he had grown up and enjoyed his first successes.* 'Arrived yesterday', noted Lotte on 26 April after they had driven round the town to visit sites familiar from her father's youth, among them the park in which as an eight-year-old he had discovered while listening to the band that he had the gift of perfect pitch. 'Papa in a good mood and very happy to see the town again, is delighted with the Hotel Vierjahreszeiten and the view [over the Binnenalster] from the windows ... it's the most beautiful spring weather. He had a good appetite and in the evening even drank a beer.'

Although he had only one concert in Hamburg, Klemperer remained in the city for almost two weeks. Thus he had time to visit, and be visited by, old friends, to take an excursion round the port and to visit a well-known tourist café on the Elbchaussee. At one moment he was observed sitting happily on a bench by the Alster and singing the city's traditional song, 'Stadt Hamburg an der Elbe Auen, Wie bist Du schön, Harmonia'.[65] On 3 May he conducted Mozart's Symphony No. 40 and Bruckner's Symphony No. 7 in the Musikhalle, where fifty-four years earlier he had conducted his very first symphony concert. The critics outstripped each other in their praise. Heinz Joachim, who had experienced Klemperer in the Berlin of the Weimar Republic, commented that a volcanic temperament that had caused difficulties in earlier days seemed to have been transformed into a source of spiritual strength.[66]

Rolf Liebermann, Intendant of the Hamburg State Opera, invited him to return to conduct some performances of *Lohengrin*, but Klemperer refused, fearful lest they should recall the scandal of 1912, when he had been whipped by an outraged husband at the end of a performance of that very work.† But that was the only shadow on a visit that had enabled him to recapture the past. 'When one is as old as you and I', he had written a few months earlier to

---

* 'Yes, I'm almost a Hamburger.' Interview in the *Hamburger Echo*, 28 September 1955.
† Klemperer suspected that Liebermann's choice of work had been made with malice aforethought, a suspicion that astonished Liebermann when he learnt of it from the author.

Anna Lippmann, one of the few survivors of his boyhood days in Hamburg, 'one sees the whole of life in a peculiar light. Sometimes I can't grasp that it was all so long ago. Do you remember how as children we used to play quartets in your parents' house? It is all so long ago that it doesn't seem true. And yet it stands quite clearly before me.'[67]

From Hamburg, Klemperer went to Berlin for what was to be his last concert there. Once again, neither the place nor the Philharmonic Orchestra gave him pleasure. 'I don't need to tell you that the orchestra is excellent', wrote Lotte before the concert. 'That's sufficiently well known, not least by the players themselves. At the first rehearsal I had an impression that they take it as a personal offence to be interrupted, which doesn't stop my father from doing it frequently.'[68] Klemperer had to admit that, after it had 'pulled it together', the orchestra had finally played 'really well'.[69]

*   *   *

Back in Zurich in mid-May 1966 Klemperer at once resumed the Italian lessons he had started earlier in the year in preparation for recording *Don Giovanni*, a work he had never previously conducted in the original language.* He also read Kierkegaard's *Tagebuch eines Verführers*, as he had done in Cologne in 1920, Alfred Einstein's *Mozart*, which he much admired, and Grabbe's *Don Juan und Faust*.† Mozart's opera seemed to him almost more wonderful than ever. 'I am overcome by its perfection', he wrote to Kruttge on 1 July in the middle of recording sessions. As soon as they were finished he flew on 12 July directly to Israel, where on the following day his younger sister, Marianne, underwent an operation for a malignant tumour.

Klemperer was impressed by the immense strides the young state had made since his last visit in 1958. But he did not warm to the militant orthodoxy that was increasingly making itself felt. A group of zealots stopped his car as he was being driven on the Sabbath to visit his sister. Though he could have walked the short distance to the hospital, he refused to do so and was driven to the hospital's door.[70] He was also irritated by the controversy as to whether or not Wagner's music should be played in a Jewish State.

Since the cancellation of the concerts Klemperer was to have given with the Israel Philharmonic in the winter of 1958–9, relations between orchestra and conductor had been cool. Negotiations in 1961 had broken down when the manager, Abe Cohen, turned down Lotte's proposal that on account of his health her father should make a longer visit than the orchestra had in

---

* Less surprising than it would be today (1991). Until the sixties and seventies even major German houses functioned essentially as repertory companies and sang all works in German.
† Christian Dietrich Grabbe (1801–36), son of the head warder of Detmold prison. *Don Juan und Faust* was successfully performed in 1829 with music by Lortzing, who played the role of Don Juan. As a forerunner of epic theatre, Grabbe's plays have attracted more attention in the second half of the twentieth century than they did in their own time.

mind, adding that 'because of ... prior cancellations [i.e. on Klemperer's part] we find it impossible to leave open an entire series, which may possibly not be fulfilled'.[71] The implication that he was regarded as an unreliable person did not dispose Klemperer to respond favourably to further overtures in 1965.

In July 1966 a new manager, Wolfgang Lewy, took the opportunity of Klemperer's presence in Israel to call on him. But Klemperer was not willing to give the orchestra the 'special terms' it expected from conductors of Jewish origin. His demands were stiff, but what put the orchestra's nose out of joint was his subsequent insistence that he should be free to conduct the Radio's Kol Israel Orchestra as well. After Klemperer's return to Zurich on 22 July, Lewy wrote to inform Lotte that 'I had really hoped that at long last our orchestra would benefit from the experience of playing under ... your father, but it seems that material circumstances are stronger'.[72] Klemperer resented the implication that his wish to conduct the Radio Orchestra stemmed from a desire to maximise his earnings. He was also vexed by Lewy's suggestion in a telephone conversation with Lotte that the Philharmonic's public would not be impressed by a conductor who was prepared to conduct such a modest band. Apart from a letter in which Lewy later attempted to excuse himself for his *faux pas*, that proved to be the last communication between Klemperer and the Israel Philharmonic Orchestra.*

* * *

During their ten-day visit to Jerusalem Lotte had observed that her father was growing increasingly restless and talkative. He had also begun to compose again. By the time he returned home it was clear that he was mildly manic.[73] It did not cause her undue concern: a similar rise in spirits after his visit to Hamburg had fizzled out of its own accord.

On 27 July Klemperer left with Lotte for a summer holiday in St Moritz, where on 8 August they were visited by Gershom Scholem,† whom Klemperer had met a few weeks earlier in Jerusalem. After tea Lotte went to fetch her father's overcoat so that he could accompany his guests to their car. Unwilling to wait for her return, Klemperer started to negotiate a brief flight of steps without a handrail, when he suddenly slipped and broke his good hip. His high spirits had made him incautious.

The surgeons at the Samedan Cantonal Hospital feared to operate at a height of over 5,000 feet on a man in his eighties. A helicopter proved impracticable owing to Klemperer's great length, so that he had to endure a seven-hour

---

* In a letter to Klemperer (23 May 1967) Lewy claimed that it was only after agreements had been reached on fees and expenses that Lotte had informed him of her father's intention also to conduct the Radio Orchestra.
† Gershom Scholem (1897–1982). German-born Jewish scholar. Leading authority on Jewish mysticism. Author of a biography (1957) of the manic-depressive Shabbetai Javi (1628–64).

journey to Zurich by ambulance. There on 16 August he underwent an operation for the insertion of a plastic cap in the upper femur of the right leg. A week later he was able to sit on the edge of his bed. Thereafter his recovery was speedy and by the end of November he had discarded his crutches and wheelchair and was walking as well as he had done before the accident.[74] However, the surgeon would not allow him to resume conducting until February 1967.

Meanwhile a cook-housekeeper, Frau Anna Hesch, was engaged. There was also a new nurse, Sister Ruth Vogel, who was employed on a permanent basis; although she did not live in, she always travelled with Klemperer. Both women were to remain with the family until Klemperer's death. The winter in Zurich passed uneventfully. There were occasional outings to the opera and the cinema. There were also visitors, among them Carlos Kleiber, who asked Klemperer to take him through the score of *Das Lied von der Erde*, which he was to conduct in Vienna. Together they worked on it for several hours. Klemperer was impressed by his visitor's musicianship, less sure of his character.

At the end of January 1967 Lotte went to Budapest for nine days to visit a friend who was ill. During her absence Klemperer resolved to leave the Roman Catholic Church. It was not a sudden decision. In recent years his attendances at Mass had grown infrequent. There were aspects of Catholicism that he found increasingly hard to swallow, such as an appearance on television of Pope Paul VI with relics of St Andrew.[75] There were also dogmas he could no longer accept, for example the Church's concept of grace and the doctrine of free will, which had been a stumbling block at the time of his conversion.[76]

Klemperer had also come to find the Church's failure to dissociate itself from the anti-Semitism endemic in Christian society increasingly unacceptable. What, however, brought his decision to leave it to a head was the information that had emerged about Pope Pius XII's failure to take a stand against the Third Reich, especially during the latter stages of the war, when Rome (though not the Vatican City) was under German occupation. One incident in particular outraged Klemperer. On 23 March 1944 a resistance group assassinated 33 German soldiers in the centre of Rome. On Hitler's direct order, the SS in retribution massacred 335 Italians (70 of them Jewish) in the Ardeatine caves on the city's outskirts. Though forewarned of German intentions, the Pope refused to put pressure on the occupying authorities to prevent or even to postpone the massacre, while condemning the action of the resistance.* The fact that these equivocal policies had been pursued by a man

---

* These events are dealt with in detail in Robert Katz's *Death in Rome*, which Klemperer read at this time. The Pope had reasons for acting as he did: he was involved in delicate negotiations with the Germans to have Rome declared an open city. Less to his credit was his fear that left-wing resistance groups would seize power when the Germans were finally obliged to withdraw.

Klemperer had known in Berlin and twice visited in the Vatican made them no easier to accept.

Klemperer reached his decision without discussing it with Lotte, but there was no question of his acting on impulse. He was quite clear about his intentions.[77] On 6 February he addressed a letter to the president of the Catholic community in Zurich, informing him that he was leaving the Church. Three weeks later he wrote to tell Werner what he had done:

> I have left the Roman Catholic Church ... The reasons were of course only inward (*innerlich*). That outside considerations (political, etc.) were also an influence is clear ... It was only over the years that it came to the final step. Only one request: tell no one apart from your wife. I have only informed Marianne and Herman. I don't want it to become a matter of gossip in musical circles or in the papers.[78]

Later Klemperer wrote to inform Soma Morgenstern, who ten years earlier had sent him his novel *Blutsäule*, in the hope that it might incline Klemperer to his Jewish heritage. On receiving the news, Morgenstern replied, 'You have always belonged to us.'[79] In a real sense that was true. In his eighty-third year Klemperer had taken a decisive step towards returning to the faith of his fathers.

14

The shadows lengthen

For several months Klemperer had been planning to perform and record Mahler's Symphony No. 9, a work he had not conducted for forty years. EMI, whose catalogue already contained Barbirolli's version, was not over-enthusiastic about the idea, but was prepared to go along with it in view of what Peter Andry called Klemperer's 'scarcely veiled threat' to record the symphony for another company. EMI's German subsidiary, Electrola, was patronising. 'Let old Dr Klemperer do as he wishes', wrote its artistic director, Dr Helmut Storjohann. 'As you know, there is little interest in Mahler in Germany.'[1] The final go-ahead was not given by EMI's International Classical Recording Committee until 23 January 1967, scarcely more than two weeks before Klemperer was due to arrive in London to begin the recording sessions. The committee reported that a recording would show 'a distinct loss' over the first three years and continued:

> Normally, such a proposal would not be approved, but we are forced to take it very seriously as Dr Klemperer has set his heart on it, and he is our most important conductor ... [and] our best selling classical artist at present in the UK and USA. His records account for approximately 10 per cent of EMI Records' classical LP business and 15 per cent of Angel's business.*
>
> Klemperer has been exclusive to EMI since 1955 and it would be most damaging to our prestige if he were now to record for another company.[2]

Klemperer arrived in London on 8 February and began to record the Mahler symphony three days later. 'From the very start we were amazed by the old boy', wrote Laurence Taylor.

> He came in shuffling as before, with his big wooden walking stick, supported by another man, but supported only in the most nominal way ... It was clear he was in terrific condition ... he looked better, better color, and such spirit! He was filled with humor, impatience and energy in a way exceeding anything anyone could remember for years.[3]

At one of the early sessions Klemperer idly picked up a baton that happened to be lying around. Though he had not used a stick for over thirty years, he started to play with it and wondered whether he should not use one

---
* The label under which EMI sold its classical catalogue in America.

22 Klemperer in London, March 1967. Photo: G. MacDomnic

again. In Lotte's view his hand was more effective, but he asked the orchestral players for their opinion, which was divided more or less equally. Klemperer opted for the baton, which he continued to use until the end of his career.[4]

The Mahler recording was completed on 24 February and three days later Klemperer gave the first of two performances at the Festival Hall. A year had passed since he had last appeared in public in London. Once he had negotiated the steps up to the platform, he shrugged off his assistant's arm and walked slowly to the rostrum unaided. The audience rose to greet him, but all it got in response was the usual perfunctory nod. In a programme note, Klemperer described Mahler's Ninth Symphony as 'his last but greatest achievement'. Critics complained of untidy detail, but there was general agreement that Klemperer's performance had thrown new light on the work. Ronald Crichton wrote in the *Musical Times* (April 1967):

> We know what to expect from Klemperer's Mahler: big outlines, rock-like rhythms, structure before detail, no lingering by the wayside, no attempt to soften or to blend the crystal-clear and often searing orchestration. This performance ran true to form. The first movement was blocked out with awesome grandeur, the scherzo was gruff. The Rondo burleske started drily but about halfway through (at the D major section that anticipates the finale) moved on to a higher plane altogether; the New Philharmonia's already excellent playing now became superlative. Klemperer moulded the long phrases of the final Adagio with Olympian tranquillity drawn from formidable inner strength ... There was a strange accident in the last few bars, but in retrospect this seems unimportant beside the profound impression made by the performance as a whole.

Klemperer was so pleased by the success of the performance* that he decided that in the following season he would perform Mahler's vast Symphony No. 8, the so-called 'symphony of a thousand', in the Royal Albert Hall; he would also record it. He had attended the first performance in 1910, under the composer's own direction, but had never conducted it himself. EMI was wary in view of the huge costs involved, while Lotte was concerned that a work on this scale might prove to be beyond her father's physical powers. Eventually, Klemperer was persuaded by EMI to postpone the project 'until such time as it can be set up with sufficient funds available'.[5]

*   *   *

In the afternoon of 4 March 1967 the 24-year-old Daniel Barenboim presented himself at the Hyde Park Hotel to play his cadenza for Mozart's Piano Concerto in C major, K.503, which he was to perform with Klemperer three days later at the Festival Hall. That same evening Klemperer wrote approvingly to Kruttge, 'I could see at once what a remarkable pianist he is.' In spite of the almost sixty years' difference in their ages, he also warmed to Barenboim as a man. In particular, he liked the intelligence and the *chutzpah* that enabled Barenboim to stand up to the conversational sparring Klemperer so much relished. It was not always Klemperer who got the better of their

---

* In the coming years Mahler's Ninth Symphony was to feature prominently in Klemperer's programmes. Between 1967 and 1970 he conducted performances in Paris, Vienna, Edinburgh, Lucerne and Jerusalem, as well as in London.

exchanges. Later in 1967, Barenboim was summoned to the hotel, where he found a singer and accompanist, who proceeded to make their way through a pile of Klemperer's songs. When the recital had ended, the following exchange took place:

Klemperer: Do you like my compositions, Mr Barenboim?
Barenboim: No, Dr Klemperer.

After his visitor had left, Klemperer turned to Lotte: 'I like that boy, he is honest. But he is no judge of music.'[6]

No other musician of Barenboim's generation came so close to Klemperer in his last years, though paradoxically Mozart's C major concerto remained the only occasion on which they appeared together in public. Barenboim had for his part expected to encounter in Klemperer a forbidding disciplinarian of the old German school, but he soon learnt that a teasing wit lay behind a daunting exterior. At the first recording session for the Mozart concerto later in the month, Barenboim, who was already beginning to make his mark as a conductor, was disconcerted by the persistency with which Klemperer turned round to observe him. Eventually, Barenboim stopped and asked whether something was wrong. 'I want to make sure you are not conducting behind my back', came the prompt reply.[7] At the end of the final session, Klemperer, who made no secret of his admiration for the pianist, remarked (in Barenboim's hearing) to a Jewish member of the orchestra: 'This boy plays well, but not *so* well. He is too young – not mature. But what can you expect? After all, he is a Jew.' Everyone laughed, including Laurence Taylor. 'You stay out of it', Klemperer told him. 'You are a Methodist.' The collaboration with Barenboim went so smoothly that Klemperer agreed to record all Beethoven's piano concertos with him in the autumn. Henceforth Barenboim and his wife, the cellist Jacqueline du Pré, were among his most frequent visitors in London.

Another was Lord Harewood, an admirer ever since he had heard Klemperer conduct Mahler's Second Symphony in Holland in 1951, and the main instigator of the decision to invite him to conduct *Fidelio* at Covent Garden. In January 1966, Harewood had become the New Philharmonia's artistic adviser. As such he soon became the main link between the orchestra and its president. Their regular meetings in Klemperer's suite overlooking Hyde Park were 'lively, informative and always illuminating'.[8] Business completed, Klemperer would often invite his visitors to remain for sherry. On such occasions he would show an unexpectedly genial side to his character. There would be much musical gossip, and the more scurrilous the better. Like others, Harewood found that Klemperer did not hold court or deliver monologues; what he liked was an exchange of opinions. After one of the recording sessions for the Mahler Ninth, Laurence Taylor was surprised to be called to

23   Left to right: Otto Klemperer, Lotte Klemperer, Jacqueline du Pré, Daniel Barenboim, March 1967. Photo: G. MacDomnic

the conductor's room. Klemperer, stripped to the waist, was being rubbed down by Lotte. 'Sit down, Mr Taylor', he said, 'and explain to me *all* about Vietnam.' Visitors to the Hyde Park Hotel were also liable to be regaled by records of Tom Lehrer's satirical songs.* 'Alma', a send-up of Alma Mahler's many amours, was a particular favourite, though 'The Vatican Rag' with its frenetic refrain, 'Genuflect! Genuflect! Genuflect!', in which Klemperer liked to join, ran it close.

* Thomas Andrew Lehrer (b. 1928). American university lecturer, who established a reputation as a song writer and entertainer. The records had been given to Klemperer by Thomas Mann's eldest daughter, Erika, a neighbour in Zurich.

Though Lotte described her father as being 'in quite unbelievable form', she was worried that he was becoming 'almost too lively'.[9] In spite of a taxing schedule of rehearsals, recordings and concerts, his energies seemed almost inexhaustible. On free evenings he would turn up at the Festival Hall for concerts by artists such as Barenboim, Jacqueline du Pré, Solti and Boulez.* He also attended a performance of Franco Zeffirelli's celebrated production of *Cavalleria Rusticana* at Covent Garden, as well as the concert with which Britten and Pears opened the new Queen Elizabeth Hall on the South Bank.

Meanwhile, his euphoria was growing more intense. 'It's become a madhouse', Lotte wrote to a friend,

> ... but there's *nothing* one can do ... beyond here and there averting some craziness ... and even then not always with success. At the same time he's often charming, is enjoying himself immensely, is *still* working excellently, though rehearsals bore him![10]

Although normally unwilling to deputise for sick colleagues, Klemperer accepted a proposal by Lord Harewood that he should prolong his stay in London to deputise for an indisposed Paul Kletzki on 4 April. Kletzki's programme comprised Haydn's 'Clock' Symphony, nine songs from Mahler's *Knaben Wunderhorn*, with Irmgard Seefried and Thomas Hemsley as soloists, and Brahms's First Symphony. For the Brahms Klemperer insisted on substituting Stravinsky's *Petrushka* in its 1947 version, which he had recorded a few days earlier for EMI. It was a score with which he had long been familiar, and in his younger days he had conducted it with marked success. But during the recording sessions Stravinsky's rhythms caused him great difficulty and EMI eventually decided not to release it.† The rehearsals for the concert also went badly. In the evening Klemperer pulled himself together sufficiently to get through the evening without disaster. But in her diary Lotte noted, 'concert not good ... badly prepared'.

Yet Klemperer's behaviour was less wild than it had been in earlier manic phases. That was partly a matter of age; he no longer had the physical strength for nocturnal escapades.[11] Thus, on his arrival in Paris on 21 April to conduct the New Philharmonia in a performance of Mahler's Ninth Symphony, his high spirits remained within bounds. As in London two months earlier, the press found some of the playing rough and inaccurate, but

---

* Boulez returned the compliment by attending the Mozart programme Klemperer conducted on 7 March. It ended with a performance of the 'Jupiter' Symphony that Boulez and Harewood rated among the fastest they had heard (Harewood, *The Tongs and the Bones*, p. 280). So much for the widespread belief that Klemperer's tempi were invariably slow.

† Four years later Klemperer recalled its existence and Lotte wrote to ask what had become of it. At Peter Andry's request, Diana Chapman wrote on 23 July 1971 to say that 'we feel that it would not really be in your father's interest for us to issue this recording – if you remember, he was not feeling his best at the time'. Lotte asked for a copy to be sent. After Klemperer had heard it, she wrote to say that he agreed that the recording 'is not good enough to be released' (letter to Diana Chapman, 9 August 1971).

the performance, on 24 April, made so deep an impression that Klemperer was invited to return with the orchestra in the autumn to conduct Bach's B minor Mass and a Beethoven programme, though the plans came to nothing owing to lack of funds.

Paris was at its most irresistible in brilliant spring sunshine. 'I ... can't tell you what an enormous impression the city again made on me. It was always lovely, but now it seems more beautiful than ever.'[12] At the very end of his stay an incident occurred that gave Klemperer particular pleasure. As he was leaving his hotel he was recognised by a student band that happened to be on its way to a ceremony at the Etoile, but stopped to salute him with the grand march from *Aida*. Klemperer was not a man who set much store by public recognition, but the spontaneity of the gesture delighted him.[13]

* * *

Since it had become a self-governing entity the New Philharmonia's concert work had grown at the expense of studio recordings. At the same time its playing standards had begun to slip for want of a firm hand on the helm. Meanwhile, Klemperer's advancing years were obliging him to reduce his engagements. For these reasons the NPO's council of management decided on 3 February 1967 to consider 'the appointment of a conductor who would undertake a reasonable proportion of the orchestra's concert promotions'. The recently appointed manager, George Stringer, informed the council that he and Lord Harewood planned to visit a candidate, who at this stage remained anonymous. The council gave its approval, but emphasised that 'any such discussions should be of an exploratory nature ... as the exact nature of such an appointment remained to be decided'.

On 8 February Harewood and Stringer flew to Milan, where they spent the better part of a day in discussions with the 33-year-old Claudio Abbado, a leading member of the rising generation of conductors. Much table tennis was played and Abbado, who at that time occupied no major post, showed lively interest in an appointment with the NPO. His terms were not unreasonable; he would want to determine the players and programmes of such concerts he himself conducted. He also expressed a desire to discuss the situation with Klemperer, whom he admired but had never met.

The meeting took place in April. But Stringer and Lotte recall the encounter as purely social. The issue of Abbado's appointment and the form it should take was never touched upon, so that he is said to have come away from the encounter 'bemused'.[14] On the following day Peter Andry called on Lotte. To Lotte's amazement, Andry informed her that 'Mr Stringer had hired Mr Abbado as Principal Conductor as of the fall of 1969.' In an angry letter to Gareth Morris, the orchestra's first flute and chairman of its council since 1966, she wrote,

I asked Mr Andry if he had asked Mr Stringer what Klemperer thought of that, and supposedly Mr Stringer answered that it was being put to my father that day ... As you know, it has not been put to him so far, and ... I will not put it to him. You will have to do it directly.

... it must be made unmistakably clear ... that from now on I will have nothing further to do with Mr Stringer ...

And now to the main problem: the engagement of Mr Abbado, or rather the conditions that Mr Abbado ... attaches to this engagement. As you know, my father does not know Mr Abbado as a conductor (nor do I), has heard only good things about him, and was absolutely agreeable to your giving him a large portion of your concerts. He fully understood the orchestra's need in this respect. As you also know, my father has never paid attention to what other conductors are engaged during your season ...

Now Mr Abbado wants a title, and Decca, who plans to do a series of recordings with him and the NPO, would also find that desirable. Needless to say [that] would diminish my father's position with the orchestra as well as with EMI ... In addition Mr Abbado now wants to have a say in who the other guest-conductors will be. This condition can only have one reason and that is to play the age-old game of If-you-invite-me – I'll-invite-you-back ... I – quite frankly – would be most disturbed to see my father associated with such politics.[15]

Clearly the orchestra was faced with the possibility of losing Klemperer. On 5 May, Morris flew to Milan to tell Abbado that the deal was off.

*   *   *

In London Klemperer had started to attend services at the Marble Arch Synagogue, though that did not prevent him on one occasion from also attending Mass at the Brompton Oratory. To meet Jewish requirements, he made an excursion to the East End where he acquired a cap, a ritual shroud to be worn when dead, a shawl such as male Jews are required to wear at morning prayers and a prayer book. He also bought three large volumes of the writings of the Jewish philosopher Moses Maimonides.* Henceforth all these items (apart from the books) accompanied Klemperer on his travels.

Back in Zurich, his attendance at synagogue gradually grew more sporadic. To an old friend, the philosophy professor Helmuth Plessner, it seemed as though Klemperer's return to Judaism stemmed less from faith than from a desire to show solidarity with Israel;[16] as he himself put it, 'I wanted to demonstrate that I am a Jew and am loyal to Jewish things.'[17] It was not long before an opportunity arose for him to do so.

---

* Moses Maimonides (1135–1204). Sage and philosopher who has been described as 'the most illustrious figure in Judaism in the post-Talmudic era'. Born in Cordoba, he settled in 1160 in Fez. He put medieval Jewish philosophy on a firm Aristotelian basis and also exercised influence on Christian thought.

At the end of April Klemperer learnt that his surviving sister, Marianne, was about to undergo a major operation and he decided to visit her in Jerusalem. While there he conducted a concert on 20 May for the benefit of the Hebrew University with the Radio Orchestra, which had been enlarged since he had last conducted it in 1951. The programme included Schubert's Unfinished Symphony and Mozart's 'Jupiter'. With the proceeds an endowment fund bearing Klemperer's name was set up; it still supports needy students.*

Meanwhile, tension was rising in the Middle East. The Egyptian army had moved into Sinai with the intention of blockading the Straits of Tiran, and general mobilisation was declared in Israel on the day of Klemperer's concert. On 5 June, two weeks after Klemperer had returned to Zurich, the Six Day War began. The Soviet Union and its Eastern European satellites launched a propaganda campaign against Israel. Anti-Israeli demonstrations in East Berlin touched Klemperer on an exposed nerve, for only a month before the outbreak of the Six Day War arrangements were in hand for him to spend no fewer than three months in the capital of the German Democratic Republic.[18] At the Deutsche Staatsoper he was to conduct four performances of *Fidelio*, six of *Die Entführung aus dem Serail*, both at his suggestion to be directed by Ruth Berghaus, and two concerts. There was also a plan for him to perform and record *Così fan tutte* in the following autumn.[19]

Klemperer was eager to appear again at the theatre with which his name had been so closely linked in the latter years of the Weimar Republic. He was also sympathetic to the East German regime. An increasing animus against West Germany is apparent in his correspondence in the mid-sixties. As he admitted, 'I myself was powerfully drawn to the German Democratic Republic as I became all too aware of ... the inadequacies of the democratic system in the West.'[20] But to appear at the leading opera house of a State that supported an Arab coalition bent on the destruction of Israel was quite another matter. On 9 June he wrote in no uncertain terms to inform Hans Pischner, the Intendant of the Deutsche Staatsoper, that 'I cannot ... and *will* not come to the German Democratic Republic.' To make his sympathies doubly plain, on 29 June he gave a performance of Mahler's Second Symphony with the Zurich Tonhalle Orchestra in aid of Israel.†

Klemperer's sense of anger with and disappointment in the German Democratic Republic is evident in a sharp exchange of letters with his old friend Paul Dessau, who since Eisler's death in 1962 had come to be generally

---

* Two months later Klemperer made a second visit to Jerusalem to see his sister whose condition was deteriorating. She died on 5 September 1967.
† The concert was a repeat of one he had conducted on 6 June, which marked his reconciliation with the Tonhalle Orchestra after the quarrels over the Zurich *Fidelio* of 1962.

regarded as East Germany's leading composer. On 2 July Klemperer wrote to tell him that 'in my view you are a Jew, born of a Jewish father and a Jewish mother – and circumcised'. As such, it was his duty to leave the German Democratic Republic. Dessau replied that he regarded himself as a Jew, not an Israeli. It was a distinction Klemperer would not accept:

> For six thousand years or more this people has survived. Rome fell, Greece fell, England fell as a colonial power, Germany fell deepest of all. Judaism *remains* ... It's so monstrous that words fail me ... In my view ... every Jew should be a defender of Israel.[21]

When Dessau stuck to his guns, Klemperer became still angrier.

> I have only one word to say to you. Out. Why did Ernst Bloch leave? I know why and so do you, and in spite of that you persist in putting yourself in this absolutely unworthy position ...
>
> You are a Communist and you should remain one ... Ernst Bloch still maintains that he is a Marxist ... [But] the German Democratic Republic is quite another matter, a highly dubious outfit.*

Thereafter Klemperer never again conducted in Eastern Europe and the rift was reinforced after the Soviet bloc's suppression of Dubček's 'socialism with a human face' in Prague in August 1968. Though cautious about lending his name to public protests, in this instance he allowed it to be included among the thirty-four leading musicians who joined Rafael Kubelik in stating that they would not appear in the five countries of the Warsaw Pact so long as their troops remained on Czechoslovak soil.[22]

*   *   *

At the end of July 1967 Klemperer went to Bayreuth for three days. He had not visited the festival since 1930, when Siegfried Wagner's funeral provided an opportunity for him to hear Toscanini conduct *Tristan und Isolde*. Wieland Wagner's plan for him to give a performance in Bayreuth of Beethoven's Ninth Symphony with the Philharmonia in 1963, in celebration of the 150th anniversary of his grandfather's birth, had collapsed when the festival orchestra threatened to strike. But in 1966 Boulez's interpretation of *Parsifal* had aroused much interest – and controversy – and Klemperer was determined to go and hear it in the following year. There could be no question of him travelling to Bayreuth alone. In the course of the summer of 1967, he had become increasingly manic; on one occasion in Zurich he had returned from a nocturnal expedition in a bedraggled condition.[23] Lotte, who was in any case no Wagnerian, needed a break. It was therefore agreed that he

---

* Letter to Paul Dessau, Zurich, 5 August 1967. Less than three weeks later Klemperer advised Helene Hirschler to leave the United States on account of its policies in Vietnam (letter of 25 August 1967).

THE SHADOWS LENGTHEN

24 Left to right: Pierre Boulez, Erwin Jacobi, Otto Klemperer, Anna Hesch (the Klemperers' housekeeper), Bayreuth 1967

should be accompanied by his housekeeper, Frau Anna, and a friend from Zurich, the musicologist, Erwin Jacobi.

The visitors were received in style. A car, which remained at their disposal throughout the visit, met them at Munich airport and they were lodged in a sanatorium conveniently close to the Festspielhaus, where Wolfgang Wagner's daughter, Eva, attended to their needs. Klemperer attended performances of *Tannhäuser* and *Lohengrin*, as well as *Parsifal*. But he did not see eye to eye with Boulez when they discussed *Parsifal* over lunch. To a man of Klemperer's religious temperament, Wagner's theatrical exploitation of Christian ritual was offensive. In his view it was at best a parody. The agnostic Boulez had no such qualms. There were, he admitted, aspects of the work he did not care for, but he was content to take the music at its face value.

During the visit, Klemperer visited Wahnfried, the villa Wagner had built in the town. In the big drawing-room he sat down at the piano that Steinway had presented to Wagner in 1873 and played the prelude to *Tristan* with extraordinary intensity. For a while he continued to sit in silence before the keyboard, and then – not by chance – started to play music that seemed vaguely familiar to his audience, though nobody could put a name to it. It proved to be 'O Tod, wie bitter bist Du', the third of Brahms's *Vier ernste Gesänge*. During Cosima's long reign little Brahms had been heard within Wahnfried's sacred portals.[24]

After one performance at the Festspielhaus, Klemperer insisted on going in search of Bayreuth's almost non-existent night-life. He concocted a plan to stage Mozart's five most famous operas in the town's exquisite Markgräfliches Opernhaus.[25] He was so taken by Anja Silja in the role of Elisabeth that, in spite of the fact two other sopranos had already been approached, he told Peter Andry that 'we should make every effort to get her' for the recording and concert performance of *Der fliegende Holländer* he was scheduled to conduct in London in the coming winter. 'Musically and dramatically', he said, 'she is extraordinary.'[26]

*   *   *

In his earlier days in Germany, Klemperer had gained a well-merited reputation as a champion of contemporary music, but with advancing years he had indeed come to feel that 'my season for experimenting is over'.[27] He was predictably out of sympathy with aleatory music.[28] When he attended a rehearsal in London of Henze's agitprop cantata, *Versuch über Schweine*, he found its combination of *Sprechstimme* and orchestra 'alien' and 'passé'.* He even found difficulty in coming to terms with a score as conservative in idiom as Britten's War Requiem.[29] Yet he felt uncomfortable in a reactionary role. After listening to Strauss's late opera *Daphne* on the radio, he observed, 'I prefer any experimental music to that.'[30]

On 22 September 1967, at a ceremony at the West German embassy in Berne, Klemperer was invested with Germany's highest honour, the Pour le Mérite, which is limited to thirty members.† A speech was expected of him and in preparation he put some of his views on contemporary music on paper. In spite of his reservations, he was not prepared to associate himself with the blanket condemnation of new musical developments such as Hindemith had delivered in 1963, the last year of his life, when he had been admitted to the same order. While admitting that he had become estranged from new developments, they were, he insisted, inevitable. 'I am thinking, for example, of Boulez and Stockhausen.‡ I cannot say that their works always appeal to

---

* Letter to Paul Dessau, London, 21 March 1969. Henze later expressed surprise to the author that Klemperer made no reference to the music when they met in the interval. Klemperer's letter to Dessau makes it clear that his omission was intentional.

† Honours were beginning to accrue. In November 1966 Klemperer had received the Lower Saxon Art Prize. The City of Leipzig's Artur Nikisch Medal followed in April 1967. Towards the end of Klemperer's life, Lord Harewood recommended him for a British award in belated recognition of his contribution to British musical life. Klemperer died before the official machinery had cranked into action.

‡ After hearing a rehearsal of *Gruppen* in London on 21 February 1968, he wrote in a letter to Rolf Liebermann (25 February 1968) that the work '*very* much impressed' him.

me, but I am convinced by their seriousness. In other words, the movement as a whole is all right by me.'

* * *

For Klemperer, Bach's Mass in B minor was 'the greatest and most unique music ever written';[31] he approached no other work with such care and caution. In a career of almost sixty years he had performed it only once before, in Berlin in December 1932, when he had described it as 'the hardest thing I have as yet had to conduct'. That diffidence did not diminish with age. In Berlin he had used the 250-strong Philharmonic Chorus. When the possibility arose of recording and performing the Mass in London in 1962, Walter Legge wanted to use the Philharmonia Chorus, but over the years Klemperer had become convinced that the work called for a professional chorus of some fifty voices. Partly to convince himself and partly to placate Legge, he agreed to trial recording sessions with the Philharmonia Chorus. The results confirmed his preference for small forces and, much to Legge's irritation, he cancelled the projected performance. In May 1966 he met the German scholar Friedrich Smend, whose controversial edition of the Mass had caused a furore on its publication in the Neue Bach-Ausgabe in 1956. Smend confirmed Klemperer's belief about the required forces, and in the autumn of the following year Klemperer recorded the work with a chorus of forty-eight and an orchestra consisting of thirty-three strings and twelve woodwind.

Klemperer insisted on recording the work in its proper order, so that his soloists (who included Agnes Giebel, Janet Baker and Nicolai Gedda) had to fly to London as and when required. To Peter Andry he seemed concerned above all with structure.[32] Told from the control room that a passage was not together, Klemperer shouted out, 'Then let it not be together.'[33] Following Smend's edition, he used a flute in place of the more usual violin in the Benedictus and a Mander positive organ in the continuo. At the final rehearsal for performances of the work in the Festival Hall on 14 and 17 November, Kruttge, who had come to London from Cologne for the occasion, felt that Klemperer had achieved exceptional contrapuntal lucidity, but the press reaction was mixed. In the *Financial Times* (15 November) Ronald Crichton found a welcome contrast to the hearty English choral style of the day, but several critics commented on Klemperer's slow tempi. In the *Musical Times* (January 1968) Stanley Sadie challenged Klemperer's claim in a programme note that the performances were 'experimental'; the use of chamber forces, he pointed out, was no longer so rare in the B minor Mass as the conductor seemed to suppose.

Klemperer was not dissatisfied with what he had achieved and declared that he would never again perform the work with a large orchestra and chorus. He had found the task strenuous, but, as he observed in a letter to a friend, 'Work is of course the best thing of all, for it's what gives old folk like us a hold on life.'[34] Lotte noted, however, that a long period of work now strained her father more than before, and as a result some engagements were cancelled to enable him to remain at home until his return to London almost three months later.

*   *   *

Der fliegende Holländer was recorded in London between 17 February and 14 March 1968, followed by a concert performance in the Festival Hall on 19 March. Klemperer's letters of this period are full of delighted references to his Senta, Anja Silja, though the critics were in two minds about her merits: William Mann, for example, praised her vocal attack, but found her 'careless about pitch and breathing'.[35] But the dramatic impact of her performance was indisputable. As at the Kroll almost forty years earlier, Senta was portrayed not as the conventional dreamer, but as a woman possessed. At moments orchestral ensemble was precarious and in at least one passage disaster was only narrowly averted. But such imperfections were of little account. 'From the opening bars of the overture', wrote the author, 'one [was] plunged into a world where man is at the mercy of wind and water, and against this tumultuous background there ... unfolded a story, not of cosy sentimentality and true love, but of an obsessive and self-destructive passion that can only be consummated in annihilation.'[36] As in Berlin, Klemperer again used the original Dresden version of the opera, a decision in line with his somewhat eccentric view that Wagner's early works were to be preferred to those that came later. 'Young Wagner', he later wrote to Dessau, 'was already a great composer. With advancing years he developed backwards. *Der fliegende Holländer, Tannhäuser* and *Lohengrin* are surely more appealing than *Siegfried* and *Götterdämmerung*.'[37]

After again performing Mahler's Symphony No. 9 on 28 March, he started to record Strauss's *Don Quixote*. It was not a score he much cared for,* and only his affection for Jacqueline du Pré, who played the solo cello part, led him to attempt it on this occasion. During the sessions Klemperer seemed weary and uninvolved, so much so that he twice fell asleep during a playback.[38] Lotte suspected that her father's fatigue reflected his lack of enthusiasm for the work. The recording was cancelled, and Klemperer withdrew from the concert that was to have followed. Sir Adrian Boult conducted in his place. On 9 April Klemperer returned to Zurich, exhausted by his two-month stint in London.

The break was necessary, for in May he was due to conduct the Vienna Philharmonic Orchestra on its home ground in a series of five concerts with programmes that included works ranging from Bach to Stravinsky. He looked

---

* He had previously conducted it only in Los Angeles, 3/4 March 1938.

forward to the engagement, because the Vienna Philharmonic remained his favourite orchestra. As it played at the State Opera in the evening, the concerts took place on successive Sunday mornings in the Musikverein. Klemperer's Beethoven interpretations in particular were hailed by Karl Löbl (*Express*, 27 May) as being 'right without being didactic, clean without being sterile, full of tension yet free of effects', even though the Fifth Symphony had lasted ten minutes longer than usual and suffered from imprecise playing in the finale. Klemperer's account of Bruckner's Symphony No. 5 on 2 June was also greeted with enthusiasm.

At this point, however, the visit started to go sour. In rehearsals for his fourth concert, which consisted of Mahler's Symphony No. 9, Klemperer became aware that the orchestra was less familiar with the score than he had expected. In *Die Presse* (11 June) Franz Endler attributed the blame for a disappointing performance to Klemperer, who, he insisted, had on this instance bitten off more than he could chew. Endler waspishly added, 'in a great ... but rarely performed work such as this, the orchestra not only requires occasional firm (*grossartig*) direction but ... a clear beat'. In Karl Löbl's view the deficiencies of the performance stemmed from the orchestra's 'hardly disguised aversion' to the music. Helmut Hermann went further and asked whether it did not spring from 'latent anti-Semitism'.*[39] In the light of the difficulties they had experienced in Mahler, the players asked Klemperer to end his final concert on 16 June with a few familiar Wagner excerpts instead of *Petrushka*, as had been planned. He raised no objection to the change, which *Express* (12 June) welcomed 'after the experiences of last weekend'.

What was to prove his last visit to Vienna none the less gave him much pleasure. The weather was fine and a number of old friends who had joined him for the occasion accompanied him on excursions. David Oistrakh, who had recently taken up conducting, was also in the city. After attending some of his rehearsals, Klemperer told the great violinist that it was a pleasure to be able to greet him as a colleague. 'Oh', answered Oistrakh, 'I didn't know that you now play the violin.'[40]

Klemperer took the opportunity to visit Ferdinand Onno, an actor who had come to be a close friend during their early days together in Prague. Now widowed, old and poor, Onno lived with a retarded son in a fifth-floor apartment that had no lift. Klemperer insisted on climbing the stairs, only to find the door barred: Onno had developed mild paranoia. When finally admitted, they were confronted by a scene of disorder that to Lotte's eye

---

* The fact that in the twenty-three years that had passed since the end of the Third Reich, when Mahler's music had been banned, the Vienna Philharmonic had only twice performed the symphony, on both occasions under foreign conductors (Kubelik, 2 and 3 March 1957 and Mitropoulos, 1 and 2 October), does not suggest much eagerness to renew acquaintanceship with it.

evoked a set for a Beckett play. When Klemperer returned the following day, the meeting took place in the street; Onno perched on an upturned box while Klemperer remained in the wheelchair that had by now become his usual conveyance. The two old gentlemen were so engrossed in each other's company that they remained blithely unaware of the bizarre spectacle they presented to passers-by.[41]

* * *

Since his return to London in February 1967 Klemperer had started to compose again. Erwin Jacobi had drawn his attention to a gavotte by Rameau that he had played as a small boy, and on it Klemperer wrote a modest set of variations for a small group of wind instruments and strings. Though it aroused little enthusiasm, he included it in concerts in Vienna, London and Paris, and recorded it with the NPO.*

During the summer of 1967 he also returned to a symphony, his second, that he had first begun five years earlier, but had put aside. He performed it for the first time on 22 March 1968 before a small audience of friends in EMI's Abbey Road studios. The programme also included the Rameau variations and the short choral work *J'accuse*, written in 1933. Gareth Morris wrote on behalf of the New Philharmonia to tell Klemperer that it would not be sending him a bill for its services.[42] Klemperer was greatly touched by this act of generosity, particularly as the orchestra had financial problems of its own. In a letter of thanks he wrote to tell the players how rewarding it had been for him to hear his work: 'You see, any composer can study as long as he will, but the real test is the hearing. I enjoyed this rehearsal very much, and thanks to your letter my joy is even greater. Please tell the whole orchestra of all my gratitude.'[43] Yet he did not deceive himself about the significance of his music. 'It's easy enough to put down ideas', he wrote to Aladár Tóth. 'The difficulty is to realise them.' Later in the year, however, he sent the score of the symphony to a number of radio stations and conductors. The only person to react positively was the American conductor Dean Dixon, who conducted it at a studio concert with the Frankfurt Radio Orchestra.

Klemperer gave the symphony its first public performance at a concert in the Festival Hall on 30 September 1969. The critics were not impressed. In the *Guardian* (1 October) Meirion Bowen described it as 'the product of an outstanding conductor musing on the works of composers he has championed throughout his career, notably Mahler, Bruckner and Strauss ... What it does not reflect is their grasp of large-scale structure.' The *Neue Zürcher Zeitung* dismissed the symphony as 'post-Mahlerian *Kapellmeistermusik*'.[44] But a hall full of admirers gave the work such a warm reception that, much to

---

* Bärenreiter toyed with the idea of publishing the score, but it collapsed when Klemperer abruptly withdrew it (Lotte Klemperer, memo to the author, 30 January 1985).

Klemperer's delight, Peters Edition decided to publish the score, while EMI agreed to record the work, along with the Rameau variations, as a tribute on his approaching eighty-fifth birthday.[45] As he wrote to Bloch, 'Der Eine acht's, der Andere verlacht's, was macht's?' ('One praises, the other mocks. What does it matter?')*

The Second Symphony was not the only work in which Klemperer's interest had revived. By the spring of 1969 he had completed the score of his biblical opera *Der verlorene Sohn*, which he had sketched out during his last days in Germany in 1933. He sent it to a number of opera houses, including Vienna and the Deutsche Oper in West Berlin, but nothing happened. Klemperer bore such setbacks philosophically. To Max Hofmüller, a friend from his early days in Strasbourg during the First World War, who had attempted to interest the Bavarian State Opera in the work, he wrote, 'Much greater men than myself have had to show even more patience.'[46] Thereafter his interest in his biblical operas seems to have dwindled.

A similar fate finally befell *Das Ziel*, a score whose origins went back to 1915. Of all Klemperer's operas, it was the one in which he retained confidence. He revised and completed the score in the winter of 1928–9, only to withdraw it from the publishers in the following summer. Then in April 1931 he had performed it privately in Berlin. Nearly thirty-six years later, in March 1967, the author was surprised to receive a summons to hear a run-through of the work in the Hyde Park Hotel. It proved an unnerving experience. Klemperer's assistant, Otto Freudenthal, played the piano, while the composer himself sang all the parts, frequently missing the entries. At the work's conclusion the conductor turned to his visitor and announced with glee, 'And now the Herr *Kritikus* will tell us what he thinks of my opera.' Some days later Lord Harewood underwent a similar ordeal.

Thereafter Klemperer again lost interest in the piece. To an enquiry, he replied that the score 'lies ... in my desk, waiting for Godot'.† 'Naturally', he told the author, 'I would be glad to be remembered as a conductor *and* a composer. But, without wanting to be arrogant, I would only want to be remembered as a *good* composer. If people find my compositions weak, then it is better not to be remembered.'[47]

---

* A paraphrase of an inscription (1492) in the town hall of Wernigrode, Harz (letter to Ernst Bloch, 2 October 1969). Eighteen months later Klemperer was still trying to interest his colleagues in the work, among them Colin Davis, Kubelik, Kletzki, Dorati, Bernstein and Stokowski.

† Letter to C.M. Gruber, 27 November 1968. In his eighties Klemperer had become an admirer of Samuel Beckett's plays.

15

The final years

In spite of his frailty, Klemperer's hold on his audiences showed no sign of declining. That he now scarcely conducted in the usual meaning of the word did not trouble his public. On the contrary, at the end of what by most accounts was a less than compelling account of Mahler's Symphony No. 9 with the NPO at the Edinburgh Festival on 30 August 1968, he received an ovation such as the veteran critic Neville Cardus claimed to have seldom heard in a concert hall before.[1]

Karl-Heinz Wocker, London representative of the North and West German Radios, was disturbed by the low standard of playing at the concert: 'One observes the destiny of this once famous orchestra with concern ... The performance of Mahler's Symphony No. 9 was a musical non-event ... One could not tell who was the rider and who the horse.'[2] Yet when a few days later Klemperer conducted the NPO in the same work at the Lucerne Festival, Willi Schuh, writing in the *Neue Zürcher Zeitung*, brushed aside complaints of slow tempi and minimal gestures: 'What is essential is that out of this ... level-headed approach there emerges a spiritual experience (*Durchgeistigung*) such as one rarely encounters.'[3]

EMI and the NPO could not afford to share such enthusiasm. EMI feared that recordings as unsatisfactory as that of *Petrushka* might, if issued, damage Klemperer's reputation.[4] *Der fliegende Holländer*, in which EMI had for the first time introduced sound effects, had also occasioned some disappointment on artistic as well as technical grounds, so much so that EMI considered postponing its release until after the important pre-Christmas period.[5] Klemperer's desire to record Beethoven's Symphony No. 7 for the third time was a further source of friction. Peter Andry saw no alternative but to let him have his way, but J.K.R. Whittle, general manager of EMI's classical division, took a more robust view: 'It is really quite foolish I think to consider a third round of Beethoven symphonies with Klemperer. The second lot compared unfavourably with the first, and now I imagine the situation would be worse still.' Whittle returned to the attack three weeks later: 'I take the view that Dr Klemperer should do what we want and we should not do what Dr Klemperer wants. We pay him.'[6] Robert Myers, director of Angel Records' classical repertory in America, echoed Whittle's worries:

> To my ears at least, the recent Klemperer recordings have lacked the grandeur and nobility of his earlier efforts. I also believe that the mystique associated with his name has lessened, at least here in the United States ... But we shall see.[7]

However, it was decided that it would be politic to fall in with Klemperer's wishes and the recording of the Seventh was duly made in October 1968.*

*   *   *

The 1968–9 season did not start promisingly. Two days after Klemperer's arrival in London on 10 September 1968 a piano rehearsal for Bach's B minor Mass left him so exhausted that he was obliged to cancel an orchestral rehearsal arranged for the following day. Perhaps as a result, the performance of the work at the Festival Hall on 15 September caused widespread disappointment.

Mahler's Symphony No. 7 fared scarcely better on 1 October. Klemperer had been present when the work had received its first performance under its composer's direction in Prague in 1908, but had always been distinctly ambivalent about its merits. Though he found the three short central movements 'deeply affecting in their simplicity',[8] he had reservations about the longer and more rhetorical outer movements. It was for this reason that he had conducted it only once before, in Cologne in 1922.† As though to confirm his doubts about the work, the London performance misfired. The Festival Hall was far from full and, above all in the huge opening allegro, the extremely measured tempi were widely criticised. When Klemperer's recording of the work was issued later in the season it was coolly received.

At an all-Mendelssohn concert at the Festival Hall on 22 January 1969 Klemperer caused surprise by leaving out the coda of the last movement of the 'Scottish' Symphony. He justified his action in a programme note:

> In Heinrich Edward Jacob's book, *Felix Mendelssohn und seine Zeit* (S. Fischer, 1959), I found the following sentence: 'Mendelssohn was so much worried over the male-chorus character of the ending (of the last movement) that he asked Ferdinand David (the leader of the orchestra) whether he should not leave out the drums, reinforce the horns and greatly reduce the violins.' In other words, he was not satisfied at all with the coda of this symphony. This coda is, indeed, very strange. Mendelssohn uses the 6/8 time to introduce a theme which is not Scottish at all and finishes *fortissimo*. Is it not possible that here the clever Gewandhaus Kapellmeister Mendelssohn got the better of the great composer Mendelssohn? I therefore believe that this gives me the right to

---

* Whittle's and Myers's fears proved justified. As Klemperer's 1956 mono version of the Seventh Symphony is widely regarded as being musically superior to the 1960 stereo version, so the 1968 version is generally considered the least satisfactory of the three.

† Thirty years later the Concertgebouw Orchestra had tried to persuade him to perform the symphony at the Holland Festival. After long hesitation Klemperer turned the proposal down.

> alter this coda radically. But every single note in my version is by Mendelssohn. I simply continue with the beautiful second subject and thus arrive at an ending which is (for me personally) satisfying. I know I shall be much criticised for this alteration but I still believe that it is right.

Klemperer had gauged the critics' reaction accurately. They were not impressed. Nor were they enchanted by what one of them called a 'slow and leaden'[9] performance of the *Midsummer Night's Dream* incidental music, a score Klemperer particularly loved and had often conducted with great success. However, matters improved six days later when a Brahms programme, with Vladimir Ashkenazy as soloist in the B flat piano concerto, was greeted with general enthusiasm, as was a performance of Schumann's 'Rhenish' Symphony on 11 February. Towards the end of a recording session for the symphony a few days earlier Klemperer had fallen asleep, as he had done during *Don Quixote* the previous season. After the orchestra had completed the take, the librarian, Clem Relf, gently shook Klemperer. 'Wake up, Doctor', he said. 'It's all over.' Klemperer opened his eyes. 'And was it good?' he asked, quite undisconcerted.[10]

Klemperer rounded off his visit to London with a revival of *Fidelio* at Covent Garden, with Anja Silja in the title-role. The house was sufficiently concerned about his physical condition to arrange for a doctor to be on call during the six performances. Many of the production rehearsals took place at Klemperer's suite at the Hyde Park Hotel. In spite of his difficulty in walking, he sometimes took an active part in demonstrating the moves he wanted, much to the alarm of members of the cast, who were in constant fear that he would trip and fall. At the time he was much exercised by the danger of major hostilities breaking out in the Middle East. Israel had bombed Arab guerrilla positions in Jordan and in retaliation the Popular Front for the Liberation of Palestine had attacked an El Al airliner at Zurich airport. He harped on the situation constantly during the rehearsals. But there was plenty of good-humoured banter, as well as evidence that Klemperer's priapic inclinations had not been dulled. Told by Margaret Price, the Marzelline, that she had a cold and was not feeling well, he advised her: 'Then you must go to bed – with me.'[11]

The first night took place on 5 March. Klemperer's slow tempi came in for the usual criticism from the press, but Donald McIntyre, who sang the role of Pizarro, felt that, although the performance 'was not very tidy, there was something about Klemperer's conducting that was block-like. I thought it was quite extraordinarily powerful. No one else could have done it at those sort of tempi.' Richard Armstrong, who acted as prompter, recalled in particular the Leonora No. 3 Overture, which Klemperer again chose to conduct between the two scenes of the final act: 'Many conductors treat it as an orchestral showpiece, but with Klemperer it was more like a meditation – a summing-up of what had gone before and a preparation for what was to come.'[12] Klemperer was enthralled by the Leonore of Silja, whose singing was described by *The Times* (6 March) as 'a mixture of the thrilling and careless'. For Klemperer it counted for more that her performance was 'quite free of the usual sentimentality'.[13]

Klemperer was overjoyed by the news that his old friend and champion, Ira Hirschmann, with whom he had broken during a manic phase almost thirty years earlier, might be able to attend the last *Fidelio* on 24 March. He wrote to Hirschmann: 'I always hoped to see you once more in this life. Now there is the possibility. Please do your best to come. Then we can talk of the past – also the future which is not cheering. I have not and never will forget all you did for me, when things were very bad in my life.'[14] Hirschmann did manage to attend the performance and after it the two men talked until late into the night. It proved to be the last occasion on which Klemperer conducted in an opera house.

Before leaving for Zurich on the following day, he suggested to Covent Garden that he might direct and conduct a new production of *Carmen*, with Silja in the title-role, but the offer was not taken up. The Opera House can hardly be blamed for showing no interest in such a project, for it is unlikely that Klemperer would have had the physical strength to carry it through. In *Fidelio* there had been problems of contact between stage and pit and, in the interests of ensemble, Armstrong had been instructed to conduct the chorus from the prompt box.

However, for all his physical limitations, Klemperer was still able to rise to an occasion, such as the three concerts he gave in Paris with the Orchestre de Paris on 6, 7 and 10 May. In spite of their unfamiliarity with his gestures, the players seemed to have little difficulty in following him. Grubb described the performance of the 'Eroica' Symphony on 7 May as 'without question the finest I have heard either from Klemperer or any other conductor'.[15] Both in London and in Paris enthusiasm ran so high that EMI at one point toyed with a plan to record Klemperer with the French orchestra.[16] Even Klemperer himself admitted to a degree of satisfaction. 'The orchestra was excellent', he wrote to Paul Dessau on 18 May, adding uncharacteristically, 'Of course it was also on account of me. I don't think I've ever conducted the "Eroica" so well.'

The success he enjoyed in Paris brought out the more optimistic side to his character, as can be seen in the reflections he put on paper shortly before his eighty-fourth birthday on 14 May:

> Good heavens! . . . You are eighty-four. You have come a long way and you are moving steadily closer to your death. But today you are in Paris – a real birthday treat! Go to the Bois and stay there until sundown. Enjoy the earth that will soon enfold you. Be happy, at least on *this* day. You know there is an endless coming and going. An endless dance. How can death frighten you?

25   Klemperer and his nurse Ruth Vogel in 1969

Lotte noted that her father had entered a peaceful phase mentally. There was no sign of a depression, nor of a manic mood. It was a phase that was to last for some time.

On the day after his birthday Klemperer flew to Munich, where on 23 May he conducted the Bavarian Radio Orchestra in the same Mendelssohn programme he had given earlier in the year in London. The German critics took a more favourable view of it than their English colleagues, perhaps because Klemperer's appearances in the Federal Republic were sufficiently rare to be considered events. However, a Beethoven programme given on 29 May, and repeated the following day, fared less well. The weather was hot and Munich's notorious wind, the *Föhn*, had its usual debilitating effect. By the final rehearsal there were doubts as to whether Klemperer would be well enough to conduct.[17] In the event he did so, but the performances were considered to be lacking in concentration.

While he was in Munich Klemperer visited his wife's grave. On the way to the airport for the journey home he was asked when he hoped to return to the city. He replied sadly that probably he would not be coming back, a prophecy that turned out to be accurate.[18] A few days later he wrote to Helene Hirschler: 'I shall conduct less next season. The concerts are not so bad. It's the steps to the auditorium and all that goes with it ("drum und dran") that are such a strain.'[19]

*   *   *

At the beginning of September 1969 Peter Heyworth recorded a series of radio interviews with Klemperer for the Canadian Broadcasting Commission in anticipation of the conductor's eighty-fifth birthday. When, earlier in the summer, Heyworth had written to Lotte asking whether her father would agree to such an undertaking, he had not been optimistic that it would ever take place. However, to Heyworth's surprise, Lotte replied that if he could spare a few days Klemperer would be willing to talk at length about his life. There were, however, certain matters he would not discuss. He would also want to exercise some control over what was to be used in the final version. A few days later Lotte wrote again: 'Were I you, I would not wait, because [my father] is in exceptionally good form at the moment in every respect.'

As the appointed day drew nearer, Klemperer became increasingly apprehensive. He had always drawn a sharp line between his professional and private life, and there were some events, notably the Schumann scandal in Hamburg, that he did not wish to discuss. To put his mind at rest, he had a trial run with Lotte as interrogator.

On 2 September Heyworth arrived as planned at the simple two-bedroom flat in Dufourstrasse that had been Klemperer's home since 1956. During the intervening years recordings had made him comparatively wealthy. Yet it never seems to have occurred to him to move into more spacious, not to mention more luxurious, accommodation. The sitting-room, in which meals were taken, contained a Steinway grand piano and a well-lit armchair in which Klemperer spent much of the day, surrounded by newspapers, books and scores, pipes, matches and ashtrays. The modern furniture was practical rather than elegant. There were few decorative items. Such pictures as hung on the wall – a print by Picasso, reproductions of portraits of Mozart and Goethe – were small to the point of unobtrusiveness. Frau Anna, Klemperer's cook and housekeeper, occupied the second bedroom. Lotte lived in a flat directly opposite her father's.

The interviews lasted four days. Sometimes Klemperer's answers were terse, even monosyllabic: he was a man who talked as he wrote, in short sentences. Any attempt to extract more information than he was willing to provide was firmly rebuffed. Heyworth became conscious of the wide expressive range of Klemperer's voice. At one moment it was harsh and rasping, at the next mocking, quizzical or plaintive. It was also capable of great tenderness. However, Klemperer's slurred speech was not always easy to decipher and at moments he tired. Heyworth would then withdraw to another room, while Klemperer read a book until the session was resumed.*

To the end of his life Klemperer was a voracious reader who never travelled without a volume of Shakespeare, Goethe's poems and the Bible in Luther's translation.[20] He was an avid consumer of newspapers and television programmes, particularly on current affairs. Nor did his interests shrink with advancing years. After he had been visited by Anna Freud in London in the autumn of 1969 he read three of her father's works, including the epoch-making *Traumdeutung*. Until then, he admitted to Anna Freud, he had not 'taken psychoanalysis quite seriously, probably because I knew too little about it'.[21]

*   *   *

A week after the CBC interviews with Heyworth had been completed, Klemperer flew to London to begin a two-month stint of concerts and recordings with the NPO. His biggest undertaking was a recording of Act One of *Die Walküre*. Acts Two and Three were to follow in 1971, with, at Klemperer's request, Anja Silja as Brünnhilde, Theo Adam as Wotan and Janet Baker as Fricka. The project had for some time been a source of friction between Klemperer and EMI, which, together with its satellite companies in Germany and America, had at first opposed it.[22] But Klemperer had got his way and the recording of Act One was completed successfully on 24 October. For a fee of £120 Reginald Goodall, who had assisted Klemperer on his Covent Garden productions, rehearsed the orchestra.

Four days later Klemperer conducted a concert performance of the act at the Festival Hall with the same cast of young singers that he had used in the recording: Helga Dernesch, who was making her London début, as Sieglinde, William Cochran as Siegmund and Hans Sotin as Hunding. Several reviewers noted imprecisions in the orchestral playing; some expressed the hope that the recording might prove to be a more vivid experience than the concert. Andrew Porter, writing in the *Financial Times*, felt that the performance 'never quite took wing. Klemperer's reading was more "monumental" than picturesque or particularly dramatic ... Even on the concert platform the first act of *Die Walküre* should be more moving than this.'[23]

On the day of the concert there was a meeting of the NPO's Council of Management. Anxiety was expressed about playing standards, at any rate as

---

* Peter Heyworth had drafted this account of the CBC interviews before he died. Although it has been edited and added to, it is basically as he left it. Heyworth conducted further interviews with Klemperer, for West German radio, in November 1969. Three days before they were due to begin, Klemperer had a bad fall while getting out of a friend's car. In spite of the shock, and of cuts and bruises to his face, Klemperer insisted on meeting Heyworth as planned. The two sets of interviews were later combined and edited by Heyworth for publication in *Conversations with Klemperer* – J.L.

far as Klemperer's concerts were concerned, and it was agreed that Gerald McDonald, the orchestra's new general manager, should discuss the matter with Peter Andry, who had shown similar concern. There were grounds for worry about Klemperer himself. Both his sight and hearing were deteriorating.*

In order to help Klemperer conserve his strength, EMI had taken to hiring an assistant conductor to rehearse the New Philharmonia for the first half-hour of each three-hour recording session. Klemperer could in any case manage only one session a day, be it for a rehearsal, a recording session or a concert. This meant that the final rehearsal for a Festival Hall concert could no longer take place on the day itself and had to be held on the previous day. It was an additional financial burden for an orchestra that was far from enjoying the strong position it had held in the time of Walter Legge. The players had come to feel great affection for their president, but even the most devoted among them admitted that playing under him could be an unnerving experience.

*   *   *

Klemperer spent November and December 1969 in Zurich. On his return to London in January 1970 he embarked on a recording of *Le Nozze di Figaro*, followed by a concert performance at the Festival Hall on 3 February. The event failed to catch the public interest – the hall was only two-thirds full – but it aroused fierce controversy in the press. William Mann, senior critic of *The Times*, found the performance so heavy-handed that he left in the middle of the last act. He had done so, he explained in his review the following morning, 'because Otto Klemperer was conducting in his most didactic, humourless, tortoise-like manner'. In the *Daily Telegraph*, Peter Stadlen described the performance as 'the kind of reading one was apt to encounter in pre-Hitler Germany, when people were expected, by Dr Klemperer for instance, to take their Mozart seriously ... Comedy does not depend on speed, Dr Klemperer seemed to insist defiantly.'[24] Desmond Shawe-Taylor, on the other hand, congratulated Klemperer on avoiding 'the kind of speed that so often turns the music ... into an ill-articulated gabble', though he complained of the lack of appoggiaturas.†[25]

---

* He had been deaf in his right ear since his years in Los Angeles. By the late sixties he was starting to suffer from cataracts.
† The preliminary rehearsals at the beginning of each recording session for *Figaro* were conducted by the 26-year-old Richard Armstrong. He had been warned by members of the NPO that Klemperer did not always take kindly to the assistants hired by EMI; he could be uncooperative and had been known to shout out critical remarks from the back of the hall. Armstrong, however, found Klemperer consistently helpful and encouraging. He took pains to reproduce Klemperer's tempi as accurately as possible. Klemperer seemed to have only one criticism. 'Why', he asked the producer, Suvi Raj Grubb, 'does he take it all so slowly?' (Richard Armstrong, interview with J.L., May 1994).

When Klemperer returned to Zurich at the end of February 1970 he was in a philosophical mood. He wrote in his sketch book:

> How was it seventy years ago? Ah well, comme ci, comme ça. The fulfilment was still to come. Today after seventy years there's nothing more to come. That's a bad disappointment. Ah well. Bear it with dignity.

But there *was* more to come. He had much enjoyed conducting *Figaro* and now his mind turned to another Mozart opera, *Così fan tutte*, for which he had an affection rare in conductors of his generation. He was also seized with a desire to record Weber's *Euryanthe*, a score he greatly admired, but had not conducted for almost half a century. EMI was not interested in either work. Now that it had Act One of *Walküre* in the can, a complete recording of Wagner's opera seemed a better commercial proposition. It was decided that Grubb should be dispatched to Zurich to persuade Klemperer to record the last two acts. He got no closer than a telephone conversation with Lotte, who told him that her father would not complete *Walküre*, but was willing to record the closing scene of the opera, so as to fill a fourth LP side of the recording of Act One.* Otherwise, the only major projects he was prepared to consider were *Così* and *Euryanthe*. If EMI refused to accept either one, there would be no point in Grubb coming to Zurich.[26] After discussing the matter with his superiors, Peter Andry decided not to record either opera.[27] The scene was set for a battle of wills.

EMI was the first to reconsider its position. On 20 May Andry wrote to inform Klemperer that, while *Euryanthe* would be prohibitively expensive, *Così fan tutte* might be reconsidered in the autumn despite its poor sales prospects. Annoyed that EMI should attach more importance to profit than to artistic merit, Klemperer told Andry that

> I have definitely decided not to try to do the 2nd and 3rd acts of *Walküre* because at this age I no longer have the physical strength for such a project. *Euryanthe* and *Così* [are] both much easier works.
>
> I have suggested *Euryanthe*, not only because it is very good music, but also because it does not exist on recordings. I thought EMI would be proud to be the first to do that ...
>
> You will certainly understand that at my time of life I will only do what I want – and not what a Company wants. Until now our interests have met – the future nobody can tell.[28]

This barely disguised threat that he might look to EMI's competitors for the realisation of his plans was followed on 12 June by a letter from Lotte in which she informed Andry that her father wanted to vary a clause in his contract, so that in future he could 'conduct any orchestra for any recording company of any work', provided it had not been recorded for EMI during the

---

* Klemperer eventually recorded the scene in October 1970, with Norman Bailey as Wotan.

previous seven years. Such a clause would have spelt the end of Klemperer's exclusivity to EMI. At first the company took a tough line. On 7 July Andry informed L.G. Wood, head of EMI's recording activities, that the deficits on *Euryanthe* and *Così* were now estimated at £23,000 and £5,000 respectively. He and his colleagues did not consider it to be in EMI's interests 'to incur massive losses to keep Klemperer exclusive when he is rapidly coming to the end of being commercially viable'.

It seems to have been only at this point that EMI heard that Gerald McDonald had made an approach to Deutsche Grammophon on Klemperer's behalf. On 8 July McDonald was summoned to Andry's office for what McDonald described as 'a grilling'. Andry was taken aback when told by McDonald that DGG had discussed with him the possibility of recording *Euryanthe*, and that it had taken a more favourable view than had EMI of its sales potential, at any rate in Germany. DGG would accordingly be interested in such a project and 'in Dr Klemperer in general'.[29]

The prospect filled EMI's senior management with alarm, so much so that on 15 July Wood considered it advisable to inform EMI's chief executive, J.E. Read, that the company was in danger of losing its most prestigious classical artist: 'I think this is [an] instance where we have to bend for the purpose of retaining the goodwill of an old and highly respected EMI recording artist and additionally to avoid the adverse publicity which would undoubtedly follow his signing up with anyone else.' Andry was therefore instructed to negotiate with Klemperer on the basis that EMI would record *Così*. Andry was still unhappy, however. No one, he told Read, wanted a recording of *Così* that might expose the company to criticism. It was a 'witty, light-hearted, fast-moving opera – Klemperer is the very opposite of this'.[30]

EMI tried to interest Klemperer in other projects that looked profitable, for example a recording of Gluck's *Orfeo*, with Grace Bumbry in the title-role. Klemperer told Andry that he felt she was not the 'ideal protagonist for this role'. He would prefer Janet Baker.[31] But Baker was not available and the project was shelved for the time being. EMI realised that if it wanted to keep Klemperer, it had no alternative but to record *Così*. On 12 August Andry flew to Zurich to inform Klemperer that EMI would record the work during the following season. In return Klemperer agreed to sign a new one-year exclusive contract. But any idea of recording *Euryanthe* was dropped for good.

*   *   *

Three weeks before his eighty-fifth birthday, which fell on 14 May 1970, Klemperer wrote to a friend, 'I find birthday celebrations ghastly ... Thank goodness I have a concert on that day so I can't be visited.'[32] At first the New Philharmonia had toyed with the idea of giving concert performances of Klemperer's biblical operas, *Der verlorene Sohn* and *Juda*, but it had proved impractical and eventually Klemperer opted for a performance at the Festival Hall of *Das Lied von der Erde*, with Janet Baker and Richard Lewis as soloists. It was the sole work on the programme. The NPO had not performed it for some time and the first rehearsal did not go smoothly. 'The orchestra was at sea ', Lotte wrote in her diary,

> ... and Papa also seemed unsure of himself. That evening McDonald telephoned: the players thought that it might be good to engage a conductor to take the first half-hour of the rehearsals – as in recording sessions ... Papa accepted [the suggestion] quietly and at once proposed Shapirra.* But afterwards he grew pensive ...
>
> When Shapirra came the following morning, he was icily received. All attempts on S's part to make contact were in vain. OK sat before him like the Stone Guest. One could almost see the ... great struggle going on inside him – on the one hand his awareness of the necessity, on the other his intense resentment of it. After coffee, I left them alone to work. When I came in afterwards the atmosphere was relaxed, almost jolly as a result of their work together. When S had gone [my father] praised his musicality and intelligence.

Characteristically, the concert itself was far from being a sentimental occasion. As Klemperer was helped on to the platform, the audience rose to greet him. All it got in return was a curt nod before Klemperer sat down on the conductor's chair. John Warrack wrote in the *Sunday Telegraph* that

> despite some slips, and even the partial misfire of a whole movement, 'Der Trunkene im Frühling', which for some reason Klemperer and the tenor, Richard Lewis, let slip through their grasp, it was the most profound and starkly moving performance I can remember. Barely stirring himself, his stick for long stretches merely quavering before him, the huge hands sometimes seeming not so much to give a beat as to shake the whole orchestra into sound, Klemperer still manages to diminish all problems of ensemble and impose his complete will upon his players.
>
> Above all, there is a knowledge of darkness in Klemperer's performance which stands behind Mahler's painful awareness of the earth's beauty, and which reaches heroic stature. 'Dunkel ist das Leben': life's darkness is never forgotten. Klemperer plays the last chord of this opening song as if it were some huge bond finally snapping.[33]

After the concert it fell to Gareth Morris as chairman to present Klemperer with an inscribed Georgian salver on behalf of the orchestra. Hardly had he embarked on a brief speech when Klemperer's huge hand shot out, as though to take possession of the gift and bring the ceremony to an end. Morris stood his ground: 'Now, now, you'll have to wait!'[34]

The following day friends and relatives who had come to London for the occasion gathered at the Hyde Park Hotel. At one point in the informal

---

* Elyakum Shapirra (b. 1926), Israeli conductor.

festivities Klemperer raised his glass in memory of Tante Hélène, the French cousin who had financed his early musical education.[35] His birthday present from Lotte took the shape of a performance by the Bartók Quartet of his String Quartet No. 7 at St John's, Smith Square. The players' attempts to offer congratulations after the concert were cut short with the dry comment, 'Very cleanly played' ('Sehr sauber gespielt').[36]

A week later Klemperer and the NPO embarked on what was to be his last Beethoven cycle, which was filmed for television by the BBC. In the past, with the single exception of the NPO's inaugural concert in 1964, Klemperer had set his face against his concerts being televised. But in the case of the Beethoven cycle, John Culshaw, head of BBC TV's music programmes, managed to allay his (and Lotte's) fears and reservations. Filming would cease should Klemperer be taken ill, and there should not be too many shots from the right-hand, paralysed, side of his face. Nor would he be seen acknowledging applause or making his laborious way across the Festival Hall's platform, supported as always on such occasions by Clem Relf.

Reactions to the televised cycle varied. One reviewer described the visual side of the programmes as 'a disaster', if only because the eye took precedence over the ear.[37] Many viewers found it painful to witness Klemperer's physical frailty at close quarters; at times he seemed barely aware of his surroundings. But as the cycle progressed such moments proved less distracting. 'If every now and then', reported the *Neue Zürcher Zeitung*, 'Klemperer seemed lost to the world, at musically important moments he was ... wide awake ... and his gestures were as pregnant as an orchestra could wish.'[38]

Inevitably, there was a good deal of comment about the generally slow tempi adopted by Klemperer. Festival Hall timings show that the 'Eroica' took 58′47″ as against 47′59″ in the 1959 cycle. Yet, paradoxically, the First and Sixth Symphonies were a shade faster than they had been in either 1959 or 1963. Many listeners were entranced by the tenderness and lyricism of the 'Pastoral' – not qualities usually associated with Klemperer.

In the course of time his approach to music-making had indeed undergone far-reaching changes. In younger days an intimidating martinet, he later became increasingly uninterested in technical perfection as an end in itself, perhaps in part because it was hardly within his reach. 'A few mistakes don't matter ... It isn't a disaster if a horn player gets a bit of saliva on his lips and his tone goes wrong. Good heavens, he's a human being ... that's the most important thing of all.'[39]

Klemperer had come to regard the essential function of the conductor as allowing the music to breathe. 'It's important to observe the pauses, to keep the ... measure of every phrase. This is what breath is to a human being. You must let the music breathe when it needs to.' A conductor should 'exercise his influence on the players without them noticing it'.[40]

In later years Klemperer also grew more pragmatic in his attitude to orchestral retouchings. As a young conductor in Cologne in the early twenties, he had shared the general view that the use of double woodwind was unavoidable in Beethoven. In 1930, however, he had performed the Ninth Symphony with the number of instruments specified in the score, and for many years afterwards he remained committed to the principle of *Werktreue* ('faithfulness to the original') in Beethoven. By 1970 his attitude had changed again, and he asked the BBC to include in its spoken introduction to the televised Beethoven cycle a note he had written on the subject. It was printed in the programme.

> Great musicians like Wagner, Mahler, Pfitzner, Strauss and others wrote about the possibility or impossibility of *rétouches* in the original orchestrations of Beethoven. Their suggestions and changes differed greatly. The most courageous and at the same time questionable *rétouches* are those of Mahler. I believe such alterations are dependent on the orchestra, the acoustics of the hall and, last but not least, on the conductor's own momentary interpretative ideas. For instance I double the woodwind and horns in some of the symphonies and make other minor changes. I have not always done so and will probably change my mind again in the future, as I find it impossible to be dogmatic on the questions of orchestral changes.[41]

*   *   *

In July 1970 Klemperer paid another visit to Israel for a concert with the Jerusalem Radio Orchestra. When the invitation had been issued earlier in the year, it had been suggested that his programme might consist of Mozart's G minor Symphony and Mahler's Fourth. Klemperer insisted on something more challenging and after some argument settled for Mahler's Symphony No. 9. There was a snag, however, for the Radio Orchestra consisted of only fifty-four players. Additional forces had to be sought, and eventually it was decided to call on the services of an Israeli youth orchestra, the Gadna Symphony Orchestra. Its playing standards were not high, but Klemperer warmed to its enthusiasm and was touched by the presence of a twelve-year-old boy sitting alongside the leader of the cello section. His doctor in Zurich had regarded the journey as being not without risk, but agreed that if he wanted to go he should do so, though all unnecessary effort should be avoided. That did not prevent him from making two visits to the Wailing Wall.

A day or two before the concert, which took place on 4 August, Klemperer casually asked his driver if it was easy to acquire an Israeli passport. Supposing the question to be a serious one, the driver reported it to

THE FINAL YEARS

26 Klemperer being presented with his Israeli passport by the Director Genereal of the Interior Ministry, August 1970. Behind Klemperer is his assistant Otto Freudenthal. Photo: K. Weiss, Jerusalem

the authorities, who telephoned Klemperer. Lotte took the call. Would her father like to become an Israeli? She put the question to him. 'Why not?' he replied, somewhat amazed by the offer. At a reception after the concert he was presented with a passport. Back in Zurich, he gave a statement to the press: 'At a time like today, I feel the need as a Jew to obtain this citizenship and I am grateful to the State of Israel for this great honour.' But, he added cautiously, 'I shall retain my citizenship of the German Federal Republic and permanent Swiss residency.' An Israeli passport was not without its disadvantages, as in most countries it necessitated visas.

Some weeks later the West German consulate in Zurich wrote to warn Klemperer that if, as the *Jewish Chronicle* in London had claimed, he himself had asked for Israeli citizenship, he had offended against German regulations and should forfeit his German passport. The storm eventually blew over after the Israeli government provided a document certifying that the passport had been issued under the Return Law, which for undivulged reasons obviated any expression of intention on Klemperer's part.

*   *   *

In 1970 Bonn, Beethoven's birthplace and capital of the German Federal Republic, celebrated the bicentenary of the composer's birth with a series of concerts. The Vienna Philharmonic came under Karl Böhm, Karajan brought the Berliners and Klemperer was invited to give two concerts with the New Philharmonia. It was a signal honour, but Klemperer was at first unwilling to accept it because his concerts were scheduled to take place on consecutive days, which would put a considerable strain on him. Gerald McDonald arranged for Colin Davis to conduct instead.[42] On hearing this news Klemperer decided to go to Bonn after all. When he entered the city's Beethovenhalle on 25 September, he was given a standing ovation.

In the first half of the programme his restrained account of the Symphony No. 1 aroused respect rather than enthusiasm. But after the interval there followed a performance of the 'Eroica' that one reviewer described as 'rising to a level of greatness such as no other interpreter can rival today'.[43] There was general surprise that a conductor who barely gestured was able to exercise control over a performance so packed with detail. At the end of the concert Klemperer bowed briefly and left the platform. In spite of long and frenetic applause, he did not return. Eventually Gerald McDonald appeared and explained that Klemperer was tired. He thanked the audience for its appreciation and expressed the hope that conductor and orchestra might one day be invited back to Bonn. There were shouts from the audience of 'You will be.'[44] The programme was repeated on the following evening. It was the last occasion on which Klemperer conducted in his native country, and the last occasion on which he conducted a symphony by Beethoven. Gareth Morris recalled the concerts as among the best Klemperer had given for a long time. It was a remarkable triumph for a man in his eighty-sixth year.

*   *   *

Klemperer had a busy recording schedule with the NPO lined up for the 1970–1 season. EMI had agreed to consider a group of Bach cantatas, Bruckner's Symphony No. 2 and Schoenberg's arrangement of the Brahms G minor Piano Quartet. The idea of recording *Orfeo* was revived, with Janet Baker as Orfeo, Heather Harper as Euridice and Margaret Price as Amor. But for one reason or another none of the projects came to fruition. Klemperer was particularly disappointed by the loss of the Brahms-Schoenberg work, for he had conducted its first performance in Los Angeles in 1938.[45] EMI estimated that a recording of it would fail to recover its costs.[46] None the less, Peter Andry was able to give a firm commitment that *Così* would be recorded in February 1971. Klemperer was delighted by the news.[47] Another major undertaking was a recording of Bruckner's Symphony No. 8, which Klemperer completed on 14 November 1970. Three days later he conducted

THE FINAL YEARS

the work at the Festival Hall. Peter Heyworth wrote in the *Observer* (22 November) that it was a performance he would 'not readily forget':

> I do not mean that it was flawless; far from it. In the opening bars the woodwind played phrases marked piano as mezzoforte and thus flattened out what should be a crescendo, while the drastic cuts that Klemperer imposed on the last movement did nothing to solve the perennial problems of Bruckner's finales. A colleague found the scherzo heavy-footed: I can only say that to my mind its relentless tread exactly caught the music's peasant-like gait and massive power.

Klemperer contributed another of his notes to the programme: 'In the last movement of Bruckner's Eighth Symphony I have made cuts. In this instance it seems to me that the composer was so full of musical invention that he went too far. Brucknerians will object, and it is certainly not my intention that these cuts should be considered as a model for others. I can only take the responsibility for my own interpretation.' To EMI's chagrin he made cuts in the recording of the symphony, too. When Suvi Raj Grubb, with Gerald McDonald's backing, remonstrated with him, Klemperer replied, 'If you want a complete, uncut fourth movement, find yourself another conductor.'[48]

During the course of the Bruckner recording sessions Klemperer had also conducted a Mozart concert at the Festival Hall on 8 November and, with Grubb, auditioned both Elizabeth Harwood and Margaret Price at the Hyde Park Hotel for the role of Fiordiligi in the *Così* recording. Price herself had asked Klemperer if she could audition for the role. He had agreed to hear her, but initially was not convinced that she was ready to take on the role. Harwood was auditioned first. Price's turn came the following day. After she had sung she was asked to wait outside the room. A heated debate then ensued, with Grubb making it clear that EMI wanted Harwood, and Klemperer remaining adamant that he preferred Price. 'Well, Miss Price', said Klemperer, after she had been called back in. 'I want you, but EMI does not.' There was an awkward silence. Lotte decided to take the initiative. 'But you're the conductor', she told her father. Price got the job.[49] The Fiordiligi was to mark a major step forward in her career.

* * *

In an attempt to raise playing standards and provide the New Philharmonia with a new dynamic and sense of purpose, it was now decided by the orchestra's management that an associate principal conductor should be appointed. At first Klemperer was put out, but he soon accepted the need for such a post, which, with his approval, was given to the American conductor Lorin Maazel. On 22 October Gerald McDonald was able to report to the orchestra's council that at a meeting with Klemperer he had found him 'in great form'. Lotte had also been present and McDonald had noted the good-humoured backchat between father and daughter:

> [Klemperer] repeated that he was very much in favour of Maazel ... The idea had obviously stimulated him into taking a much greater interest in the way we run our affairs and he was full of wanting to be present at the audition of 'a new principal viola', not to mention leader and other personnel! In other words, he wants to exercise his rights as Chief Conductor.

In a postscript, McDonald noted that 'Klemperer wants to be considered to take over one or two concerts on every tour!'

As far as Klemperer was concerned, his rights included having the first choice of works to be performed. For the 1971–2 season, he told McDonald, he had in mind Mahler's Symphony No. 8 and Mendelssohn's *Die erste Walpurgisnacht*. 'Unsinn, Wahnsinn' ('stuff and nonsense'), said Lotte, aghast at the idea of such a huge undertaking. Klemperer laughed. 'You see, Mr McDonald, my only enemy is my daughter!' Lotte had the last word. By the following season, she said, 'you will be eighty-seven and even more foolish than you are now!'[50]* Those who saw only Klemperer's stern, public face were often surprised to discover his sense of fun. He enjoyed playing practical jokes, particularly if they were at Lotte's expense. In Zurich one morning in 1970 she received a telegram which read:

> The Jewish women's committee yesterday appointed you an honorary member stop Many congratulations stop Jehuda Manasse.†

She hastened to her father and waved the telegram at him in fury. She had no wish to join a committee of any kind. Klemperer looked at her sympathetically. He was well aware that, ever since he had re-embraced the Jewish faith, Lotte had had to deal with an avalanche of mail from Jewish organisations; it took up a lot of her time. The committee was probably the last straw for her. 'What do I do now?' Lotte demanded. Klemperer could contain himself no longer and burst out laughing. He had composed the telegram himself and had dispatched Frau Anna to the post office to send it. It was April Fool's Day.

*   *   *

The recording sessions for *Così fan tutte* began in London on 24 January 1971 and were spread over a period of three weeks. A concert performance

---

* In fact the New Philharmonia took up the idea of the Mendelssohn work and EMI agreed to record it, with Beethoven's *Meeresstille und Glückliche Fahrt* as a filler. However, as the months went by, EMI began to get cold feet about the project on cost grounds and it was finally dropped when the New Philharmonia Chorus asked to be excused from taking part because of other commitments (Suvi Raj Grubb, letter to Klemperer, 23 March 1971).

† 'Jüdischer Frauenverein ernannte Sie gestern zum Ehrenmitglied stop herzliche Gratulation stop Jehuda Manasse'.

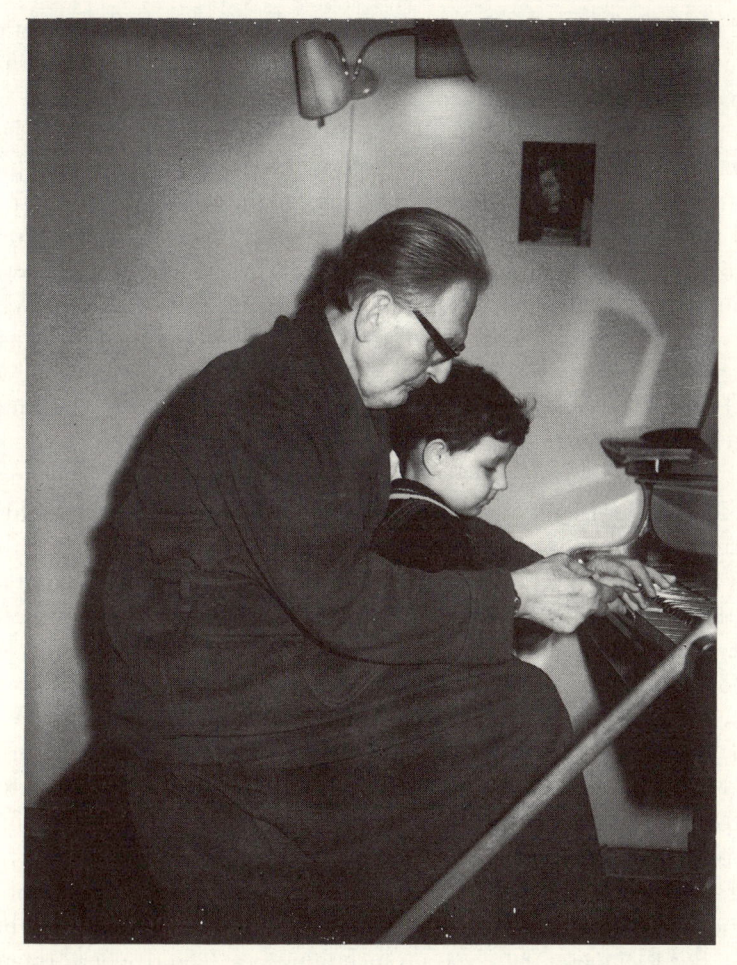

27 Klemperer with his cleaner's small son, Zurich, 21 March 1970

followed on 21 February. Critical reaction was not overenthusiastic, but at least the controversy sparked off by Klemperer's *Figaro* was not repeated. Two days later Klemperer flew home to Zurich, where he began taking Hebrew lessons with Abraham Kuflik, a stern Orthodox Jew of Polish origin. The two had long discussions on theological, philosophical and literary matters. Lotte noted that the erudite Kuflik could not help but smile at some of the ideas of his strictly unorthodox pupil.

There were many other visitors to Dufourstrasse. Klemperer's regular assistant, Otto Freudenthal, came to discuss arrangements for what was to prove the conductor's last visit to Israel, in the following June. Rafael Kubelik sought Klemperer's advice as to whether or not he should accept the post of musical director of the Metropolitan Opera in New York. Klemperer thought he should refuse the offer. But Kubelik did not follow the advice, unwisely as it turned out: after only six months in the post, he resigned following sharp disagreements with the management.

On Saturdays, Peter, the small son of the Klemperers' cleaning lady, would arrive to watch *Tarzan* on the colour television. At first Klemperer watched too, but later he was bothered by the programme's violence ('That's supposed to be for children?' he asked Lotte) and immersed himself in his books while Peter ate potato crisps in front of the television set. It was a period of tranquillity for Klemperer, though he was greatly affected by news of Stravinsky's death in New York on 6 April. He telephoned many friends to talk to them about it. He watched the funeral in Venice on television and was impressed by the ceremonial, but he could not understand why Stravinsky should have wanted his body to be transported to Europe.

On 10 May, four days before his eighty-sixth birthday, Klemperer returned to London for two performances at the Festival Hall of Mahler's 'Resurrection' Symphony. By chance, the sixtieth anniversary of Mahler's death fell between the performances, and Klemperer asked for the fact to be noted in the programme. The concerts marked a break with tradition in that Klemperer wore a dark suit for them and, at his request, the men of the New Philharmonia Orchestra and Chorus followed his example. The women wore short black dresses. Klemperer had never cared for evening dress. In the *Financial Times* (17 May), Gillian Widdicombe summed up the first of the two performances: 'Much of it was magnificent, powerful; parts of it were wilful, eccentric; odd moments were poorly executed, unsuccessful; but in all the performance was intensely memorable, evidently possessed by one of the most extraordinary musicians of our time.' Klemperer was well aware of the imperfections. By the second performance, on 20 May, most of them had been sorted out. For Klemperer there was no such thing as a definitive performance. He regarded each performance as a preparation for the next one.

Twelve days later Klemperer flew to Israel with Lotte, Freudenthal and his nurse, Sister Ruth. He was to give three concerts of works by Bach and Mozart with the Radio Orchestra in Jerusalem. There had been difficulties from the start. Klemperer had been irritated to learn that the concerts were to be given in the 650-seat Wise Auditorium of the Hebrew University, which he regarded as too small. The radio would not change the venue on the grounds that there was no suitable alternative. Jerusalem's main concert hall had already been booked for conferences.[51] Klemperer accepted the situation, but, on arrival in Jerusalem, Lotte discovered that access to the Auditorium's platform involved more stairs than her father could negotiate. Klemperer insisted that the concerts be moved to the Edison Cinema, where he had first conducted twenty years earlier, but which had not housed a concert since 1958 and was now neglected and in need of a clean.

Rehearsals gave rise to further annoyances. Players arrived late without offering apologies. The date of one of the concerts was given wrongly in press advertisements, as were details of the works to be performed. Klemperer took exception to the sound of the harpsichord. The Israel Philharmonic refused to release a trumpet player needed for the Brandenburg Concerto No. 2, even though the player in question had been loaned to the Philharmonic by the Radio Orchestra in the first place.[52] The heat was oppressive, reaching 35 °C at one point. The series was a success, however, and the orchestra played well. At the end of the last concert the director of the broadcasting organisation came to the stage to present Klemperer with an old map of Jerusalem. 'For many reasons', said Klemperer, 'I am always so touched when I can conduct in the land of my fathers – so I thank you very much.'[53] None the less he was not sorry when the visit was over and, as the plane for Zurich took off, he and Freudenthal broke into a loud and joyful rendering of Handel's 'Hallelujah Chorus'.

During the following three months Klemperer was generally unwell, tired and apparently slipping into a depression. He went to the cinema to see Visconti's *Death in Venice*, but left in the interval having taken exception to the use of Mahler's Fifth Symphony as background music. He stopped smoking (always a sign of depression), found it difficult to sleep and lost his appetite. He began to feel that, professionally, he was not wanted any more. He read a good deal and went through his own manuscripts, destroying several scores in the process. He told Lotte that, as far as composing was concerned, he was actually 'just a conductor, at any rate in the first place. Sometimes I think I belong to those who are only shown the Promised Land, but are not allowed to live there.' Lotte replied that that in itself was something, for most people were not even vouchsafed a glimpse of that land. Klemperer laughed in agreement. He had plans to record his opera *Das Ziel* at his own expense when he was next in London, but, when he read the text again, he admitted that he did not think much of it. When a few days later he went through the score with Freudenthal at the piano, he made a few changes, but finally decided to cancel the sessions. He studied scores for the forthcoming season in London, but complained that he found it hard to memorise them.[54]

Klemperer flew to London on 15 September and three days later began to record Haydn's 'Oxford' Symphony. He was nervous, because it was the first time that he had recorded a work that he had never conducted in public. He completed it in two sessions. The orchestra applauded. It was generally agreed among the players that he was in exceptionally good form (he had even dispensed with the services of a rehearsal conductor). After the second session he went to the Purcell Room, where the Epsilon Quartet, made up of young players from the New Philharmonia, gave his Quartet No. 7. Klemperer thought they played it excellently, but found he no longer cared for the work, apart from its last movement.[55] The following day he was back at EMI's

Abbey Road studios to start recording Mozart's Wind Serenade, K.375, with the New Philharmonia Wind Ensemble.* On 26 September, only eleven days after he had arrived in London, Klemperer continued his heavy schedule with a concert at the Festival Hall which included two works by Beethoven, the *King Stephen* Overture and the Fourth Piano Concerto, with the young Israeli, Daniel Adni, as soloist. Brahms's Symphony No. 3 completed the programme. The concerto brought differences of opinion over tempo between pianist and conductor. In the finale, noted *The Times* critic, Adni 'quite deliberately pushed on now and again, which was all to the good in making up the conductor's lost time'.[56] Klemperer was not pleased.

The performance of the Brahms symphony, however, was magisterial. With Klemperer's permission, it was filmed for television by the Dutch documentary-maker Philo Bregstein. The film shows Klemperer launching into the symphony with vigour. His gestures, though limited, are clear and unambiguous, his command of the orchestra throughout undeniable. The performance left him exhausted, but the next morning he was back at Abbey Road to complete the recording of the serenade. After talks with Andry and Grubb about future plans he flew back to Zurich on 30 September. It had been an extraordinary fortnight.

In mid-October Klemperer recovered from yet another attack of cystitis, though it left him weak. He was still bedevilled by depression, which lifted only occasionally. Meanwhile, his relations with EMI had reached a low point. The company had been disappointed by the poor critical reaction to the release of the Bach Suites, while the recording of *Le Nozze di Figaro*, in spite of winning a coveted Deutsche Schallplatten prize, had been greeted with very mixed reviews. A plan for Klemperer to record Sibelius's Symphony No. 4 had been dropped and he now feared that another promised recording, of Mozart's *Entführung aus dem Serail*, was also in danger of being cancelled. However, when Peter Andry visited Zurich in October 1971, he told Klemperer that, provided he would sign a new two-year contract, *Entführung* would be recorded in the first half of 1972 and Bach's *St John Passion* would follow in the autumn.[57] There were promises of further recordings in 1973. Eventually Klemperer signed.

*   *   *

On 15 January 1972 Klemperer returned to London, where, six days later, he was to conduct a performance of Bruckner's Symphony No. 7 at the Festival Hall. Still weak as a result of cystitis, he found the journey arduous and the following morning asked for his London physician, Dr Peter Meyer,

---

* The players were Richard Morgan and Michael Winfield (oboes), John McCaw and Archibald Jacob (clarinets), Gwydion Brooke and Ronald Waller (bassoons), Nicholas Busch and Ian Beers (horns).

to be called in. Meyer examined him. He could find nothing seriously wrong, but observed that conducting was a considerable strain for a man of Klemperer's age. Perhaps, said Meyer, he should cancel the forthcoming concert; indeed, it would be wise if he were to stop conducting in public altogether. Meyer had offered Klemperer such advice in the past, but it had been ignored. This time Klemperer accepted it. He asked to be put through to Gerald McDonald on the telephone immediately. Klemperer told McDonald that he was withdrawing from the Bruckner concert. In future he would only conduct at recording sessions.* That afternoon McDonald went to the Hyde Park Hotel to discuss a brief press statement. The orchestra was mortified by the news. But Klemperer, Lotte noted, was hugely relieved at his decision. That night he slept better than he had done for a long time.[58]

Two days later Klemperer returned to Zurich, where he planned to stay for a month before returning to London for the *Entführung* recording, which had been arranged to start in mid-February. Once home, however, his depression deepened. He also remained very frail. He was pleased about his decision to give up concerts, but at the same time found it hard to come to terms with the fact that he had only a limited amount of work ahead of him. He was distressed to hear that Gareth Morris, principal flute of the New Philharmonia and chairman of its council, had been forced to resign following a complicated feud involving other members of the orchestra. Klemperer regarded Morris as a confidant and good friend, and he wrote a letter, addressed to all members of the orchestra, pleading with them to withdraw their criticisms of Morris, which, he said, 'seem unbelievable to me'. But his words fell on deaf ears. He was in effect no longer their chief conductor. Meanwhile he studied the score of the *Entführung* ceaselessly, but his eyes were bad and he had to resort to listening to recordings of the opera instead. He began to dread the thought of going to London. However, just when it seemed that he might have to call off the recording, a solution to his dilemma came from an unexpected quarter. Britain's coal-miners had gone on strike and the government had declared a state of emergency. The country was being paralysed by electricity black-outs lasting up to nine hours and EMI had no alternative but to postpone the recording. The decision gave Klemperer a much needed respite.

Throughout the next few weeks Klemperer suffered a succession of ailments – cystitis, a cold, bronchitis and a high fever which lasted into March. When his temperature finally dropped he started to work again on both the *Entführung* and the *St John Passion*. He was much preoccupied with the phenomenon of death and read once again Schopenhauer's *Über den Tod*. Each day Lotte wheeled him down to the lake to enjoy the mild spring weather. Werner came for a visit, at the end of which Klemperer accompanied

---
* Charles Groves took over the performance of the Bruckner Seventh.

him to the airport. The short journey tired him and the doctor was called to give him a vitamin injection.

In mid-April the depression began to lift and Lotte noted a general change for the better.[59] On 2 May, Klemperer attended a rehearsal of the Tonhalle Orchestra at which Michael Gielen conducted Lutoslawski's Second Symphony and Heinz Holliger's *Siebengesang*. Nine days later Lotte was able to report that her father's 'sense of humour is again making timid appearances'.[60] In early June EMI wrote with the encouraging news that the *Entführung* had been re-scheduled for September and October, with, it was hoped, a cast headed by Lucia Popp as Constanze and Werner Hollweg as Belmonte.[61] Klemperer welcomed a host of visitors – Deszö Ernster, the Hungarian bass who had sung Rocco for him in Budapest; Hans Curjel, his *Dramaturg* at the Kroll Oper; Heinrich Wollheim, once a member of the Kroll orchestra, who now copied scores for him; Lotte Lehmann, by now so crippled with arthritis that she could hardly walk; Gottfried Reinhardt, the film director, son of Max Reinhardt; Peter Heyworth, who went through the proofs of his book *Conversations with Klemperer*; the young Swiss conductor Karl Anton Rickenbacher, who corrected mistakes in the *Entführung* parts. Klemperer read aloud to Rickenbacher the first chapter of Ecclesiastes: 'Vanity of vanities, saith the Preacher; all is vanity. What profit hath a man of all his labour which he taketh under the sun? One generation passeth away, and another generation cometh; but the earth abideth for ever.' Rickenbacher felt strongly that the passage was Klemperer's credo.

In the second week of July there was a welcome two-day visit from Werner's wife Susan, who was on holiday in Europe with the children, Mark, now twelve, and nine-year-old Erika. 'Papa', Lotte wrote to Werner, 'is enchanted with both of them.' Klemperer inspected their camper-van and there was an expedition to a restaurant by the lakeside for ice-creams. Lotte suggested to her father that he should give each of his grandchildren something personal by which to remember him. To her surprise he chose to give Mark something of which he was particularly proud, his Goethe Medal. The silver was tarnished and Sister Ruth was asked to polish it up. Klemperer told Mark not to lose it, 'because, you see, it is a little bit historical'. For Erika he chose a Mahler medal that had been presented to him in Vienna. Later Klemperer joined in a game of draughts with the children. 'You are always welcome to visit me', Klemperer told them as they left. 'Always.'[62]

On 22 July Klemperer was driven over to Lucerne, where Lotte Lehmann was staying. It was an enjoyable visit and there was a good deal of laughter, but Klemperer found the expedition a strain physically. Two days later he began to feel unwell. He refused to eat and retired to bed at noon. The following day he began to run a fever and the doctor was called. He diagnosed pneumonia. For the next few weeks Klemperer was seriously ill.

THE FINAL YEARS

28 Klemperer with Lotte Lehmann, Lucerne, 22 July 1972

Lotte moved into his flat and slept in the next room with the doors between them left open. She was never to return to her own apartment. By the end of the month the fever had subsided and Klemperer's lungs had cleared, but he never fully regained his strength.

In early September EMI decided that, for various reasons, it would have to postpone the *Entführung* recording yet again, and it was proposed that Klemperer and the NPO should use the October sessions to record Beethoven's *Grosse Fuge*, Mozart's *Serenata notturna* and Brahms's St Antony Variations.[63] Klemperer at first agreed to the schedule, but in mid-September he had to inform the New Philharmonia that he was not strong enough to undertake it. EMI made one last attempt to set up the *Entführung*, this time for January/February 1973. It was to no avail. On 1 December, Klemperer wrote to Peter Andry,*

> Today I have to write you a letter which is for me a very sad one, but one which is unfortunately vital. As you can imagine, it concerns the *Entführung* project

* Original letter in German.

and my ability to carry it out. It is now the beginning of December, and I really do not feel that I shall be up to travelling by 24 January.

Therefore I am withdrawing completely from this project, since I realise that at my age a further postponement can only result in another situation like today's, and in these circumstances and in everybody's interest I want to avoid this.

I had hoped so much that all would be well and, as you can imagine, this letter is very hard for me to write.

Naturally I can show you a medical certificate, should this be necessary.

Although I cannot promise anything, I hope from the bottom of my heart that I shall be able to work again, but naturally on a less important project.

Hoping that you will understand, and with best greetings,

Yours respectfully

Otto Klemperer

Lotte asked McDonald to make sure that Klemperer's name as chief conductor was removed from all New Philharmonia literature.[64] She had made a similar request the previous February, when her father had given up his concert engagements, but the orchestra had not had the heart to comply.

Klemperer never did work again. He endured the remaining months of his life with an extraordinary stoicism. His circulation was poor and for some time he had had to accept the need for a permanent catheter; having it changed was a painful experience for him. He went out regularly in his wheelchair, however, and even managed to walk up and down the steps of the house. He continued to study, but his eyes had grown even worse. Lotte read to him. He dozed a good deal. Occasionally, to his annoyance, he lost track of time and place, but on the whole he remained alert and his wit was undiminished.

On 24 April the New Philharmonia gave a performance of Klemperer's Second Symphony under Lorin Maazel at the Festival Hall as a tribute to its former chief. Klemperer was invited to attend, but he was not strong enough to make the journey to London. He was touched to receive a copy of the programme signed by all those who had taken part. He read the reviews and grudgingly conceded to Lotte that the general reaction to the symphony 'could have been much worse'.[65]

Klemperer's eighty-eighth birthday on 14 May passed quietly: a few old friends called, among them Hans Curjel. Klemperer was fully aware of his approaching death and accepted it with composure. He had made his will in 1967 and in it had left instructions for his funeral. He was to be buried in a Jewish cemetery according to the plain Jewish rite. The officiating rabbi was not to say any other words apart from the usual prayers. The coffin was to be of the cheapest materials.

Meanwhile, Klemperer's breathing had become increasingly difficult

THE FINAL YEARS

29   Klemperer with his daughter Lotte, Zurich, November 1972

and he slept almost constantly. On 28 June he slipped into a coma. Werner arrived from America the following day, but Klemperer never recovered consciousness. He died, very gently, at 6.15 p.m. on 6 July during a thunderstorm. Werner and Lotte were with him, together with Frau Anna, Sister Ruth and Otto Freudenthal. Lotte believed that the thunderstorm, and the sudden change of pressure it brought, had triggered the end.

Klemperer was buried four days later in the Jewish cemetery at Friesenberg, high up in the hills overlooking Zurich. As he requested, the headstone that marks his grave bears only his name and dates.

OTTO

KLEMPERER

14. MAI 1885

6. JULI 1973

NOTES

1. Into exile

1. Lotte Klemperer, interview with Philo Bregstein II/3, p. 15.
2. Strasser, *Und dafür wird man noch bezahlt*, p. 106.
3. *Neue Wiener Presse* and *Der Abend*, 25 April 1933.
4. 'Vienna's Great Conductors', interview with B.H. Haggin, *Encounter*, July 1977.
5. Undated letter.
6. Letter from Schoenberg to Webern, Paris, 19 May 1933. Gertrud Schoenberg's reminiscences. Brochure accompanying *The Music of Arnold Schoenberg*, Volume IV (CBS 73459/60).
7. Nicky Mariano, *Forty Years with Berenson*, p. 214.
8. Letter from Miss Eva Einstein, 14 December 1981.
9. Made available by Mrs Alice von Hildebrand.
10. *Berliner Tageblatt*, 4 April 1933 (evening edition).
11. *Völkischer Beobachter* (6 April 1933).
12. Fred K. Prieberg, *Kraftprobe*, pp. 74–5.
13. Correspondence between Gustav Spiess and Friedrich Krebs. Stadtarchiv, Frankfurt am Main.
14. Undated draft of letter retained by Mrs Dorothea Alexander-Katz, who typed Klemperer's correspondence in Fiesole.
15. Author's interview with Klemperer, London, 11 February 1970.
16. *Los Angeles Times*, 9 August 1936.
17. Vilmos Tátrai, interview with the author, 2 October 1984.
18. *Ajarilott*, p. 7.
19. Interview with Louis Kentner, 13 February 1980.
20. Aládar Tóth, *Pesti Napló*, 3 June 1933.
21. Aládar Tóth, 'Klemperers Tätigkeit in Ungarn', Electrola brochure, 1965.
22. Heyworth (ed.), *Conversations*, p. 88.
23. Aládar Tóth, *Pesti Napló*, 9 June 1933.
24. Reported in *Usjág*, 3 June 1933.
25. Klemperer's file at the Berlin State Opera.
26. Archives of the Vienna Philharmonic Orchestra.
27. Rosenzweig, letter to Ernst Krenek, 1 September 1947.
28. Klemperer, *Autobiographische Skizze*, p. 25.
29. Unpublished letters, made available by Robert Craft and published by permission of the Stravinsky Estate.
30. Letter from Willy Strecker to Stravinsky, 20 July 1933.
31. Vera Stravinsky and Robert Craft, *Stravinsky in Pictures and Documents*, p. 662.
32. Klemperer's letter to Joseph Wulf, 25 June 1962, reprinted in *Musik im dritten Reich*, p. 21.
33. Letter to Hermann Wisler, Montreal, 15 December 1951.
34. Related to the author by Mr Eric Simon.
35. Letter of 24 August 1933, Budapest.

36 Ibid.
37 *Documents on British Foreign Policy*, 2nd Series, Volume VI, pp. 538–40 (quoted in Elisabeth Barker, *Austria 1918–1972*, p. 80).
38 Norbert Schausberger, *Der Griff nach Oesterreich*, p. 256, and Barker, pp. 80–1.
39 Thomas Michaels, OSB, in an interview with the author on 20 June 1978.
40 Information provided by both by Eric Simon and Karl Trötzmüller, musicians who were close to Klemperer.
41 Information provided by Trötzmüller.
42 Obituary notice. The *Guardian*, 9 July 1973.
43 Letter to Johanna Klemperer, Vienna, 3 September 1933.
44 Thomas Michaels, OSB, in interview with the author.

2. 'A cloudburst of non-sequiturs'

1 Caroline Estes Smith, *The Philharmonic Orchestra*, pp. 39–43.
2 José Rodriguez, *Rob Wagner's Script*, 21 October 1933.
3 C. Sharpless Hickman, *Musical Courier*, August 1954.
4 *Los Angeles Times*, 19 June 1934.
5 *Los Angeles Herald and Express*, 12 and 14 January 1933; *Los Angeles Times*, 15 January 1933.
6 *Los Angeles Times*, 11 February 1933.
7 Heyworth (ed.), *Conversations*, p. 89.
8 Letter to Johanna Klemperer, Los Angeles, 25 November 1933.
9 Carey McWilliams, *Southern California*, pp. 233 and 249.
10 Letter to Johanna Klemperer, Los Angeles, 17 October 1933.
11 Letter to Johanna Klemperer, Los Angeles, 31 October 1933.
12 Interview with Gottfried Reinhardt, 20 June 1978.
13 Information provided by Lotte Klemperer, David Brunswick and Gottfried Reinhardt.
14 Taped interview with Alfred Wallenstein, UCLA (Long Beach), William Weber.
15 Interview with Frederick Moritz, November 1977.
16 Interview with Jack Pepper, December 1978.
17 *Los Angeles Times*, 6 and 8 February 1934.
18 W.A. Clark, letter to George Leslie Smith, Paris, 19 February 1934.
19 *Musical Courier*, 28 October 1933.
20 *Rob Wagner's Script*, 28 October 1933.
21 *Beverly Hills Town Topics*, 25 October 1933.
22 Interview with Sven Reher, April 1980.
23 Carl Bronson, *Herald-Express*, 20 October 1933.
24 Gottfried Reinhardt, *Der Liebhaber*, p. 273, and interview with the author, 20 June 1978.
25 Gilbert Brown, *The Record*, 20 October 1933.
26 *Rob Wagner's Script*, 25 November 1933.
27 *Musical Courier*, 16 December 1933.
28 Letter to Johanna Klemperer, Los Angeles, 15 December 1933.
29 *Hollywood Citizens News*, 5 February 1934.
30 Letter to Dorothea Alexander-Katz, Los Angeles, 9 November 1933.
31 Letter to Johanna Klemperer, Los Angeles, 13 November 1933.
32 Letter to Johanna Klemperer, Los Angeles, 17 October 1933.
33 Letter to Johanna Klemperer, Los Angeles, 6 November 1933.
34 Letter to Johanna Klemperer, Los Angeles, 31 October 1933.
35 Letter to Johanna Klemperer, Los Angeles, 25 November 1933.
36 Letter to Johanna Klemperer, 19 January 1934.
37 Abram Chasins, *Stokowski*, p. 126.
38 Philip Hart, *Orpheus in the New World*, pp. 72, 79–92; Howard Shanet, *Philharmonic*, pp. 248–9.

39 Letter to Roger Sessions, Los Angeles, 12 March 1934.
40 Letters to and from Rudolf Mengelberg, 19 February and 7 March 1934.
41 Letter to Dorothea Alexander-Katz, Los Angeles, 3 March 1934.
42 Letter of 27 March 1934.
43 *New York Herald-Tribune*, 6 May 1934.
44 *Musical America*, 10 May 1934.
45 *Encounter*, July 1977.
46 *Neues Wiener Journal*, 15 May 1934.
47 Letter from Berg to Kleiber, 29 May 1934.
48 Letter from Heinsheimer to Berg, 30 June 1934.
49 Bloch, *Briefe*, p. 472.
50 Letter from Berg to Heinsheimer, 14 June 1934.
51 Letter from Heinsheimer to Berg, 11 July 1934.
52 Quotation from Klemperer's letter to Universal Edition in letter from Heinsheimer to Berg, 16 August 1934.
53 Unpublished memoirs of Dietrich von Hildebrand.
54 Letter to Johanna Klemperer, Zurich, 14 August 1934.
55 Undated draft in Sessions's hand.

3. Bread and work

1 *New York Times*, 29 September 1934.
2 *New York Herald-Tribune*, 5 October 1934.
3 *New York Times*, 12 October 1934.
4 *Los Angeles Times*, 23 December 1934.
5 *New York Times*, 26 October 1934.
6 *Los Angeles Times*, 3, 4 and 7 October 1934.
7 *New Yorker*, 13 October 1934.
8 José Rodriguez, *Rob Wagner's Script*, 24 November 1934.
9 Richard Saunders, *Hollywood Citizens News*, no date.
10 Issue of 9 December 1934.
11 Letter to Peter and Micha Konstam, 28 December 1934.
12 Interview with Henry Pleasants, 29 March 1985.
13 Edward H. Schloss, *The Record*, 18 January 1935.
14 *New York Times*, 30 January 1935.
15 *Brooklyn Eagle*, 20 February 1935.
16 *Philadelphia Inquirer*, 21 January 1935.
17 Letter to Johanna Klemperer, Philadelphia, 28 January 1935.
18 Letter to Johanna Klemperer, Rome, 7 March 1935.
19 CBC transcripts, IX, p. 15.
20 New York Philharmonic Orchestra archives (minutes of the 1934 board). Library of the Performing Arts, New York.
21 *Los Angeles Times*, 1 May 1935.
22 Letter from Harvey S. Mudd to Walter S. Hilborn, 15 July 1935.
23 Viertel, *The Kindness of Strangers*, p. 210 (German edition, p. 314).
24 Hertha Glaz, conversation with the author, February 1986.
25 Koopal, *The Miracle of Music*, pp. 168–71.
26 *Conversations*, pp. 90 and 98.
27 Isabel Morse Jones, *Hollywood Bowl*, pp. 185–6.
28 Howard S. Swan, *Music in the Southwest*, pp. 242–3.
29 Lawrence Morton, *Rob Wagner's Script*, 29 July 1944.
30 C. Sharpless Hickson, 'The Los Angeles Philharmonic Orchestra Today', *Musical America*, August 1954.
31 Letter to Johanna Klemperer, Rome, 3 March 1935.
32 *Musical Courier*, 5 October 1935.

33 Letter to Johanna Klemperer, New York, 25 April 1935.
34 Letter to Johanna Klemperer, Los Angeles, 17 May 1935.
35 New York Philharmonic Archives.
36 Letter (written in English) to Ira Hirschmann, Los Angeles, undated (September 1935?).
37 Hilborn files.
38 *New York Times*, 5 May 1935.
39 *Brooklyn Eagle*, 15 September 1935.
40 *Brooklyn Eagle*, 13 October 1935.
41 *The Stage*, November 1935.
42 *New York Times*, 13 October 1935.
43 *World Telegram*, 12 October 1935.
44 *World Telegram*, 18 October 1935.
45 *Brooklyn Eagle*, 18 October 1935.
46 *New York Times*, 18 October 1935.
47 *New York Herald-Tribune*, 18 October 1935.
48 *Brooklyn Eagle*, 25 October 1935.
49 Oscar Levant, *A Smattering of Ignorance*, pp. 29–30.
50 Saul Goodman, Columbia University Oral History Program, No. 1221, p. 87.
51 Heyworth (ed.), *Conversations*, p. 90.
52 *New York Times*, 29 November 1935.
53 *New York Herald-Tribune*, 29 November 1935.
54 Letter to Mark Brunswick, 20 December 1941.
55 Interview given to the author, 20 October 1977.
56 *Modern Music*, January–February 1936.
57 *Musical America*, 25 December 1935.
58 *Brooklyn Eagle*, 22 December 1935.
59 *Musical America*, 25 December 1935.
60 *Die Staatszeitung*, 13 December 1935.
61 Telegram, 13 December 1935.
62 Dr Ida Halpern. Interview with Mr Robert Chesterman.
63 *Newsweek*, 21 December 1935.
64 Information provided by Lotte Klemperer.
65 *World Telegram*, 2 January 1936.
66 *Los Angeles Times*, 8 January 1936.
67 Philip Hart, *Orpheus in the New World*, p. 89; Howard Shanet, *Philharmonic*, pp. 283–4.
68 *Deutsche Allgemeine Zeitung*, 25 November 1934.
69 Fred K. Prieberg, *Kraftprobe*, pp. 186–94.
70 Bertha Geissmar, *The Baton and the Jackboot*, p. 158.
71 Letter from Hirschmann to Klemperer, New York, 3 December 1936.
72 Heyworth (ed.), *Conversations*, p. 78.
73 Harvey Sachs, *Toscanini*, p. 254.
74 *Los Angeles Times*, 9 August 1936.
75 Letters from Regi Elbogen to Marianne Joseph, 14 and 24 May 1936.
76 Letters to Natalia Satz, Fiesole, 27 July 1933, and Los Angeles, 21 December 1933.
77 Sofia Khentova, *Shostakovich*, pp. 163 and 435. Also I.D. Glikman, who was also present, in conversation with Stuart Campbell, April 1988.
78 *Sovetskoyo isskustvo*, 5 June 1936.
79 Yudin, *Za gran'ya proshlikh*, pp. 107–20.
80 *Sovetskoyo isskustvo*, 29 May 1936.
81 *Der Wiener Tag*, 9 June 1936.
82 Letter to Johanna Klemperer, SS *Normandie*, 5 October 1936.
83 Letter to Johanna Klemperer, Vienna, 12 October 1936.
84 Moldenhauer, *Anton von Webern*, pp. 679–80 (German edition).

85 Ibid., pp. 426–80.
86 Heyworth (ed.), *Conversations*, p. 94.
87 Moldenhauer, *Anton von Webern*, pp. 679–80 (German edition).
88 *Neues Wiener Journal*, 17 October 1936.
89 Peter Stadlen, 'Serialism Reconsidered', *The Score*, February 1958.
90 Letter from Webern to Schoenberg, Mödling, 12 December 1936.
91 Letter from Webern to Edward Steuermann, 6 December 1936.
92 Heyworth (ed.), *Conversations*, p. 94.
93 Letter to Johanna Klemperer, Vienna, 20 October 1936.
94 *Modern Music*, May–June 1937.
95 Files of the Reichsministerium für Volksaufklärung und Propaganda.
96 Gauk, pp. 91–4.
97 Letter to Schnabel, Los Angeles, 24 December 1936.
98 Ginzburg, pp. 84–6.
99 *Deutsche Zentral Zeitung*, 11 November 1936; *Sovjetskaya musika*, January 1937.
100 Letter to Schnabel, Los Angeles, 12 April 1937.
101 Letter to Ernest Ansermet, Los Angeles, 29 July 1937.
102 Letter to Schnabel, Los Angeles, 14 July 1937.

4. In the wrong place

1 *Los Angeles Times*, 26 July 1936.
2 Anderson (ed.), *Klemperer on Music*, pp. 69–80.
3 *Los Angeles Times*, 20 August 1936.
4 *Rob Wagner's Script*, 5 September 1936.
5 Letter to Lonny Epstein, Los Angeles, 12 August 1936.
6 William McKelvey Martin, interview, April 1980.
7 Heyworth (ed.), *Conversations*, p. 98.
8 Letter to Lonny Epstein, Los Angeles, 20 June 1937.
9 Robert Knudsen, interview, 6 June 1984.
10 Werner Klemperer, interview with the author, 15 May 1985.
11 *Los Angeles Times*, 27 September 1936.
12 Heyworth (ed.), *Conversations*, p. 99.
13 Letter to Roger Sessions, Los Angeles, 23 October 1933.
14 Undated draft letter from Roger Sessions to Klemperer, *c.* 1 November 1933.
15 *Rob Wagner's Script*, 22 October 1938.
16 *Rob Wagner's Script*, 5 November 1938.
17 *Rob Wagner's Script*, 18 March 1939.
18 Oscar Levant, *A Smattering of Ignorance*, p. 189.
19 Charles Schwartz, *Gershwin*, p. 277.
20 *New York World-Telegram*, 2 January 1936.
21 Maurice Zam, interview with the author.
22 Gottfried Reinhardt, interview with the author, 20 June 1978.
23 Heyworth (ed.), *Conversations*, p. 99.
24 Lawrence Stewart and Edward Jablonski, *The Gershwin Years*, p. 275.
25 Letter from Stravinsky to Alexander Kall, December 1936. *Selected Correspondence*, Volume I, p. 171 (footnote).
26 Telegram to Stravinsky, Los Angeles, 9 February 1937.
27 Letter from Hindemith to his wife, Los Angeles, 22 March 1939, in Rexnoth (ed.), *Briefe*, pp. 219–20.
28 Letter of 8 November 1934.
29 Hertha Glaz, undated letter to the author.
30 Stuckenschmidt, *Schoenberg* (German edition, p. 376).
31 Letter to the President of UCLA, Los Angeles, 4 January 1936 (UCLA archives).
32 Heyworth (ed.), *Conversations*, pp. 91–2.

33 Edmund Cykler, letter to the author, 14 January 1978.
34 Gerald Strang, interview with the author.
35 Communication of 18 March 1938 to Alfred Frankenstein, music critic of the *San Francisco Chronicle* (Rufer, *The Works of Arnold Schoenberg*, pp. 95–6).
36 Letter to Schoenberg, New York, 24 November 1940.
37 Heyworth (ed.), *Conversations*, p. 90.
38 Letter from Schoenberg to Klemperer, Los Angeles, 23 November 1940.
39 Letter from Schoenberg to Alma Mahler-Werfel, 12 September 1948.
40 *Rob Wagner's Script*, 14 May 1938.
41 Incident related to the author by Lotte Klemperer.
42 Letter from Schoenberg to Klemperer, 18 March 1936.
43 Heyworth (ed.), *Conversations*, p. 91.
44 Interview with an unidentified Viennese newspaper, June 1936.
45 Letter to Clare Riess, Los Angeles, 6 July 1937.
46 Letter to Ira Hirschmann, Los Angeles, 5 May 1937 (English original).
47 Letter, 20 December 1941.
48 Letter to Johanna Klemperer, Pittsburgh, 6 August 1937.
49 Letter to Ira Hirschmann, Los Angeles, 19 November 1937 (English original).
50 Ur-CBC transcripts. Tape No. 10, p. 1.
51 Interview with the author.
52 *Pacific Coast Musician*, 1 May 1937.
53 Letter from Isabel Morse Jones to Klemperer, 20 October 1937.
54 *Rob Wagner's Script*, 5 February 1938.
55 *Pacific Coast Musician*, 21 May 1938.
56 *Los Angeles Times*, 10 September 1939.
57 Undated letter addressed to Mrs Brandes, July 1938.
58 Letter to Fritz Stiedry, Los Angeles, 23 February 1938.
59 Author's interviews with Sol Babitz and Frederick Moritz.
60 Undated letter to Helene Hirschler.
61 Letter from Georg Klemperer, Boston, 2 July 1939.
62 Hugo Strelitzer, interview with the author.
63 Undated letter to Helene Hirschler, Arrowhead Springs, July 1939.
64 Letter to Helene Hirschler, Los Angeles, 19 August 1939.
65 Gustave Arlt, Werner Klemperer and William McKelvey Martin, interviews with the author.
66 Letter from Regi Elbogen to Marianne Joseph, New York, 14 November 1939.
67 Communications from Lotte Klemperer.

5. On the road to self-destruction

1 Letter from Georg Klemperer to Helene Hirschler, Boston, 18 September 1939.
2 Letter from Georg Klemperer to Helene Hirschler, Boston, 22 September 1939.
3 Letter from Georg Klemperer to Helene Hirschler, Boston, 12 October 1939.
4 Letter from Johanna Klemperer to her children, Boston, 18 September 1939.
5 Letter from Regi Elbogen to Marianne Joseph, New York, 21 February 1940.
6 Letter from Georg Klemperer to Ulrich Friedemann, Boston, 14 February 1940.
7 Letter from Regi Elbogen to Marianne Joseph, New York, 8 February 1940.
8 Letter to Marianne Joseph, Great Neck, 27 March 1940.
9 Interview with Max Friedemann, November 1977.
10 Vera Stravinsky's diary, 3 May 1940 (unpublished).
11 Letter from Georg Klemperer to Helene Hirschler, Boston, 12 May 1940.
12 Letter from Elisabeth Schumann to Helene Jung, New York, 19 May 1940.
13 Axel Hubert, typescript, October 1977.
14 'Meine Begegnung mit Otto Klemperer' (typescript), on which the account of the relationship is partly based.

15 Interview with Maria Schacko, 8 December 1985.
16 Information provided by Robert Craft.
17 Letter to Helene Hirschler, Los Angeles, 6 June 1940.
18 Letter to Helene Hirschler, Arrowhead Springs, 3 July 1940.
19 Interview with Thea Dispeker, March 1980.
20 Information provided by Lotte Klemperer, 31 July 1985.
21 Letter to Johanna Klemperer, Santa Barbara, undated.
22 Letter from Ernst Bloch to Max and Helene Hirschler, Marlboro, 29 August 1940.
23 Conversation with Mrs David Frisina, April 1980.
24 Undated letter from Etta Dahl to Raymond and Daphne Spottiswood, Los Angeles, September 1940.
25 Edmund Cykler, letter to the author, 14 January 1978.
26 Interviews with Fritz Zweig and Tilly de Garmo, August 1972 and August 1974.
27 Letter from Vicki Baum to Grete Fischer, Los Angeles, 14 December 1940.
28 Letter from Johanna to Werner Klemperer, Los Angeles, 3 October 1940.
29 Letter from Walter S. Hilborn to Klemperer, Los Angeles, 16 July 1940.
30 Letter from Harvey S. Mudd to Walter S. Hilborn, Los Angeles, 16 September 1940.
31 All quotations from documents in the Hilborn files.
32 The letter, written in early April 1940, has not survived.
33 Although the letter is headed 2 April 1940, the latter part of it was written on 9 April, after Schoenberg had received the letter referred to above from Klemperer. Stiedry replied on 12 April.
34 Dika Newlin, *Schoenberg Remembered*, pp. 248–52.
35 The letter has not survived.
36 Letter from Schoenberg to Klemperer, 25 September 1940.
37 Letter from Klemperer to Schoenberg, New York, 29 September 1940.
38 Letter from Klemperer to Schoenberg, New York, 24 November 1940.
39 Interview with Rudolf Kolisch, November 1977.
40 The information in this paragraph is drawn from interviews and conversations with, among others, Thomas Scherman, Rudolf Kolisch, Thea Dispeker and Felicia Dayrup.
41 Interview with Eva Heinitz, November 1977.
42 Conversation with Professor Alfred B. Mann, February 1981.
43 Interview with Werner Klemperer, 16 May 1985.
44 *New York Times*, 31 October 1940.
45 Letter from Ernst Bloch to Max and Helene Hirschler, 31 January 1941.
46 Interview with Karl Ulrich Schnabel, March 1980.
47 Interview with John Barnett, November 1977; and letter to the author, 24 March 1986.
48 Letter from Regi Elbogen to Marianne Joseph, New York, 3 November 1940.
49 Stresemann, ... *und Abends in der Philharmonie*, pp. 98–9.
50 Interview with Nathan Milstein, 16 May 1985.
51 Transcript of interview with Philo Bregstein, p. 4.
52 Interview with John Barnett, October 1977; letter to the author, 16 February 1986.
53 *New York Daily Mirror*, 27 January 1941.
54 Letter from Ernst Bloch to Helene Hirschler, 11 November 1940.
55 Based on information provided by, among others, Hugo Burghauser, Thea Dispeker, Axel Hubert, Mrs Paul Klemperer, Irving Kolodin, Louis Krasner, Mrs Mercedes Meyerhof.
56 Letter from Ira Hirschmann to Mark Brunswick, 20 December 1941.
57 Typescript reminiscences of Axel Hubert.
58 Interviews with Hans Heinsheimer and Mrs Dorle Soria.
59 Information provided by Howard Taubman and Thomas Lask.
60 Letter from Ernst Bloch to Max and Helene Hirschler, 20 November 1940.
61 Typescript reminiscences of Axel Hubert.

62 Letter to Helmut and Marianne Joseph, New York, 27 February 1941.
63 Information provided by Lotte Klemperer.
64 Letter from Ernst Bloch to Max and Helene Hirschler, 31 January 1941.
65 Letter from Georg Klemperer to Helene Hirschler, 5 March 1941.
66 Letter from Ernst Bloch to Helene Hirschler, 20 November 1940.
67 Memo provided by Lotte Klemperer.
68 *New York Daily News*, 4 March 1941.
69 *New York Times*, 4 March 1941.
70 The greater part of the account that follows is based on reports in the *New York Times* and *New York Herald-Tribune*, 2, 3 and 4 March 1941.

6. 'Ajax fell through Ajax's hand'

1 Letter from Elisabeth Schumann to Helene Jung, 21 August 1941.
2 Letter from Lotte Klemperer to Gertrud Schoenberg, New York, 15 April 1941.
3 *New York Times*, 19 March 1941.
4 Letter to Hindemith, New York, 30 March 1941.
5 Letter from Hindemith to Ernest Voigt, New Haven, *c.* 25 April 1941.
6 Interview with Eric Simon, November 1977.
7 Letter from Georg Klemperer to Helene Hirschler, 3 May 1941.
8 Letter (written in English) to Serge Koussevitzky, New York, 19 December 1941.
9 *New York Times*, 28 April 1941.
10 *New York Times*, 18 April 1941.
11 Hilborn files.
12 Gustave O. Arlt, UCLA Oral History Program 300/133.
13 Interview with Gustave O. Arlt, November 1978.
14 Bruno Ussher, *Los Angeles Examiner*, 29 May 1941.
15 Letter to the author from Richard T. Andrews, 5 January 1985.
16 *Daily News*, 11 June 1941.
17 Conversation with Mrs Florence Caylor, the Rehearsal Orchestra's manager, April 1980.
18 Lawrence Morton, *Rob Wagner's Script*, 11 October 1941.
19 Letter from Edmund Cykler to the author, 14 January 1978.
20 Maria Schacko, unpublished typescript and interviews with the author.
21 Hilborn file, 12 November 1941.
22 *Aufbau*, 7 March 1942.
23 Letter from Morton Estrin to the editor of *Keynote*, 18 April 1985.
24 Letter from Ernst Bloch to Helene Hirschler, 6 May 1943.
25 Recollections of Hanns Eisler's son, Georg, in an interview with Philo Bregstein.
26 Letter from Regi Elbogen to Marianne Joseph, 29 June 1942.
27 Letter from Harvey S. Mudd to Walter S. Hilborn, 25 June 1942.
28 Letter from Harvey S. Mudd to Walter S. Hilborn, 26 September 1942.
29 Interviews with Lotte Hammerschlag.
30 Anderson (ed.), *Klemperer on Music*, pp. 91–3.
31 Letter to Johanna Klemperer, New York, *c.* 15 December 1942.
32 Undated letter from Johanna to Lotte Klemperer, early December 1942.
33 Klemperer's reminiscences on 5 October 1969, noted at that time by Lotte Klemperer.
34 Excerpts from two undated letters from Johanna to Lotte Klemperer.
35 Communication from Lotte Klemperer.
36 Interview with Robert Mann.
37 Letter to Helene Hirschler, Los Angeles, 11 May 1943.
38 Letter from Georg to Johanna Klemperer, Boston, 28 March 1943.
39 Letter from Lotte to Johanna Klemperer, 22 March 1943.
40 Klemperer's reminiscences on 5 October 1969, noted at the time by Lotte Klemperer.

41 Letter from Lotte to Johanna Klemperer, New York, 15 December 1942.
42 Letter from Thomas Mann to Jonas Lesser, 27 August 1944.
43 *Rob Wagner's Script*, 26 September 1942.
44 Interview with John Edwards, assistant manager of the Los Angeles Orchestra and Hollywood Bowl (1942/4).
45 *Hollywood Citizens News*, 18 August 1943.
46 Letter from Stravinsky to Stokowski, Los Angeles, 16 February 1944.
47 Klemperer, *Minor Recollections*, p. 45.
48 Letter to Johanna Klemperer, New York, 22 March 1944.
49 Letter to Johanna Klemperer, New York, 30 March 1944.
50 Letter from Johanna to Lotte Klemperer, Los Angeles, 18 June 1944.
51 Letter from Johanna to Lotte Klemperer, Los Angeles, 27 May 1944.
52 Letter to Lonny Epstein, Los Angeles, 26 August 1944.
53 Letter from Georg Klemperer to Helene Hirschler, Boston, 6 February 1945.
54 Alfred Price Quinn, *B'nai B'rith Messenger*, 16 February 1945.
55 *Rob Wagner's Script*, 3 March 1945.
56 Alfred Price Quinn, *B'nai B'rith Messenger*, 16 February 1945.
57 Letter to Helene Hirschler, Los Angeles, 15 February 1945.
58 Letters to Helene Hirschler, Los Angeles, 1 and 18 May 1945.
59 Hilborn files. Draft income return.
60 Interview with Sol Babitz, November 1978.
61 Interview with Kalman Bloch, 15 February 1986.
62 This and much other information about the Music Guild concerts was provided by Alfred Leonard in a letter (1 October 1978) to the author.
63 Ingolf Dahl's diary, entry of 25 October 1945.
64 *Rob Wagner's Script*, 3 November 1945.
65 Vera Stravinsky in R. Craft (ed.), *Dearest Bubushkin*, p. 133. Entry of 22 October 1945.
66 Letter to Helene Hirschler, Los Angeles, 18 October 1945.
67 Letter to Helene Hirschler, Los Angeles, 16 September 1945.
68 Letters to Helene Hirschler, Los Angeles, 9 and 18 December 1945.
69 *The Desert News*, Salt Lake City, 31 December 1945.
70 Pencilled estimate in the Hilborn file.

7. Europe remains Europe

1 *L'Unità*, 16 April 1946.
2 Letter to Helene Hirschler, Paris, 11 June 1946.
3 *Carrefour*, 30 May 1946.
4 Letter to Fritz Fischer, Paris, 2 July 1946.
5 Letter to Fritz Fischer, Paris, 22 June 1946.
6 Letter to Helene Hirschler, Interlaken, 30 July 1946.
7 Undated letter from Hilde Strobel to her brother.
8 *Badener Tageblatt*, 29 June 1946.
9 Lotte Klemperer, communication to the author, 28 August 1988.
10 Philo Bregstein's interviews with Jan Bresser, Hubert Barwehser, Louis Metz, 1972.
11 Letter to Fritz Fischer, Paris, 21 August 1946.
12 Letters (in English) to Helene Hirschler and Olin Downes, Interlaken, 30 July 1946.
13 Letter to Richard Strauss, Zurich, 10 August 1946.
14 Letter from Ernst Bloch to Joachim Schumacher, Boston, 3 September 1946.
15 Letter from Regi Elbogen to Marianne Joseph, New York, 8 September 1946.
16 Details from Dr Eugene Ziskind's notes on two consultations, 17 and 25 September 1946.
17 Interview with Regina Resnik, New York, 8 February 1986.
18 Mrs Victor White, interview with Robert Chesterman.

19 Ian Docherty, letter to the author, 3 May 1978.
20 Communication from Lotte Klemperer to the author, January 1986.
21 Jarmila Novotna, letter to the author, 16 November 1985.
22 Letter from Lilly Toch to Julius Steinfeld, Santa Monica, 14 November 1946.
23 Klemperer's reminiscences, noted by Lotte Klemperer, 1966.
24 Lilly Toch, letter to Helene Hirschler, Santa Monica, 18 November 1946.
25 Letter to Marcel Mihalovici, Los Angeles, 2 January 1947; letter to Stravinsky, 10 January 1947.
26 *Musical Courier*, 1 February 1947.
27 *Rob Wagner's Script*, 18 January 1947.
28 Thomas Mann, *Tagebücher*, 14 January 1947.
29 Regi Elbogen, letter to Marianne Joseph, New York, 26 January 1947.
30 Lilly Toch, letter to Helene Hirschler, Santa Monica, 17 February 1947.
31 Letter to Lilly Toch, 6 February 1947.
32 Lotte Klemperer's memo on the incident.
33 Correspondence between the US Department of State (Passport Division) and André Mertens, Columbia Artists Inc., January–March 1947.
34 *Die Furche*, 12 April 1947.
35 Karl Trötzmüller, interview with the author, January 1979.
36 Peter Lafitte, 4 April 1947.
37 Otto Strasser, *Und dafür wird man noch bezahlt*, p. 107.
38 Board meeting of 24 June 1947, Vienna Philharmonic Orchestra's archives.
39 *Dagens Nyheter*, 27 April 1947.
40 *New York Herald Tribune*, 18 and 19 May 1947.
41 Olga Demetriescu-von Liechtenstein, 'Meine Begegnung mit Otto Klemperer', an account of a brief relationship that had originated in Stockholm in April 1947.
42 Interviews with Hilde Strobel and Jean Fonda.
43 Karl Schouten, 'Zo was het ook', *Preludium*, February 1982.
44 Interviews with J.H.H. Poth and Kappeyne van de Cappello (16 June 1987), among others.
45 *Musical Times*, August 1947; Grete Fischer, *Dienstbote Brechts und anderen*, p. 84.
46 Ida Haendel, *Woman with Violin*, p. 175.
47 Letter from Alfred Rosenzweig to Ernst Krenek, London, 1 September 1947.
48 Letter to Alfred Schlee, 29 October 1946.
49 *Die Furche*, 12 July 1947.
50 Lotte Klemperer, communication to the author, 28 August 1988.
51 Vaughan, *Herbert von Karajan*, p. 222.
52 Article from unknown source, 15 April 1947. Reprinted in Saathen, *Einem Chronik*, pp. 137–8.
53 Information provided by Helmut Grohe and Eva Morel.
54 Klemperer, *Minor Recollections*, p. 63.
55 Bruno Walter, *Briefe*, pp. 289–90.
56 Heyworth (ed.), *Conversations*, p. 55.
57 Letter from Lotte Klemperer to J. Beek, 1 July 1947.
58 Karl Schouten, 'Zo was het ook', *Preludium*, February 1982.
59 Karl Schouten and Jan Boon, among others.
60 Dispatch (1 August) that provided material for the article that appeared in *Time* on 11 August 1947.
61 Information provided by Robert Mayer, Eric Simon, Jean Fonda, Irene Eisinger and Eleanor Warren-Susskind.
62 Among others by Gustav Pichler, *Oesterreichische Musikzeitung*, October 1947.
63 Norbert J. Schneider, 'Phasen der Hindemith-Rezeption 1945/55', *Hindemith Jahrbuch*, 1984/XII, pp. 122–6.
64 Heyworth (ed.), *Conversations*, p. 78.
65 Letter from Lotte Klemperer to J. Beek, Salzburg, 28 August 1947.

66 Letter to Olga Demetriescu, 22 September 1947.

8. Behind the Curtain

1 *New York Times*, 9 March 1947.
2 Interview with Annie Fischer, 9 April 1986.
3 Interview with Annie Fischer, 24 April 1987.
4 Keesing's Archives. Stanley M. Max, *The United States, Great Britain and the Sovietisation of Hungary*, pp. 76–116. François Fejtö, *La tragédie hongroise*.
5 Interview with Miklós Lukács, 3 October 1984.
6 Attila Boros, *Klemperer Magyarországon* (second edition), pp. 24–6.
7 Unidentified Hungarian newspaper and *Világ*, 11 October 1947.
8 Interview with János Kerekes, 18 October 1986.
9 Boros, p. 23.
10 Boros, p. 22.
11 Boros, pp. 64–5.
12 Interview with Ede Banda, 20 October 1986.
13 Observation made by Ligeti to the author, Hamburg, November 1982.
14 Interview with Vilmos Tátrai, Boros, pp. 64–70; interview with Ede Banda, 20 October 1986.
15 Interview with Pál Varga, Boros, pp. 93–6; interview with János Kerekes, 18 October 1986.
16 *Time*, 18 October 1948.
17 *Uj Hirék*, 2 November 1947.
18 *Magyar Nemzet*, 11 November 1947.
19 Letter to Fritz Fischer, 9 November 1947.
20 Endre Gaál, *Magyar Nemzet*, 25 November 1947.
21 Interview with András Mikó, 19 October 1986.
22 Interviews with Maria Curzio, Dr Evert Cornelius, Peter Diamand, Helmuth Plessner, Lex van Delder.
23 *Het Parool*, 8 December 1947.
24 *Het Parool*, 21 November 1947.
25 Testimonial written by Klemperer in English on 1 December 1947 (Archives of the Concertgebouw Orchestra).
26 Letter from Johanna to Lotte Klemperer, Sils-Maria, 13 August 1951.
27 *Szabad Nép*, 27 January 1948.
28 *Magyar Nemzet*, 2 March 1948.
29 Boros, pp. 39–40.
30 Sándor Jemnitz, *Népszava*, 22 February 1948. *Szivárvány*, 28 February 1948.
31 *Kis Ujság*, 21 February 1948.
32 Aladár Tóth, 'Klemperers Tätigkeit in Ungarn', Electrola Records (1965).
33 Anderson (ed.), *Klemperer on Music*, p. 86.
34 Boros, pp. 34–5.
35 Thomas Blum, interview with Philo Bregstein.
36 Boros, p. 69.
37 *Radioújság*. April 1940.
38 *A Reggel*, 19 April 1948.
39 *Time*, unpublished dispatch, 8 October 1948.
40 Letter from Johanna Klemperer, 26 December 1947.
41 Letter of 8 March 1948, Hilborn files.
42 Lotte Klemperer, undated memorandum.

9. Caught in the crossfire

1 Letter, Paris, 8 March 1946.
2 Legge/Schwarzkopf, *On and Off the Record*, p. 177.

3 EMI internal memorandum (Leonard Smith), 7 December 1948.
4 Undated BBC internal memorandum.
5 BBC internal memorandum, 12 July 1946.
6 BBC internal memoranda, 10, 16 and 24 March 1948.
7 *New Statesman and Nation*, 13 March 1948.
8 Lotte Klemperer, communication to the author, 28 January 1986.
9 Letter to Lotte Klemperer, Budapest, 2 February 1948.
10 Lotte Klemperer, communication to the author, 23 November 1986.
11 Letter from Alfred Rosenzweig to Ernst Krenek, London, 1 April 1948.
12 Letters to Fritz Fischer, 7 June 1948, and Imre Kun, 4 May 1949.
13 Letter to Fritz Fischer, Budapest, 6 June 1948.
14 Lotte Klemperer, communication to the author.
15 W. Philipps Davison, *The Berlin Blockade*; Ann and John Tusa, *The Berlin Blockade*.
16 Hans Adler, interview with the author, July 1981.
17 Walther Harth, *Der Kurier*, 3 May 1948.
18 Kurt Westphal, *Berliner Zeitung*, 4 May 1948.
19 *Magyar Nemzet*, 2 September 1948.
20 *Új Hirek*, 17 May 1948. The dancer's comment is quoted in an unpublished *Time* dispatch, 8 October 1948.
21 *Kis Ujság*, 23 May 1948.
22 Interview with Tamás Major, Boros, *Klemperer Maggarországon*, pp. 59–64.
23 *Die Neue Zeitung*, 21 September 1948.
24 *Telegraf*, 5 May 1948.
25 'Geht die Kunst nach Brot?', *Die Welt*, 31 December 1948.
26 Josef Rufer, interview with the author.
27 Heyworth (ed.), *Conversations*, p. 102.
28 Lotte Klemperer, communication to the author, 2 April 1982.
29 *Magyar Nemzet*, ? 3 September 1948; *Népszava*, 9 November 1948.
30 Interviews with members of the cast, Boros, pp. 76–8.
31 *Népszava*, 7 November 1948.
32 Boros, p. 97.
33 Attila Boros, sleeve note to Hungaroton recording.
34 *Népszava*, 9 November 1948.
35 Walther Felsenstein and Siegfried Melchinger, *Musiktheater*, pp. 57–8.
36 Heyworth (ed.), *Conversations*, pp. 102–3.
37 Letter from Felsenstein to Jack Abrams, Berlin, 1 April 1974.
38 Letter to Fritz Fischer, Berlin, 8 January 1949.
39 *Neue Zeitung*, 8 January 1949.
40 Boroslaw Barlog, interview with the author, 4 April 1988.
41 Walther Felsenstein, interview with Philo Bregstein (*c.* 1972).
42 Letters to Diana Eustrati, Budapest, 19, 22 and 24 January 1949.
43 Vilmos Somogli, *Világ*, 23 January 1949.
44 Pál Varga, Boros, p. 95.
45 Sándor Jemnitz, unpublished diaries, 24 and 25 March 1949.
46 Lotte Klemperer, communication to the author, 27 November 1987.
47 Boros, p. 94.
48 Boros, sleeve note to Hungaroton recording (LPX 122340/1).
49 *Szinház ès Mozi*, 10 November 1948.
50 Lotte Klemperer, communication to the author, 8 October 1983.
51 Letter to Helene Hirschler, Los Angeles, 24 June 1945.
52 Letter to Helene Hirschler, Los Angeles, 9 December 1945.
53 Letter to Stravinsky, Los Angeles, 10 January 1947.
54 *Szinház ès Mozi*, 10 November 1948.
55 Ernst Bloch, letter to Adolf Lowe, Cambridge, MA, 19 February 1949.
56 *Der Tagesspiegel*, 8 January 1949.

57 Letter from Beek (agent) to the Concertgebouw Orchestra, Amsterdam, 4 June 1949.
58 Lotte Klemperer, communication to the author, 7 February 1986.
59 Letter to Lotte Klemperer, Melbourne, 21 August 1949.
60 Conversations with Brenton Langbein (28 April 1986) and Eldon Fox (13 October 1988), among others.
61 Letter to Lotte Klemperer, Melbourne, 19 September 1949.
62 Information supplied by Sir Charles Moses.
63 *The Canon*, September 1949.
64 *Szinház és Mozi*, 25 November 1949.
65 Letter from Johanna to Lotte Klemperer, Budapest, ? 11 May 1950.
66 Tamas Aczel and Tibor Meray, *The Revolt of the Mind*, pp. 76–86.
67 Diaries, *Kritika*, 1983, No. 8.
68 Annie Fischer, interview with the author, 19 October 1986.
69 Sándor Jemnitz, unpublished diaries, 1 December 1949.
70 Hans Adler, interview with the author, July 1981.
71 István Szenthogyi, *Kis Ujság*, 31 May 1950; *Független Magyarország*, 5 June 1950.
72 Information provided by Lotte Klemperer, who was present.
73 Letter to Aladár Tóth, Sydney, 30 September 1950.

10. A sea of troubles

1 Johanna Klemperer, letter to Lotte Klemperer, Melbourne, 15 August 1950.
2 Letter of 6 November 1950. Stravinsky, *Selected Correspondence, Volume Three*, p. 338.
3 C. Sharpless Hickman, *B'nai B'nai Messenger* (Los Angeles), 3 November 1950.
4 Pierre Béique, recorded interview with Eric McLean, Montreal, 4 August 1984.
5 Alexander Brott (concert-master), letter to the author, Montreal, 29 February 1988.
6 Eric McLean, *Daily Star* (Montreal), 22 May 1965.
7 *Daily Star*, 15 November 1950.
8 Undated letter to Lotte Klemperer, Brussels, *c.* 22 November 1950.
9 Report of the Californian Committee on Un-American Activities, 1948 (pp. 310–16).
10 FBI file 105–8695.
11 Lotte Klemperer, communication to the author, 6 January 1989.
12 *New York Times*, 10 November 1950.
13 Letter from Walther Felsenstein, Berlin, 14 October 1950.
14 Letter from Dr Hans J. Reichhardt (Berliner Landesarchiv) to the author, 15 November 1988.
15 *Het Parool*, 12 December 1950.
16 Peter Diamand, interview with the author, 26 August 1986.
17 Daniel Schorr, *New York Times*, 2 February 1951.
18 *New York Times*, 28 and 29 January 1951.
19 *New York Times*, 13 February 1951.
20 *Die Weltpresse* (Vienna), 22 March 1951.
21 Lotte Klemperer, communication to the author, 14 November 1988.
22 Letter to Aladar Tóth, Montreal, 1 January 1952.
23 *Der Abend* (Vienna), 17 May 1951.
24 Lotte Klemperer, communication to the author, 14 November 1988.
25 Shabtai Petrushka, 'Encounters with Otto Klemperer', programme book of Klemperer centenary concerts given by the Jerusalem Symphony Orchestra, 12–13 May 1985.
26 Letter from Marianne Joseph to Lene Rosenbaum, Jerusalem, 7 May 1951.
27 Letter from George de Mendelssohn-Bartholdy, New York, 4 January 1951.
28 Otto Glastra van Loon, *Onder de Stenen Lier*, p. 43.

29 *Preludium*, February 1982.
30 *Het Parool*, 30 March 1951.
31 *De Groene Amsterdammer*, 14 April 1951.
32 *Wiener Tageszeitung*, 21 May 1951.
33 Letter to Helene Hirschler, Vienna, 25 May 1951.
34 Kathleen Ferrier, letter to John Newmark, 24 September 1951. Maurice Leonard, *Kathleen*, p. 194.
35 Legge/Schwarzkopf, *On and Off the Record*, p. 100.
36 *The Times*, 26 June 1951.
37 Letter to Aladár Tóth, Montreal, 1 February 1952.
38 John Denison (music director, Arts Council), conversation with the author, 14 September 1988.
39 *Daily Telegraph*, 30 June 1951.
40 *The Times*, 30 June 1951.
41 Legge/Schwarzkopf, p. 100.
42 Peter Heyworth, 'The English Connection' in Peter Csobadi (ed.), *Karajan oder die kontrollierte Ekstase*, pp. 125–35.
43 Legge/Schwarzkopf, pp. 177–8.
44 Concertgebouw archives, Book 132.
45 EMI internal memo, 10 July 1951.
46 Letter to Lotte Klemperer, 22 July 1951.
47 Letter to Therese Schnabel, 26 August 1951.
48 Summary of medical papers provided by the Royal Victoria Hospital, Montreal, 20 July 1987.
49 Letter to George de Mendelssohn-Bartholdy, Montreal, 13 November 1951.
50 EMI internal memo, 26 February 1952.
51 Letters to Fritz Fischer, Montreal, 23 and 28 November and 6 December 1951.
52 Lotte Klemperer, letter to Helene Hirschler, 3 March 1952.
53 Lotte Klemperer, communication to the author, 7 April 1987.
54 *Variety*, 2 July 1952.
55 Letter to Walter Legge, Montreal, 25 August 1952.
56 Letter from Walter Legge to Mrs Beek, London, 18 September 1952.
57 Letter from Walter Legge to Klemperer, London, 3 July 1953.
58 Letter to Marianne Joseph, New York, 3 February 1953.
59 Eric McLean, letter to the author, Montreal, January 1988.
60 Anderson (ed.), *Klemperer on Music*, p. 184.
61 Letter to Fritz Fischer, New York, 25 May 1953.
62 Lotte Lenya, interview with the author, 1980.
63 Letter from R.J.F. Howgill to Mrs John Beek, 26 October 1953.
64 Jan Bresser, interview with Philo Bregstein, c. 1972.
65 Letters of 2 May, 20 June and 27 August 1952 (Concertgebouw Archives, Book 12A).
66 Johanna Klemperer, letter to Lotte Klemperer, Montreal, 14 October 1953.
67 Letter to Lotte Klemperer, Montreal, 23 October 1953.
68 Philip Hart, *Musical Courier*, September 1961.
69 Philip Hart, letter to the author, 14 June 1987.
70 Johanna Klemperer, letter to Lotte Klemperer, Portland, ? 3 November 1953.
71 *Musical Courier*, September 1961.
72 Letter to the author, 14 June 1987.
73 Letter to Lotte Klemperer, Montreal, 9 November 1953.
74 Johanna Klemperer, letter to Lotte Klemperer, Buffalo, 17 November 1953.

11. The high ground regained

1 Lotte Klemperer, letter to Helene Hirschler, 26 January 1954.
2 Letter to Regi Elbogen, Berlin, 11 February 1954.

3 Letter to Johanna Klemperer, Rome, 10 March 1954.
4 Bernard Berenson, *Sunset and Twilight*, entry for 9 March 1954.
5 *Times Educational Supplement*, 26 March 1954.
6 Letter to Johanna Klemperer, The Hague, 22 March 1954.
7 *The Scotsman*, 12 April 1954.
8 Letter to Else Nürnberg, Montreal, 18 January 1952.
9 Legge/Schwarzkopf, *On and Off the Record*, p. 179.
10 Lotte Klemperer, letter to Hanns Hartmann, Scheveningen, 14 July 1954.
11 Lotte Klemperer, letter to Loli Hatvány, Zurich, 20 August 1954 (in English).
12 Lotte Klemperer, communication to the author, 22 July 1989.
13 Legge/Schwarzkopf, pp. 180–1.
14 Lotte Klemperer, interview, Radio France, 19 October 1988.
15 Gerald Jackson, *First Flute*, p. 77.
16 *Daily Telegraph*, 21 April 1955.
17 Neville Cardus, *Manchester Guardian*, 22 April 1955.
18 Letter to Ernst and Lilly Toch, 1 May 1955.
19 Letter from J. Beek to Concertgebouw Orchestra, 27 December 1954.
20 Matthijs Vermeulen, *De Groene Amsterdammer*, July 1955.
21 Letter to Johanna Klemperer, London, 4 October 1955.
22 Letter from Maurice Johnstone (BBC) to E.M. Tillett, London, 11 October 1955.
23 BBC internal memo, 21 November 1955.
24 *Christian Science Monitor*, 28 January 1956.
25 Letter to Johanna Klemperer, Berlin, 9 February 1956.
26 Lotte Klemperer, comment on diary entry of 12 February 1956.
27 E.M., *Das Tagesspiegel*, 25 March 1958.
28 Letter to Johanna Klemperer, Cologne, 6 January 1956.
29 Letter of Johanna to Lotte Klemperer, Bad Gastein, 22 September 1956.
30 Letter from Regi Elbogen to Marianne Joseph, New York, 21 November 1956.
31 The account of Johanna Klemperer's last illness, death and burial is based mainly on Lotte Klemperer's letters and information provided by her.
32 Lotte Klemperer, letter to Arthur Judson, Zurich, 20 November 1956.
33 Lotte Klemperer, letter to Louise Schwab, London, 5 October 1957.
34 *The Times*, 1 October 1956.
35 *New Statesman and Nation*, 6 October 1956.
36 John Amis, communication to the author, 20 April 1989.
37 Martin Cooper, *Daily Telegraph*, 23 March 1957.
38 *The Times*, 23 March 1957.
39 *The Times*, 11 April 1958.
40 Karl Schouten, 'Zo was het ook', *Preludium*, February 1957.
41 Marius Flothuis, letter to Lotte Klemperer, Amsterdam, 22 March 1957.
42 Marius Flothuis, interview with the author, Amsterdam, 3 May 1987.
43 Letter from Lotte Klemperer to Marius Flothuis, Rome, 13 April 1957.
44 Letter to Hans van Leeuwen, Zurich, 27 April 1957.
45 Letter to Aladar Tóth, Zurich, 25 March 1957.
46 Annelien Kappeyne, Notizen, 14 May 1958.
47 *Het Parool*, 24 May 1958.
48 *Het Parool*, 18 September 1958.
49 Heyworth (ed.), *Conversations*, p. 91.
50 Heyworth (ed.), *Conversations*, p. 71.
51 Desmond Shawe-Taylor, *New Statesman and Nation*, 7 September 1957.
52 Klemperer. *Autobiographische Skizze*, p. 29; letter to Helene Hirschler, Zurich, 1 September 1957.
53 Christopher Grier, *The Scotsman*, 31 August 1957.
54 Legge/Schwarzkopf, p. 181.
55 Mosco Carner, *Evening News*, 13 November 1957.

56 Desmond Shawe-Taylor, *New Statesman and Nation*, 23 November 1957.
57 John Amis, *The Scotsman*, 18 November 1957.
58 Lotte Klemperer, letter to Louise Schwab, London, 20 November 1957.
59 Letter to Helene Hirschler, London, 17 November 1957.
60 Lotte Klemperer, letter to Louise Schwab, Zurich, 3 December 1957.
61 Walter Legge, internal EMI memo, 1 January 1958.
62 Lotte Klemperer, letter to Loli Hatvány, London, 23 November 1957.
63 Letter from Lotte Klemperer to Loli Hatvány, Vienna, 24 February 1958.
64 Heyworth (ed.), *Conversations*, p. 114.
65 *Die Presse*, 1 March 1958.
66 Lotte Klemperer, letter to Loli Hatvány, Stockholm, 17 April 1958.
67 Letter to Helene Hirschler, Stockholm, 19 April 1958.

12. Ordeal by fire

1 Lotte Klemperer, communication to the author, 3 January 1990.
2 *Express* (Vienna), 16 June 1958.
3 *Express* (Vienna), 13 June 1958.
4 Letter from David Webster, 25 November 1957.
5 Geoffrey Skelton, *Wieland Wagner*, pp. 144–5.
6 Lotte Klemperer, letter to Wieland Wagner, Zurich, 9 November 1958.
7 Lotte Klemperer, letter to Loli Hatvány, Vienna, 16 June 1958.
8 Correspondence, 1 July–3 October 1958; Israel Philharmonic archives.
9 Rolf Kienberger, letter to the author, 24 March 1986.
10 Lotte Klemperer, letter to Loli Hatvány, Zurich, 20 August 1958.
11 Peter Diamand, interview with the author, 7 September 1989.
12 Robert Ponsonby, interview with the author, 21 November 1989.
13 Clem Relf, incident recounted to John Lucas, November 1978.
14 Walter Legge, *The Gramophone*, May 1960.
15 Letter to Charlotte Naef, Zurich, 20 September 1958.
16 Lotte Klemperer, letter to Helene Hirschler, Zurich, 27 September 1958.
17 Lotte Klemperer, letter to Micha May, Zurich, 18 October 1958.
18 Lotte Klemperer, diaries and pastoral letter, Zurich, 15 October 1958.
19 Lotte Klemperer, letter to Loli Hatvány, Zurich, 21 November 1958.
20 Lotte Klemperer, pastoral letter, 31 December 1958.
21 Lotte Klemperer, pastoral letters, Zurich, 5 and 12 March 1959.
22 Lotte Klemperer, pastoral letter, Zurich, 17 March 1959.
23 Bürgerspital, Solothurn, medical papers.
24 Legge/Schwarzkopf, *On and Off the Record*, p. 183.
25 EMI internal memo, Legge/Bicknell, 7 April 1959.
26 Lotte Klemperer, pastoral letters, 23 and 29 April 1959.
27 Peter Diamand, interview with the author, 7 September 1989.
28 Lotte Klemperer, pastoral letter, Solothurn, 7 May 1959.
29 Lotte Klemperer, pastoral letter, Zurich, 21 May 1959.
30 Peter Erös, 'Otto Klemperer', *Applause*, November 1978.
31 Peter Diamand, interview with the author, 26 August 1986.
32 Lotte Klemperer, pastoral letter, The Hague, 10 June 1959.
33 Undated letter from Wieland Wagner, subsequently published in a 1959 Bayreuth Festival programme book.
34 Hans van Leeuwen, interview with the author, 4 May 1987.
35 Letter from Lotte Klemperer to Loli Hatvány, St Moritz, 24 July 1959.
36 Herbert Downes, interview with Philo Bregstein, c. 1971.
37 Lotte Klemperer, letter to Charlotte Naef, Zurich, 29 December 1958.
38 Lotte Klemperer, letter to Basil and Antoine Verkholanzeff, London, 19 October 1959.

39 Mosco Carner, *Evening News*, 27 October 1959.
40 Neville Cardus, *Manchester Guardian*, 11 November 1959.
41 Adam Bell, *Evening Standard*, 1 December 1959.
42 Letter to Werner and Susan Klemperer, Zurich, 8 December 1959.
43 Letter to Lotte Klemperer, London, 23 January 1960.
44 Hilde Firtel, Diaries and communications to the author.
45 Hilde Firtel, letter to Lotte Klemperer, 17 January 1960.
46 Information provided by Else Mayer-Lismann.
47 Letter to Lotte Klemperer, London, 26 February 1960.
48 Letter to Käthe Tannhauser, London, 8 March 1960.
49 Letter to Erich Maschat, London, 13 May 1960.
50 David Cairns (Adam Bell), *Evening Standard*, 4 May 1960.
51 Desmond Shawe-Taylor, *Sunday Times*, 15 May 1960.
52 Wieland Wagner, Bayreuth, 15 March 1960.
53 Heinrich Kralik, *Die Presse*, 1 June 1960.
54 Karl Löbl, *Express* (Vienna), 8 June 1960.
55 Lotte Klemperer, pastoral letter, St Moritz, 7 July 1960.
56 Lotte Klemperer, letter to Loli Hatvány, Zurich, 8 September 1960.
57 *Luzerner Neueste Nachrichten*, 3 September 1960.
58 Rudolf Firkušný, communication to the author, 20 August 1990.
59 Lotte Klemperer, pastoral letter, Zurich, 7 September 1960.
60 Memorandum from Michael Allen to Richard Dawes, 22 December 1960.
61 David Cairns, *The Spectator*, 21 October 1960.
62 Andrew Porter, *Financial Times*, 16 November 1960.
63 Adam Kuratin, communication to the author.
64 Walter Legge, internal EMI memo, 22 December 1960.
65 The interview was recorded on 27 November 1960 and broadcast by the BBC on 8 January 1961.
66 Lotte Klemperer, pastoral letter, London, 16 January 1961.
67 Jon Vickers, letter to the author, 27 February 1990.
68 Lotte Klemperer, letter to Antoine Verkholantzeff, London, 8 February 1961.
69 CBC interviews, uncut tapes, XIII, p. 6.
70 John Warrack, *Sunday Telegraph*, 26 February 1961.
71 Desmond Shawe-Taylor, *Sunday Times*, 26 February 1961.
72 Mosco Carner, *Time and Tide*, 2 March 1961.
73 David Cairns, *The Spectator*, 3 March 1961.
74 Letter to Aladár Tóth, London, 2 April 1961.
75 Letter to the editor, *Observer*, 16 April 1961.
76 Letter to Lotte Lehmann, London, 1 March 1961.
77 Lotte Klemperer, diary note, 18 March 1961.
78 Letter to Walter Legge, London, 28 April 1961.
79 Walter Legge, letter to Klemperer, London, 2 May 1961.
80 EMI internal memo, 26 May 1961.
81 Dietrich Fischer-Dieskau, *Nachklang*, pp. 132–3.
82 Regina Resnik, interview with the author, 8 February 198?.
83 John Amis, *The Scotsman*, 21 April 1961.
84 Letter to William Malloch, London, 6 September 1962.
85 *Volksrecht* (Zurich), 9 June 1961.
86 H. Morel, *De Linie*, 1 July 1961.
87 *The Scotsman*, 11 September 1961.
88 Lotte Klemperer, communication to the author, 31 March 1982; Eric Guignand, interview with the author, Zurich, 3 April 1989.
89 Lotte Klemperer, communications to the author, 19 January 1974 and 28 December 1986.
90 Letter to Helene Hirschler, Zurich, 4 December 1959.

91 Georg Eisler, interview with Philo Bregstein, *c.* 1972.
92 Walter Jellinek, interview with Philo Bregstein, *c.* 1971.
93 Peter Pears, interview with the author, 18 January 1984.
94 George Malcolm, interview with the author, 5 September 1990.
95 Gareth Morris, interview with the author, 8 August 1990.
96 *The Times*, 26 February 1962.
97 Letter to Oskar Kokoschka, London, 3 May 1961.
98 Lotte Klemperer, letter to Sir David Webster, Zurich, 19 May 1961.
99 Letter to Oskar Kokoschka, Zurich, 19 May 1961.
100 Legge/Schwarzkopf, p. 189.
101 Philip Hope-Wallace, *Guardian*, 5 January 1962.
102 Peter Branscombe, *Musical Times*, February 1962.
103 Desmond Shawe-Taylor, *Sunday Times*, 7 January 1962.
104 Professor Hans Landau, interview with the author, 10 May 1974.
105 David Cairns, *The Spectator*, 12 January 1962.
106 Norma Major, *Joan Sutherland*, p. 81.
107 Andrew Porter, *Financial Times*, 17 January 1962.
108 Walter Legge, EMI memo to J.D. Bicknell, 23 January 1962.
109 J.D. Bicknell, memo to Walter Legge, 31 January 1962; notes of discussion with Legge, 22 February 1962.
110 *The Times*, 5 May 1962.
111 Benjamin Britten, Aldeburgh, 4 December 1961.
112 *The Times*, 8 May 1962.
113 Albert Simon, interview with the author, Budapest, 18 October 1986.

13. Exit Legge

1 Lotte Klemperer, letter to Herbert Graf, Zurich, 3 May 1962.
2 *Tagesanzeiger*, 26 and 29 May 1962.
3 *Die Tat*, 1 June 1962.
4 *Tagesanzeiger*, 6 June 1962.
5 *Süddeutsche Zeitung*, 9 June 1962.
6 Lotte Klemperer, diary, 25 July 1962.
7 Letter to Eugene Ormandy, Zurich, 28 September 1961.
8 Letter to Arthur Judson, Zurich, 28 September 1961.
9 Memorandum, Walter Legge to J.D. Bicknell, 6 October 1961.
10 Lotte Klemperer, undated communication to the author.
11 Werner Klemperer, interview with the author, New York, December 1978.
12 Winthrop Sargeant, *New Yorker*, 3 November 1962.
13 David Cairns, *Financial Times*, 12 February 1963.
14 Letter to Sir David Webster, Zurich, 6 August 1962.
15 Royal Opera House, Covent Garden, Board minutes, 26 June 1962.
16 Letter to Lotte Klemperer, Salzburg, 11 August 1951.
17 Arianna Stassinopoulos, *Maria*, p. 105.
18 Memorandum to J.D. Bicknell, 27 March 1962.
19 Letter to Sir David Webster, London, 7 April 1962.
20 Sir David Webster, letter to Klemperer, 6 February 1963.
21 Desmond Shawe-Taylor, *Sunday Times*, 14 April 1963.
22 Martin Cooper, *Daily Telegraph*, 9 April 1963.
23 Letter to Helene Hirschler, Zurich, 3 June 1963.
24 Lotte Klemperer, pastoral letter, Zurich, 18 June 1963.
25 David Cairns, *Financial Times*, 3 December 1963.
26 Lotte Klemperer, pastoral letter, 24 December 1963.
27 Heyworth (ed.), *Conversations*, p. 90.
28 Ibid., p. 120.

29 Ibid., p. 123.
30 EMI internal memo (Legge/R. Dawes) 13 June 1963.
31 EMI internal memo (Bicknell/Legge) 20 June 1963.
32 EMI internal memos (Legge/Bicknell) 19 and 26 March 1962.
33 Suvi Raj Grubb, *Music Makers on Record*, pp. 12–13.
34 Ibid., p. 42.
35 John Culshaw, obituary, *High Fidelity/Musical America*, November 1979.
36 Grubb, *Music Makers on Record*, p. 42.
37 EMI internal memo (Peter Andry/David Bicknell) 20 November 1963.
38 David Bicknell, letter to Lotte Klemperer, Hayes, 10 February 1964.
39 Lotte Klemperer, letter to David Bicknell, London, 19 February 1964. EMI minutes, meeting, 26 February 1964.
40 Gareth Morris, interview with the author, Bristol, 6 August 1990.
41 Heyworth (ed.), *Conversations*, p. 106.
42 *The Times*, 24 March 1964.
43 Pettitt, *Philharmonia*, p. 128.
44 Lotte Klemperer, letter to the author, Zurich, 29 June 1964.
45 Suvi Raj Grubb, interview with the author, London, 1 December 1990.
46 Dr H. Storjohann (Electrola), letter to Legge, Cologne, 11 March 1964.
47 Walter Legge, letter to Dr H. Storjohann, London, 18 March 1964.
48 Suvi Raj Grubb, interview with the author, London, 1 December 1990.
49 Lotte Klemperer, communications to the author, 26 July 1982 and 6 October 1990; also interview in BBC TV's Omnibus programme, May 1985.
50 Telegram to Peter Andry, London, 28 March 1964.
51 Walter Legge, telegram to Klemperer, London, 29 March 1964.
52 John Amis, letter to the author, 14 August 1979.
53 Letter to Aladár Tóth, Zurich, 8 December 1966.
54 Streseman, ... *und Abends in der Philharmonie*, pp. 101–2; interview with the author, Berlin, 3 April 1988.
55 Laurence Taylor, letter to his parents, London, 18 October 1964.
56 Peter Beavan, *Klempererisms*, p. 6.
57 Andrew Porter, *Financial Times*, 4 February 1965.
58 Desmond Shawe-Taylor, *Sunday Times*, 7 February 1965.
59 Letter to Helene Hirschler, Zurich, 13 February 1965.
60 Lotte Klemperer, diary, 20 March 1965.
61 Lotte Klemperer, memo, 26 March 1965.
62 Letter to Helene Hirschler, Zurich, 24 July 1965.
63 Letter to Fritz Fischer, London, 31 January 1966.
64 Letter to Erik Maschat, Zurich, 20 May 1966.
65 Eigel Kruttge, communication with the author, 20 November 1973.
66 Heinz Joachim, *Die Welt*, 5 May 1966.
67 Letter to Anna Lippmann, Zurich, 17 January 1966.
68 Lotte Klemperer, letter to Erik Maschat, Berlin, 10 May 1966.
69 Letter to Eigel Kruttge, Zurich, 20 May 1966.
70 Lotte Klemperer, Diary, 16 July 1966.
71 Lotte Klemperer, letter to Abe Cohen, Zurich, 9 February 1961; Abe Cohen, letter to Lotte Klemperer, Tel Aviv, 24 March 1961.
72 Wolfgang Lewy, letter to Lotte Klemperer, Tel Aviv, 4 August 1966.
73 Lotte Klemperer, diary, 14–22 July 1966.
74 Lotte Klemperer, letter to Loli Hatvány, Zurich, 25 November 1966.
75 Lotte Klemperer, diary, 25 September 1964.
76 Lotte Klemperer, diary, 20 September 1964.
77 Lotte Klemperer, communication to the author, 19 August 1987.
78 Letter to Werner Klemperer, London, 27 February 1967.
79 Soma Morgenstern, letter to Klemperer, New York, 21 April 1967.

14. The shadows lengthen

1. Electrola (Storjohann/ICRC), Cologne, 12 December 1966.
2. EMI internal memo, Michael Allen to L.G. Wood, 23 January 1967.
3. Laurence Taylor, letter to his parents, London, 7 March 1967.
4. Lotte Klemperer, communications to Stephen J. Pettitt, 21 August 1986, and to the author, 4 March 1987.
5. Peter Andry, memorandum to J.D. Bicknell, 5 April 1967.
6. Peter Beavan, *Klempererisms*, pp. 9–10.
7. Grubb, *Music Makers on Record*, p. 76.
8. Lord Harewood, programme of Klemperer commemorative concert, Royal Albert Hall, 14 January 1974.
9. Lotte Klemperer, letter to Karola Bloch, London, 7 March 1967.
10. Lotte Klemperer, letter to Loli Hatvány, London, 1 April 1967.
11. Lotte Klemperer, communication to the author, 10 July 1985.
12. Klemperer, letter to Hans Pischner, Zurich, 27 April 1967.
13. P.V. de Jongh, letter to David Bicknell, 3 May 1967.
14. George Stringer, interview with the author, 4 June 1991.
15. Lotte Klemperer, letter to Gareth Morris, Zurich, 27 April 1967.
16. Helmuth Plessner, interview with the author, January 1974.
17. Interview with Philo Bregstein (II, pp. 9–10), 1971.
18. Deutsche Staatsoper, internal memo, 2 May 1967.
19. Hans Pischner, letter to Klemperer, Berlin, 25 May 1967.
20. Letter to Paul Dessau, Zurich, 2 July 1967.
21. Letter to Paul Dessau, Zurich, 25 July 1967.
22. *New York Times*, 26 August 1968.
23. Lotte Klemperer, diary, 4 July 1967.
24. Erwin Jacobi, interview with the author, 23 November 1972.
25. Letter to Peter Diamand, Zurich, 3 August 1967.
26. Letter to Peter Andry, Zurich, 2 August 1967.
27. Louis Metz, *Over dirigieren*, pp. 141–3.
28. Letter to Jan Bresser, Zurich, 16 January 1967.
29. Letter to Fritz Fischer, London, 8 November 1964.
30. Lotte Klemperer, diary, 22 August 1966.
31. Anderson (ed.), *Klemperer On Music*, p. 97.
32. Peter Andry, Klemperer's B minor Mass, *The Gramophone*, April 1968.
33. Eigel Kruttge, letter to Heinrich Knabben, Bonn, 18 December 1967.
34. Letter to Anna Lippmann, Zurich, 22 November 1967.
35. William Mann, *The Times*, 20 March 1968.
36. The author, *Observer*, 24 March 1968.
37. Letter to Paul Dessau, London, 23 February 1969.
38. Lotte Klemperer, diary, 7 April 1968.
39. *Express* (Vienna), 10 June 1968; *Kleine Zeitung*, 15 June 1968.
40. V.A. Yuzeovich, *Conversations with Igor Oistrakh*, p. 237.
41. Lotte Klemperer, diary, 21 May 1968, and undated memo to the author.
42. Gareth Morris, letter to Lotte Klemperer, London, 30 March 1968.
43. Letter to Gareth Morris, London, 1 April 1968.
44. *Neue Zürcher Zeitung*, 27 November 1969.
45. EMI internal memos, 17 and 30 October 1969.
46. Letter to Max Hofmüller, Zurich, 16 October 1969.
47. Heyworth (ed.), *Conversations*, p. 99.

15. The final years

1. Neville Cardus, *Guardian*, 2 September 1968.

2 Karl-Heinz Wocker, *Neue Zeitschrift für Musik*, October 1968.
3 Willi Schuh, *Neue Zürcher Zeitung*, 10 September 1968.
4 Michael Allen (EMI) in conversation with Peter Heyworth, 8 March 1991.
5 EMI internal memo (Smith/Bicknell), 19 August 1968.
6 EMI internal memos (Andry/Bicknell), 24 July 1968; (Whittle/Andry), 31 July 1968; (Whittle/Allen), 21 August 1968.
7 Letter from Robert E. Myers to Michael Allen, Hollywood, 1 October 1968.
8 Klemperer, *Minor Recollections*, p. 19.
9 Noel Goodwin, *Daily Express*, 23 January 1969.
10 Grubb, *Music Makers on Record*, p. 93.
11 Sir Donald McIntyre, conversation with John Lucas, 1992.
12 Richard Armstrong, conversation with John Lucas, 5 May 1994.
13 Interview with Alan Blyth, *The Gramophone*, May 1970.
14 Letter to Ira Hirschmann, London, 15 March 1969.
15 EMI internal memo (Grubb/Bicknell), 9 May 1969.
16 EMI internal memo (Whittle/Locantro), 13 May 1969.
17 Hilde Viertel, diary, 28 May 1969.
18 Erich Mauermann, conversation with Peter Heyworth, Munich, 7 May 1990.
19 Letter to Helene Hirschler, Zurich, 15 June 1969.
20 Lotte Klemperer, interviews with Philo Bregstein, III/5, Zurich.
21 Letter to Anna Freud, Zurich, 12 November 1969.
22 EMI internal memo (Locantro/Andry), 31 March 1969.
23 *Financial Times*, 30 October 1969.
24 *Daily Telegraph*, 4 February 1970.
25 *Sunday Times*, 8 February 1970.
26 EMI internal memo (Grubb/Andry), 26 March 1970.
27 EMI internal memo (Andry/Grubb), 3 April 1970.
28 Letter to Peter Andry, London, 29 May 1970.
29 Memorandum in Philharmonia Orchestra's archives, 9 July 1970.
30 EMI internal memos (Andry/Wood), 15 July 1970; (Wood/Andry), 15 July 1970; (Andry/Wood), 17 July 1970.
31 Letter to Peter Andry, Zurich, 17 July 1970.
32 Letter to Soma Morgenstern, Zurich, 23 April 1970.
33 *Sunday Telegraph*, 17 May 1970.
34 Gareth Morris, communication to Peter Heyworth, 3 May 1991.
35 Jacqueline Bensard, interview with Peter Heyworth, 28 April 1975.
36 David Pickett, interview with Peter Heyworth, 19 August 1986.
37 Henry Pleasants, *International Herald-Tribune*, 7 July 1970.
38 *Neue Zürcher Zeitung*, 1 August 1970.
39 Heyworth (ed.), *Conversations*, p. 124.
40 Interview with Alan Blyth, *The Gramophone*, May 1970.
41 The original copy of the note, signed and dated May 1970, is in the Philharmonia Orchestra's archives.
42 Letter from Gerald McDonald to Hans Ulrich Schmid, London, 10 March 1970.
43 Werner Oehlmann, *Berliner Tagesspiegel*, 29 September 1970.
44 Gerald McDonald, NPO internal memo, 22 October 1970.
45 Lotte Klemperer, letter to Peter Andry, Zurich, 24 July 1970.
46 EMI internal memo (Allen/Andry), 21 July 1970.
47 Lotte Klemperer, letter to Gerald McDonald, Zurich, 13 August 1970.
48 EMI internal memo (Grubb/Andry), 19 November 1970.
49 Lotte Klemperer, diary, 12 November 1970.
50 Gerald McDonald, memo to New Philharmonia Council, 22 October 1970.
51 Letters, Michal Smoira-Cohn to Lotte Klemperer, Jerusalem, 1 February and 31 March 1971; Lotte Klemperer to Michal Smoira-Cohn, Zurich, 24 March and 7 April 1971.

52 Johanan Boehm, *Jerusalem Post*, 2 and 6 August 1971.
53 Lotte Klemperer, diary, 23 June 1971.
54 Lotte Klemperer, précis of her diary, June–September 1971.
55 Lotte Klemperer, diary, 20 September 1971.
56 Joan Chissell, *The Times*, 27 September 1971.
57 EMI internal memo (Andry/Wood), 16 November 1971.
58 Lotte Klemperer, diary, 16 January 1972.
59 Lotte Klemperer, diary, 28 April 1972.
60 Letter to Peter Heyworth, Zurich, 11 May 1972.
61 Diana Chapman (EMI), letter to Lotte Klemperer, London, 5 June 1972.
62 Lotte Klemperer, letter to Werner Klemperer, Zurich, 10 July 1972.
63 Diana Chapman, letter to David Richard (NPO), London, 12 September 1972.
64 Letter to Gerald McDonald, Zurich, 1 December 1972.
65 Lotte Klemperer, letter to Gerald McDonald, 4 May 1973.

BIOGRAPHICAL GLOSSARY

Maurice Abravanel (1903–94). Conductor, composition pupil and friend of Kurt Weill. Abravanel conducted the first performance of *Die sieben Todsünden* (Paris, 1933) and the premières of most of Weill's American musicals. Conductor of the Utah Symphony Orchestra, 1947–79.

Peter Andry (b. 1927). Joined EMI in 1956 and three years later became commercial manager of its International Classical Recording Committee. Further promotions within the company led to his becoming president of EMI's International Classical Division. In 1989 Andry joined Warner Music International as senior vice-president, Warner Classics, with responsibility for the Teldec, Erato and Nonesuch labels.

Ernest Ansermet (1883–1969). Swiss conductor who in 1918 founded the Suisse Romande Orchestra, which he continued to conduct until 1966. Closely associated with Stravinsky during the composer's neo-classical period and conducted a number of premières, notably of *L'Histoire du soldat* and *Pulcinella*. Also championed the music of Bartók, Honegger, Martin and Britten, among others.

Richard Austin (1903–89). Conductor of the Carl Rosa Opera Company (1929–31) and the Bournemouth Municipal Orchestra (1934–40). Director of the New Era Concert Society (1948–58).

Sol Babitz (1911–82). American violinist and musicologist. Flesch pupil. After four years in the Los Angeles Philharmonia (1933–7), Babitz played mainly in film studio orchestras. In 1948 he founded the Early Music Laboratory to promote 'historical accuracy in performance' (*New Grove*). He also edited Stravinsky's string parts for a number of years.

John Barbirolli (1899–1970). British conductor whose career was largely in opera until he was appointed sole conductor of the New York Philharmonic Orchestra in 1937, a post he held until 1942. From 1943 until his death he was conductor of Manchester's Hallé Orchestra.

Ruth Berghaus (b. 1927). German producer and wife of Paul Dessau. In 1971 she succeeded Brecht's widow, Helene Weigel, as Intendant of the Berliner Ensemble, a position she held until 1977. Since then she has devoted herself largely to opera production.

Gertrud Bing (1892–1964). One of Klemperer's oldest friends, who in 1922 joined Aby Warburg's celebrated Hamburg Institute, where she was professor of the history of the classical tradition. In 1934 she moved with the Institute to London, where she became its director (1955–9). After her death Klemperer described her as a person 'I could talk to about everything' (*Gertrud Bing*, The Warburg Institute, 1965).

Marc Blitzstein (1905–64). American composer who, after studying with both Nadia Boulanger and Schoenberg, came under the influence of Hanns Eisler and developed a form of left-wing music theatre.

Ernst Bloch (1885–1977). Not to be confused with the composer, *Ernest* Bloch, he was one of the most idiosyncratic Marxist thinkers of his time. After emigrating to America after 1933, Bloch returned in 1948 to what was still the Soviet Zone of occupied Germany, where he was appointed professor of philosophy in Leipzig. In

1961 he moved to West Germany, where he held a guest professorship at Tübingen for the remainder of his life. Bloch was one of Klemperer's few close friends and on Klemperer's death delivered at the age of eighty-eight a lengthy extempore eulogy on German television. He was a versatile essayist and a knowledgeable music lover.

Mark Brunswick (1902–71). May have been introduced to Klemperer by their mutual friend Roger Sessions. Though he studied with Ernest Bloch and Nadia Boulanger, Brunswick's small musical output has left little lasting impression. Married to Ruth Mack, an American psychiatrist who had undergone a training analysis with Freud and become one of his favourite pupils, he was friendly with Webern among a number of other Viennese composers. The wealthy Brunswicks' substantial villa in the fashionable 'Cottage' district on the edge of the Wienerwald provided a meeting place for the city's musical and intellectual circles.

Richard Buhlig (1880–1952). Pupil, alongside his friend Schnabel, of Leschetitsky. Studied in Berlin (1901–5), where he got to know Busoni, who dedicated to him the 1912 edition of his *Fantasia Contrappuntistica*. In 1912 he gave the first performance in London of Schoenberg's Three Piano Pieces, Op. 11. After settling in southern California, Buhlig confined his activities to lecture recitals, in which he coupled Bach with modern composers, such as Hindemith, Krenek, Chavez and Cowell. He explained his disenchantment with the life of a keyboard virtuoso in an (unpublished) article, 'The Decline of the Concert, with some references to cookery'. Buhlig also taught John Cage the piano. (Nancy Wolbert, 'Richard Buhlig', thesis, Californian State University, Long Beach, 1978.)

Adolf Busch (1891–1952). Noted German-born violinist, who before 1933 on several occasions appeared with Klemperer as soloist and in 1939 emigrated to America. As the founder of the Marlboro School of Music in 1950, two years before his death, Busch did much to instigate the subsequent flowering of string quartet playing in the USA.

Elizabeth Sprague Coolidge (1864–1953). Established the Berkshire Festivals of Music and commissioned works from, among others, Bartók, Prokofiev, Schoenberg, Stravinsky and Webern. Financed the cycle of Schoenberg's string quartets, including the first performance of the Fourth, which the Kolisch Quartet gave at UCLA in 1937.

Robert Craft (b. 1923). American conductor, writer and close friend of Stravinsky in the last two decades of his life, during which period he exercised far-reaching influence on the composer, notably by opening his mind to the possibilities of twelve-note technique.

Ingolf Dahl (1912–70). German-born (of Swedish parentage) conductor and composer, who had settled in Los Angeles in 1939. Member of the music faculty of the University of Southern California, 1945–70.

William Dieterle (1893–1972). German-born director, who in 1931 moved to Hollywood, where he made films such as *Zola* and *Louis Pasteur*, with Paul Muni in the title-roles. He co-directed Reinhardt's film version of *A Midsummer Night's Dream*.

Walther Felsenstein (1901–75). Intendant of the Komische Oper. Under his leadership the house became celebrated for a style of production that was to have widespread influence and owed much to Stanislavski's naturalism. Felsenstein himself termed it 'realistic music theatre'. His assistants included Götz Friedrich and Joachim Herz.

Annie Fischer (1914–95). Hungarian pianist, renowned for her interpretative penetration and prowess. Frequently performed with Klemperer, with whom she also recorded.

Otto Freudenthal (b. 1934). Swedish composer, pianist and teacher. Met Klemperer for the first time in February 1960 when the conductor heard him playing chamber music in London. Two months later Klemperer turned up unannounced at a piano recital that Freudenthal was giving in Zurich. Freudenthal was invited to lunch the following day and from then on, until Klemperer's death in 1973, acted as his assistant.

Ferenc Fricsay (1914–63). From 1945 musical director of the Budapest Opera and the Budapest Philharmonic Orchestra. His appearance at Salzburg to conduct *Dantons Tod* made his international reputation. In 1948 he was appointed musical director of the Städtische Oper and the RIAS Orchestra in Berlin, where he mainly worked until his premature death.

Wilhelm Furtwängler (1886–1954). By 1920 Furtwängler had emerged in the front rank of German conductors as director of the concerts of Berlin Staatskapelle. Two years later he was appointed conductor of both the Gewandhaus Orchestra and the Berlin Philharmonic Orchestra. In 1925 he made his transatlantic début with the New York Philharmonic Orchestra and in 1936 was invited to succeed Toscanini as its permanent conductor. By this time, however, he had become involved in political issues and, in spite of the fact that he had defended Hindemith's music and colleagues such as Walter and Klemperer, he withdrew after a storm of protest. The Allies forbade him to conduct in Germany after the war and he did not resume his activities until May 1947. His last years continued to be clouded by controversy over the equivocal role he had played in the Third Reich.

Alexander Vasil′yevich Gauk (1893–1963). Ukrainian conductor and composer. Conductor of the Leningrad Opera (1923–31), Leningrad Philharmonic Orchestra (1930–4), the USSR State Symphony Orchestra (1936–41) and the All-Union Radio Symphony Orchestra (1953–63).

Sir William Glock (b. 1908). After studying with Schnabel in Berlin, where he regularly attended Klemperer's concerts, Glock at first pursued careers as a pianist, critic (*The Observer*, 1934–45) and administrator (he ran the celebrated Bryanston, later Dartington, Summer School, 1948–79). As Controller of Music at the BBC (1959–72) he brought about far-reaching reforms in programme planning, notably in the field of contemporary music.

Herbert Graf (1904–73). Austrian-born, later American producer, who worked for many years at the New York Met. Director of the Zurich Stadttheater (1960–3) and the Grand Théâtre, Geneva (1965–72).

Dietrich von Hildebrand (1889–1977). Professor of philosophy at Munich University. After 1933 he obtained a chair at Vienna, where he became a champion of a Catholic and independent Austria. After the *Anschluss* he moved to America. Hildebrand was a son-in-law of the composer Walter Braunfels.

Hans Hinkel (1901–60). In 1930 he was a member of the Reichstag, and active in Rosenberg's Kampfbund für deutsche Kultur. In 1933 he became Commissioner in the Prussian Ministry of Education and the Arts, and 'Leiter der Abteilung für besondere Kulturaufgaben' ('head of the department for special cultural tasks') in Goebbels's Propaganda Ministry, in which capacity he exercised supervision over Jews active in intellectual or cultural life. From 1943, SS Gruppenführer on Himmler's staff. In the *Frankfurter Zeitung* of 27 August 1935 Hinkel was reported as expressing his sense of outrage that 'Christian churches actually exist in Germany ... where the organ has for years been played by Jews ...'

Helene Hirschler (1888–1977). One of Klemperer's oldest friends, having first met him in 1909. A practising doctor, in 1914 she married another, Max Hirschler, who was a school friend of the German philosopher Ernst Bloch (q.v.). The Hirschlers emigrated to the United States in 1938 and settled in Maine. Klemperer's letters to Helene Hirschler are particularly numerous during and after the Second World War.

Ira A. Hirschmann (1901–89). United States business executive, philanthropist and author. Vice-president, Saks Fifth Avenue, 1935–8; vice-president, Bloomingdale Bros., 1938–46. Co-founder and chairman of the board of the University in Exile

BIOGRAPHICAL GLOSSARY

(New School of Social Research, New York), 1933. Founder and president, New Friends of Music, 1936. Special Inspector-General, UNRRA, 1946.

Bronislaw Huberman (1882–1947). Polish violinist, who, together with William Steinberg, established the Palestine Symphony Orchestra, later the Israel Philharmonic.

Theodore Innitzer (1875–1955). From 1932 Archbishop of Vienna. After the *Anschluss* of 1938 Innitzer was for a short period sympathetic to the Nazis. Thereafter he opposed them.

Erwin Jacobi (1909–78). After study in Israel and the United States, where he was a pupil of Wanda Landowska (harpsichord), Hindemith (composition) and Curt Sachs (musicology), he received a doctorate from Zurich University (whose music faculty he joined in 1961) for a dissertation on the development of musical theory in Britain after the death of Rameau. Jacobi's speciality lay in the field of baroque music.

Alvin Johnson (1874–1951). The son of a Danish immigrant, he had studied at Heidelberg under the eminent sociologist Max Weber and preserved close ties with European intellectual life. He was appointed director of the New School of Social Research in 1923.

Carlos Kleiber (b. 1930). Son of Erich Kleiber and perhaps the outstanding conductor of his generation, in spite of the narrowness of his repertory and the infrequency of his appearances. In 1964–6 Kleiber was on the staff of the Zurich Opera House.

Rudolf Kolisch (1896–1978). Violinist and leader of the celebrated string quartet that bore his name. Brother-in-law of Schoenberg.

Erich Wolfgang Korngold (1897–1957). Austrian-born composer, son of Julius Korngold, principal critic of the *Neue Freie Presse* (Vienna). At the age of ten was pronounced a talent by Mahler, who recommended that he studied composition with Zemlinsky. His other operas included *Violanta* and *Der Ring des Polykrates*. In 1934 Max Reinhardt invited him to Hollywood, where he composed scores for *Sea Hawk*, *The Adventures of Robin Hood* etc. Klemperer conducted the first European performance of his Violin Concerto in Vienna in 1947.

Julius Korngold (1860–1945). Hanslick's successor as music critic of the leading Viennese newspaper. Father of the composer Erich Wolfgang Korngold.

Clemens Krauss (1893–1954). Austrian conductor. Appointed Intendant of the Frankfurt City Opera in 1928 at the early age of thirty-five, Krauss became director of the Vienna State Opera in 1929. In 1935 he moved to Berlin, taking with him several leading members of the Vienna ensemble, a step that cost him the directorship of the Vienna State Opera after the war. From 1937 to 1945 Krauss was Intendant of the Bavarian State Opera in Munich, where a friendship ripened with Strauss, for whom Krauss wrote the libretti of his final operas, *Capriccio* and *Die Liebe der Danae*. Krauss was an outstanding interpreter of Strauss's music.

Walter Legge (1906–79). Joined His Master's Voice (a part of the Gramophone Company, subsequently EMI) in 1926 in a modest capacity. From writing publicity material he graduated to recording. He made his name with the Hugo Wolf Society albums and began to supervise Thomas Beecham's recordings. In 1938 he became assistant to Beecham at Covent Garden, where he was put in charge of casting. In the immediate post-war years Legge engaged for EMI a notable roster of Central European artists, including Herbert von Karajan and Elisabeth Schwarzkopf, whom he married in 1953. In 1945 Legge founded the Philharmonia Orchestra, which was followed by the Philharmonia Chorus in 1957, with Wilhelm Pitz as chorus master. In 1964 Legge retired and, in a manner that brought much criticism on his head, announced that he was dissolving his orchestra. It survived as the New Philharmonia Orchestra, however.

Richard Lert (1885–1980). Austrian-born, subsequently American, conductor, with whom Klemperer had in July 1914 planned a series of popular performances of

Der Ring des Nibelungen in Berlin. The plan was abandoned when the Hofkapelle (the orchestra of the Berlin Court Opera) proved to be unavailable. Lert was married to the well-known novelist Vicki Baum.

Oscar Levant (1906–72). Known for what *Baker's Biographical Dictionary of Musicians* describes as his 'authentic' performance of Gershwin's *Rhapsody in Blue* and Piano Concerto in F, also composed music of 'considerable complexity'. His lively volumes of reminiscences, *A Smattering of Ignorance* and *The Memoirs of an Amnesiac*, contain a number of anecdotes about Klemperer, some of them apocryphal.

Rolf Liebermann (b. 1910). Composer, musical administrator and opera director. Intendant, Hamburg State Opera (1959–73), a period that marked the height of its post-war reputation; director of the Paris Opéra (1973–80).

Sir Joseph Lockwood (1904–91). Chairman, EMI Ltd (1954–74). Chairman, the Royal Ballet (1971–85). Member of the Arts Council of Great Britain (1967–70) and of the boards of numerous cultural institutions.

György Lukács (1885–1971). Leading Marxist philosopher, who in 1919 had served as Commissar for Education in Béla Kun's short-lived regime. During the uprising of 1956 he occupied a similar position in Imre Nagy's (also short-lived) government. A close friend of Ernst Bloch since their student days.

Alma Mahler (1879–1964) née Schindler. When Mahler in 1901 met and fell in love with this talented daughter of the Austrian landscape painter E.J. Schindler, she was studying composition with Alexander von Zemlinsky. They married in the following year. After Mahler's death, Alma remarried, first the architect Walter Gropius and subsequently the Czech expressionist writer Franz Werfel.

Tamás Major (1910–86). Actor, producer and director of the National Theatre in Budapest (1945–52). As a member of the Central Committee of the Hungarian Socialist Workers' (Communist) party (1957–66), Major was for over twenty years a powerful and latterly much criticised figure in the country's theatrical life.

Joseph Marx (1882–1964). Late romantic composer, best remembered for his many songs. Principal critic of the *Neues Wiener Journal*.

Heinrich Neuhaus (Gennikh Neygauz) (1888–1964). Celebrated pianist and pedagogue, who numbered Sviatoslav Richter and Emil Gilels among his pupils. In 1936 Neuhaus was rector of the Moscow Conservatory. According to Yudin, Neuhaus insisted that all members of its conducting class should attend Klemperer's rehearsals.

Ferdinand Onno-Wolschek (1879–?19). Started his career under Reinhardt in Berlin. In 1906 he was engaged by the Landestheater in Prague, and in 1930 joined the Vienna Burgtheater.

Eugene Ormandy (1899–1985). American conductor of Hungarian birth. Minneapolis Orchestra 1931–6. Continued until 1980 as conductor of the Philadelphia Orchestra. His performances were more notable for their technical finish than for their interpretative insights.

Hans Pischner (b. 1914). German musicologist and harpsichordist. Director of the music department of the East German Ministry of Culture (1954–6), Deputy Minister of Culture (1956–62). Intendant of the Deutsche Staatsoper, Berlin (1963–89).

Wilhelm Pitz (1897–1973). German chorusmaster and conductor. At the Aachen Opera he had in the thirties worked under Karajan, who in 1951 recommended him to Bayreuth, where he remained chorusmaster until shortly before his death. Chorusmaster of the Philharmonia Chorus, 1957–71.

Rudolf Réti (1885–1957). Critic, analyst and pianist, who in 1911 gave the first performance of Schoenberg's Three Piano Pieces, Op. 11, and was one of the founders of the International Society for Contemporary Music in 1923.

József Révai (1898–1959). Avant-garde expressionist poet, who in 1918 became a founding member of the Hungarian Communist party. In 1944 he returned to

Hungary in the wake of the Red Army as No. 3 in the party hierarchy, and in the following year became editor in chief of *Szabad Nép*, the official party organ, in which position he played an increasingly crucial role in cultural life. In 1950 Révai was appointed deputy secretary-general of the party and thus in effect Mátyás Rákosi's deputy. At the second party congress in 1951 he attacked Bartók's music as containing elements 'alien to the people'. On Rákosi's fall, he was denounced as 'a Jewish leftist adventurer' and on 20 July 1953 lost both his membership of the Politbüro and his ministerial post. During the uprising of 1956, he escaped to the Soviet Union.

Artur Rodzinski (1892–1958). American conductor of Polish descent. After a period as Stokowski's assistant in Philadelphia, Rodzinski was appointed conductor in Los Angeles in 1929. After four years in Cleveland, he was engaged at Toscanini's request in 1937 to form and train the National Broadcasting Company's new orchestra. From 1942–7 he was conductor of the New York Philharmonic-Symphony Orchestra.

Arnold Rosé (1863–1946). Austrian violinist. Leader of the Vienna Court (later State) Opera Orchestra from 1881 until 1938, when he emigrated to London. Founder of the celebrated Rosé Quartet, which gave first performances of works ranging from Brahms to Schoenberg. Rosé was a close collaborator of Mahler (whose sister, Justine, he married) during the latter's decade as director of the Vienna Opera.

Thomas K. Scherman (1917–79). American conductor, who in 1947 set up in New York the Little Orchestral Society, which for almost thirty years presented much new and little-known music.

Karl Schmid-Bloss (1884–1956). Celebrated bass, who, after singing at the Zurich City Theatre from 1919 until 1932, became its director, a position he occupied until his death. During his regime the first performances of Berg's *Lulu* and Hindemith's *Mathis der Maler* were staged in Zurich. In each case Schmid-Bloss produced.

Elisabeth Schumann (1888–1952) joined the Hamburg company in 1901 and remained there until 1919, when at Strauss's request she joined the Vienna State Opera. She continued to sing there until the *Anschluss*, after which she lived in New York until her death.

Roger Sessions (1896–1985). Leading US composer. At first strongly influenced by his teacher, Ernest Bloch, he later adopted a serial style of composition. The winner of two consecutive Guggenheim fellowships, he lived mostly in Europe from 1926 to 1933. On returning to the United States, he took up a series of important teaching posts, including Boston University (1933–5), Princeton University (1935–45 and 1953–65) and Harvard University (1968–9).

Peter Stadlen (b. 1910). Austrian, subsequently British, pianist and critic. Gave the first performance of Webern's Variations for Piano, Op. 27, in Vienna in 1937.

Wolfgang Stresemann (b. 1904). Son of Gustav Stresemann, Chancellor and Foreign Minister during the Weimar Republic. Assistant conductor of the National Orchestral Association, New York, 1939–45, and conductor of the Toledo Orchestra of Ohio, 1949–55. After the war Stresemann returned to Berlin, where he served two terms as Intendant of the Berlin Philharmonic Orchestra, 1959–78 and 1984–86.

Heinrich Strobel (1898–1970). As music critic of the *Berliner Börsen Courier* Strobel had prior to 1933 been a champion of Hindemith, of whose music he had published a study as early as 1928. Although employed in France on cultural tasks by the German occupation authorities during the war, Strobel, who had earlier fled to Paris with his Jewish wife, had won the confidence of French musical circles (his biography of Debussy was published in Paris in 1943). He later jettisoned his Hindemithian allegiance and became an equally dogmatic champion of the post-war avant-garde, notably of Boulez, who came to live in Baden-Baden in 1959. As director of the Donaueschingen Festival Strobel was responsible for many important premières. In 1946 he became editor of the reconstituted periodical

Melos. More than any other single man, Strobel was responsible for the avant-gardism that dominated post-war German musical life.

Ernst Toch (1887–1964). Austrian, later American, composer, who first emigrated to England, where he wrote film scores for Alexander Korda. Klemperer conducted his Cello Concerto in Berlin in 1931. In Los Angeles he performed his Music for Baritone and Orchestra (23 September 1936), the overture, *Pinocchio* (10 December 1936) and a suite, *The Idle Stroller* (20 April 1939). In 1951 he conducted his Symphony No. 1 in Amsterdam.

Arturo Toscanini (1867–1957). Italian conductor. Music director of the Teatro alla Scala, Milan (1898–1903) and of the New York Metropolitan Opera House (1908–15). Artistic director of the Scala (1920–9), conductor of the New York Philharmonic-Symphony Orchestra (1928–36) and of the NBC Orchestra (1937–54).

Aladár Tóth (1908–68). Leading Hungarian music critic. In 1937 he married the pianist Annie Fischer (q.v.), with whom he emigrated to Sweden in 1940. On returning to Hungary after the Second World War, he became director of the Budapest State Opera (1946–56).

V.I. Vaynonen (1901–64). Dancer and choreographer at the Kirov (Leningrad) Opera until 1938, thereafter at the Bolshoi. His outstanding achievement is considered to have been his choreography for Asaf'yev's *The Flames of Paris* (1932), which he also staged in Budapest in 1950. In this work 'the people is for the first time the principal hero' (*Ballet Encyclopedia*, ed. Yu. N. Grigorovich, Moscow, 1951). Vaynonen's disapproval of the explicit sexuality of *The Miraculous Mandarin* led to its withdrawal from the repertory a month after his arrival in Budapest.

Salka Viertel (1891–1978). Bridged the worlds of music, film and theatre. The sister of Eduard Steuermann and aunt of the conductor Michael Gielen, she came of a musical Galician family. As the writer of scenarios for some of Garbo's most celebrated films, she was one of the Swedish star's few intimates. Herself originally an actress, she was married to the Austrian producer, dramatist and poet Berthold Viertel (1885–1953), the original of the memorable central character in Christopher Isherwood's *Prater Violet*. Her autobiography, *The Kindness of Strangers*, gives a vivid picture of life in Los Angeles during the years that Klemperer spent there.

Wieland Wagner (1917–66). Elder son of Siegfried and grandson of Richard Wagner, producer and stage designer, who was the artistic director of the Bayreuth Festival from its post-war reopening in 1951 until his death. His largely abstract and symbolic productions were strongly influenced by Appia and marked a complete break with the naturalism that had previously prevailed at Bayreuth.

Alfred Wallenstein (1898–1983). Started his career as a cellist with the Los Angeles Orchestra and subsequently became first cellist of the New York Philharmonic under Toscanini. Musical director in Los Angeles 1943–56.

Bruno Walter (1876–1962). Walter's international career flowered in the early twenties when he became a popular and highly esteemed visitor to New York, London and Paris. In 1925 he became a notably successful music director of the Berlin Städtische Oper and began a close association with the Salzburg Festival that lasted until the *Anschluss* of 1938. In 1929 he succeeded Furtwängler as conductor of the Gewandhaus concerts in Leipzig, while in Berlin he also established an annual series of concerts that bore his own name and formed a counterpart to those conducted by Furtwängler and Klemperer. On leaving Germany in 1933 he held positions with the Amsterdam Concertgebouw Orchestra and the Vienna State Opera. In 1939 he settled in America where he conducted regularly at the New York Metropolitan Opera between 1941 and 1957, as well as acting as musical adviser to the New York Philharmonic Orchestra from 1947 to 1949.

BIOGRAPHICAL GLOSSARY

Sir David Webster (1903–71). In the course of a commercial career, became chairman of the Liverpool Philharmonic Society (1940–5). General administrator of the Covent Garden Trust (1945–70), which established the Royal Opera House as a state-subsidised theatre.

Franz Werfel (1890–1945). Prague-born expressionist poet and novelist, who married Mahler's widow in 1929. Best known outside Central Europe for his novel *The Song of Bernadette* (1941).

DISCOGRAPHY: THE RECORDINGS OF OTTO KLEMPERER

By Michael H. Gray

Introduction

This discography of Otto Klemperer's gramophone recordings has been divided into two parts. Recordings made for Polydor/Deutsche Grammophon, Parlophone and His Master's Voice were included in the first volume of this biography; those made for American VOX, the Hungaroton label and for EMI appear in this volume. Recordings from concerts and broadcasts, if issued commercially, have also been included in this discography (prefixed L). Those made for the conductor's personal use, or those he did not pass for issue or which he left incomplete, however, have been omitted. References to them may be found in Stephen J. Pettit's *Philharmonia Orchestra: Complete Discography 1945–1987*, published by John Hunt in 1987.

An index to composers and their works and to key performers is provided in this volume.

Acknowledgements

A full list of acknowledgements for this discography appears in Volume I of this biography. In the intervening years since that list was compiled, Ruth Edge of the EMI Archives contributed immeasurably to the refinement and correction of this section. John Lucas also reviewed and corrected the draft of this section. Kjell Moseng contributed valuable information on an obscure Danish LP issue. Any errors or omissions, however, remain my own.

Abbreviations used in Part Two

Record Labels	Ang.	Angel (applies to all countries using this trademark)
	Col.	Columbia
	Elec.	Electrola (Germany)
	Poly.	Polydor (all countries)
Countries	Arg.	Argentina
	Aust.	Australia
	Ger.	Germany
	Eng.	United Kingdom
	It.	Italy
	Neth.	Netherlands
	Russ.	USSR
	US	United States

Roman numerals in entries for symphonies and concertos signify movement numbers

Part Two
L-1   Verdi: *I Vespri Siciliani*. Overture

L-2   Beethoven: Symphony No. 5 in c, Op. 67

L-3   Wagner: *Die Meistersinger von Nürnberg*. Act I: Prelude
Los Angeles Philharmonic Orchestra; recorded from a broadcast 1 January 1934
Release: **CD = archiphon forthcoming.**

L-4   Puccini: *La Bohème*. Act I: Che gelida manina; O soave fanciulla; Si, mi chiamano Mimi

L-5   Gounod: *Faust*. Act III: Salut! demeure

L-6   German: 'Who'll buy my sweet lavender?'

L-7   Massenet: *Manon*. Act III: Obéissons quand leur voix appelle ('Gavotte')
Los Angeles Philharmonic Orchestra; Lucrezia Bori, soprano, Joseph Bentonelli, tenor; recorded from a broadcast at the Hollywood Bowl, 6 June 1937
Release: US = EJS 292 (L-1 and L-2); EJS 295 (L-3); EJS 425 (Si, mi chiamano Mimi; Who'll buy my sweet lavender?); EJS 541 (O soave; Si, mi chiamano; Obéissons); MDP 033 (O soave; Who'll buy my sweet lavender?) Eng. = Symposium 1007 (O soave).

L-8   Gershwin: Second Prelude (arr. Dave Broekman)
Los Angeles Philharmonic Orchestra; recorded from a broadcast at the Hollywood Bowl, 8 September 1937
Release: US = Citadel CT 7025; Radio Years **CD** RY9; Eng. = Symposium 1007
Note: From a concert memorialising the death of George Gershwin.

L-9   Berlioz: *Benvenuto Cellini*, Op. 23. Overture

L-10   Mozart: Symphony No. 35 in D, K. 385, 'Haffner'

L-11   Debussy: *Prélude à l'après-midi d'un faune*
Los Angeles Philharmonic Orchestra; recorded from a CBS broadcast at the Paramount Studios, Hollywood, 1 January 1938
Release: Eng. = Symposium 1004.

L-12   Handel-Schoenberg: Quartet Concerto (freely transcribed from the Concerto Grosso Op. 6, No. 7; excerpts)
Los Angeles Philharmonic Orchestra; with the Kolisch Quartet; recorded during public performances at Philharmonic Auditorium, Los Angeles, 6 or 7 January 1938
Release: Eng. = Symposium 1007
CD–archiphon forthcoming.

L-13   Brahms-Schoenberg: Piano Quartet in g, Op. 25 (excerpts from movements 1 and 4)
Los Angeles Philharmonic Orchestra; recorded during a public performance at Philharmonic Auditorium, Los Angeles, 7 May 1938
Release: Eng. = Symposium 1007
CD = archiphon forthcoming.
Note: This was the world-première performance.

L-14   Strang: Intermezzo
Los Angeles Philharmonic Orchestra; recorded at rehearsals for performances 9 and 10 February 1939
Release: **CD = archiphon forthcoming.**

- L-15   Thomas: *Mignon*. Overture

- L-16   Liszt: Totentanz for Piano and Orchestra, G. 126

- L-17   Strauss, Johann, II: *Die Fledermaus*. Overture

- L-18   Bach: 'Bist du bei mir', BWV 508 (arr. Klemperer from Notenbuch für Anna Magdalena Bach)
  Los Angeles Philharmonic Orchestra; Bernardo Segall, piano; recorded from a broadcast of The Standard Hour, NBC Network, 11 February 1945
  Release: US = P.A.A.R.V. PRV 3501; Eng. = Symposium 1007 (Strauss only).

- L-19   Corelli: Sonata in d for Violin, Op. 5, No. 2, 'La Folia' (arr. Hubert Léonard)
  Los Angeles Philharmonic Orchestra; Joseph Szigeti, violin; recorded from a broadcast of The Standard Hour, 16 December 1945
  Release: **CD = Music & Arts CD-720.**

- 1   Bach: Brandenburg Concerto No. 3 in G, BWV 1048
  Pro Musica Orchestra, Paris; recorded 2–7 July 1946, Apollo Studio, Paris

Matrix	
1214-1 CPP	I
1215-3 CPP	I
1237-1 CPP	II

  Release: Fr. = Poly. 566214/5, A 6214/5; US = Vox set 620, PL 6200 (late issues are labelled Vienna Pro Musica).

- 2   Bach: Brandenburg Concerto No. 4 in G, BWV 1049
  Pro Musica Orchestra, Paris; recorded 2–7 July 1946, Apollo Studio, Paris

Matrix	
1216-2 CPP	I
1217-2 bis CPP	I
1218-3 CPP	II
1219-1 CPP	III

  Release: Fr. = Poly. 566216/7, A 6216/7; US = Vox set 621 (626/7), PL 6200 (late issues are labelled Vienna Pro Musica)
  Note: Matrix 1218 is also reported to contain take -2 on some copies.

- 3   Bach: Chorale 'Nun komm' der Heiden Heiland', BWV 659 (arr. Klemperer)
  Pro Musica Orchestra, Paris; recorded 2–7 July 1946, Apollo Studio, Paris

  Matrix
  1220-2 CPP

  Release: Fr. = Poly. 566211, A 6209; US = Vox set 618.

- 4   Bach: Brandenburg Concerto No. 1 in F, BWV 1046
  Pro Musica Orchestra, Paris; recorded 2–7 July 1946, Apollo Studio, Paris

Matrix	
1222-1 CPP	I
1221-2 CPP	II
1225-1 CPP	III
1224-1 bis CPP	IV
1223-1 bis CPP	V

  Release: Fr. = Poly. 566209/11, A 6209/11; US = Vox set 618, PL 6180 (late issues are labelled Vienna Pro Musica).

5   Bach: Brandenburg Concerto No. 6 in B-Flat, BWV 1051
Pro Musica Orchestra, Paris; recorded 2–7 July 1946, Apollo Studio, Paris

    Matrix
    1248-2 CPP   I
    1249-1 CPP   I
    1230-1 CPP   II
    1231-3 CPP   II
    1228-1 CPP   III
    1229-3 CPP   III

Release: Fr. = Poly. 566221/3, A 6221/3; US = Vox set 623, PL 6220 (late issues are labelled Vienna Pro Musica).

6   Mozart: Serenade No. 13 in G, K. 525, 'Eine kleine Nachtmusik'
Pro Musica Orchestra, Paris; recorded 2–7 July 1946, Apollo Studio, Paris

    Matrix
    1232-3 CPP   I
    1233-1 CPP   II
    1234-1 CPP   III
    1235-2 CPP   IV

Release: Fr. = Poly. 566224/5, A 6224/5; It. = Celson DC 1000/1; US = Vox set 169 (12022/3); VLP 1690, PL 11870; MS 5000H in set MS 5000; Jap. = Col. DXM-167 (labelled Vienna Symphony Orchestra)

Note: Matrix 1232 is also reported to carry take -2 on some copies.

7   Bach: 'Bist du bei mir', BWV 508 (arr. Klemperer from Notenbuch für Anna Magdalena Bach)
Pro Musica Orchestra, Paris; recorded 2–7 July 1946, Apollo Studio, Paris

    Matrix
    1236-2 CPP

Release: Fr. = Poly. 566215, A 6214; US = Vox set 620.

8   Bach: Brandenburg Concerto No. 5 in D, BWV 1050
Pro Musica Orchestra, Paris; M. Roesgen-Champion, harpsichord, R. Cortet, flute, H. Merckel, violin; recorded 2–7 July 1946, Apollo Studio, Paris

    Matrix
    1238-2 CPP   I
    1239-2 CPP   I
    1240-2 CPP   I
    1241-2 CPP   II
    1242-4 CPP   II
    1243-2 CPP   III

Release: Fr. = Poly. 566218/20, A 6218/20; US = Vox set 622, PL 6220 (labelled Vox Chamber Orchestra; late issues are labelled Vienna Pro Musica).

Note: Matrix 1243 is also reported to carry take -3 on some copies.

9   Bach: Brandenburg Concerto No. 2 in F, BWV 1047
Pro Musica Orchestra, Paris; M. Mule, soprano saxophone; recorded 2–7 July 1946, Apollo Studio, Paris

    Matrix
    1244-2 CPP   I
    1245-3 CPP   I
    1247-1 CPP   II
    1246-2 CPP   III

Release: Fr. = Poly. 566212/3, A 6212/3; US = Vox set 619, PL 6180 (late issues are labelled Vienna Pro Musica).

L-20 Mahler: *Lieder eines fahrenden Gesellen*
Concertgebouworkest, Amsterdam; Hermann Schey, baritone; recorded from a broadcast at the Concertgebouw, 3 or 4 December 1947
Release: **CD = archiphon ARC 109.**

10 Schubert: Symphony No. 8 in b, D. 759, 'Unfinished'
Budapest Symphony Orchestra; recorded from a broadcast of the Hungarian Radio, 18 June 1948
Release: Hungary = Hungaroton LPX 12379 (Klemperer in Budapest, Vol. 6).

11 Mozart: *Don Giovanni*, K. 527 (excerpts)
Hungarian State Opera Orchestra and Chorus; recorded during a performance at the State Opera House, Budapest, 22 October 1948 (sung in Hungarian)
György Losonczy, baritone (Don Giovanni), Mihály Székely, bass (Leporello), Lajos Tóth, baritone (Commendatore), Júlia Osváth, soprano (Donna Anna), Endre Rösler, tenor (Don Ottavio), Sándor Reményi, baritone (Masetto), Mária Gyurkovics, soprano (Zerlina), Júlia Orosz, soprano (Donna Elvira)

*Act I: Overture; Duet: Fuggi crudele, fuggi; Aria: Ah chi mi dice mai; Catalogue Aria; Aria: Or sai chi l'onore; Aria: Fin ch'han dal vino; Aria: Batti, batti bel Masetto; Two excerpts from Finale

*Act II: Trio: Ah taci, ingiusto core; Canzonetta – Deh vieni alla finestra; Sextet; Aria: Il mio tesoro; Duet: O statua gentilissima; Excerpt from Finale: Don Giovanni! A cenar teco

Release: Hungary = *Hungaroton LPX 12450 (Klemperer in Budapest, vol. 5); Finale: Don Giovanni! A cenar teco only in Hungaroton LPX 12004/6 (Stars of the Hungarian Opera Houses, Vol. II) Act I: Fin ch'han an dal vino and Act II: Second Finale in disc accompanying book *Klemperer in Hungary* by A. Boros (Budapest: Zenemükiado, 1973).

12 Wagner: *Lohengrin* (excerpts)
Hungarian State Opera Orchestra and Chorus; recorded during a performance at the State Opera House, Budapest, 24 October 1948 (sung in Hungarian)
György Losonczy, baritone (Henry, King of Germany), József Simándy, tenor (Lohengrin), Magda Rigó, soprano (Elsa), László Jambor, baritone (Frederick of Telramund), Ella Némethy, mezzo-soprano (Ortrud), Sándor Reményi, baritone (King's Herald)

Act I: Prelude; Dank, König dir ... Seht hin! Sie naht ... Einsam in trüben Tagen

Act II: Sie naht, die Engelgleiche; Mein Held, entgegne

Act III: Introduction; Das süsse Lied verhallt; Lohengrin's narrative

Release: Hungary = Hungaroton LPX 12436 (Klemperer in Budapest, vol. 4)

Other excerpts
Act II: Duet in disc accompanying book *Klemperer in Hungary* by A. Boros (Budapest: Zenemükiado, 1973)

Act II: Entweihte Götter!

Release: Hungary = Hungaroton LPX 12004/6 (Stars of the Hungarian Opera Houses, Vol. II).

13 Beethoven: *Fidelio*, Op. 72

Hungarian State Opera Orchestra and Chorus; recorded during a performance at the State Opera House, Budapest, 8 November 1948 (sung in Hungarian)

István Koszó, bass (Don Fernando), Oszkár Maleczky, baritone (Pizarro), Endre Rösler, tenor (Florestan), Anna Báthy, soprano (Leonore), Mihály Székely, bass (Rocco), Mária Mátyás, soprano (Marzelline), Gyula Angyal Nagy, tenor (Jaquino), László Külkey, tenor (First Prisoner), Jeno Vermes, bass (Second Prisoner)

Release: Hungary = Hungaroton SLPX 12428/9 (Klemperer in Budapest, Vol. 3)

Other excerpt

Act I: Pizarro's Aria in disc accompanying book *Klemperer in Hungary* by A. Boros (Budapest: Zenemükiado, 1973).

14 Mozart: *Die Zauberflöte*, K. 620

Hungarian State Opera Orchestra and Chorus; recorded during a performance at the State Opera House, Budapest, 30 March 1949 (sung in Hungarian)

Mihály Székely, bass (Sarastro), László Nagypál, tenor (Tamino), Júlia Osváth, soprano, (Pamina), Mária Mátyás, soprano (First Woman), Judit Sándor, mezzo-soprano (Second Woman), Magda Tiszay, contralto (Third Woman), Sándor Farkas, baritone (Speaker), Pál Fekete, tenor (Monostatos), Ödön Mindszenti, baritone (Papageno), Edina Pavlánszky, soprano (Papagena), Lajos Somogyvári, tenor (First Priest), Ervin Galsay, bass (Second Priest), Sári Gencsy, soprano (First Child), Valéria Koltay, soprano (Second Child), Ida Jurenák, contralto (Third Woman), Zoltán Köles, tenor (First Guard) Lajos Tóth, baritone (Second Guard)

Release: Hungary = Hungaroton LPX 12705/6 (Klemperer in Hungary, vol. 9); Excerpt: *Act I*: Der Vogelfänger bin ich ja; Wo willst du, kühner Fremdling, hin? in Hungaroton LPX 12004/6 (Stars of the Hungarian Opera Houses, Vol. II).

15 Offenbach: *Les Contes d'Hoffmann* (excerpts)

Hungarian State Opera Orchestra and Chorus; recorded during a performance at the State Opera House, Budapest, 2 April 1949 (sung in Hungarian)

Pál Fehér, tenor (Hoffmann), Lajos Somogyvári, tenor (Hermann), Margit Szilvássy, mezzo-soprano (Giulietta), Pál Fekete, tenor (Franz)

Act I: Légende de Kleinzack
Act III: Vous me quittez ... O dieu de quelle ivresse
Act IV: Eh bien! Quoi? ... Nuit et jour

Release: Hungary = Hungaroton LPX 12004/6 (Stars of the Hungarian Opera Houses, Vol. II); Septet in disc accompanying book *Klemperer in Hungary* by A. Boros (Budapest: Zenemükiado, 1973)

16 Wagner: *Die Meistersinger von Nürnberg* (excerpts)

Hungarian State Opera Orchestra and Chorus; recorded during a performance at the State Opera House, Budapest, 11 April 1949 (sung in Hungarian)

György Losonczy, baritone (Sachs), Mihály Székely, bass (Pogner), József Somló, tenor (Vogelgesang), Lajos Katona, baritone (Nachtigall), Oszkár

Maleczky, baritone (Beckmesser), István Koszó, bass (Kothner), József Joviczky, tenor (Zorn), Lajos Somogyvári, tenor (Eisslinger), Gyula Toronyi, tenor (Moser), Pál Rissay, bass (Ortel), Endre Várhelyi, bass (Schwarz), Ervin Galsay, bass (Foltz), József Simándy, tenor (Stolzing), János Sárdy, tenor (David), Júlia Osváth, soprano (Eva), Mária Budanovits, mezzo-soprano (Magdalena); László Pless, chorusmaster.

Act I: Prelude; Das schöne Fest, Johannistag; Am stillen Herd; Fanget an! So rief der Lenz ... (to end of Act I)

Act II: Lass sehn, ob Meister Sachs zu Haus!; Fliedermonolog; Den Tag seh'ich erscheinen

Act III: Prelude; Am Jordan Sankt Johannes stand ... Wahnmonolog Grüss Gott, mein Evchen ... Selig wie die Sonne; Sankt Krispin! ... Wach' auf; Morgendlich leuchtend (to end of opera)

Release: Hungary = Hungaroton LPX 12340/1 (Klemperer in Budapest, vol. 2); Act I: Mein Herr! Der Singer Meisterschlag in LPX 12004/6 (Stars of the Hungarian Opera, Vol. II)

Two unspecified excerpts sung by Losonczy and Simándy in disc accompanying book *Klemperer in Hungary* by A. Boros (Budapest: Zenemükiado, 1973).

17 Bach: Orchestral Suite No. 4 in D, BWV 1069

18 Mozart: Symphony No. 39 in E-Flat, K. 543
Hungarian Radio Symphony Orchestra; recorded from a broadcast at the Hungarian Radio Studios, 17 April 1949
Release: Hungary = Hungaroton LPX 12667 (Klemperer in Budapest, Vol. 8)

19 Bach: Orchestral Suite No. 2 in b, BWV 1067
Hungarian Radio Symphony Orchestra; János Szebenyi, flute; recorded for a Hungarian Radio broadcast, 19 June 1949
Release: Hungary = Hungaroton LPX12379 (Klemperer in Budapest, Vol. 6)
Note: The date given on the record sleeve (24 June) is not correct.

20 Bach: Brandenburg Concerto No. 5 in D, BWV 1050
Hungarian Radio Symphony Orchestra; Tibor Ney, violin, János Szebenyi, flute, Annie Fischer, piano; recorded 20 January 1950, Studio No. 6, Hungarian Radio, Budapest
Release: Hungary = Hungaroton LPX 12160 (Klemperer in Budapest, Vol. 1).

21 Bach: Magnificat in D, BWV 243
Hungarian Radio Symphony Orchestra; Budapest Chorus; Anna Báthy, soprano, Judit Sándor, soprano, Magda Tiszay, contralto, Lajos Somogyvári, tenor, György Littasy, bass.; Olivér Nagy, piano, Sándor Margittay, organ, continuo; recorded from a broadcast at Studio No. 6, Hungarian Radio, 20 January 1950
Release: Hungary = Hungaroton LPX 12160 (Klemperer in Budapest, Vol. 1)

22 Mozart: Symphony No. 36 in C, K. 425, 'Linz'
Pro Musica Orchestra, Paris; recorded mid-February 1950, Salle Pleyel

Matrix
0289.1 GCP	I
0290.1 GCP	I
(0291 GCP)	II
(0292 GCP)	II
0293.1 GCP	III
0294.2 GCP	IV

Release: Fr. = Poly. 566329/31, A 6329/31; 545001; US = Vox PLP 6280, PL 11820; MS 5000F in set MS 5000; Turnabout THS-65093; Jap. = Col. DXM-172

Note: PL 11820, THS-65093 and DXM-172 are all labelled Vienna Pro Musica.

23   Mozart: Symphony No. 25 in g, K. 183
Pro Musica Orchestra, Paris; recorded mid-Feburary 1950, Salle Pleyel

Matrix
0310.1 GCP   I
0311.2 GCP   II
0312.2 GCP   III
0313.2 GCP   IV

Release: Fr. = Poly. 566345/6, A 6345/6; 545001; US = Vox PLP 6280, PL 11820 (labelled Vienna Pro Musica); MS 5000E in set MS 5000; Jap. = Col. DXM-172 (labelled Vienna Pro Musica)

Note: Some copies of matrix 0312 are designated 312.2 GCP.

24   Mozart: *Die Entführung aus dem Serail*, K. 384.
Hungarian State Opera Orchestra and Chorus; recorded during a performance at the State Opera House, Budapest, 20 March 1950 (sung in Hungarian)

Mária Gyurkovics, soprano (Constanze), Sári Gencsy, soprano (Blonde), Endre Rösler, tenor (Belmonte), Arpád Kishegyi, tenor (Pedrillo), Mihály Székely, bass (Osmin)

Release: Hungary: Hungaroton LPX 12636/7 (Klemperer in Budapest, Vol. 7)
Overture only in disc accompanying book *Klemperer in Hungary* by A. Boros (Budapest: Zeneműkiado, 1973)

25   Schubert: Symphony No. 4 in c, D. 417, 'Tragic'
Lamoureux Orchestra; recorded 19–20 November 1950, Salle Pleyel

Release: Fr. = Vox PL 6800, PL 7860; MS 5000D in set MS 5000; Eng. = Vox PL 7860, GBY 11060; Ger. = Vox GBY 11060; US = Vox PLP 6800, PL 7860, PL 11880; Jap. = Col. DXM-161
CD = Enterprise Documents LV 939/40, Enterprise Palladio PD 4147.

L-21   Mozart: *Don Giovanni*, K. 527. Overture
RIAS Sinfonie-Orchester, Berlin; recorded 19 December 1950

Release: It. = I grandi della classica 93.5121
CD = Grandi Opere Curcio Concerto CON-01.

L-22   Mozart: Symphony No. 25 in g, K. 183
RIAS Sinfonie-Orchester, Berlin; recorded Jesus Christus-Kirche, 20 December 1950

Release: It. = Movimento Musica 01.033; I Grandi Concerti/Valentine Records GCL 30; in set 9097/4
CD = Frequenz Memoria CMC 1, Hunt CD-572.

L-23   Mozart: Symphony No. 29 in A, K. 201
RIAS Sinfonie-Orchester, Berlin; recorded Jesus Christus-Kirche, 20 December 1950

Release: It. = Movimento Musica 01.033; I Grandi Concerti/Valentine Records GCL 21; in set 9097/4; Jap. = Laudis RCL 3309; Melodram MEL 215 (incorrectly cites a recording date of 18 February 1956)
CD = Frequenz Memoria CMC 1, Hunt Classica Music

> 34001 (erroneously cites a recording date of 18 February 1956), **Hunt CD-572, Armando Curcio Editore CD (rel. 1991).**

L-24   Mozart: Symphony No. 38 in D, K. 504, 'Prague'
RIAS Sinfonie-Orchester, Berlin; recorded 22–23 December 1950
Release: It. = Movimento Musica 01.019; I Grandi Concerti/Valentine Records GCL 21; in set 9097/4; Jap. = Laudis RCL 3309
CD = Frequenz Memoria CMC 1, Hunt CD-572.

L-25   Mozart: Serenade No. 6 in D, K. 239, 'Serenata Notturna'
RIAS Sinfonie-Orchester, Berlin; recorded 21–22 December 1950
Release: **CD = Hunt CD-572, Hunt CD-729.**

L-26   Mozart: Serenade No. 11 in E-Flat, K. 375
Members of RIAS Sinfonie-Orchester, Berlin; recorded from a broadcast December 1950 (?)
Release: It. = I Grandi Concerti/Valentine Records GCL 63
Note: Although dated September 1952, Klemperer did not appear in Berlin in 1952. This recording is therefore tentatively assigned to the conductor's RIAS recording sessions of December 1950.

L-27   Bartók: Concerto for Viola and Orchestra, Sz. 120
Concertgebouworkest, Amsterdam; William Primrose, viola; recorded from a broadcast at the Concertbegouw, 10 or 11 January 1951
Release: **CD = archiphon ARC 101, Music & Arts CD-752.**

L-28   Janáček: Sinfonietta
Concertgebouworkest, Amsterdam; recorded from a broadcast at the Concertgebouw, 10 or 11 January 1951
Release: **CD = archiphon ARC 101, Music & Arts CD-752.**

L-29   Mozart: Symphony No. 25 in g, K. 183
Concertgebouworkest, Amsterdam; recorded from a broadcast at the Concertgebouw, 18 January 1951
Release: **CD = archiphon ARC 109.**

L-30   Mozart: Concerto for Violin and Orchestra in A, K. 219
Concertgebouworkest, Amsterdam; Jan Bresser, violin; recorded from a broadcast, 18 January 1951
Release: Ger. = archiphon 1.5.

26   Beethoven: Symphony No. 6 in F, Op. 68, 'Pastoral'
Wiener Symphoniker; recorded 19–23 March 1951, Vienna
Release: US = Vox PL 6960, STPL-56960, PL 16070, VXLS/VVX 2203; MS 5000I/J in set MS 5000; Music Appreciation MAR 577; Classics International CIS-1802; Eng. = Vox 100, GBY, PL 6960; Fr. = Pathé-Vox VP-100; Panthéon XVP 1071; Ger. = Vox GBY 6960; Intercord 125.803, 120.923; Jap. = Vox 5508, 511/2; Col. DXM-168
CD = Allegro ACD8000.

27   Bruckner: Symphony No. 4 in E-Flat (ed. Haas 1944)
Wiener Symphoniker; recorded 19–23 March 1951, Vienna
Release: US = Vox PL 6930, PL 11200, VSPS-5, VSPS-14; Turnabout THS-65019; Eng. = Vox PL 6930, GBY 11200; Turnabout TV 37073S; Ger. = Vox GBY 11200; Turnabout 37073; Intercord 120.925,

DISCOGRAPHY

120.805; Fr. = Vox PL 6930; Panthéon XP 2890; Aust. = Festival CFR 12-196; Jap. = Col. DXM-158
CD = Enterprise Documents LV 939/40, Enterprise Palladio PD 4147.

28   Beethoven: Mass in D, Op. 123 (*Missa solemnis*)
Wiener Symphoniker; Ilona Steingruber, soprano, Else Schuerhoff, contralto, Erich Majkut, tenor, Otto Wiener, bass; Akademiechor, Vienna; recorded 19–23 March 1951, Vienna

Release: US = Vox set PL 6992, PL 11430; Turnabout THS-65015/6; Eng. = Vox and set PL 6992, PL 11430; Turnabout TV 37072S; Ger. = Vox PL 11430; Turnabout 37072; Eurodisc 70748XK; Intercord 155.803; Fr. = Vox PL 6992; Aust. = Festival CFR 12-86; Jap. = Col. DXM-164.

29   Mahler: *Das Lied von der Erde*
Wiener Symphoniker; Elsa Cavelti, mezzo-soprano, Anton Dermota, tenor; recorded 28–30 March 1951, Vienna

Release: US = Vox PL 7000, VBX-115, PL 11890, VSPS-16, VSPS-12M; Turnabout THS-65089; Eng. = Vox 130, PL 7000, GBY 11890; Fr. = Pathé-Vox VP 130; Ger. = Vox VBX 115, GBY 118980; Intercord 125.806, 120.926; Aust. = Festival CFR 12-508; Jap. = Col. DXM-150.

L-31   Falla: *Nights in the Gardens of Spain*
Concertgebouworkest, Amsterdam; Willem Andreissen, piano; recorded from a broadcast at the Concertgebouw, 26 March 1951

Release: **CD = Music & Arts CD-752.**

L-32   Beethoven: Symphony No. 7 in A, Op. 92
Concertgebouworkest, Amsterdam; recorded from a broadcast at the Concertgebouw, 26 April 1951

Release: **CD = archiphon ARC 109.**

L-33   Beethoven: *Ah, perfido!*
Concertgebouworkest, Amsterdam; Gre Brouwenstijn, soprano; recorded from a broadcast at the Concertgebouw, 26 April 1951

Release: **CD = Music & Arts CD-752.**

30   Beethoven: Symphony No. 5 in c, Op. 67
Wiener Symphoniker; recorded April–May 1951, Vienna

Release: US = Vox PL 7070, PL 11870, STPL-513190, VXLS/VVX 2203; MS 5000G/H in set MS 5000; Allegro ACS-8039; Eng. = Vox PLP 7070; Fidelio ATL 4107; Delta TQD 3029; Ger. = Intercord 125.802, 120.922; Fr. = Pathé-Vox VP-150; Panthéon XVP 1068, MV 217; Aust. = Festival CFR 12-122; Jap. = Col. DXM-167
CD = Allegro 8039.

Note: Vox STPL-513190 and the Allegro CD contain a performance of Beethoven's *Leonore Overture No. 3* that is not credited to Klemperer, according to a Vox internal memorandum it is led by Jósef Krips.

31   Mendelssohn: Symphony No. 4 in A, Op. 90, 'Italian'
Wiener Symphoniker; recorded April–May 1951, Vienna

Release: US = Vox PL 6980, PL 7860, PL 11880; MS 5000C in set MS 5000;

Eng. = Vox PLP 6980; Fidelio ATL 1043; Great Musicians TGM 33; Fr. = Pathé-Vox VP-290, Vox PL 7860; It. = Grandi Musicisti IGM 52; Jap. = Col. DXM-161

CD = **Enterprise Documents LV 939/40, Enterprise Palladio PD 4147.**

32   Mahler: Symphony No. 2 in c, 'Resurrection'

Wiener Symphoniker; Ilona Steingruber, soprano, Hilde Rössl-Majdan, contralto; Akademie Kammerchor and Singverein der Musikfreunde, Vienna; recorded before 18 May 1951, Vienna

Release: US = Vox set PL 7010, PL 7012, VBX-115, VSPS-12M; Turnabout 34249/50, THS-65087/8; Eng. = Vox set PL.7012, TVS 34249/50; Vox 382; Fr. = Vox PL-7012, VBX 115, VUX 2014; Ger. = Vox VUX 2014; Intercord 155.804; Aust. = Festival set 12-83; Jap. = Col. DXM-160

CD = **Tuxedomusic TUXCD 1036.**

33   Mendelssohn: Symphony No. 3 in A, Op. 56, 'Scottish'

Wiener Symphoniker; recorded before 16 June 1951, Vienna

Release: US = Vox PL 7080, PL 11840; MS 5000A/B in set MS 5000; Eng. = Vox 320, PL 7080; Ger. = Vox PL 11840; Fr. = Pathé-Vox VP-320; Panthéon XPV 1046; Aust. = Festival CFR 12-146; Jap. = Col. DXM-166

Note: Per Lotte Klemperer, the final two movements in this recording are led by Prof. Herbert Haefner, who completed the symphony after the conductor had departed for concerts in Greece. The composited recording was issued in November 1951 without Klemperer's approval and led to the break between Vox's George Mendelssohn and the conductor.

34   Beethoven: Concerto No. 4 in G for Piano and Orchestra, Op. 58

Wiener Symphoniker; Guiomar Novaes, piano; recorded before 16 June 1951, Vienna

Release: US = Vox PL 7090, VBX-1, Vox VXLS/VVX 2203; Eng. = Vox PL 7090; Fr. = Pathé-Vox VP-400; Panthéon XVP 1017

CD = **VOX CDX2-5501.**

35   Chopin: Concerto No. 2 in f for Piano and Orchestra, Op. 21

Wiener Symphoniker; Guiomar Novaes, piano; recorded before 16 June 1951, Vienna

Release: US = Vox PL 7100, PL 11380; Music Appreciation MAR 571; Eng. = Vox PL 7100; Fr. = Pathé-Vox VP-160; Panthéon XVP-1019; Jap. = Col. TD-3032.

CD = **VOX CDX2-5501.**

36   Schumann: Concerto in a for Piano and Orchestra, Op. 54

Wiener Symphoniker; Guiomar Novaes, piano; recorded before 16 June 1951, Vienna

Release: US = Vox PL 7110, VXLS/VVX 2203, STPL-513.420; Fr. = Pathé-Vox VP-310; Panthéon XVP 1010

CD = **VOX CDX2-5501.**

L-34   Mahler: Symphony No. 2 in c, 'Resurrection'

Concertgebouworkest and Chorus, Amsterdam; Jo Vincent, soprano, Kathleen Ferrier, contralto; recorded from a broadcast at the Concertgebouw, 12 July 1951

Release: US = IGI-374; Eng. = Decca D264D2, K264K22; Fr. = Decca 592132; Jap. = London L40C-1406/7
CD = **London 425-970-2, Verona 27062/3, Jap. London K1CC6059/72**

Urlicht only: CD = **Verona 27076**.

L-35 Mahler: *Kindertotenlieder*
Concertgebouworkest, Amsterdam; Kathleen Ferrier, contralto; recorded from a broadcast at the Concertgebouw, 12 July 1951
Release: Eng. = Decca 417-634-1, -4; Ger. = Teldec 6.43895
CD = **Jap. London K1CC6059/72, Decca/London 425-995-2**.

L-36 Mozart: Symphony No. 29 in A, K. 201
Det Kongelige Kapel; recorded from a concert given at Odd Fellow Palaeets Store, Copenhagen, 29 January 1954
Release: Denmark = Polygram EBTL 83.

L-37 Beethoven: Symphony No. 6 in F, Op. 68, 'Pastoral'
RIAS Sinfonie-Orchester; recorded from a broadcast at the Titania Palast, 15 February 1954
Release: It. = Movimento Musica 01.030
Note: Erroneously labelled 'Berliner Philharmoniker', according to Dr Werner Unger and the Philharmonic's performance records, which contain no Klemperer appearance on this date.

L-38 Mahler: Symphony No. 4 in G
Kölner Rundfunk-Sinfonie-Orchester; Elfriede Trötschel, soprano; recorded from a broadcast 21 February 1954
Release: It. = Movimento Musica 01.054
CD = **Frequenz Memoria CME 1**.

L-39 Brahms: Concerto No. 2 in B-Flat for Piano and Orchestra, Op. 83
L-40 Bruckner: Symphony No. 4 in E-Flat
Kölner Rundfunk-Sinfonie-Orchester; Géza Anda, piano; recorded from a broadcast at the Grosser Sendesaal, 5 April 1954
Release: It. = I grandi della classica 93.5121; Movimento Musica 01.051 (Brahms) and 01.052 (Bruckner)
CD = **Arkadia CDHP 591** (Bruckner), **Hunt CD-733** (Brahms).

L-41 Mendelssohn: Concerto in a for Violin, Op. 64
Residentie Orkest, Den Haag; Johanna Martzy, violin; recorded from a broadcast at the Kurhaus, The Hague, 23 June 1954
Release: Ger. = archiphon 1.5.

37 Mozart: Symphony No. 41 in C, K. 551, 'Jupiter'
Philharmonia Orchestra; recorded 5–6 October and 24 November 1954, Kingsway Hall, London
Release: Eng. = Col. 33CX1257; Ger. = Col. 33WCX1257, 33WC516, 33WSX610; Elec. C 90427, C 70368, C 80115; Fr. = Col. 33FC25105, 33FCX426; It. = Col. 33QCX10177; US = Ang. 35209; Jap. = Col. ZL-133, RL-3024; Arg. = Col. LPC-11819

38 Hindemith: *Nobilissima Visione*
Philharmonia Orchestra; recorded 7–8 October 1954, Kingsway Hall, London

DISCOGRAPHY

   Release: Eng. = Col. 33CX1241; Ger. = Col. 33WCX1241, 33WC514;
   Elec. C 70366, SF 35490; Fr. = Col. 33FCX418; US = Ang. 35221;
   Seraphim 60004.

39 Mozart: Symphony No. 29 in A, K. 201
   Philharmonia Orchestra; recorded 8–9 October 1954, Kingsway Hall, London
   Release: Eng. = Col. 33CX1257; Ger. = Col. 33WCX1257, WCX523/SAXW
   2356; Elec. C 90427, C 91148, STC 90548, C(STC)91069; Fr. = Col.
   33FCX426; US = Ang. 35209; Arg. = Col. LPC-11819.

40 Brahms: Variations on a theme of Haydn, Op. 56a
   Philharmonia Orchestra; recorded 9 October 1954, Kingsway Hall, London
   Release: Eng. = Col. 33CX1241; Ger. = Col. 33WCX1241, 33WC514; Elec.
   C 70366; Fr. = Col. 33FCX418; Neth. = Col. HC 116; US = Ang.
   35221; Seraphim 60004
   CD = EMI CDM 764146-2.

L-42 Chopin: Concerto No. 1 in e for Piano and Orchestra, Op. 11
   Kölner Rundfunk-Sinfonie-Orchester; Claudio Arrau, piano;
   recorded from a broadcast in the Grosser Sendesaal, 25 October 1954
   Release: It. = I grandi della classica 93.5121; Cetra LO-507, Doc 37; Jap. =
   Cetra SFL 5002 (gives – incorrectly – the performance date as 23
   October)
   CD = Cetra CDE 1004, Hunt HPCD 511.

41 Beethoven: *Leonore Overture No. 1*, Op. 138
   Philharmonia Orchestra; recorded 17 November 1954, Kingsway Hall, London
   Release: Eng. = Col. 33CX1270; HMV in sets SLS 873 (Intl. OC 191-01526/8)
   and EX 29 0457-3; Ger. = Col. 33WCX1270; Elec. C 90440;
   Fr. = Col. 33FCX446; It. = Col. 33QCX10237; US = Ang. 35258;
   Jap. = Col. XL-5254
   CD = EMI CDM 764143-2.

42 Beethoven: *Fidelio*, Op. 72. Overture
   Philharmonia Orchestra; recorded 18 November 1954, Kingsway Hall, London
   Release: Eng. = Col. 33CX1270; HMV in set SLS 873 (Intl. OC 191-01526/8);
   EX 29 0457-3 Ger. = Col. 33WCX1270; Elec. C 90440; Fr. = Col.
   33FCX446; It. = Col. 33QCX10237; US = Ang. 35258; Jap. = XL-
   5154.

43 Beethoven: *Leonore Overture No. 3*, Op. 72a
   Philharmonia Orchestra; recorded 18 November 1954, Kingsway Hall, London
   Release: Eng. = Col. 33CX1270; HMV in sets SLS 873 (Intl. OC 191-01526/8)
   and EX 29 0457-3; Ger. = Col. 33WCX1270; Elec. C 90440;
   Fr. = Col. 33FCX446; It. = Col.33QCX10237; US = Ang. 35258;
   Jap. = Col. XL-5154
   CD = EMI CDM 763855-2.

44 Beethoven: *Leonore Overture No. 2*, Op. 72a
   Philharmonia Orchestra; recorded 18 and 24 November 1954, Kingsway Hall, London

Release: Eng. = Col. 33CX1270; HMV in set SLS 873 (Intl. OC 191-01526/8); Ger. = Col. 33WCX1270; Elec. C 90440; Fr. = Col. 33FCX446; It. = Col. 33QCX10237; US = Ang. 35258; Jap. = Col. XL-5154
CD = EMI CDM 763855-2.

45 Bach: Orchestral Suite No. 2 in b, BWV 1067
Philharmonia Orchestra; Gareth Morris, flute; recorded 19–20 and 22 November 1954, Kingsway Hall, London
Release: Eng. = Col. 33CX1239; Ger. = Col. 33WCX1239; Fr. = Col. 33FCX433; It. = Col. 33QCX10137; US = Ang. 35234 in set 3536B-L; Jap. = Col. XL-5118.

46 Bach: Orchestral Suite No. 1 in C, BWV 1066
Philharmonia Orchestra; recorded 19–20 November and 4 December 1954, Kingsway Hall, London
Release: Eng. = Col. 33CX1239; Ger. = Col. 33WCX1239; Fr. = Col. 33FCX433; It. = Col. 33QCX10137; US = Ang. 35234 in set 3536B-L.

47 Bach: Orchestral Suite No. 3 in D, BWV 1068
Philharmonia Orchestra; recorded 22–23 November and 4 December 1954, Kingsway Hall, London
Release: Eng. = Col. 33CX1240; Ger. = Col. 33WCX1240, 33WSX610; Elec. C 80115, C 90415; Fr. = Col. 33FCX434; It. = Col. 33QCX10139; US = Ang. 35235 in set 3536B-L; Jap. = Col. XL-5118.

48 Bach: Orchestral Suite No. 4 in D, BWV 1069
Philharmonia Orchestra; recorded 23 November and 3–4 December 1954, Kingsway Hall, London
Release: Eng. = Col. 33CX1240; Ger. = Col. 33WCX1240; Elec. C 90415; Fr. = Col. 33FCX434; It. = Col. 33QCX10139; US = Ang. 35235 in set 3536B-L.

L-43 Mozart: *Don Giovanni*, K. 527
Kölner Rundfunk-Sinfonie-Orchester and Chorus; recorded from a broadcast 17 May 1955
George London, bass (Don Giovanni), Ludwig Weber, bass (Commendatore), Léopold Simoneau, tenor (Don Ottavio), Hilde Zadek, soprano (Donna Anna), Maud Cunitz, soprano (Donna Elvira), Benno Kusche, baritone (Leporello), Horst Günter, baritone (Masetto), Rita Streich, soprano (Zerlina)
Release: US = BWS RR-478
CD = Frequenz Memoria CMA 3.

L-44 Beethoven: Mass in D, Op. 123 (*Missa solemnis*)
Kölner Rundfunk-Sinfonie-Orchester; Hamburg and Köln Radio Choruses; Annelies Kupper, soprano, Sieglinde Wagner, mezzo-soprano, Rudolf Schock, tenor, Josef Greindl, bass; Hans Bachem, organ; recorded from a broadcast in the Grosser Sendesaal, 6 June 1955
Release: It. = Cetra LO-532; Movimento Musica 02.012;
CD = Frequenz Memoria CMB 2.

L-45 Mendelssohn: *A Midsummer Night's Dream*. Overture, Op. 21 and Incidental Music, Op. 61
Kölner Rundfunk-Sinfonie-Orchester and Chorus; Käthe Möller-Siepermann, soprano, Hanna Ludwig, mezzo-soprano; from a broadcast recording made 8–11 June 1955

Release: It. = Movimento Musica 01.040; US = Priceless cassette XY 2227
CD = Priceless D-14252

Note: The recording date on the sleeve reads 8 May 1955; the date noted is taken from Köln Radio files.

L-46 Schoenberg: *Verklärte Nacht*

Concertgebouworkest, Amsterdam; recorded from a broadcast at the Concertgebouw, 7 July 1955

Release: Ger. = archiphon ARCH-1
CD = Memories CDHR 42489; archiphon ARC 101.

49 Beethoven: Symphony No. 3 in E-Flat, Op. 55, 'Eroica'

Philharmonia Orchestra; recorded 3–4 October and 17 December 1955, Kingsway Hall, London

Release: Eng. = Col. 33CX1346, CAT.292; HMV in sets SLS 873 (Intl.OC 191-01526/8) and EX 29 0457-3; Ger. = Col. 33WCX1346; Elec. C 90493, C 90413; Fr. = Col. 33FCX557; US = Ang. 35328; Jap. = Col. XL-5175
CD = EMI CDM 763855-2.

50 Beethoven: Symphony No. 7 in A, Op. 92

Philharmonia Orchestra; recorded 5–6 October and 17 December 1955, Kingsway Hall, London

Release: Eng. = Col. 33CX1379, CAT.293/BTA.114; HMV in sets SLS 873 (Intl. OC 191-01526/8) and EX 29 0457-3; Ger. = Col. 33WCX1379; Elec. C(STC)90512; Fr. = Col. 33FCX587; US = Ang. 35330; Jap. = Col. XL-5178
CD = EMI CDM 769183-2, EMI CDM 763868-2, Jap. Ang. CE28-5153.

51 Beethoven: Symphony No. 5 in c, Op. 67

Philharmonia Orchestra; recorded 6–7 October and 17 December 1955, Kingsway Hall, London

Release: Eng. = Col. 33C1051, CBT.562; HMV in sets SLS 873 (Intl.OC 191-01526/8) and EX 29 0457-3; Ger. = Col. 33WC1051; Elec. C 70101, C 90157; Fr. = Col. 33FC25037; It. = Col. 33QC5037; US = Ang. 35329
CD = EMI CDM 763868-2.

L-47 Mahler: *Kindertotenlieder*

Kölner Rundfunk-Sinfonie-Orchester; George London, bass; recorded from a broadcast in the Grosser Sendesaal, 17 October 1955

Release: It. = Cetra LO-510; Jap. = Cetra SLF 5005
CD = 2Hunt CD-578.

L-48 Brahms: Symphony No. 1 in c, Op. 68

Kölner Rundfunk-Sinfonie-Orchester; recorded from a broadcast in the Grosser Sendesaal, 17 October 1955

Release: It. = Cetra LO-515; Canada = Rococo 2096 (the label credits the Dresden Staatskapelle/Hans Knappertsbusch, though, in fact, the recording is this one)
CD = Frequenz 041.013, Bella Musica BMF 89964.

L-49 Mendelssohn: *A Midsummer Night's Dream*. Overture, Op. 21

Concertgebouworkest, Amsterdam; recorded from a broadcast in the Concertgebouw, 3 November 1955

DISCOGRAPHY

Release: Ger. = archiphon 1.4
   CD = **Memories HD 42489**.

L-50   Mahler: Symphony No. 4 in G
   RIAS Sinfonie-Orchester, Berlin; Elfriede Trötschel, soprano; recorded 13 February 1956, Hochschule für Musik, Berlin
   Release: It. = Melodram MEL 215
      CD = **2HuntCD-563**
   Note: Both the Melodram and Hunt note an incorrect recording date, 18 February 1956.

L-51   Brahms: *Ein deutsches Requiem*, Op. 45
   Kölner Rundfunk-Sinfonie-Orchester and Chorus; Elisabeth Grümmer, soprano, Hermann Prey, baritone; Hans Bachem, organ; recorded from a broadcast, 20 February 1956
   Release: **CD = Hunt CD-716**.

L-52   Beethoven: Concerto No. 4 in G for Piano and Orchestra, Op. 58
   Kölner Rundfunk-Sinfonie-Orchester; Leon Fleisher, piano; recorded from a broadcast in the Grosser Sendesaal, 27 February 1956
   Release: **CD = Hunt CD-733, Enterprise Palladio PD 4189**.

L-53   Strauss, Richard: *Don Juan*, Op. 20
   Kölner Rundfunk-Sinfonie-Orchester; recorded from a broadcast in the Grosser Sendesaal, 27 February 1956
   Release: **CD = Hunt CD-725**.

52   Mozart: Serenade No. 13 in G, K. 525, 'Eine kleine Nachtmusik'
   Philharmonia Orchestra; recorded 25 March 1956, Studio No. 1, Abbey Road
   Release: Eng. = Col. 33C1053/SBO 2751, BTB.303; Ger. = Col. 33WC1053/SBOW 2751, 33WC544/SBOW 8504; Elec. C 50517, C(STC)70102, C(STC)70461, Fr. = Col. SBOF 1001; It. = Col. SEBQ194/ESLQ 1001; Jap. = Col. ZL-97; Ang; AA-7087.

53   Mozart: Serenade No. 6 in D, K. 239, 'Serenata Notturna'
   Philharmonia Orchestra; Manoug Parikian and David Wise, violins, Herbert Downes, viola, James Edward Merrett, double-bass; recorded 25 March 1956, Studio No. 1, Abbey Road
   Release: Eng. = Col. 33CX1438, BTB.306; Ger. = Col. 33WC514, 33WCX1438; Elec. C 70366, C 90450, C 70102; in set 1C 197-53714/38; Sp. = HMV LALP 320; Neth. = Col. HC 116; US = Ang. 35401; Jap. = Ang. AA-7087
      CD = EMI CDM 764146-2.

54   Beethoven: Quartet: *Grosse Fuge* in B-Flat, Op. 133 (arr. orch.)
   Philharmonia Orchestra; recorded 26–27 March 1956, Studio No. 1, Abbey Road
   Release: Eng. = Col. 33CX1438; HMV in set SLS 873 (Intl. OC 191-01526/8) (artificial stereo from mono tape); ED 290271-1; EX 29 03799; Ger. = Col. 33WCX1438; Elec. C90540; in sets 1C 147-, 197-53400/19 and 1C 137-29 0379-3; Fr. = HMV in set 2C 147-50298/318; US = Ang. 35401; AE–, 4AE-34424
      CD = EMI CDC 747186-2, CDM 763356-2, CDZG 568057-2; Jap. Ang. **CC33-3243, TOCE6116**.

DISCOGRAPHY

55 Mozart: Adagio and Fugue in c, K. 546
Philharmonia Orchestra; recorded 27 March 1956, Studio No. 1, Abbey Road
Release: Eng. = Col. 33CX1438, 33CX1948/SAX 2587, BTB.306; HMV in set SLS 5048 (Intl. OC 147-01842/7); EX 29 0482-3; Ger. = Col.33WCX1438; Elec. C 90540, SME 80933; in sets 1C 153-01842/7, 1C 147-50229/318 and 197- 53714/38; Fr. = HMV 2C 061-, 069-00602; 100602-4; in set 2C 147-50298/318; It. = Col. ESLQ 1010; US = Ang. (S)36289, 35401, RL-32099, AE–, 4AE-34462, AEW 34470; Jap. = Ang. AA-7087, AA-7596, AA-8578, EAC-40044
CD = EMI CDM 763620-2.

56 Handel: Concerto Grosso in a, Op. 6, No. 4
Philharmonia Orchestra; recorded 28 March and 26 July 1956, Studio No. 1, Abbey Road
Release: Eng. = Col. 33C1053/SBO 2751, 33CX(SAX)5252, SEL 1594/ESL 6254; Ger. = Col. 33WC1053/ESLW 6254, 33WC544/SOBW 8504; Elec. C(STC)70102, C(STC)70461, STC 50517; Fr. = Col. SBOF 1001; It. = Col. ESLQ 1001, SBO 2751; Jap. = Col. ZL-97
CD = EMI CDM 764146-2.

L-54 Bruckner: Symphony No. 7 in E
Symphonie-Orchester des Bayerischen Rundfunks; recorded from a broadcast in the Herkules-Saal, Munich, 12 April 1956
Release: **CD = Hunt CD-708.**

L-55 Beethoven: Symphony No. 4 in B-Flat, Op. 60
Concertgebouworkest, Amsterdam; recorded from a broadcast at the Concertgebouw, 9 May 1956
Release: **CD = Arkadia forthcoming.**

L-56 Beethoven: Symphony No. 6 in F, Op. 68, 'Pastoral'
Concertgebouworkest, Amsterdam; recorded from a broadcast in the Concertgebouw, 13 May 1956
Release: **CD = Music & Arts CD-246.**

L-57 Beethoven: Symphony No. 7 in A, Op. 92
Concertgebouworkest, Amsterdam; recorded from a broadcast in the Concertgebouw, 13 May 1956
Release: **CD = archiphon ARC 109.**

L-58 Beethoven: Symphony No. 8 in F, Op. 93

L-59 Beethoven: Symphony No. 9 in d, Op. 125, 'Choral'
Concertgebouworkest, Amsterdam; Gré Brouwenstijn, soprano, Annie Hermes, alto, Ernst Haefliger, tenor, Hans Wilbrink, bass; Amsterdam Toonkunst Choir; recorded from a broadcast in the Concertgebouw, 17 May 1956
Release: It. = AS 115 (Eighth Symphony)
CD = Music & Arts CD-246, AS Disc AS 115 (Eighth Symphony); **Curtain Call CD-242** (Ninth Symphony).

L-60 Mozart: Concerto No. 22 in E-Flat for Piano and Orchestra, K. 482
Concertgebouworkest, Amsterdam; Annie Fischer, piano; recorded from a broadcast in the Concertgebouw, 12 July 1956
Release: US = Recital Records RR-527
CD = Memories CDHR 42489.

DISCOGRAPHY

57 Mozart: Symphony No. 36 in C, K. 425, 'Linz'
    Philharmonia Orchestra; recorded 19–20 July 1956, Kingsway Hall, London
    Release: Eng. = Col. 33CX1786/SAX 2436; HMV in sets SLS 5048 (Intl. OC 147-01842/7) and EX 29 0482-3; Ger. = Elec. C(STC)91143, SMC 110000/1-3; in sets 1C 197-53714/38, 153-01842/7 and 137-29 0482-3; Fr. = Col.33FCX918/SAXF 236, 33FC25101; HMV 2C 061-01190; Neth. = HMV 1A 137-53556/7; US = Ang. (S)36128, Jap. = Col. ZL-159, OS- 3116; Ang. SCA-1021 AA-7404, AA-8136, EAA-93083/4, EAC-40047
    CD = EMI CMS 763272-2; Ger. Zweitausendeins 60625; Jap. Ang. TOCE6093/6.

58 Mozart: Symphony No. 38 in D, K. 504, 'Prague'
    Philharmonia Orchestra; recorded 20, 23 and 24 July 1956, Kingsway Hall, London
    Release: Eng. = Col. 33CX1486; Ger. = Col. 33WCX1486, 33WCX523/SAXW 2356; Elec. C 90916, C(STC)91069; Fr. = Col. 33FC25102; It. = Col. 33QCX10284; US = Ang. (S)35408; Jap. = Col. ZL-120, XL-5211; Ang. SCA-1005.

59 Mozart: Symphony No. 40 in g, K. 550
    Philharmonia Orchestra; recorded 21 and 23 July 1956, Kingsway Hall, London
    Release: Eng. = Col. 33CX1457/SAX 2278; HMV in set SLS 5048 (Intl. OC 147-01842/7); Ger. = Col. 33WC521/SBOW 8504, 33WCX1457/SAXW 2278; Elec. C(STC)90548, C(STC)70376; in sets 1C 153-01842/7 and 197-53714/38; Fr. = Col. 33FC25104; HMV 2C 059-, 259-01847; It. = Col. 33QCX 10274; US = Ang. (S)35407; Jap. = Col. ZL-128, RL-3024/OS-3086; Ang. AA-7280, EAC-40049, EAC-55033
    CD = EMI CDC 747852-2, CMS 763272-2; Ger. Zweitausendeins 60625; Jap. Ang. TOCE6093/6, CC33-3795.

60 Beethoven: Overture *Zur Weihe des Hauses*, Op. 124 (Consecration of the House)
    Philharmonia Orchestra; recorded 21 and 25 July 1956, Kingsway Hall, London
    Release: Eng. = EMI EX 29 0457-3; US = Ang. 35329; Jap. = Ang. AA-7061.

61 Mozart: Symphony No. 39 in E-Flat, K. 543
    Philharmonia Orchestra; recorded 23–24 July 1956, Kingsway Hall, London
    Release: Eng. = Col. 33CX1486; Ger. = Col. 33WCX1486; Elec. C 90916; Fr. = Col. 33FC25103; It. = Col. 33QCX10284; US = Ang. (S)35408; Jap. = Col. ZL-124.

62 Mozart: Symphony No. 25 in g, K. 183
    Philharmonia Orchestra; recorded 24–25 July 1956, Kingsway Hall, London
    Release: Eng. = Col. 33CX1457/SAX 2278, 33CX(SAX)5252, SEL 1594/ESL 6254; HMV in sets SLS 5048 (Intl. OC 147-01842/7) and EX 29 0482-3; Ger. = Col.33WCX1457/SAXW 2278; Elec. C(STC)90548, C 91148, C(STC)70736; in sets 1C 197-53714/38, 153-01842/7 and 137-29 0482- 3; It. = HMV 33QCX10274; US = Ang. (S)35407; in set AEW- 34470; Jap. = Col. XL-5211, OS-3086; Ang. AA-7087, AA-8083, SCA-1005, EAA-93083/4, EAC-40044
    CD = EMI CDMD 763272-2, CMS 763272-2; Ger. Zweitausendeins 60625; Jap. Ang. TOCE6093/6.

L-61   Mozart: Concerto No. 27 in B-Flat for Piano and Orchestra, K. 595
Kölner Gürzenich Orchester; Clara Haskil, piano; recorded from a broadcast at the Pavilion des Sports, Montreux, Switzerland, 9 September 1956
Release: US = Recital Records RR-545; Fr. = unnumbered circulation premium cassette issued by *Diapason- Harmonie* magazine, autumn 1987; It. = I grandi della classica 93.5121; Jap. = Col. OS 7079
CD = AS Disc AS 612, Legend LGD 113, PGP 11023.

L-62   Haydn: Symphony No. 101 in D, 'Clock'
Symphonie-Orchester des Bayerischen Rundfunks; recorded from a brodcast at the Herkules-Saal, Munich, 19 October 1956
Release: It. = Melodram MEL 215; I Grandi Concerti/Valentine Records GCL 62; Jap. = Laudis RCL 3301
CD = Disques Refrain DR 910002.
Note: GCL 62 is erroneously dated 12 February 1956 and credited to the RIAS Radio-Sinfonie Orchester, Berlin; the Melodram credits the same orchestra, but wrongly dates the performance 18 February 1956.

L-63   Mahler: Symphony No. 4 in G
Symphonie-Orchester des Bayerischen Rundfunks; Elisabeth Lindermeier, soprano; recorded from a broadcast at the Herkules-Saal, Munich, 19 October 1956
Release: I Grandi Concerti/Valentine Records GCL 67
CD = Arkadia 2CDHP 590.
Note: The Valentine label credits the wrong orchestra (Kölner Rundfunk-Sinfonie) and furnishes an incorrect recording date, 12 February 1956.

63   Brahms: Symphony No. 2 in D, Op. 73
Philharmonia Orchestra; recorded 29–30 October 1956, Kingsway Hall, London
Release: Eng. = Col. 33CX1517/SAX 2362; HMV ASD 2706; in set SLS 804 (Intl. OC 163-50034/7), SXLP 30238 (Intl. OC 053-00470); Ger. = Col. 33WCX1517/SAXW 2362, SMC 91632; Elec. C(STC)90920, 1C 053-, 063-00470; in sets 1C 137- and 153-, 197-50034/7; Fr. = Col. 33FCX693/SAXF 202; HMV 2C 065-00470; in set 2C 197-50034/7; It. = Col. 33QCX10322/SAXQ 7311; US = Ang. (S)35532, RL- 32049, AE-34413; in set (S)3614D; Time-Life STL-142; Jap. = Col. RL-3008/OS-3062; Ang. SCA-1069, AA-7412, EAA-93087/8, EAC-40051, EAC-55060
CD = EMI CDM 769650-2; Ger. Zweitausendeins 60625; Jap. Ang. TOCE-6088, TOCE-1567.

64   Brahms: Symphony No. 1 in c, Op. 68
Philharmonia Orchestra; recorded 29 and 31 October 1956, 1 November 1956 and 28–29 March 1957, Kingsway Hall, London
Release: Eng. = Col. 33CX1504/SAX 2262, BTA 130; HMV ASD 2705; in set SLS 804 (Intl. OC 163-50034/7), SXLP 30217 (Intl. OC 053-00466); Ger. = Col. 33WCX1504/SAXW 2262; Elec. C(STC)90570, 1C 037-, 053-, 063-00466; in sets 1C 137-, 153-, 197-50034/7; Fr. = Col. 33FCX692/SAXF 201; HMV in set 2C 197-50034/7; It. = Col. 33QCX10310/SAXQ 7262; US = Ang. (S)35481; in set (S)3614D; Jap. = Col. RL-3007/OS-3061; Ang. SCA-1084, AA-7414, AA-8105, EAA-93087/8, EAC-40050, EAC-55059
CD = EMI CDM 769651-2, CZS 479885-2; Ger. Zweitausendeins 60625; Jap. Ang. TOCE-6086, TOCE-1566.

DISCOGRAPHY

65   Brahms: Symphony No. 4 in e, Op. 98

       Philharmonia Orchestra; recorded 1 November 1956 and 27–28 March 1957, Kingsway Hall, London

       Release: Eng. = Col. 33CX1591/SAX2350, HMV ASD 2708; in set SLS 804 (Intl. OC 163-50034/7), SXLP 30214 (Intl. OC 053-00487); TC-EXE 196; Ger. = Col. 33WCX1591, SMC 91634; Elec. C(STC)90968, 1C 063-00487; in sets 1C 153-, 197-50034/7; Fr. = Col. 33FCX695/SAXF 204; HMV in set 2C 197-50034/7; It. = Col. 33QCX10393/SAXQ 7289; US = Ang. (S)35546; AE-34413; in set (S)3614D; Jap. = Col. RL-3010/OS-3064; Ang. SCA-1052, AA-7408, AA-8084, EAA-93089/90, EAC-40053, EAC-55087

       CD = EMI CDM 769649-2; Jap. Ang. TOCE-6087, TOCE-1568.

L-64   Beethoven: Symphony No. 1 in C, Op. 21

L-65   Schubert: Symphony No. 8 in b, D. 759, 'Unfinished'

L-66   Wagner: *Die Meistersinger von Nürnberg*. Act I: Prelude.

       RAI Symphony Orchestra, Turin; recorded 17 December 1956 in the Auditorium RAI, Turin for broadcast 27 January 1957

       Release: It. = Cetra LAR 37; Jap. = Cetra K22C324 (Beethoven and Schubert), Cetra K22C325 (Wagner).

L-67   Haydn: Symphony No. 101 in D, 'Clock'

L-68   Strauss, Richard: *Till Eulenspiegels lustige Streiche*, Op. 28

L-69   Stravinsky: *Pulcinella* Suite

L-70   Shostakovich: Symphony No. 9 in e, Op. 70

       RAI Symphony Orchestra, Turin; recorded from a broadcast 21 December 1956

       Release: It. = Cetra LAR 37; Replica RPLC 2481 (Shostakovich) Jap. = Cetra K22C325 (Haydn and Strauss only)

       Note: Incorrectly dated in the notes for these recordings as December 1955.

L-71   Brahms: Symphony No. 2 in D, Op. 73

       RIAS Sinfonie-Orchester, Berlin; recorded from a broadcast at the Hochschule für Musik, Berlin, 21 January 1957

       Release: **CD = Enterprise Palladio PD 4189.**

L-72   Bach: Cantata No. 202, 'Weichet nur, betrübte Schatten'

       Concertgebouworkest, Amsterdam; Elisabeth Schwarzkopf, soprano; recorded from concerts in the Concertgebouw on 6 and 7 February 1957

       Release: US = Recital Records RR-537 and RR-208 (side 2)

            CD = Hunt CD-727, AS Disc AS 533, Music & Arts CD-751, Legend LGD 103.

L-73   Brahms: Variations on a theme of Haydn, Op. 56a

       Concertgebouworkest, Amsterdam; recorded from a broadcast in the Concertgebouw, 6 February 1957

       Release: **CD = Music & Arts CD-247** (gives an incorrect recording date 7 February 1957), **Disc AS 113, Hunt CD-709.**

L-74   Mendelssohn: *Hebrides Overture*, Op. 26

       Concertgebouworkest, Amsterdam; recorded from a broadcast in the Concertgebouw, 21 February 1957

       Release: Ger. = archiphon 1.4

            CD = Memories CDHR 42489.

L-75 Schubert: Symphony No. 4 in c, D. 417, 'Tragic'
Concertgebouworkest, Amsterdam; recorded from a broadcast in the Concertgebouw, 21 February 1957
Release: Ger. = archiphon 1.4
   CD = Memories CDHR 42489, Frequenz 041.013, Bella Musica BMF 89964, 31.6005.

L-76 Beethoven: Symphony No. 7 in A, Op. 92
Orchestre de la Suisse Romande; recorded from a broadcast in Victoria Hall, Geneva, 6 March 1957
Release: It. = Movimento Musica in set O8.001
Note: The recording date given in the liner notes (5 March 1955) is incorrect.

66 Brahms: Symphony No. 3 in F, Op. 90
Philharmonia Orchestra; recorded 26–27 March 1957, Kingsway Hall, London
Release: Eng. = Col. 33CX1536/SAX 2351; HMV ASD 2707; in set SLS 804 (Intl. OC 163-50034/7); SXLP 30255 (Intl. OC 053-00473); Ger. = Col. 33WCX1536/SAXW 2351; Elec. SMC 91633, C(STC)90933, 1C 053-, 063-00473; in sets 1C 137-, 153-, 197-50034/7; Fr. = Col. 33FCX694/SAXF 203; HMV 2C 065-00473; in set 2C 197-50034/7; It. = Col. 33QCX10402/SAXQ 7314; US = Ang. (S)35545, RL-32050; in set (S)3614D; Jap. = Col. RL-3009/OS-3063; Ang. SCA-1060, AA-7409, EAA-93089/90, EAC-40052, EAC-55086
CD = EMI CDM 769649-2; Ger. Zweitausendeins 60625; Jap. Ang. TOCE, TOCE-1568 6087; It. = I grandi della classica 93.5121.

67 Brahms: *Tragic Overture*, Op. 81
Philharmonia Orchestra; recorded 29 March 1957, Kingsway Hall, London
Release: Eng. = Col. 33CX1517/SAX 2362; HMV ASD 2706; in sets SLS 821 (Intl. 1E 153-01295/6) and SLS 804 (Intl. OC 163-50034/7); SXLP 30238 (Intl. OC 053-00470); TC-SXLP 30238; Ger. = Col. 33WCX1517/SAXW 2362, SMC 91632; Elec. C(STC)90920, STC 91224S/5, 1C 053-00470; in sets 1C 137-, 153-, 197-50034/7 and 153-01295/6; Fr. = Col. 33FCX693/SAXF202; HMV 2C 065-00470; in sets 2C 167-01295/6 and 197-50034/7; It. = Col. 33QCX10322/SAXQ 7311; US = Ang. (S)35532, RL-32049; in set (S)3614D; Jap. = Col. RL-3008/OS-3062; Ang. SCA-1069, AA-7412, AA-8097, AA-8328/9, EAA-93087/8, EAC-40051, EAC-55060
CD = EMI CDM 769651-2, CZS 479885-2; Jap. Ang. TOCE-6086, TOCE-1566; It. = I grandi della classica 93.5121.

68 Brahms: *Academic Festival Overture*, Op. 80
Philharmonia Orchestra; recorded 29 March 1957, Kingsway Hall, London
Release: Eng. = Col. 33CX1536/SAX 2351; HMV ASD 2707; in set SLS 804 (Intl. OC 163-50034/7), SXLP 30255 (Intl. OC 053-00473); Ger. = Col. 33WCX1536/SAXW 2351, SMC 91633; Elec. C(STC)90933, 1C 053-, 063-00473; in sets 1C 137-, 153-, 197-50034/7; Fr. = Col. 33FCX694/SAXF 203; HMV 2C 065-00473; in set 2C 197-50034/7; It. = Col. 33QCX10402/SAXQ 7314; Neth. = HMV 1A 137-53562/3; US = Ang. (S)35545, RL-32050; in set (S)3614D; Jap. = Col. RL-3009/OS-3063; Ang. SCA-1060, AA-7409, AA-8105, EAA- 93089/90, EAC-40052, EAC-55086
CD = EMI CDM 769651-2, CZS 479885-2; Ger. Zweitausendeins 60625; Jap. Ang. TOCE-6086, TOCE-1566; It. = I grandi della classica 93.5121.

DISCOGRAPHY

L-77   Beethoven: Symphony No. 3 in E-Flat, Op. 55, 'Eroica'
        Det Kongelige Kapel; recorded from a concert given at the Tivolis Koncertsal, Copenhagen, 26 April 1957
        Release: Denmark = Polygram EBTL 83.

L-78   Bruckner: Symphony No. 8 in c
        Kölner Rundfunk-Sinfonie-Orchester; recorded from a broadcast in the Grosser Sendesaal, 7 June 1957
        Release: It. = Movimento Musica 02.023
            CD = Hunt CD-704.

L-79   Bach: Orchestral Suite No. 3 in D, BWV 1068

L-80   Brahms: Symphony No. 4 in e, Op. 98
        Symphonie-Orchester des Bayerischen Rundfunks; recorded from a broadcast at the Herkules-Saal, Munich, 27 September 1957
        Release: Ger. = Orfeo MC201 891
            CD = Orfeo CD201 891A; Jap. Orfeo OCD2041.

69   Beethoven: Symphony No. 2 in D, Op. 36
        Philharmonia Orchestra; recorded 4–5 October 1957, Kingsway Hall, London
        Release: Eng. = Col. 33CX1615/SAX 2331; HMV ASD 2561; in set SLS 788 (Intl. OC 177-00794/802); TC-SLS 788; ED 29 0252-1; EX 29 0379-3; Ger. = Col. 33WCX1615/SAXW 2331, SMC 91623; Elec. C 100000, C(STC)91000, 1C 053-00488; in sets 1C 147-, 197-53400/19, 29 0379-3 and 137-, 181-50187/94; Fr. = Col. 33FCX880/SAXF 197; HMV 2C 069- 00795; in set 2C 147-50298/318; It. = Col. 33QCX10342/SAXQ 7336; US = Ang. (S)35658, AE-34425, AEW-34469; (S)35954/61 in set (S)3619H; Jap. = Col. OS-3072; Ang. AA-7023, AA-8135, AA-41/3, EAA-93077/8, EAC-40055; in set AA-5131/9
            CD = EMI CDC 747185-2, CDM 763355-2, CDZG 568057-2; Jap. Ang. CC30-3272/7, TOCE6115, TOCE7363/8.

70   Beethoven: Symphony No. 6 in F, Op. 68, 'Pastoral'
        Philharmonia Orchestra; recorded 7–8 October 1957, Kingsway Hall, London
        Release: Eng. = Col. 33CX1532/SAX 2260, TA-33CX1522; HMV ASD 2565; in set SLS, TC-SLS 788 (Intl. OC 177-00794/802); ED 29 0253-1; EX 29 03793; Ger. = Col. 33WCX1532/SAXW 2260; Elec. C 100000, C(STC)90915, 1C 053-00472; in sets 1C 137-, 181-50187/94, 147-, 197-53400/19 and 137-29 0379-3; Fr. = Col. 33FCX784/SAXF 104; HMV 2C 069-00799; 100472-1, -4; in set 2C 147-50298/318; It. = Col. 33QCX10317/SAXQ 7265; US = Ang. (S)35711, 8XS-, 4XS-35711, AE-34426; (S)35954/61 in set (S)3619H and set AEW-34469; Jap. = Col. RL3040/OS-3076; Ang. SCA-1014, AA-7403, AA-8087, EAA-93073/4, EAC-40059; in set AA-5131/9
            CD = EMI CDC 747188-2, CDM 763358-2, CDZG 568057-2; Jap. Ang. CC30-3272/7, CC33-3245, TOCE6118, TOCE7363/8.

71   Beethoven: *Coriolan Overture*, Op. 62
        Philharmonia Orchestra; recorded 21 October 1957, Kingsway Hall, London
        Release: Eng. = Col. 33CX1615/SAX 2331, 33CX1930/SAX 2570, TA-33CX1930; HMV ASD 2564; in set SLS, TC-SLS 788 (Intl. OC 177-00794/802), TC-SLS 788 and SXLP 30322 in set SXDW 3032 (Intl. OC 153-03103/4); ED 29 02701; EX 29 0379-3; Ger. = Col.

33WCX1615/SAXW 2331, SMC 91623, SMC 80995, SMC 80944; Elec. C(STC)91000, SME 2037/8, 1C 053-00488; in sets 1C 137-, 181-50187/94, 197- 03103/4, 147-, 197-53400/19 and 137-29 0379-3; Fr. = Col. 33FCX880/SAXF 197; HMV 2C 069-00798; in set 2C 147-50298/318; It. = Col. 33QCX10342/SAXQ 7336; I Grandi Concerti GCL 24; US = Ang. (S)35658, AE-34426; in set AEW-34469; in set SBR-3800; Jap. = Col. OS-3072; Ang. AA-8097, AA-7384, AA-7023, AA-8369, EAC-40055; in set AA-5131/9
CD = EMI CDC 747190-2, CDM 763611-2, CDZG 568057-2, CZS 479562-2; Jap. Ang. CC33-3247, CE25-5671.

72   Beethoven: *Egmont*, Op. 84. Overture and Incidental Music (Nos. 2, 5 and 8)

Philharmonia Orchestra; Birgit Nilsson, soprano; recorded 21 October (Overture) and 21 and 25 November (Incidental music) 1957, Kingsway Hall, London

Release: Eng. = Col. 33CX1574/5//SAX 2276/7; SEL 1609 (Overture, No. 2 & 5); HMV ASD 2563; in set SLS, TC-SLS 788 (Intl. OC 177-00794/802); ED 29 0253-1, -4, EX 29 0379-3; Ger. = Col. 33WCX1575/SAXW 2277, SMC 80995; Elec. C(STC)90982; in sets 1C 147-, 197-53400/19; Fr. = Col. 33FCX873/4//SAXF 167/8; HMV 2C 069-00797; in set 2C 147-50298/318; It. = Col. 33QCX10332; US = Ang. (S)3577B-L; AE-34426; Jap. = Ang. AA-24/7
CD = EMI CDC 747188-2, CDM 763358-2, CDZG 568057-2; Jap. = Ang. CC33-3245
Overture only: Eng. = Col. 33CX1930/SAX 2570; HMV SXLP 30321 in set SXDW 3032 (Intl. OC 153-03103/4); Ger. = Elec. in sets 1C 197-03103/4 and 137-29 0379-3; Neth. = HMV 1A 137-53562/3; US = Angel in set AEW-34469; Jap. = Ang. AA-7364, AA-8103, AA-8369; in set AA-5131/9
CD = Jap. Ang. CD25-5671
Overture and Nos. 2 & 5 only: It. = Col. SEBQ 227.

73   Beethoven: Symphony No. 4 in B-Flat, Op. 60

Philharmonia Orchestra; recorded 21–22 October 1957, Kingsway Hall, London

Release: Eng. = Col. 33CX1702/SAX 2354; HMV ASD 2563; in set SLS, TC-SLS 788 (Intl. OC 177-00794/802); ED 29 0270-1, EX 29 0379-3; Ger. = Col. 33WCX1702/SAXW 2354, SMC 91625; Elec. C 100000, C(STC)91070, 1C 053-00500; in sets 1C 137-, 181-50187/94, 147-, 197-53400/19 and 137-29 0379-3; Fr. = Col. 33FCX881/SAXF 198; HMV 2C 069-00797; in set 2C 147-50298/318; It. = Col. 33QCX10438/SAXQ 7339; US = Ang. (S)35661; AE-34423; (S)35954/61 in set (S)3619H and in set AEW-34469; Jap. = Col. OS-3074; Ang. AA-7061, AA-8134, EAA- 93077/8, EAC-40057; in set AA-5131/9
CD = EMI CDC 747185-2, CDM 763355-2, CDZG 568057-2; Jap. Ang. CC30-3272/7, TOCE6115, TOCE7363/8.

74   Beethoven: Symphony No. 1 in C, Op. 21

Philharmonia Orchestra; recorded 28–29 October 1957, Kingsway Hall, London

Release: Eng. = Col. 33CX1554/SAX 2318; HMV ASD 2560; in set SLS, TC-SLS 788 (Intl. OC 177-00794/802); ED 29 0270-1; EX 29 0379-3; Ger. = Col. 33WCX1554/SAXW 2318; Elec. C 100000, C(STC)90967, 1C 053-, 063-00476; in sets 1C 137-, 181-50187/94,

DISCOGRAPHY

147-, 197-53400/19 and 137-29 0379-3; Fr. = Col. 33FCX776/ SAXF189; HMV 2C 069-00794; in set 2C 147-50298/318; It. = Col. 33QCX10379/SAXQ 7269; US = Ang. (S)35657, AE-34423; (S)35954/61 in set (S)3619H and in set AEW-34469; Time-Life STL-141; Jap. = Col. RL-3066/OS-3071; Ang. AA-7011, AA-8134, AA-41/3, EAA-93077/8, EAC-40054; in set AA-5131/9
CD = EMI CDC 747184-2, CDM 763354-2, CDZG 568057-2; Jap. Ang. CC30-3272/7, TOCE6114, TOCE7363/8.

75 Beethoven: Symphony No. 8 in F, Op. 93

Philharmonia Orchestra; recorded 29–30 October 1957, Kingsway Hall, London

Release: Eng. = Col. 33CX1554/SAX 2318, BTB.308; HMV ASD 2560; in set SLS, TC-SLS 788 (Intl. OC 177-00794/802); ED 29 0328-1; EX 29 0379-3; Ger. = Col. 33WCX1554/SAXW 2318; Elec. C 100000, C(STC)90967, 1C 053-, 063-00476; in sets 1C 137-, 181-50187/94, 147-, 197-53400/19, 137-01370/1 and 137-29-03793; Fr. = Col. 33FCX776/SAXF 189; HMV 2C 069-006794; in set 2C 147-50298/ 318; It. = Col. 33QCX10379/SAXQ 7269; US = Ang. (S)35657, AE-34427; (S)35954/61 in set (S)3619H and in set AEW-34469; Jap. = Col. RL-3066/OS-3071; Ang. AA-7011, AA-7051, AA-8135, EAA-93077/8, EAC-40054; in set AA-5131/9
CD = EMI CDC 747187-2, CDM 763357-2, CDZG 568057-2; Jap. Ang. CC30-3272/7, CC33-3244, TOCE6117, TOCE7363/8.

76 Beethoven: Symphony No. 9 in d, Op. 125, 'Choral'
Philharmonia Orchestra and Chorus; Aase Nordmo-Lövberg, soprano, Christa Ludwig, mezzo-soprano, Waldemar Kmentt, tenor, Hans Hotter, baritone; recorded 30–31 October and 21–23 November (with chorus and soloists) 1957, Kingsway Hall, London

Release: Eng. = Col. 33CX1574/5//SAX 2276/7; HMV ASD 2567/8; in sets SLS, TC-SLS 788 (Intl. OC 177-00794/802), SLS 790 (Intl. 0C 153-00801/2) and SXLP 30511/2 in set SXDW 3051 (Intl. OC 151-00801/2); ED 29 0272-1; EX 29 0379-3; Ger. = Col. 33WCX1574/5//SAXW 2276/7, SMC 91629/30S; Elec. C 100000, C(STC)90981/2, STC 91047/8, 1C 153-00949/50S, 1C 245-01341, STE 9047; in sets 1C 137-, 181-50187/94, 147-, 197-53400/19, 137-29 0379-3, and 137-01370/1; Fr. = Col. 33FCX873/4//SAXF 167/8; HMV 2C 153-00801/2, 101381-1; in set 2C 147-50298/318; 2C 1003811, 2C 1003814; It. = Col. 33QCX10331/2//SAXQ 7266/7; US = Ang. AE-34428; (S)35662/3 in set (S)3577B- L; (S)35954/61 in set (S)3619H and in set AEW-34469; Jap. = Col. OL-3037/8//OS-3078/9; Ang. SCA-1105/6, AA- 7294/5, AA-8094/5, EAA-93073/4, EAC-40060/1; in set AA-5131/9
CD = EMI CDC 747189-2, CDM 763359-2, CDZG 568057-2; Jap. Ang. CC30-3272/7, CC33-3246, TOCE6119, TOCE7363/8.
Fourth movement only: US = Ang. S-36815.

77 Beethoven: *Die Geschöpfe des Prometheus*, Op. 43. Overture

Philharmonia Orchestra; recorded 25 November 1957, Kingsway Hall, London

Release: Eng. = Col. 33CX1615/SAX 2331, 33CX1930/SAX 2570, TA-33CX1930; HMV ASD 2561; in set SLS, TC-SLS 788 (Intl. OC 177-00794/802), ED 29 1341-1; Ger. = Col. 33WCX1615/SAXW 2331, SMC 91623, SMC 80995; Elec. C(STC)91000, SME 2037/8, 1C

053-00488; Fr. = Col. 33FCX880/SAXF 197; HMV 2C 069-00795; in set 2C 147-50298/318; It. = Col. 33QCX10342/SAXQ 7336; US = Ang. (S)35658; Jap. = Col. OS-3072; Ang. AA-7023, AA-8369, EAC-40055; in set AA-5131/9
CD = EMI CDM 769183-2, CDM 763358-2, CDZG 568057-2; Jap. Ang. CC33-3245, CE28-5183.

L-81 Beethoven: Symphony No. 3 in E-Flat, Op. 55, 'Eroica'
RIAS Sinfonie-Orchester, Berlin; recorded from a broadcast at the Hochschule für Musik, Berlin, 29 March 1958
Release: **CD = Hunt Classica Music 34001** (gives the performance date as 28 March).

L-82 Brahms: *Ein deutsches Requiem*, Op. 45
Wiener Philharmoniker; Singverein der Gesellschaft der Musikfreunde; Wilma Lipp, soprano, Eberhard Waechter, baritone; recorded from a broadcast at the Musikvereinssaal, 15 June 1958
Release: **CD = Disques Refrain DR 920034.**

L-83 Beethoven: Overture *Zur Weihe des Hauses*, Op. 124 (Consecration of the House)
Philharmonia Orchestra; recorded from a broadcast at the Usher Hall, Edinburgh, 24 August 1958
Release: US = P.A.A.R.V. PRV 3501.

L-84 Bruckner: Symphony No. 7 in E
Berliner Philharmoniker; recorded 3 September 1958 during a performance at the Kunsthaus, Lucerne, Switzerland
Release: It. = Movimento Musica 01.057
CD = Frequenz Memoria CMD 1, Music & Arts CD-7561; First Movement only in **Relief LR 1883.**

L-85 Mozart: Concerto No. 20 in d for Piano and Orchestra, K. 466
Philharmonia Orchestra; Clara Haskil, piano; recorded 8 September 1959 at a performance in the Kunsthaus, Lucerne, Switzerland
Release: US = BWS RR-545; Jap. = Col. OS 7079
CD = CLS ARPCL 22046, AS Disc AS 61, I grandi della classica 93.5121, Legend LGD 113, PGP 11023.

78 Beethoven: Symphony No. 5 in c, Op. 67
Philharmonia Orchestra; recorded 22–24 and 29 October 1959, Studio No. 1, Abbey Road
Release: Eng. = Col. 33CX1721/SAX 2372; HMV ASD 2564, ED 29 0252-1, EX 29 0379-3 in set SLS, TC-SLS 788 (Intl. OC 177-00794/802); Ger. = Col. SAXW 9550; Elec. C 100000, STC 91137, 1C 053-, 063-, 243-, 345-00736; in sets 1C 137-, 181-50187/94, 147-, 197-53400/19 and 137-29 0379-3; Fr. = HMV 2C 069-00798, 100736-1, -4; in set 2C 147-50298/318; It. = Col. 33QCX10410/SAXQ 7306; I Grandi Concerti GCL 24; US = Ang. (S)35843, AE-34425; (S)35954/61 in set (S)3619H and in set AEW-34469; Jap. = Col. OS-3075; Ang. AA-7051, AA-7002, AA-8081, EAA-93075/6, EAC-40058; in set AA-7131/9
CD = EMI CDC 747187-2, CDM 763357-2, CDZG 568057-2; Jap. Ang. CC30-3272/7, TOCE6117, TOCE7363/8.

79 Beethoven: Overture *Zur Weihe des Hauses*, Op. 124 (Consecration of the House)

Philharmonia Orchestra; recorded 28 October 1959, Studio No. 1, Abbey Road

Release: Eng. = Col. 33CX1930/SAX 2570, 33CX1702/SAX 2354; HMV ASD 2566, ED 29 0328-1; in set SLS, TC-SLS 788 (Intl. OC 177-00794/802) and SXLP.30321 (Intl. OC 147-03103/4); Ger. = Col. 33WCX1702/SAXW 2354, SMC 91625; Elec. C(STC)91070, 1C 053-, 069-00800; in sets 1C 197-03103/4, 147-, 197-53400/19 and 137-29 0379-3; Fr. = Col. 33FCX881/SAXF 198; HMV 2C 069-00800; in set 2C 147-50298/318; It. = Col. 33QCX10438/SAXQ 7339; US = Ang. (S)35661, AE-34426; in set AEW-34469; Jap. = Col. OS-3074; Ang. AA-7061, AB-7061, AA-8134, EAA-93077/8, AA-41/3, AA-8369, EAC-40057; in set AA-5131/9

CD = EMI CDC 747190-2, EMI CDM 763611-2, CDZG 568057-2, CZS 479562-2; Jap. Ang.CC33-3247.

80 Beethoven: *König Stefan*, Op. 117. Overture

Philharmonia Orchestra; recorded 29 October 1959, Studio No. 1, Abbey Road

Release: Eng. = Col. 33CX1721/SAX 2373, TA-33CX1721, 33CX1930/SAX 2570; HMV ASD 2567/8, ED 29 0401-1; in set SLS, TC-SLS 788 (Intl. OC 177-00794/802) and SLS 790 (Intl. 1C 153-00801/2); SXLP 30321 in set SXDW 3032 (Intl. OC 153-03103/4) and SXLP 30512 in set SXDW 3051 (Intl. OC 151-00801/2); Ger. = Col. SMC 80995; Elec. 1C 053-, 069-00800; in sets 1C 147-, 197-53400/19; Fr. = HMV 2C 153-00801/2; in set 2C 147-50298/318; It. = Col. 33QCX10410/SAXQ 7306; US = Ang. (S)35843, RL-32032, AE- 34441; Jap. = Col. OS-3075; Ang. AA-7002, AA-7364, AA- 8369, EAC-40058; in set AA-5131/9

CD = EMI CDM 763611-2, CDZG 568057-2, CZS 479562-2.

81 Beethoven: Symphony No. 3 in E-Flat, Op. 55, 'Eroica'

Philharmonia Orchestra; recorded 29 October and 11–13 November 1959, Studio No. 1, Abbey Road

Release: Eng. = Col. 33CX1710/SAX 2364, TA-33CX1710; HMV ASD 2562, SXLP 30310 (Intl. OC 053-00796), ED 29 0271-1, EX 29 0379-3 in set SLS, TC-SLS 788 (Intl. OC 177- 00794/802); Ger. = Col. SAXW 2364, SMC 91624; Elec. C 100000, C(STC)90943, 1C 053-, 243 345-00501; in sets 1C 137-, 181-50187/94, 147-, 197-53400/19 and 137-29 0379-3; Fr. = Col. 33FCX943/SAXF 261; HMV 2C 069-00796, 100501-1, -4; in set 2C 147-50298/318; It. = Col. 33QCX10435/SAXQ 7338; US = Ang. (S)35853, RL-32052, AE-34424; (S)35954/61 in set (S)3619H and in set AEW- 34469; Time-Life STL-143; Jap. = Col. OS-3073; Ang. SCA-1039, AA-7406, AA-8103, EAA-93075/6, EAC-40056; in set AA-5131/9

CD = EMI 747186-2, CDM 63356-2, CDZG 568057-2; Jap. Ang. CC30-3272/7, CC33-3243, TOCE6116, TOCE7363/8.

82 Haydn: Symphony No. 101 in D, 'Clock'

Philharmonia Orchestra; recorded 18–19 January 1960, Studio No. 1, Abbey Road

Release: Eng. = Col. 33CX1748/SAX 2395; Ger. = Col. 33WCX1748/SAXW

2395; Elec. C(STC)91130, C(STC)91409; Fr. = Col. 33FCX901/
SAXF 208; HMV 2C 069-01505; It. = Col. 33QCX10454/SAXQ
7354; US = Ang. (S)35872; Jap. = Col. OL-3171; Ang. SCA-1034,
AA-7291, AA-8090,
EAA-93079/80, EAC-70201, EAC-81047
CD = EMI CDMC 763667-2; Jap. Ang. TOCE6566/8.

83   Haydn: Symphony No. 98 in B-Flat
Philharmonia Orchestra; recorded 19–21 January 1960, Studio No. 1, Abbey Road
Release: Eng. = Col. 33CX1748/SAX 2395; Ger. = Col. 33WCX1748/
SAXW 2395; Elec. C(STC)91130, C(STC)91409; Fr. = Col.
33FCX901/SAXF 208; It. = Col. 33QCX10454/SAXQ 2395;
US = Ang. (S)35872; Jap. = Col. OL-3171; Ang. SCA-1034, AA-7291
CD = EMI CDMC 763667-2; Jap. Ang. TOCE6566/8.

84   Mendelssohn: Symphony No. 3 in A, Op. 56, 'Scottish'
Philharmonia Orchestra; recorded 22, 25 and 27–28 January 1960, Studio No. 1, Abbey Road
Release: Eng. = Col. 33CX1736/SAX2342; Ger. = Col. 33WCX524/SAXW
9541; Elec. C(STC)91131, 1C 037-, 051-, 225-, 237-00518; Fr. = Col.
33FCX838/SAXF 190; It. = Col. 33QCX10427/SAXQ 7327;
US = Ang. (S)35880, RL-32072; Jap. = Col. OL-3175/OS-3019; Ang.
SCA-1033, EAA-127, EAA-93081/2, AA-7258, AA-8082, EAC-81062
**CD = EMI CDM 763853-2, CZS 479885-2; Jap. Ang. CC33-3264,
TOCE7009**

Note: Both the Klemperer and Mendelssohn endings were recorded at these sessions.

85   Mendelssohn: *A Midsummer Night's Dream*. Overture, Op. 21 and Incidental Music, Op. 61 (No. 1, 2a, 3, 5, 7, 9, 10a, 11 and 12a only)
Philharmonia Orchestra and Chorus; Heather Harper, soprano, Janet Baker, mezzo-soprano; recorded 28–29 January and 16 and 18–19 February 1960, Studio No. 1, Abbey Road
Release: Eng. = Col. 33CX1746/SAX 2393; HMV SXLP 30196 (Intl. OC
053-00521); Ger. = Col. 33WCX1746/SAXW 2393; Elec.
C(STC)91180, CVB 897, 1C 037-, 237-, 053-00521; Fr. = Col.
33FCX897/SAXF 209; HMV 2C 053-, 059-00521; It. = Col.
33QCX10428/SAXQ 7329; Neth. = HMV 1A 137-53562/3;
US = Ang. (S)35881, AE-34445; Jap. = Col. OS-3090; Ang.
AA-7066, AA-8104, EAA-93081/2, EAA-189, EAC-81083
**CD = EMI CDC 747230-2, CDM 764144-2; Jap. Ang. CC33-3757,
TOCE7028**
Overture only: Eng. = HMV SXLP 30227 in set SLS 5073;
Jap. = Ang. SCA-1022, AA-7289
Nocturne and Wedding March only: Eng. = Col. SEL.1708.

86   Mendelssohn: *Hebrides Overture*, Op. 26
Philharmonia Orchestra; recorded 15 February 1960, Studio No. 1, Abbey Road
Release: Eng. = Col. 33CX1736/SAX 2342; Ger. = Col. 33WCX524/SAXW
9541; Elec. C(STC)91131, 1C 037-, 051-, 225-, 237-00518; Fr. = Col.
33FCX838/SAXF 190; Neth. = HMV 1A 137-53562/3; It. = Col.
33QCX10427/SAXQ 7327; US = Ang. (S)35880, RL-32072;
Jap. = Col. OL-3176/OS-3019; Ang. SCA-1033, AA-8104, AA-8097,
EAA-189, EAA-93081/2, EAC-81063.

DISCOGRAPHY

87 Mendelssohn: Symphony No. 4 in A, Op. 90, 'Italian'

Philharmonia Orchestra; recorded 15 and 17–18 February 1960, Studio No. 1, Abbey Road

Release: Eng. = Col. 33CX1751/SAX 2398; HMV SXLP 30178 (Intl. OC 047-00524); Ger. = Col. 33CX550/SBOW 854, SMC 91274; Elec. C(STC)70437, 1C 037-, 053-, 237-00524, 037-, 237-29 0643; Fr. = Col.33FCX896/SAXF 218; HMV 2C 037-, 053-00524; Neth. = Col. HC(SHC)149; It. = Col. 33QCX10438/SAXQ 7340; US = Ang. (S)35629, AE–, 4AE-34453; Jap. = Col. OL-3178/OS-3027; Ang. SCA-1022, AA-7289, AA-8082, EAA-127, EAC-70132, EAA-93081/2, EAC-81062

CD = EMI CDM 763853-2, CZS 479885-2; Jap. Ang. 33CC-3264, TOCE7009; I grandi della classica 93.5121.

88 Schumann: Symphony No. 4 in d, Op. 120

Philharmonia Orchestra; recorded 19 February and 4–5 May 1960, Studio No. 1, Abbey Road

Release: Eng. = Col. 33CX1751/SAX 2398; HMV SXLP 30178 (Intl. OC 047-00524); Ger. = Col. SMC 91274; Elec. C(STC) 70478, 1C 037-, 053-, 237-00524; 037-, 237-290643; in set 1C 197-52497/9; Fr. = Col. 33FCX896/SAXF 218; HMV 2C 037-, 053-00524; It. = Col. 33QCX10438/SAXQ 7340; US = Ang. (S)35629, AE–, 4AE-34453; Jap. = Col. OL- 3178/OS-3027; Ang. AA-8017, EAA-152, EAA-93095/6, EAC- 81064, EAC-70171

CD = EMI CDM 763613-2, CZS 479885-2.

Note: The session on the 19th was held for experimental purposes only.

89 Wagner: *Tannhäuser*. Overture.

Philharmonia Orchestra; recorded 23–24 February 1960, Kingsway Hall, London

Release: Eng. = Col. 33CX1697/SAX 2347, CMS.837/SMS.1007; HMV ASD 2695, SXLP 30436 (Intl. OC 053-00498); TC-SXLP 30436; in set SLS 5075 (Intl. OC 153-50347/9); Ger. = Elec. 1C 037-03459; in sets 1C 187-00498/9 and F668- 525/33; Fr. = Col. 33FCX868/9//SAXF 187/8; HMV 2C 069-, 269-00498; It. = Col.33QCX10391/2//SAXQ 7280/1, 33QCX10503; US = Ang. (S)36187, RL-32039, AE-34418; (S)35875/6 in set (S)3610B; Jap. = Col. OS-3003/4, OL- 3226; Ang. SCA-1087, AA-7417, AA-8089, EAA-93099/100, EAC-85038, EAC-55066

CD = EMI CDC 747254-2, CDM 763617-2; Jap. Ang. CC33-3266, TOCE6559, TOCE1514.

90 Wagner: *Der fliegende Holländer*. Overture

Philharmonia Orchestra; recorded 24–25 February 1960, Kingsway Hall, London

Release: Eng. = Col. 33CX1697/SAX 2347, TA-33CX1697, CMS.837/SMS.1007; HMV ASD 2695, SXLP 30436 (Intl. OC 053-00498); TC-SXLP 30436; in set SLS 5075 (Intl. OC 153-50347/9); Ger. = Elec. 1C 037-03459; in sets 1C 187-00498/9 and F668-525/33; Fr. = Col. 33FCX868/9//SAXF 187/8; HMV 2C 069, 269-00498; It. = Col. 33QCX10391/2//SAXQ 7280/1; US = Ang. (S)36187, RL-32039, AE-34418; (S) 35875/6 in set (S)3610B; Jap. = Col.OS-3003/4, OL-3226; Ang. SCA-1087, AA-7417, AA-8089, EAA-93099/100, EAC- 85038, EAC-55066

CD = EMI CDC 747254-2, CDM 763617-2; Jap. Ang. CC33-3266, TOCE6559, TOCE1514.

91 Wagner: *Lohengrin*. Act I: Prelude.

Philharmonia Orchestra; recorded 25 February and 3 March 1960, Kingsway Hall, London

Release: Eng. = Col. 33CX1698/SAX 2348, CMS.837/SMS.1007; HMV ASD 2695, SXLP 30436 (Intl. OC 053-00498); TC-SXLP 30436; in set SLS 5075 (Intl. OC 153-50347/9); Ger. = Elec. 1C 037-03459; in sets 1C 187-00498/9 and F668- 525/33; Fr. = Col.33FCX868/9//SAXF 187/8; HMV 2C 069-, 269-00498; It. = Col.33QCX10391/2//SAXQ 7280/1; US = Ang. (S)36188, RL-32057; (S)35875/6 in set (S)3610B; Jap. = Col. OS-3003/4, OL-3227; Ang. SCA-1109, AA-7296, AA-8597, EAA-93099/100, EAC-55067

CD = EMI CDC 747254-2, CDM 763617-2; Jap. Ang. CC33-3266, TOCE6559, TOCE1514.

92 Wagner: *Lohengrin*. Act III: Prelude.

Philharmonia Orchestra; recorded 27 February 1960, Kingsway Hall, London

Release: Eng. = Col. 33CX1698/SAX 2348, CMS.837/SMS.1007, SCD. 2178; HMV ASD 2696, SXLP 30525 (Intl. OC 053-00499); in set SLS 5075 (Intl. OC 153-50347/9); Ger. = Elec. 1C 037-03459; in sets 1C 187-00498/9 and F668-525/33; Fr. = Col. 33FCX868/9//SAXF 187/8; HMV 2C 069-00499; It. = Col. 33QCX10391/2//SAXQ 7280/1, SEBQ 260; US = Ang. (S)36188, RL-32057; (S)35875/6 in set (S)3610B; Jap. = Col. OS-3003/4, OL-3227; Ang. SCA-1109, AA-7296, AA-8089, EAA-93099/100; EAC-55067

CD = EMI CDC 747254-2, CDM 763617-2; Jap. Ang. CC33-3266, TOCE6559, TOCE1514.

93 Wagner: *Die Götterdämmerung*. Act III: Siegfrieds Trauermusik

Philharmonia Orchestra; recorded 27 February 1960, Kingsway Hall, London

Release: Eng. = Col. 33CX1698/SAX 2348, CMS.837/SMS.1007, SEL.1677/ESL 6283; HMV ASD 2696, SXLP 30525 (Intl. OC 053-00499); in set SLS 5075 (Intl. OC 153-50347/9); Ger. = Elec. C(STC)91281, 1C 037-00567; in sets 1C 187- 00498/9 and F668-525/33; Fr. = Col. 33FCX868/9//SAXF 187/8; HMV 2C 069-00499, 069-, 269-01356; It. = Col. 33QCX10391/2//SAXQ 7280/1, SEBQ 234; US = Ang. (S)36188, RL-32057, AE-34407; (S)35875/6 in set (S)3610B; Jap. = Col. OS-3003/4, OL-3227; Ang. SCA- 1109, AA-7296, AA-7402, AA-8089, EAA-93099/100, EAC-55067

CD = EMI CDC 747255-2, CDM 763618-2; Jap. Ang. CC33-3267, TOCE6560, TOCE1515.

94 Wagner: *Die Meistersinger von Nürnberg*. Act I: Prelude.

Philharmonia Orchestra; recorded 1–2 March 1960, Kingsway Hall, London

Release: Eng. = Col. 33CX1698/SAX 2348, CMS.837/SMS.1007; HMV ASD 2696, SXLP-30525 (Intl. OC 053-00499); in set SLS 5075 (Intl. OC 153-50347/9); Ger. = Elec. SMC 80944, SME 2037/8; in sets 1C 187-00498/9 and F668-525/33; Fr. = Col. 33FCX868/9//SAXF 187/8; HMV 2C 069-, 269-01356, 069-00499; It. = Col. 33QCX10391/2//SAXQ 7280/1; US = Ang. (S)36187, RL-32039, AE-34418; (S)35875/6 in set (S)3610B; Time-Life STL-142; Jap. = Col. OS-3003/4, OL-3227; Ang. SCA-1109, AA-7296, AA-8089, EAA-93099/100, EAC-85038; EAC-55067

CD = EMI CDC 747255-2, CDM 763618-2; Jap. Ang. CC33-3267, TOCE6560, TOCE1515.

DISCOGRAPHY

95   Wagner: *Tristan und Isolde*. Prelude and Liebestod
     Philharmonia Orchestra; recorded 1–3 March 1960, Kingsway Hall, London
     Release: Eng. = Col. 33CX1698/SAX 2348, CMS.837/SMS.1007; HMV ASD 2696, SXLP 30525 (Intl. OC 053-00499); in set SLS 5075 (Intl. OC 153-50347/9); Ger. = Elec. 1C 037-03459; in sets 1C 187-00498/9 and F668-525/33; Fr. = Col. 33FCX868/9//SAXF 187/8; HMV 2C 069-, 269-01356, 069- 00499; It. = Col. 33QCX10391/2//SAXQ 7280/1, 33QCX10503; US = Ang. (S)36188, RL-32057; (S)36875/6 in set (S)3610B; Jap. = Col. OS-3003/4, OL-3227; Ang. SCA-1109, AA-7296, AA-8597, EAA-93099/100, EAC-55067
     CD = EMI CDC 747254-2, CDM 763617-2; Jap. Ang. CC33-3266, TOCE6559, TOCE1514.

96   Wagner: *Rienzi*. Overture
     Philharmonia Orchestra; recorded 2–3 March 1960, Kingsway Hall, London
     Release: Eng. = Col. 33CX1697/SAX 2347, TA-33CX1697, CMS.837/SMS1007; HMV ASD 2695, SXLP 30436 (Intl. OC 053- 00498); TC-SXLP 30436; in set SLS 5075 (Intl. OC 153- 50347/9); Ger. = Elec. in sets 1C 187-00498/9 and F668-525/33; Fr. = Col. 33FCX868/9//SAXF 187/8; HMV 2C 069-, 269-00498; It. = Col. 33QCX10391/2//SAXQ 7280/1, 33QCX10503; US = Ang. (S)36187, RL-32039, AE-34418; (S)35875/6 in set (S)3610B; Jap. = Ang. SCA-1087, AA- 7417, AA-8597, EAA-93099/100, EAC-55066
     CD = EMI CDC 747254-2, CDM 763617-2; Jap. Ang. CC33-3266, TOCE6559, TOCE1514.

97   Wagner: *Tannhäuser*. Act III: Prelude.
     Philharmonia Orchestra; recorded 3 March 1960, Kingsway Hall, London
     Release: Eng. = Col. 33CX1820/SAX 2464; HMV ASD 2697, SXLP 30528 (OC 053-00567); in set SLS 5075 (Intl. OC 153-50347/9); Ger. = Elec. C(STC)91281, 1C 037-00567; in set F668-525/33; Fr. = Col. 33FCX937/SAXF 254; HMV 2C069-, 269-00567; It. = Col. 33QCX10479; US = Ang. (S)35947, RL-32058, AE-34407; Jap. = Col. OS-3003/4; Ang. SCA-1011, AA-7402, EAA-93101/2, EAC-55068
     CD = Jap. Angel TOCE1514.

98   Strauss, Richard: *Salome*, Op. 54. Salomes Tanz
     Philharmonia Orchestra; recorded 5 March 1960, Kingsway Hall, London
     Release: Eng. = Col. 33CX1715/SAX 2367; HMV SXLP 30298 (Intl. 0C 053-03538), TC-SXLP 30298, TCC2-POR 54296; Fr. = Col. 33FCX809/SAXF 185; HMV 2C 181-50557/8; It. = Col. 33QCX10404/SAXQ 7299; US = Ang. (S)35737, AE-34472; Jap. = Col. OL-3172/OS3016; Ang. SCA-1042, AA-7407, AA-8086
     CD = EMI CDM 763350-2; Jap. Ang. CC33-3758, TOCE6126, TOCE 7036, TOCE 1524.

99   Wagner: *Die Meistersinger von Nürnberg*. Act III: Aufzug der Meistersinger and Tanz der Lehrbuben
     Philharmonia Orchestra; recorded 8 March 1960, Kingsway Hall, London
     Release: Eng. = Col. 33CX1698/SAX 2348, CMS.837/SMS.1007, SEL1677/ESL 6283; HMV ASD 2696, SXLP 30525 (Intl. OC 053-00499); in set SLS 5075 (Intl. 0C 153-50347/9); Ger. = Col. 33WCX600/SAXW 9880; Elec. in sets 1C 187- 00498/9 and F668-525/33; Fr. = Col. 33FCX868/9//SAXF 187/8, SEBQ 234; HMV 2C 069-, 269-01356;

US = Ang. (S)36188, RL-32057; (S)35875/6 in set (S)3610B; Jap. = Col. OS-3003/4, OL-3227; Ang. SCA- 1109, AA-7296, AA-8597, EAA-93099/100, EAC-55067
CD = EMI 747255-2, CDM 763618-2; Jap. Ang. CC33-3267, TOC-E6560, TOCE1515 (Dance of the Apprentices only).

100 Strauss, Richard: *Till Eulenspiegels lustige Streiche*, Op. 28
Philharmonia Orchestra; recorded 8–9 March 1960, Kingsway Hall, London
Release: Eng. = Col. 33CX1715/SAX 2367; HMV SXLP 302988 (Intl. 0C 053-03538), TC-SXLP 30298, TCC2-POR 54296; Fr. = Col. 33FCX809/SAXF 185; HMV 2C 181-50557/8; It. = Col. 33QCX10404/SAXQ 7299; US = Ang. (S)35737, AE-34472; Jap. = Col. OL-3172/OS-3016; Ang. SCA-1042, AA-7407, AA-8086
CD = EMI CDM 764146-2; Jap. Ang. CC33-3758, TOCE7036, TOCE1524.

101 Strauss, Richard: *Don Juan*, Op. 20
Philharmonia Orchestra; recorded 9–10 March 1960, Kingsway Hall, London
Release: Eng. = Col. 33CX1715/SAX 2367; HMV SXLP 302988 (Intl. 0C 053-03538), TC-SXLP 30298, TCC2-POR 54296; Fr. = Col. 33FCX809/SAXF 185; HMV 2C 181-50557/8; It. = Col. 33QCX10404/SAXQ 7299; US = Ang. (S)35737, AE-34472; Jap. = Col. OL-3172/OS-3016; Ang. SCA-1042, AA-7407, AA-8086
CD = EMI CDM 763350-2; Jap. Ang. CC33-3758, TOCE6126, TOCE7036, TOCE1524.

102 Wagner: *Die Walküre*. Act III: Walkürenritt
Philharmonia Orchestra; recorded 10 March 1960, Kingsway Hall, London
Release: Eng. = Col. 33CX1820/SAX 2464, SCD.2178; HMV in set SLS 5075 (Intl. 0C 153-50347/9), ASD 2697, SXLP 30258 (Intl. 0C 053-00567); Ger. = Elec. STC 91281, 1C 037-, 237-00567; in set F668-525/33; Fr. = Col. 33FCX937/SAXF 254; HMV 2C 069-, 269-00567; It. = Col. 33QCX10479; US = Ang. (S), 4XS-, 8XS-35947, RL-32058, AE-34407; Jap. = Ang. SCA-1011, AA-7402, AA-8089, EAA-93101/2, EAC-55068
CD = EMI CDC 747255-2, CDM 763618-2; Jap. Ang. CC33-3267, TOCE6560, TOCE1515.

103 Weber: *Der Freischütz*. Overture
Philharmonia Orchestra; recorded 5–6 May 1960, Kingsway Hall, London
Release: Eng. = Col. 33CX1770/SAX 2417; US = Ang. (S)36175, RL-32079; Time-Life 143; Jap. = Col. OL-3190/OS-3097; Ang. AA-8097
CD = EMI CDM 763917-2.

104 Weber: *Oberon*. Overture
Philharmonia Orchestra; recorded 6 May 1960, Kingsway Hall, London
Release: Eng. = Col. 33CX1770/SAX 2417; Ger. = Elec. SMC 80944; US = Ang. (S)36175, RL-32079; Jap. = Col. OL-3190/OS-3097; Ang. AA-7038
CD = EMI CDM 763917-2.

105 Mozart: Concerti for Horn and Orchestra, K. 412, 417, 447, 496
Philharmonia Orchestra; Alan Civil, horn; recorded 11–12 (Nos. 1–2) and 18–19 May (Nos. 3–4) 1960, Studio No. 1, Abbey Road
Release: Eng. = Col. 33CX1760/SAX 2406; HMV SXLP 30207 (Intl. 0C 053-00530); Ger. = Elec. STC 91205, 1C 037-00530; in set 1C

197-53714/38; Fr. = Col. 33FCX899/SAXF 211; HMV 2C 037-, 061-00530; US = Ang. (S)35689, RL-32028, AE- 34410; Jap. = Col. OL-3190/OS-3099; Ang. SCA-1027, AA- 7283, AA-8708
CD = EMI CDZ 767012-2, CDM 767032-2; Jap. Ang. TOCE6807 No. 4 only: Eng. = HMV in set SLS 5073.

106 Schumann: Concerto in a for Piano and Orchestra, Op. 54

Philharmonia Orchestra; Annie Fischer, piano; recorded 22–24 May 1960 and 9–10 and 16 August 1962, Studio No. 1, Abbey Road

Release: Eng. = Col. 33CX1842/SAX 2485; Ger. = Elec. C(STC)91284; in set 1C 197-52497/9; Fr. = Col. 33FCX(SAXF)967; US = Ang. 4XG-60440; Jap. = Ang. AA-7006
CD = Priceless C 16442, EMI CDM 764145-2.

107 Liszt: Concerto No. 1 in E-Flat for Piano and Orchestra, G. 124

Philharmonia Orchestra; Annie Fischer, piano; recorded 24 May 1960 and 10 and 31 May 1962, Studio No. 1, Abbey Road

Release: Eng. = Col. 33CX1842/SAX 2485; Ger. = Elec. C(STC)91284; Fr. = Col. 33FCX(SAXF)967; US = Ang. 4XG-60440; Jap. = Ang. AA-7006
CD = EMI CDM 764144-2.

L-86 Beethoven: Overture *Zur Weihe des Hauses*, Op. 124 (Consecration of the House)

Philharmonia Orchestra; recorded in the Musikvereinssaal, Vienna, 29 May 1960

Release: **CD = Fonit-Cetra CDE 1038.**

L-87 Beethoven: Symphony No. 2 in D, Op. 36

Philharmonia Orchestra; recorded in the Musikvereinssaal, Vienna, 29 May 1960

Release: **CD = Fonit Cetra CDE 1033, Arkadia CDGI 756.1.**

L-88 Beethoven: Symphony No. 3 in E-Flat, Op. 55, 'Eroica'

Philharmonia Orchestra; recorded in the Musikvereinssaal, Vienna, 29 May 1960

Release: **CD = Fonit-Cetra CDE 1007, Arkadia CDGI 755.1, I grandi della classica 93.5121.**

L-89 Beethoven: *Egmont*, Op. 84. Overture

Philharmonia Orchestra; recorded in the Musikvereinssaal, Vienna, 31 May 1960

Release: **CD = Fonit Cetra CDE 1008, Virtuoso 22697042, Arkadia CDGI 757.1; I grandi della classica 93.5121.**

L-90 Beethoven: Symphony No. 4 in B-Flat, Op. 60

Philharmonia Orchestra; recorded in the Musikvereinssaal, Vienna, 31 May 1960

Release: **CD = Fonit Cetra CDE 1038, Arkadia CDGI 757.1, I grandi della classica 93.5121.**

L-91 Beethoven: Symphony No. 5 in c, Op. 67

Philharmonia Orchestra; recorded in the Musikvereinssaal, Vienna, 31 May 1960

Release: **CD = Virtuoso 2697042, Cetra CDE 1067, Arkadia CDGI 758.1, Frequenz 041.018.**

L-92 Beethoven: *Die Geschöpfe des Prometheus*, Op. 43. Overture
Philharmonia Orchestra; recorded in the Musikvereinssaal, Vienna, 2 June 1960
Release: CD = **Fonit Cetra CDE 1038, Virtuoso 2697042, Arkadia CDGI 757.1.**

L-93 Beethoven: Symphony No. 6 in F, Op. 68, 'Pastorale'
Philharmonia Orchestra; recorded in the Musikvereinssaal, Vienna, 2 June 1960
Release: CD = **Cetra CDE 1068, Arkadia CDGI 758.1, I grandi della classica 93.5121.**

L-94 Beethoven: Symphony No. 7 in A, Op. 92
Philharmonia Orchestra; recorded in the Musikvereinssaal, Vienna, 2 June 1960
Release: CD = **Cetra CDE 1008, Arkadia CDGI 756.1, I grandi della classica 93.5121.**

L-95 Beethoven: *Coriolan Overture*, Op. 62
Philharmonia Orchestra; recorded in the Musikvereinssaal, Vienna, 4 June 1960
Release: CD = **Cetra CDE 1008, Virtuoso 2697042, Arkadia CDGI 759.1, I grandi della classica 93.5121.**

L-96 Beethoven: Symphony No. 8 in F, Op. 93
Philharmonia Orchestra; recorded in the Musikvereinssaal, Vienna, 4 June 1960
Release: CD = **Cetra CDE 1033, Arkadia CDGI 756.1.**

L-97 Beethoven: Symphony No. 1 in C, Op. 21
Philharmonia Orchestra; recorded in the Musikvereinssaal, Vienna, 7 June 1960
Release: CD = **Cetra CDE 1067, Arkadia CDGI 755.1.**

L-98 Beethoven: Symphony No. 9 in d, Op. 125, 'Choral'
Philharmonia Orchestra and Chorus of the Singverein, Vienna.
Wilma Lipp, soprano, Ursula Boese, mezzo-soprano, Fritz Wunderlich, tenor, Franz Crass, bass; recorded in the Musikvereinssaal, Vienna, 7 June 1960
Release: CD = **Stradivarius STR 10003, Cetra, CDE 1051, Arkadia CDGI 759.1, I grandi della classica 93.5121.**

108 Brahms: Concerto in D for Violin and Orchestra, Op. 77 (Joachim cadenzas)
Orchestre National de la Radiodiffusion Française; David Oistrakh, violin; recorded 17–19 June 1960 in the Salle Wagram, Paris
Release: Eng. = Col. 33CX1765/SAX 2411, TA-33CX1765; HMV SXLP 30264 (Intl. 0C 053-00534); in set SLS 5004 (Intl. 0C 177-05777/81); CFP 4398; Ger. = Col. 33WCX560/SAXW 9542; Elec. C(STC)91134, 1C 037-, 063-, 237-00534; Fr. = Col. 33FCX879/SAXF 196; HMV 2C 059-, 065, 259- 00534; in set 2C 181-52289/90; It. = Col. 33QCX10447/SAXQ 7347; US = Ang. (S)35836, RL-32031; Jap. = Col. OS-3084; Ang. SCA-1090, AA-8032, EAC-85052
CD = **EMI CDM 769034-2, CZS 479890-2; Jap. Ang. CE28-5049, CE25-5678.**

109   Humperdinck: *Hänsel und Gretel*. Overture and Act II: Dream Pantomime
      Philharmonia Orchestra; recorded 27–29 September 1960, Kingsway Hall, London
      Release: Eng. = Col. 33CX1770/SAX 2417; US = Ang. (S)36175, RL-32079; Jap. = Col. OL-3190/OS-3097; Ang. AA-7038, AA-8097
      CD = EMI CDM 763917-2
      Dream Pantomime only: Eng. = Col. SCD.2239.

110   Weber: *Euryanthe*. Overture
      Philharmonia Orchestra; recorded 28 September 1960, Kingsway Hall, London
      Release: Eng. = Col. 33CX1770/SAX 2417; US = Ang. (S)36175, RL-32079; Jap. = Col. OL-3190/OS-3097; Ang. AA-7038, AA-8097
      CD = EMI CDM 763917-2.

111   Gluck: *Iphigénie en Aulide*. Overture (Wagner concert ending)
      Philharmonia Orchestra; recorded 29 September 1960, Kingsway Hall, London
      Release: Eng. = Col. 33CX1770/SAX 2417; US = Ang. (S)36175, RL-32079; Time-Life STL-141; Jap. = Col. OL-3190/OS-3097; Ang. AA-7038, AA-8090
      CD = EMI CDM 764143-2.

112   Mozart: *Die Entführung aus dem Serail*, K. 384. Overture
      Philharmonia Orchestra; recorded 29 September 1960, Kingsway Hall, London
      Release: Eng. = Col. 33CX1948/SAX 2587, 33CX1786/SAX 2436; HMV in sets SLS 5048 (Intl. 0C 147-01842/7) and EX 29 0482-3; Ger. = Elec. SME 80933, STC 91332, SMC 80944, C(STC) 91136; in sets 1C 153-01842/7, 197-53714/38 and 137-29 0482-3; Fr. = Col. 33FCX918/SAXF 236; HMV 2C 061-, 069-00602, 100602-4; Neth. = HMV 1A 137-53556/7; US = Ang. (S)36128, (S)36289, RL-32099, AE-34462; in set AEW-34470; Jap. = Col. OS-3116; Ang. SCA-1021, AA- 7404, AA-8097, AA-8578, AA-7596
      CD = EMI CDM 763619-2; Jap. Ang. TOCE-6574, TOCE-1574.

113   Bach: Six Brandenburg Concerti, BWV 1046-1051
      Philharmonia Orchestra; Hugh Bean, violin; Gareth Morris and Arthur Ackroyd, flutes; Sidney Sutcliffe, Stanley Smith and Peter Newbury, oboes; Cecil James, bassoon; Alan Civil, and Andrew Woodburn, horns; Adolf Scherbaum, trumpet; George Malcolm, harpsichord
      Recorded as follows in Studio No. 1, Abbey Road:
      No. 1: 3–4 October 1960
      No. 2: 30 September and 1 and 11 October 1960
      No. 3: 4–5 October 1960
      No. 4: 6–7 October 1960
      No. 5: 1 and 7–8 October 1960
      No. 6: 5, 8 and 9 October 1960
      Release: Eng. = Col. 33CX1763/4//SAX 2408/9; Ger. = Elec. 1C 187-00532/3, 1C 197-54135/45; Fr. = Col. 33FCX910/1//SAXF 224/5; HMV 2C 181-00532/3; It. = Col. SAXQ 7341/2; US = Ang. (S)35845/6 in (S)3627B-L, AE-34401 (Nos. 1, 2, and 6) and AE-34002 (Nos. 3, 4, and 5); Jap. = Col. OS-3081/2; Ang. AA-7125/6, EAC-93093/4
      CD = EMI CDM 764150-2
      No. 3 only: Ger. = Elec. C(STC)50586.

DISCOGRAPHY

114   Mozart: Symphony No. 35 in D, K. 385, 'Haffner'
      Philharmonia Orchestra; recorded 22–23 October 1960, Studio No. 1, Abbey Road
      Release: Eng. = Col. 33CX1786/SAX 2436; HMV in sets SLS 5048 (Intl. 0C 147-01842/7) and EX 29 0482-3; Ger. = Elec. C(STC)91143, SMC 110000/1-3; in sets 1C 153-01842/7, 197-53714/38 and 137-29 0482-3; Fr. = Col. 33FCX5005; HMV 2C 061-01190; Neth. = HMV 1A 137-53556/7; US = Ang. (S)36128; in set AEW-34470; Jap. = Col. OS-3116; Ang. SCA-1021, AA-7404, AA-8136, EAA-93083/4, EAC-40097
      CD = EMI CMS 763272-2; Ger. Zweitausendeins 60625; Jap. Ang. TOCE6093/6.

115   Beethoven: Symphony No. 7 in A, Op. 92
      Philharmonia Orchestra; recorded 25 October (I–II), 19 November (II–IV) and 3 December 1960, Kingsway Hall, London
      Release: Eng. = Col. 33CX1769/SAX 2315; HMV ASD 2566; ED 29-03281, EX 29 0379-3; in set SLS 788 (Intl. 0C 177- 00794/802), TC-SLS 788; Ger. = Col. SMC 91628; Elec. C 100000; in sets 1C 181-50187/94, 137-29 0379-3 and 147-, 197-53400/19; Fr. = Col. 33FCX895/SAXF 217; HMV 2C 069-00800, 100538-1, -4; in set 2C 147-50298/318; It. = Col. 33QCX10434/SAXQ 7337; US = Ang. (S)35945, AE-34427; (S)35954/61 in set (S)3619H and in set AEW-34469; Jap. = Col. OS-3077; Ang. SCA-1105/6, AA-7294, AA-8094/5, EAA-93075/6, EAC-40061/2; in set AA-5131/9
      CD = EMI CDC 747184-2, CDM 763354-2, CDZG 568057-2; Jap. Ang. CC30-3272/7, TOCE6114, TOCE7363/8.

116   Bruckner: Symphony No. 7 in E (1885 version)
      Philharmonia Orchestra; recorded 1–5 November 1960, Kingsway Hall, London
      Release: Eng. = Col. 33CX1808/9//SAX 2454/5; HMV ED 29004-1, -4; Ger. = Elec. C(STC)912120/1s, 037-, 237-29 0004; Fr. = Col. 33FCX(SAXF)945/6; HMV CCA 945/6; It. = Col. 33QCX10475/6; US = Ang. (S)35785/6 in (S)3626B, AE-34420; Jap. = Col. OS-3126/7; Ang. SCA-1061/2, AA-7410/1, AA-8091/2, EAA-93097/8, EAC-50044/5
      CD = EMI CDM 769126-2, CZS 479885-2; Jap. Ang. CE28-5155, TOCE-1571.

117   Schubert: Symphony No. 9 in C, D. 944
      Philharmonia Orchestra; recorded 16–19 November 1960, Kingsway Hall, London
      Release: Eng. = Col. 33CX1754/SAX 2397; HMV ED 29 0426; Ger. = Elec. SHZE 381, CVB 900, 1C 037-, 237-00527; 037-, 237-29 0426; Fr. = Col. 33FCX900/SAXF 212; HMV 2C 059-, 259-00527; It. = Col. 33QCX10429/SAXQ 7330; US = Ang. (S)35946, RL-32001, AE-34463; Jap. = Col. OS- 3108; Ang. SCA-1070, AA-7413, EAC-40066
      CD = EMI CDM 763854-2, CZS 479885-2.

118   Bach: *Matthäus-Passion*, BWV 244
      Philharmonia Orchestra and Chorus; Hampstead Parish Church Choir; Elisabeth Schwarzkopf, soprano; Janet Baker, Christa Ludwig, mezzo-sopranos; Helen Watts, contralto; Peter Pears, Nicolai Gedda, Wilfred

Brown, tenors; Dietrich Fischer-Dieskau, Otakar Kraus, Geraint Evans, baritones; Walter Berry, John Carol Case, basses

Recorded 21 November (Studio No. 1, Abbey Road) and 25–26 November 1960; 3–4 January, 14–15 April, 4–6, 8, 10–12 May and 28 November 1961, Kingsway Hall, London

Release: Eng. = Col. 33CX1799/803//SAX 2446/50; HMV SLS 827 (Intl. 1E 191-01312/5); Ger. = Elec. C(STC)91200/3, 1C 153-01312/5; in set 1C 197-54135/45; Fr. = Col. 33FCX9241/5//SAXF 243/7; HMV C 153-, 167-01312/5; It. = Col. 33QCX10458S/62//SAXQ 7358S/62; US = Ang. (S)35801/5 in (S)3699E-L; Jap. = Col. OS-3120/4; Ang. AA-9027/31, AA-9366/9, EAC-77245/8

CD = EMI CMS 763058-2; Jap. Ang. CE25-5711/3

Arias for soprano and mezzo-soprano (Nos. 10, 12, 19, 33, 47, 58 and 61)

Release: Eng. = Col. 33CX(SAX)5253; US = Ang. (S)36163

CD = EMI Eminence CD EMX 2223 (CDM 565210-2)

Choruses and chorales (Nos. 1, 16, 21, 31, 35, 44, 48, 53, 55, 63, 72 and 78)

Release: Eng. = Col. 33CX1881/SAX 2525; Ger. = Col. SMC 81021; Elec. 1C 037-00580; Fr. = HMV 2C 037-00580; US = Ang. (S)36162

CD = EMI Eminence CD EMX 2223 (CDM 565210-2)

Other excerpts: Eng. = Col. SEL 1707; Ger. = Elec. C(STC)80693/4; US = Time-Life STL-144

Note: A further session was held on 4 December 1961 to superimpose Schwarzkopf and Berry in No. 45 A & B and in No. 77.

119 Brahms: *Ein deutsches Requiem*, Op. 45

Philharmonia Orchestra and Chorus; Elisabeth Schwarzkopf, soprano, Dietrich Fischer-Dieskau, baritone, Ralph Downes, organ; recorded 2 January; 21, 23 and 25 March; 26 April 1961, Kingsway Hall, London

Release: Eng. = Col. 33CX1781/2//SAX 2430/1; HMV ASD 2789/90 in set SLS 821 (Intl. 0E 153-01295/6); Ger. = Col. STC 91224s/5; Elec. 1C 161-00545S/6, 153-01295/6; Fr. = Col. 33FCX915/6S//SAXF 233/4s; HMV 2C 167-01295/6; 29 0279-3, -5; It. = Col. 33QCX104555/6//SAXQ 7355/6; US = (S)35911/2 in Ang. (S)B3624-L, 4XS-3624; Jap. = Col. OS-3091/2; Ang. SCA 1117/8, AA-8328/9, AA-9092/3

CD = EMI CDC 747238-2; Jap. Ang. CC33-3759

Excerpt: US = Ang. S-3754.

L-99 Bruckner: Symphony No. 6 in A

BBC Symphony Orchestra; recorded from a BBC broadcast at Studio No. 1, Maida Vale, London, 12 January 1961

Release: **CD = Hunt CD-725** (the recording date given in the notes – 21 March 1967 – refers to a performance of the Bruckner Fifth Symphony with the New Philharmonia Orchestra, not the one recorded here).

L-100 Bruckner: *Te Deum*

BBC Symphony Orchestra and Chorus; Heather Harper, soprano, Janet Baker, mezzo-soprano, Richard Lewis, tenor, Marian Nowakowski, bass; recorded from a BBC broadcast at Studio No. 1, Maida Vale, London, 12 January 1961

Release: It. = Melodram MEL 214.

L-101 Beethoven: *Fidelio*, Op. 72

Orchestra and Chorus of the Royal Opera House, Covent Garden; recorded from a BBC broadcast, 7 March 1961

Forbes Robinson, bass (Don Fernando), Hans Hotter, bass (Don Pizarro), Jon Vickers, tenor (Florestan), Sena Jurinac, mezzo-soprano (Leonore), Gottlob Frick, bass (Rocco), Elsie Morison, soprano (Marzelline), John Dobson, tenor (Jacquino), Joseph Ward, tenor (First Prisoner), Victor Godfrey, baritone (Second Prisoner)

Release: It. = Melodram MEL 407
  CD = Melodram 27076.

120   Mahler: Symphony No. 4 in G
      Philharmonia Orchestra; Elisabeth Schwarzkopf, soprano; recorded 6–7, 10 and 25 April 1961, Kingsway Hall, London
      Release: Eng. = Col. 33CX1793/SAX 2441; HMV ASD 2799 (Intl. 0C 063-00553); Ger. = Elec. C(STC)91191, 1C 063-00553; Fr. = Col. 33FCX941/SAXF 259; HMV 2C 065-, 069-00553, 100553-4; in set 2C 165-52519/26; It. = Col. 33QCX10473; US = Ang. S-35829; 76966-4; Sera. S-60356; Jap. = Col. OS-3125; Ang. AA-7001, AA-8085, EAA-93091/2, EAC-50035
        CD = EMI CDM 769667-2; Jap. Ang. CE25-5657, TOCE-1510.

L-102 Klemperer: Symphony No. 1

L-103 Bruckner: Symphony No. 6 in A
       Concertgebouworkest, Amsterdam; recorded from a broadcast at the Concertgebouw, 22 June 1961
       Release: Ger. = archiphon ARCH-1 (Klemperer); It. = Movimento Musica 01.056 (Bruckner)
         CD = Music & Arts CD-247 (Bruckner), Memories CDHR 42489 (Klemperer).

121   Tchaikovsky: Symphony No. 6 in b, Op. 74, 'Pathétique'
       Philharmonia Orchestra; recorded 18–20 October 1961, Kingsway Hall, London
       Release: Eng. = Col. 33CX1812/SAX 2458, HMV in set SLS 5003 (Intl. 0C 191-52130/4), EM 29 0282-3; Ger. = Col. SAXW 2458; Elec. SHZE 296, 1C 037-00564, 037-, 237-29 0747; Fr. = Col. 33FCX937/SAXF 248; US = Ang. (S)35787, 4XG-60416; in set (S)3711G; Jap. = Ang. SCA-1001, AA-7346, EAC-40062
         CD = EMI CDMB 763838-2.

122   Strauss, Johann, II: *Kaiser-Walzer*, Op. 427
       Philharmonia Orchestra; recorded 20 October 1961, Kingsway Hall, London
       Release: Eng. = Col. 33CX1814/SAX 2460; HMV SXLP 30226, SXLP 30277 in set SLS 5073; Fr. = HMV 2C 069-00565; It. = Col. 33QCX10480; US = Ang. (S)35927; Jap. = Ang. SCA-1024, AA-7405
         CD = EMI CDM 764146-2.

123   Strauss, Johann, II: Waltz, *Wiener Blut*, Op. 354
       Philharmonia Orchestra; recorded 20 October 1961, Kingsway Hall, London
       Release: Eng. = Col. 33CX1814/SAX 2460; HMV SXLP 30226, SXLP 30277 in set SLS 5073; Fr. = HMV 2C 069-00565; It. = Col. 33QCX10480; US = Ang. (S)35927; Jap. = Ang. SCA-1024, AA-7405.

124   Strauss, Richard: *Tod und Verklärung*, Op. 24
       Philharmonia Orchestra; recorded 23 October and 13 November 1961, Kingsway Hall, London

Release: Eng. = Col. 33CX1789/SAX 2437; HMV TCC2-POR 54296, ED 29 0616-1; Ger. = Elec. C(STC)91190; Fr. = Col. 33FCX939/SAXF 258; HMV 2C 181-50557/8; It. = Col. 33QCX10465/SAXQ 7363; US = Ang. (S)35796, AE-34472; Jap. = Col. OS-3117; Ang. AA-7039, AA-8086
CD = EMI CDM 63350-2; Jap. Ang. CC33-3758, TOCE6126, TOCE6162, TOCE7036, TOCE1524.

125 Wagner: *Das Rheingold*. Einzug der Götter in Walhall
Philharmonia Orchestra; recorded 24 October 1961, Kingsway Hall, London
Release: Eng. = Col. 33CX1820/SAX 2464; HMV ASD 2697, SXLP 30528 (Intl. 0C 053-00567); in set SLS 5075 (Intl. 0C 153-50347/9); Ger. = Elec. 1C 037-, 237-00567; in set F668-525/33; Fr. = Col. 33FCX937/SAXF 254; HMV 2C 069-, 269-00567; It. = Col. 33QCX10479; US = Ang. (S), 4XS-, 8XS-35947, RL-32058, AE-34407; Jap. = Ang. SCA-1011, AA-7402, AA-8597, EAA-93101/2, EAC-55068
CD = EMI CDC 747255-2, CDM 763618-2; Jap. Ang. CC33-3267, TOCE6560, TOCE1515.

126 Wagner: *Siegfried*. Act II: Waldweben
Philharmonia Orchestra; recorded 24 October and 13 November 1961, Kingsway Hall, London
Release: Eng. = Col. 33CX1820/SAX 2464; HMV ASD 2697, SXLP 0528 (Intl. 0C 053-00567); in set SLS 5075 (Intl. C 153-50347/9); Ger. = Col. 33WCX600/SAXW 9880; Elec. C(STC)91281, 1C 037-, 237-00567; in set F668-525/33; Fr. = Col. 33FCX937/SAXF 254; HMV 2C 069-00567; It. = Col. 33QCX10479; US = Ang. (S), 4XS-, 8XS-35947, RL-32058, AE-34407; Jap. = Ang. SCA-1011, AA-7402, EAA-93101/2, EAC-55068
CD = EMI CDC 747255-2, CDM 763618-2; Jap. Ang. CC33-3267, TOCE6560, TOCE1515.

127 Wagner: *Siegfried Idyll*
Philharmonia Orchestra; recorded 25 October 1961, Kingsway Hall, London
Release: Eng. = Col. 33CX1808/9//SAX 2454/5; Ger. = Elec. C(STC)91281; in set F668-525/33; Fr. = Col. 33FCX(SAXF)945/6; HMV 2C 069-, 269-01356; It. = Col. 33QCX10475/6; US = Ang. (S) 35786 in (S)3626B = Col. OS-3126/7; Ang. SCA-1061/2, AA-7410/1, EAA-93101/2, AA-8091/2, EAC-50044/5
CD = EMI CMS 763277-2; Ger. Zweitausendeins 60625; Jap. Ang. TOCE6091/2.
Note: Klemperer uses the original version for thirteen instruments.

128 Klemperer: *Merry Waltz* and *One-Step*.
Philharmonia Orchestra; recorded 30 October 1961, Kingsway Hall, London
Release: Eng. = Col. 33CX1814/SAX 2460; HMV SXLP 30226, ED 29 0332-1; Fr. = HMV 2C 069-00565; It. = Col. 33QCX10480; US = Ang. (S)35927; Jap. = Ang. AA-7405
CD = EMI CDM 763917-2.

129 Strauss, Johann, II: *Die Fledermaus*. Overture.
Philharmonia Orchestra; recorded 30 October and 2 December 1961, Kingsway Hall, London

Release: Eng. = Col. 33CX1814/SAX 2460; HMV SXLP 30226, SXLP 30277 in set SLS 5073; Fr. = HMV 2C 069-00565; It. = Col. 33QCX10480; US = Ang. (S)35927; Jap. = Ang. AA-7405.

130 Weill: *Kleine Dreigroschenmusik* (omits the 3rd movement)
Philharmonia Orchestra; recorded 31 October and 2 December 1961, Kingsway Hall, London

Release: Eng. = Col. 33CX1814/SAX 2460; HMV SXLP 30226, ED 29 0332-1; Fr. = HMV 2C 069-00565; It. = Col. 33QCX10480; US = Ang. (S)35927; Jap. = Ang. SCA-1024, AA-7405
CD = EMI CDM 764142-2.

131 Strauss, Richard: *Metamorphosen*
Philharmonia Orchestra; recorded 3–4 November 1961, Kingsway Hall, London

Release: Eng. = Col. 33CX1789/SAX 2437; HMV TCC2-POR 54296, ED 29 0616-1; Ger. = Elec. C(STC)91190; Fr. = Col. 33FCX939/SAXF 258; HMV 2C 181-50557/8; It. = Col. 33QCX10465/SAXQ 7363; US = Ang. (S)35796, AE-34472; Jap. = Col. OS-3117; Ang. AA-7039, AA-8091/2
CD = EMI CDM 763350-2; Jap. Ang. TOCE6126.

132 Wagner: *Parsifal*. Prelude
Philharmonia Orchestra; recorded 14 November 1961, Kingsway Hall, London

Release: Eng. = Col. 33CX1820/SAX 2464; HMV ASD 2697, SXLP 30528 (Intl. 0C 053-00567); in set SLS 5075 (Intl. 0C 153-50347/9); Ger. = Col. 33WCX600/SAXW 9880; Elec. C(STC)91281, 1C 037-, 237-00567; in set F668-525/33; Fr. = Col. 33FCX937/SAXF 254; HMV 2C 069-00567; It. = Col. 33QCX10479, 33QCX10503; US = Ang. (S), 4XS-, 8XS-35947, RL-32058, AE-34407; Time-Life STL 155; Jap. = Ang. SCA-1011, AA-7402, AA-8597, EAA-93101/2, EAC-55068; Russ. = Melodyia D 020747/50
CD = EMI CDC 747255-2, CDM 763618-2; Jap. Ang. CC33-3267, TOCE6560, TOCE1515.

133 Wagner: *Die Götterdämmerung*. Siegfrieds Rheinfahrt
Philharmonia Orchestra; recorded 22 November 1961, Kingsway Hall, London

Release: Eng. = Col. 33CX1820/SAX 2464; HMV ASD 2697, SXLP 30528 (Intl. 0C 053-00567); in set SLS 5075 (Intl. 0C 153-50347/9); Ger. = Col. 33WCX600/SAXW 9880; Elec. SME 2037/8; 1C 037-, 237-00567; in set F668-525/33; Fr. = Col. 33FCX937/SAXF 254; HMV 2C 069-, 269-00567; It. = Col. 33QCX10479; US = Ang. (S), 4XS-, 8XS-35947, RL-32058, AE-34407; Time-Life STL 155; Jap. = Ang. SCA-1011, AA-7402, AA-8089, EAA-93101/2, EAC-55068
CD = EMI CDC 747255-2, CDM 763618-2; Jap. Ang. CC33-3267, TOCE6560, TOCE1515.

134 Mahler: Symphony No. 2 in c, 'Resurrection'
Philharmonia Orchestra and Chorus; Elisabeth Schwarzkopf, soprano; Hilde Rössl-Majdan, contralto; recorded 22–24 November 1961 and 15 and 24 March 1962, Kingsway Hall, London

Release: Eng. = Col. 33CX1829/30//SAX 2473/4; HMV ASD 2691/2, SLS 806 (Intl. 1C 191-00570/1); TCC2-POR 54293; Ger. = Elec.

C(STC)91268/9, 1C 163-00570/1; Fr. = Col. 33FCX(SAXF)948/9; HMV CCA 948/9, 2C 181-00570/1; 100570-3, -5; in set 2C 165-52519/26; US = Ang. (S)35991/2 in (S)B3634; Jap. = Ang. SCA-1085/6, AA- 7415/6, AA-8098/9, EAC-77257/8, EAC-50033/4
CD = EMI CDM 769662-2; Ger. Zweitausendeins 60625; Jap. Ang. TOCE-6089.

L-104 Mozart: *Die Zauberflöte*, K. 620 (excerpts)
Orchestra of the Royal Opera House, Covent Garden; Joan Sutherland, soprano, and other performers; recorded from a BBC broadcast at the Royal Opera House, 4 January 1962
Release: US = UORC 147
CD = **Gala GL 319** (Der Hölle Rache)
Note: Includes the Queen of the Night's two arias and 'Stille, stille . . .'

135 Beethoven: *Fidelio*, Op. 72
Philharmonia Orchestra and Chorus; recorded 6–10, 12–15 and 17 and 19 February 1962, Kingsway Hall, London
Franz Crass, bass (Don Fernando), Walter Berry, bass (Don Pizarro), Jon Vickers, tenor (Florestan), Christa Ludwig, mezzo-soprano (Leonore), Gottlob Frick, bass (Rocco), Ingeborg Hallstein, soprano (Marzelline), Gerhard Unger, tenor (Jaquino), Kurt Wehofschitz, tenor (First Prisoner), Raymond Wolansky, baritone (Second Prisoner)
Release: Eng. = Col. 33CX1804/6//SAX 2451/3, CMS(SMS) 1014, BTA 133/5; HMV ASD 3068/70, SLS, TC-SLS 5006 (Intl. 0C 153-00559/61); Ger. = Elec. C(STC)91206/8, 1C 149-, 163-00559/61; in sets 1C 147-, 197-53400/19; Fr. = Col. 33FCX921/3//SAXF 240/2; HMV 2C 149-, 167-00559/61; in set 2C 147-50298/318; It. = Col. 33QCX10467/9//SAXQ 7364/8; US = Ang. (S)35741/3 in (S)CL3625; Jap. = Col. OS-3130/2; Ang. SCA-1081/3, AA-9342/4, AA-24/7
CD = **EMI CMS 769324-2, CDS 555170-2; Ger. Zweitausendeins 60625; Jap. Ang. TOCE6097/8**
Excerpts: Eng. = Col. 33CX1907/SAX 2547; HMV SXLP 30307 (Intl. 0C 053-00586), HQS 1408 (No. 10, prisoner's Chorus); Ger. = Elec. C(STC)80775, 1C 063- 00831; US = Ang. (S)36168, AV-34003
Overture only: Eng. = Col. 33CX1902/SAX 2542; HMV ASD 2562, SXLP, TC-SXLP 30310 (Intl. 0C 053-00796), ED 29 0272-1; in sets SLS 788 (Intl. 0C 177-00794/802) and SXLP 30322 in SXDW 3032 (Intl. 0C 153-03103/4); Ger. = Elec. SMC 80898, 1C 063-00583; in sets 1C 197-03103/4 and 147-, 197-53400/19; Fr. = Col. FCX(SAXF)1016; HMV 2C 069-00796; in set 2C 147-50298/318; US = Ang. (S)36209, 4XS-, 8XS-35711; AE-34428; in set AEW-34469; Sera. S-60261; Jap. = Ang. AA-7207, AA-41/3
CD = **EMI CDC 747190-2, CDM 763611-2, CDZG 568057-2, CZS 479565-2; Jap. Ang. CC33-3247, CE25-5671**
Note: A test session for this recording was also held on 3 March.

136 Mozart: Symphony No. 41 in C, K. 551, 'Jupiter'
Philharmonia Orchestra; recorded 6–7 March 1962, Kingsway Hall, London
Release: Eng. = Col. 33CX1843/SAX 2486; HMV in sets SLS 5048 (Intl. 0C 147-0142/7) and EX 29 0482-3; Ger. = Elec. C(STC)91147, SMC 110000/1-3, 1C 053-00574; in sets 1C 153-01842/7, 197-53714/38 and

137-29 0482; Fr. = Col. 33FCX5007, 33FCX(SAXF)942; HMV 2C 061- 00574, 069-, 259-01847; Neth. = HMV 1A 137-53556/7; US = Ang. (S)36183, RL-32098, AE-34405; in set AEW- 34470; Jap. = Ang. SCA-1075, AA-8088, EAA-93085/6, EAC-40049, EAC-55033
CD = EMI CDC 747852-2, CMS 763272-2; Ger. Zweitausendeins 60625; Jap. Ang. CC33-3795, TOCE6093/6.

137 Mozart: Symphony No. 40 in g, K. 550
Philharmonia Orchestra; recorded 8 and 28 March 1962, Kingsway Hall, London
Release: Eng. = Col. 33CX1843/SAX 2486; HMV in set SLS 5003 (Intl. 0C 191-52130/4) and EX 29 0482-3; Ger. = Elec. C(STC)91147, 1C 053-00574; in sets SMC 110000/1-3, 1C 137-29 0482; Fr. = Col. 33FCX5007, 33FCX(SAXF)942; HMV 2C 061-00574; Neth. = HMV 1A 137-53556/7; US = Ang. (S)36183, RL-32098, AE-34405; in set AEW-34470; Jap. = Ang. SCA-1075, AA-8088, EAA-93085/6.

138 Brahms: *Alt Rhapsodie*, Op. 53
Philharmonia Orchestra and Chorus; Christa Ludwig, mezzo-soprano; recorded 21 and 23 March 1962, Kingsway Hall, London
Release: Eng. = Col. 33CX1817/SAX 2462; HMV ASD 2391; ASD 2789/90 in set SLS 821 (Intl. 1E 053-01295/6); SXLP 27 0000-1; Ger. = Col. 33WCX907/SAXW 9587; Elec. SME 91365, STC 91224/5S, 1C 063-00826; in sets 1C 161-00545S/6 and 153-01295/6; Fr. = Col. 33FCX935/SAXF 252; HMV 2C 063- 00826, 29 0279-3,-5; US = Ang. (S)35923; Jap. = Ang. AA-8084, AA-8468, EAC-40118
CD = EMI Classics CZS 479885-2; Jap. Ang. TOCE-6088, TOCE-1567.

139 Wagner: *Wesendonck-Lieder*
Philharmonia Orchestra and Chorus; Christa Ludwig, mezzo-soprano; recorded 22–23 March 1962, Kingsway Hall, London
Release: Eng. = Col. 33CX1817/SAX 2462; HMV ASD 2391, SXLP 270000-1; Ger. = Col. 33WCX907/SAXW 9587; Elec. SME 91365, 1C 063-00826; in sets 1C 161-00545S/6 and F668-525/33; Fr. = Col. 33FCX935/SAXF 252; HMV 29 0279-3, -5; It. = Col. 33QCX10507; HMV 2C 063-00826; It. = Col. 33QCX10507; US = Ang. (S)35923; Jap. = Ang. SCA-1003, AA-8468, AA-8098/9, EAA-93101/2, EAC-40118
CD = EMI CDM 764074-2.

140 Wagner: *Tristan und Isolde*. Isolde's Liebestod
Philharmonia Orchestra; Christa Ludwig, mezzo-soprano; recorded 23 March 1962, Kingsway Hall, London
Release: Eng. = Col. 33CX1817/SAX 2462; HMV SXLP 27 0000-1; Ger. = HMV 1C 063-00826; in set F668-525/33; Fr. = Col. 33FCX935/SAXF 252; HMV 2C 063-00826 It. = Col. 33QCX10507; US = Ang. (S)35923; Jap. = Ang. SCA-1003, AA-7296, AA-8597, EAA-93101/2, EAC-85038
CD = EMI CDM 764074-2.

141 Mozart: Symphony No. 39 in E-Flat, K. 543
Philharmonia Orchestra; recorded 26–28 March 1962, Kingsway Hall, London

DISCOGRAPHY

Release: Eng. = Col. 33CX1824/SAX 2468; HMV in set SLS 5048 (Intl. 0C 147-01842/7) and EX 29 0482-3; Ger. = Elec. C(STC)91145, SMC 110000/1-3; 1C 053-00569; in sets 1C 153-01842/7, 197-53714/38 and 137-29 0482-3; Fr. = Col. 33FCX5006, 33FCX938/SAXF 255; HMV 2C 061-00569; US = Ang. (S)36129; in set AEW-34470; Jap. = Ang. SCA-1005, AA- 7401, AA-8102, EAA-93085/6, EAC-40048
CD = EMI CMS 763272-2; Ger. Zweitausendeins 60625; Jap. Ang. TOCE6093/6.

142   Mozart: Symphony No. 38 in D, K. 504, 'Prague'

Philharmonia Orchestra; recorded 27 March 1962, Kingsway Hall, London

Release: Eng. = Col. 33CX1824/SAX 2468; HMV in set SLS 5048 (Intl. 0C 147-01842/7) and EX 29 0482-3; Ger. = Elec. C(STC)91145, SMC 110000/1-3, 1C 053-00569; SME 2037/8; in sets 1C 153-01842/7, 197-53714/38 and 137-29 0482-3; Fr. = Col. 33FCX5006, 33FCX938/SAXF 255; HMV 2C 061-00569; US = Ang. (S)36129; in set AEW-34470; Jap. = Ang. SCA-1005, AA-7401, AA-8102, EAA-93085/6, EAC-40048
CD = EMI CMS 763272-2; Ger. Zweitausendeins 60625; Jap. Ang. TOCE6093/6.

143   Stravinsky: Symphony in Three Movements

Philharmonia Orchestra; recorded 28 and 30 March and 16 May 1962, Kingsway Hall, London

Release: Eng. = Col. 33CX1949/SAX 2588; Fr. = Col. 33FCX(SAXF)1054; US = Ang. (S)36238; Sera. S-60188; Jap. = Ang. AA-7374
CD = EMI CDM 764142-2.

L-105   Schumann: Symphony No. 4 in d, Op. 120

Philadelphia Orchestra; recorded from a performance at the Academy of Music, 27 October 1962

Release: **CD = AS Disc AS 533; Legend LGD 103.**

L-106   Bach: Brandenburg Concerto No. 1 in F, BWV 1046

Philadelphia Orchestra; recorded from a performance at the Academy of Music, 3 November 1962

Release: **CD = AS Disc AS 533; Legend LGD 103.**

144   Tchaikovsky: Symphony No. 5 in e, Op. 64

Philharmonia Orchestra; recorded 16–19 and 21 January 1963, Kingsway Hall, London

Release: Eng. = Col. 33CX1854/SAX 2497; HMV EM 29 0282-3; Ger. = Elec. C(STC)91245, 1C 037-, 237-00577; It. = Col. 33QCX10490; US = Ang. (S)36141, 4XG-60415; in set (S)3711C; Jap. = Ang. AA-7010
CD = EMI CDM 763838-2.

145   Tchaikovsky: Symphony No. 4 in f, Op. 36

Philharmonia Orchestra; recorded 23–25 January and 2 February 1963, Kingsway Hall, London

Release: Eng. = Col. 33CX1851/SAX 2494, TA-33CX1851; HMV EM 29 0282-3; Ger. = Elec. C(STC)91241; US = Ang. (S)36134; in set (S)3711C; Jap. = Ang. AA-7022
CD = EMI CDM 763838-2.

DISCOGRAPHY

146   Schubert: Symphony No. 8 in b, D. 759, 'Unfinished'

Philharmonia Orchestra; recorded 4 and 6 February 1963, Kingsway Hall, London

Release: Eng. = Col. 33CX1870/SAX 2514, TA-33CX1870; HMV ED 29 0460-1, EMX-, TC-EMX 2135; in set SLS 5003 (Intl. 0C 191-52130/4); Ger. = Elec. C(STC)91306, 1C 037-, 237-, 063-00579, 1C 037-29 1165, SME 2037/8; Fr. = HMV 2C 069-00579; US = Ang. (S)36164, AE-34444, RL-32038; Jap. = Ang. AA-7051, AA-8081
CD = EMI CDM 763854-2, CZS 479885-2.

147   Stravinsky: *Pulcinella* Suite

Philharmonia Orchestra; recorded 18 February and 14 and 18 May 1963, Kingsway Hall, London

Release: Eng. = Col. 33CX1949/SAX 2588; Fr. = Col. 33FCX(SAXF)1054; US = Ang. (S)36238; Sera. S-60188; Jap. = Ang. AA-7374
CD = EMI CDM 764142-2.

148   Berlioz: *Symphonie fantastique*, Op. 14

Philharmonia Orchestra; recorded 23–26 April and 17–18 September 1963, Kingsway Hall, London

Release: Eng. = Col. 33CX1898/SAX 2537, TA-33CX1898; HMV EMX, TC-EMX 2030; in set SLS 5003 (Intl. 0C 191-52130/4); Ger. = Elec. STC 91352; It. = Col. 33QCX(SAXQ)7375; US = Ang. (S)36196; Jap. = Ang. AA-7158, EAC-40067
CD = EMI CDM 764143-2.

149   Schubert: Symphony No. 5 in B-Flat, D. 485

Philharmonia Orchestra; recorded 13 and 15–16 May 1963, Kingsway Hall, London

Release: Eng. = Col. 33CX1870/SAX 2514, TA-33CX1870; HMV 29 04601, EMX, TC-EMX 2135; Ger. = Elec. C(STC)91306, 1C 037-, 237-, 063-00579; 037-, 237-29 1165; Fr. = HMV 2C 069-00579; US = Ang. (S)36164, AE-34444, RL-32038; Time-Life STL-143; Jap. = Ang. AA-7051
CD = EMI CDM 763869-2.

L-107   Beethoven: *Coriolan Overture*, Op. 62

L-108   Beethoven: Symphony No. 3 in E-Flat, Op. 55, 'Eroica'

Wiener Symphoniker; recorded from a broadcast at the Theater an der Wien, 16 June 1963

Release: Ger. = Orfeo MC233901
CD = Orfeo CD233901; Jap. Orfeo PHC5224.

150   Bruckner: Symphony No. 4 in E-Flat (1878/80 version ed. Nowak)

Philharmonia Orchestra; recorded 19–20 and 24–26 September 1963, Kingsway Hall, London

Release: Eng. = Col. 33CX1928/SAX 2569, TC-EXE-, 8X-EXE-75; HMV SXLP 30167 (Intl. 0C 047-00593); Ger. = Col. SMC 91356; HMV 1C 037-, 237-, 063-00593; Fr. = HMV CCA 1039; US = Ang. (S)36245, RL-32059, AE-24456; Time-Life STL-142; Jap. = Ang. AA-7170, AA-8101, EAA- 93097/8, EAC-50040
CD = EMI CDM 769127-2, CZS 479885-2; Jap. Ang. CE28-5154, CE25-5611, TOCE-1570.

151 Mozart: Symphony No. 31 in D, K. 297, 'Paris'

Philharmonia Orchestra; recorded 16–18 October 1963, Kingsway Hall, London

Release: Eng. = Col. 33CX1906/SAX 2546; HMV in set SLS 5048 (Intl. 0C 147-01842/7) and EX 29 0482-3; Ger. = Elec. STC 91332; in sets 1C 153-01842/7, 197-53714/38 and 137-29 0482-3; Fr. = Col. 33FCX-(SAXF)1015; US = Ang. (S)36216; in set AEW-34470; Jap. = Ang. AA-7193, AA-8093, EAA-93083/4

CD = EMI CMS 763272-2, CMGD 763585-2; Ger. Zweitausendeins 60625; Jap. Ang. TOCE6093/6.

152 Mozart: Symphony No. 34 in C, K. 338

Philharmonia Orchestra; recorded 18–19 October 1963, Kingsway Hall, London

Release: Eng. = Col. 33CX1906/SAX 2546; HMV in sets SLS 5048 (Intl. 0C 147-01842/7) and HMV EX 29 0482-3; Ger. = Elec. STC 91332; in sets 1C 153-01842/7, 197-53714/38, and 137-29 0482-3; Fr. = Col. 33FCX(SAXF)1015; US = Ang. (S)36216; in set AEW-34470; Jap. = Ang. AA-7193, EAC-40046

CD = EMI CMS 763272-2; Ger. Zweitausendeins 60625; Jap. Ang. TOCE6093/6.

153 Dvorak: Symphony No. 9 in e, Op. 95, 'From the New World'

Philharmonia Orchestra; recorded 30 October–2 November 1963, Kingsway Hall, London

Release: Eng. = Col. 33FX1914/SAX 2554; HMV in set SLS 5003 (Intl. 0C 191-52130/4); Ger. = Col. SAX 2554; Elec. 1C 063-, 243-00587; US = Ang. (S)36246, RL-32003; Jap. = Ang. AA-7203, AA-8205, EAC-40069

CD = EMI CDM 763869-2.

154 Beethoven: *Leonore Overture No. 3*, Op. 72a

Philharmonia Orchestra; recorded 4–5 November 1963, Kingsway Hall, London

Release: Eng. = Col. 33CX1902/SAX 2542; HMV ASD 2567/8; ED 29 0401-1; in sets SLS 788 (Intl. 0C 177-07794/802) and SLS 790 (Intl. 1C 153-00801/2) and SXLP 30322 in SXDW 3032 (Intl. 0C 151-00801/2); Ger. = Col. SMC 80898, SMC 80944; HMV SME 2037/8, 1C 063-00583; in sets 1C 197-03103/4 and 147-, 197-53400/19; Fr. = HMV in sets 2C 153-00801/2 and 147-50298/318; Neth. = HMV 1A 137- 53562/3; US = Ang. (S)36209, AE-34441; Sera. S-60261; Time-Life STL-143; Jap. = Ang. AA-7207, AA-8087, AA-8094; in set AA-5131/9

CD = EMI CDC 747190-2, CDM 763611-2, CDZG 568057-2, CZS 479562-2; Jap. Ang. CC33-3247, CE25-5671.

155 Beethoven: *Leonore Overture No. 2*, Op. 72a

Philharmonia Orchestra; recorded 5–6 November 1963, Kingsway Hall, London

Release: Eng. = Col. 33CX1902/SAX 2542; HMV ASD 2561, ED 29 0401-1; in set SLS 788 (Intl. 0C 177-07794/802) and SXLP 30322 in SXDW 3032 (Intl. 0C 151-00801/2); Ger. = Col. SMC 80898; Elec. 1C 063-00583; in sets 1C 197- 03103/4 and 147-, 197-53400/19; Fr. = HMV 2C 069-00795; in set 1C 147-50298/318; Neth. = HMV 1A 137-53562/3; US = Ang. (S)36209, AE-34441; Sera. S-60261;

Jap. = Ang. AA-7207, AA-41/3; in set AA-5131/9
CD = **EMI CDC 747190-2, EMI CDM 763611-2, CDZG 568057-2, CZS 479885-2; Jap. Ang. CC33-3247, CE25-5671.**

156 Beethoven: *Leonore Overture No. 1*, Op. 138
Philharmonia Orchestra; recorded 6–7 November 1963, Kingsway Hall, London
Release: Eng. = Col. 33CX1902/SAX 2542; HMV ASD 2565; ED 29 0401-1; in set SLS 788 (Intl. 0C 177-00794/802) and SXLP 30322 in SXDW 3032 (Intl. 0C 151-00801/2); Ger. = Col. SMC 80898; Elec. 1C 063-00583; in sets 1C 197-03103/4 and 147-, 197-53400/19; Fr. = HMV 2C 069-00795; in set HMV 2C 147-50298/318; Neth. = HMV 1A 137-53562/3; Ang. = (S)36209, AE-34441; Sera. S-60261; Jap. = Ang. AA-7207, AA-8097, AA-41/3; in set AA-5131/9
CD = **EMI CDC 747190-2, EMI CDM 763611-2, CDZG 568057-2, CZS 479562-2; Jap. Ang. CC33-3247, CE25-5671.**

157 Mozart: Serenade 'Gran Partita' in B-Flat, K. 361
London Wind Quintet and Ensemble; recorded 26 November and 10–13 December 1963, Studio No. 1, Abbey Road
Release: Eng. = Col. CX(SAX)5259; HMV SXLP 30501 in set SXDW 3050 (Intl. 0C 151-53528/9); Ger. = Col. SMC 91335; Elec. in set 1C 197-53714/38; Fr. = HMV CCA 1095, 2C 069-00609; US = Ang. (S)36247; Jap. = Ang. AA-8011
CD = **EMI CDM 763349-2; Jap. Ang. TOCE6125, TOCE6575.**

158 Mahler: Lieder aus 'Des Knaben Wunderhorn' (No. 5 and 9)
Philharmonia Orchestra; Christa Ludwig, mezzo-soprano; recorded 17–18 February 1964, Kingsway Hall, London
Release: Eng. = HMV ASD 2391, SXLP 27 0000-1; US = Ang. (S)3704B; Jap. = Ang. AA-8468, EAC-40118.

159 Mahler: Rückert-Lieder (Nos. 1, 4, and 5)
Philharmonia Orchestra; Christa Ludwig, mezzo-soprano; recorded 17–19 February 1964, Kingsway Hall, London
Release: Eng. = HMV ASD 2391, 27 0000-1; US = Ang. (S)3704B; Jap. = Ang. AA-8468, EAC-40118
Um Mitternacht only: US = Ang. Sera. S-6072.

160 Mahler: *Das Lied von der Erde*
Philharmonia and New Philharmonia Orchestras; Christa Ludwig, mezzo-soprano; Fritz Wunderlich, tenor; recorded 19–22 February 1964, Kingsway Hall, London, 7–8 November 1964 (Wunderlich in Studio No. 1, Abbey Road) and 6–9 July 1966 (Ludwig in Studio No. 1)
Release: Eng. = Ang. AN(SAN)179 (Intl. 0C 065-00065), EL 29 0441; Ger. = Elec. SME 91639, 1C 065-00065; Fr. = HMV 2C 069-00065, 100065-1; in set 2C 165-52519/26; US = Ang. (S)36407/8 in (S)B3704; S-, 4XS-38234; Jap. = Ang. AA-8100, EAA-93091/2, EAC-70226, EAC-81017
CD = **EMI CDC 747231-2; Jap. Ang. CC30-9061, TOCE7022**
Note: The Philharmonia Orchestra was employed for the February and November 1964 sessions, the New Philharmonia for the July 1966 dates.

161 Handel: *Messiah* (omits Nos. 33–35 and 47–49)
Philharmonia Orchestra and Chorus; Elisabeth Schwarzkopf, soprano,

Grace Hoffman, contralto, Nicolai Gedda, tenor, Jerome Hines, bass; recorded 24–25 February, 9-14 and 16–19 March, 20–22 (Hines) and 28–29 September (Gedda), 1–2 and 8–9 October (Chorus) and 2–3 November (Hoffman) 1964, Kingsway Hall, London

Release: Eng. = Ang. AN(SAN)146/8; HMV RLS(SLS)915; Ger. = Ang. CAN 146/8; Fr. = HMV 2C 167-00037/9, 101393-1; Ang. (S)36276/8 in (S)CL3657, X4S-3657; Jap. = Ang. AA-9117/9, AA-9326/8
CD = EMI CMS 763621-2; Jap. Ang. TOCE6563/5

Excerpts: (Nos. 3, 6, 12, 15, 19, 20, 23, 24, 26, 31, 39, 42, 44, 51 and 52)

Release: Eng. = HMV ALP(ASD)2288; Ger. = Col. SMC 80936; Elec. 1C 063-01430; Fr. = HMV 2C 061-, 069-01393; US = Ang. (S)-, 4XS-, 8XS-36324, AE-34465; Jap. = Ang. AA-8401

Note: Additional sessions with tenor Peter Pears (on 13 March, Nos. 1, 2, 25, 40 and 41) and with soprano Ursula Boese (on 16 and 17 March, Nos. 5, 7–9, 12 and 21) were held but not included in the approved recording.

162   Mozart: *Die Zauberflöte*, K. 620 (without spoken dialogue)

Philharmonia Orchestra and Chorus; recorded 24–26 and 31 March and 1–4, 6–8 and 10 April 1964, Kingsway Hall, London

Gottlob Frick, bass (Sarastro), Nicolai Gedda, tenor (Tamino), Franz Crass, bass (Speaker, Second Armed Man), Gerhard Unger, tenor (First Priest, Monostatos), Lucia Popp, soprano (Queen of the Night), Gundula Janowitz, soprano (Pamina), Elisabeth Schwarzkopf, soprano (First Lady), Christa Ludwig, mezzo-soprano (Second Lady), Marga Höffgen, contralto (Third Lady), Walter Berry, bass (Papageno), Ruth-Margret Pütz, soprano (Papagena), Agnes Giebel, soprano (First Boy), Anna Reynolds, mezzo-soprano (Second Boy), Josephine Veasey, mezzo-soprano (Third Boy), Karl Liebel, tenor (First Armed Man)

Release: Eng. = Ang. AN(SAN)137/9; HMV RLS(SLS)912 (Intl. 1E 153-00031/3); Ger. = Elec. STA 91368/70, 1C 157-, 165-00031/3, CVPM 130557; in set 197-53714/38; Fr. = HMV 2C 165-, 295-00031/3; 143547-1, -4; US = Ang. (S)36228-S/30 in (S)CL3651; Jap. = Ang. AA- 9102/4, AA-9438/40
CD = EMI CDMS 769971-2, CDS 555173-2; Jap. Ang. TOCE6099/ 100, TOCE7341/2

Excerpts: Eng. = HMV ALP(ASD)2314, ESD-, TC-ESD 1003261; Ger. = Elec. 1C 061-, 261-, 069-00835, SMC 80858; US = Ang. (S)36315; CDC 76056-4; Jap. = Ang. AA-8489
CD = Ang. 763747-2; Jap. Ang. CE28-5052.

Overture only: Eng. = Col. 33CX1949/SAX 2587; HMV EX 29 04823; Ger. = Col. SME 80933; Fr. = HMV 2C 061-, 069-00602, 100602-4; US = Ang. (S)36289, RL-32099, AE- 34462; in set AEW-34470; Jap. = Ang. AA-7596, AA-8097, AA-8578
CD = EMI CDM 763619-2; Jap. Ang. TOCE6574.

L-109   Bach: Orchestral Suite No. 3 in D, BWV 1068. Air

Berliner Philharmoniker; recorded from a broadcast at the Philharmonie, Berlin, 29 May 1964

Release: It. = I Grandi Concerto/Valentine Records GCC 41; Jap. = Laudis RCL 3332.

163   Haydn: Symphony No. 88 in G
New Philharmonia Orchestra; recorded 12–14 October 1964, Studio No. 1, Abbey Road

Release: Eng. = Col. 33CX1931/SAX 2571; Ger. = Col. SMC 91409; Elec. 1C 063-01196; Fr. = Col. 33FCX(SAXF)1040; US = Ang. (S)36346; Jap. = Ang. AA-7317, AA-8570, EAA- 93079/80
CD = **EMI CDMC 763667-2; Jap. Ang. TOCE-6566/8.**

164   Haydn: Symphony No. 104 in D
New Philharmonia Orchestra; recorded 14–16 October 1964, Studio No. 1, Abbey Road
Release: Eng. = Col. 33CX1931/SAX 2571; HMV ED 29 03571; Ger. = Col. SMC 91409; Elec. 1C 063-01196; Fr. = Col. 33FCX(SAXF)1040; US = Ang. (S)36346, AE-34464; Jap. = Ang. AA-7317, AA-8570, EAA-93079/80
CD = **EMI CDMC 763667-2; Jap. Ang. TOCE-6566/8.**

165   Mozart: *Così fan tutte*, K. 588. Overture
New Philharmonia Orchestra; recorded 16 and 29 October 1964, Studio No. 1, Abbey Road
Release: Eng. = Col. 33CX1948/SAX 2587; HMV in sets SLS 5048 (Intl. 0C 147-01842/7) and EX 29 0482-3; Ger. = Elec. SME 80933; in sets 1C 153-01842/7 and 137-29 0482-3; Fr. = HMV 2C 061-, 069-00602, 100602-4; US = Ang. (S)36289, RL-32099, AE-34462; in set AEW-34470; Time-Life STL-143; Jap. = Ang. AA-7596, AA-8088, AA-8578, EAC-40044
CD = **EMI CDM 763619-2; Jap. Ang. TOCE-6574, TOCE-1574.**

166   Mozart: *Don Giovanni*, K. 527. Overture
New Philharmonia Orchestra; recorded 29–30 October 1964, Studio No. 1, Abbey Road
Release: Eng. = Col. 33CX1948/SAX 2587; HMV in sets SLS 5048 (Intl. 0C 147-01842/7) and EX 29 0482-3; Ger. = Elec. SME 80933; in sets 1C 153-01842/7 and 137-29 0482-3; Fr. = HMV 2C 061-, 069-00602, 100602-4; US = Ang. (S)36289, RL-32099, AE-34462; in set AEW-34470; Jap. = Ang. AA-7596, AA-8088, AA-8578, EAC-40047
CD = **EMI CDM 763619-2; Jap. Ang. TOCE-6574, TOCE-1574.**
Note: The version recorded here uses Klemperer's own concert ending.

167   Mozart: *Le nozze di Figaro*, K. 492. Overture
New Philharmonia Orchestra; recorded 30 October and 9 November 1964, Studio No. 1, Abbey Road
Release: Eng. = Col. 33CX1948/SAX 2587; HMV in sets SLS 5048 (Intl. 0C 147-01842/7) and EX 29 0482-3; Ger. = Elec. SME 80933; in sets 1C 153-01842/7 and 137-29 0482-3; Fr. = HMV 2C 061-, 069-00602, 100602-4; US = Ang. (S)36289, RL-32099, AE-34462; in set AEW-34470; Jap. = Ang. AA-7596, AA-8088, AA-8578, EAC-40048
CD = **EMI CDM 763619-2; Jap. Ang. TOCE-6574, TOCE-1574.**

168   Mozart: Serenade No. 13 in G, K. 525, 'Eine kleine Nachtmusik'
New Philharmonia Orchestra; recorded 30 October and 4 November 1964, Studio No. 1, Abbey Road
Release: Eng. = Col. CX(SAX)5252; HMV in sets SLS 5048 (Intl. 0C 147-01842/7) and EX 29 0482-3; Ger. = Elec. in set 1C 147-53714/38; US = Ang. in set AEW-34470; Jap. = AA-8102, EAC-40045
CD = **EMI CDM 763619-2; Jap. Ang. TOCE-6574, TOCE-1574.**

169   Bruckner: Symphony No. 6 in A (Original version)
New Philharmonia Orchestra; recorded 6, 10–12 and 16–19 November 1964, Kingsway Hall, London

DISCOGRAPHY

Release: Eng. = Col. 33CX1943/SAX 2582; HMV SXLP 30448 (Intl. OC 053-00599); Ger. = Col. SMC 91437; Elec. 1C 063-00599; US = Ang. (S)36271; 4XG-60501; Jap. = Ang. AA-7370, AA-8096, EAC-85023, EAC-50043
CD = EMI CDM 763351-2; Jap. Ang. TOCE-6127.

170   Mozart: *La Clemenza di Tito*, K. 621. Overture
New Philharmonia Orchestra; recorded 9 and 14 November 1964, Studio No. 1, Abbey Road
Release: Eng. = Col. 33CX1948/SAX 2587; HMV in set SLS 5048 (Intl. OC 147-01842/7); EX 29 0482-3; Ger. = Elec. SME 80933; in sets 1C 153-01842/7, 197-53714/38, and 147-30636/7, 137-29 0482-3; Fr. = Col. 33FCX(SAXF)1057; HMV 2C 061-, 069-00602, 100602-4; US = Ang. (S)36289, RL-32099, AE-34462; in set AEW-34470; Jap. = Ang. AA- 7596, AA-8578
CD = EMI CDM 763619-2; Jap. Ang. TOCE-6574, TOCE-1574.

171   Mozart: Masonic Funeral Music in c, K. 477
New Philharmonia Orchestra; recorded 14 November 1964, Studio No. 1, Abbey Road
Release: Eng. = Col. 33CX1948/SAX 2587; HMV in set SLS 5048 (Intl. OC 147-01842/7); EX 29 0482-3; Ger. = Elec. SME 80933; in sets 1C 153-01842/7, 197-53714/38, and 147-30636/7, 137-29 0482-3; Fr. = HMV 2C 061-, 069- 00602, 100602-4; US = Ang. (S)36289, RL-32099, AE-34462; in set AEW-34470; Jap. = Ang. AA-7596, AA-8578, EAC-40045
CD = EMI CDM 763619-2; Jap. Ang. TOCE-6574, TOCE-1574.

L-110   Mahler: Symphony No. 2 in c, 'Resurrection'
Symphonie-Orchester des Bayerischen Rundfunks; Heather Harper, soprano, Janet Baker, mezzo-soprano; Chorus of the Bayerischen Rundfunk, Wolfgang Schubert, chorusmaster; recorded from a broadcast in the Herkules-Saal, Munich, 29 January 1965
Release: **CD = Nuova Era 6714-DM, Hunt CD-703**.

172   Mozart: Symphony No. 40 in g, K. 550. Fourth Movement (excerpt)
Stockholm Philharmonic Orchestra; recorded during a rehearsal, 11 May 1965
Release: **CD = BIS CD-424A**.

173   Mozart: Symphony No. 29 in A, K. 201
New Philharmonia Orchestra; recorded 20–21 September 1965, Studio No. 1, Abbey Road
Release: Eng. = Col. CX(SAX)5256; HMV in sets SLS 5048 (Intl. OC 153-01842/7), EX 29 0482-3; Ger. = Col. SMC 91336; Elec. in sets 1C 153-01842/7, 197-53714/38, and 137-29 0482-3; Fr. = Col. 33FCX-(SAXF)1030; US = Ang. (S)36329; 4XG-60481; in set AEW-34470; Jap. = Ang. AA-7614, AA-8083, EAA-93083/4, EAC-40044
CD = EMI CMS 763272-2; Ger. Zweitausendeins 60625; Jap. Ang. TOCE6093/6.

174   Mozart: Symphony No. 33 in B-Flat, K. 319
New Philharmonia Orchestra; recorded 22–23 September 1965, Studio No. 1, Abbey Road
Release: Eng. = Col. CX(SAX)5256; HMV in sets SLS 5048 (Intl. OC 153-01842/7), EX 29 0482-3; Ger. = Col. SMC 91336; Elec. in sets 1C

153-01842/7, 197-53714/38, and 137-29 0482-3; Fr. = Col. 33FCX-(SAXF)1030; US = Ang. (S)36329; in set AEW-34470; Jap. = Ang. AA-7614, AA-8136, EAA-93083/4, EAC-40046
CD = EMI CMS 763272-2; Ger. Zweitausendeins 60625; Jap. Ang. TOCE6093/6.

175 Haydn: Symphony No. 102 in B-Flat
New Philharmonia Orchestra; recorded 25–26 September and 19 October 1965, Studio No. 1, Abbey Road
Release: Eng. = Col. CX(SAX)5266; Ger. = Col. SMC 91433; Elec. 1C 063-01196; Fr. = HMV CCA 1091; US = Ang. (S)36364; Jap. = Ang. AA-8025
CD = EMI CDMC 763667-2; Jap. Ang. TOCE6566/8.

176 Beethoven: Mass in D, Op. 123 (*Missa solemnis*)
New Philharmonia Orchestra and Chorus; Elisabeth Söderstrom, soprano, Marga Höffgen, contralto, Waldemar Kmentt, tenor, Martti Talvela, bass; recorded 30 September, 1, 4–8 and 11–13 October 1965, Kingsway Hall, London
Release: Eng. = Ang. AN(SAN)165/6; HMV RLS(SLS)922 (Intl. OC 193-00056/7), TC-SLS 922; Ger. = Ang. CAN 165/6; Elec. SMA 91489/90; in sets 1C 147-, 197-53400/19; Fr. = HMV 2C 167-, 181-00627/8, 29 0944-3; in set 2C 147-50298/318; US = Ang. (S)36348/9 in (S)B3679; Jap. = Ang. AA-9257/8, AA-71/5, EAC-77255/6
CD = EMI CMS 769538-2; Jap. Ang. CE25-5719/20.

177 Haydn: Symphony No. 100 in G
New Philharmonia Orchestra; recorded 20–21 October 1965, Studio No. 1, Abbey Road
Release: Eng. = Col. CX(SAX)5266, ED 29 03571; Ger. = Elec. SMC 91433, 1C 063-01196; Fr. = HMV CCA 1091, 2C 069-01505; US = Ang.(S)36364, AE-34464; Jap. = Ang. AA-8090, AA-8025, AA-8093, EAA-93097/8, EAC-70201, EAC-81047
CD = EMI CDMC 763667-2; Jap. Ang. TOCE6566/8.

178 Schumann: Symphony No. 1 in B-Flat, Op. 38, 'Spring'
New Philharmonia Orchestra; recorded 21–23, 25 and 27 October 1965 Studio No. 1, Abbey Road
Release: Eng. = Col. CX(SAX)5269; Ger. = Elec. 1C 063-00613; in set 1C 197-52497/9; Fr. = HMV CCA 1095; US = Ang. (S)36353, RL-32063; 4XG-60482; Jap. = Ang. AA-8017, EAA-151, EAA-93095/6, EAC-70203, EAC-81036
CD = EMI CDM 763613-2, CZS 479885-2.

179 Schumann: *Manfred*, Op. 115. Overture.
New Philharmonia Orchestra; recorded 27 October 1965 and 14–15 February 1966, Studio No. 1, Abbey Road
Release: Eng. = Col. 33CX(SAX)5269; Ger. = Elec. 1C 063-00613; in set 1C 197-52497/9; Fr. = HMV CCA 1095; US = Ang. (S)36353, RL-32063; 4XG-60482
CD = EMI CDM 763917-2.

180 Beethoven: Concerto in D for Violin and Orchestra, Op. 61 (Kreisler cadenzas)
New Philharmonia Orchestra; Yehudi Menuhin, violin; recorded 21–22 and 24–25 January 1966, Kingsway Hall, London

DISCOGRAPHY

        Release: Eng. = HMV ALP(ASD)2285, EG 29 0274; Ger. = Elec. CVB 1921, 1C 063-00307, 055-, 255-29 0274; in sets 1C 127-53644/8, 147-, 197-53400/19 and 127-153644-; Fr. = HMV 2C 063-00307, 100307-1, -4; in set 2C 147- 50298/381; Neth. = HMV 1A 137-53550/1; US = Ang. (S)36369, RL-32100, AM-34714; 769001-4 Jap. = Ang. AA-9963B
        CD = EMI CDC 769001-2; Jap. Ang. CC28-3816.

L-111   Berlioz: *Symphonie fantastique*, Op. 14
        New Philharmonia Orchestra; recorded from a broadcast at the Royal Festival Hall, 30 January 1966
        Release: **CD = Disques Refrain DR 910007.**

181   Franck: Symphony in d
        New Philharmonia Orchestra; recorded 10–12 and 15 February 1966, Studio No. 1, Abbey Road
        Release: Eng. = Col. CX(SAX)5276; HMV in set SLS 5003 (Intl. OC 191-52130/4); Ger. = Col. SMC 91609; Elec. 1C 063-00616; Fr. = HMV CCA 1106; US = Ang. (S)36416; Jap. = Ang. AA-8090, EAC-40068
        CD = EMI CDM 764145-2.

L-112   Beethoven: *Grosse Fuge*, Op. 133

L-113   Beethoven: Symphony No. 7 in A, Op. 92
        New Philharmonia Orchestra; recorded from a broadcast at the Royal Festival Hall, 20 February 1966
        Release: **CD = Disques Refrain DR 920037.**

L-114   Beethoven: *Leonore Overture No. 3*, Op. 72a
        Kölner Rundfunk-Sinfonie-Orchester; recorded from a broadcast in the Grosser Sendesaal, 17 March 1966
        Release: **CD = Cetra CDE 1068.**

L-115   Schubert: Symphony No. 8 in b, D. 759, 'Unfinished'

L-116   Bruckner: Symphony No. 4 in E-Flat, 'Romantic'
        Symphonie-Orchester des Bayerischen Rundfunks; recorded from a broadcast in the Herkules-Saal, Munich, 1 April 1966
        Release: **CD = Hunt CD-701 (Schubert), Hunt CD-732 (Bruckner), Arkadia 2CDHP 591 (Bruckner).**

L-117   Beethoven: *Leonore Overture No. 3*, Op. 72a

L-118   Beethoven: Symphony No. 4 in B-Flat, Op. 60

L-119   Beethoven: Symphony No. 5 in c, Op. 67
        Berliner Philharmoniker; recorded during broadcasts of concerts in the Philharmonie, 11–13 May 1966
        Release: **CD = Hunt CD-732 (Overture only), Hunt CD-571 (Symphonies).**

182   Mozart: *Don Giovanni*, K. 527
        New Philharmonia Orchestra and Chorus; recorded 16–19, 22–25, 27–30 June, and 3–4 July 1966, Studio No. 1, Abbey Road
        Nicolai Ghiaurov, bass (Don Giovanni), Franz Crass, bass (Commendatore), Claire Watson, soprano (Donna Anna), Nicolai Gedda, tenor (Don Ottavio), Christa Ludwig, mezzo-soprano (Donna Elvira), Walter Berry, bass (Leporello), Mirella Freni, soprano (Zerlina), Paolo Montarsolo, bass (Masetto); Henry Smith, continuo

DISCOGRAPHY

Release: Eng. = Ang. AN(SAN)172/5; HMV RLS(SLS)923, SLS-, TC-SLS 143 462-3; Ger. = Elec. SMA 91494/7, 1C 165-00061/4; in sets 1C 197-53714/38 and 157-143462-3; US = Ang. (S)36389/92 in (S)DL3700; Jap. = Ang. AA-9318/21
CD = EMI CDM 769055-2, EMI CMS 763841-2; Jap. Ang. CE28-5062, TOCE7335/7

Excerpts: Ang. HMV ASD 2508; Ger. = Elec. 1C 061-063-00836; US = Ang. 769055-4.

183 Mahler: Symphony No. 9
New Philharmonia Orchestra; recorded 15–18 and 21–24 February 1967, Kingsway Hall, London
Note: Rehearsals for this recording were also recorded 11 and 13 February 1967 in Kingsway Hall.
Release: Eng. = Col. SAX 5281/2; HMV SXLP 30211/2 in set SXDW 3021 (Intl. OC 147-00617/8); Ger. = Elec. 1C 153-00617/8; Fr. = HMV CCA 1108/9, 2C 181-00617/8, 143462-3; in set 165-52519/26; US = Ang. S-36432/3 in S-3708B; Jap. = Ang. AA-8222/3, EAC-50038/9
CD = EMI CMS 763277-2; Ger. Zweitausendeins 60625; Jap. Ang. TOCE6091/2.

184 Bruckner: Symphony No. 5 in B-Flat
New Philharmonia Orchestra; recorded 9–11 and 14–15 March 1967, Kingsway Hall, London
Release: Eng. = Col. SAX 5288/9; Ger. = Col. SMC 91663/4; Elec. 1C 163-00621/2; Fr. = HMV CVB 2064/5; US = Ang. S-36444/5 in SB-3709; Jap. = Ang. AA-8186/7, EAC-85003/4, EAC-50041/2
CD = EMI CDM 763612-2.

185 Mozart: Serenade No. 12 in c, K. 388
New Philharmonia Wind Ensemble; recorded 14–15 March 1967, Kingsway Hall, London
Release: Eng. = Col. 33CX(SAX)5290; HMV SXLP 30502 in set SXDW 3050 (Intl. OC 151-53528/9); CFP 41 4448; Ger. = Elec. SME 91696, CVB 2058, 1C 037-, 163-00400; in set 1C 197-53714/38; Fr. = HMV 2C 037-00400; US = Ang. (S)36536; Jap. = Ang. AA-8572
CD = EMI CDM 763620-2.

186 Mozart: Concerto No. 25 in C for Piano and Orchestra, K. 503
(Barenboim cadenzas)
New Philharmonia Orchestra; Daniel Barenboim, piano; recorded 17–18 March 1967, Studio No. 1, Abbey Road
Release: Eng. = Col. 33CX(SAX)5290; Ger. = Elec. SME 91696, CVB 2058, 1C 037-, 063-00400; in set 1C 197-53714/38; Fr. = HMV 2C 037-00400; US = Ang. (S)36536; Jap. = Ang. AA-8572
CD = EMI CDM 763620-2.

187 Beethoven: Concerto No. 5 in E-Flat for Piano and Orchestra, Op. 73, 'Emperor'
New Philharmonia Orchestra; Daniel Barenboim, piano; recorded 4–5 and 9 October 1967, Studio No. 1, Abbey Road
Release: Eng. = Ang. in set SAN 238/41; HMV ASD 2500; in sets SLS 5180 (Intl. OC 157-01890/3) and SLS 941; Ger. = Elec. 1C 063-01982; in sets SME 91766/70, 1C 187-, 197-01890/3 and 147-, 197-53400/19;

Fr. = HMV 2C 069-01982; in sets 2C 197-01890/3, 147-50298/318 and 29 1325-1, -4; Neth. = HMV 1A 137-53550/1; US = Ang. S-3752D-L; Jap. = Ang. AA-8794, EAA-128, EAA-93117/8, EAC-70210
CD = EMI CDMC 763360-2; Jap. Ang. TOCE6120/2.

188 Beethoven: Concerto No. 4 in G for Piano and Orchestra, Op. 58 (Beethoven cadenzas)
New Philharmonia Orchestra; Daniel Barenboim, piano; recorded 9 and 10 October 1967, Studio No. 1, Abbey Road
Release: Eng. = Ang. in set SAN 238/41; HMV ASD 2550; in sets SLS 5180 (Intl. OC 157-01890/3) and SLS 941; Ger. = Elec. 1C 063-01981; in sets SME 91766/70 1C 187-, 197-01890/3, and 147-, 197-53400/19; Fr. = HMV 2C 069-01980; in sets 197-01890/3, 147-50298/318 and 29 1325-1, -4; US = Ang. S-3752D-L; Jap. = Ang. AA-8796
CD = EMI CDMC 763360-2; Jap. Ang. TOCE6120/2.

189 Beethoven: Concerto No. 3 in c for Piano and Orchestra, Op. 37 (Beethoven cadenzas)
New Philharmonia Orchestra; Daniel Barenboim, piano; recorded 10–11 and 14 October 1967, Studio No. 1, Abbey Road
Release: Eng. = Ang. in set SAN 238/41; HMV ASD 2579; in sets SLS 5180 (Intl. OC 157-01890/3) and SLS 941; Ger. = Elec. 1C 063-01980; in sets SME 91766/70, 1C 187-, 197-01890/3 and 147-, 197-53400/19; Fr. = HMV 2C 069-01980; in sets 197-01890/3, 147-50298/318 and 29 1325-1, -4; US = Ang. S-3752D-L; Jap. = Ang. AA-8795, EAA-169, EAA-93117/8, EAC-70209
CD = EMI CDMC 763360-2; Jap. Ang. TOCE6120/2.

190 Beethoven: Concerto No. 1 in C for Piano and Orchestra, Op. 15 (Beethoven cadenzas)
New Philharmonia Orchestra; Daniel Barenboim, piano; recorded 11, 14 and 28 October and 4 November 1967, Studio No. 1, Abbey Road
Release: Eng. = Ang. in set SAN 238/41; HMV ASD 2616; in sets SLS 5180 (Intl. OC 157-01890/3) and SLS 941; Ger. = Elec. 1C 063-01978; in sets SME 91766/70, 1C 187-, 197-01890/3 and 147-, 197-53400/19; Fr. = HMV 2C 069-01978; in sets 197-01890/3, 147-50298/318 and 29 1325-1, -4; US = Ang. S-36605, S-3672D-L; Jap. = Ang. AA-8797
CD = EMI CDMC 763360-2; Jap. Ang. TOCE6120/2.

191 Bach: Mass in b, BWV 232
New Philharmonia Orchestra and BBC Chorus; Agnes Giebel, soprano, Janet Baker, mezzo-soprano, Nicolai Gedda, tenor, Hermann Prey, baritone, Franz Crass, bass; recorded 18–20, 23–26 and 30–31 October and 6–7, 9–10 November 1967, Kingsway Hall, London; an unpublished rehearsal session with the chorus was recorded 2–3 March 1967 in Studio No. 1, Abbey Road.
Release: Eng. = Ang. SAN 195/7; HMV SLS, TC-SLS 930 (Intl. OC 065-00090/2; Ger. = Elec. 1C 157-, 165-00090/2, SMA 91691/3; 1C 197-54135/45; Fr. = HMV 2C 165-00090/2; US = Ang. (S)36744/6 in SC3720; Jap = Ang. AA-9496/8, EAC-77249/51
CD = EMI CDMB 763364-2; Jap. Ang. TOCE6123/4.
Excerpt: No. 21, Sanctus: Eng. = HMV HQS 1407; another excerpt with Giebel and Baker in US = Ang. SPRO 4515 (Angel New Release Promotional disc issued April 1968).

DISCOGRAPHY

L-120 Bach: Mass in b, BWV 232

New Philharmonia Orchestra and BBC Chorus; Agnes Giebel, soprano, Janet Baker, mezzo-soprano, Nicolai Gedda, tenor, Hermann Prey, baritone, Franz Crass, bass; recorded from a concert broadcast at the Royal Festival Hall, 16 November 1967

Release: **CD = 2Hunt CD-727.**

192 Beethoven: Concerto No. 2 in B-Flat for Piano and Orchestra, Op. 19 (Beethoven cadenzas)

New Philharmonia Orchestra; Daniel Barenboim, piano; recorded 3–4 November 1967, Studio No. 1, Abbey Road

Release: Eng. = Ang. in set SAN 238/41; HMV ASD 2608; in sets SLS 5180 (Intl. OC 157-01890/3) and SLS 581; Ger. = Elec. 1C 063-01979; in sets SME 91766/70, 1C 187-, 197-01890/3 and 1C 147-, 197-53400/19; Fr. = HMV 2C 069-01979; in sets 2C 197-01890/3, 147-50298/318 and 29 13244-1, -4; US = Ang. S-3752D-L; Jap. = Ang. AA-8796 **CD = EMI CDMC 763360-2; Jap. Ang. TOCE6120/2.**

193 Beethoven: Fantasia in c, Op. 80

New Philharmonia Orchestra; John Alldis Choir; Daniel Barenboim, piano; recorded 3–4 November 1967, Studio No. 1, Abbey Road

Release: Eng. = Ang. in set SAN 238/41; HMV ASD 2608; in sets SLS 5180 (Intl. OC 157-01890/3) and SLS 581; Ger. = Elec. 1C 063-01979; in sets SME 91766/70, 187-, 197- 01890/3 and 147-, 197-53400/19; Fr. = HMV 2C 069- 01979, 053-78220 and 29 1325-1, -4; in sets 197-01890/3 and 147-50298/318; US = Ang. S-36815, S- 3752D-L; Jap. = Ang. AA-8795, EAA-169, EAA-93117/8, EAC-70209 **CD = EMI CDMB 769538-2, EMI CDMC 763360-2; Jap. Ang. TOCE6120/2.**

194 Wagner: *Der fliegende Holländer* (1843 Dresden version)

New Philharmonia Orchestra; BBC Chorus; recorded 17–19, 21–24, 28 February and 8–11 and 13–14 March 1968, Studio No. 1, Abbey Road

Theo Adam, bass-baritone (Holländer), Anja Silja, soprano (Senta), Martti Talvela, bass (Daland), Ernst Kozub, tenor (Erik), Annelies Burmeister, mezzo-soprano (Mary), Gerhard Unger, tenor (Steuermann)

Release: Eng. = Ang. SAN 207/9; HMV SLS 934; Ger. = Elec. SMA 91763/5, 1C 157-, 165-00104/6; in set F668-525/33; Fr. = HMV 2C 167-00104/6; US = Ang. S-36533/5 in SCL- 3730; Jap. = Ang. AA-9554/6
CD = EMI CDMS 763344-2, CDS-555179-2; Ger. Zweitausendeins 60625; Jap. Ang. TOCE6101/3

Excerpts: Eng. = HMV ASD 2724; Ger. = Elec. 1C 061-, 063-00828; Jap. = Ang. EAC-80195; Senta's Ballad in Fr. = HMV 29 0841-3, -5.

L-121 Wagner: *Der fliegende Holländer* (1843 Dresden version)

New Philharmonia Orchestra; BBC Chorus; recorded from a broadcast at the Royal Festival Hall, 19 March 1968

Theo Adam, bass-baritone (Holländer), Anja Silja, soprano (Senta), Martti Talvela, bass (Daland), James King, tenor (Erik), Annelies Burmeister, mezzo-soprano (Mary), Kenneth MacDonald, tenor (Steuermann)

Release: **CD = Hunt CD-561.**

DISCOGRAPHY

L-122   Mozart: Serenade No. 12 in c, K. 388
Wiener Philharmoniker; recorded from a broadcast in the Musikvereinssaal, 19 May 1968
Release: **CD = Disques Refrain DR 910019.**

L-123   Mozart: Symphony No. 41 in C, K. 551, 'Jupiter'
Wiener Philharmoniker; recorded from a broadcast in the Musikvereinssaal, 19 May 1968
Release: **CD = Disques Refrain DR 910019.**

L-124   Beethoven: Symphony No. 5 in c, Op. 67
Wiener Philharmoniker; recorded from a broadcast in the Musikvereinssaal, 26 May 1968
Release: **CD = DG 435-327-2; Jap. DG POCG-2626.**

L-125   Bruckner: Symphony No. 5 in B-Flat
Wiener Philharmoniker; recorded from a broadcast in the Musikvereinssaal, 2 June 1968
Release: **CD = Hunt CD-569; Jap. King K1CC-2078.**

L-126   Rameau/Klemperer: Gavotte with Six Variations
Wiener Philharmoniker; recorded from a broadcast in the Musikvereinssaal, 2 June 1968
Release: **CD = Disques Refrain DR 910019.**

L-127   Mozart: Masonic Funeral Music in c, K. 477
Wiener Philharmoniker; recorded from a broadcast in the Musikvereinssaal, 9 June 1968
Release: **CD = Hunt CD-578**
Note: Performed in memory of Senator Robert F. Kennedy.

L-128   Mahler: Symphony No. 9
Wiener Philharmoniker; recorded from a broadcast in the Musikvereinssaal, 9 June 1968
Release: **CD = Nuova Era 033.6709, Hunt CD-578.**

L-129   Schubert: Symphony No. 8 in b, D. 759, 'Unfinished'
Wiener Philharmoniker; recorded from a broadcast in the Musikvereinssaal, 16 June 1968
Release: **CD = DG 435-327-2; Jap. DG POCG-2626**
Note: Contrary to published reviews of this performance, Klemperer does not salute the orchestra at the conclusion of the symphony with the remarks attributed to him.

L-130   Wagner: *Siegfried Idyll*
Wiener Philharmoniker; recorded from a broadcast in the Musikvereinssaal, 16 June 1968
Release: **CD = Hunt CD-708.**

L-131   Wagner: *Tristan und Isolde.* Act I: Prelude
Wiener Philharmoniker; recorded from a broadcast in the Musikvereinssaal, 16 June 1968
Release: **CD = Hunt CD-578.**

L-132   Wagner: *Die Meistersinger von Nürnberg.* Act I: Prelude

DISCOGRAPHY

              Wiener Philharmoniker; recorded from a broadcast in the Musikvereinssaal, 16 June 1968
              Release: CD = **Hunt CD-578.**

L-133   Mahler: Symphony No. 9
              New Philharmonia Orchestra; recorded from a broadcast at Usher Hall, Edinburgh, 30 August 1968
              Release: CD = **Hunt CD-563.**

195   Mahler: Symphony No. 7
              New Philharmonia Orchestra; recorded 19–21 and 24–28 September 1968, Kingsway Hall, London
              Release: Eng. = HMV ASD 2491/2, SLS 781; CDP 41 4442; Ger. = Elec. 1C 163-01931/2; Fr. = HMV 2C 163-01931/2; in set 165-52519/26; US = Ang. S-3740B; Jap. = Ang. AA-8581/2, EAC-50036/7
              CD = **EMI CDMS 764147-2**
              Note: A further session devoted to tests only was held on 18 September.

196   Schumann: Symphony No. 2 in C, Op. 61
              New Philharmonia Orchestra; recorded 5–6 October 1968, Studio No. 1, Abbey Road
              Release: Eng. = HMV ASD 2454; Ger. = Elec. 1C 063-01918; in set 197-52497/9; US = Ang. S-36606; Jap. = Ang. AA-8552, EAA-151, EAA-93095/6, EAC-70203, EAC-81036
              CD = **EMI CDM 763613-2, CZS 479885-2.**

197   Schumann: *Genoveva*, Op. 81. Overture
              New Philharmonia Orchestra; recorded 3, 6–7 October 1968, Studio No. 1, Abbey Road
              Release: Eng. = HMV ASD 2454; Ger. = Elec. 1C 063-01918; US = Ang. S-36606; Jap. = Ang. AA-8552
              CD = **EMI CDM 763917-2.**

198   Rameau/Klemperer: Gavotte with Six Variations
              New Philharmonia Orchestra; recorded 7 and 13 October 1968, Studio No. 1, Abbey Road
              Release: Eng. = HMV ASD 2537; Ger. = Elec. 1C 063-02003
              CD = **EMI CMS 764150-2; Jap. YMCD-1004.**

199   Beethoven: Symphony No. 7 in A, Op. 92
              New Philharmonia Orchestra; recorded 12–14 October 1968, Studio No. 1, Abbey Road
              Release: Eng. = HMV ASD 2537; Ger. = Elec. 1C 063-02003; Jap. = Ang. AA-8761, AA-44/7
              CD = **Jap. YMCD-1004.**

L-134   Brahms: Concerto No. 2 in B-Flat for Piano and Orchestra, Op. 83
              New Philharmonia Orchestra; Vladimir Ashkenazy, piano; recorded from a broadcast at the Royal Festival Hall, 28 January 1969
              Release: CD = **Hunt CD-709.**

200   Schumann: Symphony No. 3 in E-Flat, Op. 97, 'Rhenish'
              New Philharmonia Orchestra; recorded 5–7 February 1969, Studio No 1, Abbey Road

DISCOGRAPHY

>Release: Eng. = HMV ASD 2547; Ger. = Elec. 1C 037-, 063-02011; in set 1C 197-52497/9; Fr. = HMV 2C 063-02011; US = Ang. S-36689, RL-32064; 4XG-60483; Jap. = Ang. AA-8656, EAA-152, EAA-93095/6, EAC-70101, EAC-81064
>**CD = EMI CDM 763613-2, CZS 479885-2.**

201   Schumann: *Scenes from Faust*. Overture
>New Philharmonia Orchestra; recorded 8 February 1969, Studio No. 1, Abbey Road
>Release: Eng. = HMV ASD 2547; Ger. = Elec. 1C 037-, 063-02011; Fr. = HMV 2C 063-02011; US = Ang. S-36689, RL-32064; 4XG-60483; Jap. = Ang. AA-8656
>**CD = EMI CDM 763613-2.**

L-135   Mendelssohn: *Hebrides Overture*, Op. 26
>Symphonie-Orchester des Bayerischen Rundfunks; recorded from a broadcast at the Herkules-Saal, Munich, 23 May 1969
>Release: **CD = 2HuntCD-701, Grandi Opere Curcio Concerto CON-03.**

L-136   Mendelssohn: Symphony No. 3 in a, Op. 56, 'Scottish'
>Symphonie-Orchester des Bayerischen Rundfunks; recorded from a broadcast at the Herkules-Saal, Munich, 23 May 1969
>Release: **CD = 2Hunt CD-701**
>Note: Uses Klemperer's revised ending.

L-137   Mendelssohn: *A Midsummer Night's Dream*. Overture, Op. 21 and Incidental Music, Op. 61
>Symphonie-Orchester des Bayerischen Rundfunks and Chorus; Edith Mathis, soprano, Brigitte Fassbaender, contralto; recorded from a broadcast at the Herkules-Saal, Munich, 23 May 1969
>Release: **CD = 2HuntCD-701, Grandi Opere Curcio Concerto CON-2** (Overture and Wedding March only).

L-138   Beethoven: *Coriolan Overture*, Op. 62

L-139   Beethoven: Symphony No. 4 in B-Flat, Op. 60

L-140   Beethoven: Symphony No. 5 in c, Op. 67
>Symphonie-Orchester des Bayerischen Rundfunks; recorded from a broadcast at the Herkules-Saal, Munich, 29 May 1969
>Release: **CD = Disques Refrain DR 920038** (Overture and Symphony No. 4), **Disques Refrain DR 910002** (Symphony No. 5), **Enterprise PD 4189** (Symphonies).

202   Bach: Orchestral Suites, BWV 1066–1069
>New Philharmonia Orchestra; Gareth Morris, flute (in Suite No. 2); recorded as follows in Studio No. 1, Abbey Road:
>Suite No. 1, 15–16 October;
>Suite No. 2, 17 September and 6 October; Suite No. 3, 17 September and 17 October;
>Suite No. 4, 18–19 September 1969

Release: Eng. = HMV ASD 2604/5; in set SLS 808; Ger. = Elec. 1C 163-, 187-02102/3; 1C 197-54135/45; Fr. = HMV 2C 181-02102/3; US = Ang. S-3763; Jap. = Ang. AA-8759/60
CD = EMI CDM 764145-2.

203 Beethoven: *Die Geschöpfe des Prometheus*, Op. 43. Overture, No. 5, Adagio and No. 16, Finale
New Philharmonia Orchestra; recorded 18 October 1969, Studio No. 1, Abbey Road
Release: Eng. = HMV SXLP 30321 in SXDW 3032 (Intl. OC 153-03103/4; ED 29 0401-1; Ger. = Elec. 1C 197-03103/4; in set 1C 147-197-53400/19; Fr. = HMV in set 2C 147-50298/318; US = Ang. AE-34441
CD = EMI CDC 747188-2.

204 Wagner: *Die Walküre*. Act I
New Philharmonia Orchestra; recorded All Saints Church, Tooting, 22-24, 30–31 October and 3 November 1969
Helga Dernesch, soprano (Sieglinde), William Cochran, tenor (Siegmund), Hans Sotin, bass (Hunding)
Release: Eng. = Ang. SAN 334/5; HMV SLS 968; Ger. = Elec. 1C 193-02222/3; in set F668 525/33; US = Ang. S-3797B-L; Jap. = Ang. EAA-90051/2
Excerpts: Ger. = Elec. 1C 037-02887.

205 Klemperer: Symphony No. 2
New Philharmonia Orchestra; recorded 3 November 1969, Studio No. 1, Abbey Road
Release: Eng. = HMV ASD 2575, ED 29 03321; Ger. = Elec. 1C 063-02043; Jap. = Ang. EAA-80035
CD = EMI CDMS 764147-2.

206 Mozart: *Le Nozze di Figaro*, K. 492
New Philharmonia Orchestra; John Alldis Choir; recorded 8, 10–13, 15–16, 19–22, 25–26 and 29–31 January 1970, Studio No. 1, Abbey Road
Gabriel Bacquier, baritone (Count Almaviva), Elisabeth Söderstrom, soprano (Countess), Reri Grist, soprano (Susanna), Geraint Evans, baritone (Figaro), Teresa Berganza, mezzo-soprano (Cherubino), Annelies Burmeister, mezzo-soprano (Marcellina), Werner Hollweg, tenor (Basilio), Willi Brokmeier, tenor (Don Curzio), Michael Langdon, bass (Bartolo), Clifford Grant, bass (Antonio), Margaret Price, soprano (Barbarina), Teresa Cahill and Kiri Te Kanawa, sopranos (Two Maidens); Henry Smith, continuo
Release: Eng. = Ang. SAN 283/6; HMV SLS 955; Ger. = Elec. 1C 157-, 191-02134/7; in set 197-53714/38; Fr. = HMV 2C 191-02134/7; Jap. = Ang. AA-9652/5
CD = EMI CDMC 763849-2; Jap. Ang. TOCE7332/4
Excerpts: Ger. = Elec. 1C 037-, 063-02232; Jap. = Ang. EAC-80196.

207 Bruckner: Symphony No. 9 in d (Nowak edn)
New Philharmonia Orchestra; recorded 6–7, 18–21 February 1970, Kingsway Hall, London
Release: Eng. = HMV ASD 2719; Ger. = Elec. SHZE 360; US = Ang. S-36873; Jap. = Ang. EAA-181, EAA-80034, EAC-70173, EAC-81037
CD = EMI CDM 763916-2, CZS 479885-2; Jap. = Aug. TOCE-1572.

208 Haydn: Symphony No. 95 in c
New Philharmonia Orchestra; recorded 9–10 February 1970, Studio No. 1, Abbey Road
Release: Eng. = HMV ASD 2818; Ger. = Elec. 1C 063-02268; Fr. = HMV 2C 065-02268; US = Ang. S-36919; Jap. = Ang. EAA-80053
CD = EMI CDMC 763667-2; Jap. Ang. TOCE6566/8.

209 Klemperer: Quartet No. 7 (recorded under the composer's supervision)
Philharmonia Quartet; recorded 16–17 February 1970, Studio No. 1, Abbey Road
Release: Eng. = HMV ASD 2575; Ger. = Elec. 1C 063-02043; Jap. = Ang. EAA-80035
CD = EMI CDMS 764147-2.

L-141 Beethoven: Symphony No. 1 in C, Op. 21

L-142 Beethoven: Symphony No. 3 in E-Flat, Op. 55, 'Eroica'
New Philharmonia Orchestra; recorded at a concert at the Beethovenhalle, Bonn, 25 September 1970
Release: **CD = Arkadia 2CDHP 591.**

210 Wagner: *Die Walküre*. Act III: Wotan's Farewell and Magic Fire Music
New Philharmonia Orchestra; Norman Bailey, bass-baritone (Wotan); recorded 24, 26–27 October 1970, Wandsworth School and All Saints' Church, Tooting
Release: Eng. = Ang. SAN 334/5; HMV SLS 968; Ger. = Elec. 1C 193-02222/3; in set F668 525/33; US = Ang. S-3797B-L; Jap. = Ang. EAA-90051/2
Excerpts: Ger. = Elec. 1C 037-02887
CD = EMI CDM 763835-2 (Wotan's Farewell only).

211 Bruckner: Symphony No. 8 in c (1890 version ed. Nowak)
New Philharmonia Orchestra; recorded 29–30 October and 2–4, 10–11 and 14 November 1970, Kingsway Hall, London
Release: Eng. = HMV ASD 2943/4; in set SLS 872; Ger. = Elec. 1C 191-02259/60; US = Ang. S-3799B; Jap. = Ang. EAA-80041/2, EAC-85012/3, EAC-50046/7
CD = EMI CDM 763835-2
Note: There are two cuts in the fourth movement.

L-143 Mozart: Concerto No. 25 in C for Piano and Orchestra, K. 503

L-144 Mozart: Symphony No. 40 in g, K. 550
New Philharmonia Orchestra; Alfred Brendel, piano; recorded from a concert, 8 November 1970
Release: **CD = Hunt CD-729, Foyer ICF 2037.**

212 Mozart: *Così fan tutte*, K. 588
New Philharmonia Orchestra; John Alldis Choir; recorded 25, 27–30 January and 3–4, 6, 8–10, 12–13, 15–18 February 1971, Kingsway Hall, London
Margaret Price, soprano (Fiordiligi), Yvonne Minton, mezzo-soprano (Dorabella), Geraint Evans, baritone (Guglielmo), Luigi Alva, tenor (Ferrando), Lucia Popp, soprano (Despina), Hans Sotin, bass (Don Alfonso); Otto Freudenthal, continuo

DISCOGRAPHY

              Release: Eng. = Ang. SAN 310/3; HMV SLS 961; Ger. = Elec. 1C 191-02249/52; in set 197-53714/38; Fr. = HMV 2C 165-02249/52; Jap. = EAA-90011/4
              CD = **EMI CDMC 763845-2; Jap. Ang. TOCE7338/40**
        Excerpts: Ger. = Elec. 1C 037-, 063-02368; Fr. = HMV 2C 037-02368
        Note: Omits Nos. 7 and 24; some other numbers are cut.

L-145   Mahler: Symphony No. 2 in c, 'Resurrection'
        New Philharmonia Orchestra and New Philharmonia Chorus; Anne Finley, soprano, Alfreda Hodgson, contralto; recorded from a broadcast in the Royal Festival Hall, 16 May 1971
        Release: **CD = Arkadia 2CDHP-590, I grandi della classica 93.5121.**

213   Haydn: Symphony No. 92 in G, 'Oxford'
        New Philharmonia Orchestra; recorded 18–19 September 1971, Studio No. 1, Abbey Road
        Release: Eng. = HMV ASD 2818; Ger. = Elec. 1C 063-02268; Fr. = HMV 2C 065-02268; US = Ang. S-36919; Jap. = Ang. EAA-80053
            CD = **EMI CDMC 763667-2; Jap. Ang. TOCE6566/8.**

214   Mozart: Serenade No. 11 in E-Flat, K. 375
        New Philharmonia Wind Ensemble; recorded 20–21 and 28 September 1971, Studio No. 1, Abbey Road
        Release: Eng. = HMV SXLP 30502 in SXDW 3050 (Intl. OC 151-53528/9); Ger. = Elec. in set 1C 197-53714/38; US = Ang. AE-34410
            CD = **EMI CDM 763349-2; Jap. Ang. TOCE6125, TOCE6575**
        Note: The session on the 28th was Klemperer's last as a conductor; his final concert appearance occurred on September 26th.

Unconfirmed or misattributed recordings:

1937
Gershwin: Rhapsody in Blue (excerpts)
Los Angeles Philharmonic Orchestra; José Iturbi, piano.
Release: Eng. = Symposium 1007
Conducted by Alexander Smallens or by Iturbi himself.

1964
Beethoven: *Fidelio*. Leonore's Air and Leonore/Florestan Duet
Release: Fr. = Rodolphe RP 22445/6; ('Régine Crespin sur Scène')
with Vilém Pribyl, tenor; the conductor is Norman del Mar.

Composer index

Auber: *Fra Diavolo* Overture, 19

Bach: 'Bist du bei mir', BWV 508, L-18, 7
Bach: Brandenburg Concerto No. 1 in F, BWV 1046, L-106, 4, 113
Bach: Brandenburg Concerto No. 2 in F, BWV 1047, 9, 113
Bach: Brandenburg Concerto No. 3 in G, BWV 1048, 1, 113
Bach: Brandenburg Concerto No. 4 in G, BWV 1049, 2, 113
Bach: Brandenburg Concerto No. 5 in D, BWV 1050, 8, 20, 113

Bach: Brandenburg Concerto No. 6 in B-Flat BWV 1051, 5, 113
Bach: Cantata No. 202, 'Weichet nur, betrübte Schatten', L-72
Bach: Chorale 'Nun komm' der Heiden Heiland', BWV 559, 3
Bach: Magnificat in D, BWV 243, 21
Bach: Mass in b, BWV 232, L-120, 191
Bach: Matthäus-Passion, BWV 244, 118
Bach: Orchestral Suite No. 1 in C, BWV 1066, 46, 202
Bach: Orchestral Suite No. 2 in b, BWV 1067, 19, 45, 202

DISCOGRAPHY

Bach: Orchestral Suite No. 3 in D, BWV 1068, L-79, 47, 202
    Air: L-109
Bach: Orchestral Suite No. 4 in D, BWV 1069, 17, 48, 202
Bartók: Concerto for Viola and Orchestra, Sz. 120, L-27
Beethoven: *Ah, perfido!*, L-33
Beethoven: Concerto No. 1 in C for Piano and Orchestra, Op.15, 190
Beethoven: Concerto No. 2 in B-Flat for Piano and Orchestra, Op. 19, 192
Beethoven: Concerto No. 3 in c for Piano and Orchestra, Op. 37, 189
Beethoven: Concerto No. 4 in G for Piano and Orchestra, Op. 58, L-52, 34, 188
Beethoven: Concerto No. 5 in E-Flat for Piano and Orchestra, Op. 73, 187
Beethoven: Concerto in D for Violin and Orchestra, Op. 61, 180
Beethoven: *Coriolan Overture*, Op. 62, 8, L-95, L-107, L-138, 71
Beethoven: *Die Geschöpfe des Prometheus*, Op. 43
    Overture, L-92, 77
Beethoven: *Die Geschöpfe des Prometheus*, Op. 43
    Overture, Nos. 5 and 16, 203
Beethoven: *Egmont*, Op. 84
    Overture, 9, L-89
    Overture and Incidental Music, 72
Beethoven: Fantasia in c, Op. 80, 193
Beethoven: *Fidelio*, Op. 72, L-101, 13, 135
    Overture, 42
Beethoven: *König Stefan*, Op. 117
    Overture, 80
Beethoven: *Leonore Overture No. 1*, Op. 138, 41, 156
Beethoven: *Leonore Overture No. 2*, Op. 72a, 44, 155
Beethoven: *Leonore Overture No. 3*, Op. 72a, 10, L-14, L-117, 43, 154
Beethoven: Mass in D, Op. 123 (*Missa solemnis*), L-35, 28, 176
Beethoven: Overture *Zur Weihe des Hauses*, Op. 124, L-82, L-86, 60, 79
Beethoven: Quartet: *Grosse Fuge* in B-Flat, Op. 133, L-112, 54
Beethoven: Symphony No. 1 in C, Op. 21. L-64, L-97, L-141, 74
Beethoven: Symphony No. 2 in D, Op. 36, L-87, 69
Beethoven: Symphony No. 3 in E-Flat, Op. 55, 'Eroica', L-81, L-88, L-108, L-142, 49, 81
Beethoven: Symphony No. 4 in B-Flat, Op. 60, L-56, L-90, L-118, L-139, 73
Beethoven: Symphony No. 5 in c, Op. 67, L-2, L-91, L-119, L-119, L-124, L-140, 30, 51, 78

Beethoven: Symphony No. 6 in F, Op. 68, 'Pastoral', L-37, L-56, L-93, 26, 70
Beethoven: Symphony No. 7 in A, Op. 92, L-32, L-57, L-76, L-94, L-113 50, 115, 199
Beethoven: Symphony No. 8 in F, Op. 93, 4, 6, L-58, L-96, 75
Beethoven: Symphony No. 9 in d, Op. 125, 'Choral', L-59, L-98, 76
Berlioz: *Benvenuto Cellini*, Op. 23 Overture, L-9
Berlioz: *Symphonie fantastique*, Op. 14, L-111, 148
Brahms: *Academic Festival Overture*, Op. 80, 15, 68
Brahms: *Alt Rhapsodie*, Op. 53, 138
Brahms: Concerto in D for Violin and Orchestra, Op. 77, 108
Brahms: Concerto No. 2 in B-Flat for Piano and Orchestra, Op. 83, L-39, L-134
Brahms: *Ein deutsches Requiem*, Op. 45, L-51, L-82, 119
Brahms: Symphony No. 1 in c, Op. 68, 17, L-48, 64
Brahms: Symphony No. 2 in D, Op. 73, L-71, 63
Brahms: Symphony No. 3 in F, Op. 90, 66
Brahms: Symphony No. 4 in e, Op. 98, L-80, 65
Brahms: *Tragic Overture*, Op. 81, 67
Brahms: Variations on a theme of Haydn, Op. 56a, L-73, 40
Brahms-Schoenberg: Piano Quartet in g, Op. 25, L-13
Bruckner: Symphony No. 4 in E-Flat, 'Romantic', L-40, L-116, 27, 150
Bruckner: Symphony No. 5 in B-Flat, L-125, 184
Bruckner: Symphony No. 6 in A, L-99, L-103, 169
Bruckner: Symphony No. 7 in E, L-54, L-71, 116
Bruckner: Symphony No. 8 in c, L-78, 211
    Adagio, 2
Bruckner: Symphony No. 9 in d, 207
Bruckner: *Te Deum*, L-100

Chopin: Concerto No. 1 in e for Piano and Orchestra, Op. 11, L-42
Chopin: Concerto No. 2 in f for Piano and Orchestra, Op. 21, 35
Corelli: Sonata in d for Violin, Op. 5, No. 2, 'La Folia', L-19

Debussy: *Prélude à l'après-midi d'un faune*, L-11
Debussy: Two Nocturnes, 7
Dvorak: Symphony No. 9 in e, Op. 95, 'From the New World', 153

Falla: *Nights in the Gardens of Spain*, L-31
Franck: Symphony in d, 181

German: 'Who'll buy my sweet lavender?', L-6
Gershwin: Second Prelude, L-8
Gluck: *Iphigénie en Aulide*. Overture, 111
Gounod: *Faust*
  Act II: Salut! demeure, L-5

Handel: Concerto Grosso in a, Op. 6, No. 4, 56
Handel: *Messiah*, 161
Handel-Schoenberg: Quartet Concerto, L-12
Haydn: Symphony No. 88 in G, 163
Haydn: Symphony No. 92 in G, 'Oxford', 213
Haydn: Symphony No. 95 in c, 208
Haydn: Symphony No. 98 in B-Flat, 33
Haydn: Symphony No. 100 in G, 177
Haydn: Symphony No. 101 in D, 'Clock', L-62, L-67, 82
Haydn: Symphony No. 102 in B-Flat, 175
Haydn: Symphony No. 104 in D, 164
Hindemith: *Nobilissima Visione*, 38
Humperdinck: *Hänsel und Gretel*
  Overture and Act II: Dream Pantomime, 109

Janáček: Sinfonietta, L-28

Klemperer: *Merry Waltz* and *One-Step*, 128
Klemperer: Quartet No. 7, 209
Klemperer: Symphony No. 1, L-102
Klemperer: Symphony No. 2, 205

Liszt: Piano Concerto No. 1 in E-Flat, G. 124, 107
Liszt: Totentanz for Piano and Orchestra, G. 126, L-16

Mahler: *Kindertotenlieder*, L-35, L-47
Mahler: *Das Lied von der Erde*, 29, 160
Mahler: Lieder aus 'Des Knaben Wunderhorn', 158
Mahler: *Lieder eines fahrenden Gesellen*, L-20
Mahler: Rückert-Lieder, 159
Mahler: Symphony No. 2 in c, 'Resurrection', L-34, L-110, L-145, 32, 134
Mahler: Symphony No. 4 in G, L-38, L-50, L-63, 120
Mahler: Symphony No. 7, 195
Mahler: Symphony No. 9, L-128, L-133, 183
Massenet: *Manon*
  Act III: 'Gavotte', L-7
Mendelssohn: Concerto in a for Violin and Orchestra, Op. 64, L-41

Mendelssohn: *Hebrides Overture*, Op. 26, L-74, L-135, 86
Mendelssohn: *A Midsummer Night's Dream*.
  Overture, Op.21 and Incidental Music Op. 61, L-45, L-137, 85
  Overture, Op.21, 12, L-49
Mendelssohn: Symphony No. 3 in A, Op. 56, 'Scottish', L-136, 33, 84
Mendelssohn: Symphony No. 4 in A, Op. 90, 'Italian', 31, 87
Mozart: Adagio and Fugue in c, K. 546, 55
Mozart: *La Clemenza di Tito*, K. 621
  Overture, 170
Mozart: Concerti for Horn and Orchestra, 105
Mozart: Concerto No. 20 in d for Piano and Orchestra, K. 466, L-85
Mozart: Concerto No. 22 in E-Flat for Piano and Orchestra, K. 482, L-60
Mozart: Concerto No. 25 in C for Piano and Orchestra, K. 503, L-143, 186
Mozart: Concerto No. 27 in B-Flat for Piano and Orchestra, K. 595, L-61
Mozart: Concerto in A for Violin and Orchestra, K. 219, L-30
Mozart: *Così fan tutte*, K. 588, 212
  Overture, 165
Mozart: *Don Giovanni*, K. 527, L-34, 182
  Excerpts, 11
  Overture, L-21, 166
Mozart: *Die Entführung aus dem Serail*, K. 384, 24
  Overture, 112
Mozart: Masonic Funeral Music in c, K. 477, L-127, 171
Mozart: *Le nozze di Figaro*, K. 492, 206
  Overture, 167
Mozart: Serenade 'Gran Partita' in B-Flat, K. 361, 157
Mozart: Serenade No. 6 in D, K. 239, 'Serenata Notturna', L-25, 53
Mozart: Serenade No. 11 in E-Flat, K. 375, L-26, 214
Mozart: Serenade No. 12 in c, K. 388, L-122, 185
Mozart: Serenade No. 13 in G, K. 525, 'Eine kleine Nachtmusik', 6, 52, 168
Mozart: Symphony No. 25 in g, K. 183, L-22, L-29, 23, 62
Mozart: Symphony No. 29 in A, K. 201, L-23, 39, 173
Mozart: Symphony No. 31 in D, K. 297, 'Paris', 151
Mozart: Symphony No. 33 in B-Flat, K. 319, 174
Mozart: Symphony No. 34 in C, K. 338, 152
Mozart: Symphony No. 35 in D, K. 385, 'Haffner', L-10, 114
Mozart: Symphony No. 36 in C, K. 425, 'Linz', 22, 57

DISCOGRAPHY

Mozart: Symphony No. 38 in D, K. 504, 'Prague', L-23, 58, 142
Mozart: Symphony No. 39 in E-Flat, K. 543, 18, 61, 141
Mozart: Symphony No. 40 in g, K. 550, L-144, 59, 137, 172
Mozart: Symphony No. 41 in C, K. 551, 'Jupiter', L-123, 37, 136
Mozart: *Die Zauberflöte*, K. 620, 14, 162
  Excerpts, L-104

Offenbach: *Les Contes d'Hoffmann*
  Excerpts, 15
Offenbach: *La Belle Hélène*
  Overture, 20

Puccini: *La Bohème*
  Excerpts, L-4

Rameau/Klemperer: Gavotte with Six Variations, L-126, 198
Ravel: Alborada del gracioso, 5

Schoenberg: *Verklärte Nacht*, L-46
Schubert: Symphony No. 4 in c, D. 417, 'Tragic', L-75, 25
Schubert: Symphony No. 5 in B-Flat, D. 485, 149
Schubert: Symphony No. 8 in b, D. 759, 'Unfinished', 3, 10, L-65, L-115, L-129, 146
Schubert: Symphony No. 9 in C, D. 944, 'The Great', 117
Schumann: Concerto in a for Piano and Orchestra, Op. 54, 36, 106
Schumann: *Genoveva*, Op. 81
  Overture, 197
Schumann: *Manfred*, Op. 115
  Overture, 179
Schumann: *Scenes from Faust*
  Overture, 201
Schumann: Symphony No. 1 in B-Flat, Op. 38, 'Spring', 178
Schumann: Symphony No. 2 in C, Op. 61, 196
Schumann: Symphony No. 3 in E-Flat, Op. 97, 'Rhenish, 200
Schumann: Symphony No. 4 in d, Op. 120, L-75, L-105, 88
Shostakovich: Symphony No. 9 in e, Op. 70, L-70
Strang: Intermezzo, L-14
Strauss, Johann, II: *Die Fledermaus*
  Overture, L-17, 129
Strauss, Johann, II: *Kaiser-Walzer*, Op. 427, 122
Strauss, Johann, II: Waltz, *Wiener Blut*, Op. 354, 123
Strauss, Richard: *Don Juan*, Op. 20, 22, L-53, 101
Strauss, Richard: *Metamorphosen*, 131

Strauss, Richard: *Salome*, Op. 54. Salomes Tanz, 18, 98
Strauss, Richard: *Till Eulenspiegels lustige Streiche*, 21, L-53, 100
Strauss, Richard: *Tod und Verklärung*, Op. 24, 124
Stravinsky: *Pulcinella* Suite, L-69, 147
Stravinsky: Symphony in Three Movements, 143

Tchaikovsky: Symphony No. 4 in f, Op. 36, 145
Tchaikovsky: Symphony No. 5 in e, Op. 64, 144
Tchaikovsky: Symphony No. 6 in b, Op. 74, 'Pathétique', 121
Thomas: *Mignon*
  Overture, L-15

Verdi: *I Vespri Siciliani*
  Overture, L-1

Wagner: *Der fliegende Holländer*, L-121, 194
  Overture, 90
Wagner: *Die Götterdämmerung*
  Siegfrieds Rheinfahrt, 133
  Act III: Siegfrieds Trauermusik, 93
Wagner: *Lohengrin*
  Excerpts, 12
  Act I: Prelude, 91
  Act III: Prelude, 92
Wagner: *Die Meistersinger von Nürnberg*
  Excerpts, 16
  Act I: Prelude, L-3, L-66, L-132, 94
  Act III: Aufzug der Meistersinger and Tanz der Lehrbuben, 99
Wagner: *Parsifal*
  Prelude, 132
Wagner: *Das Rheingold*
  Einzug der Götter in Walhall, 125
Wagner: *Rienzi*
  Overture, 96
Wagner: *Siegfried*
  Act II: Waldweben, 47
Wagner: *Siegfried Idyll*, 11, L-130, 127
Wagner: *Tannhäuser*
  Overture, 89
  Act III: Prelude, 97
Wagner: *Tristan und Isolde*
  Act I: Prelude, L-131, 16, 118
  Isolde's Liebestod, 140
  Prelude and Liebestod, 95
Wagner: *Die Walküre*
  Act I, 204
  Act III: Walkürenritt, 102
Wagner: *Wesendonck-Lieder*, 139
Weber: *Euryanthe*
  Overture, 13, 110

Weber: *Der Freischütz*
  Overture, 103

Weber: *Oberon*
  Overture, 104
Weill: *Kleine Dreigroschenmusik*, 14, 130

Performer index

Ackroyd, Arthur (flute)
  113
Adam, Theo (bass-baritone)
  L-121, 194
John Alldis Choir
  193, 206, 212
Alva, Luigi (tenor)
  212
Anda, Géza (piano)
  L-39
Andreissen, Willem (piano)
  L-31
Arrau, Claudio (piano)
  L-42
Ashkenazy, Vladimir (piano)
  L-134

BBC Chorus
  L-100, L-120, L-121, 191, 194
Bachem, Hans (organ)
  L-44, L-51
Bacquier, Gabriel (baritone)
  206
Bailey, Norman (baritone)
  210
Baker, Janet (mezzo-soprano)
  L-100, L-110, L-120, 85, 118, 191
Barenboim, Daniel (piano)
  186, 187, 188, 189, 190, 192, 193
Báthy, Anna (soprano)
  13, 21
Bean, Hugh (violin)
  113
Bentonelli, Joseph (tenor)
  L-4, L-5, L-6, L-7
Berganza, Teresa (mezzo-soprano)
  206
Berry, Walter (baritone)
  118, 135, 162, 182
Boese, Ursula (soprano)
  L-98, 161
Bori, Lucrezia (soprano)
  L-4, L-5, L-6, L-7
Brendel, Alfred (piano)
  L-143
Bresser, Jan (violin)
  L-30
Brokmeier, Willi (tenor)
  206
Brouwenstijn, Gré (soprano)
  L-59, 33
Brown, Wilfred (tenor)
  118
Budanovits, Mária (mezzo-soprano)
  16

Burmeister, Annelies (mezzo-soprano)
  L-121, 194, 206

Cahill, Teresa (soprano)
  206
Case, John Carol (baritone)
  118
Cavelti, Elsa (mezzo-soprano)
  29
Civil, Alan (horn)
  105, 113
Cochran, William (tenor)
  204
Cortet, R. (flute)
  8
Crass, Franz (bass)
  L-98, L-120, 135, 162, 182, 191
Cunitz, Maud (soprano)
  L-43

Dermota, Anton (tenor)
  29
Dernesch, Helga (soprano)
  204
Dobson, John (tenor)
  L-101
Downes, Herbert (viola)
  53
Downes, Ralph (organ)
  119

Evans, Geraint (baritone)
  118, 206, 212

Farkas, Sándor (baritone)
  14
Fassbaender, Brigitte (soprano)
  L-137
Fehér, Pál (tenor)
  14, 15
Fekete, Pál (tenor)
  15
Ferrier, Kathleen (contralto)
  L-34, L-35
Finley, Anne (soprano)
  L-145
Fischer, Annie (piano)
  L-60, 20, 106, 107
Fischer-Dieskau, Dietrich (baritone)
  118, 119
Fleisher, Leon (piano)
  L-52
Freni, Mirella (soprano)
  182

DISCOGRAPHY

Freudenthal, Otto (continuo)
    212
Frick, Gottlob (bass)
    L-101, 135, 162

Galsay, Ervin (bass)
    14, 16
Gedda, Nicolai (tenor)
    L-120, 118, 161, 162, 182, 191
Gencsy, Sári (soprano)
    14, 24
Ghiaurov, Nicolai (bass)
    182
Giebel, Agnes (soprano)
    L-120, 162, 191
Godfrey, Victor (baritone)
    L-101
Grant, Clifford (bass)
    206
Greindl, Josef (bass)
    L-44
Grist, Reri (soprano)
    206
Grümmer, Elisabeth (soprano)
    L-51
Günter, Horst (bass)
    L-43
Gyurkovics, Mária (soprano)
    11, 24

Haefliger, Ernst (tenor)
    L-59
Hallstein, Ingeborg (soprano)
    135
Harper, Heather (soprano)
    L-100, L-110, 85
Haskil, Clara (piano)
    L-61, L-85
Hermes, Annie (mezzo-soprano)
    L-59
Hines, Jerome (bass)
    161
Hodgson, Alfreda (contralto)
    L-145
Höffgen, Marga (contralto)
    162, 176
Hoffman, Grace (contralto)
    161
Hollweg, Werner (tenor)
    206
Hotter, Hans (baritone)
    L-101, 76

Jambor, László (baritone)
    12
James, Cecil (bassoon)
    113
Janowitz, Gundula (soprano)
    162
Joviczky, József (tenor)
    16

Jurenák, Ida (contralto)
    14
Jurinac, Sena (soprano)
    L-101

Katona, Lajos (baritone)
    16
King, James (tenor)
    L-121
Kishegyi, Arpád (tenor)
    24
Kmentt, Waldemar (tenor)
    76, 176
Köles, Zoltán (tenor)
    14
Kolisch Quartet
    L-12
Koltay, Valéria (soprano)
    14
Koszó, István (bass)
    13, 16
Kozub, Ernst (tenor)
    194
Kraus, Otakar (baritone)
    118
Külkey, László (tenor)
    13
Kupper, Annelies (soprano)
    L-44
Kusche, Benno (bass)
    L-43

Langdon, Michael (bass)
    206
Lewis, Richard (tenor)
    L-100
Liebel, Karl (tenor)
    162
Lindermeier, Elisabeth (soprano)
    L-63
Lipp, Wilma (soprano)
    L-82, L-98
Littasy, György (bass)
    21
London, George (bass-baritone)
    L-43, L-47
Losonczy, György (baritone)
    11, 12, 16
Ludwig, Christa (mezzo-soprano)
    76, 118, 135, 138, 139, 140, 158, 159, 160,
        162, 182
Ludwig, Hanna (mezzo-soprano)
    L-45

MacDonald, Kenneth (tenor)
    L-121
Majkut, Erich (tenor)
    28
Malcolm, George (harpsichord)
    113

DISCOGRAPHY

Maleczky, Oszkár (baritone)
13, 16
Margittay, Sándor (organ)
21
Martzy, Johanna (violin)
L-41
Mathis, Edith (soprano)
L-137
Mátyás, Mária (soprano)
13, 14
Menuhin, Yehudi (violin)
180
Merckel, H. (violin)
8
Merrett, James Edward (double-bass)
53
Mindszenti, Ödön (baritone)
14
Minton, Yvonne (mezzo-soprano)
212
Möller-Siepermann, Käthe (soprano)
L-45
Montarsolo, Paolo (baritone)
182
Morison, Elsie (soprano)
L-101
Morris, Gareth (flute)
45, 113, 202
Mule, M. (saxophone)
9

Nagy, Gyula Angyal (tenor)
13
Nagy, Olivér (piano)
21
Nagypál, László (tenor)
14
Némethy, Ella (mezzo-soprano)
12
Newbury, Peter (oboe)
113
Ney, Tibor (violin)
20
Nilsson, Birgit (soprano)
72
Nordmo-Lövberg, Aase (soprano)
76
Novaes, Guiomar (piano)
34, 35, 36
Nowakowski, Marian (bass)
L-88

Oistrakh, David (violin)
108
Orosz, Júlia (soprano)
11
Osváth, Júlia (soprano)
11, 14, 16

Parikian, Manoug (violin)
53

Pavlánszky, Edina (soprano)
14
Pears, Peter (tenor)
118, 161
Pless, László (chorus master)
16
Popp, Lucia (soprano)
162, 212
Prey, Hermann (baritone)
L-51, L-120, 191
Price, Margaret (soprano)
206, 212
Primrose, William (viola)
L-27
Pütz, Ruth-Margaret (soprano)
162

Reményi, Sándor (baritone)
11, 12
Reynolds, Anna (mezzo-soprano)
162
Rigó, Magda (soprano)
12
Rissay, Pál (bass)
16
Robinson, Forbes (bass)
L-101
Roesgen-Champion, M. (harpsichord)
8
Rösler, Endre (tenor)
11, 13, 24
Rössl-Majdan, Hilde (contralto)
32, 134

Sándor, Júdit (mezzo-soprano)
14, 21
Scherbaum, Adolf (trumpet)
113
Schey, Hermann (bass)
L-20
Schock, Rudolf (tenor)
L-44
Schubert, Wolfgang (chorus-master)
L-110
Schuerhoff, Else (contralto)
28
Schwarzkopf, Elisabeth (soprano)
L-72, 118, 119, 120, 134, 161, 162
Segall, Bernardo (piano)
L-16
Silja, Anja (soprano)
L-121, 194
Simándy, József (tenor)
12, 16
Simoneau, Léopold (tenor)
L-43
Smith, Henry (continuo)
182, 206
Smith, Stanley (oboe)
113

DISCOGRAPHY

Söderström, Elisabeth (soprano)
176, 206
Somló, József (tenor)
16
Somogyvári, Lajos (tenor)
14, 15, 16, 21
Sotin, Hans (bass)
204, 212
Steingruber, Ilona (soprano)
28, 32
Streich, Rita (soprano)
L-43
Sutherland, Joan (soprano)
L-104
Sutcliffe, Sidney (oboe)
113
Szebenyi, János (flute)
19, 20
Székely, Mihály (bass)
11, 13, 14, 16, 24
Szigeti, Joseph (violin)
L-19
Szilvássy, Margit (mezzo-soprano)
15

Talvela, Martti (bass)
L-121, 176, 194
Te Kanawa, Kiri (soprano)
206
Tiszay, Magda (contralto)
14, 21
Toronyi, Gyula (tenor)
16
Tóth, Lajos (baritone)
11, 14
Trötschel, Elfriede (soprano)
L-38, L-50

Unger, Gerhard (tenor)
135, 162, 194

Várhelyi, Endre (bass)
16
Veasey, Josephine (mezzo-soprano)
162
Vermes, Jeno (bass)
13
Vickers, Jon (tenor)
L-101, 135
Vincent, Jo (soprano)
L-34

Waechter, Eberhard (baritone)
L-82
Wagner, Sieglinde (contralto)
L-44
Ward, Joseph (tenor)
L-101
Watson, Claire (soprano)
182
Watts, Helen (contralto)
118
Weber, Ludwig (bass)
L-43
Wehofschitz, Kurt (tenor
135
Wiener, Otto (baritone)
28
Wilbrink, Hans (bass)
L-59
Wise, David (violin)
53
Wolansky, Raymond (bass)
135
Woodburn, Andrew (horn)
113
Wunderlich, Fritz (tenor)
L-98, 160

Zadek, Hilde (contralto)
L-43

Orchestra index

BBC Symphony Orchestra,
L-99, L-100

Berliner Philharmoniker,
L-84, L-109, L-117, L-118, L-119

Budapest Symphony Orchestra,
10

Concertgebouworkest, Amsterdam,
L-20, L-27, L-28, L-29, L-30, L-31, L-32, L-33, L-34, L-35, L-46, L-49, L-55, L-56, L-57, L-58, L-59, L-60, L-72, L-73, L-74, L-75, L-102, L-103

Hungarian Radio Symphony Orchestra,
17, 18, 19, 20, 21

Hungarian State Opera Orchestra and Chorus,
11, 12, 13, 14, 15, 16, 24

Kölner Gürzenich Orchester,
L-61

Kölner Rundfunk-Sinfonie-Orchester,
L-38, L-39, L-40, L-42, L-43, L-44, L-45, L-47, L-48, L-51, L-52, L-53, L-63, L-78, L-114

Det Kongelige Kapel,
L-36, L-77

Lamoureux Orchestra,
25

London Wind Quintet,
157

Los Angeles Philharmonic Orchestra,
L-1, L-2, L-3, L-4, L-5, L-6, L-7, L-8, L-9, L-10, L-11, L-12, L-13, L-14, L-15, L-16, L-17, L-18, L-19

Mitglieder der Staatskapelle Berlin,
    14, 17, 19, 20, 21, 22

New Philharmonia Orchestra,
    L-111, L-112, L-113, L-120, L-121, L-133,
    L-134, L-141, L-142, L-143, L-144, L-145,
    160, 163, 164, 165, 166, 167, 168, 169, 170,
    171, 173, 174, 175, 176, 177, 178, 179, 180,
    181, 182, 183, 184, 185, 186, 187, 188, 189,
    190, 191, 192, 193, 194, 195, 196, 197, 198,
    199, 200, 201, 202, 203, 204, 205, 206, 207,
    208, 210, 211, 212, 213, 214

Orchester der Staatskapelle Berlin,
    1, 2, 3, 4, 5, 6, 7, 8, 9, 10, 11, 12, 13

Orchester der Staatsoper Berlin,
    15, 16, 17

Orchestra and Chorus of the Royal Opera House, Covent Garden,
    L-101, L-104

Orchestre de la Radiodiffusion Française,
    108

Orchestre de la Suisse Romande,
    L-76

Philadelphia Orchestra,
    L-105, L-106

Philharmonia Orchestra,
    L-83, L-85, L-86, L-87, L-88, L-89, L-90,
    L-91, L-92, L-93, L-94, L-95, L-96, L-97,
    L-98, 37, 38, 39, 40, 41, 42, 43, 44, 45, 46,
    47, 48, 49, 50, 51, 52, 53, 54, 55, 56, 57, 58,
    59, 60, 61, 62, 63, 64, 65, 66, 67, 68, 69, 70,
    71, 72, 73, 74, 75, 76, 77, 78, 79, 80, 81, 82,
    83, 84, 85, 86, 87, 88, 89, 90, 91, 92, 93, 94,
    95, 96, 97, 98, 99, 100, 101, 102, 103, 104,
    105, 106, 107, 109, 110, 111, 112, 113, 114,
    115, 116, 117, 118, 119, 120, 121, 122, 123,
    124, 125, 126, 127, 128, 129, 130, 131, 132,
    133, 134, 135, 136, 137, 138, 139, 140, 141,
    142, 143, 144, 145, 146, 147, 148, 149, 150,
    151, 152, 153, 154, 155, 156, 157, 158, 159,
    160, 161, 162

Philharmonia Quartet,
    209

Pro Musica Orchestra, Paris,
    1, 2, 3, 4, 5, 6, 7, 8, 9, 22, 23

RAI Symphony Orchestra,
    L-64, L-65, L-66, L-67, L-68, L-69, L-70

Residentie Orkest, Den Haag,
    L-41

RIAS Sinfonie-Orchester, Berlin
    L-21, L-22, L-23, L-24, L-25, L-26, L-37,
    L-50, L-71, L-81

Stockholm Philharmonic Orchestra,
    172

Symphonie-Orchester des Bayerischen Rundfunks,
    L-54, L-62, L-63, L-79, L-80, L-110, L-115,
    L-116, L-135, L-136, L-137, L-138, L-139,
    L-140

Wiener Philharmoniker,
    L-82, L-122, L-123, L-124, L-125, L-126,
    L-127, L-128, L-129, L-130, L-131, L-132

Wiener Symphoniker,
    L-107, L-108, 26, 27, 28, 29, 30, 31, 32, 33,
    34, 35, 36

OTTO KLEMPERER ON FILM

By Charles Barber

There is a great deal more of Klemperer on film than is generally known. The earliest visual record of his work dates from 1934 with the Los Angeles Philharmonic, and the last with London's New Philharmonia in 1971. In these films, he may be seen in rehearsal, in concert and in conversation.

From this evidence, it appears that the brain tumour surgery of 1939, leaving a residual facial and a slight right-side paralysis, changed somewhat his conducting technique. In his last performances, at 86, it is also clear that age had exacted its price.

Even so, these films provide indisputable evidence of means and approach and of the semaphore he employed to signal his intentions. Film tells us much about the grand style of Klemperer, confirming aural impressions, reawakening memory, recreating for generations his remarkable work. Preserved forever is the image of power and command, the sudden flash of anger, the warmth of response, his rehearsal strategies, his ironic wit.

Unfortunately, most of this visual documentation is not publicly available. With the growing market penetration of home VCRs, and a growing awareness of the commercial value of this rare footage, the several owners of copyright are determined to ascertain and acquire financial compensation, and/or to honour original restrictions on use.

This filmography indicates, where known, the sources of these materials. No suggestion is made that these films are presently available, save as noted.

Otto Klemperer
Rehearsal and Performance Films

1934
Los Angeles Philharmonic, Hollywood Bowl   3:00
repertoire unknown, in rehearsal
with Lotte Lehmann et al.
black and white, silent
SOURCE: Film and Television Archive, UCLA

Los Angeles Philharmonic, Huntington Library   2:00
black and white, silent
25 December 1934, radio broadcast
SOURCE: Film and Television Archive, UCLA
NOTE: An audio record of this performance exists. It has not been possible to match it to the film which has survived.

1936
Los Angeles Philharmonic, Forest Lawn at Glendale, California
Wagner, *Parsifal*, fragment; et al.   9:00
black and white, sound

Blythe Taylor Burns, soprano; Glendale Community Chorus, Joseph Klein, conductor; Albert Hay Malotte, Gaylord Carter, accompanists; William Farnum, speaker
Easter sunrise service, 5:20 a.m., 12 April 1936
SOURCE: Hearst-Metrotone Archive, UCLA (newsreel)
NOTE: The surviving film is in rough-cut form only

1946
Radio Symphony Orchestra, Baden-Baden
Beethoven, Symphony No. 5, rehearsal   1:00
black and white, sound
30 June 1946
SOURCE: Blick in die Welt, Frankfurt am Main (newsreel)
NOTE: Defective synchronicity

1958
Concertgebouw Orchestra, Amsterdam
Beethoven cycle, in rehearsal   25:00
black and white, silent
12 May–1 June 1958
SOURCE: Private

1960
Philharmonia Orchestra, Musikvereinssaal, Vienna
Beethoven, *Egmont* overture, in rehearsal   1:30
black and white, sound
31 May 1960
SOURCE: Private (newsreel)

1964
New Philharmonia Orchestra, Royal Albert Hall, London
Beethoven, Symphony No. 9   90:00
Agnes Giebel, Marga Hoffgen, Ernst Haefliger, Gustav Neidlinger;
New Philharmonia Chorus
television programme; Anthony Craxton, director
black and white, sound
27 October 1964; broadcast on BBC, 8 November 1964
SOURCE: BBC, London
NOTE: Commercially available on EMI Classics home video and laser disc

1970
New Philharmonia Orchestra, Festival Hall, London
Beethoven symphony cycle
television programmes; colour, sound (stereo recording)
broadcast by BBC on dates indicated

Symphony No. 1   27:00
26 May 1970

Symphony No. 2   36:00
9 June 1970

Symphony No. 3   57:00
26 May 1970

Symphony No. 4   38:00
2 June 1970

Symphony No. 5   35:00
2 June 1970

Symphony No. 6   44:00
9 June 1970

Symphony No. 7   43:00
21 June 1970

Symphony No. 8   30:00
21 June 1970

Symphony No. 9   82:00
30 June 1970
Teresa Zylis-Gara, Janet Baker, George Shirley, Theo Adam; New Philharmonia Chorus
SOURCE: BBC, London

Otto Klemperer
Documentaries

1960
Face to Face   30:00
Klemperer interviewed by John Freeman
black and white, sound
filmed 27 November 1960 in Lime Grove Studios
broadcast on BBC, 8 January 1961
SOURCE: BBC, London

1971
Otto Klemperer's Long Journey Through His Times   96:00
TV documentary, Holland/Germany, 1971/1984
Philo Bregstein, director
German with English subtitles
black and white, colour, sound

Beethoven, Piano Concerto No. 4, rehearsal   3:00
Daniel Adni, piano; New Philharmonia Orchestra, 1971

Brahms, Symphony No. 3, rehearsal   3:00
New Philharmonia Orchestra, 1971

Haydn, Symphony No. 92, rehearsal   3:00
New Philharmonia Orchestra, 18 and 19 September 1971
NOTE: These were among Klemperer's last sessions, and the only occasions on which he recorded a work he had never performed publicly.

Mahler, Symphony No. 2, rehearsal   3:00
New Philharmonia Orchestra, 1971

Mozart, Serenade K.375, rehearsal   1:00
New Philharmonia Orchestra, 1971
SOURCE: Facets Multi-Media, 1517 W. Fullerton, Chicago Illinois 60614, USA (800) 331-6197

Otto Klemperer in Rehearsal   42:00
TV documentary, Holland/London, September 1971
Philo Bregstein, director
black and white, colour, sound

Beethoven, Overture to *King Stephen* 2:00
New Philharmonia Orchestra, Royal Festival Hall, 1971

Beethoven, Piano Concerto No. 4 3:00
Daniel Adni, piano; ibid.

Brahms, Symphony No. 3, rehearsal and concert 34:00
ibid.
SOURCE: Philo Bregstein, Paris

1985
Omnibus – 100th Anniversary of Otto Klemperer 52:00
Keith Cheetham, producer
broadcast on BBC, 14 June 1985
black and white, colour, sound

Beethoven, Symphony No. 3, New Philharmonia, 1970 1:00

Beethoven, Symphony No. 5, Baden-Baden, 1946 1:00

Beethoven, Symphony No. 9, New Philharmonia, 1964 2:00
SOURCE: BBC, London

1990
Bei Kroll 28:00
The Kroll Opera during Klemperer's tenure, 1927 to 1931
Jörg Moser-Metius, director
black and white, colour, sound
SOURCE: Jörg Moser-Metius, Berlin

1991
Die Deutsche Mitte: Kroll und der Platz der Republik 58:00
A social and architectural history of the Kroll Oper, its site and uses, featuring Klemperer and his circle
Jörg Moser-Metius, director
black and white, colour, sound
SOURCE: Jörg Moser-Metius, Berlin

1994
The Art of Conducting 2:00:00
IMG/BBC television documentary
broadcast on BBC, January 1994
black and white, colour, sound
Volume 1:   Bernstein, Beecham, Barbirolli, Nikisch, Weingartner, Busch, Strauss, Walter, Klemperer, Furtwängler, Toscanini
Volume 2:   Toscanini, Stokowski, Koussevitsky, Reiner, Szell, Karajan, Bernstein, Klemperer

        These one-hour films include Klemperer conducting the 1946 Fifth, 1960 *Egmont*, 1964 Ninth, and excerpts from his interview with John Freeman.
SOURCE: IMG/BBC, London
NOTE: Commercially available on Tel Dec home video and laser disc.

BIBLIOGRAPHY

Aczel, Tamas, and Meray, Tibor, *The Revolt of the Mind*. London 1960
Adamy, Bernard, *Hans Pfitzner. Literatur und Zeitgeschehen in seinem Weltblick and Musik*. Tutzing 1980
Anderson, Martin (ed.), *Klemperer on Music*. London 1986
Armitage, Merle (ed.), *Schoenberg*. New York 1937

Barker, Elisabeth, *Austria 1918–1972*. London 1973
Baum, Vicki, *I Know What I'm Worth*. London 1964
Beavan, Peter, *Klempererisms*. London 1974 (privately printed)
Berenson, Bernard, *Sunset and Twilight. Diaries 1947–1958*. London 1964
Bertin, Celia, *Marie Bonaparte*. New York 1982
Bloch, Ernst, *Briefe 1903–1975*. Frankfurt 1985
Bloch, Karola, *Aus meinem Leben*. Pfullingen 1971/1981
Bónis, Ferenc, *Tizenházom találkozas Ferencsik Jánossol*. Budapest 1984
Boros, Attila, *Klemperer Magyarországon*. Budapest 1984
Bracher, Karl Dietrich, *The German Dictatorship*. London 1978 (paperback edn.)
Brecht, Bertolt, *Briefe*. Frankfurt 1981
Buder, Marianne, and Gonschorek, Dorette (eds.), *Tradition ohne Schlendrian: 100 Jahre Philharmonischer Chor, Berlin, 1882–1982*. Berlin 1982
Burghauser, Hugo, *Erinnerungen eines Philharmonikers*. Zurich/Freiburg 1979
   Philharmonische Begegnungen. Zurich 1979
Buschbeck, E.H., *Austria*. London 1949
Butt, John, *Bach: Mass in B minor*. Cambridge 1991
Cairns, David, *Responses*. New York 1980
Cassirer, Toni, *Mein Leben mit Ernst Cassirer*. Hildesheim 1981
Chasins, Abram, *Leopold Stokowski*. London 1981
Craft, Robert (ed.), *Dearest Bubushkin: Selected Letters and Diaries of Vera and Igor Stravinsky*. London 1985
Csicsery-Rónay, István, *The Russian Penetration of Hungary*. New York 1952
Csobadi, Peter, *Karajan oder die kontrollierte Ekstase*. Vienna 1988
Culshaw, John, *Putting the Record Straight*. London 1981
Daniel, Oliver, *Stokowski: A Counterpoint of Views*. New York 1982
Davison, W. Philipps, *The Berlin Blockade*. Princeton 1958
Emmons, Shirley, *Tristanissimo (Melchior)*. New York 1990
Evans, Geraint, *A Knight at the Opera*. London 1984
Felsenstein, Walther, and Melchinger, Siegfried, *Musiktheater*. Bremen 1961
Fischer, Grete, *Dienstbote Brechts und anderen*. Freiburg i.B 1966
Fischer-Dieskau, Dietrich, *Nachklang*. Stuttgart 1987
Furtwängler, Wilhelm, *Aufzeichnungen*. Wiesbaden 1980
Gallup, Stephen, *A History of the Salzburg Festival*. London 1987
Gauk, A.V., *Memuari. Izbranniye stut'i. Vospominaniya souvemannikov*. Moscow 1975
Geissmar, Bertha, *The Baton and the Jackboot*. London 1944

Gelatt, Roland, *The Fabulous Phonograph*, 2nd edition. London 1977
Gillis, Daniel, *Furtwängler and America*. New York 1970
Ginsburg, Leo M., *Izbrannoye. Dirizhori i orkestri*. Moscow 1981
Goodwin, F.K., and Jamison, K.R., *Manic-Depressive Illness*. Oxford 1990
Grubb, Suvi Raj, *Music Makers on Record*. London 1986
Haendel, Ida, *Woman with Violin*. London 1970
Harewood, Earl of, *The Tongs and the Bones*. London 1981
Hart, Philip, *Orpheus in the New World*. New York 1973
Heilbuth, Anthony, *Exiled in Paradise*. New York 1983
Heyworth, Peter (ed.), *Conversations with Klemperer*. London 1973
Hildebrandt, Dietrich von, Unpublished memoirs.
Hilmar, Ernst, *Catalogue of Schoenberg Memorial Exhibition*. Vienna 1974
Hindemith, Paul (ed.), Dieter Rexnoth, *Briefe*. Frankfurt 1982
    Jahrbuch 1984/XIII. Mainz 1985
Hiscocks, Richard, *The Rebirth of Austria*. London 1953
Horowitz, Joseph, *Conversations with Arrau*. London 1982
    Understanding Toscanini. London 1987
Ignatus, Paul, *Hungary*. London 1972
Jackman, Jarrell C., and Borden, Carla M., *The Muses Flee Hitler*. Washington (DC) 1983
Jackson, Gerald, *First Flute*. London 1968
Jones, Isabel Morse, *Hollywood Bowl*. New York/Los Angeles 1936
Kantorowicz, Alfred, *Deutsches Tagebuch, Erster Band*. Munich 1959
Katz, Robert, *Death in Rome*. London 1967
Khentova, Sofia, *Shostakovich, His Life and Works*. Leningrad 1985
Klemperer, Otto, *Autobiographische Skizze* ('Autobiographical sketch'). Unpublished 1962
    Minor Recollections. London 1964
    Über Musik und Theater. Berlin (DDR) 1982
Koopal, Grace G., *The Miracle of Music*. Los Angeles 1972
Kortner, Fritz, *Aller Tage Abend*. Munich 1959
Legge, Walter (ed. Elisabeth Schwarzkopf), *On and Off the Record*. London, 1982
Leonard, Maurice, *Kathleen: The Life of Kathleen Ferrier*. London 1988
Levant, Oscar, *A Smattering of Ignorance*. New York 1940
Lewy, Guenter, *The Catholic Church and Nazi Germany*. New York 1964
Macartney, C.A., *A History of Modern Hungary*. Edinburgh 1961
McWilliams, Carey, *Southern California: An Island on the Land*. Santa Barbara 1973
Major, Norma, *Joan Sutherland*. London 1987
Mann, Thomas, *Dr Faustus*. Frankfurt 1980
    Die Entstehung des Doktor Faustus. Amsterdam 1949
    Tagebücher, 1946/8. Frankfurt 1989
Mariano, Nicky, *Forty Years with Berenson*. London 1966.
Max, Stanley M., *The United States, Great Britain and the Sovietization of Hungary*. Boulder 1985
Metz, Louis, *Over dirigieren, dirigenten en orkesten*. Lochem (Holland) 1956
Monson, Karen, *Alma Mahler*. Boston 1983
Morgenstern, Soma, *Memoirs*. (unpublished)
Nelson, Walter Henry, *The Berliners*. London 1969
Newlin, Dika, *Schoenberg Observed*. New York 1980
Newman, Ernest, *The Life of Richard Wagner*. 4 vols. London 1933–47
Northcott, John Orlando, *The Hollywood Bowl Story*. Hollywood 1962
Pettitt, Stephen J., *Dennis Brain*. London 1976
    Philharmonia Orchestra: A Record of Achievement 1945–1985. London 1985
Prieberg, Fred K., *Musik im NS-Staat*. Frankfurt 1982
    Kraftprobe: Wilhelm Furtwängler im Dritten Reich. Wiesbaden 1986

BIBLIOGRAPHY

Radkan, Joachim, *Die deutsche Emigration in den USA*. Düsseldorf 1971
Reinhardt, Max, *Der Liebhaber*. Munich 1973
Rozhdestvensky, Gennadi, *Mïsli o musike*. Moscow 1975
Rufer, Josef, *The Works of Arnold Schoenberg*. London 1962
Saathen, Friedrich, *Einem Chronik*. Graz 1982
Sachs, Harvey, *Toscanini*. New York 1978
    Music in Fascist Italy. London 1987
Saunders, Alan, *Walter Legge: A Discography*. London 1984
Schausberger, Norbert. *Der Griff nach Oesterreich*. Vienna 1978
Schoenberg, Arnold, *Selected Letters*. London 1964
Schuh, Willi, *Richard Strauss: A Chronicle of the Early Years (1864–98)*. Cambridge 1982
Schwartz, Charles, *Gershwin: His Life and Music*. Indianapolis 1973
Schwarz, Boris, *Musical Life in the Soviet Union, 1917–1970*. London 1972.
Seefehlner, Egon, *Die Musik meines Lebens*. Vienna 1983
Skelton, Geoffrey, *Wieland Wagner: The Positive Sceptic*. London 1971
Smith, Caroline Estes, *The Philharmonic Orchestra: The First Ten Years*. Los Angeles 1930
Spalek, John M., *Guide to the Archival Materials of the German Speaking Emigration to the United States after 1933*. Charlottesville (Virginia) 1978
Stader, Maria, *Nehmt mein Dank*. Munich 1979
Stassinopoulos, Arianna, *Maria: Beyond the Callas Legend*. London 1980
Stewart, Lawrence, and Jablonski, Edward, *The Gershwin Years*. London 1974
Strasser, Otto, *Und dafür wird man noch bezahlt*. Vienna 1974
Stravinsky, Igor (ed. Robert Craft), *Selected Correspondence, Volumes 1–3*. London 1982, 1984 and 1985
Stravinsky, Igor, and Craft, Robert, *Diologues and a Diary*. London 1968
Stravinsky, Vera, and Craft, Robert, *Stravinsky in Pictures and Documents*. London 1979
Stresemann, Wolfgang, ... *und Abends in der Philharmonie*. Munich 1981
Stuckenschmidt H.H., *Schoenberg, Leben, Umwelt, Werk*. Zurich 1974
Swan, Howard S., *Music in the Southwest, 1825–1950*. San Marino (California) 1952
Tawa, Nicholas E., *Serenading the Reluctant Eagle*. New York 1984
Taylor, John Russell, *Strangers in Paradise*. New York 1983
Tusa, Ann and John, *The Berlin Blockade*. London 1988
Vaughan, Roger, *Herbert von Karajan: A Biographical Portrait*. London 1986
Viertel, Salka, *The Kindness of Strangers*. New York 1969
Walter, Bruno, *Theme and Variations*. London 1947
    Briefe, 1894–1962. Frankfurt 1969
Wulf, Joseph, *Musik im dritten Reich*. Gütersloh 1963
Yates, Frances Mullen, *Chronicle of the Evenings on the Roof/Monday Evening Concerts*. Unpublished typescript
Yudin, G. Ya., *Za gram'yu proshlikh dney*. Moscow 1978
Yuzeovich, V.A., *David Oistrakh*. Stuttgart 1977

Historie en Kronick van het Concertgebouw en het Concertgebouworkest. Zutphen 1988

INDEX

The name of Otto Klemperer appears on almost every page of the text. Many references to him have therefore been placed under other relevant headings, and his name abbreviated to 'OK'.

Italic page numbers indicate illustrations; **bold** page numbers, which precede other page numbers, indicate an entry in the bibliographical glossary. Where footnotes are referred to they are indicated by '*n*'/'& *n*'; where endnotes are referred to they are indicated by note number following the page on which the referent occurs.

An asterisk (*) following a page reference indicates a performance by/under Klemperer. Where the subheading 'recording' appears, the recording was conducted by Klemperer.

The discography is indexed separately on pp. 452–60 and there are no references to it below.

Abbado, Claudio, 327–8
Abbiati, Franco, 145–6
Abend, Der (Vienna), 2
Abendroth, Walter, 166
Abravanel, Maurice, **386**, 105
Achron, Joseph: Violin Concerto No. 2, 78*n**; Violin Concerto No. 3, 79*n**
Adam, Theo, 344
Adelaide, 211
Adler, Hans, 195*n*
Adni, Daniel, 358
Adorno, Theodor, 113
Alexander-Katz, Dorothea, 3–4, 14, 28, 31
Algemeen Handelsblad, 225
American Federation of Musicians, 25, 93*n*, 239, 241, 249
American Guild for German Cultural Freedom, 96 & *n*, 104*n*
American Hebrew, 56
Amis, John, 248, 265, 291
Amsterdam, 177, 243, 246, 248, 251, 257
  Concertgebouw Orchestra, 30, 31, 147–8, 167, 168, 177–8, 179, 192, 207, 224–6, 229–30, 237, 243, 254, 261–3, 269, 292, 339*n*; OK on, 149, 178, 261, 262
  Tonkunst Chorus, 262
Anda, Géza, 248
Andry, Peter, **386**, 311*n*, 321, 326*n*, 327–8, 332, 333, 338, 345, 346, 347, 352, 358, 361–2
Angel Records, 265 & *n*, 321, 338
Angeles, Victoria de los, 304
Ansermet, Ernest, **386**, 7–8, 71, 170
Appia, Adolphe, 217*n*
Arlt, Gustave O., 126
Armstrong, Richard, 340–1, 345*n*
Arrau, Claudio, 202, 264 & *n*
Arts Council, 231, 232

Ashkenazy, Vladimir, 340
Association for Contemporary Music (Russia), 62
Astaire, Fred, 79, 80*n*
Auden, W.H., 221*n*
Aufbau, 115 & *n*
Augenfeld, Felix, 12 & *n*
Aurora Health Institute, 121, 122, 132
Austin, Richard, **386**, 190, 212
Australia, 210–12, 219, 220
Australian Broadcasting Commission, 210, 220
Austria, political situation, 11, 14–15, 16, 18*n*, 19, 29, 30, 37, 46, 69–70, 94–5, 158, 159, 164, 165, 193, 335 & *n*

Babitz, Sol, **386**, 142
Bach, Johann Sebastian, 132–3, 142–3
  OK's arrangements of works by, 93*, 113*, 125*; recording, 147
  'Bist Du bei mir', 258
  Brandenburg Concertos, 90, 178*, 217, 287*, 291*; recording, 147, 287
    No. 1, 42*, 113*, 221*, 286*, 302*n*
    No. 2, 113*, 287*, 357*
    No. 3, 113*, 221*, 287*
    No. 4, 113*, 287*
    No. 5, 113*, 221*
    No. 6, 128*, 133*, 287*
  cantatas, 90, 352; 'Ich hatte viel Bekümmernis', 18*; 'Tritt auf die Glaubensbahn', 113*; 'Vergnügte Ruh', 113*; 'Weichet nur, betrübte Schatten', 113*
  Concerto for two violins in D minor, 113*, 161*, 162
  keyboard concertos, recording, 147
  Mass in B minor, 145, 327, 333–4*, 339*; recording, 333

INDEX

Musikalische Opfer, Ricercare, Webern's arrangement of, 67*n*
orchestral suites, 50*, 148*; recording, 252, 358
   No. 2 in B minor, 113*, 133*, 221*
   No. 3 in D, 190*, 212*n**, 312*
   Prelude and Fugue in E flat, Schoenberg's transcription, 39*
St John Passion, 93*, 159*, 358, 359
St Matthew Passion, 146*, 276, 295–6* & *n**; recording, 294–5
Toccata in C minor (arr. Weiner), 25*
Violin Concerto in A minor, 142*
'Wenn ich einmal muss scheiden', 259
Backhaus, Wilhelm, 293–4
Baden-Baden, 146–7, 148, 161
Badener Tageblatt, 161
Bailey, Norman, 346*n*
Baker, Janet, 333, 344, 347, 348, 352
Banda, Ede, 174, 175(n14)
Barber, Samuel: Adagio for Strings, 79*n**; Essay for Orchestra No. 1, 79*n*
Barbirolli, John, **386**, 60, 138, 232*n*, 307, 321
Barenboim, Daniel, 323–4, 325, 326
Bärenreiter (publishers), 336*n*
Barnett, John, 116, 117*n*
Bartók, Béla, 4, 8–9 & *n*, 215
   Concerto for Orchestra, 237
   Divertimento for strings, 287*
   Miraculous Mandarin, The, 215 & *n*
   Piano Concerto No. 2, 8–9*, 8 & *n*, 9
   Piano Concerto No. 3, 212*, 216
   Viola Concerto, 230*
   Violin Concerto No. 2, 182*
Bartók Quartet, 349
Barwahser, Hubert, 148
Basler National-Zeitung, 148, 160*n*, 168
Baum, Vicki, 23, 108
Bavarian Radio Symphony Orchestra, 263, 313, 316, 342
Bayreuth, 269–70, 277, 330–2
BBC, 191–2, 243, 255–6, 260, 287, 305, 349; television, 287
BBC Symphony Orchestra, 191, 212 & *n*, 308*n*, 310*n*
Bean, Hugh, 286, 309*n*, 313
Bean, T. Ernest, 308–9
Beard, Paul, 260
Becher, Johannes, 204 & *n*
Beckett, Samuel, 337 & *n*
Beecham, Thomas, 261, 279, 290–1 & *n*, 311*n*
Beek, John, 251
Beek, Mrs John, 192, 243(n63)
Beers, Ian, 358*n*
Beethoven, Ludwig van, 61, 62–4, 85, 137, 252, 350
   'Ah, perfido!', 304*n*
   arias, 150*
   Coriolan Overture, 286*
   Egmont Overture, 231*, 248*, 302*n*

Fidelio, 13, 15, 151, 200–1* & *n*, 227–8, 269, 278, 288–90*, 293*, 296*, 297*, 299–300*, 303*, 324*, 329*, 340–1*; inclusion of *Leonore* No. 3 Overture in performances, 201 & *n*, 288–9, 340–1; OK asks Bloch for article on, 294; recording, 175*n*, 201*n*, 297, 308
Grosse Fuge, 212*, 361
King Stephen Overture, 262*, 358*
Leonore No. 3 Overture, 201 & *n*, 222*, 288–9, 340–1
Missa solemnis, 92, 107, 254*, 260*, 262*, 273, 287*, 315*; recording, 229, 254, 315
Piano Concerto No. 3 in C minor, 70*, 202*, 257*, 293*
Piano Concerto No. 4 in G, 161–2*, 306, 358*
Piano Concerto No. 5 in E flat ('Emperor'), 200*n**, 232*, 264*, 286*, 293*
symphonies
   complete cycles, 32–3*, 46*, 64–5*, 207*, 224*, 230*, 257*, 259*, 261–2*, 263, 264–5*, 267, 273, 275*, 279*, 285*, 305–6*, 349*; recording, 264–5
   No. 1 in C, 2*, 175*, 313*, 349*, 352*
   No. 3 in E flat ('Eroica'), 18*, 44, 56*, 63*, 125*, 163*, 167*, 168*, 178*, 191*, 229*, 239*, 247*, 248*, 253*, 264*, 286*, 302* & *n*, 341*, 349*, 352*; recording, 255, 259, 290
   No. 4 in B flat, 279*
   No. 5 in C minor, 25*, 33*n**, 40*, 43* & *n*, 53*, 64*, 114*, 131*, 141*, 145*, 231–2*, 335*; recording, 255
   No. 6 in F ('Pastoral'), 127*, 247*, 254*, 279*, 302* & *n*, 312*, 349*; recording, 229
   No. 7 in A, 40*, 60 & *n*, 116*, 174–5*, 212*n**, 244*, 262*, 264*, 270*, 302*n*; recording, 255, 338–9 & *n*
   No. 8 in F, 163; recording, 313
   No. 9 in D minor ('Choral'), 6, 33*, 40–1*, 43*, 50*, 54, 60, 63*, 65*, 160*, 182*, 207*, 219, 255, 265*, 279*, 285*, 287*, 291–2*, 313*, 330, 350*
Violin Concerto, 163*, 315*; recording, 315
violin sonatas, 152
Beinum, Eduard van, 224, 225 & *n*
Béique, Pierre, 221, 235
Bekker, Paul, 52 & *n*, 55
Belgian National Orchestra, 202
Bell, Adam, *see* Cairns, David
Bellini, Vincenzo, *Norma*, 249
Beneš, Eduard, 194
Berenson, Bernard, 4, 247
Berg, Alban, 4, 34–6, 54 & *n*
   Chamber Concerto, 29*n*
   Lulu, 34–5, 90 & *n*; suite, 34, 35–6, 39, 54*
   Lyric Suite, 79
   Violin Concerto, 67*, 68–9*, 69, 90, 143*, 177–8*

INDEX

Wozzeck, 34; suite, 34
Berghaus, Ruth, 386, 329
Berlin, 194–5, 197–9, 204, 246, 247, 329;
    Akademie der Künste, 10n; Festival, 5, 6,
    256; Hochschule für Musik, 10n;
    Staatskapelle, 35
Berlin, opera houses: Komische Oper, 198,
    202–3, 204, 217, 223–4; Kroll, 10,
    31 & n, 34, 77, 146, 205, 228, 234, 270;
    Städtische Oper, 195; State Opera
    (Linden Opera), 1, 5–6, 7, 9–11, 34, 36,
    58, 59, 198, 250, 329
Berlin Philharmonic Chorus, 6, 7–8
Berlin Philharmonic Orchestra, 194, 195,
    196–7, 217, 234n, 242, 251, 256, 259,
    273, 312, 317; and divided Berlin, 198;
    OK on, 3n
Berlin Radio, 8
Berliner Börsen-Courier, 31n
Berliner Lokal-Anzeiger, 7, 10
Berliner Tageblatt, 31n
Berlioz, Hector, 33–4, 292; *Symphonie
    fantastique*, 27*, 72*, 152*, 297*
Bernstein, Leonard, 139, 337n; *Jeremiah
    Symphony*, 139
Berry, Walter, 295n
Berton, Pierre, 148n
Bicknell, David, 289, 290, 297, 307, 308n, 309
Bing, Gertrud, 386, 303
Bing, Rudolf, 11n
Bircher-Benner clinic, 1, 37
Bird, Remsen D., 41
Bizet, Georges: *L'Arlésienne* incidental
    music, 152*; *Carmen*, 198 & n, 202–3*,
    203*, 217*, 341
Blech, Leo, 10n
Blitzstein, Marc, 386, 55
Bloch, Ernest: *Schelomo*, 28*; *Voice in the
    Wilderness, A*, 78n*; *Winter–Spring*, 28*
Bloch, Ernst, 386–7, 48, 96 & n, 103–4 & n,
    107, 113, 120–1, 148, 149, 199, 208,
    224n, 294, 337; on *Fidelio*, 294; on
    Johanna Klemperer, 120; on OK, 36,
    117, 118, 119, 130, 137–8
Blum, Tamás (Thomas), 176 & n, 180
Boese, Ursula, 285
Böhm, Karl, 352
Bóka, László, 183, 185
Bolshoi Theatre, 62
Bonaparte, Princess Marie, 19 & n
Bonn, 352
Boon, Jan, 168(n59)
Borodin, Alexander, *Prince Igor*, 215n
Boros, Attila, 205
Boston, Malkin Conservatory, 79
Boston Symphony Orchestra, 20, 45, 138
Boulez, Pierre, 239n, 306 & n, 326 & n, 330,
    331, 331, 332–3; *Marteau sans maître,
    Le*, 306; *Soleil des eaux, Le*, 306
Boult, Adrian, 191–2, 212n, 310, 334
Bowen, Meirion, 336

Brahms, Johannes, 37
    German Requiem, 255*, 267, 269*, 291*;
    recording, 290
    Piano Concerto No. 2 in B flat, 248*, 340*
    Piano Quartet in G minor, Schoenberg's
    arrangement, 87–8* & n, 150*, 352
    symphonies, 259*, 260*, 280*; recording,
    258
        No. 1 in C minor, 70n*, 115*, 127*,
        146*, 148*, 211*, 212–13*, 326
        No. 2 in D, 85*
        No. 3 in F, 145*, 247*, 302n, 358*
        No. 4 in E minor, 255*
    Variations on a theme of Haydn
    (St Antony Variations), 116*, 361;
    recording, 252
    Vier ernste Gesänge, 'O Tod, wie bitter
    bist Du', 332*
    Violin Concerto, recording, 285
Brain, Alfred, 24n
Brain, Dennis, 251–2 & n
Branscombe, Peter, 296
Brecht, Bertolt, 136, 198, 204 & n, 279, 280;
    *Aufstieg und Fall der Stadt Mahagonny,
    Der* (Weill), 36, 74n
Breisach, Paul, 151
Bresser, Jan, 243
Britten, Benjamin, 297–8, 326; *Peter Grimes*,
    185; *War Requiem*, 332
Broekman, Dave, transcription of Gershwin
    Piano Prelude No. 2, 79–80*
Brooke, Gwydion, 358n
Brown, Lindsay, 211, 220
Bruckner, Anton, 55
    symphonies
        No. 2, 352
        No. 4 ('Romantic'), 27*, 162–3*, 253*,
        303*, 316*; recording, 229
        No. 5, 2–3*, 15*, 44*, 66–7*, 335*;
        editions, 66
        No. 6, 292*
        No. 7, 45 & n, 158*, 173, 176*, 211*,
        254*, 267*, 287*, 316*, 358–9* & n;
        recording, 287
        No. 8, 2, 15*, 352–3*; recording, 352,
        353
        No. 9, 17–18*, 40*, 305*
    performing versions and editions, 66,
    176 & n
Brunswick, David, 23, 150
Brunswick, Mark, 387, 3, 12, 18, 19, 28, 38,
    67 & n, 69–70, 90, 302
Brunswick, Ruth (Ruth Mack), 18, 19
Brussels, 27n
Brussels Philharmonic Society, 176
Büchner, Georg, *Dantons Tod*, 169
Buckerfield, Amy, 150, 152
Buckwitz, Harry, 298n
Budapest, 34, 70, 170, 171–6, 177, 178–90,
    208, 218; Concert Orchestra, 8–9 & n,
    61–2; Municipal Orchestra, 174–5;

INDEX

Radio, 188–9; State Opera, 172, 173–6, 179–80, 184–6, 195–6, 199–201, 204–6, 215–17, 218–19
Buffalo, 245
Buhlig, Richard, **387**, 23, 137
Bumbry, Grace, 347
Burghauser, Hugo, 1–2, 3, 11, 12, 16, 17, 34
Busch, Adolf, **387**, 139
Busch, Fritz, 12, 172, 235
Busch, Nicholas, 358*n*
Busoni, Ferruccio, 63

Cairns, David, 279, 282, 287, 288, 296, 297, 303, 305–6
Callas, Maria, 249, 303–4 & *nn*, 307
Canadian Broadcasting Commission, 343–4 & *n*
Cantor, Eddie, 22
Capell, Richard, 212, 232
Cardus, Neville, 18, 253, 280, 338
Carner, Mosco, 264, 265, 279
Carnera, Primo, 26 & *n*
Carosio, Margherita, 218
Carpenter, Edward, *Danza*, 78*n**
Carpenter, John Alden, Violin Concerto, 78*n**
Carter, Tom, 190
Casella, Alfredo, 30, 31
Cassirer, Ernst, 1
Chaplin, Charlie, 25, 204
Chapman, Diana, 326*n*
Charpentier, Gustave, *Louise*, 49*
Chéreau, Pierre, 160
Chicago, 242
Chicago Symphony Orchestra, 20, 92–3 & *n*, 208–9, 239
Chopin, Frédéric, 264*n*; Piano Concerto No. 1 in E minor, 264*n**
Chotzinoff, Samuel, 41
Christian Science Monitor, 68–9, 128
Cimini, Pietro, *80*
Clair, René, 22
Clark, Raymond, 313
Clark, William Andrews, 20–2 & *n*, 24, 25, 26, 27, 28, 33, 72, 73
Cleveland Orchestra, 20
Cochran, William, 344
Cohen, Abe, 317–18
Cologne, 34, 246–7, 248, 251, 254, 264*n*; Gürzenich Orchestra, 254 & *n*, 256–7; Opera, 254 & *n*; Radio Orchestra, 254, 313, 316
Columbia Artists, 20, 144, 244*n*, 301
Columbia Records (EMI), 233 & *n*, 234
Cooke, Deryck, 291*n*
Coolidge, Elizabeth Sprague, **387**, 86–7
Cooper, Martin, 260–1, 265, 305
Copenhagen, 160
Copland, Aaron, 78; *El Salón México*, 78
Cossmann, Paul Nikolaus, 166
Craft, Robert, **387**, 221

Crain, Hal D., 42, 128
Crass, Franz, 285, 290, 295*n*
Crespin, Régine, 304
Crichton, Ronald, 323, 333
Crosby, Bing, 80*n*
Csillag, Miklós, 216 & *n*
Culshaw, John, 307, 309, 349
Curjel, Hans, 77, 306, 360, 362
Curzio, Maria, 177
Curzon, Clifford, 306
Cushing, George, 183*n*
Cushing, Harvey, 99 & *n*, 100
Cykler, Edmund, 74, 86
Czech Philharmonic Orchestra, 61
Czechoslovakia, political situation, 194

Dahl, Etta, 107–8
Dahl, Ingolf, **387**, 105, 107–8, 142–3
Daily News (Los Angeles), 24
Daily Star, 222
Daily Telegraph, 192, 212, 232, 265, 345
D'Albert, Eugen, 232
Darmstadt Summer School, 170
Davenport, Marcia, 52
Davis, Colin, 278*n*, 337*n*, 352
Death in Venice (film), 357
DeBusscher, Henri, 24*n*
Debussy, Claude, 26, 33–4; *Fêtes*, 70*n**; *Mer, La*, 50*; *Nocturnes*, 255*; *Nuages*, 70*n**
Decca, 290, 307, 309
Defauw, Desiré, 222
Delden, Lex van, 292
Dermota, Anton, 159
Dernesch, Helga, 344
Dessau, Paul, 103, 199, 315, 329–30, 332*n*, 334, 341
Deutsche Grammophon, 309, 347
Deutsche Musikbühne, 11
Deutsche Zentral Zeitung, 70
Diamand, Peter, 177 & *n*, 225, 269, 271–2, 276
Dieterle, William, **387**, 85
Dietrich, Marlene, 50
Dimitrov, Georgi, 209
Dispeker, Thea, 104 & *n*
Dixon, Dean, 336
Dobson, John, 290
Dollfuss, Engelbert, 2, 16, 19, 30, 37
Donizetti, Gaetano, *Lucia di Lammermoor*, 280
Dorati, Antal, 337*n*
Downes, Herbert, 278(n36)
Downes, Olin, 32, 39, 40, 41, 44, 46, 52, 54, 55–6, 84, 115–16, 121, 124, 133, 148–9
Dreifuss, Willy, drawing of OK, *283*
Drogheda, Earl of, 280, 296
Druckner, Vladimir, 24*n*
Dryden, John, 21*n*
du Pré, Jacqueline, 324, *325*, 326, 334
Dushkin, Samuel, 13

INDEX

Dvořák, Antonin: Cello Concerto, 72*; Symphony No. 8, 244*

Edinburgh, 212, 272–3, 323*n*
Edinburgh Festival, 165, 169, 263, 264, 271, 272–3, 292–3, 338
Egli, Sister Käthi, 276, 277
Ehlers, Alice, 142
Einem, Gottfried von, *Dantons Tod*, 165, 169
Einstein, Alfred, 4–5
Eisenhower, Dwight David, 240
Eisinger, Irene, 169
Eisler, Georg, 296
Eisler, Hanns, 112, 113, 131, 136, 198–9, 204
Elbin, Herman (OK's nephew), 66, 281, 320
Elbogen, Ismar (OK's brother-in-law), 61, 66*n*, 95–6, 241
Elbogen, Regi (Regina) (OK's sister), 61, 66*n*, 93, 95–6, 118, 122, 131–2, 134, 149, 157, 241, 281; and Johanna Klemperer, 140, 258; on OK, 101, 102, 103, 114, 129, 155, 212; death, 314
Electrola (record company), 147*n*
Elgar, Edward, *Enigma Variations*, 52*, 232* & *n*
EMI, 147*n*, 191, 233 & *n*, 234, 236–7, 239, 241, 249, 251, 265*n*, 266, 278, 284, 286, 289–90, 297, 304, 307–8 & *n*, 309, 315*n*, 321, 326 & *n*, 337, 338, 341, 344–5 & *n*, 346–7, 352, 353, 354*n*, 358
Endler, Franz, 335
Enesco, Georges, 21, 161, 162
Epsilon Quartet, 357
Epstein, Jacob, 265, 312
Epstein, Lonny, 45, 51, 59–60, 72, 74, 103, 141, 193, 264, 302; death, 314
Erkel, Ferenc, 215
Ernster, Deszö, 360
Erös, Peter, 277
Essen City Orchestra, 246
Estrin, Morton, 129–30(n23)
Eustrati, Diana, 202*n*, 203, 205
Evans, Geraint, 296–7
Evening News (London), 264
Evening Standard (London), 311
Express (Vienna), 269, 285, 335

Fairbanks, Douglas, 49
Falla, Manuel de, *Nights in the Gardens of Spain*, 230*
FBI, 222
Fehling, Jürgen, 7
Felsenstein, Walther, **387**, 198 & *n*, 202–3, *203*, 205, 224, 303
Ferencsik, János, 185 & *n*, 223
Ferrier, Kathleen, 224, 231
Ferrir, Emile, 24*n*
Festival of Britain, 231–4
Feuchtwanger, Lion, 136
Feuchtwanger, Martha, 136
Feuermann, Emmanuel, 45, 60, 86

Fiechtner, Helmut, 158, 164
Fiesole, 4–5, 13
Figaro, Le, 146
Financial Times, 333, 344, 356
Firkušny, Rudolf, 286
Firtel, Hilde, 3, 12, 279–80, 298*n*
Fischer, Annie, **387**, 145, 172, 173, *183*, 200*n*, 257, 280
Fischer, Edwin, 193
Fischer, Fritz, 146, 180, 184, 188, 190, 210, 237, 238, 241, 250, 269, 313
Fischer-Dieskau, Dietrich, 263, 290, 291, 295
Florence, 4–5, 13, 146; Maggio Musicale festival, 4, 92, 93 & *n*; Maggio Musicale Orchestra, 247, 314
Flothuis, Marius, 230, 243, 254, 261–2
Forest Sanatorium, 152
Fournier, Pierre, 161, 169
Franck, César, Symphony in D minor, 27*
Frank, Hans, 15, 166*n*
Frankfurt am Main, 7, 298*n*
Frankfurt Radio Orchestra, 336
Freeman, John, 287
Freud, Anna, 344
Freud, Sigmund, 12*n*, 19 & *n*, 344
Freudenthal, Otto, **387**–8, 337, 351, 355, 357, 363
Frick, Gottlob, 290
Fricsay, Ferenc, **388**, 165–6
Friedemann, Gertrud, 102, 103, 104 & *n*, 110, 118
Friedemann, Ulrich, 102–3, 110
Frigerio, Maria, 217
Független Magyarország, 200
Furtwängler, Elisabeth, 193*n*
Furtwängler, Wilhelm, **388**, 3, 11 & *n*, 34–5, 39, 46, 57–60 & *n*, 166, 192–3, 296; and the Nazis, 6–8, 58–60, 142, 148 & *n*, 161, 192–3; OK and, 6–8, 30, 58–60, 161 & *n*, 195*n*, 209, 241–2; OK compared to, 3, 53, 56, 64, 148, 195, 260, 269; death, 253, 259

Gaál, Endre, 184, 185
Gadna Symphony Orchestra, 350
Gauk, Alexander Vasil'yevich, **388**, 70
Gedda, Nicolai, 290, 295*n*, 297*n*, 333
Geissler (Metzner), Carla (Johanna Klemperer's daughter), 186 & *n*
Geissler, Johanna, *see* Klemperer, Johanna
Geissmar, Bertha, 58
Germany, political situation, 5–8, 14, 23*n*, 29–30, 59, 61, 95, 146–7, 194–5, 197–8, 199, 224, 267, 281 & *n*
Gershwin, George, 79–80, 150, 207; Piano Concerto, 79; Piano Prelude No. 2, transcription by Broekman, 79–80*; *Porgy and Bess*, 79
Ghiringelli, Antonio, 218
Gibson, James, 305
Giebel, Agnes, 295*n*, 333

INDEX

Gielen, Josef, 303
Gielen, Michael, 360
Gieseking, Walter, 193
Gilels, Emil, 70
Gilman, Lawrence, 39, 53, 54 & n
Gimpel, Bronislaw, 93n, 107, 164
Giulini, Carlo Maria, 278n
Glasgow, 200n, 212
Glasgow Herald, 200n
Glaz, Hertha, 48, 85, 113, 151
Glock, William, **388**, 190
Gluck, Christoph Willibald, *Orfeo*, 347, 352
Godard, Benjamin, 27n; 'Sérénade à Mabel' (*Scènes Ecossaises*), 27* & n*
Goebbels, Joseph, 6, 7, 8, 70, 222
Goering, Hermann, 58
Goethe, Johann Wolfgang: *Faust*, 208, 250; *Wilhelm Meister*, 28
Goldschmidt, Berthold, 291n
Gollancz, Victor, 118n
Goltz, Christel, 228
Goodall, Reginald, 305, 344
Goodman, Saul, 53
Gorlinsky, S.A., 163
Gorr, Rita, 304
Graf, Herbert, **388**, 293, 299, 300
Graf, Max, 17, 18n, 63–4
Graz Festival, 164–5
Gregor, Hans, 202
Grier, Christopher, 292–3
Grillparzer, Franz, 130
Grinberg, Matias, 63
Groene Amsterdammer, De, 225, 226
Groves, Charles, 359n
Grubb, Suvi Raj, 311, 341, 345n, 346, 353, 358
Gruber, C.M., 337n
Gruenberg, Louis, *Serenade to a Beauteous Lady*, 78n*
Gründgens, Gustav, 193
Guardian, The, 59, 336
Gyurkovics, Mária, 173 & n, 174

Haas, Robert, 17n, 66
Haefner, Herbert, 236 & n
Haendel, Ida, 163
Hagemann, Carl, 217n
Haggin, B.H., 52, 53
Hague Residentie Orchestra, 147, 161–3, 246, 250, 254
Hallstein, Ingeborg, 297n
Hamburg, 316–17, 343
Hammond, Joan, 163
Hampton, Lionel, 150
Handel, George Frideric
  Concerti Grossi, 87, 178*
  Messiah, 143*, 154*, 155*, 291*; recording, 310 & n
Hanekroot, Leo, 162–3
Harewood, Earl of, 280 & n, 324, 326 & n, 327, 332n, 337

Harper, Heather, 284, 352
Harris, Roy, 78; Symphony No. 3, 168 & n*, 170*; *When Johnny Comes Marching Home*, 78*
Harrison, Jay, 302
Hart, Philip, 244–5
Harth, Walther, 195
Harwood, Elizabeth, 353
Hassell, Ulrich von, 46 & n
Haydn, Joseph
  Cello Concerto, 161*
  symphonies, 90
    No. 45 in F sharp minor ('Farewell'), 26*, 116*, 157*
    No. 88 in G, 53*
    No. 92 in G ('Oxford'), recording, 357
    No. 99 in E flat, 279
    No. 101 in D ('Clock'), 26*, 326*
    No. 103 in E flat ('Drumroll'), 42*
  OK says his compositions in spirit of, 188
Hearst, Siegfried, 249
Heath, Edward, 311
Hedrick, E.R., 127
Heger, Robert, 11, 12
Heifetz, Jascha, 50 & n, 164, 207
Heine, Heinrich, 189
Heinitz, Eva, 113, 133n
Heinsheimer, Hans, 34, 35–6
Hemsley, Thomas, 326
Henderson, W.J., 54
Henkemans, Hans, 225n
Henze, Hans Werner, 161; *Versuch über Schweine*, 332 & n
Hepburn, Katharine, 48
Herald-Express, 157
Herbage, Julian, 191
Hermann, Helmut, 335
Hesch, Anna, 319, 331, *331*, 343, 354
Hess, Myra, 51 & n, 232
Heyworth, Peter, 234n, 248, 306, 310, 312–13, 337, 343–4 & n, 353, 360
Hilborn, Walter S., 33 & n, 101, 105, 108, 109, 126, 128, 129, 130, 131, 132, 134
Hildebrand, Dietrich von, **388**, 5, 37
Hill, Edward Burlingame, Symphony No. 1 in B flat, 79n*
Hill, Hainer, 303
Hindemith, Paul, 81–3, 170, 252, 332; and the Nazis, 81 & n; on OK, 118
  Cardillac, 170
  Funeral Music, 82n*
  Harmonie der Welt, Die, 170, 263
  Horn Concerto, 251–2
  Long Christmas Dinner, The, 170
  Mathis der Maler (opera), 39, 58, 81n, 90
  Mathis der Maler symphony, 39*, 42*, 58
  Nobilissima Visione suite, 82 & n*, 125*, 170*, 254*; recording, 252
  Symphonic Dances, 82n*
Hinkel, Hans, **388**, 5–6
Hinrichsen (publisher), 298

INDEX

Hirsch, Georges, 160 & *n*
Hirschler, Helene, **388**, 99–100, 101, 104, 107, 118, 119, 120, 130, 149, 152, 154, 155, 238, 246, 267, 272, 303; OK's letters to, 96, 97, 104*n*, 105, 106, 135, 136, 137, 138–9, 141, 142, 143, 144, 148, 208, 210, 224*n*, 230–1, 256, 257, 264, 265, 267, 314, 315, 330*n*, 342–3
Hirschmann, Ira, **388–9**, 51(n36), 54, 57, 59, 60, 90, 92, 112 & *n*, 118, 132, 134, 341
Hitler, Adolf, 20, 58, 166, 276*n*, 294
HMV, 233, 234
Hoffmann, Rolf, 23
Hofmannsthal, Hugo von, *Jedermann*, 15
Hofmuller, Max, 337
Holland Festival, 231, 257, 269, 271, 292, 339*n*
Holliger, Heinz, *Siebengesang*, 360
Hollweg, Werner, 360
Hoover, J. Edgar, 222–3
Hope-Wallace, Philip, 296
Hopf, Hans, 304–5
Horenstein, Jascha, 112
Horrax, Gilbert, 99–100 & *n*, 101, 102, 104, 106, 109*n*, 135
Hotter, Hans, 289, 290
Howes, Frank, 232 & *n*
Hubay, Jenö, 8 & *n*
Huberman, Bronislaw, **389**, 40, 59, 65, 138
Hugel, Marguerite, 64–5 & *n*
Hungary, political situation, 172–3, 206–7, 213–14, 215–16, 257
Huxley, Aldous, 136

Ibbs and Tillett, 191, 255(n22)
Independent International Opera, 11 & *n*, 13–14
Infantino, Luigi, 218
Innitzer, Theodore, **389**, 17
Inquirer, The, 43
Interlaken, 147–8, 167
Irish, Mrs Leland Atherton, 48–9, 72, 137, 140
Isherwood, Christopher, 136
Israel, 228–9, 317–18, 329, 350–1; *see also* Palestine
Israel Philharmonic Orchestra, 270–1 & *n*, 317–18, 357
Israeli Radio Orchestra, 228–9, 329
Iturbi, José, 51 & *n*, 80
Ives, Charles, 78

Jacob, Archibald, 358*n*
Jacobi, Erwin, **389**, 331, *331*
Jacobs, Victor, 243
Janáček, Leoš, *Sinfonietta*, 39*
Jellinek, Walter, 251, 295
Jemnitz, Sándor, 188, 201, 215, 216, 217
Jerusalem, 323*n*; Radio Orchestra, 350, 356–7
Jerusalem Post, 291

Jewish Chronicle, 351
Joachim, Heinz, 316
Jochum, Eugen, 8, 170, 259 & *n*
Johnson, Alvin, **389**, 112
Johnson, Horace, 115, 116, 117
Johnstone, Maurice, 255
Jolson, Al, 80*n*
Jones, Isabel Morse, 94
Joseph, Helmuth (OK's brother-in-law), 50, 65
Joseph, Marianne (OK's sister), 50, 65, 131, 170, 178 & *n*, 228–9, 270, 317, 320, 329; death, 329*n*
Judson, Arthur, 20, 22, 30–2, 31 & *n*, 32, 37, 38, 43, 46–7, 51, 54, 56, 57, 60–1, 134, 138, 144, 244*n*, 259, 260, 301 & *n*
Juilliard Quartet, 134*n*
Jurinac, Sena, 289, 290 & *n*, 293, 297

Kallman, Chester, 221*n*
Kantorowicz, Alfred, 204
Karajan, Herbert von, 165 & *n*, 170, 193, 231, 233, 259, 264, 266, 269, 273, 278, 311*n*, 312, 352
Katholikentag, Allgemeine Deutsche, 16–18, 115
Kaufman, Oszkár, 210
Kayser, Kay, 118
Kelly, Daniel J., 121, 122, 123, 126
Kempe, Rudolf, 300, 309
Kempen, Paul van, 225–6
Kentner, Lajos (Louis), 8 & *n*, 9
Képes Figyelö, 196
Kerekes, János, 175(n15)
Khrennikov, Tikjon, 215
Khuner, Felix, 111, 113
Kipnis, Alexander, 10*n*
Kis Ujsák, 201
Kleiber, Carlos, **389**, 319
Kleiber, Erich, 30, 34, 35, 36, 192, 209, 259
Klemperer, Abraham (OK's grandfather), 61
Klemperer, Erika (OK's granddaughter), 305, 315, 360
Klemperer, Georg (OK's cousin), 77, 93*n*, 96–7, 98, 99–100, 101, 102–3, 104, 106–7, 118, 120, 130 & *n*, 135, 140*n*, 149, 154
Klemperer, Johanna (Johanna Geissler, OK's wife), 1, 28–9, 44, 50, 75–7, 91, 95, 101*n*, 110*n*, 128, 138, 178, 186–7, 209*n*, 210–11, 228, 234, 235, 235, 242, 249 & *n*, 250, 257; career, 77 & *n*; drinking, 75–6, 82, 83, 135; health, 102, 107, 220, 238, 244; on OK, 211, 212, 217–18, 244, 245; relationship with OK, 4, 14, 18, 22, 28–9, 39, 41, 43, 46, 48, 75–6, 82, 83, 101–2, 106, 108, 119–20, 121, 122–3, 128–9, 132, 133, 134, 135–6, 139–40, 149, 150, 151, 157, 167, 186–9, 210, 257–8, 259; and OK's health, 98, 99, 100–2, 150, 153, 157, 253; and OK's Hungarian

decoration, 207; OK's letters to, *see under* OK; and OK's relations with other women, 3; support for OK, 124–5, 126, 160; and OK's career, 137, 144, 211; and politics, 214, 223–4; social behaviour, 57n, 74; death, 220, 258–9, 263, 314; OK visits grave, 342

Klemperer, Lotte (OK's daughter), 119, 120, 122, 123, 124, 128, 133, 139–40, 158, 178, 187, 188, 218, 223, 228, 237–8, 240, 248–51 *& n*, 256, 257, 258, 259, 286, 297, 310 *& n*, 312, 325, 330, 343, 353–4, 355, 359, 363; childhood, 1, 29, 74–5, 76, 91, 110n; on OK, 239, 246, 250–1, 253, 257, 265, 266, 268, 269, 270, 272, 277, 278–9, 285, 286, 288, 305, 306, 322, 326, 334, 342, 348, 360; and OK's decision to leave Catholic Church, 319, 320; taking responsibility for OK, 106, 132, 134, 135–6, 139, 150, 151, 152, 153–4, 157, 167, 251, 252, 254, 256, 259–60, 261–2, 263, 269, 271, 273–5, 276, 277–8, 299, 317–18, 327–8, 343, 346, 361–3; and politics, 1, 214

Klemperer, Marianne (OK's sister), *see* Joseph, Marianne

Klemperer, Mark (OK's grandson), 279, *283*, 285, 315, 360

Klemperer, Nathan (OK's father), 11

Klemperer, Otto Nossan

Section 1: the man

and anti-Semitism, 94, 115 *& n*; attitude to setbacks, 61; attitudes concerning his children, 29, 47, 74–5; busts of, 163n, 265, 312; endowment fund named for in Israel, 329; and his family, 74–7, 76, 91, 93; and films, 22; photographs of him, 80, 95, *181*, *183*, *227*, *235*, *283*, *284*, *289*, *295*, *331*, *342*, *355*, *361*, *363*; portrayed in fiction, 137; puritanism, 36; reading, 28, 317, 328, 344, 359, 360; social behaviour, 57 *& n*, 65n, 74; wit, 291, 313, 324, 354

FINANCES, 108–10 *& nn*, 119, 120, 125–6, 128–9, 130, 131, 134, 143, 151, 154, 178, 186, 208, 235, 238, 244, 269, 343; fees and salaries, 43, 47, 50, 94, 141, 142, 183, 184, 210, 234, 244n, 249, 251, 254; German state and, 14, 250

HEALTH, 1, 92

manic-depressive illness, 1n, 93 *& n*, 103, 147n

depressive phases, 92, 131–2, 135–6, 143, 144, 157, 238, 241, 244, 250, 257, 258, 268, 302, 315, 359

manic phases, 1, 4–5, 101 *& n*, 107–10, 117–31, 149–54, 155–7, *156*, 167–8, 177, 209–10, 230 *& n*, 269, 270, 271–3, 274, 276, 280, 285–6, 300, 318, 326, 330; appears with water pistols, 112, 114, 128; injuries sustained during, 155, *156*, 157; police alert, 121–4, 126; pursuit of women, 105, 106, 116, 119, 126, 150–1, 152, 169, 209–10, 211, 272–3; takes taxis without fare, 112, 114, 115

treatments for, 152–4

other illnesses/accidents/problems: appendicitis, 253; bladder infection and tumour, 253; brain tumour, 96–104, 107, 157n; bronchitis, 273, 274, 275; burns himself, 274–6; bursitis, 36–7; circulatory problem, 263; cystitis, 275, 305, 358, 359; falls, 344n; femur and hip injuries, 235–6, 237, 238, 239, 240, 318–19; pericarditis, 279; pleurisy and pneumonia, 140, 237, 238, 360–1; prostate problems, 238, 245, 253; stomach problems, 37, 220, 237–8; problems with hearing, 311 *& n*, 312, 345 *& n*; problems with sight, 345 *& n*; thoughts of his own death, 314, 341, 359, 362; death and funeral, 352–3

HONOURS AND DECORATIONS, 267 *& n*, 332 *& n*; Goethe Medal, 360; honorary degrees, 74; Hungarian decoration, 206, 207, 226

LETTERS: to Dorothea Alexander-Katz, 28; to Ernst Bloch, 337; to Paul Dessau, 329–30, 332n, 334, 341; to Olin Downes, 148–9; to Herman Elbin, 66; to Lonny Epstein, 51, 59–60, 72, 74, 141, 193, 264; to Fritz Fischer, 180, 184, 188, 190, 237, 238, 241, 250, 313; to Lawrence Gilman, 54n; to Helene Hirschler, *see under* Hirschler; to Ira Hirschmann, 51(n36), 57, 92, 341; to Bronislaw Huberman, 40; to Arthur Judson, 60–1; to Johanna Klemperer, 1, 3, 4, 15, 22, 24, 27 *& n*, 28–9, 30, 32, 37, 44, 45, 46, 47, 69, 92–3, 133, 138, 139, 143, 186, 193, 247, 255, 257; to Micha Konstam, 47–8; to Anna Lippmann, 316–17; to Micha May, 241; to Natalia Satz, 41; to Schnabel, 86; to Schoenberg, 54, 55; to Elisabeth Schumann, 27, 28; to Tóth, 262, 336

LIVING SITUATIONS, 1, 12, 15–16, 18, 24, 41, 76–7, 139, 184, 187, 188, 208, 238–9, 240, 249, 257–8, 263, 286, 343

NATIONAL/POLITICAL OUTLOOK, 209, 226

concerning Austria, 37, 46

concerning Czechoslovakia, 330

concerning Germany, 4–5, 14, 29–30, 59–60, 61, 66, 105, 142, 146–7, 148 *& n*, 158, 192–4, 199, 267, 280–1, 329–30

INDEX

Klemperer, Otto Nossan (*cont.*)
    concerning Hungary, 207, 213–14, 216, 223–4 & *n*
    concerning Palestine/Israel, 66, 317, 328–9, 350–1
    concerning the USA, 207, 223, 330*n*; views on living in the USA, 22, 28, 43, 46, 47–8, 74
    concerning the USSR, 207–8
    denial of radicalism, 2
    other political interests, 117, 118*n*
    German citizenship, 248–50, 351; Israeli passport, 350–1, *351*; US citizenship and passport situation, 47, 95, 96*n*, 158, 170, 209, 213 & *n*, 222–3, 240–1, 243–4, 248, 249 & *n*
    RELATIONSHIPS WITH AND OPINIONS OF OTHERS, 118–19, 136–7; Arrau, 264*n*; Backhaus, 293–4; Barbirolli, 60; Barenboim, 323–4; Bartók, 9; Beecham, 290–1; Beethoven, 41; Berg, 34–6, 54 & *n*, 143; Berlioz, 27; Bernstein, 139; Ernst Bloch, 294; Boulez, 306, 332–3; Brecht, 204; Copland, 78; Alice Ehlers, 142; Eisler, 204; Edwin Fischer, 193; Franck, 27; Freud, 344; Furtwängler, 6–8, 30, 58–60, 142, 161 & *n*, 192–3, 195*n*, 207, 209, 241–2; Gershwin, 79–80, 207; Gieseking, 193; Henze, 332 & *n*; Myra Hess, 51 & *n*, 232; Hindemith, 170, 263; Ira Hirschmann, 341; Carlos Kleiber, 319; Erich Kleiber, 209; Koestler, 280; Kubelik, 299; Legge, 234 & *n*, 312; Leoncavallo, 23–4; Mahler, 34, 169*n*, 170, 201*n*, 339, 357, 360; Mendelssohn, 339–40; Mengelberg, 229; Gareth Morris, 212*n*, 359; Pfitzner, 166–7; Poulenc, 225; Prokofiev, 141; Schoenberg, 83–9, 85, 110–12, 138, 141, 212, 216, 220–1, 263; Schwarzkopf, 211; Shostakovich, 208; Stockhausen, 332–3; Stokowski, 43 & *n*; Strauss, 22, 27, 37, 77, 142, 206, 332; Stravinsky, 14, 138, 212, 220, 221, 237, 241, 356; Tchaikovsky, 53; Tietjen, 195 & *n*; Toscanini, 45, 60; Tóth, 145, 216, 219; Richard Wagner, 41, 331, 334; Wieland Wagner, 276 & *n*; Walter, 139, 193, 285; Weill, 118*n*
    RELIGION, 61, 74, 228, 270, 271 & *n*; and his children's upbringing, 75; Catholic observance, 105, 117, 149, 152, 269, 270, 271, 277, 328; relations with Austrian hierarchy, 2, 16, 17; decision to leave Catholic Church, 319–20; and Judaism, 246–7, 320; return to Judaism, 328–9, 354, 362; Hebrew lessons, 355

    Section 2: the musician
    and contemporary music, 32, 35, 39, 52, 54, 67–8, 77–82, 164, 165, 170, 182, 221, 243, 263, 332–3; and die Neue Sachlichkeit, 2, 57
    attitudes concerning agents, 30; attitudes concerning authenticity, 17; attitudes concerning consistency, 289; attitudes concerning encores, 199–200 & *n*; attitudes concerning interpretation, 53; attitudes concerning opera, 202*n*, 228, 254; attitudes concerning orchestral sound, 93; attitudes concerning ornamentation, 125, 287, 295, 345; attitudes concerning performance practice, 25*n*, 90, 112–13, 125, 133, 142, 207, 287, 333; attitudes concerning rehearsal, 9, 70, 162, 163, 167, 173–4, 175, 180, 182, 252, 271; attitudes concerning re-orchestration and doublings, 40–1, 350
    musical memory, 182
    AS A COMPOSER, 105, 117, 127, 188–9, 269, 271, 276, 292, 300, 324, 336–7, 357; reactions to his work, 105, 108, 297–8, 336–7; broadcast of compositions, 188
    arrangements of works by Bach, 93*, 113*, 125*; recording, 147
    Bathseba, 5, 105
    Fugato for strings, 292*
    Humoresque for wind instruments, 128*
    J'accuse, 336*
    Juda, 298*n*, 347–8
    Little Overture, 211–12*
    Merry Waltz, 114*, 115*n*, 126, 277, 292*; recording, 147
    1933, 4, 5 & *n*
    songs, 18*n*, 104, 119*, 127*, 284–5*; 'Gebet', 151*n*; 'Ich weiss nicht, was soll es bedeuten', 189
    string quartets, 161 & *n*, 188; No. 7, 349*, 357*
    Symphony No. 1/Symphony in Two Movements, 292*, 297–8*, 302; Britten on, 297–8
    Symphony No. 2, 298*, 336–7*, 362*
    Thamar, 285 & *n*
    Trinity (*America*), 106, 108, 114–15*
    Valse for violin and piano, 127–8*
    variations, 298*
    Variations on a theme by Rameau, 336*, 337; recording, 336
    verlorene Sohn, Der, 5, 17, 337, 347–8
    Weber, Die, 188–9
    Ziel, Das, 337*, 357*; One-Step, 293*
    AS A CONDUCTOR, 69, 162, 179, 194, 203, 282, 301, 322
    at the Kroll and the Lindenoper, 28, 34, 77

INDEX

audience reactions, 17–18, 25–6, 33, 42, 44, 116, 129, 142, 212, 220, 230, 242, 245, 254, 286, 288, 338
  of choirs, 105
  compared with others, 192; Beecham, 261; Busoni, 63; Furtwängler, 3, 53, 56, 64, 148, 195, 260, 269; Karajan, 269; Mahler, 53, 172; Mengelberg, 55; Muck, 53; Nikisch, 172; Schuricht, 269; Stokowski, 43; Strauss, 3; Toscanini, 33n, 52, 56, 148, 248, 260, 265, 286, 302; Walter, 3, 64, 148, 230, 261, 264; Weingartner, 3
  conducting recitatives, 159, 295; conducting seated, 238, 239, 246; disputes over operatic productions, 160; educational concerts and introductions, 26, 74; forms orchestra for Carnegie Hall concert, 125, 129; on function of conductor, 349–50; ideas on orchestral sound, 3, 40–1, 43, 56; insistence on conducting without a score, 54; limitations, 8–9, 36, 67–8, 79, 175, 182, 298, 326 & n; need for breaks from work, 51, 54; and orchestral seating arrangements, 43
  relations with orchestral musicians, 25, 43, 44, 53–4, 64–5, 70, 93–4, 113, 114, 126–7, 129–30, 134, 146–7, 148, 160, 162–3, 168, 173, 175, 205–6, 229, 244–5, 252, 262, 266, 293, 312, 313; dispute in Zurich, 292, 299–300, 329; and unions, 25, 93n, 239, 241, 249, 299, 300
  relations with soloists, 175, 178, 182, 228, 288, 296
  repertoire, 26–8, 183–4, 237
  spoken introductions to programmes, 26
  tempi, 113, 145, 174, 175 & n, 178, 179–80, 195, 201 & n, 206, 221, 252, 255, 260, 262, 285, 287, 295, 302, 326n, 335, 339, 340, 345, 349; view of his own tempi, 345n
  use/non-use of baton, 112n, 321–2
  works without fee, 196
AS AN OPERA PRODUCER, 205, 217–18, 227, 270
PIANO/KEYBOARD PLAYING, 89n, 136, 264n, 275, 325, 331–2; continuo playing/accompanying recitative, 113, 128, 159, 174, 175, 178, 179; one-handed playing, 103, 119, 152, 174; performances, 119, 127–8, 150; plays duets, 65 & n
RECORDING CONTRACTS, 147 & n, 234 & n, 236–7, 239, 241, 251, 290, 309, 358
RECORDINGS, 147, 149, 229, 230, 231, 244, 251–2, 255, 258, 285, 286–7, 290, 293, 294–5, 297, 298, 303, 306, 311–12, 315, 357–8; tempi and timings, 175n; views on dialogue in opera, 311

REVIEWS IN THE PRESS
  of compositions, 18, 188, 284–5*, 292, 298, 336, 362
  of concerts, 2–3, 15, 17, 18, 25, 26, 27n, 34, 39, 40, 41, 43–4, 52, 53, 54, 55–6, 62–4, 113, 114, 115–16, 125, 128, 137, 141, 142, 143, 146, 148, 158–9, 162–3, 168, 178, 182, 190, 192, 195, 197, 207, 211, 212–13, 221, 222, 225, 230, 231–3, 239, 246, 247, 248, 253, 254, 255, 260, 261, 262, 263–4, 265, 267, 269, 273, 279, 282–3, 285, 286, 287, 291, 292–3, 295–6, 297, 302, 303, 305–6, 314, 316, 323, 326–7, 333, 334, 335, 338, 340, 342, 348, 352, 353, 356, 358
  of operas, 159, 174, 177, 179–80, 196, 201, 203, 218, 288, 296–7, 305, 340, 341, 344, 345
  of television appearances, 349
  tributes to his German career, 10
Schoenberg's view of his musical limitations, 89
as a teacher, 118, 141–2 & n
television appearances, 287, 313 & n, 349, 350, 358
WRITINGS, 35n, 40–1, 74, 201, 339–40, 350, 353; memoirs of Mahler, 280 & n; political writings, 117, 199; stories, 280
Klemperer, Paul (OK's cousin), 107
Klemperer, Regina (OK's sister), see Elbogen, Regi
Klemperer, Susan (OK's daughter-in-law), 279, 285, 360
Klemperer, Werner (OK's son), 1, 61, 113, 119, 122, 123, 143, 235, 257, 258, 259, 271, 273, 283, 285, 302, 305, 315, 320, 359–60, 363; childhood, 74–5, 76, 91; adolescence, 29; piano lessons, 29 & n; in the Army, 133–4, 143; career, 133, 143, 251, 285, 315
Kletzki, Paul, 326, 337
Knopf, Alfred, 138–9 & n
Knopf, Blanche, 138–9 & n
Kodály, Zoltán, 4, 172, 216n
Koestler, Arthur, 280 & n, 294
Kohnstamm, Oskar, 92, 121
Kokoschka, Oskar, 296
Kol Israel Orchestra, 318 & n
Kolisch, Rudolf, 389, 4, 101, 112, 113
Kolisch Quartet, 87
Kolodin, Irving, 113, 125
Konstam, Micha, 43(n11), 47
Konya, Sandor, 304–5
Korngold, Erich Wolfgang, 389, 45n, 80, 118n; tote Stadt, Die, 80*; Violin Concerto, 164*
Korngold, Julius, 389, 2, 17
Korodi, András, 173
Kortner, Fritz, 136
Koussevitzky, Serge, 45, 52, 54, 104, 129, 138, 271n

INDEX

Kralik, Heinrich, 267, 285
Krasner, Louis, 67, 68, 69, 87
Krauss, Clemens, **389**, 11–12
Krenek, Ernst, 2*n*, 4, 67; realisation of Mahler's symphony No. 10, 291*
Krips, Josef, 12 *& n*
Kruttge, Eigel, 246, 247, 249, 253–4, 317, 323, 333
Kubelik, Rafael, 212*n*, 224, 234, 299, 330, 335*n*, 337*n*, 355–6
Kuflik, Abraham, 355
Kunz, Erich, 159, 179
Kurtz, Efrem, 125

Labate, Bruno, 53
Lafitte, Peter, 159, 230
Landré, Guillaume, 243, 254
Lang, Paul Henry, 302
Laux, Karl, 203
League of Composers (New York), 89–90
Leeds Triennial Festival, 273
Leeuwen, Hans van, 276, 277
Legal, Ernst, 198
Legge, Walter, **389**, 165*n*, 190–1, 233–4 *& n*, 248, 249, 259, 261, 264–5 *& n*, 267*n*, 287, 288, 293–4, 295, 295*n*, 296, 297 *& n*, 299, 304 *& n*, 333; and EMI, 233, 236–7, 241, 251–3, 278, 307–8 *& n*, 311; on OK, 266, 273, 275–6, 287, 289–90, 300, 303; and Philharmonia Orchestra, 231, 233, 247, 255, 283, 307, 308–11
Lehmann, Lotte, 30, 60, 149, 289, 298*n*, 360, 361
Lehrer, Tom, 325 *& n*; 'Alma', 325; 'Vatican Rag, The', 325
Leitner, Ferdinand, 276, 277
Leningrad, 27*n*, 62–3
Lenya, Lotte, 241
Leonard, Alfred, 142
Leoncavallo, Ruggero, *I Pagliacci*, 23–4
Lert, Richard, **389–90**, 23, 80, 82, 83
Levant, Oscar, **390**, 79, 80*n*
Lewis, Richard, 348
Lewy, Wolfgang, 318 *& n*
Liebermann, Rolf, **390**, 316 *& n*, 332*n*
Lier, Bertus van, 178, 207, 225, 230, 262
Ligeti, György, 175
Lipatti, Dinu, 169
Lipp, Wilma, 269, *284*, 285
Lippmann, Anna, 317
Lisbon, 249
List, Emanuel, 10*n*
Löbl, Karl, 285, 335
Lockwood, Joseph, **390**, 307–8
Loewenstein, Hubertus, 104*n*
London, 163, 247–8, 251
  Covent Garden, 269, 278, 288–90, 296–7, 303–5, 324, 340–1
  Festival Hall, 231–4, 248, 260, 322–3
  Harringay Arena, 163
  London Philharmonic Orchestra, 192, 308*n*
  London Symphony Orchestra, 163, 253, 308*n*
  New Era Concert Society, 190, 212
  New Philharmonia Chorus, 354*n*, 356
  New Philharmonia Orchestra, 310–11, 313–14, 324, 326–8, 336, 338, 344–5, 347–8, 349, 352, 353–4 *& n*, 356, 359, 361–2
  Philharmonia Chorus, 265–6, 333
  Philharmonia Orchestra, 190–2, 212–13, 231–4, 247, 248, 251–3, 255, 257, 260–1, 263, 264–6, 271, 272–3, 278, 285, 286, 290–1, 292–3, 298, 300; end of and re-formation as New Philharmonia, 306–13; OK as 'principal conductor for life', 278, 310, 362
  Queen's Hall, 18*n*
  relations between orchestras in, 308, 310
  Royal Philharmonic Orchestra, 253, 308*n*
London County Council, 265
London, George, 254*n*
Lorre, Peter, 136
Los Angeles, 22–4, 28, 32–3, 66, 82, 136, 220–1, 242; Assistance League, 127–8; Auditorium, 24 *& n*, 141; Dorothy Chandler Pavilion, 24*n*; Easter Sunrise Services, 73–4, 141; Evenings on the Roof/Monday Evening Concerts, 136–7 *& n*; Hollywood Bowl, 48, 49–50 *& n*, 137, 140, 141, 242; Hollywood Youth Orchestra, 107; Junior Philharmonic, 74; Music Guild, 142, 157; Rehearsal Orchestra, 127; Shrine Auditorium, 49; Southern California Symphony Association, 43, 48, 126 *& n*, 128, 131, 137; UCLA, 74, 86, 126, 127, 138
Los Angeles Examiner, 127
Los Angeles Philharmonic Orchestra, 20–2, 24–8, 30, 33, 41–3, 48–50, 53, 72–4, 77–9, 93–4, 110, 126*n*, 137, 140–1, 143, 154–5; finances, 20–2, 27, 30, 33, 41, 42, 48–9, 72, 94; OK arranges other conductors for, 45 *& n*, 81–2, 85*n*
Los Angeles Times, 22, 33, 42, 92, 94, 142, 157
Losonczy, Géza, 215 *& n*
Losonczy, György, 173, 174
Lubitsch, Ernst, 23
Lucerne, 273, 286, 323*n*
Lucerne Festival, 278, 338
Ludwig, Christa, 291, 295*n*, 297*n*, 303
Lukács, György, **390**, 214
Lukács, Miklós, 173
Lutosławski, Witold, Symphony No. 2, 360
Lympany, Moura, 163

Maag, Otto, 148, 168
Maazel, Lorin, 353–4, 362

INDEX

McCaw, John, 358*n*
McCracken, James, 293
McDonald, Gerald, 344–5, 347, 348, 352, 353–4, 359, 362
McDonald, Harl, Rhumba movement, 79*n**
MacDonald, Jeanette, 50
McIntyre, Donald, 340
Mack, Ruth (Ruth Brunswick), 18, 19
McLean, Eric, 222, 237
Madách, Imre, 184 & *n*
Magyar Nemzet, 184, 185, 213, 215*n*
Mahler, Alma, 390, 4, 17, 18, 56, 118, 136, 167, 325
Mahler, Anna, 163 & *n*
Mahler, Gustav, 21, 55, 111, 185, 200, 230, 231, 280–1, 323, 335 & *n*, 339, 350; as a conductor, 60 & *n*; OK and, 34, 53, 169*n*, 170, 172; on opera, 201 & *n*
   Kindertotenlieder, 44*, 231*
   Knaben Wunderhorn, Des, 326*
   Lied von der Erde, Das, 37, 48*, 85*, 93*, 224–5*, 229*, 263–4*, 286*, 291*, 319, 348*; OK on, 264; recording, 229, 306
   symphonies
     No. 2 ('Resurrection'), 38, 51*, 54–6*, 60, 84*, 197*, 198*, 220*, 231*, 305*, 313*, 314*, 324*, 329*, 356*; recording, 220, 230, 307
     No. 4, 169–70* & *n*, 195*, 211*, 247*, 253*, 285; recording, 307
     No. 5, 357
     No. 7, 34, 339* & *n*
     No. 8, 169*n*, 323, 354
     No. 9, 307, 322–3* & *n**, 326–7*, 334*, 335*, 338*; recording, 321–2
     No. 10, 291* & *n*
   performing versions, 169 & *n*
Maimonides, Moses, 328 & *n*
Major, Tamás, 390, 196 & *n*
Malcolm, George, 287
Malipiero, Gian Francesco, 4
Mann, Alfred B., 113(n42)
Mann, Erika, 325
Mann, Heinrich, 136
Mann, Nelly, 136
Mann, Robert, 134 & *n*
Mann, Thomas, 104*n*, 136, 137, 155, 214; *Doktor Faustus*, 137
Mann, William, 334, 345
Mariano, Nicky, 4
Maritain, Jacques, 118
Marsick, Martin, 21
Martin, William McKelvey, 97–8
Martinů, Bohuslav, Cello Concerto, 161
Marx, Joseph, 390, 2, 9, 18 & *n*, 34, 68
Masaryk, Jan, 194
Mascagni, Pietro, *Cavalleria Rusticana*, 326
Mason, Daniel Gregory, *Lincoln Symphony*, 79*n**
Mathis, Alfred, *see* Rosenzweig, Alfred

May, Micha, 241
Mayer-Lismann, Else, 280
Melbourne, 211
Melchior, Lauritz, 105
Melos, 10, 170
Mendelssohn-Bartholdy, Felix, 33–4, 158, 188, 280–1
   erste Walpurgisnacht, Die, 354 & *n*
   Midsummer Night's Dream incidental music, 33–4*, 196*, 340*, 342*
   Symphony No. 3 in A minor ('Scottish'), 178*, 339–40*, 342*; recording attributed to OK, 236–7 & *n*
Mendelssohn-Bartholdy, George de, 147, 229, 230, 234 & *n*, 236 & *n*, 238
Ménestrel, Le, 64
Mengelberg, Rudolf, 225 & *n*, 226, 230, 243
Mengelberg, Willem, 31*n*, 55 & *n*, 178, 225, 229
Menuhin, Yehudi, 161, *162*, 280, 315–16
Metzner, Carla, *see* Geissler, Carla
Mexico City, 88, 130–1
Meyer, Peter, 358–9
Mignone, Francisco, 140*n*; Brazilian Fantasy No. 1, 140–1*
Milan, 34, 145–6, 249
   La Scala, 217–18, 227, 259; orchestra, 46, 146, 177
Milanov, Zinka, 139
Milhaud, Darius, 4, 14, 93*n*
Milstein, Nathan, 115
Mindszenty, József, 207
Mischakoff, Mischa, 129
Mitropoulos, Dimitri, 125, 244*n*, 245, 335*n*
Mödl, Martha, 277
Molinari, Bernardino, 80
Monn, Georg Matthias, 86
Monteux, Pierre, 80
Montreal, 221–2, 235, 238–9, 242, 244
Moore, Douglas, 31*n*
Moore, Grace, 22
Morgan, Richard, 358*n*
Morgenstern, Soma, 320
Morison, Elsie, *289*, 290
Moritz, Frederick, 24*n*, 25
Morris, Gareth, 212 & *n*, 298, 309*n*, 327, 336, 348, 352, 359
Morton, Lawrence, 137, 141, 143, 155
Moscow, 62, 70–1; Sofil Orchestra, 70*n*
Moses, Charles, 210, 211
Mozart, Wolfgang Amadeus, 90, 257, 278, 283; letters, 28; on opera, 201 & *n*
   arias, 150*
   Clarinet Concerto, 291*
   Clarinet Quintet, 237
   Clemenza di Tito, La, 179*n*, 304*n*
   Così fan tutte, 174*, 176*, 179*, 180*, 329, 346–7; recording, 352, 353, 354
   Don Giovanni, 159*, 173–4*, 179–80*, 199*, 218*, 254* & *n**, 278, 304*n*; recording, 175*n*, 317

INDEX

Eine kleine Nachtmusik, recording, 147
Entführung aus dem Serail, Die, 176–7*, 179*, 329, 358, 359, 360, 361–2
Idomeneo, 179*n*, 303
Impresario, The, 129
Nozze di Figaro, Le, 10*, 166, 179*, 232*, 345*, 346*; recording, 345 & *n*, 358
Piano Concerto No. 20 in D minor, K.466, 163, 178*
Piano Concerto No. 25 in C, K.503, 225*n*, 323*, 324*
Serenata notturna, 361
Sinfonia Concertante for violin and viola, 129*
symphonies
  No. 25 in G minor, 261*; recording, 225 & *n*
  No. 29 in A, 230 & *n**, 247*, 249*, 312*; recording, 225 & *n*, 252
  No. 35 in D ('Haffner'), 129*, 145*, 241
  No. 38 in D ('Prague'), 195*, 261*; recording, 225 & *n*
  No. 39 in E flat, 260–1*
  No. 40 in G minor, 46*, 116*, 134* & *n*, 260–1*, 316*
  No. 41 in C ('Jupiter'), 225*, 232*, 233*, 248*, 260–1*, 302*n*, 326*n**, 329*; recording, 251
Wind Serenade in E flat, K.357, recording, 358 & *n*
Zauberflöte, Die, 10*, 11, 179*, 180*, 195–6*, 217–18*, 291*, 296–7*, 303*, 311*n*; recording, 311–12
OK says his compositions in spirit of, 188
Muck, Karl, 53
Mudd, Harvey S., 41, 42, 48, 94 & *n*, 101, 108, 110, 126*n*, 131, 132, 188
Munich, 258–9, 263, 342
Music Review, 192
Musical America, 25, 40, 41, 42, 57, 93, 119
Musical Courier, 26, 40, 114, 116, 119
Musical Times, 323, 333
Mussolini, Benito, 29 & *n*, 37
Mussorgsky, Modest, 215*n*; *Sorochinsky Fair*, 216–17*
Myers, Robert, 338–9 & *n*

Nagy, Ferenc, 173, 215*n*
Nagypál, Laszló, 180
Naples, 146
Nash, Ogden, 23
National Youth Administration orchestra, 129–30
Nazione, La, 247
NBC Symphony Orchestra, 92
Neher, Caspar, 227*n*
Népszava, 185, 199–200
Neue Freie Presse, 9, 15, 17
Neue Wiener Presse, 2
Neue Zeitung, 198

Neue Zürcher Zeitung, 13*n*, 15, 247 & *n*, 299, 336, 338, 349
Neues Wiener Journal, 2, 9, 15, 17, 18
Neuhaus, Heinrich, 390, 63
Neunkirchen, Alfons, 246
New Friends of Music, *see under* New York
New Philharmonia Orchestra, *see under* London
New Philharmonia Wind Ensemble, 358
New Statesman, 260, 290–1
New York, 45, 57; Carnegie Hall, 30, 125; League of Composers, 89–90; Metropolitan Opera, 241, 270, 279, 355–6; Mozart Festival Committee, 129; New Friends of Music, 90, 111, 132–3, 134–5, 136; New School for Social Research, 112–13, 119
New York City Symphony Orchestra, 114, 115–17, 124
New York Herald-Tribune, 39, 55, 101, 114, 157, 302
New York Philharmonic(-Symphony) Orchestra, 20, 31–2 & *nn*, 37–8, 39–41, 45, 46–7, 50–7, 125, 138, 139, 245, 259–60; chamber orchestra from, 129
New York Post, 41, 302
New York Times, 32, 39, 40, 44(& n14), 53(n42), 55–6, 59, 60, 94, 113, 114, 115–16 & *n*, 117*n*, 124(n3), 125, 129, 133, 292, 302, 308; OK article in, 133; OK goes to offices, 118; pursues OK for debt, 129; reports OK 'sought as insane', 122
Newlin, Dika, 89*n*
Newsweek, 55
Ney, Tibor, 9
Nierendorf, Karl, 119, 120, 121
Nietzsche, Friedrich Wilhelm, 196*n*
Nieuwe Rotterdamsche Courant, 225
Nikisch, Arthur, 25, 172, 185
Nilsson, Birgit, 290, 297*n*
Noack, Sylvain, 24*n*
Norrby, Johannes, 145
North German Radio Orchestra, 316
North-West German Radio Orchestra, 246
Novaes, Guiomar, 264*n*
Novotna, Jarmila, 18–19, 152
NPO, *see* New Philharmonic Orchestra *under* London

Observer, The, 281*n*, 353
Oesterreichische Musikzeitung, 164
Offenbach, Jacques, 292; Cello Concerto, 279; *Orpheus in the Underworld*, 196*n*, 198, 202, 205*; *Périchole, La*, 129; *Tales of Hoffman, The*, 205*
Oistrakh, David, 285, 335
Oláh, Gusztáv, 180, 196, 227*
Onno-Wolschek, Ferdinand, 390, 34, 335–6
Oporto, 249

INDEX

Orff, Carl, *Kluge, Die*, 202
Ormandy, Eugene, **390**, 57, 88, 301, 302
Orwell, George, 224*n*
Osváth, Júlia, 173 *& n*, 206

Pacelli, Eugenio (Pope Pius XII), 13, 210, 228, 319–20
Pacific Coast Musician, 26, 155
Païchadze, Gavril Gavrilovich, 13–14
Palestine, 65–6, 178 *& n*; *see also* Israel
Palestine Symphony Orchestra, 65
Palestrina, Giovanni Pierluigi da, *Missa Iste Confessor*, 17*
Parikian, Manoug, 260
Paris, 146, 147, 149, 160–1, 247, 323*n*, 326–7; Conservatoire Orchestra, 146; Opéra, 160; Orchestre de Paris, 341; Orchestre National of French Radio, 146, 163–4; Orchestre Symphonique, 31
Parlophone, *see* EMI
Parmenter, Ross, 114, 116
Parool, Het, 226, 292
Paul VI, Pope, 319
Pauly, Rose, 18–19
Pears, Peter, 262, 295 *& n*, 326
Peerce, Jan, 151
Pesti Músor, 201
Peters (publishers), 337
Petrillo, James C., 239, 241
Petrushka, Shabtai, 228
Pfitzner, Hans, 166–7 *& n*, 350; *Herz, Das*, 166; *Palestrina*, 166 *& n*
Philadelphia Inquirer, 302
Philadelphia Orchestra, 20, 32, 43–5, 57, 301–2, *301*
Philharmonia Orchestra, *see under* London
Piatigorsky, Gregor, 72
Picasso, Pablo, 296
Pischner, Hans, **390**, 329
Pittsburgh, 242
Pittsburgh Orchestra, 90–2
Pitz, Wilhelm, **390**, 265, 276
Pius XI, Pope (Achille Ratti), 13
Pius XII, Pope (Eugenio Pacelli), 13, 210, 228, 319–20
Plessner, Helmuth, 328–9
Poell, Alfred, 159
Polgár, Tibor, 189 *& n*
Pollak, Egon, 315
Polnauer, Josef, 67
Pons, Lily, 80*n*
Ponsonby, Robert, 272 *& n*
Popp, Lucia, 360
Porter, Andrew, 287, 297, 314, 344
Portland Symphony Orchestra, 244–5 *& n*
Poulenc, Francis, 225; *Aubade*, 225; Piano Concerto, 225*, 230*
Powell, Dick, 33
Prague, 61, 70
Pravda, 62
Presse, Die, 170, 335

Price, Margaret, 340, 352, 353
Primrose, William, 129, 169, 230
Pro Musica Orchestra, 147
Prokofiev, Serge, 214; *Alexander Nevsky* (cantata), 141*; Symphony No. 6, 237
Puccini, Giacomo, 67

Quebec, 239

Rachmaninov, Sergei, Piano Concerto No. 3, 163
Rachmilovich, Jacques, 141–2
Rajk, László, 177, 206, 207, 214
Rákosi, Mátyás, 206, 207
Rameau, Jean-Philippe, *Paladins, Les*, 152*
Ravel, Maurice, 26; *Daphnis et Chloé*, second suite, 42*; *Tombeau de Couperin, Le*, 53*
Ravinia, 239, 242
Redondel, El, 131
Rée, Helene ('Tante Helene', OK's cousin), 349
Reger, Max, *Variations and Fugue on a theme by Mozart*, 42*
Reich, Anneliese, 92, 103
Reichsmusikkammer, 13*n*
Reiner, Fritz, 92, 93*n*, 125, 241
Reinhardt, Gottfried, 23, 360
Reinhardt, Max, 6–7, 15, 49, 205
Reitler, Josef, 9
Relf, Clem, 273, 340, 349
Renesse, George van, 178
Residentie Orchestra, *see* Hague Residentie Orchestra
Resnik, Regina, 150, 151
Réti, Rudolf, **390**, 2–3
Reuss, Prince Heinrich XLV of, 11
Révai, József, **390**–1, 214 *& n*, 215, 216 *& n*, 217, 219
RIAS Symphony Orchestra, 246, 256
Rickenbacker, Karl Anton, 360
Riegger, Wallingford, 78
Riemann, Hugo, *Musiklexicon*, 184
Riess, Claire, 89
Rob Wagner's Script, 72
Robinson, Edward G., 33, 141
Rodriguez, José, 25, 26, 42(n8), 72–3, 74, 78–9, 88, 94, 98
Rodzinski, Artur, **391**, 20, 21, 60, 92, 138, 139, 253
Rogers, Ginger, 79
Rome, 13, 146, 227–8, 247; Santa Cecilia Orchestra, 46, 146, 210, 314
Rooney, Mickey, 49
Roosevelt, Eleanor, 129
Roosevelt, Franklin D., 113, 129
Rosbaud, Hans, 8*n*
Rosé, Arnold, **391**, 68, 69
Rosenberg, Alfred, 13
Rosenzweig, Alfred, 2*n*, 11–12, 163
Rösler, Endre, 173

481

INDEX

Rostand, Claude, 146
Rothenberger, Anneliese, 290, 297*n*
Rothwell, Walter, 21
Roussel, Albert, 4
Ruggles, Carl, 78
Russia, *see* USSR
Russian Association of Proletarian Musicians, 62

Sadie, Stanley, 333
St Petersburg, *see* Leningrad
Saint-Saëns String Quartet, 21
Salt Lake City, 143, 154, 155
Salzburg, 14–15
Salzburg Festival, 14, 15, 165–6, 193, 209, 242, 259, 263, 303
Salzburg International Opera Guild, 11 *& n*, 13–14
Salzman, Eric, 302
Sanborn, Pitts, 53
Sándor, György, 212
Santa Monica Symphony Orchestra, 142
Sargeant, Winthrop, 44, 52, 53, 55, 302
Sargent, Malcolm, 164, 210
Satz, Natalia, 12, 41
Sauerbaum, Heinz, 203
Saunders, Richard, 42(n9), 137, 155
Schacko, Hedwig, 104*n*
Schacko, Maria, 104–5, 106, 107, 119–20 *& n*, 122, 127–8, 131, 132, 133, 135, 139, 140, 157, 178, 218 *& n*
Scherchen, Hermann, 69*n*
Scherman, Thomas, **391**, 112
Scheveningen, 147, 161–3, 167, 250
Schiller, Johann Christoph von, 130
Schinkel, Karl Friedrich, 296
Schlee, Alfred, 169*n*
Schloss, Edward H., 44(n13)
Schmid-Bloss, Karl, **391**, 12–13
Schnabel, Artur, 22, 65*n*, 70–1, 90, 103, 131, 139, 161–2, 169, 231, 232; OK and, 44, 45, 65, 86, 124; death, 235
Schnabel, Karl Ulrich, 29 *& n*, 116
Schnéevoigt, Georg, 21
Schneiderhan, Wolfgang, 161*n*, 194
Schneiderhan Quartet, 161*n*
Schoenberg, Arnold, 4, 10*n*, 67 *& n*, 80, 82, 83–9, 101, 136, 137, 140, 170, 212; and Gershwin, 79 *& n*; and OK, 42, 45*n*, 54, 55, 68 *& n*, 83–9, 85, 103, 110–12, 138, 216, 220–1; and Pfitzner, 167; and Rehearsal Orchestra, 127; and Stravinsky, 81*n*; and Thomas Mann, 137; teaching at UCLA, 82, 86; Webern and, 67 *& n*, 68; death, 235
arrangement of Bach Prelude and Fugue in E flat, 39*
arrangement of Brahms G minor Piano Quartet, 87–8* *& n*, 150*, 352
Cello Concerto, 86*, 89*
Chamber Symphony No. 1, 85*n*, 89*n*, 111
Chamber Symphony No. 2, 141*
Concerto for String Quartet and Orchestra, 87*, 89*
Gurrelieder, 69*n**, 86*, 89*, 111
Moses und Aron, 263
Pelleas und Melisande, 111
Pierrot Lunaire, 29*n*, 110
String Quartet No. 1, 111
String Quartet No. 2, 77*n*
String Quartet No. 3, 86
String Trio, 86
Suite for Piano, 111
Suite for String Orchestra, 53*, 67*, 84 *& n**, 88*
Theme and Variations, Op. 43b, 140, 141, 216, 220*
Verklärte Nacht, 42*, 56*, 84*, 86*, 88–9*, 254*
Violin Concerto, 86–7, 89–90, 110
Schoenberg, Gertrud, 110*n*, 124
Schoenberg, Nuria, 149
Schöffler, Paul, 159, 179
Scholem, Gershom, 318 *& n*
Schonberg, Harold, 292
Schöne, Lotte, 10*n*
Schopenhauer, Arthur, *Über den Tod*, 359
Schorr, Friedrich, 263
Schott (publishers), 20
Schouten, Karl, 168(n59), 229
Schreker, Franz, 10*n*
Schröder-Aufrichtig, Käthe, 241 *& n*
Schubert, Franz
'Krähe, Die', 314–15
piano duets, 65*
String Quintet in C, 237
symphonies
No. 4 in C minor ('Tragic'), 244*; recording, 244
No. 5 in B flat, 134* *& n*
No. 8 in B minor ('Unfinished'), 316*, 329*
No. 9 in C, 145*, 167, 168, 287*; recording, 287
Schuh, Oskar Fritz, 158, 165
Schuh, Willi, 247 *& n*, 338
Schumann, Elisabeth, **391**, 2*n*, 17 *& n*, 18 *& n*, 27, 28, 34, 105, 113, 119, 343; on OK, 124; death, 238
Schumann, Robert
Symphony No. 3 in E flat ('Rhenish'), 340*; recording, 340
Symphony No. 4 in D minor, 225*, 302*n*
Schuricht, Carl, 8, 256 *& n*, 269
Schwab, Louise, 1, 28, 47*n*, 48, 75, 77 *& n*, 260
Schwarzkopf, Elisabeth, 159, 211, 233, 290, 295*n*
Schweizerische Musikverband, 299
Scotsman, The, 264
Scottish Orchestra, 200*n*, 212

INDEX

SCSA, *see* Southern California Symphony Association
Seefehlner, Egon, 164
Seefried, Irmgard, 159, 326
Segall, Bernardo, 140
Sessions, Barbara, 32
Sessions, Roger, **391**, 30, 32, 37–8, 40, 45, 78; *Black Maskers* suite, 28*, 78*
Sevitsky, Fabian, 244n
Shakespeare, William, 21n; *Julius Caesar*, 49; *Midsummer Night's Dream, A*, 49, 196
Shawe-Taylor, Desmond, 192, 260, 263–4, 265, 280n, 283–4, 296, 305, 314, 345
Shipley, Mrs R.D., 240–1, 243–4
Shlifshteyn, Semyon Isaakovich, 62–3
Shostakovich, Dmitri, 62, 208, 214
   Lady Macbeth of Mtsensk, The, 45, 62
   symphonies
      No. 1, 52*
      No. 4, 62
      No. 5, 62n
      No. 8, 139
      No. 9, 208
Sibelius, Jean
   Swan of Tuonela, The, 27*
   symphonies
      No. 1 in E minor, 27*
      No. 2 in D, 27*, 40*
      No. 4 in A minor, 93*, 358
      No. 5 in E flat, 52*
Sievert, Ludwig, 217 & n
Silja, Anja, 332, 334, 340, 341, 344
Simándy, József, 182, 199, 200, 262
Simon, Albert, 298
Simon, Eric, 96, 97
Simoneau, Leopold, 254n
Smend, Friedrich, 333
Smith, Caroline E., 25
Söderström, Elisabeth, 290, 297n
Sollertinsky, Ivan, 62
Solti, Georg, 303, 306, 326
Sotin, Hans, 344
Sousa, John Philip, *Stars and Stripes Forever, The*, 26
South-West German Radio Orchestra, 161
Southern California Symphony Association, 43, 48, 126 & n, 128, 131, 137
Sovetskaya musika, 62–3
Spalding, Albert, 51 & n
Staatszeitung, Die (New York), 52 & n
Stadlen, Peter, **391**, 68, 345
Stadt, Die, 286
Stefan, Paul, 18n
Stein, Erwin, 68–9 & n, 255
Stein, Leonard, 111
Steinberg, Albert, 152
Steinberg, William, 244n
Steinfeld, Julius, 152–4, 155–7, 172, 186
Steuermann, Eduard, 29 & n, 48, 68, 111
Stiedry, Erika, 97, 103

Stiedry, Fritz, 36, 62, 71n, 88–9, 90, 96, 97, 101, 103, 110–11
Still, William Grant, *Kaintuck*, 79n*
Stock, Frederick, 20, 93n
Stockhausen, Karlheinz, 332–3; *Gruppen*, 332n
Stockholm, 145–6, 148, 160, 267
Stockholm Philharmonic Orchestra, 145, 267
Stokowski, Leopold, 30, 43, 45, 52, 57, 87, 112n, 138, 234, 337n
Storjohann, Helmut, 321
Strang, Gerald, 221; *Intermezzo*, 79n*
Strasbourg, 64–5, 66, 161
Strasbourg Bach Festival, 161, 162
Strauss, Johann, 292
   'Emperor' Waltz, 292*
   Fledermaus, Die, 123 & n, 196*, 202, 219*; OK composes interlude for, 188
   Wiener Blut, 161
Strauss, Richard, 4, 15, 149, 292, 350; as a conductor, 3, 206; position concerning Nazis, and boycotting of his music, 4, 22, 27, 37, 77 & n, 142
   Daphne, 332
   Don Juan, 175
   Don Quixote, 334 & n*, 340
   Intermezzo, 11
   Metamorphosen, 142, 182*
   Rosenkavalier, Der, 177*; waltzes, 293*
   Salome, 14n, 217, 279
   Tod und Verklärung, 143*, 230* & n
Stravinsky, Igor, 7, 13–14, 33–4, 81, 104n, 136, 141, 212, 244n; and OK, 13–14, 31, 45, 104, 105, 138, 143, 220, 221; and Rehearsal Orchestra, 127; and Schoenberg, 81n; death, 356
   Agon, 137n
   Apollo, 28*
   Capriccio for piano and orchestra, 81
   Concerto in D, 182, 220*
   Fairy's Kiss suite, 81
   Firebird suite, 81
   In Memoriam Dylan Thomas, 137n
   Jeu de Cartes, 81*, 182*, 185*
   Oedipus Rex, 10*, 279, 280
   Perséphone, 31
   Petrushka, 25*, 33–4*, 81, 163, 215, 326*, 335; recording, 326 & n, 338
   Piano Concerto, 81
   Pulcinella suite, 42*
   Rake's Progress, The, 221, 237, 241
   Symphonies of Wind Instruments, 306
   Symphony of Psalms, 39*, 237
   Symphony in Three Movements, 154–5* & n, 164 & n, 177*, 178*, 190–1*, 212n*, 232*, 237, 261* & n*; recording, 298
   Threni, 273
Stravinsky, Vera, 104 & n, 105, 138, 143
Strecker, Willy, 13, 20, 81
Streich, Rita, 254n

INDEX

Stresemann, Wolfgang, **391**, 115, 312
Stringer, George, 327–8
Strobel, Heinrich, **391–2**, 146, 161, 170
Strobel, Hilde, 147
Stuckenschmidt, Hans-Heinz, 197, 203
Sun, The (New York), 54, 56, 113, 125
Sun, The (Vancouver), 148*n*
Sunday Telegraph, 348
Sunday Times, 280*n*
Sutherland, Joan, 280, 296
Svedrofsky, Harry, *80*
Swarthout, Gladys, 49, 80*n*
Sydney, 211–12, 220
Sydney Morning Herald, 211, 220
Szabad Nép, 185, 215, 216
Szabolcsi, Bence, 201
Szakasits, Árpád, 206, 207
Székely, Mihály, 173 *& n*
Szell, George, 65*n*, 137, 193, 231, 234
Szenthelyi, István, 174, 201
Szervánzky, Endre, 179–80, 182
Szigeti, Joseph, 143, 169, 237
Szivárvány, 185
Szymanowski, Karol, 138

Taddei, Giuseppe, 218
Tátrai, Vilmos, 174 *& n*, 175(n14), 182, 183*n*
Taylor, Deems: *Casanova* ballet music, 78*n**;
 Through the Looking Glass suite, 78*n**
Taylor, Kendall, 164
Taylor, Laurence, 313, 321, 324–5
Tchaikovsky, Piotr Ilyich, 27, 53, 278
 1812 Overture, 116*, 282*
 Nutcracker, The, 216
 Piano Concerto No. 1, 282*
 Queen of Spades, The, 215*n*
 Romeo and Juliet Overture, 27*
 symphonies
  No. 4 in F minor, 27*n**
  No. 5 in E minor, 27*, 53*; recording, 303
  No. 6 in B minor ('Pathétique'), 27* *& n**, 49*, 116*, 155*, 164*, 200*n**, 282–3*
 Violin Concerto, 115*
Tel Aviv, 270
Telegraaf, De, 262
Temianka, Henri, 142, 237
Tenschert, Rudolf, 230
Thibaut, Jacques, 21
Thomas, Ambroise, *Mignon*, 49*
Thompson, Oscar, 40, 55
Thomson, Virgil, 114 *& n*
Tibbett, Lawrence, 49
Tietjen, Heinz, 195 *& n*, 198
Tiggers, Piet, 225
Tillett, E.M., 255(n22)
Time, 55, 125, 148, 160, 168–9, 302
Time and Tide, 190
Times Educational Supplement, 305

Times, The, 3–5, 18*n*, 163, 190, 212–13, 231–3 *& n*, 255, 260, 261, 264, 265, 279, 284–5, 287, 295–6, 297, 298, 310, 341, 345, 358
Tito (Josip Broz), 206, 214
Toch, Ernst, **392**, 80, 152, 239, 240, 257
Toch, Lilly, 152, 155, 239, 257
Toronto, 239
Toscanini, Arturo, **392**, 41, 45, 52, 57*n*, 59, 92, 259, 330; and New York Philharmonic(-Symphony) Orchestra, 31 *& n*, 32, 37, 38, 41, 50, 51–2, 57–60, 125; OK compared with, 33*n*, 56, 148, 248, 260, 265, 286, 302
Tóth, Aladár, **392**, 9, 145, 170, 172, 173–4, 176–7, 178–9, 180, 183, *183*, 184, 185–6, 199, 205, 216, 219, 227*n*, 228, 232, 257, 262, 288–9, 336
Trötschel, Elfriede, 203
Trotsky, Leon, 117
Trötzmüller, Karl, 158(n35)
Truman, Harry S., 240 *& n*
Turin, 146

Unger, Gerhard, 297*n*
UNIO (Independent International Opera), 11 *& n*, 13–14
Union of Soviet Composers, 62
Universal Edition, 34, 35–6, 69*n*, 169*n*
USA, political situation, 222, 240, 248, 330*n*
Ussher, Bruno, 25, 33
USSR, 62, 70, 71; political situation, 207–8, 214–15
USSR State Symphony Orchestra, 70–1

Van den Burg, William, *80*
Vancouver, 143, 150–2
Varèse, Edgard, 78
Varga, Pál, 175(n15), 206
Vatican, 13
Vaynonen, Vasily Ivanovich, **392**, 216, 217
Venice Festival of Contemporary Music, 31
Verdi, Giuseppe: *Aida*, 207, 217; *Otello*, 177*, 218; Requiem Mass, 51, 139, 225, 226; *Rigoletto*, 151, 306; *Traviata, La*, 217, 218*, 280
Verein Deutsche Tonkünstler und Musiklehrer, 280–1
Vermeulen, Matthijs, 225, 226, 230, 254
Vichy, 149
Vickers, Jon, 288, 290, 297
Vidor, King, 25
Vienna, 11, 15–19, 63–4, 66–70, 158–9, 247, 267, 269, 273, 285, 323*n*
 Gesellschaft der Musikfreunde, 266–7; Singverein, 269, 285
 International Festival of Contemporary Music, 164
 Katholikentag concert, 16–18, 115
 Konzertorchester, 11, 31

INDEX

State Opera, 11–12, 159, 186, 259
Tonkünstlerorchester, 2
Vienna Boys' Choir, 17
Vienna Philharmonic Orchestra, 1–3, 11, 16–18, 19, 33–4, 41, 66–9, 69, 159, 169–70, 217, 251, 269, 285, 305, 309, 334–5, 352; and Mahler, 335 & n; OK's views on, 3 & n, 69, 269, 335
Vienna Symphony Orchestra, 158–9, 164–5, 229, 236, 267–8, 305
Viertel, Salka, **392**, 23, 136
Világosság, 188
Vinay, Ramon, 277
Visconti, Luchino, 357
Vogel, Ruth, 319, *342*, 356, 360, 363
von Sternberg, Josef, 50
Vossische Zeitung, 7, 10
Vox (record company), 147, 234, 236, 239
Vroons, Frans, 225

Waarheid, De, 225, 226
Wächter, Eberhard, 269
Wagner, Cosima, 332
Wagner, Eva, 331
Wagner, Richard, 215, 350; Israel and, 317
  arias, 163*
  fliegende Holländer, Der, 332, 334*; recording, 334, 338
  Lohengrin, 160, 182*, 199–200*, 215n*, 239*, 303–5*, 316, 331, 334; recording, 199n
  Meistersinger von Nürnberg, Die, 58, 74*, 205–6*, 207*, 215n*, 239*, 270, 277, 309; recording, 175n, 206
  Parsifal, 74*, 330, 331
  Ring des Nibelungen, Der, 50*, 119n*
    Rheingold, Das, 307
    Walküre, Die, 344*; recording, 344–5, 346 & n
    Siegfried, 334
    Götterdämmerung, 334
  Siegfried Idyll, 116–17 & n
  Tannhäuser, 7, 182*, 185*, 215n*, 331, 334
  Tristan und Isolde, 129*, 239*, 269, 270, 271, 273, 276–7, 279, 303*, 304n, 330, 331*; prelude, 70n*
  version of Beethoven's symphony No. 9, 41
Wagner, Siegfried, 330
Wagner, Wieland, **392**, 269–70, 276–7 & n, 285, 303, 330
Wagner, Winifred, 276n
Wagner, Wolfgang, 211
Walker, Edyth, 119 & n
Wallenstein, Alfred, **392**, 137, 140, 141
Waller, Ronald, 358n
Wallingford House, 121–2, 126
Walter, Bruno, **392**, 11n, 12, 13, 14, 22, 41, 93n, 101n, 137–8, 165, 172, 193, 241, 259, 284, 285; and Furtwängler, 6–7, 209n; and New York Philharmonic(-Symphony) Orchestra, 31, 32, 52 & n, 125; and OK, 137, 243; OK compared with, 3, 64, 148, 230, 261, 264; OK on, 139; and OK's compositions, 105; and Pfitzner, 166, 167; and Rehearsal Orchestra, 127; death, 285
Walton, Bernard, 309n
Walton, William, 191; *Scapino* Overture, 232*
Wanamaker, Sam, 303
Warburg, Felix H., 58
Warr, Eric, 191
Warrack, John, 253, 288, 348
Warsaw, 34
Waxman, Franz, 83 & n
Weber, Carl Maria von
  arias, 163*
  Euryanthe, 247, 346–7
  Freischütz, Der, 223–4; Overture, 291*
  Oberon, 304n
Weber, Fyodor Vladimirovich, 13
Weber, Ludwig, 159, 254n
Webern, Anton, 67 & n, 69 & n, 83, 84, 85
  arrangement of Ricercare from J.S. Bach, *Musikalische Opfer*, 67n
  Six Pieces, Op. 6, 306
  Symphony, 67–8*
  Variations, 306
Webster, David, **392–3**, 269, 289, 303, 304
Wedekind, Frank, 35
Weigel, Helene, 136
Weill, Kurt, 77, 118 & n; *Aufstieg und Fall der Stadt Mahagonny, Der*, 36, 74n; *Kleine Dreigroschenmusik*, 28*
Weiner, Leo, Bach arrangements, 25 & n
Weingartner, Felix von, 3
Weiss, Hermann, 121, 122
Welitsch, Ljuba, 159
Welt am Abend, Die, 158
Werfel, Alma, *see* Mahler, Alma
Werfel, Franz, **393**, 4, 18, 56, 118, 136; *Song of Bernadette, The*, 136
Westermann, Gerd von, 256
Whewell, Michael, 255–6 & n
Whittle, J.K.R., 338, 339n
Widdicombe, Gillian, 356
Wiener Kurier, 159, 230
Wiener Tag, 2, 17, 35n
Wiener Tageszeitung, 164
Wiener Zeitung, 9, 15, 159
Wiesbaden, 27n, 264n
Wilde, Oscar, 14n, 21n
Wilford, Ronald, 244n, 301 & n
Wilson, Marie, 233
Winchell, Walter, 122
Winfield, Michael, 358n
Winterthur City Orchestra, 247
Withers, Jane, 309, 310
Wocker, Karl-Heinz, 338
Wolfes, Felix, 129
Wollheim, Heinrich, 360
World Telegram, 53, 114

485

INDEX

WPA (Works Progress Administration) orchestras, 114, 115–17, 124, 126
Wright, Kenneth, 191, 192
Wunderlich, Fritz, 285, 291
Wysor, Elizabeth, 116, 117*n*

Yudin, Gavril Yaklovlevich, 63

Zadek, Hilde, 254*n*
Zathureczky, Endre, 182
Zefirelli, Franco, 326
Zemlinsky, Alexander von, 205
Zhizn' iskusstva, 27*n*
Ziskind, Eugene, 150, 153, 154*n*, 186, 242
Zurich, 1, 37, 149, 247, 249, 257; City Opera, 263; City Theatre, 12–13, 293; Tonhalle Orchestra, 292, 293, 299–300, 329 & *n*, 360
Zurich Festival, 293, 299–300
Zweig, Fritz, 10*n*
Zweig, Stefan, 393, 11*n*, 13